More Praise for

TABLET
& PEN

Kieran, Sholeh Wolpé, Basharat Peer, Edouard Roditi, and Erdag Göknar. Great translators are almost as rare as great writers, and it is a joy to see so many of them represented in one volume."

—Brooke Allen, *Barnes & Noble Review*

"The book argues that the long-imposed colonial vision of the Middle East as exotic, savage and erotic continues to shape the way the West understands the region. It asks readers to instead examine the depictions of the region through the words of its residents. . . . The beauty of these direct sources is in their rawness, which allows the reader to draw their own conclusions. . . . Reading the literary flair of these authors, whose writings are largely unknown in the UK, makes this book a must-read." —Hannah Brenton, Politics.co.uk

TABLET & PEN

OTHER WORDS WITHOUT BORDERS ANTHOLOGIES

Literature from the "Axis of Evil": Writing from Iran, Iraq, North Korea, and Other Enemy Nations

The ECCO Anthology of International Poetry

The Wall in My Head: Words and Images from the Fall of the Iron Curtain

Words without Borders: The World Through the Eyes of Writers

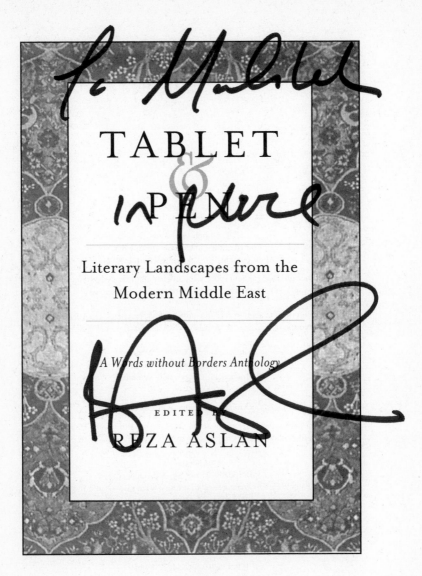

TABLET & PEN

Literary Landscapes from the Modern Middle East

A Words without Borders Anthology

EDITED BY

REZA ASLAN

W. W. NORTON & COMPANY

New York · London

Copyright © 2011 by Reza Aslan and Words without Borders

All rights reserved
Printed in the United States of America
First published as a Norton paperback 2011

Since this page cannot legibly accommodate all the copyright notices,
pages 643–48 constitute an extension of the copyright page.

For information about special discounts for bulk purchases, please contact
W. W. Norton Special Sales at specialsales@wwnorton.com or 800-233-4830

Manufacturing by Courier Westford
Book design by JAM Design
Production manager: Julia Druskin

Library of Congress Cataloging-in-Publication Data

Tablet & pen : literary landscapes from the modern Middle East :
a Words without borders anthology / edited by Reza Aslan. — 1st ed.
       p. cm.
Includes index.
ISBN 978-0-393-06585-5 (hardcover)
1. Middle Eastern literature—20th century—Translations into English.
2. Middle East—Literary collections.
I. Aslan, Reza. II. Words without borders. III. Title: Tablet and pen.
PJ409.T33 2011
808.8'9956—dc22

                                                                  2010032679

ISBN 978-0-393-34077-8 pbk.

W. W. Norton & Company, Inc.
500 Fifth Avenue, New York, N.Y. 10110
www.wwnorton.com

W. W. Norton & Company Ltd.
Castle House, 75/76 Wells Street, London W1T 3QT

1 2 3 4 5 6 7 8 9 0

This book is dedicated to the people of Iran.

Whoever keeps you and me
from being *we*,
let his house cave in.
If *I* don't become *we*, I'm alone.
If *you* don't become *we*,
you are just you.
Why not make The East
arise again?
Why not force open
the hands of the vile?
If I rise,
if you arise,
everyone will be roused.
If I sit,
if you take a seat,
who will take a stand?
Who will fight the foe,
grapple the foul enemy hand to hand?

—from "Blue, Grey, Black" by HAMID MOSADIQ (1969)

Translated from the Persian by SHOLEH WOLPÉ
and TONY BARNSTONE

TABLET AND PEN

I shall not cease to feed this pen, but still
Keep record of what things pass through the soul,
Still gather means for love to work its will,
Keep green this age round which blank deserts roll.

Though these days' bitterness must grow sharper yet,
And tyrants not renounce their tyranny,
I taste their bitter wrongs without regret,
But while breath lasts will nurse each malady—

While yet the tavern stands, with its red wine
Crimson the temple's high cold walls; and while
My heartblood feeds my tears and lets them shine,
Paint with each drop the loved one's rosy smile.

Let others live for calm indifferent peace;
I listen to earth's pangs, and will not cease.

—FAIZ AHMED FAIZ
   Pakistan

Translated from the Urdu by V. G. KIERNAN

This book would not have been possible without the contributions of the following regional editors:

Arabic: MICHAEL BEARD

Michael Beard teaches at the University of North Dakota and publishes frequently on Persian and Arabic literature. His first book, *Hedayat's Blind Owl as a Western Novel*, is a study of modernism in Iran. Among his many translations is (with Adnan Haydar) Adonis's *Mihyar of Damascus, His Poems* (Aghânî Mihyâr al-Dimashqî, 2009). He coedits the journal *Middle Eastern Literatures Incorporating Edebiyât*, as well as the series *Middle East Literature in Translation* for Syracuse University Press.

Persian: SHOLEH WOLPÉ

Sholeh Wolpé is the author of *Rooftops of Tehran* (Red Hen Press), *The Scar Saloon* (Red Hen Press), and the translator of *Sin: Selected Poems of Forugh Farrokhzad* (University of Arkansas Press), for which she was awarded the Lois Roth Translation Prize in 2010. She is the guest editor of the 2010 Iran issue of *Atlanta Review* and the poetry editor of the *Levantine Review*, an online journal about the Middle East. Her poems, translations, essays, and reviews have appeared in scores of literary journals, periodicals, and anthologies worldwide, and have been translated into several languages. Born in Iran, she now lives in Los Angeles.

Urdu: ZEENUT ZIAD

Zeenut Ziad was assistant professor of economics at the University of Karachi and the first woman executive in Pakistani banking. She also served as the director of the Staff College of a major commercial bank and as an economic consultant for the World Bank. Her publications include *The Magnificent Mughals* (Oxford University Press, 2002). She is also working on the translation of the nineteenth-century Urdu text on Sufi ethics, *The Radiant Dawn*.

Words without Borders gratefully acknowledges Amazon.com for its grant in support of the publication of *Tablet and Pen: Literary Landscapes from the Modern Middle East*.

Contents

Introduction xix

+ **PART ONE: 1910–1950**

I. The Language of Invention:
The Renaissance of Arabic Literature, 1910–1920 3

KHALIL GIBRAN
The Future of the Arabic Language 6

YAHYA HAQQI
The First Lesson 12

TAWFIQ AL-HAKIM
Diary of a Country Prosecutor 21

'ARRAR
Are You Intoxicated? 29
The Sheikh Says . . . 29
My Kinsmen Say "Leave her!" 30

'ABD AL-RAHIM MAHMUD
The Aqsa Mosque 32

II. My Country:
The Nationalization of Turkish Literature, 1920–1930 35

AZIZ NESIN
  Istanbul Boy 37

NÂZIM HIKMET
  I Love My Country 56
  The Epic of Sheikh Bedreddin 58
  Since I Was Thrown Inside 64

REFIK HALIT KARAY
  The Gray Donkey 67

III. Once Upon a Time:
Politics and Piety in Persian Literature, 1930–1940 75

MOHAMMAD ALI JAMALZADEH
  Persian Is Sugar 78

SADEGH HEDAYAT
  The Blind Owl 89

NIMA YUSHIJ
  Cold Ashes 109
  O People! 110

PARVIN E'TESAMI
  Iranian Women 112
  A Woman's Place 114

IV. Rise Up! Pakistan and the Independence
of Urdu Literature, 1940–1950 119

SA'ADAT HASAN MANTO
  For Freedom's Sake 122

ISMAT CHUGHTAI
  The Quilt 145

MUHAMMAD IQBAL
  The Houri and the Poet 155
  Heaven and the Priest 156
  God's Command to the Angels 157

MIRAJI
   Far and Near   158
   Devadasi and Pujari   158
   I Forgot   160

N. M. RASHED
   Near the Window   163
   Deserted Sheba   164
   Oil Merchants   165

✦ **PART TWO: 1950–1980**

V. I Am Arab: Arabic Literature at Midcentury   169

GHASSAN KANAFANI
   Letter from Gaza   171

ABU SALMA
   My Country on Partition Day   176
   We Shall Return   177
   I Love You More   178

MAHMOUD DARWISH
   To the Reader   179
   Identity Card   180
   Athens Airport   182
   They'd Love to See Me Dead   182

ADONIS
   The Pages of Day and Night   184
   The Wound   185
   Grave for New York   188

MOZAFFAR AL-NAWWAB
   Bridge of Old Wonders   196

ZAKARIYYA TAMIR
   The Enemies   214

YUSIF IDRIS
   The Aorta   226

HAYDAR HAYDAR
   The Dance of the Savage Prairies   233

NAGUIB MAHFOUZ
   The Seventh Heaven 247

**VI. Strangers in a Strange Land: Turkish Literature
   after Atatürk** 275

YAŞAR KEMAL
   Memed, My Hawk 277

AHMET HAMDI TANPINAR
   A Mind at Peace 294

SAIT FAIK ABASIYANIK
   Such a Story 314

MELIH CEVDET ANDAY
   The Battle of Kadesh 322
   I Became a Tree 322
   Barefoot 323
   Are We Going to Live Without Aging? 323

ORHAN VELI KANIK
   Exodus I 325
   I Am Listening to Istanbul 325

OKTAY RIFAT
   Agamemnon I 328
   Agamemnon II 337
   Agamemnon III 341

**VII. Those Days: Persian Literature Between
   Two Revolutions** 351

FORUGH FARROKHZAD
   Sin 354
   Window 355
   Wind-Up Doll 357
   Those Days 359

NADER NADERPOUR
   False Dawn 363
   Qom 364
   Faraway Star 365

SADEQ CHUBAK
  The Baboon Whose Buffoon Was Dead 367

HOUSHANG GOLSHIRI
  My China Doll 378

JALAL AL-E AHMAD
  Gharbzadegi 389

SIMIN DANESHVAR
  The Playhouse 399

AHMAD SHAMLOO
  I'm Still Thinking of That Crow 420
  The Song of Abraham in Fire 421

SIMIN BEHBAHANI
  Don't Read 424
  My Country, I Will Build You Again 425
  You Leave, I'll Stay 425

REZA BARAHENI
  I Am an Underground Man 427
  Doctor Azudi, the Professional 428
  Zadan! Nazadan! 428
  Hosseinzadeh, the Head Executioner 428
  The Shah and Hosseinzadeh 430

VIII. Between the Dusk and Dawn of History:
  Urdu Literature after Partition 433

INTIZAAR HUSSEIN
  The First Morning 435

FAIZ AHMED FAIZ
  Freedom's Dawn (August 1947) 439
  August 1952 440
  Bury Me Under Your Pavements 440

AKHTAR UL-IMAN
  Compromise 442
  The Last Stop Before the Destination 443
  The Boy 444

ALI SARDAR JAFRI
  Robe of Flame 447
  My Journey 448

ABDULLAH HUSSEIN
  The Refugees 451

GHULAM ABBAS
  The Room with the Blue Light 481

✦ **PART THREE: 1980–2010**

IX. **Ask Me About the Future:**
  The Globalization of Middle East Literature, 1980–2010 493

ZAKARIA MOHAMMAD
  Is This Home? 495

HAIFA ZANGANA
  Dreaming of Baghdad 502

ORHAN PAMUK
  The Black Book 507

MELISA GÜRPINAR
  The Bank Teller Tecelli Bey 512

FAHMIDA RIAZ
  In the City Court 518
  She Is a Woman Impure 521

AZRA ABBAS
  Today Was a Holiday 523
  A Dot Might Appear 523

KISHWAR NAHEED
  We Sinful Women 525
  Censorship 526
  To the Masters of Countries with a Cold Climate 527

ZEESHAN SAHIL
  Rome 529
  Karachi 530

ALTAF FATIMA
  Do You Suppose It's the East Wind? 532

GOLI TARAGHI
 The Grand Lady of My Soul 540

ZOYA PIRZAD
 Mrs. F Is a Fortunate Woman 550
 The Desirable Life of Mr. F 555

MANOUCHEHR ATASHI
 Nostalgia 559
 Mountain Song 560

PEGAH AHMADI
 The Dark Room 562
 The Girl Sleeping on Top of Oil 563
 Four Views of a Private Orange 565

CEMAL SÜREYA
 This Government 567
 "Dying?" 568
 I'm Dying, God 568
 After Twelve PM 568

CAN YÜCEL
 Poem X 569
 The Wall of Love 571

CEMIL KAVUKÇU
 The Route of the Crows 572

ZAYD MUTEE' DAMMAJ
 A Woman 578

NAZIK AL-MALA'IKA
 Jamilah and Us 584
 To Poetry 585
 Myths 588
 The Lover River 591

SAADI YOUSSEF
 Koofa 593
 The Bird's Last Flight 594

FARAJ BAYRAQDAR
 An Alphabetical Formation 595
 Groans 598

HAMID REZA RAHIMI
　A Quarter to Destruction　603
　Blockage　605
　Inclination　606

ALIREZA BEHNAM
　What?　607
　Hanging from the Trees of Babylon　608

Author Biographies　611

Permissions　643

Index of Works, Authors, and Translators　649

Introduction

IN MY HIGH SCHOOL's world-history book, which opened with Ancient Greece and the founding of "Western Civilization" and closed with Ronald Reagan's "Morning in America," there was a picture I will never forget: Napoleon Bonaparte astride a black horse at the edge of the Giza Plateau—hands on his reins, epaulets fluttering in the desert wind—staring at the cracked and crumbling façade of the Sphinx. The Egyptian colossus is shrouded in centuries of sand, so that only its head is visible; the angle of the portrait is such that the newly minted Master of Egypt is eye to eye with the Sphinx. In fact, the mounted Napoleon, whose army had vanquished the Egyptian forces loyal to the Ottoman sultan a few days earlier, is presented as a kind of Sphinxian figure himself—august, inscrutable, constant as the boundless desert that surrounds him.

Napoleon set sail from France in 1798, promising to free the "indigents" of Egypt from the profligate and tyrannical rule of the Ottoman Empire, which had, at least in the European imagination, led to the degeneration of Egyptian civilization. The French, as torchbearers of the Enlightenment, thought they would reestablish the splendor and glory of ancient Egypt. "The genius of liberty," Napoleon declared, "which has since its birth rendered the Republic the arbiter of Europe, is now headed toward the most distant lands."[1]

The rhetoric of invasion firmly established, Napoleon reached the shores of Alexandria on July 1, 1798; with him had sailed an armada of 50,000 men, 1,000 guns, 700 horses, and, aboard Napoleon's flagship, a handpicked cadre of artists, astronomers, geologists, botanists, engineers, and archaeologists comprising the Commission des Sciences et Arts d'Égypte. The "savants," as they were known, shadowed the French army with the aim of cataloguing all that they witnessed of Egypt: its manners and customs, its cultures and norms. The comprehensive, multivolume survey produced by the savants, *Description de l'Égypte,* would launch throughout Europe a wave of interest in "the Orient," which, though it referred to the Middle East, North Africa, and South Asia, was less a geographic designation than it was a moral, cultural, and even *civilizational* one—that is, whatever was not "the Occident" or "the West." As Edward Said wrote in his book *Orientalism,* "One could speak in Europe of an Oriental personality, an Oriental atmosphere, an Oriental tale, Oriental despotism, or an Oriental mode of production, and be understood."[2]

As most high-school history students know, Napoleon's conquest of Egypt was a short-lived and ultimately disastrous endeavor. Two years after their arrival, the French were routed by their colonial rivals, the British, and by a reconstituted Egyptian army. But the savants' depiction of "the savage nations" of the Orient as a region of indecipherable customs and irrational beliefs—a land where even the most spectacular human achievements were viewed as the result of instinct rather than talent ("like the insect whose workmanship we admire while we know it has not the power of applying the same skill to different purposes," to quote one of Napoleon's savants, Dominique Vivant Denon)[3]— would last into the present century. Indeed, from the "civilizing mission" of European colonialism to the "clash of civilizations" mentality of today, the West's perception of the Middle East as a mysterious and exotic, savage and erotic place has changed little in the more than two centuries since Napoleon's fleet set sail for Egypt. The aim of this book is to provide a different, more authentic perception of this rich and complex region, an image not fashioned by the descriptions of invaders, but rather one that arises from the diverse literatures of its most acclaimed poets and writers.

The countries that stretch along the broad horizon of the modern Middle East—from Morocco to Iran, Turkey to Pakistan—speak different languages, practice different faiths, and possess different cultures. Yet the literary landscape of this vast and eclectic region has been shaped by a common experience of Western imperialism and colonial domination: the disrupted histories and ravaged lands, the depletion of resources and inequities in wealth and status, the long struggles for sovereignty, and the vacuums of power and identity that so often followed independence from foreign rule.

Tablet and Pen spans a century of poems, short stories, novels, memoirs, and essays translated (many for the first time) from Arabic, Persian, Turkish, and Urdu—languages that too often have been neglected in the canon of world literature. This collection, which is organized both linguistically and chronologically, takes the pre–World War I period as its starting point and includes a host of material placed throughout the book to assist readers in situating the individual works in their historical context. This is not an anthology to be tasted in disparate bits but rather a single sustained narrative to be consumed as a whole, from the first page to the last.

Part One: 1910–1950 spans the tumultuous period between the two world wars, during which the boundaries of the modern Middle East were carved. Sweeping through the first decades of the twentieth century, this initial section offers a glimpse of the myriad ways in which literature became a tool for forming national identities. The writers of the period confronted profound historical changes that were reshaping the political, cultural, and literary landscape of the region: the twilight of colonialism and the arduous struggle for independence among the Arab states; the collapse of the Ottoman Caliphate and the birth of the secular Republic of Turkey; the transition from an antiquated Persian fiefdom to the modern Iranian state; the partitioning of the Indian subcontinent and the founding of Pakistan.

Part Two: 1950–1980 slows the pace of the collection as it enters midcentury, an era of regional wars (between Israel and the Arab states, between Pakistan and India) and internal conflicts (between competing visions of tradition and modernity in Turkey and Iran) that would define the postcolonial Middle East for a generation or more. These were the decades in which huge population increases, rapid urbanization, and mass unemployment created a common bond among the countries of the Middle East. This was also the era in which the poet and the writer emerged as the most powerful voices of dissent against the region's authoritarian regimes, and literature became a mirror reflecting the failure of religious and political leaders to live up to their responsibilities.

Part Three: 1980–2010 covers the era that began with the 1979 Iranian Revolution (which introduced the world to political Islam) and continues into the present with a "War on Terror" that has propelled political Islam onto the global stage. This is also an era that has witnessed the rise of a new and globalized generation of writers unburdened by many of the political and religious preoccupations of their literary forebears yet nevertheless still grappling with similar issues of personal identity and social inequality. All of this has occurred in the shadow of 9/11 and the so-called War on Terror, which, since 2001, has become the dominant framework within which relations between the West and the Middle East have been cast. Much as the borders and boundaries that partition the world have begun to blur and disintegrate in the face of globalization, the divisions of language and region that mark Parts One and Two give way in this final section to a "borderless" collage of contemporary poems, essays, and stories from across the region.

Although most of the writers in this collection hail from Muslim-majority states, and the questions posed by the role of Islam in society are ever-present themes in their writings, this is not meant to be an anthology of literature from "the Muslim world"—not only because many of the authors do not self-identify as Muslim but also because there is no such thing as a monolithic "Muslim world," save perhaps in the imaginations of some in the West. Even the term *Middle East* is a hazy geographic designation in which, an argument can be made, neither Turkey nor the countries of South Asia would be included. Yet what binds together the writers in this collection—from the famed Arab poet Khalil Gibran to the Iranian essayist Jalal Al-e Ahmad, from the Indian poet-philosopher Muhammad Iqbal to the Turkish Nobel Prize winner Orhan Pamuk—is neither borders nor nationalities, but rather intention, circumstance, and setting. (It is for this reason that Hebrew literature, which has developed along a different historical path and thus reflects certain social and historical realities that do not align with themes of imperialism, colonialism, and Western cultural hegemony that occupy so much of the literature of the modern Middle East, is not included in this anthology. See note below for two excellent available collections of Hebrew and Israeli literature of this period.)[4]

It is the preoccupation with these themes—the overwhelming sense of being cast as "foreign," as "other"—that links the individual works in this anthology. And while it may be too much to expect that a collection of literature can reframe perceptions of an entire region, it is our hope that this book can go some way toward providing a new paradigm for viewing the mosaic that is the modern Middle East. At the very least, the writings contained in these pages may help move our consciousness of the region away from the ubiquitous images of terrorists and fanatics and toward a new, more constructive set of ideas and metaphors—wrought by the region's own artists, poets, and writers—with which to understand the struggles and aspirations of this restless and multifaceted part of the world.

Readers of English, for whom many of these literary works may be unfamiliar, may find this anthology to be an especially vital companion, as will Americans seeking a window into a region with which their country is now inextricably enmeshed. Indeed, two centuries after Napoleon's invasion of Egypt, the United States has displaced the old colonial powers to become, for better or worse, a dominant and unavoidable presence in the lives of the people of the Middle East. The consequences of American involvement in the region will be felt for many years to come. But consider this: Among the first Egyptian artifacts plundered by the French was a pair of grand obelisks known as "Cleopatra's Needles." Today, the first of these obelisks stands along the River Thames in London; the second has stood for more than a century in New York's Central Park.

REZA ASLAN
Los Angeles, California

---

[1]Quoted in Juan Cole, *Napoleon's Egypt* (New York: Palgrave-Macmillan, 2007), 5.

[2]Edward Said, *Orientalism* (New York: Vintage, 1979), 32.

[3]Quoted in Terence M. Russell, *The Discovery of Egypt* (Charleston, SC: The History Press, 2005), 93.

[4]See Robert Alter, *Modern Hebrew Literature* (Springfield, NJ: Behrman House, 1962), 10-12, and Ammiel Alcalay, *Keys to the Garden: New Israeli Writing* (City Lights, 1996).

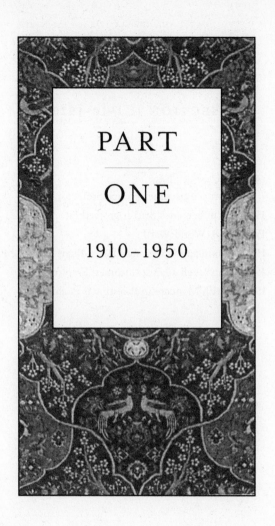

PART

ONE

1910–1950

Chronology

SECTION I: 1910–1920

1912 Italy seizes Libya
Morocco becomes French protectorate

1914 Egypt becomes British protectorate

1914–1918 World War I

1916 Britain and France sign Sykes-Picot Agreement

1918 Arab revolt against Ottoman Empire

1920 British Mandate in Palestine is established

I

The Language of Invention:
The Renaissance of Arabic Literature,
1910—1920

ARABS HAVE A LONG and proud literary tradition that extends back many centuries, from the pre-Islamic love songs of bedouin poets to the timeless tales from *A Thousand and One Nights*, which, though derived from Persian, remains the pinnacle of Arab storytelling. At the dawn of the twentieth century, however, Arabic literature experienced a renaissance when hitherto unfamiliar literary forms borrowed from Europe and North America—the novel, for instance, and the short story—began influencing a new generation of Arab writers. This renaissance coincided with a surge of Arab nationalism and a revival of the Arabic language within the Ottoman-occupied Arab lands. As the sublime Lebanese poet Khalil Gibran writes in his 1923 manifesto, *The Future of the Arabic Language*, with which our collection begins:

> Language is but one manifestation of the power of invention in a nation's totality or public self. But if this power slumbers, language will stop in its tracks, and to stop is to regress, and regression leads to death and extinction.

Just after the turn of the twentieth century, dozens of underground literary societies began cropping up all over the Middle East, led by Arab writers and intellectuals who sought to revive and modernize the Arabic literary tradition. With the 1913 publication of Husayn Haykal's

Zaynab, which chronicled the life of a young peasant girl in rural Egypt, the Arab novel was born. But it was Haykal's literary successor, the Egyptian author and playwright Tawfiq al-Hakim (*Diary of a Country Prosecutor*), who most successfully fused Arab and Western literary traditions and helped give birth to modern Arab literature. These Arab modernist authors grounded their stories in the daily lives of the mostly poor, mostly rural people struggling to reconcile their traditions and identities with the rapidly changing societies in which they lived.

The fires of Arab nationalism flared with the collapse of the Ottoman Empire at the end of World War I. The British and French, who promised the Arab peoples independence in exchange for siding with the Allies, reneged—in fact, the colonial powers had no intention of relinquishing control over the region. Two years before the end of World War I, on May 16, 1916, Britain and France had secretly signed the Sykes-Picot Agreement, parceling out the vanquished Ottoman lands among themselves. Still, the nationalist aspirations of the Arabs would not be extinguished—neither in Syria, which declared independence in 1920 under King Faisal I, nor in Egypt, where a wave of demonstrations forced Britain to grant the country its sovereignty in 1922. Of course, all of this was merely an illusion of independence. France stormed Damascus a few months after independence was declared, placing the territories of Syria and Lebanon under a French mandate, and the British did not relinquish their political and economic control over the new Egyptian state.

As the Arab countries lurched toward a nominal state of independence, a new, politically active crop of Arab writers, such as the Jordanian poet 'Arrar (pen name for Mustafa Wahbi al-Tal) and the Egyptian short-story writer Yahya Haqqi, began using the power of the written word to condemn the failures of their political and religious leaders. Establishing a theme that appears quite often throughout this volume, these criticisms of society were often veiled in metaphor, as in Haqqi's unforgettable short story "The First Lesson," in which a train—the "huge, black, strange creature" that carves a murderous path of iron and steel through Egypt's barren landscape—represents the awesomeness of an invisible, callous, and all-powerful government.

Meanwhile, reverberating in the background of these global events like a persistent drumbeat was the ever-present issue of Palestine. The

Balfour Declaration of 1917, in which Britain promised support for "the establishment in Palestine of a national home for the Jewish people," and the British Mandate of 1922, whereby the region was administered by the United Kingdom on behalf of the League of Nations, had resulted in sporadic violence between Palestine's Arab population and the increasing numbers of mostly European Jewish immigrants flooding into the Holy Land to lay the groundwork for the future state of Israel. The warning of the Palestinian poet 'Abd al-Rahim Mahmud about the troubles brewing in Palestine—"This land, this holy land, is being sold to all intruders/and stabbed by its own people!"—would, in a few short years, become impossible for the rest of the world to ignore.

KHALIL GIBRAN
(1883–1931)

The Future of the Arabic Language
(EXCERPT)
Translated from the Arabic by Adnan Haydar

What is the future of the Arabic language?

Language is but one manifestation of the power of invention in a nation's totality or public self. But if this power slumbers, language will stop in its tracks, and to stop is to regress, and regression leads to death and extinction.

Therefore, the future of the Arabic language is tied to the presence or absence of invention in all the countries that speak Arabic. Where invention is present, the future of the language will be glorious like its past, and where it is absent, the future will be like the present of its two sisters—Syriac and Classical Hebrew.

And what is this power we call invention?

It is the nation's resolve to move ever forward. It is in the nation's heart, a hunger and thirst for the unknown, and in its soul a chain of dreams that the nation seeks to realize day and night, and every time one of the links in the chain is realized, life adds another one. It is, for that individual, a yearning for brilliance and for the group enthusiasm. And what is brilliance save the ability to mold the group's hidden tendencies into clear and tangible forms. In the *Jahiliyya** the poet was always prepared because the Arabs then were in a state of readiness. Likewise, in the period bridging the *Jahiliyya* with Islam, the poet prospered and expanded his talents because the Arabs then were in a state

---

* *Jahiliyya*: "The Era of Ignorance." A reference to the period in Arabia before the rise of Islam.

6

of growth and expansion. In the post-classical period the poet split his loyalties because the Islamic nation was in a state of disunion. And the poet kept on progressing, ascending and changing his color, appearing at times as a philosopher, at other times as a physician, and, at still other times, as an astronomer, until the Arabic language was lured to drowsiness and then to sleep. And in its deep sleep the poets reverted to versifiers; the philosophers metamorphosed into scholastic theologians, the physicians into quacks; and the astronomers into fortune tellers.

If the above is correct, the future of the Arabic language is closely tied to the power of invention in all the nations that speak Arabic. And if those nations together were possessed of a private self or unity of spirit, and if the power of invention in that self were to wake up after a long sleep, the future of the Arabic language would be as glorious as its past. And if not, it will not happen.

What kind of influence would the European Civilization and the Western Spirit have on it?

As for the Western Spirit, it is but a stage in man's life and a chapter of his existence. For man's life is a formidable procession that forever moves forward. And out of that golden dust arising from the roads he travels, languages, governments, and sects are fashioned. The nations that walk in the forefront of this procession are the inventive ones, and that which is inventive is that which influences. On the other hand, the nations that walk last in the procession are the ones that imitate, and the imitator is the one who is influenced. So when the Easterners were ahead and the Westerners were behind, our civilization had a great influence on their languages. But now, since they are in the front and we have lagged behind, their civilization has necessarily exerted great influence on our language, our thinking, and our morality.

Whereas the Westerners in the past consumed what we cooked, partaking of our food, swallowing it, and transforming what was useful to their very being, the Easterners, at present, consume what the Westerners cook; they swallow their food, but it does not become part of their being. Rather, it transforms them into something similar to their counterparts in the West. This is a result that I fear and complain about because it presents the East, at times, as an old man who has lost his molars and, at other times, as an infant who has not yet sprouted them.

The Western Spirit is at once our friend and our enemy. It is a friend if we can vanquish it and an enemy if it can vanquish us, a friend if we can open our hearts to it and an enemy if we offer it our hearts, a friend if we borrow from it what suits us and an enemy if we place ourselves in situations that suit it.

What influence does the present Arab political scene have on our language?

All writers and thinkers in both the East and the West agree that the Arab countries are in a state of political, psychological, and administrative confusion, and most of them agree that this confusion is the harbinger of destruction and extinction. I, however, ask: Is it confusion or boredom?

If it is boredom, it will spell the death of every nation and the end of every people. Boredom is dying in the form of drowsiness, and death in the semblance of sleep. And if it is in reality confusion, I believe that confusion is always useful because it brings to light that which was hidden in the nation's soul, changing this soul's intoxication to sobriety and its stupor to wakefulness, precisely the way a powerful storm shakes the trees, not to uproot them but to break their dead branches and scatter their yellow leaves.

And if confusion appears in a nation that still possesses some inborn qualities, that will be the plainest proof of the presence in its individuals of the power of invention and the power of initiative in its public soul. Is not mist the first word in the book of life, not the last? And what is the mist save a life rife with confusion?

Therefore the influence of political development in the Arab countries will change these countries' confusion into order and their ambiguities and their problems into harmonious organization. But it alters their boredom neither to passion nor to excitement. For the potter may be able to fashion from clay a jug for wine or vinegar, but he cannot fashion anything from sand and pebbles.

What is the best means to revive the Arabic language?

The best and only means is to be found in the poet's heart, on his lips, and at his fingertips. The poet is the mediator between the power of invention and humanity. He is the cable that transfers what the world of the soul conceives to the world of research, and what the world of thought determines to the world of retention and writing.

The poet is both the father and the mother of language; language travels the same roads he travels and stops to rest where he stops to rest, and if the poet dies, language sits on his grave crying over the loss, wailing until another poet passes by and extends his hands to it. And if the poet is both the father and the mother of language, the imitator is the weaver of its shroud and the digger of its grave.

By poet, I mean every inventor, be he big or small, every discoverer, be he strong or weak, every creator, be he great or humble, every lover of pure life, be he a master or a pauper, and everyone who stands in awe before the day and the night, be he a philosopher or a guard at a vineyard. The imitator, on the other hand, is the one who does not discover or create anything, but rather the one whose state of mind is borrowed from his contemporaries, and his conventional garments are made from the tatters of garments worn by his predecessors.

By poet, I mean that farmer who plows his field with a plow that differs, however little, from the plow he inherited from his father, in order that someone will come after him to give the new plow a new name; I mean that gardener who breeds an orange flower and plants it between a red flower and a yellow flower, in order that someone will come after him to give the new flower a new name; or that weaver who produces on his loom patterns and designs that differ from those his neighbors weave, in order that someone will give his fabric a new name. By poet, I mean the sailor who hoists a third sail on a ship that has only two, or the builder who builds a house with two doors and two windows among houses built with one door and one window, or the dyer who mixes colors that no one before him has mixed, in order to produce a new color for someone who arrives later on to give the ship of the language a new sail, the house a new window, and the garment a new color.

As for the imitator, he is the one who travels from place to place on the roads that a thousand and one caravans have traveled, making sure he does not deviate from his course for fear he will get lost; he is the one who earns his living, eats, drinks, and wears the clothes of a thousand generations before him, and so his life remains a mere echo, his whole being a mere shadow of a distant truth he neither knows anything about nor cares to know.

By poet, I mean that worshipper who enters the temple of his own soul and kneels down crying for joy, wailing, rejoicing, listening. And when he comes out, his lips and tongue articulate nouns, verbs, letters, and new meanings for the various patterns of his own adoration that renew themselves every day, and for the many types of his own supplications that change every night. Thus he adds with this effort a silver string to the lute of the language and a perfumed branch to its hearth. The imitator, on the other hand, is the one who repeats the worshippers' prayers and their supplications without an act of will on his part, without even an emotion, and thus leaves the language where he finds it and keeps his personal rhetoric where there is neither rhetoric nor distinctive character.

By poet, I mean that lover who, when he falls in love with a woman, his soul isolates itself and walks away from all that is human in order to drape his dreams with embodiments of the day's splendor, the night's terror, the tempests' rage, and the valleys' calm, then goes on to fashion from its experiences a wreath to grace the head of the language, and mold from its contentment a necklace to adorn its neck.

The imitator, on the other hand, is the one who copies others even when he loves or flirts or celebrates his beloved in verse. So if he happens to describe his beloved's face or neck, he says "moon" and "gazelle"; if he thinks of her hair, her figure, and her glances, he says "night," "bent branch," and "arrows"; and if he complains about his love, he says "a sleepless eyelid," "a distant dawn," and "close rebuker"; and if he decides to come up with a rhetorical feat, he will say "my beloved sheds tears of pearls from her narcissus eyes in order to water her roseate cheeks, and bites her fingers of gum-arabic with her nail-like teeth." And so our friend keeps on aping this hackneyed song, not realizing that he is poisoning with his stupidity the richness of the language and insulting, with his abuse, its honor and nobility.

I have talked about the "innovative" and its benefits and the "barren" and the harm that comes from it, but I have yet to mention those who spend their lives writing dictionaries and founding language academies. I have not said a word about them because I believe that they are like the beach between the ebb and the flow of the language and that their job is limited to functioning like a sieve. Now sifting is a good job, but what can the sifter possibly sift if the nation's innovative power sows only chaff and harvests only straw, and hoards in its threshing floors only thorn and thistle?

Again I say the life of the language, its unification, its propagation, and all that has any relationship to it have been and will always be the product of the poets' imaginations. But do we have poets?

Yes, we do have poets, and every Easterner can be a poet in his field, in his garden, before his loom, in his temple, in his pulpit, and in his library. Every Easterner can free himself from the prison of imitation and tradition and emerge to meet the sun and walk in the procession of life. Every Easterner can submit to the power of innovation that lies hidden in his soul—that eternal power that transforms rock into God's children.

As for those who have devoted themselves to versifying and setting in prose their talents, to them I say: Let your personal aims prevail over your attempts to follow the tracks of those who preceded you, for it is better for you and for the Arabic language to build a poor hut made of your humble selves than to erect a lofty palace made of your borrowed selves. Let your self-esteem prevent you from composing eulogies, elegies, and occasional poems, for it is better for you and for the Arabic language to die despised and cast out than to burn the incense of your hearts before the idols and the monuments. Let your national zeal spur you to depict the mysteries of pain and the miracles of joy that characterize life in the East, for it is better for you and for the Arabic language to adopt the simplest events in your surroundings and clothe them with the fabric of your imagination than to translate the most beautiful and the most respected of what the Westerners have written.

YAHYA HAQQI

(1905–1992)

The First Lesson

Translated from the Arabic by Miriam Cooke

THE [EGYPTIAN] HAMLET of Dasunis had a small station slumbering far from the village out in the fields. Peaceful and humble, it was perfumed with the fragrance of plants. Its short platform was not enclosed, the maize stalks growing right up to it, and herds of cattle and buffalo wandered close by. The bell, which the station-master rang whenever the train was about to stop, was as quiet and muffled as the cheeping of chicks. Luxury trains passed through disdainfully, making the earth tremble and filling the air with a whistling sound which to the *fallah** represented the awesomeness of the government. At long intervals, dirty trains stopped at the station to discharge a passenger and sometimes to take on another. Then the train resumed its journey, leaving behind a cloud of smoke. But none of this robbed the station at Dasunis of its peace. Just as people are molded by their circumstances, so the station at Dasunis had a peasant's innocence. It did not like nor understand the secret of this black shining track which cut through from north to south, with no known beginning or end. It was a magic way that led everywhere and in which no traveler could get lost. The wooden huts and short platform seemed to stare fearfully at these rails, shrinking from them like a cat bewitched by a viper.

When the train was almost due, the station would gradually come to life, rousing itself at the faint sound of the bell that rang twice. Abu Dawud would go to the telephone and give the "All clear." Then he would go to the signal levers and pull them toward his chest one after the other. Then, when he came to the distance signal, he would take

---

* *Fallah*: Peasant, or agricultural laborer. Also *fellah*.

12

a large, embroidered handkerchief out of his pocket, bend over, plant his foot firmly on the ground, and give the lever a sharp pull, which would send the blood rushing to his face, and a hidden sickness would course through his veins. If you saw the arm of the signal drop, one kilometer away, you knew that Abu Dawud had succeeded and that, exhausted, he had collapsed on a chair and was mopping his brow.

At the precise moment when the signal stopped—neither before nor after—'Amm Khalil would come out from his hut, close the level crossing gates, and tell the crowd of peasants to wait for the train to pass. The pedestrians would stoop and crawl under the barriers and then walk off. Those who were riding remained seated on their mounts, complaining vociferously:

"'Amm Khalil, it's still early for the train."

But 'Amm Khalil would never accede to their wishes. If they continued to insist, he would unfurl a red flag in front of them and stand motionless. But he still heard from all sides:

"'Amm Khalil, let us go through just this once."

At that point he would look around and pick out someone who had only just arrived and had not heard the discussion. He would approach him, without turning to the others who were standing by, and address him, disregarding the expression of amazement mixed with submissiveness on the man's face:

"I am a government employee. I understand the rules. Don't you know that the donkey which the train knocked over cost my predecessor ten days' punishment? I am responsible. What do you care? You go on and that's all there is to it and all the blame lands on my shoulders."

When the train was about to appear, the station-master, Hilmi Effendi, would rush onto the platform, his paunch hanging out of his trousers, wearing a jacket with embroidered sleeves, a pencil behind his ear.

Once the train had passed, Dasunis station returned to its deep sleep. 'Amm Khalil settled into a low chair in his hut to read *The Guide to Good Deeds*.* Abu Dawud leaned against the window and dozed until the next bell. The station-master disappeared into his nearby home,

* *The Guide to Good Deeds*, or *Dala'il al-Khayrat:* A collection of sayings and prayers meant for daily recitation; collected by Sufi scholar Muhammad al-Jazuli of Morocco.

until the telegraph summoned him with its noisy, insistent clanging, forcing him to listen—like it or no.

YOU KNOW THOSE buildings which the Railway Department constructs for its employees in small stations: one-story rectangular mud huts, unpainted, narrow, with small rooms, all of the same size. Yusuf Hilmi was born in just such a building. When he was still in the cradle he had grown accustomed to the trembling of the earth and the whistling of the train and the clash of iron. When he could stand on his own, his mother would take him to a back window and hold on to him by the end of his *galabiya.** Whenever he could take advantage of his meager liberty, Yusuf would look down at the freight train, shunting backward and forward behind the house. He would breathe in the smoke of the train and not be frightened by its appearance. He imagined it to be a huge, black, strange creature driven by a man with grimy clothes, a dirty face, and dirty hands.

When his legs were strong enough for him to walk outside the front door, his mother handed him over to his father so that he might strut up and down the platform with him—the one corpulent, the other puny. But with time the little one began to move about independently. He crossed the platform to 'Amm Khalil's hut, where he found a gentle atmosphere and the love that he did not find with his father.

Hilmi Effendi was the station-master. He was very concerned with keeping his house in order. He had a gift for breeding pigeons, geese, and chickens. When you entered his house you would find cages hung up behind the door, and friendly Yemeni and fantail pigeons would greet you with their pleasant cooing. You could see Hilmi Effendi's clean, fat geese walk off slowly to a nearby ditch, bathe, and then return. When he picked up a chicken it would not be frightened. He would not put it down until he had given it—God knows from where—some bread, or a handful of barley which he scattered in front of it. If he woke up early he would go to the pigeons, geese, and chickens, and feed them. He would collect the eggs, change their water, and clean up. Perhaps you will now forgive him for neglecting

---

* *Galabiya* or *jalabiya*: Traditional full-length garment worn by Arab men and women.

his son's upbringing. Yusuf Hilmi cannot remember having ever spent more than two minutes chatting with his father, or having ever been kissed twice in a row. As soon as he had set him on the ground, his father would pat him on the back and leave, as though saying: "Get on with it."

The boy would go to his mother for tenderness. But she was a woman and could not satisfy his thirst for male company. She was, moreover, a prisoner in her own home, and just a step away beyond the threshold was the freedom of the long platform up and down which he could strut. He might as well have been an orphan!

'Amm Khalil was Sudanese. His mother had been Egyptian. He epitomized Sudanese customs and clung to his identity as though it were a religion. His clothes were clean and he ate elegantly. He despised peasants and read *The Guide* in a loud but gentle voice. The strange perfume of the Sudanese is unforgettable, and you could smell it near 'Amm Khalil's hut—a mixture of cleanliness and perfume. You knew that this was his refuge from the company of men. Only a few knew 'Amm Khalil's tragic story. In his youth he had married, with full ritual, a girl from an Arab family that loved horses. She was chaste and modest. Then she gave him his only son and died in childbirth. When his son was six years old he followed his mother and left 'Amm Khalil to weep in bitter loneliness.

One day Yusuf Hilmi felt like an adventure and he crossed the platform. It was a fortunate adventure, since it led him to 'Amm Khalil's hut. The Sudanese looked at him for a while, then took him by the hand and sat him down by his side on the low chair. Yusuf could smell his perfume, and he felt a gentle hand on his shoulder. He raised his eyes to a wrinkled face, kind eyes, and a clean white turban; the boy laughed, exposing all his teeth. The wrinkles smoothed out and the man smiled. The boy stood up, went onto the platform, and ran home.

At that time the boy was seven years old and the man was in his fifties. One by one the boy's adult teeth were emerging and one by one the man's teeth were falling out. The boy knew nothing of life other than this station platform; the man had known both its sweetness and its bitterness. And yet during this short period they spent together in the hut their hearts came close together. It was not fatherly affection, nor a son's love. The boy ached for the tenderness denied him, and the man's own loss had taken from him the joy of living—they were on an equal footing. Each took and gave, each was the victim of a cruel fate. They felt mutual trust and concern for the other's welfare. Their hearts were learning the meaning of true friendship. For the one, unfortunately, this came too late; for the other, unfortunately also, it came too early.

Until he was eight, Yusuf believed that the world ended at 'Amm Khalil's hut, which represented happiness and love. Then the monitor from the Koranic school came to collect this new recruit, and the boy found out that the world had another dimension, one that contained suffering.

But his absence during the day helped the growth of his friendship with 'Amm Khalil. The latter was very anxious not to be disturbed in his work. When Yusuf returned from school he would go home, put down his slate and copybooks, take a hunk of bread and cheese, and walk up and down the platform, nibbling. Then he would go down to 'Amm Khalil's hut, where he exhausted 'Amm Khalil with a recitation of what he had memorized, in a quiet singing voice: "Do not play with religion as the scepter plays with the ball. Safeguard it for it is the grace of the educated man."

Then in a voice that began loudly and ended quietly: "Clean your bedroom. Do not eat unripe fruit."

Then in a measured, quick tone: "Head, skull, face, hair."

These sounds mixed with the reading of *The Guide*. When a train passed, Yusuf would shriek with delight and throw himself into 'Amm Khalil's arms.

Two years passed. Yusuf memorized the section of *'Amma* and a part of *Tabarak*.* In arithmetic he had reached simple division, and in reading he had finished his spelling and reading books, and had passed into the top level. The lessons became rote. Then what?

His father did not give the matter any thought because he was busy looking after his geese, chickens, and pigeons. Were it not for his mother's ambition to see her son competing with the son of her sister-in-law, and that he should be a pupil in a suit and fez, and were it not for 'Amm Khalil's severity and his repetition of a Tradition that he had memorized and sanctified—"Look for knowledge, even if it be in

---

* *'Amma* and *Tabarak*: Sections of the Qur'an often memorized by children.

China"—were it not for all this Yusuf Hilmi would now be writing "Administrative Assistant" under his name.

His father took him by force to Damanhur, where he passed an examination and was enrolled in primary school. When people tell you the story of their school life they say how pleasant it was and what a sweet youth they had. But if Yusuf Hilmi were to tell you about his, it would be a story filled with pain.

Here he was, a small boy in trousers that exposed his knees, torn socks, his elbows sticking out of the holes in his jacket sleeves. His fez with its short tassel was faded, and he carried it under one arm with his books. In his other hand was a loaf wrapped in a kerchief. At 6 a.m., he was standing ready on the platform waiting for the No. 4 train to take him to his school in Damanhur.

No. 4! He would never forget this number—it was his unlucky number and he hated it. In winter when it rained, he would wrap his fez in his kerchief and arrive late in school with mud up to his knees. He returned home late in the evening. Yusuf Hilmi awaited Friday impatiently: he could spend the whole day with 'Amm Khalil in his hut, sitting by his side, feeling the glow of his presence.

One bitingly cold day in February, the rail repair workers arrived and overran Dasunis station. They slept under planks of old wood that they had taken out from underneath the rails and had knocked together into small shacks. They ate crackers out of the same sack. They started work as soon as the sun was up. Each man took his place in line, naked from the waist up, with the tie belts of their dirty white trousers dangling to the ground. Their faces were dark and even-featured; their hands were rough and their arms powerful; their backs were like rubber, unaffected by continual bending. At first, they hammered away without any rhythm, until someone in the middle began to sing. The others joined in the chorus loudly, hammering away even harder. The rhythm pleased them, and they would forget the hard work until they sat down during the rest periods, utterly exhausted. Then they enjoyed *mawwals** that one of them sang about al-Balina, Mazata, Na'isa, and the daughters of 'Abdallah, and each one longed for home. They drank tea as thick as ink, their faces were hard as stone, their arms like iron,

---

* *Mawwals*: Traditional Arab songs.

their backs immensely strong. When evening came, they huddled around the fire. One of them might stretch his leg over the flame as though he were about to toast it. What could the fire do to the many-layered crust that had built up upon it? After burning fragments had started to fly off it, he would stretch out the other leg.

When an express train passed through, it would slow right down. The passengers would stand at the windows to see what had delayed them, exchanging quick curious glances with the workers.

The flames cast a red gleam on the faces of the men seated on the ground. The rest of their bodies disappeared into the darkness. Their voices were raised, their looks hungry. They stared at the passengers as though they were strange beings. As they passed, standing behind the windows without a word, it seemed to the workers that they were ghosts, not of this world.

The passengers glanced at them quickly. Some ignored these creatures staring out from the darkness; some were caught up in the fragrance of the fields, the croaking of the frogs, and the night breeze. Often a passenger laughed for some reason and this laugh sounded strange to the workers, and they would laugh back—and the train moved on.

How 'Amm Khalil complained of the smell of fenugreek, onion, and sweat that these strangers exuded like vapor from a stove. He was convinced that swarms of lice had invaded and occupied his hut. He would take his wooden chair out into the sun, and wash the hut with petrol, filling it with Sudanese incense, which his little friend could smell for many days.

The workers had brought a red signal that they put at the point where the repair work began, so that the trains should slow down. The station-master instructed 'Amm Khalil to stand by this signal, and to get on every train to guide the driver past the confusion on the rails. Such are the instructions that a government employee has to obey, even if he can find no justification for them.

EVEN NOW YUSUF Hilmi can remember that cold, heavily overcast morning—the air was pale as though it were sad and weeping. As usual Yusuf stood on a particular spot on the platform waiting for the train. He saw the signal for the Alexandria-bound trains go down. He saw 'Amm Khalil come out of his hut, and as he passed him he said: "Keep your ears covered with your scarf, so as not to catch cold."

'Amm Khalil soon reached the red signal; then, in the distance where the rails disappear, a black dot appeared and gradually became clear—a train. Yusuf saw 'Amm Khalil's arm signal up and down. Then he saw 'Amm Khalil, with a red flag in his hands, jump onto the steps of the locomotive when it reached the signal. The train continued slowly, puffing out clouds of smoke. It was a freight train that did not stop at Dasunis.

The train advanced and when it came to where Yusuf was standing, 'Amm Khalil jumped to get off, but fate had decided otherwise. Does anyone know his destiny, or what has been decreed for him? 'Amm Khalil jumped, his foot slipped between the platform and the locomotive, and he fell. He stretched out his hand to the platform, trying to grab hold of something even if it meant someone else's death. But a greater power dragged it down and it dropped convulsively, the veins protruding. For a split second Yusuf saw the face of his friend sprawled on the ground, almost devouring the earth in its agony. His eyes were bulging as though they were seeing the hell they had feared all their lives.

What had happened to the kind face of 'Amm Khalil and his gentle eyes and clean turban? Could it be the same as this dusty face convulsed with pain, with its turban torn to shreds by the train?

The train continued, dragging the corpse beyond the platform where it dropped off. It rolled to within a couple of yards of the hut that was scented with Sudanese incense. There was no sound; the corpse did not respond to the cry of the home for its master.

When Yusuf's train came, his father pushed him onto it. Yusuf did not want to go to school that day.

THE TEACHER ENTERED for the first lesson and wrote on the blackboard in capitals: ARABIC COMPOSITION. And then below in cursive: The Advantages of the Railways. He explained these advantages to the pupils and then told the class to start writing. Forty small hands took hold of pens and wrote in their copybooks. Forty brains started to explore the advantages of the railways. One of them wrote: "The advantages of the railways. What do you know about the railways?" Another wrote: "God created man." A third wrote: "The train is propelled by steam and goes from village to village, and no one gets tired."

Hands moved and pens squeaked. But the hands of one of them remained motionless on a small copybook. They belonged to a pale face with a twisted glance. Yusuf had turned his face so as to look directly at his teacher wherever he might be as he moved about among the rows, as though seeking an explanation, or wanting to give one. But he felt his teacher and companions had forgotten him, and did not feel his presence among them. He was a stranger.

The class ended and only the blank sheet of paper could tell what was going on in the boy's heart.

TAWFIQ AL-HAKIM

(1898—1987)

Diary of a Country Prosecutor

(EXCERPT)

Translated from the Arabic by Abba Eban

WHEN WE GOT BACK, it was time for the session to begin. Our car approached the court, where we saw people crowded like flies at the entrance. My assistant had slumped down at my side completely prostrate and I took no further notice of him. It did not occur to me to summon him in that state of fatigue to sit through a court session with me after attending an investigation. He was not yet accustomed to a twenty-four-hour day and the instructive night which he had just spent was quite enough for him.

So I decided to deal gently with him in the early period of his service; and as soon as we came to the court, I made the driver stop and ordered him to take my assistant home.

I bade farewell to the *ma'mur** and alighted from the car, clearing a path between the serried ranks of men, women, and children. When I entered the conference room, the judge was already sitting. As soon as I saw him, my spirits dropped. There are two judges in this court and they work on alternate days. One of them lives in Cairo and travels up for the session by the first train. He always hears his cases with the utmost speed in order to catch the eleven o'clock train returning to Cairo. No matter how great the number of cases for hearing—this judge has never yet missed his train. The other judge is an excessively conscientious man who lives with his family in the district office. He is very slow in dealing with cases, for he is afraid of making mistakes through haste; and perhaps, too, he is eager to fill in time and enliven

---

* *Ma'mur.* An assistant; someone who takes orders or who is a subordinate.

21

his boredom in this provincial outpost. Moreover he has no train to catch. So from early morning he sits at his desk as though he were inseparably nailed to it; and he never leaves it till just before noon. He generally resumes the session in the evening too. These sessions have always been a nightmare to me; they are a veritable sentence of imprisonment—as though I were condemned to be tied to my desk and remain immobile the whole day long. The red and green sash placed around my neck and under my armpit seemed like a yoke. Was it divine vengeance for all the innocent people whom I had inadvertently sent to prison? Or is it that the consequences of our professional mistakes recoil upon us, so that we pay for them some time in our life without knowing when?

I said nothing when I saw the judge. It was clear to me that I was in for a merciless session after a night of continuous toil. I don't know what can have blurred my memory and made me imagine that it was the turn of the brisk judge to preside this morning. . . .

I entered the court. First of all, I glanced at the list and saw that we had to deal with seventy misdemeanors and forty felonies—quite sufficient to ensure an endless session with this particular judge. There were always more cases for him than for his colleagues; and the reason was quite simple. The conscientious judge never imposed a higher fine than twenty piastres* for a misdemeanor, whereas his colleague raised the fine to as much as fifty piastres. People charged with misdemeanors had gotten to know this, and always took special care to escape from the expensive judge and patronize his more reasonably priced colleague. Today's judge had often complained and grumbled about the way his work increased in volume from one day to the next, and had never discovered the cause. I used to say to myself, "Raise your price and you'll have a pleasant surprise."

The usher began calling out the names of the accused from a paper he was holding. Kuzman Effendi, the usher, was an old man with white hair and a white mustache, endowed with a presence and bearing fit for a Justice of the Supreme Court. Whenever he called anyone to the box, he was extremely majestic in his movements, gestures, and voice. He would turn to the court attendant with an air of supreme

---

* Piastre: A unit of currency in the Ottoman Empire.

authority, and that worthy fellow would echo the name outside the chamber just as he had heard it from the usher, except that he would introduce a long-drawn-out chant and an intonation like that of a street hawker. A certain judge had once noticed this resemblance, and said to him, "Come, Sha'ban, are you calling out the names of defendants in crime cases or selling potatoes and black dates?"

And the man replied, "Crime cases, potatoes, dates, it's all the same; it's all to make a living."

The first defendant took his place. The judge, who had plunged into his papers, now raised his head, adjusted a pair of thick spectacles on his nose, and said to the man before him, "You have contravened the Slaughter of Animals Regulations by killing a sheep outside the slaughter-house."

"Your honor, we slaughtered the sheep—saving your presence—on a very special evening (may you be granted one like it)—it was the circumcision of our little son and . . ."

"Twenty piastres fine! Next case!"

The usher called out a name. And so it went on—name after name— a whole succession of cases exactly similar to the first on which sentence had been pronounced. I left the judge to his verdicts and began to amuse myself by observing the people in the court. . . . They filled all the seats and benches and overflowed onto the floor and gangways, where they sat on their haunches like cattle gazing up humbly at the judge, while he pronounced sentence like shepherd with a staff. The judge grew weary of the succession of identical cases and shouted, "What is all this about? Is there nothing in this court except sheep outside slaughter-houses?"

He glared at the crowd with eyes like peas behind his spectacles, which bobbed up and down his nose. Nobody, not even himself, caught the implication of what he said. The usher went on calling out names. The type of charge had begun to vary and we were entering a different world, for the judge was now saying to the accused, "You are charged with having washed clothes in the canal!"

"Your honor—may God exalt our station—are you going to fine me just because I washed my clothes?"

"It's for washing them in the canal."

"Well, where else could I wash them?"

The judge hesitated, deep in thought, and could give no answer. He knew very well that these poor wretches had no washbasins in their village, filled with fresh flowing water from the tap. They were left to live like cattle all their lives and yet were required to submit to a modern legal system imported from abroad.

The judge turned to me and said, "The Legal Officer! Opinion, please."

"The state is not concerned to inquire where this man should wash his clothes. Its only interest is the application of the law."

The judge turned his glance away from me, lowered his head, shook it, and then spoke swiftly like a man rolling a weight off his shoulders: "Fined twenty piastres. Next case."

A woman's name was called. It was the village prostitute. She had blackened her eyelashes with the point of a match and smeared her cheeks with the glaring crimson color that can be seen painted on boxes of Samson cigarettes. On her bare arm was tattooed the image of a heart pierced by an arrow. She was wearing on her wrist several bracelets and armlets made of metal and colored glass.

The judge looked at her and said, "You are charged with having stood at the entrance of your house . . ."

She put her hand on her hip and shouted, "Well, darling, is it a crime for someone to stand in front of his house?"

"You were doing it to seduce the public."

"What a pity! By your honor's beard, I've never seen this Public—he's never called in at my place."

"Twenty piastres. Next case."

Kuzman Effendi summoned the next defendant. He was a middle-aged farmer of some prosperity, to judge from his blue turban, his Kashmir *galabiya*, his cloak of "imperial" pattern, and his elastic boots of screaming yellow tint. As soon as he appeared, the judge sprang the accusation upon him: "You, sir, are charged with not having registered your dog within the statutory period."

The accused coughed, shook his head, and mumbled as though reciting a religious formula, "A fine age we're living in—dogs have to be 'registered' like plots of land, and a great fuss is made over them!"

"Twenty piastres fine. Next case. . . ."

The hearing of the misdemeanors continued, all in the same vein.

Not a single one of the defendants showed any sign of believing in the real iniquity of whatever he had done. It was merely that fines had fallen upon them from heaven, whence all disasters proceed; they had to be paid, for so the law required. I had often tried to convince myself of the purpose of these sessions. Could one claim that these judgments had a deterrent effect when the delinquent had not the least idea of what fault he had committed?

We got through the misdemeanors and the usher called out, "Cases of Felony." He glanced at the list and shouted, "Umm as-Sa'ad, daughter of Ibrahim al-Jarf."

An old peasant woman walked slowly down the center of the room until she reached the dais, where she stood in front of Kuzman Effendi the usher. He directed her toward the judge, at whom she gazed weakly for a while. Soon she turned away from him and stood once more with her eyes fixed on the aged usher.

The judge buried his face in the papers and asked, "Your name?"

"Umm Sa'ad, sir."

She appeared to address this reply to the usher, who made a sign directing her once more to face the dais. The judge questioned her: "Your profession?"

"Woman, your honor!"

"You are charged with biting the finger of Sheikh Hasan Imara."

She left the dais and addressed the usher again: "I swear to you, by the honor of your white hair, that I haven't done any wrong—I swore, I gave a sacred oath that my daughter wouldn't be married for a dowry of less than twenty gold pieces."

The judge raised his head, adjusted his spectacles, looked at her, and said sharply, "Now then, speak to me. I'm the judge here. Did you bite him? Answer yes or no!"

"Bite him? God forbid! I've got a temper, I admit—but I don't go as far as biting people!"

"Call the witness," the judge said to the usher.

The victim appeared—his finger bound in a sheath. The judge asked him his name and occupation, made him swear that he would tell nothing but the truth, and asked him to elucidate what had happened.

"Your honor, I wasn't on one side or on the other, and the matter arose because I generously offered to mediate."

He relapsed into silence, as though he had completely clarified the whole matter.

The judge glared at him in repressed anger, and then upbraided him to recount in detail what had happened. The man made a full statement to this effect:

The accused woman had a daughter called Sitt Abuha; she was wooed by a peasant named Horaisha, who offered a dowry of fifteen gold pieces. The mother refused and demanded twenty. The matter stood there until one day the suitor's brother, a young boy called Ginger, came along on his own accord and informed the bride's family, quite falsely, that the suitor had accepted their terms. He then went back to his brother and told him that the girl's family had agreed to reduce the dowry and to accept his offer. As a result of this cunning joke played on both parties, a day was appointed for reciting the Fatiha at the bride's house, and the bridegroom deputed Sheikh Hasan and Sheikh Faraj to be his witnesses.

Everybody came together and the girl's mother killed a goose. Scarcely had the meal been made ready and served to the guests when the dowry was mentioned and the trick was revealed. It was evident that the deadlock had not been solved and a quarrel flared up between the two parties. The girl's mother began to shout and wail in the yard: "What a dreadful calamity! How our enemies would rejoice. By the life of the Prophet, I will not let my daughter go for less than twenty gold pieces." The woman, half-crazed, rushed in among the menfolk to defend her daughter's interests, fearing that the men would settle the matter in an unsatisfactory way. Sheikh Hasan was moved by the spirit of devoted zeal and did not touch the food. He began to argue with the woman, vainly trying to convince her, while his colleague, Sheikh Faraj, stretched out his hand toward the goose and began to guzzle it avidly, without entering into the impassioned dispute. It appears that the enthusiasm on each side went beyond the limits of verbal discussion, and soon Sheikh Hasan saw that his hand was not in the plate of goose but in the woman's mouth. He let forth a resounding shriek and soon the whole house was turned upside down in chaotic confusion. Sheikh Hasan grabbed his companion, pulled him violently away from the goose, and went out, gnashing his teeth with rage. His companion, who had not said a single word, had been rewarded with an excellent meal; whereas he, after all his zeal, had left the banquet hungry, with his finger bitten by the old woman. . . .

The plaintiff went on at great length. Suddenly the judge was seized with agitation. His conscientious scruples had come to life, and he interrupted the witness, saying, as though in a soliloquy, "I wonder if I made the witness take the oath!"

He turned to me and inquired, "Prosecuting Counsel, did I make the witness take the oath?"

I tried hard to remember, but the judge could not banish his doubts. He shouted at the witness, "Take the oath, sir. Say: 'By almighty God, I swear to speak the truth!'"

The man swore the oath—whereupon the judge called out, "Begin your evidence from the beginning!"

I saw that we would never finish the session. I was utterly bored and sank, yawning, into my seat. Sleep began to play with my eyelids and there elapsed an interval the length of which I cannot surmise. Suddenly I heard the judge's voice calling to me: "Prosecution! What is the request of Prosecuting Counsel?"

I opened a pair of bloodshot eyes that requested nothing but sleep and was informed by the judge that he had just studied the medical report, which said that the injury had left a permanent infirmity—the loss of the medial parallax of the third finger. I sat up in my seat and immediately demanded a ruling of *ultra vires*.* The judge turned to the old woman and said, "The case has become a felony and within the jurisdiction of the Criminal Court."

The old lady showed no sign of understanding this subtle distinction. In her view, a bite was a bite. How could it suddenly be transformed from a misdemeanor into felony? (What an accursed law it is—far beyond the comprehension of these simple folk!)

The next case was called. It dealt with a violent quarrel, leading to blows, which had broken out between the father of Sitt Abuha and the family of the husband, Sayyid Horaisha—for eventually the marriage had taken place. The bridegroom had sent some of his relatives with a camel to take the bride from her father's house, bur her father had

---

* *Ultra vires*: Latin term meaning "beyond the scope" or "in excess of legal power or authority."

received them with sharp abuse, shouting in their faces, "What? A camel? My daughter leave here on a camel? Not likely! There must be a Tuombeel."*

The two parties began to argue about who was to pay for this new-fangled device provided by modern scientific development. The argument led to the raising of sticks and the effusion of a few drops of blood—quite inevitable in a situation of this kind. Finally, a well-intentioned person produced a banknote from his pocket and hired one of the taxis that plied the country roads.

The judge gave his ruling on the dispute, and remarked, "Thank heavens, we've finished with the joys of matrimony. Next case."

* Toumbeel: An automobile.

'ARRAR*
(1897—1949)

Selected Poems

Translated from the Arabic by Noel Abdulahad

Are You Intoxicated?

Drunk again!
In God's name I am so
and shall not cease from getting intoxicated.

Time has made a fool of me
and I shall make a fool of time itself
thanks to this overflowing cup of wine.

The Sheikh Says . . .

The Sheikh ordered me to repent,
to abstain from singing
or flirting with Laila or Kalvadara.

Most respected Sheikh!
Is there a divine text
justifying seeing my reason gone
or behaving like a silly ass?

* 'Arrar: Pen name for Mustafa Wahbi al-Tal.

My Kinsmen Say "Leave her!"

My kinsmen say: "Do, please repent
and leave her."
Surely, I shall report and turn from her
—if God wills!
God suffices as my guardian.

I shall desert the bars
ignore my boon companions
cast off the veil of sin
cling to sobriety
scorn the glances of coquettes
and enticements of those sweet gazelles
until my kinsmen can say,
" 'Arrar has indeed repented.
Great is the anguished sufferer
who stakes his soul's desires."

And they will add:
"Be happy, 'Arrar, for you did well.
The reckless and the diligent
are thus not two, there's clear distinction."

To my God I adjure
the valley of shelter and its lovely maidens,
The love-lorn damsels of Wadi as-Sir*
God is the beloved one!

Do tell me, please! How can one thrill
without agony's passion or ardent kisses
or consoling pleasant music
and a goblet of refreshing wine?

---

* Wadi as-Sir: A small village in Jordan south of Amman.

The love-afflicted beauty
beckons my worn-out age,
so how can the elderly's outpourings
yield with vigor to love-lorn youth?
I shall respond to the call of yearning
even as I trespass my eightieth year.

O my throbbing, love-sick heart,
consumed by fire.
To God and God alone shall I deliver
this heart of mine with all its wounds
inflicted by intense incitements.

Who dares deny that the most precious things of man
are his tongue and his heart?
So what would my kinsmen say to me
if my heart ceases to throb
or to ring out its tender melodies?

'ABD AL-RAHIM MAHMUD
(1913–1948)

The Aqsa Mosque

*Translated from the Arabic by Sharif Elmusa and
Naomi Shihab Nye*

The Aqsa Mosque

Honorable Prince![*] Before you stands a poet
whose heart harbors bitter complaint.
Have you come to visit the Aqsa mosque![†]
or to bid it farewell before its loss?
This land, this holy land, is being sold to all intruders
and stabbed by its own people!
And tomorrow looms over us, nearer and nearer!
Nothing shall remain for us but our streaming tears,
our deep regrets!

Oh, Prince, shout, shout! Your voice
might shake people awake!
Ask the guards of the Aqsa: are they all agreed to struggle
as one body and mind?
Ask the guards of the Aqsa: can a covenant with God
be offered to someone, then lost?
Forgive the complaint, but a grieving heart needs to complain
to the Prince, even if it makes him weep.

---

[*] The poem is addressed to Prince Saud Ibn 'Abd al-'Aziz, who visited the
poet's town, 'Anabta, on August 14, 1935.
[†] Aqsa mosque: The silver-topped mosque that stands near the Dome of the
Rock on the Temple Mount (*Haram al-Sharif*) in Jerusalem.

Chronology

SECTION II: Ottoman Empire/ Turkey (1908–1928)

1908 Young Turk revolt

1914 Ottoman Empire allies with Central Powers in World War I

1919–1923 Turkish War of Independence

1923 Republic of Turkey established, with Mustafa Kemal Atatürk as first president

1924 Ottoman Caliphate abolished

1928 New Turkish alphabet established

II

My Country: The Nationalization of Turkish Literature, 1920–1930

AS THE TWENTIETH century began, Turkish literature, like the Ottoman Empire itself, had become stagnant; much of it was far too imitative of Western literary styles. The lyric and epic poetry that for centuries formed the basis of the Ottoman literary tradition had become stilted and bogged down in empty romanticism and obscure vocabulary that only the educated elite could understand and appreciate. But in 1908, a nationalist uprising of military students, army officers, progressive intellectuals, artists, and writers—dubbed the Young Turks— forced the Ottoman sultan, Abdülhamid II, to initiate a series of social and political reforms throughout the empire. At the same time, Turkish literature also underwent a transformation. A new crop of writers, reacting to their predecessors' blind imitation of Western literature, began laying the foundation for a distinctly Turkish literary style.

The Young Turk revolt, with its emphasis on the principles of nationalism, liberalism, and constitutionalism, hastened the dissolution of the Ottoman Empire and laid the foundation for the nationalist uprising led by Mustafa Kemal Atatürk in 1919. The most capable commander of the ill-fated Ottoman forces during World War I, Atatürk led the Turkish resistance against Allied attempts to carve up the Ottoman Empire as spoils of war. Under his command, the remaining members of the Ottoman army were able to repel Allied advances into the Turkish heartland until 1923, when the five-hundred-year-old

Ottoman Empire was dismantled and replaced by the Republic of Turkey, with Atatürk ("Father of the Turks") as its first president.

In the following decade, Atatürk embarked upon a series of political, economic, and cultural reforms intended to forcibly modernize, Westernize and secularize the new nation. These sweeping reforms included the establishment of the Turkish Language Association, whose purpose was to "cleanse" the Turkish language of its foreign (read: Persian and Arabic) elements. The emphasis on Turkish language and literature under Atatürk proved a boon to a new generation of postwar literary stars: Yakup Kadri Karaosmanoğlu, Reşat Nuri Güntekin, and perhaps the most renowned of all Turkish short-story writers, Sait Faik Abasınayık (see section VI), were all part of what was known as the National Literature Movement. Many of these writers focused their work on themes of naturalism and realism, as is evident in Refik Halit Karay's short story "The Gray Donkey," dealing with life in a traditional rural region of Turkey, far from cosmopolitan Istanbul.

These poets and writers would soon discover that the new Turkish Republic would be even less tolerant of political dissent than were the Ottoman sultans. Nevertheless, as the 1930s progressed and opposition to Atatürk's reforms grew, the loudest voices of dissent would belong to Turkey's literati. There were the superb memoirs of the great Turkish satirist Aziz Nesin (*Istanbul Boy*), whose works vividly portrayed the conflicts between East and West, between tradition and modernity. Perhaps the most influential writer of the time was the leftist poet Nâzım Hikmet, whose poetic style (he introduced free verse in Turkish poetry with such long-form poems as *The Epic of Sheikh Bedreddin*), political pronouncements ("I love my country:/I have swung on its plane trees, I have stayed in its prisons"), and revolutionary themes led to the censorship of his books and long periods of imprisonment. As we shall see, no other writer would leave a more lasting imprint on Turkish literature.

AZIZ NESIN

(1915—1995)

Istanbul Boy: A Memoir

(EXCERPT)

Translated from the Turkish by Joseph S. Jacobson

Peris and Demons

They often ask me, "How can you write so much?"

They say that some artists have *peris** which blow art on their souls. When *peris* are mentioned, I see an airmaid—something like a mermaid, whose upper part is girl and the bottom fish—she is bird below, and above, a ravishing beauty with golden hair. This half-bird, half-girl *peri* whispers inspiration into the ear of the artist on whose shoulder she perches. She gives him the copy.

I have no *peri*, but I have inspirational demons, witches, and fiends. Mine are not half-bird, half-girl; they are, at best, one-tenth human and the balance, monster. They don't perch on my shoulder, they climb on my back; I double up under them in blood and tears, tired and exhausted. I don't have just one demon or witch, I have herds and herds. If two of them get off, three more climb on my back.

Peris are of matchless beauty; witches, demons, of matchless ugliness.

Peris caress; demons strike, pinch, bite.

The inspirational fairy breathes into the ear of the artist on whose shoulder she perches; she inspires him.

---

* *Peri*: A fairy or supernatural being; derived from Persian mythology.

The witches, demons, and monsters who are on my back, who hurl themselves on me, ceaselessly command, force, and rebuke me.

"Write! Write, you! Don't stop; write! Why do you stop? Do you have the right to sleep, you? Wake up! Don't sit down—get up, quick! You can't get sick—pssst, come on, get up—write!"

My demons, witches, and monsters are the ones who demand the rent, those who ask for money, my creditors, my inexhaustible necessities.

If I didn't write, what would I do?

In all this world, there is nothing that will inspire and force an artist to work as much as holes in the soles of his shoes.

If it had been in my hands, I would have had the Universal Declaration of Human Rights add the following article:

"The right to get sick is man's most indisputable, irrefutable, natural, and social right; every human may get sick."

I have always envied the happy people who can lie down on their backs in bed when they get sick. In my life, which has extended half a century, I haven't used my right to get sick for even one small day; my inspirational witches and monsters won't leave me alone. They are in my dream at night, my daytime fancies, in my whole world.

"Write!"

I write.

"Write more."

I write more.

If I look at the emerald green meadows in the morning dew with longing in my heart, I want to stretch out at full length on the grass. If only I could stroll there in my bare feet, the fifty years of weariness would quickly flow from my feet through and under the skin of the earth.

Someday, somehow, I will take the final rest—but what a pity—then, I won't be able to know I am at rest.

When someone asks me, "How can you write so much?" really, I feel an anger that can't be shown.

"After all, do I write for pleasure? I am forced to, for I am in dire straits."

But if I were to be born again (something I don't believe in at all), if again I came to this world, I would like to be exhausted and go in the same way, in the same happy fatigue of such work.

If I write in very different genres, novel forms, and treat varied subjects, I think it is because of my living together with mixed people of different levels of our society and from different circles. Well, here are a few of the jobs I've done up to now: peddler, shepherd, soldier, accountant, painter, newsboy, bookstore clerk, private teacher, photographer, writer, newspaperman, groceryman, convict (that's a job, too, and one of the most difficult), unemployed (that's the hardest job of all), shoeshine boy, barber, and other jobs.

My memories are not great; I know that they don't ever have the smallest importance in themselves. But from the view of the lives of all of you, as a reflection of our society and the period in which we have lived, with the hope that this may attract your interest, I will relate my recollections to you, without falsehood or deceit.

The Koran, Sewing Machine, and Potty

I opened my eyes to a world on fire. My first recollection was of crimson flames covering the blackened sky. I can't recall anything before then. But that first memory, in all its detail, was indelibly etched on my mind. The fire awoke my mother. She took the blue satin, silver-embroidered sack containing the Holy Koran, which was hanging from the brass knob by the head of the bed, kissed it, and pressed it to her forehead. Then she hung the sack around my neck. She snatched my baby sister from the hammock.

From the window with open curtains could be seen a fire-red sky, belching fire, erupting flames, squirting sparks. On the ceiling, floor, walls, red lights were playing, expanding, contracting, long, then short. I looked in the mirror—it was filled with burning sky.

Someone was banging at the front door. Outside a senseless roar, yells and cries. Now and then the cry of a child or a woman's scream split the roar. I saw the sparks from the fire striking the window panes like great bugs . . . crackling sound, the voice of the fire. . . . The window pane suddenly vanished; it either melted or broke. A blast of heat hit my face.

The door broke and a gang of men poured in. They grabbed anything that came to hand and left. My mother thought these men were good Samaritans, trying to help us save our goods from the fire.

With me under one arm and my sister under the other, Mother took us down the stairs, put us outside the open door on the threshold, and dashed back into the house.

The men from the street crowded into the house, and as the ones inside came out with their loot, they trampled all over us. My mother hurried out, with the sewing machine under one arm and the potty in her hand. All that my eighteen-year-old mother could save from that fire was her two children, the Koran, the sewing machine, and the potty. The sewing machine was her dowry, which she had earned through her own hard labor. She had saved my sister's potty from the fire in her confusion.

These things that happened frightened me not a bit; we were at an evening celebration, it seemed to me like a holiday entertainment, and that's how it remained in my memory.

After the scene at the front door, the film snapped. I really don't know what happened between there and the cemetery.

When I awoke the next morning, we were at the cemetery. Evidently we'd spent the night in the open there. The cemetery was filled with the poor and their household goods that had been saved from the fire—bewildered people and crying children. My sister was lying in the hammock stretched between two cypresses.

Much later, I learned that the place where our house burned was above the Kasımpaşa quarter, in an area called New Fountain. This rented house we lived in was spoken of for years: "We, too, had a house in New Fountain."

The year would be 1919. My father wasn't around. He'd long since left us like that and gone to Anatolia. The War of Deliverance* was going on in Anatolia.

---

* War of Deliverance: A reference to the Greek-Turkish war of 1919–22.

Baby Mice in Olive Oil

After the cemetery, we were in a small one-story house. I don't know if it was the house of someone we knew, or if we had been taken from the cemetery to the house of someone who felt sorry for us.

The charitable family who gave us shelter in their poor little house was a man and wife. The man sold spices, such as black and red pepper, thyme and ginger, in the marketplace in the Kasımpaşa quarter of Istanbul.

It was winter and the man was splitting wood in the small yard by the house. As I watched him, his wife called, "Come away from there; you'll get hit by a flying chip!"

I backed off a short distance but still watched.

He set the wood to be split on a stump. First, he'd open a crack in the wood with the axe, then he'd stick a wedge, like a piece of wood, in the crack and strike this wedge with the heel of the axe so the log would split in half.

The sharp face of the axe gleamed as he raised it in the air. When the axe struck the log, there was a noise, "chop." He held the wood with one foot to keep it from jumping.

Again he raised the axe and struck . . . but he missed the wood and hit his foot. Blood spurted. I saw that his foot was split open.

Bottles were hanging from nails in the wooden siding of the little house. They poured thick fluid from one of those bottles on the wound and bound it up.

There were lots of mice in the house, baby mice too. They threw the newborn baby mice, which couldn't run away, into a bottle of olive oil. The bottle was hung on the outside wall of the house. In the sun, the baby mice dissolved in the olive oil and formed a thick liquid. This solution quickly healed cuts and wounds and knitted broken bones. It healed the man's cut foot and it got better.

We moved from that house, where we were guests, to a single room on the bottom floor of a two-story house in Kasımpaşa. The house stood beside a filthy stream, and in front there was a vegetable garden.

Two steps led to the double door of the front entrance. On the two doors were round iron plates with mounted rings, and flowers engraved on them. The entrance had been painted long, long ago. Now, all that remained of the paint were scales and blisters. When one of the rings was raised and struck, "knock knock," a voice would come from inside:

"Who is it?"

This was a liquid, moist, humid, woman's voice, coming from a far away.

I knew very well how the door was opened. Usually they said to me, "Run and open the door."

I would run. In order to open the front door, I went up the three sandstone stair steps. Since I wasn't tall enough to reach the iron bolt on the door, I would reach up on tiptoes to pull the latch.

The door opened and coolness would strike your face. You could smell cooking onions and, usually, dried beans too. If the three renters who lived on the ground floor all planned to cook beans, one would wash and soak them, the second boil them, and the third add them to the pot with the rest of the ingredients.

Walk down three sandstone steps to a wide stone courtyard paved with cracked and broken flagstones. Some are pitted in the middle. The room where we live is located to the left. A wooden five-step stair leads to it. On the right is a gate leading to the garden. Before entering the garden one sees another room. There "Uncle" Hasan and his wife, Eve, live. Directly opposite the courtyard is the kitchen. My "Aunt" Sarah lives to the right of the kitchen.

The owners of the house live upstairs. Our landlord is a stevedore steward, his wife is a black.

One wall of our room contains two windows that look out on the thinly flowing stream. Beyond that stream lies a garden, surrounded by a wall plated with rusty cans.

Sister's hammock cords stretch from wall to wall in the room, dividing it in two. Along the windowed wall is a wooden window seat upon which I climb to look outside.

On the opposite wall is a big cabinet. During the daytime, our bedding is stored inside.

My mother sets her sewing machine on a low wooden box and

sits in front on a hassock. She sews "ticker da ticker" American cloth enters the machine on her right side and long-legged men's underwear comes out on the left, army underwear. We can't manage on the money Mama earns from the army underwear. When it becomes dark—I mean really dark—my mother lights the no. 5 oil lamp. She then lifts the bedding from the cabinet and spreads it on the floor. She washes my face and feet and puts me to bed. She kisses me and says:

"Go to sleep now, my son."

She goes to her sewing machine and ceaselessly cranks the handle. If my sister in the hammock whimpers, she pulls the string, rocks her, and croons, "Sleep, my girl."

I pull the quilt over my head. My sister sleeps. Mother softly hums a plaintive tune.

Mama feeds us with the money she makes sewing army underwear from American cloth on her sewing machine. Later, she crocheted lace and did the embroidery used to decorate the edges of the kerchiefs with which the women of that day covered their heads. Because she couldn't see well at night under the economy oil lamp (called the night lamp), she crocheted the lace and embroidered during the day, and sewed underwear at night. I would drop off to sleep in my bed to the "ticker da ticker" of the sewing machine.

Nowadays you'll not find that kerchief embroidery anywhere. That multicolored thread embroidery is considered a valuable antique.

I used to imagine that my eighteen-year-old mother embroidered not with colored thread but with her tears and the light from her eyes. For a single one of those pieces of embroidery from my mother's hand I would now give all my books and all I will ever write.

The husband of Aunt Eve, who lives in the room across from us, is Black Sea Hasan, who works as a gardener at the Navy Yard.

They have a nursing baby, too. They, like us, have a hammock stretched from wall to wall in the single room where they live. The hammock cuts the room in two.

Aunt Eve would say, "Will you rock the hammock?" I rocked it while she cooked. At that time, they had me memorize *Kulhuwallahi* (Say, He is God). I didn't like to sing lullabies, so when no one was in the room I would keep saying over and over, *"Kulhuwallahi,"* as I rocked the hammock. When the baby went to sleep, Aunt Eve would give me a slice of bread spread with curds.

The Child Promised unto God

My three-year-old sister became sick; her legs wouldn't hold her. Years later, I realized that it was the bone disease, rickets, caused by nutritional deficiency and want of proper care.

How about the doctor, the medicine? We had heard only the doctor's name. To us, he seemed a creature of luxury, unattainable for consultation, whose voice we probably would never hear. When a child died it was said, "Allah giveth and Allah taketh away." If my sister had received proper nourishment—food and medicine under a doctor's care—she would have been well long before this. They tried all the quack medicines, the home remedies that could be prepared without spending money. When those failed, my mother was told of another way to cure her:

"In the evening, when the evening prayers are to be recited, take the child to the cemetery and leave her by a gravestone, then return home without looking back and without shedding a single teardrop. Someone will follow you and bring the child back home."

Mama explained to Sister that in order to get well, to be able to walk like she used to, in order to run and play, it would have to be done this way. She must not cry when she was left in the graveyard. My sister was an intelligent, beautiful girl.

Every evening, Mother would take my sister in her arms and me by the hand. We would go to the Çürüklük cemetery, which lies between Kasımpaşa and Beyoğlu. The dense cypresses at the cemetery made the evening shadows even deeper; in this gloominess the gravestones loomed larger. When sounds of the evening prayer spread out from the minarets, Mother would leave my sister by a gravestone, take my hand, and, without looking back, hurry away. It went on like this for months, until winter. Not once did Mother turn and look back, nor did my three-year-old sister, left at the foot of a gravestone, cry or make a sound.

I couldn't see my mother's face beneath her veil, but who knows what she suffered to keep from crying on the way. Upon coming home, she would throw herself on the mattress and sob her eyes out until someone brought my sister home later.

I've thought a great deal about the consequences of leaving a sick child in a graveyard as a last resort for making him well. The poor, without doctors and medicines, who don't even have the power to feed their children, beg of God:

"Oh God! Here, I've left my child to you; bury my youngster's sickness in the earth; give him back to me alive and well!"

The Wishing Well

There was no news from my father. We didn't know where he was or what he was doing. Perhaps he had even died in battle. The women were discussing the situation among themselves: There was the Wishing Well . . . When you looked down that well, if the lost person still lived, he would appear. If he were dead, either nothing would appear or a coffin would be seen.

Two neighbor women and my mother went to the Wishing Well, taking me along. (Years later, I revisited the well, which was located on the hill in the Eyup quarter behind the Pierre Loti Coffeehouse.) When they arrived at the well, my mother said, "Don't come further; you wait back here!"

They walked up to the well and leaned their heads over the rather high, round stone abutment surrounding the wellhead. Slowly I sidled up to them and, among the skirts of their black *charshafs*,* I too, leaned over the stone abutment and gazed down. I saw my father distinctly; he passed by in a boat in the water at the bottom of the well. This was definitely an illusion created by a child's mind, but I was convinced I'd seen my father in the flesh, alive.

Mother and the other women hadn't been able to see my father. But, because I had gone to the well without their permission, I couldn't tell them, "I saw my father."

---

* *Charshaf:* A black garment that covers a woman from head to toe.

Wild Plum and Pine Needle Remedies

One day, when someone knocked, I opened the front door. Facing me stood a decrepit man with burned and crinkled eyebrows, eyelashes, and hair. I was scared and yelled, "Mother!" But the man at the door said, "My son! Don't you know me?" and grabbed me and held me in his arms.

My father had barely escaped with his life from a mosque filled with people, doused with gasoline and set afire by the retreating enemy.

The day my father came home, he fell into bed and lay there, out of his head for months. Mother, sewing more soldiers' underwear and crocheting more lace than ever before, also took care of my father.

Papa had become extremely weak. He couldn't get up from the bed, which was spread on the floor by the wall-bench. He made a medicine from a number of herbs. From time to time, the fever would come, but, burning in the heat, he shivered and yelled at Mother: "Cover me, Ma'am!" Even when he was angriest, he still called my mother "Ma'am."

I can't remember just what my mother said to my father or how she addressed him. She simply didn't say anything; I heard her say nothing at all. However, when she talked with other women, she spoke of him as *Bizim Efendi* (Our Sir) or *Efendi* (The Gentleman). Sometimes, when talking with someone she considered very close, she would call him *Bizimki* (Ours).

"Cover me, Ma'am! Quick! Cover me up."

She covered Father with blankets and quilts, coats, overcoats, and anything else there was for covers. The top of the bed would turn into a small hill. But Father, as if the cause of his chill was my mother, still yelled at her in anger: "Ma'am, I said cover me up!"

One day he was shaking so much in that bed that it seemed to me the floorboards were creaking.

"Hurry, get me some green plums—unripe wild plums—"

Father was a very stern, hot-tempered man. Whatever his wish, he would certainly see it done. He probably wanted some sour plums to eat because his insides burned from the high fever.

Mother went to the nearby orchard, picked some wild plums, and returned. Father ate those tiny plums with his face all puckered up. The following day he got to his feet; he had become well. He knew that his getting well was due to the wild plums. For years afterward, he proclaimed: "The wild plums saved me from the sickness. Otherwise I would have died."

And he loved to exaggerate: "That day I ate two pecks of plums!" What he ate was one handful of plums.

During those times, my father suffered frequent headaches. When his head ached, he stuck pine needles up his nose. When the blood started to flow, the headaches would stop and he felt better.

First Death

One day, Papa brought apples home. "Turn your back," he told me. I turned my face to the wall, and an apple fell in front of me, then one more.

Then Father said, "Look! God sent you these apples. Pray."

The God who sent the apples didn't make my sister well. My sister died.

When father carried the tiny coffin across the stone threshold, I thought it was a game, and I laughed toward Aunt Sarah, who stood at the room door. This was going to be a game; they would leave my sister in this little wooden box at the graveyard. There, she would get well and come running home.

"Take the boy inside!" they said.

They put me in the room. Crying, my mother came to me and kissed me.

"Your sister died; you shouldn't laugh!" she told me.

Understanding that I had done something bad, I was ashamed.

Always I'm asked why, or how, I became a humorist—I don't know. But I think the thing that made me a humorist must be my own life. My way here was along a path of tears.

The First Unrequitted Love

Uncle Hasan, our neighbor in the next room, worked as a gardener at the Kasımpaşa Naval Headquarter, called the Divanhane. He raised flowers and vegetables in the yard. Because I tried to imitate him in hoeing the garden, he used to hang the hoe out of my reach on top of a long pole that was stuck in the ground. When no one was looking, I would shake the pole to bring down the hoe and dig in the garden.

At the rear of the garden, the landlord kept chickens in a coop, and their continual meandering and scratching in their tiny screened run made me feel sad for them, so I would open their gate and let them loose. As soon as they got out, the rooster would rush at me and scratch and peck my face. His shiny red feathers and great comb were very beautiful, but he was a monster of a rooster, who knew nothing of love or compassion. He would bristle up—the feathers of his puffed-out chest and thick neck shimmering and changing color in the sunlight—and when he attacked me I would run inside the coop and close the gate. Though he couldn't take revenge on me, he jumped again and again at the gate; definitely, he was my enemy.

I used to give the rooster the slice of bread that Aunt Eve gave me for swinging her baby to sleep in the hammock. After he'd attacked me, leaving scratches and wounds on my face from his beak and claws, and chased me inside the coop, he would eat the bread. No one but me ever let him outside his prison cage or gave him bread.

One day he made such a brutal attack on me, clawed and scratched me so unjustly and treacherously, that I fell to the ground in trying to get away. The landlord's son came to my rescue. My face was covered with blood. When I learned of their decision to butcher the rooster, I went into the laundry closet, where no one was, and started to cry. They were trying to catch the rooster and he was fleeing for his life. He was squawking in the garden—I was bawling indoors.

I went to Uncle Hasan and begged and also promised the landlord's son:

"I will never go out in the yard again."

"I will never again open the chicken-coop door."

"May bread strike me; may the Koran strike me (if I lie)."

When they saw my tears, they didn't butcher the rooster.

Yet I sneaked into the garden again one day. I shook and shook the pole until the hoe fell down. It fell, but right on me; the pointed end stuck in my forehead. I pulled the hoe out with my hand. I was all bloody. I went to our room. All the women from the house were there. When they saw me in all that blood, they screamed together. Their screams scared me, so I began to cry. They pressed a handful of salt, and on top of that some tobacco, on the place where the blood was flowing, and bandaged it.

Because I never went out into the garden after that, they said, "Look how smart he got since he bashed his head."

As a matter of fact, it wasn't because I hurt my head that I didn't go out, but because I was afraid they would slaughter the rooster.

I Came to the World to Laugh; I Cry and Don't Know Why

The most beautiful house along Crap Creek is the house where Hafiz Recep Efendi lives; its outside is painted a very light yellow. Hafiz Recep's voice is also very beautiful. He's quite a famous person; he sings, too.

An old woman, who seemed rather rich to us, lived in the house next to Hafiz Recep's house. She liked me a lot.

Our landlord's son, Mehmet Efendi, is to be married. The bride is a Circassian maiden—what a beauty, a delicate beauty! You know those henna spots on the skins of Yapıncak grapes? . . . Well, there were some of those little Yapıncak henna freckles on the bride's face. The wedding was scheduled to be held in the garden by the house.

I was well over the age for circumcision. My mother kept thinking about it. How could she arrange for my circumcision? It would cost a lot of money.

At the time of the wedding between the handsome Kurdish youth, Mehmet Efendi, and the lovely Circassian maiden, my circumcision suddenly came about.

We had no bedstead in our house. We slept on beds spread on the floor. In the morning, the bedclothes were gathered up and put in the storage chest. (When we moved to another place with no storage space, we folded the bedding, piled it in a corner of the room, and covered it with a spread.

For my circumcision, we borrowed a nightgown and bedstead from a neighbor. Another neighbor lent a set of bedding. The circumcision bed was set up in a corner of the garden.

If it had been up to my father, there wouldn't have been anything. He wasn't unconcerned, but he acted as if he were because he didn't want to reveal our destitution and poverty.

My mother placed a circumcision cap on my head; *Mashallah* (God wills it!) was embroidered on it. She must have borrowed that from someone too. Then I put on my holiday clothes: velvet pants, satin shirt, a red-bowed sash. My mother took me to the house of that rather rich woman, who lived next to Hafiz Recep, for hand-kissing.

In the evening the celebration began. It was a very rich celebration for that neighborhood. There was a magician, singing, dancing— something like a theater—lots of things.

Mehmet Efendi became my *kirve* (godfather). In Eastern provinces, godfatherhood meant being above, and closer than, relatives. The one who smears the boy's circumcision blood on his hand becomes the godfather. The godfather protects his godson throughout his lifetime; that's the tradition.

I suffered for months after the circumcision. My circumcision was one of those they called "membranous". . . . Days and days of boric acid solution dressings. You know how very old trees rot, get hollow and full of toadstools? You rub this between your fingers and it makes a brown powder. That dry tree-rot powder was also sprinkled on the wound.

The only person who gave me a present at my circumcision celebration was that rather rich neighbor woman. It was a small camel, carved of wood—a waxed, brown, shiny camel. The hump was a lid that had two tiny yellow hinges. When you raised the hump there was an inkwell inside. When I saw the camel inkwell, I forgot the pain of the circumcision. I took the camel to bed with me. My father gave me a silver Mejid.*

---

* Mejid: An Ottoman coin.

A woman was singing; she was likely Jewish. It seems that I can still hear her voice, a cracked, hoarse, muffled, deep voice:

I came to the world to laugh;
I cry and don't know why.
. . . Where are you my tiny camel inkwell? . . .
I cry and don't know why.
. . . I came to the world—my little camel, my little camel inkwell,
where are you now; where, oh where did you go? . . .

Fergap Fesini Kap (Fergap, Grab His Fez)

I was enrolled in the neighborhood school, far from our home. You go along the creek to Uzun Caddesi, walk its length, and turn left past the police station; from there, you continue on up the hill opposite the Greek grocery on your right. Our neighborhood school is a house there. My *hoca* (religious teacher) is a Tatar woman. And she has three grown daughters who seem pretty to me.

It was during the time of the White Russian exodus into Istanbul.* I know this from two things: First, my father brought home very large banknotes. They had Latin numbers on them, and beside those numbers were several zeros—three, five, or six zeros—it was Russian money. After the revolution, as the White Russians were escaping, they smuggled out sack after sack of this money. Father had bought two or three of these banknotes. Others had purchased a lot more.

They figured the czar was destined to be reinstated and they would become millionaires with this money. Though the revolutionaries had invalidated this currency, there were people who hadn't lost their hope of becoming millionaires by hoarding these czarist banknotes for a short time.

Father bought one of them, with a whole string of zeros on it, for a nickel.

---

* While Russian exodus: A reference to the mass migration of non-Communist (dubbed "White" as opposed to the Communist "Red") Russians after the Bolshevik Revolution of 1917.

I learned also of the White Russians' coming to Istanbul from a beautiful Russian woman who stayed at the school. She was very talented and made big lampshades decorated with silken cloth and floss. When we schoolkids saw one of those big lampshades on the ceiling, we were astounded; it seemed to us, at that time, something like a spaceship.

As in all the neighborhood schools, we students sat on the floor cross-legged before low writing desks, with fezzes on our heads. I wore my first fez while going to the school.

We learned how to tack letter to letter; then we recited and memorized the prayer verses from the *Amme Cuzu*.*

Tracing the words on paper with a reed dipped in the sooty ink, we started the writing class with this prayer:

"*Rabbi yessir vela tuassir, Rabbi temmim, bilhyar!*"

In Turkish: "Oh Creator! Make my work easy, don't make it difficult! Have me finish my work auspiciously!"

At the beginning of every writing class, we recited this Arabic prayer we'd memorized, without even knowing what it meant.

The day came when it was my turn at the board, and I rocked from side to side and recited the "*Elem neshrah leke.*" (This, I later learned, was the "Chapter of Gladness.")

Why, and how, did we little boys memorize all those Arabic words without knowing what any of them meant nor understanding what the passages conveyed? What things they filled our heads with!

As five-year-olds, we memorized:

"*Elem neshrah leke sadrek. Ve veda'na anke vizrek. Ellezi enkade zahrek. Ve refa'na leke zikrek. Fe'inne ma'al'usri yusra. Inne ma'al'usri yusra Fe'iza feragte fensab. Ve ila Rabbike fergap.*"

Maybe you're curious; in Turkish it means:

"Oh Muhammed! Have we not opened Thy heart? Of course we have opened it. We bent our backs and took the burden from Thy shoulders. We raised Thy glory. Because with strength in unity there is doubtless a means. Therefore, one work's completion is the beginning

---

* *Amme Cuzu*: A section of the Qur'an from chapter 78 to the end, used as an Arabic reading book in schools.

of the next. And what thou hopest for, expect only from God."

We weren't taught the Turkish version of these chapters we were required to memorize. Was it because the Turkish was more difficult than the Arabic?

In class one day, I was reciting this chapter and as soon as I said the last line, "*Ve ila Rabbike fergap!*" my fez suddenly flew into the air. Startled, I looked up; there my fez was on the end of the *hoca*'s stick. How on earth did the fez jump off my head to hang by its tassel on the stick?

As soon as I had said "*fergap*," my *hoca* had responded "*Fesini kap*" (snatch his fez) and whipped the fez from my head.

I had no idea what was going on, and in my fear and embarrassment didn't want to ask for the return of my fez. When I get home my mother will raise hell, I thought. If I said the *hoca* took it, would she believe me? Those days, buying another fez for me was something like buying a new cabinet stereo now.

I came home crying. I didn't wish them to see me crying, so I wiped my face and eyes. I confessed hesitantly to my mother, "Mother, the *hoca* took my fez."

Exclaiming, "*Mashallah, Mashallah!*" Mama kissed and hugged me in delight.

That was the tradition: As a boy, learning to recite the Qur'an, mastered the Inshirah chapter and pronounced the word *fergap*, the *hoca* would say, "*Fesini kap*" and take his fez from his head. This was the way he informed the parents that the boy had passed. It was something like the promotion report card of today. One must then take a tray of *börek* (cheese pastry) or *helva* (honeycake) to the *hoca* to retrieve the fez. My mother made a tray of the cheaper *böreks*, took them to the *hoca*, and got my fez back.

Mother was very sad that she could not take a tray of the more expensive *helva*. Somehow I can't make my own children understand now what that sadness meant.

The Cloth Bag

The neighborhood school is far . . . winter, cold, snow . . . I don't have an overcoat. . . . I am cold, my hands are freezing.

Mother sewed a khaki-colored bag from thick cloth to put my book and notebook in. Since my hand was so cold that I couldn't hold the bag, I stuck it under my arm. And to shield my hands from the cold, I held them under the bag.

Going to and from school, my hands ached continually. When I came home one afternoon, Mother asked, "Where's your bag?"

I looked down under my arm: there was no bag. On the way, my hands had gone numb, my fingers lost their feeling, and I'd been unaware of the bag's falling. I retraced my steps—searched and searched: there was no bag.

Father, however, related the incident in a much different fashion:

"I had bought my son a brand new bag—a very expensive bag—a very nice bag—a sturdy bag. The bag had three pockets . . . the bag had a lock . . . He dropped that nice bag the very first time he took it to school, and just because his hands were cold . . . Shame on you, son! And when I asked, 'Where is your bag?' and he couldn't see it under his arm, he started to cry. 'Don't cry, my boy; I'll get you a better one,' I said. So I bought him a nicer bag."

That's the way Father told it. Through repeating and repeating it, he really came to believe what he said. Father was prone to state as fact that which actually existed only in his heart—what he hoped. He spoke of his wishes, believing they had become truth. Never could I say, "Father, that's not how it was." He could narrate the story with a smile and, smiling, I would listen.

Most of us are ashamed of our poverty, as if it were our own fault. I too was ashamed of my poverty for years, right up until I became a writer. Upon beginning my work as a writer, I finally understood that in a country where the majority is poor, it isn't poverty that is to be ashamed of, but wealth.

There are some people who are ashamed of being rich and hide their wealth. One year, a week or so after the holiday of the 27th of May, a friend of mine (a newspaper owner) and I were on the car ferry, seated in his Cadillac.

"I'm going to sell this Cadillac," he announced.

"What for?"

"Well, when we're going down the road, those on foot look at this car in such a way that I'm ashamed of being seen in it. I'm going to sell it and buy a cheap car."

For us poor people, being ashamed of wealth doesn't last long—only one or two days out of twenty or thirty years.

On that snowy winter day when I lost my cloth bag, Father hadn't bought me a new one; on the contrary, Mother immediately sewed another bag from some old thick cloth.

NÂZIM HIKMET

(1901–1963)

Selected Poems

Translated from the Turkish by
Fuat Engin
Randy Blasing and Mutlu Konuk
Deniz Perin

I Love My Country

I love my country:
I have swung on its plane trees, I have stayed in its prisons.
Nothing can overcome my spleen
as the songs and tobacco of my country.

My country:
Bedreddin, Sinan, Yunus Emre,[*] and Sakarya,[†]
lead domes and factory chimneys
are all the work of my people
who even hiding from themselves
smile under their drooping mustaches.

My country.
My country is so large:
it seems that it is endless to go around.

---

[*] Bedreddin: A preacher and theologian who launched a rebellion against
Ottoman rule in the early 1400s. Sinan: Chief architect under Ottoman Sultans
Süleyman I, Selim II, and Murad III. Yunus Emre: Thirteenth-century poet
and Sufi dervish.
[†] Sakarya: Turkish province in the Marmara region.

Edirn, Izmir, Ulukıshla, Marash, Trabzon, Erzurum.*
I know the Erzurum plateau only in its songs
and I am ashamed
not to have crossed Tauruses even once
to go to the cotton pickers
                              in the south.

My country:
camels, train, Fords and sick donkeys,
poplar
              willow
                          and red earth.

My country.
The trout which likes
pine forests, best freshwaters and the lakes
                              at the top of mountains,
              and at least half a kilo,
                          with red reflections on its scaleless, silver skin
                                        swims in the Abant lake of Bolu.

My country:
goats on the Ankara plain:
the sheen of blond, silky, long furs.
The fat plump hazelnuts of Giresun.
The fragrant red-checked apples of Amasya,
olive
              fig
                          melon
and of all colors
                          bunches and bunches of grapes
and then the plow

* Edirn, etc.: Cities and provinces in Turkey.

and then the black ox
and then: ready to accept
                        everything
            advanced, beautiful and good
                        with the joyous admiration of a child
my hard-working, honest, brave people
                        half hungry, half full
                                        half slave. . . .

Translated by Fuat Engin

The Epic of Sheikh Bedreddin (excerpt)

1.

On the divan, Bursa silk in green-branching red boughs;
a blue garden of Kütahya tiles on the wall;
wine in silver pitchers;
and lambs in copper pots roasted golden brown.
Strangling his own brother with a bowstring
— anointing himself with a gold bowl of his brother's blood—
Sultan Memet* had ascended the throne and was sovereign.
Memet was sovereign,
but in the land of Osman[†]
the wind was a fruitless cry, a death song.
The peasants' work done by the light of their eyes
and the sweat of their brows
                        was a fief.
The cracked water jugs were dry—
at the springs, horsemen stood twirling their mustaches.
On the roads, a traveler could hear the wail of men without land
                        and land without men.

* Sultan Memet (Mehmet II): Ottoman sultan from 1444 to 1446 and 1451 to 1481.
† Sultan Osman: Founder of the Ottoman Empire (1258–1326).

And as foaming horses neighed and swords clashed
                    outside the castle door where all roads led,
the marketplace was in chaos,
                    the guilds had lost faith in their masters.
In short, there was a sovereign, a fief, a wind, a wail.

2.

This is Iznik Lake.*
Still.
Dark.
Deep
It's like a well
        in the mountains.

Around here lakes
are smoky.
Their fish taste flat,
their marshes breed malaria,
and the men die
        before their beards turn white.

This is Iznik Lake.
Beside it stands the town of Iznik.
In the town of Iznik
the blacksmith's anvil is a broken heart.
The children go hungry.
The women's breasts are like dried fish.
And the young men don't sing. . . .

This is the town of Iznik.
This is a house in the workers' quarter.
In this house
lives an old man named Bedreddin.

* Iznik Lake: Lake in northwestern Turkey near which Sheikh Bedreddin was
exiled and from which he launched his insurrection.

Small build,
      big beard—
           white.
Eyes like a child's, sly and slanted,
and yellow fingers like reeds.
Bedreddin
sits
on a white sheepskin.
He's writing *Foundations*[*]
           in Persian script.
Down on their knees, they sit across from him.
And from a distance
they look at him as if staring at a mountain.
Head shaved
eyebrows bushy,
he looks:
tall and rangy Mustafa.
He looks:
hawk-nosed Kemal.[†]
They don't tire of looking
and cannot look enough—
they gaze at the Iznik exile Bedreddin.

9.

It was hot
The clouds were full.
The first drop was about to fall like a sweet word.
All
     of a sudden,
as if streaming down from the rocks,
        raining down from the sky,
               and springing up from the ground,

---

[*] *The Foundations*: Treatise written by Bedreddin while in exile at Iznik.
[†] Kemal: Mustafa Kemal Atatürk, founder of the modern Turkish Republic in 1923.

Bedreddin's braves faced the Prince's army
like the last act of this earth.
With flowing white robes,
       bare heads,
            bare feet, and bare swords. . . .

A great battle took place.

Turkish peasants from Aydın,
      Greek sailors from Chios,
          Jewish tradesmen,
Mustafa's ten thousand heretical comrades
plunged into the forest of enemies like ten thousand axes.
The ranks of green-and-red flags,
      inlaid shields,
         and bronze helmets
were torn apart,
but when the day descended into night in pouring rain,
the ten thousand were two thousand.

That they might sing as one voice
and together pull the nets from the water,
that they might all work iron like lace
and all together plow the earth,
that they might eat the honeyed figs together,
that they might say,
         "Everywhere
            all together
       in everything
           but the lover's cheek,"
the ten thousand lost eight thousand. . . .

They were defeated.

The victors wiped their bloody swords
on the flowing white robes
         of the defeated.

And the earth brothers had worked all together
like a song sung together
was ripped up
     by the hooves of horses bred in the Edirn palace.

Don't say
     it's the necessary result
          of historical, social, and economic conditions—
                    I know!
My head bows before the thing you mention.
But my heart
     doesn't speak that language.
It says,
"O fickle Fate,
O cruel Fate!"
And they pass one by one,
shoulders slashed by whips,
          faces bloodied—
in a flash they pass,
bare feet crushing my heart—
the defeated of Karaburun pass through Aydın. . . .

10.

They stopped at dark.
It was he who spoke:
"The city of Seljuk has set up shop.
Now whose neck, friends,
       whose neck is it now?"

The rain
     kept up.
They spoke
     and told him:
"It isn't
     set up—
         it will be.

The wind hasn't
    quit—
        it will.
His throat isn't
    Slit—
        it will be."

As rain seeped into the folds of darkness,
I appeared at their side
and said:
"Where are Seljuk's city gates?
        Show me, so I can go!
Does it have a fortress?
Tell me, and I'll raze it!
Is there a toll?
    Speak, so I don't pay it!"

Now it was he who spoke:
"Seljuk's gates are narrow.
        You can't come and go.
It has a fortress
    not so easy to raze.
Go away, roan-horsed brave,
        go on your way. . . ."

I said: "I can come and go!"
I said: "I can raze and set fires!"
He said: "The rain has ended,
      it's getting light.
    The headsman Ali
        is calling
          Mustafa!
Go away, roan-horsed brave, yiğit,*
        go on your way. . . ."

Translated by Randy Blasing and Mutlu Konuk

---

* *Yiğit*: A hero or brave warrior.

Since I Was Thrown Inside

Since I was thrown inside,
        the earth has orbited the sun ten times.
If you ask it:
    "Not even worth mentioning,
      a microscopic time."
If you ask me:
    "Ten years of my life."

I had a pencil
        the year I was thrown inside.
I used it all up in a week.
If you ask it:
    "A whole life."
If you ask me:
    "Come on now, just one week."

Since I was thrown inside,
        Osman, doing time for murder,
           finished his seven and a half years and left,
           drifted around for a while,
           was thrown back inside for smuggling,
           did six months and was rereleased,
           his letter came yesterday, he's married,
           his child will be born in the spring.

They're ten years old now,
      the children who were conceived
        the year I was thrown inside.
And that year's trembling, long-legged colts
      have long turned into confident, wide-rumped mares.
But the olive seeds are still olive seeds,
        they're still children.

New squares have cropped up in my faraway city
        since I was thrown inside.

And my loved ones
   are living on a street I don't know
      in a house I've never seen.

Bread was white, fluffy as cotton
     the year I was thrown inside.
Then it was rationed
and here, inside, the people beat each other
    for a pitch-black, fist-size piece.
Now it flows freely again,
but dark and tasteless.

The year I was thrown inside,
    the second war hadn't started yet,
the ovens at Dachau weren't lit,
the atom bomb hadn't dropped on Hiroshima.

Time flowed like the blood of a child whose throat's been slit.
Then that chapter officially ended,
and now the U.S. dollar speaks of a third.

Yet, in spite of everything, the days have shone
     since I was thrown inside,
and from the edges of darkness,
    the people, pressing their heavy hands to the pavement,
       have begun to rise.

Since I was thrown inside
     the earth has orbited the sun ten times
and just as passionately I repeat
    what I wrote
     the year I was thrown inside:
"The people, who are plentiful as ants on the ground
     as fish in the sea
       as birds in the sky,
who are cowardly, courageous,
    ignorant, supreme

              and childlike,
it is they who crush
    and create,
it is but their exploits sung in songs."
        And as for the rest,
             my ten-year incarceration, for instance,
                  it's all meaningless words.

Translated by Deniz Perin

REFIK HALIT KARAY

(1888—1965)

The Gray Donkey

Translated from the Turkish by Robert P. Finn

THE CHILDREN CARRYING water from the river brought the news that there was an old man lying on the mountain road. There was a gray donkey there, too, wandering about by himself. Hüsmen *Hoca**　said:

"Let's go and see."

It was near evening. A thick, pungent cloud rose from the ricefields and spread toward a swampy, malaria-infested hollow where two creeks united. From behind the split, charred trunks of five or ten old, lifeless willows, the sun extended a dim light that glinted here and there on the stagnant waters. These lighted patches looked like open stretches in a cloudy sky above the middle of a gray, damp plain. Slowly, they became cloudy and closed and were swallowed up.

Three villagers climbed up the broken, muddy footpath with difficulty, one behind the other. One of them coughed very heavily, like a horse with parasites.

First they saw the gray donkey. It was standing in the middle of the heath, in a dirty, dusty spot. No doubt it had been jumping about, rolling, and playing; now it was taking its ease with a pleased expression, nonchalantly surveying the setting sun.

The *hoca* called out:

"Well, where are you, traveler?"

On the other side an old, exhausted man was sitting with his back to a tired-out wild pear tree and breathing heavily. He looked at the newcomers with lusterless eyes and pointed with his hands to his chest.

---

* *Hoca:* A teacher or master.

He answered the questions "What's the matter?" and "What's wrong, Pop?" with incomprehensible answers in a gasping rattle that resembled breathing or sighing more than speech.

The villagers, thinking that he was dying, sank down beside him and waited all together. But the sick man was recovering and becoming more lively. He was poorly dressed, with a cotton turban and a purple robe. The part of his face that was left uncovered by his rough, gray beard had been roasted by the sun and was covered with wrinkles and folds. Underneath his loose, thick eyelids, his small eyes were such a light shade of blue that they were almost white. They stared out at people with the openness of a child's glance. Gradually, color came to his face and brightness to his eyes. At the same time, he said some things in an exhausted voice with his back still supported against the pear tree, no doubt relating how he had come from great distances and would travel on to the same. At Hüsmen *Hoca*'s proposal—"Take him to the guest room, and let him lie there!"—they all helped him to mount the donkey. They descended with a thousand difficulties, sliding over stones and earth and holding on to both sides to give him no opportunity to fall.

The sun had gone, and the waters behind it shone no more. Putting their giant heads wrapped with smoke and clouds toward one another, the large, steep mountains surrounding them had long since gone to sleep.

The village lay buried in layers of shadows of cliffs, waiting for darkness, with neither a light in a window nor a sound in the road.

An occasional face extended itself from a window in response to the uproar of those arriving. The oxen were lowing in the stables. Hüsmen shouted the news:

"Where are you, everybody? Come on out, we have a guest!"

Then a number of people, wearing their white underwear, emerged with illuminated lamps in their hands and went straight toward the guest room of the village. They moved puzzledly in a haze of smoke and light, sending flashes of light into darkened corners with their lamps and, inadvertently, kicking hardened lumps of manure. This was one of the naked, trackless, wretched villages of Anatolia, two days by road from the nearest town. Sometimes, when the weather was very dry and allowed the opportunity to ford the Kızılırmak, travelers passing on foot from one province to another would leave the highway, pass by this village, and thereby save themselves two days' travel. By this means, then, five or ten people in a year—five or ten poor, exhausted strangers—would come at a dismal hour like this and knock at the doors of the villagers. At that time Hüsmen, the headman, would send word to the person whose turn it was to put up the visitors and that person would settle the travelers in his guest room, where, whether it was winter or summer, an oven would be burning seemingly inexhaustible chips of fuel. The village would learn of the state of the world from the lies and misinformation brought by these arrant, ignorant people.

The sick man quieted down.

"It's the chest," he said. "Every once in a while it pulls."

One of the villagers hung a copper bucket filled with milk on the hook of the fireplace. The flames of the chips beat on it, and the liquid inside began to rise in colors like a soap bubble. The villagers took it down and gave a cup of it to the old man. He drank it greedily, blowing on it as he did so. As soon as the milk was finished, the old codger began to cry. His whole body was shaking. The villagers sat cross-legged across from him and waited impatiently for an opportunity to speak. The young men stood in front of the door, their eyes narrowed with sleep. They could understand nothing of this silent, sick guest. His crying didn't stop. On the contrary, it became more frequent, and deeper. At one point the sick man motioned with his hands for the men to come nearer. With Hüsmen first and the other, older men behind him, they surrounded the old man. The youths remained at the door, full of curiosity but not daring to approach any nearer; the traveler was probably relating some problem with difficulty. Perhaps he was making his will. Every once in a while, they heard Hüsmen say:

"Don't worry. Relax, we'll take care of you." Suddenly the old men quickly bent down to the floor. Then they suddenly stood up. Hüsmen muttered:

"He's gone to his rest!" One of the logs in the fireplace fell and illuminated the face of the dead man with a sharp light, then went out. Outside, a donkey brayed continuously.

The traveler had found time to make his last request. He was donating the eight pieces of gold he had stuck in his belt, together with his gray donkey, to the Hejaz.*

The villagers, returning from the cemetery, couldn't figure out what they would do with the donkey and the money remaining in their hands, or how they would carry out the old man's request. They stood discussing this under the grape arbor. Finally, they decided to go to town and seek information from the judge. Within the week, Hüsmen would take the donkey with him and set off.

The animal achieved some importance; generous supplies of grain were placed in front of him, and corn husks spread for him. This was done uncomplainingly, respectfully, promptly, as if it were a religious duty. The villagers would frequently remember and ask one another, "Has the gray donkey been taken to be watered? Has he been given barley?"

One morning, at first light, they all accompanied Hüsmen *Hoca* as far as the mill and bade him farewell. The gray donkey, tied to the *hoca*'s donkey, went happily, unburdened, his tail waving. The silver rays of the sun made Hüsmen's faded felt sheath glow like velvet.

The road was a long and boring one. Once the blades of rice protruding from still waters and the green of the reeds growing along the banks of the ditches were hidden behind the slopes, the dry and straight way continued, desolate and scorched, for over two days, without passing by a village, a mill, or even a waterhole shaded by two undersize willows. Then an ascent with steep cliffs and a fearful pass presented itself. At the top of the hill, a cool breeze and a pleasant view appeared. A narrow creek gleamed like the back of a short sword from the middle of the groups of quince and apple trees; it seemed lush, green, and fertile. The white, flat road, outlined by telegraph poles, stretched in coils toward the mountains.

Hüsmen set out for the government building early in the morning, after he had spent the night in an inn.

The tiny town had a mansion with balconies and towers that looked like a pavilion in a park. It had, however, never been completed. The unplastered brick walls had opened in spots and become nesting places

---

* Hejaz: The region of the Arabian Peninsula that includes the holy cities of Mecca and Medina.

for pigeons. The top floor stood waiting with its scaffolding, windowless and plasterless. On one side there was an abandoned limestone quarry, and a little to the other side stood an open shed remaining from when the workers had been there, with everything left just as it had been. The building had long since begun to fall apart.

A police sergeant with no hat or jacket asked Hüsmen what he wanted. The *hoca* started to tell the story of the old man from the very beginning, relating how the children coming from the stream carrying water had brought the news that they had found him. Before Hüsmen had reached the halfway point in his story, the policeman casually walked away from him and began to throw bread to the ducks swimming in the river, then turned to a turbaned old man smoking a *nargile** in the hut in the corner and asked:

"What's that, *hoca efendi*, your morning pick-me-up?"

When Hüsmen learned that the judge had gone to Istanbul on leave, he wanted to at least tell his business to the *kaymakam*.† Leaving his shoes at the door and walking humbly in the ripped socks that exposed his toes, he folded his hands before him and began his story.

The *kaymakam* was a nasal, toothless kind of person, who wore a discolored, indigo blue jacket and dyed his mustache. Without showing the forbearance of even listening to the entire story, he said:

"Call the sergeant!"

For five days, Hüsmen *Hoca* wandered around the town, telling his tale to all he came across. The police sergeant would neither take the donkey nor let him go. At last, someone emerged who sympathized with Hüsmen and who persuaded the sergeant by saying: "Let him go and come back in two weeks. Let's leave the whole thing up to the judge."

The judge from this place was well known. The townspeople called him Judge Melonhead. He solved every problem and unraveled every knot. When coming from the market with his orange cape and red umbrella, he would place his hand to his chest and smile so benignly at all whom he met that the people were crazy about him.

Hüsmen returned to his village by the road by which he had come,

---

* *Nargile*: A waterpipe.
† *Kaymakam*: A district chief in a province.

with the donkey again tied to his saddle. He had gone through a great deal of money in the town, where bread and barley were expensive, both for himself and for the donkey, who had to be fed well. The villagers who constituted the council paid little attention to the matter of expenses, saying:

"The donkey is related to sacred things. Therefore, it's our duty to look after it!"

And Hüsmen never complained of his tiredness, since working for God made him forget the vicissitudes of travel.

In the week of the second trip to town, however, he was obliged to return home again with the donkey behind him. The judge had still not arrived. The police sergeant scolded the *hoca*:

"You dumb lout, what's your hurry?"

The villagers doubted whether a donkey that had been donated to charity could be used in work or not, so they would have nothing to do with it.

Hüsmen's third journey home was like the previous ones, with the donkey trailing behind him. Someone with a sharp eye saw from the distance that the gray donkey had returned, and he spread the news to the village. Everyone was waiting with bewilderment and concern. Before Hüsmen even got down from his donkey, he said with a happy voice:

"Well, what the hell, we were supposed to bring a witness."

He explained the matter in one burst. Really, how had they not thought of this? But, there was no loss; the judge would accept the donkey. He'd write out the deed, three people would go in a week, and, if they had to, they'd swear an oath. . . .

The gray donkey became fat from eating the fodder they spread before him as recompense for the occasional loadless journeys he had made. When they took him to be watered, he would run over to the female donkeys, and, gradually, he became more and more ill-tempered. In this way, two and one-half months passed by.

Finally, preparations for the last trip were completed. As the travelers were saying goodbye in front of the mill, the newly dawned sun illuminated the particles of dust caused by the small caravan. The villagers trailing toward the rise looked to those who remained behind as if they were rising in a gilded cloud toward the heavens.

The gray donkey did not return again. The people of the village, looking at the deeds and the stamps affixed to them, finally decided that, according to the worth and honor of the donation of the donkey, it would go as far as the Hejaz without a load or any hardship, and that there it would carry water from the sacred well of Zemzem.* In fact, one night in a dream Hüsmen saw the saddle of the donkey covered with green velvet, and completely believed it.

Anyway, they all spoke often about the donkey with the enthusiasm that is felt when one is doing something other than one's job. Forgetting how it had mounted the mares, they would fool one another and tell one another how, when left by itself, it would move its head from side to side and start to recite a litany.

In the same year as this event, however, Hüsmen *Hoca* went to town to sell rice and returned looking foolish. Just when the market was most crowded, he had heard someone shouting in the distance, "Get out of the way! Don't get hit!" The crowd divided in two, and Judge Melonhead, with the gray donkey beneath him and the familiar orange cape on his back, passed through the throng of well-wishers that surrounded him at a pace that shook his large body.

---

* Zemzem (or Zamzam): A spring in Mecca located near the Ka'aba.

Chronology

SECTION III: Iran (1920–1941)

1921 Reza Khan carries out military coup in Iran

1925 Reza Khan declared shah, launching Pahlavi dynasty

1935 Persia's name changed to Iran

1939–1945 World War II
   Iran declares neutrality

1941 Britain and Russia depose Reza Pahlavi and replace him with son, Muhammad Reza Pahlavi

III

Once Upon a Time:
Politics and Piety in Persian Literature,
1930—1940

PERSIAN LITERATURE IS perhaps the oldest and most accomplished premodern literature of the Middle East. Yet under the reign of the Qajar dynasty, whose kings (or *shahs*) had ruled Iran since 1794, Persian literature experienced a steep decline in both quality and influence. Until the early twentieth century, Iran's literary elites were little more than employees of the court, composing sycophantic odes to Qajar princes.

At the start of the twentieth century, however, as Iran was divided into Russian and British zones of influence and the country's weak and corrupt shahs became pawns in the global chess game being played out by superpowers, Persian literature underwent a revolution of sorts. A new breed of young, politically active poets and writers began to break with the ornamental style of traditional Persian literature to adopt a simpler, more colloquial form of prose geared toward "the common man." Books written in Persian became less florid, more secular, and far more concerned with the daily lives of regular Iranians. The Persian language itself was refined and stripped of its Arabic influences as lyric poets such as Nima Yushij and novelists such as Sadegh Hedayat (*The Blind Owl*) broke with their predecessors and insisted on writing in the vernacular of regular Iranians.

By far the most influential of this new group of writers was Mohammad Ali Jamalzadeh, whose book *Once Upon a Time* essentially gave birth to the short story in Iran. Published in 1921, the book is a collection of short stories that paints a scathing picture of a society controlled by foreign powers, enthralled by a buffoonish clerical class, and subjugated by an ineffectual and increasingly paranoid government. Ironically, the country Jamalzadeh described so humorously collapsed the year of the book's publication. On February 21, 1921, Iran's minister of war and the country's most decorated officer, Reza Khan (1878–1944), seized control of the government in a bloodless coup backed by the Russian and British governments, thus putting an end to Qajar rule.

A simple, semiliterate man who rose through the ranks of the military, Reza Khan was a fervent nationalist dedicated to freeing Iran from foreign influence. He renegotiated Iran's economic relationships with Britain and the Soviet Union, giving the country a greater financial stake in its own natural resources, and fashioned a strong, centralized, and fairly independent government. Yet despite his populist facade and his ostensible commitment to nationalism, Reza Khan could not resist the temptations of absolute power. In 1925, he declared himself Shah of Iran, thus inaugurating the Pahlavi dynasty, which, in the years to come, would become even more brutal and authoritarian than the dynasty it had replaced.

An avid admirer of Mustafa Kemal Atatürk, Reza Shah Pahlavi instituted a series of reforms meant to modernize Iran, including banning the veil for women and forcing men to wear "Western" clothes, such as top hats and ties. He promoted advances in women's rights and encouraged Iranian women to earn degrees and hold jobs in the fields of medicine and law. The ensuing Women's Awakening Movement provided female writers, such as the celebrated poet Parvin E'tesami, with an unprecedented opportunity to write about issues never previously tackled in Iranian literature. ("Formerly a woman in Iran was almost non-Iranian," E'tesami wrote, in her most famous work, "Iranian Women." "All she did was struggle through dark and distressing days.")

At the same time, Reza Shah established an oppressive regime that stifled the press, reduced Parliament to little more than a rubber stamp, and dealt ruthlessly with any opposition, all while enriching himself and the fortunate few in his inner circle. As in Turkey and the Arab states, it fell to Iran's writers and poets to call society to account for its failings. "O people who are sitting, cheerful and laughing,/ on the shore," cried Nima Yushij, the father of modern Iranian poetry. "Someone is losing his life in the sea;/ Someone is struggling in the rough, dark/and formidable sea."

By the 1940s, Iran had become a police state, one brought frighteningly to life by Sadegh Hedayat in his novel *The Blind Owl* (widely recognized as one of the most important literary works of the twentieth century), the protagonist of which exists in a nightmare reality devoid of all reason and purpose, where the only person he can trust with his thoughts is his own shadow.

In August 1941, the same powers that encouraged Reza Khan's coup in 1925 forced him to abdicate the throne in favor of his untried, ill-prepared, and far more easily controlled son, Muhammad Reza Pahlavi, whose own tyrannical rule would bring about an even greater change in Iran near the end of the twentieth century.

MOHAMMAD ALI JAMALZADEH
(1892–1997)

Persian Is Sugar

Translated from the Persian by
Heshmat Moayyad and Paul Sprachman

NOWHERE ON EARTH do they make the good suffer along with the bad the way they do in Iran. After five years of knocking about Europe and suffering so, I hadn't yet gotten a glimpse of Iranian soil from the deck of the ship, when I heard the sounds of Gilaki spoken by the Enzeli* ferrymen. Singing, "My dear child! My soul," they had surrounded the ship like ants around the carcass of a dead locust and were badgering the passengers to death; each of us was at the mercy of several oarsmen, boatmen, and bearers. Of all the passengers, however, I was the worst off. The others were generally peddlers from Baku and Rasht in long, quilted coats and short caps, whose purse strings would have remained closed to the lethal blows of clubs and mallets and who would sooner have delivered their souls to Azrael† than let anyone see the color of their money. As for me, poor bastard, I hadn't had a chance to change the bowler hat that had remained on my head since I left Europe. These fellows, thinking that I was some *hajji*'s son and a good catch, surrounded me saying, "Sahib, Sahib." Every scrap of my baggage became a *casus belli* for the herd of ten bearers and fifteen merciless ferrymen who hollered and shouted so much that I thought the racket would never end. As I stood dumbfounded, appalled, trying to think of how to finesse my way out of the grasp of these bandits, their

* Gilaki: Language spoken by the people in Iran's Gilan Province along the Caspian Sea. Enzeli: A person from the city of Bandar-e Anzali in Gilan Province (northwest Iran).
† Azrael: The Angel of Death in Islamic mythology.

ranks parted, and like twisted images in a fun-house mirror, the frowning, surly faces of two passport officers emerged—you'd think they were the two Interrogating Angels* themselves. With them were several scowling, red-liveried attendants in imperial lion-and-sun-insignia† hats, with handlebar mustaches that went beyond their earlobes and fluttered in the sea breeze like the twin banners of hunger and starvation. When they saw my passport, it was as if someone had handed them word of the shah's assassination or as if they had received Azrael's inescapable commandment; they started, wrinkled their noses, and then stared at me, looking me up and down several times. They were, as native Tehranis say, "measuring me for an outfit they had already tailored." Finally, one of them said, "What! You're Iranian?"

I said, "Good God! That's an odd question, your honor. Where do you think I'm from? Why, of course I'm Iranian, seven generations back Iranian! It'd be a cold day in hell before you'd find anyone in all of Sangelaj who doesn't know your humble servant." These amiable words were lost on him, and it was clear that this was no laughing matter. He ordered his notorious attendants to detain the "Khan Sahib" for the time being so that "the necessary investigations could be carried out." One of the attendants, whose billy club emerged like a sword hilt about a foot and a half from his ragged sash, reached out, grabbed my wrist, and said, "Get moving!" I considered the situation and decided to go along obediently. My first urge was to play the sahib, to rant and rave, but I saw that this was not the time and that it was best simply to behave. May the good Lord keep even the infidels out of the hands of this tribe of attendants! Take it from me: I know what these bastards are capable of doing at the drop of a hat. I was only able to rescue two of my possessions intact: my bowler and my faith, neither of which, evidently, were of any use to them—otherwise there wasn't a pocket crevice or cavity that they did not empty that instant. After they had performed their official duties to the letter, they took me behind the Enzeli customs shed and threw me into a dark hole that would have made the first night in the grave seem like a sunny day, for the door

---

* Interrogating Angels: Known as Munkar and Nakir, they question the dead in order to allow entry into Paradise.

† Lion-and-sun: The imperial symbol of the shahs of Iran.

and walls of the shed had been curtained off by a troop of spiders. The attendants locked the door from the outside and left me to my fate.

Earlier, as I was leaving the ship, going ashore on the tender, I had learned from bits and pieces of people's conversations with the boatmen, that the shah and the Assembly were at loggerheads once more and that a new wave of arrests and imprisonment had begun.* The capital had decreed that travelers were to receive special scrutiny. Clearly, this was what was behind the arrests—especially when you consider that a supernumerary had arrived that morning from Rasht expressly for this purpose. In order to display his utility, his talent, and his expertise, he was making good and bad suffer alike and turning on the defenseless like a mad dog. In the meantime, he had even displaced the hapless provincial governor and was paving the way for his own administration of Enzeli: reports of his services had been keeping the telegraph lines between Enzeli and Tehran busy every minute since morning.

I was so dismayed at first that I could barely see, but, as I gradually got used to the darkness, I sensed that I wasn't the only guest in the cell. I first noticed one of those notorious "Western-oriented gentlemen" who will serve as monuments to coddling, idiocy, and illiteracy in Iran until the Resurrection, and who will surely keep audiences rolling in the aisles of local theaters (I hope the devil's not listening) for another century. My Wog† companion was perched in an arched alcove wearing a collar as tall as a samovar chimney and, from the black smoke of some Caucasus diesel train, as sooty. Pinched by the collar, which propped up his neck like a pillory, he was immersed in a French novel, reading in the light and shadow of the cell. I was going to step forward and, with a stock "Bonjour, monsieur," show him that I was also one of the *cognoscenti*, when I heard a hissing sound coming from one of the corners of the jail. I looked in that direction and something that I first took for a shiny white cat curled up sleeping on a sack of

---

* The shah and the Assembly: Jamalzadeh refers to the Constitutional Revolution of 1905, in which Mozzafar-al-Din Shah was forced to allow the drafting of a constitution and the creation of a parliament.

† Wog: Western-oriented gentleman. A disparaging term for non-Westerners who spent a great deal of time in Europe and North America and returned to their native lands totally "Westernized."

charcoal caught my eye. It was actually a sheikh who had wrapped himself from ear to ear in his cloak and was sitting seminary-style: cross-legged, his arms hugging his knees. The shiny white cat was his rumpled turban, part of which had come loose under his chin and assumed the shape of a cat's tail. The hissing sounds I heard turned out to be the salutations in his prayers.

So there were three of us. I took this number as a good omen. I was going to strike up a conversation with my cellmates (perhaps if we knew each other's plight we might find a way out) when the door to the makeshift jail suddenly opened, and they very noisily hurled a poor young provincial in a pressed felt cap into the cell and shut the door. Apparently, to terrorize the populace of Enzeli, the special functionary from Rasht had arrested this innocent young man, charging him with having been a lackey for someone or other from the Caucasus several years back during the beginning of the struggle between the constitutionalists and the monarchists. Realizing that groaning and grumbling were not going to do him any good, the new arrival wiped his eyes with the soiled hem of his cloak, and, sensing that there wasn't a guard or anyone posted outside the door, he let out a string of those undiluted obscenities that are like the melons of Gorgab and the tobacco of Hakkan: they flourish only in Iranian soil. He cursed the ancestors of this one and that and kicked the door and the walls two or three times with his bare foot. When he found that the cell door, however worm-eaten, was even harder than the special functionary's heart, he gave in with a spit, glanced around the cell, and noticed that he wasn't alone. He knew right off that there was no question of getting help from me, a "foreigner," and that there was likewise little to hope for from the Wog, so he tiptoed over to the sheikh. After gaping at him for a while, the boy, his voice shaking, said, "Reverend Sheikh, for Imam 'Abbas's sake, tell me, what the hell have *I* done? I swear to God, the only way to get them off your back is to kill yourself!"

These words caused the reverend sheikh's turban to glide slowly like a wisp of cloud. A pair of eyes emerged from it and peered feebly at the felt-hatted provincial. From the phonic defile that, though not visible, must have been below the eyes, with perfect declamation and composure these words made their way slowly and deliberately to his assembled audience: "Believer! Deliver ye not the reins of thy rebellious and weak soul to anger and rage, for 'Those who control their wrath and are forgiving toward mankind. . . .'"

The sheikh's speech stunned the felt-hatted boy. Recognizing only the word "Kazem" in "Those who control . . .," he said, "No, Reverend, your servant's name isn't Kazem, it's Ramazan. I only meant to say that we could at least know why we've been buried alive."

This time, with the same consummate declamation and composure, these words emanated from the holy precinct: "May God reward ye who believe. The point is well taken by your advocate's intellect. 'Patience is the key to release.' *Spero* that the object of our imprisonment shall become manifest *ex tempore*; but whatever the case, whether sooner or later, it most assuredly will reach our ears. *Interea,** while we wait, the most profitable occupation is to recite the name of the Creator, which in any event is the best of endeavors."

Ramazan, poor bastard, didn't catch a word of the reverend sheikh's sweet Persian. He thought that His Eminence was communing with *jinns* or spirits or was busy reading Scripture to the dead; terror and dread marked his face. He said "*Bismillah*"† faintly and prepared to retreat, but it appeared that the sheikh's venerable jaw was just getting warmed up. Without addressing anyone in particular, he stared at a spot on the wall and, again with the customary declamation, picked up the thread of his thoughts, "Perhaps," he pontificated, "our arrest was a matter of expedience or perhaps it was essentially unintentional, in which case it is strongly hoped that it will come to an end, if not immediately, shortly. Or, perhaps, considering this humblest of beings *quasi nullus essem*,‡ they will expose me in the worst way possible to gradual ruin and perdition without heeding my dignity or station; therefore it is up to us to appeal to higher authorities in whatever way, with intermediaries or without others' intervention, in writing or verbally, openly or in secret—and, without doubt, confirming the adage 'seek and ye shall find,' upon getting a favorable hearing and accomplishing our goals, we shall be released, and our innocence shall be as clear to our peers as the sun in the midday sky."

---

* *Spero*: "I hope"; *ex tempore*: "forthwith"; *interea*: "meanwhile."
† *Bismillah*: Muslim invocation: "In the name of God."
‡ *Quasi nullus essem*: "as though I did not exist."

Ramazan, poor child, now really desperate, drew back slowly from the sheikh's side of the cell and, as if having a fit, shot terrified glances at him. He kept cursing the devil under his breath and, reciting something resembling the "Throne Verse"* (at least his version of it), began to blow in all directions. It was clear that, with his wits gone and abetted by darkness, Ramazan's resolve was about to melt away from pure fright. I really felt sorry for him. But His Eminence's tongue, as though fitted with an enema or, as the preachers themselves say, as if it were "flowing freely," would not let up. He raised his blessed arms which, bare to the elbow and matted with hair, were not unlike (may you be spared such arms!) sheep trotters, from his knees and brushed back his cloak. With weird gestures and movements and without lifting his fierce and fiery stare from that innocent spot on the wall, he directed the fullest possible volleys of reproach at the absent passport officer. As though addressing an envelope to the official, he reeled off appellatives one after another: "clot of flesh," "obscure of origin," "corrupt of belief," "drinker of wine," "forsaker of prayer," "cursed of both parents," "son of adultery," and so on, any one of which—and I only remember a hundredth of them—was enough to justify making one's life and property fair game or one's wife an anathema in any Muslim house. For a time he commented with composure and dignity, anguish and commiseration on "slights to scholars and the servants of pure doctrine"; "the defaming and demeaning to which time and time again, every hour" they are subject; and "the evil consequences in this world and the next" of this defamation. Gradually his sermonizing became so tangled and obscure that not just Ramazan, but Ramazan's grandfather could never have understood one word of it. Even your humble servant, who boasts such a fine knowledge of Arabic, having spent many years of my precious youth siccing "Amr" and "Zayd"† on one another, and, in the name of education, from dawn to dusk having become under various pretexts the stem and the direct object of the verbs "to beat," "to summon," and other verbs of reproach; having conjugated my regular, perfect self in this mood and that, moved by

---

* "Throne Verse": Verse 256 of the second sura (chapter) of the Qur'an.
† "Amr" and "Zayd": The principal characters in the model sentences of traditional Arabic grammar as learned by children.

the irregular and hollow voices and the oaths and imperatives of persons with defective minds; having brought about a declension in my self-esteem and having listened to indirect discourse; and having parsed a portion of my childhood into "would that" and "maybe," "aye and nay," actively arguing syntax and impassively learning both explicit and implicit subjects—even I couldn't by any means follow the reverend sheikh's sermon.

The Wog, perched in the same alcove and, making a full set of faces, engrossed in his sweet French novel, paid absolutely no attention to what was happening around him. Occasionally he would push his jaw forward and chomp on one end of the two strands of his mustache, which twined around the corners of his mouth like two whip scorpions. He would also occasionally take out his watch and look at it as if to see whether it was time for *café au lait* or not.

The browbeaten Ramazan, who was both angry and in need of a heart-to-heart talk, having been denied the sheikh's indulgence, saw the Wog as his only way out and took heart. Like a hungry child who approaches his stepmother for food, he went over to the Wog and in a faint, trembling voice greeted him: "Sir, forgive me for interrupting you! Simple folk like me are a bit slow. As for the sheikh, it's obvious that he's possessed, having a fit, and besides, he doesn't even speak our language; he's an Arab. I beg you, for God's sake, would you be so kind as to tell me why they've thrown us into this death cell."

At this the Wog flew down from his perch, closed his book, and crammed it into the wide pocket of his overcoat. Smiling, he went over to Ramazan and saying, "Brother! Brother!" offered him his hand. Not understanding this gesture, Ramazan retreated a bit, and the gentleman was forced to stroke his mustache for no good reason. Just so his suit would not be empty, he brought his other hand into play; placing both hands on his chest and putting his thumbs through the armholes of his vest, with the tips of his eight other fingers he began to drum on his starched shirt front and, in a fetching accent, said, "My dear friend and compatriot! Why have they put us here? I, too, however much I excavate my head, find *absolument* nothing, nothing *positif*, nothing *negative. Absolument!* Is it not very *comique* that they take me, a young licentiate from the best family, for a . . . a . . . *criminal* and treat me as they would a parvenu? But this is not surprising from a thousand-year *despotisme* and the lawlessdom [*sic*] and *arbitraire* that are its fruits. A country that boasts of being *constitutionnel* must have legal tribunals so that no one will be indentured to tyranny. O brother in adversity, do you not find it so?"

How could poor Ramazan possibly grasp these lofty notions? The French words aside, how, for example, could he understand "excavate the head," which is a literal translation of the French meaning "to ponder"? In Persian they say "no matter how much I knock myself out . . ." or "no matter how much I beat my head against the wall. . . ." And how could he understand "indentured to tyranny," the literal translation of another French idiom meaning "to become the object of tyranny"? Hearing the words "indentured" and "tyranny," Ramazan with his imperfect understanding thought that the Wog imagined he was a peasant victimized by a tyrannical landlord. He said, "No sir, your humble servant is not indentured; I'm the apprentice at the coffee house just half a block from the customs shed."

The monsieur shrugged and drummed eight fingers firmly on his chest, and, whistling, he began to pace. Paying no attention to Ramazan, he rejoined his train of thought and said, "*Révolution* without *évolution* is something the idea of which cannot enter the head. We young people must make a duty for ourselves as regards the guidance of the nation. As for that which regards me, I have written a long article on this *sujet* in which I have proved with blinding light that no one dare count on others, and that everyone must, to the extent of their . . . their . . . *possibilité*, serve their country, so that everyone does their duty. This is the path of progress! Otherwise decadence will threaten us. But, unfortunately, my words have no effect on people. Lamartine* speaks well in this respect. . . ." Monsieur Philosophe began to recite some French poetry, which I happened to know (having heard it once) had nothing to do with Lamartine but belonged to Victor Hugo.

These weird and baffling words caused Ramazan to lose control of himself completely; he scurried behind the cell door and began to howl and wail. A crowd soon gathered outside the door from which there

* Lamartine: French poet and politician Alphonse Marie Louis de Prat de Lamartine (1790–1869).

came an abrasive, splintery voice that would make Shemr's* rasp sound like Nakisa's† lute, "Mother . . . what the hell's eating you? Is somebody yanking on your . . .? What's the noise all about? If you don't stop playing the Jew and going on like a gypsy, we'll have them put a muzzle on your . . . !" Ramazan began to beg and plead in a frail whimper, "Will some good Muslim please tell me what I've done? If I'm a thief, here, let them chop off my hand; if I'm guilty, they can club me, pull out my fingernails, poke my eyes out, nail my ear to a gateway, horseshoe me, impale my fingers with a stick, put out candles on me, but for the love of God and his Prophet, get me out of this hole, away from these madmen and *jinns*. By the Saints, by the Prophet, I'm losing my mind. You've buried me in here with three people. One of them, may he drop stone-dead, is a damned foreigner—just looking at his face is a sin, it makes you want to repent—standing there in the corner like a scowling owl that'll swallow you with his evil eyes. The other two don't understand a word people say—both of them are possessed, and if it ever crossed their minds to strangle a poor bastard like me, who'd answer to God for it?"

Ramazan could no longer speak; his throat clogged with anger, he began hiccuping his sobs. And once again that same gruff voice came from behind the door and laced the boy with a string of our notorious, extra-strength obscenities. I really pitied Ramazan and stepped forward, put my hand on his shoulder, and said, "Dear boy, how do you figure me for a foreigner? To hell with all the foreigners! I'm Iranian and a brother Muslim. Why have you gone to pieces? After all, what's really happened? You're a strong young man, how can you lose control of yourself this way?"

As soon as Ramazan saw that I really and truly understood the vernacular and that I was even speaking honest-to-God Persian with him, he grabbed my hand and kissed it as if there were no tomorrow. He got so excited that you would think he had just inherited the earth, and kept saying, "Thank God! Someone I can understand! You must be an angel! The Lord Himself has sent you to save me." "Steady,

---

* Shemr: The Umayyad general who killed the Prophet Muhammad's grandson, Hosayn, at the battle of Karbala in the year 680.
† Nakisa: Pre-Islamic court minstrel.

son," I said, "I'm no angel; sometimes I even doubt whether I'm human myself. But a man mustn't lose heart. Why the tears? If your buddies ever heard about this, they'd tease you, you'd never hear the end of it. . . ."

He said, "May the Lord take your suffering and pain and give it to these lunatics. God, I swear I came that close to going to pieces. Did you see how it's impossible to get these madmen to understand anything; they're always speaking some devil tongue." "Little brother," I said, "they're neither devils nor madmen, only Iranians with the same country and faith as you and I." Ramazan probably thought that I had a screw loose also; he looked at me sideways, burst out laughing, and said, "For Imam 'Abbas's sake! Please, no more kidding, not from you, sir! If they're really Iranians, why do they speak languages that have nothing to do with human speech?" "Ramazan," I said, "what they're speaking is Persian, but . . ." But it was clear that Ramazan didn't believe it, and, to tell the truth, he had every right not to; he wouldn't have believed it in a thousand years. I realized that I was wasting my time and was going to change the subject when the door to the shed opened suddenly. An orderly entered and said, "You all owe me a tip for bringing the good news. You're free to go, good-bye."

Instead of being happy, Ramazan latched onto me and said, "I swear I know whenever they want to hand a prisoner over to the hangman, they talk this way. Lord, save me!" But it didn't turn out that way; Ramazan's fears were groundless. That morning's passport officer was replaced by a new official who was just as well placed and presumptuous as the first and who also had his eyes on the governorship of Rasht. In order to undo what the morning's official had done, his first act after reaching Enzeli was to release us. We thanked God and were about to leave the cell when we saw the same attendants of that morning escorting a young man toward us. Judging by his accent, his dress, and his looks, he seemed to be from Salmas or Khoi.* The boy, in his own brand of Persian, which later on I gathered was a souvenir of Istanbul, kept making "protestations of his situation" in the strongest terms and "appeals for mercy" to the people and expressions of optimism that they would listen to what he had to say. Ramazan stared at him and,

---

* Salmas, Khoi: Turkish-speaking regions of Iran.

completely bewildered, said, "In the name of God, the Beneficent, the Merciful, another one! Lord, today you've blessed us with all the screwballs and lunatics you had. I thank you both for what you've given us and for what you've withheld." I wanted to tell him that the new arrival was also an Iranian and that he was speaking Persian, but I feared that he would think I was teasing him and this would break his heart, so I didn't mention it.

I went to make preparations for the droshky* ride to Rasht. A few minutes later, a droshky carrying the reverend sheikh, the Wog, and me was about to get going when I saw Ramazan running toward us. He handed me a handkerchief filled with dried fruit and whispered, "Forgive me, I talk too much, but, God! it seems to me that their madness has also gotten to you, otherwise how could you have the nerve to ride with these two?" I said, "Ramazan, I'm not a coward like you." He said, "May the Lord protect you! Whenever you get fed up with not understanding one another, just have some of this fruit and think of your servant." The droshky driver flicked his whip and we were on our way. I must say we enjoyed ourselves very much (wish my friends had been there). Especially when, on the way, we saw yet another passport official racing toward Enzeli and, ecstatic, we nearly split our sides laughing.

---

* Droshky: A vehicle drawn by horses.

SADEGH HEDAYAT

(1903—1951)

The Blind Owl

(EXCERPT)

Translated from the Persian by D. P. Costello

IT WAS THE thirteenth day of Nouruz.* Everyone had gone out to the country. I had shut the window of my room in order to be able to concentrate on my painting. It was not long before sunset and I was working away when suddenly the door opened and my uncle came into the room. That is, he said he was my uncle. I had never seen my uncle in my life, for he had been abroad ever since his early youth. I seem to remember that he was a sea captain. I imagined he might have some business matter to discuss with me, since I understood that he was interested in commerce as well. At all events my uncle was a bent old man with an Indian turban on his head and a ragged yellow cloak on his back; his face was partly concealed by a scarf wrapped around his neck; his shirt was open and revealed a hairy chest. It would have been possible to count the hairs of the sparse beard protruding from under the scarf which muffled his neck. His eyelids were red and sore and he had a hare-lip. He resembled me in a remote, comical way like a reflection in a distorting mirror. I had always pictured my father something like this. On entering the room he walked straight across to the opposite wall and squatted on the floor. It occurred to me that I ought to offer him some refreshment in honor of his arrival. I lit the lamp and went into the little dark closet that opens off my room. I searched every corner in the hope of finding something suitable to offer him, although I knew there was nothing of the sort in the house—I had no

---

* Nouruz: Literally, "new day"; the Persian New Year, celebrated on the first day of spring.

opium or drink left. Suddenly my eye lighted on the topmost of the shelves on the wall. It was as though I had had a flash of inspiration. On the shelf stood a bottle of old wine that had been left me by my parents. I seem to remember hearing that it had been laid down on the occasion of my birth. There it was on the top shelf. I had never so much as given it a thought and had quite forgotten there was such a thing in the house. To reach the shelf I got up onto a stool that happened to be there. As I reached toward the bottle, I chanced to look out through the ventilation-hole above the shelf. On the open ground outside my room I saw a bent old man sitting at the foot of a cypress tree with a young girl—no, an angel from heaven—standing before him. She was leaning forward and with her right hand was offering him a blue flower of morning glory. The old man was biting the nail of the index finger of his left hand.

The girl was directly opposite me but she appeared to be quite unaware of her surroundings. She was gazing straight ahead without looking at anything in particular. She wore on her lips a vague, involuntary smile as though she was thinking of someone who was absent. It was then that I first beheld those frightening, magic eyes, those eyes that seemed to express a bitter reproach to mankind, with their look of anxiety and wonder, of menace and promise—and the current of my existence was drawn toward those shining eyes charged with manifold significance and sank into their depths. That magnetic mirror drew my entire being toward it with inconceivable force. They were slanting, Turkoman eyes of supernatural, intoxicating radiance that at once frightened and attracted, as though they had looked upon terrible, transcendental things that it was given to no one but her to see. Her cheekbones were prominent and her forehead high. Her eyebrows were slender and met in the middle. Her lips were full and half-open as though they had broken away only a moment before from a long, passionate kiss and were not yet sated. Her face, pale as the moon, was framed in the mass of her black, disheveled hair and one strand clung to her temple. The fineness of her limbs and the ethereal unconstraint of her movements marked her as one who was not fated to live long in this world. No one but a Hindu temple dancer could have possessed her harmonious grace of movement.

Her air of mingled gaiety and sadness set her apart from ordinary mankind. Her beauty was extraordinary. She reminded me of a vision seen in an opium sleep. She aroused in me a heat of passion like that which is kindled by the mandrake root. It seemed to me as I gazed at her long, slender form, with its harmonious lines of shoulder, arms, breasts, waist, buttocks, and legs, that she had been torn from her husband's embrace, that she was like the female mandrake that has been plucked from the arms of its mate.

She was wearing a black pleated dress that clung tightly to her body. Gazing at her, I was certain that she wished to leap across the stream that separated her from the old man but that she was unable to do so. All at once the old man burst into laughter. It was a hollow, grating laugh, of a quality to make the hairs of one's body stand on end; a harsh, sinister, mocking laugh. And yet the expression of his face did not change. It was as though the laughter was echoing from somewhere deep within his body.

In terror I sprang down from the stool with the bottle in my hand. I was trembling, in a state of mingled horror and delight such as might have been produced by some delicious, fearful dream. I set the bottle of wine down on the floor and held my head in my hands. How many minutes, how many hours I remained thus, I do not know. When I came to myself I picked up the bottle and went back into my room. My uncle had gone and had left the room door agape like the mouth of a dead man. The sound of the old man's hollow laughter was still echoing in my ears.

It was growing dark. The lamp was burning smokily. I could still feel the aftermath of the delicious, horrible fit of trembling that I had experienced. From that moment the course of my life had changed. With one glance that angel of heaven, that ethereal girl, had left on me the imprint of her being, more deeply marked than the mind of man can conceive.

At that moment I was in a state of trance. It seemed to me that I had long known her name. The radiance of her eyes, her complexion, her perfume, her movements, all appeared familiar to me, as though, in some previous existence in a world of dreams, my soul had lived side by side with hers, had sprung from the same root and the same stock and it was inevitable that we should be brought together again. It was inevitable that I should be close to her in this life. At no time did I desire to touch her. The invisible rays that emanated from our bodies and mingled together were sufficient contact. As for the strange fact that she appeared familiar to me from the first glance, do not lovers always experience the feeling that they have seen each other before and that a mysterious bond has long existed between them? The only thing in this mean world that I desired was her love; if that were denied me I wanted the love of nobody. Was it possible that anyone other than she should make any impression upon my heart? But the hollow grating laughter, the sinister laughter of the old man had broken the bond that united us.

All that night I thought about these things. Again and again I was on the point of going to look through the aperture in the wall, but fear of the old man's laughter held me back. The next day also I could think of nothing else. Would I be able to refrain altogether from going to look at her? Finally on the third day I decided, despite the dread that possessed me, to put the bottle of wine back in its place. But when I drew the curtain aside and looked into the closet I saw in front of me a wall as blank and dark as the darkness that has enshrouded my life. There was no trace of aperture or window. The rectangular opening had been filled in, had merged with the wall, as though it had never existed. I stood upon the stool but, although I hammered on the wall with my fists, listening intently, although I held the lamp to it and examined it with care, there was not the slightest trace of any aperture. My blows had no more effect upon the solid, massive fabric of the wall than if it had been a single slab of lead.

Could I abandon the hope of ever seeing her again? It was not within my power to do so. Henceforth I lived like a soul in torment. All my waiting, watching, and seeking were in vain. I trod every hand's-breadth of ground in the neighborhood of my house. I was like the murderer who returns to the scene of his crime. Not one day, not two days, but every day for two months and four days I circled around our house in the late afternoon like a decapitated fowl. I came to know every stone and every pebble in the neighborhood but I found no trace of the cypress tree, of the little stream or of the two people whom I had seen there. The same number of nights I knelt upon the ground in the moonlight, I begged and entreated the trees, the stones, and the moon—for she might have been gazing at that moment at the moon—

I sought aid from every created thing, but I found no trace of her. In the end I understood that all my efforts were useless, because it was not possible that she should be connected in any way with the things of this world: the water with which she washed her hair came from some unique, unknown spring; her dress was not woven of ordinary stuff and had not been fashioned by material, human hands. She was a creature apart. I realized that those flowers of morning glory were no ordinary flowers. I was certain that if her face were to come into contact with ordinary water it would fade; and that if she were to pluck an ordinary flower of morning glory with her long fine fingers they would wither like the petals of a flower.

I understood all this. This girl, this angel, was for me a source of wonder and ineffable revelation. Her being was subtle and intangible. She aroused in me a feeling of adoration. I felt sure that beneath the glance of a stranger, of an ordinary man, she would have withered and crumpled.

Ever since I had lost her, ever since the aperture had been blocked and I had been separated from her by a heavy wall, a dank barrier as massive as a wall of lead, I felt that my existence had become pointless, that I had lost my way for all time to come. Even though the caress of her gaze and the profound delight I had experienced in seeing her had been only momentary and devoid of reciprocity—for she had not seen me—yet I felt the need of those eyes. One glance from her would have been sufficient to make plain all the problems of philosophy and the riddles of theology. One glance from her and mysteries and secrets would no longer have existed for me.

From this time on I increased my doses of wine and opium, but alas, those remedies of despair failed to numb and paralyze my mind. I was unable to forget. On the contrary, day by day, hour by hour, minute by minute, the memory of her, of her body, of her face, took shape in my mind more clearly than before.

How could I have forgotten her? Whether my eyes were open or closed, whether I slept or woke, she was always before me. Through the opening in the closet wall, like the dark night that enshrouds the mind and reason of man, through the rectangular aperture that looked onto the outside world, she was ever before my eyes.

Repose was utterly denied me. How could I have found repose?

It had become a habit with me to go out for a walk every day just before sunset. For some obscure reason I wanted desperately to find the little stream, the cypress tree, and the vine of morning glory. I had become addicted to these walks in the same way as I had become addicted to opium. It was as though I was compelled by some outside force to undertake them. Throughout my walk I would be immersed in the thought of her, in the memory of my first glimpse of her, and I desired to find the place where I had seen her on that thirteenth day of Nouruz: if I should find that place, if it should be granted to me to sit beneath that cypress tree, then for sure I should attain peace. But alas, there was nothing but sweepings, burning sand, horse bones, and refuse heaps around which dogs were sniffing. Had I ever really encountered her? Never. All that had happened was that I had looked furtively, covertly at her through a hole, a cursed aperture in my closet wall. I was like a hungry dog sniffing and rooting in a refuse heap: when people come to dump garbage on the pile he runs away and hides, only to return later to renew his search for tasty morsels. This was the state that I was in. But the aperture in the wall was blocked. For me the girl was like a bunch of fresh flowers that has been tossed onto a refuse heap.

On the last evening when I went out for my usual walk, the sky was overcast and a drizzling rain was falling. A dense mist had fallen over the surrounding country. In the fine rain that softened the intensity of the colors and the clarity of the outlines I experienced a sense of liberation and tranquillity. It was as though the rain was washing away my black thoughts. That night what ought not to have happened did happen.

I wandered, unconscious of my surroundings. During those hours of solitude, during those minutes that lasted I know not how long, her awe-inspiring face, indistinct as though seen through cloud or mist, void of motion or expression like the paintings one sees upon the covers of pen cases, took shape before my eyes far more clearly than ever before.

By the time I returned home I should think that a great part of the night was spent. The mist had grown denser, so much so that I could not see the ground immediately in front of my foot. Nevertheless, by force of habit and some special sense that I had developed, I found my way back to the house. As I came up to the entrance I observed a female form clad in black sitting on the stone bench outside the door.

I struck a match to find the keyhole and for some reason glanced involuntarily at the figure in black. I recognized two slanting eyes, two great black eyes set in a thin face of moonlight paleness, two eyes that gazed unseeing at my face. If I had never seen her before I should still have known her. No, it was not an illusion. This black-robed form was she. I stood bemused, like a man dreaming, who knows that he is dreaming and wishes to awake but cannot. I was unable to move. The match burned down and scorched my fingers. I abruptly came to myself and turned the key in the lock. The door opened and I stood aside. She rose from the bench and passed along the dark corridor like one who knew the way. She opened my door and I followed her into the room. I hurriedly lit the lamp and saw that she had gone across and lain down upon my bed. Her face was in shadow. I did not know whether or not she could see me, whether or not she could hear my voice. She seemed neither to be afraid nor to be inclined to resist. It was as though she had come to my room independently of any will of her own.

Was she ill? Had she lost her way? She had come like a sleepwalker, independently of any will of her own. No one can possibly imagine the sensations I experienced at that moment. I felt a kind of delicious, ineffable pain. No, it was not an illusion. This being who without surprise and without a word had come into my room was that woman, that girl. I had always imagined that our first meeting would be like this. My state of mind was that of a man in an infinitely deep sleep. One must be plunged in profound sleep in order to behold such a dream as this. The silence had for me the force of eternal life; for on the plane of eternity without beginning and without end there is no such thing as speech.

To me she was a woman and at the same time had within her something that transcended humanity. When I looked at her face I experienced a kind of vertigo that made me forget the faces of all other people. Gazing at her, I began to tremble all over and my knees felt weak. In the depths of her immense eyes I beheld in one moment all the wretchedness of my life. Her eyes were wet and shining like two huge black diamonds suffused with tears. In her eyes, her black eyes, I found the everlasting night of impenetrable darkness that I had been seeking and I sank into the awful, enchanted blackness of that abyss. It was as though she was drawing some faculty out of my being. The ground rocked beneath my feet and if I had fallen I should have experienced an ineffable delight.

My heart stood still. I held my breath. I was afraid that if I breathed she might disappear like cloud or smoke. Her silence seemed something supernatural. It was as though a wall of crystal had risen between her and me, and that second, that hour, or that eternity was suffocating me. Her eyes, weary perhaps with looking upon some supernatural sight that it is not given to other people to see, perhaps upon death itself, slowly closed. Her eyelids closed and I, feeling like a drowning man who after frantic struggle and effort has reached the surface of the water, realized that I was feverish and trembling and with the edge of my sleeve wiped away the sweat that was streaming from my forehead.

Her face preserved the same stillness, the same tranquil expression, but seemed to have grown thinner and frailer. As she lay there on my bed she was biting the nail of the index finger of her left hand. Her complexion was pale as the moon and her thin, clinging black dress revealed the lines of her legs, her arms, her breasts—of her whole body.

I leaned over her in order to see her more plainly. Her eyes were closed. However much I might gaze at her face, she still seemed infinitely remote from me. All at once I felt that I had no knowledge of the secrets of her heart and that no bond existed between us.

I wished to say something but I feared that my voice would offend her ears, her sensitive ears that were accustomed, surely, to distant, heavenly, gentle music.

It occurred to me that she might be hungry or thirsty. I went into the closet to look for something to give her, although I knew there was nothing in the house. Then it was as though I had had a flash of inspiration. I remembered that on the top shelf was a bottle of old wine that had been left to me by my father. I got up onto a stool and took it down. I walked across on tiptoe to the bed. She was sleeping like a weary child. She was sound asleep and her long, velvety eyelashes were closed. I opened the bottle and slowly and carefully poured a glassful of the wine into her mouth between the two locked rows of teeth.

Quite suddenly, for the first time in my life, a sensation of peace took possession of me. As I looked upon those closed eyes it was as though the demon that had been torturing me, the incubus that had been oppressing my heart with its iron paw, had fallen asleep for a while. I brought my chair to the side of the bed and gazed fixedly at her face. What a childlike face it was! What an unworldly expression it wore! Was it possible that this woman, this girl, or this angel of hell (for I did not know by what name to call her), was it possible that she should possess this double nature? She was so peaceful, so unconstrained!

I could now feel the warmth of her body and smell the odor of dampness that rose from her black, heavy tresses. For some reason unknown to me I raised my trembling hand—my hand was not under my control—and laid it upon a strand of her hair, that lock that always clung to her temple. Then I thrust my fingers into her hair. It was cold and damp. Cold, utterly cold. It was as though she had been dead for several days. I was not mistaken. She *was* dead. I inserted my hand into the front of her dress and laid it upon her breast above the heart. There was not the faintest beat. I took a mirror and held it before her nostrils, but no trace of life remained in her.

I thought that I might be able to warm her with the heat of my own body, to give my warmth to her and to receive in exchange the coldness of death; perhaps in this way I could infuse my spirit into her dead body. I undressed and lay down beside her on the bed. We were locked together like the male and female of the mandrake. Her body was like that of a female mandrake that had been torn apart from its mate and she aroused the same burning passion as the mandrake. Her mouth was acrid and bitter and tasted like the stub end of a cucumber. Her whole body was as cold as hail. I felt that the blood had frozen in my veins and that this cold penetrated to the depths of my heart. All my efforts were useless. I got off the bed and put on my clothes. No, it was not an illusion. She had come here, into my room, into my bed, and had surrendered her body to me. She had given me her body and her soul.

So long as she lived, so long as her eyes overflowed with life, I had been tortured by the mere memory of her eyes. Now, inanimate and still, cold, with her eyes closed, she had surrendered herself to me— with her eyes closed.

This was she who had poisoned my whole life from the moment that I first saw her—unless my nature was such that from the beginning it was destined to be poisoned and any other mode of existence was impossible for me. Now, here, in my room, she had yielded to me her body and her shadow. Her fragile, short-lived spirit, which had no affinity with the world of earthly creatures, had silently departed from under the black, pleated dress, from the body that had tormented it, and had gone wandering in the world of shadows and I felt as though it had taken my spirit with it. But her body was lying there, inanimate and still. Her soft, relaxed muscles, her veins and sinews and bones were awaiting burial, a dainty meal for the worms and rats of the grave. In this threadbare, wretched, cheerless room that itself was like a tomb, in the darkness of the everlasting night that had enveloped me and that had penetrated the very fabric of the walls, I had before me a long, dark, cold endless night in the company of a corpse, of her corpse. I felt that ever since the world had been the world, so long as I had lived, a corpse, cold, inanimate and still, had been with me in a dark room.

At the moment my thoughts were numbed. Within me I felt a new and singular form of life. My being was somehow connected with that of all the creatures that existed about me, with all the shadows that quivered around me. I was in intimate, inviolable communion with the outside world and with all created things, and a complex system of invisible conductors transmitted a restless flow of impulses between me and all the elements of nature. There was no conception, no notion that I felt to be foreign to me. I was capable of penetrating with ease the secrets of the painters of the past, the mysteries of abstruse philosophies, the ancient folly of ideas and species. At that moment I participated in the revolutions of earth and heaven, in the germination of plants, and in the instinctive movements of animals. Past and future, far and near had joined together and fused in the life of my mind.

At such times as this every man takes refuge in some firmly established habit, in his own particular passion. The drunkard stupefies himself with drink, the writer writes, the sculptor attacks the stone. Each relieves his mind of the burden by recourse to his own stimulant and it is at such times as this that the real artist is capable of producing a masterpiece. But I, listless and helpless as I was, I, the decorator of pencase covers, what could I do? What means had I of creating a masterpiece when all that I could make were my lifeless, shiny little pictures, each of them identical with all the rest? And yet in my whole being I felt an overflowing enthusiasm, an indescribable warmth of inspiration. I desired to record on paper those eyes that had closed forever; I would keep the picture by me always. The force of this desire compelled me to translate it into action. I could not resist the impulsion. How could I have resisted it, I, an artist shut up in a room with a dead body? The thought aroused in me a peculiar sensation of delight.

I extinguished the smoky lamp, brought a pair of candles, lighted them, and set them above her head. In the flickering candlelight her face was still more tranquil than before; in the half-dark of the room it wore an expression of mystery and immateriality. I fetched paper and the other things necessary for my task and took up my position beside her bed—for henceforth the bed was hers. My intention was to portray at my leisure this form that was doomed slowly and gradually to suffer decomposition and disintegration and that now lay still, a fixed expression upon its face. I felt that I must record on paper its essential lines. I would select those lines of which I had myself experienced the power. A painting, even though it be summary and unpretentious, must nevertheless produce an emotional effect and possess a kind of life. I, however, was accustomed only to executing a stereotyped pattern on the covers of pen cases. I had now to bring my own mind into play, to give concrete form to an image that existed in my mind, that image which, emanating from her face, had so impressed itself upon all my thoughts. I would glance once at her face and shut my eyes. Then I would set down on paper the lines that I had selected for my purpose. Thereby I hoped to create from the resources of my mind a drug that would soothe my tortured spirit. I was taking refuge in the end in the motionless life of lines and forms.

The subject I had chosen, a dead woman, had a curious affinity to my dead manner of painting. I had never been anything else than a painter of dead bodies. And now I was faced with the question: Was it necessary for me to see her eyes again, those eyes that were now closed? Or were they already imprinted upon my memory with sufficient clarity?

I do not know how many times I drew and redrew her portrait in the course of that night, but none of my pictures satisfied me and I tore them up as fast as I painted them. The work did not tire me and I did not notice the passage of time.

The darkness was growing thin and the windowpanes admitted a gray light into my room. I was busy with a picture that seemed to me to be better than any of the others. But the eyes? Those eyes, with their expression of reproach as though they had seen me commit some unpardonable sin—I was incapable of depicting them on paper. The image of those eyes seemed suddenly to have been effaced from my memory. All my efforts were useless. However much I might study her face, I was unable to bring their expression to mind.

All at once as I looked at her a flush began to appear upon her cheeks. They gradually were suffused with a crimson color like that of the meat that hangs in front of butchers' shops. She returned to life. Her feverish, reproachful eyes, shining with a hectic brilliance, slowly opened and gazed fixedly at my face. It was the first time she had been conscious of my presence, the first time she had looked at me. Then the eyes closed again.

The thing probably lasted no more than a moment but this was enough for me to remember the expression of her eyes and to set it down on paper. With the tip of my paintbrush I recorded that expression and this time I did not tear up my picture.

Then I stood up and went softly to the bedside. I supposed that she was alive, that she had come back to life, that my love had infused life into her dead body. But at close quarters I detected the corpse smell, the smell of a corpse in process of decomposition. Tiny maggots were wriggling on her body and a pair of blister-flies were circling in the light of the candles. She was quite dead. But why, how, had her eyes opened? Had it been a hallucination or had it really happened?

I prefer not to be asked this question. But the essential was her face, or, rather, her eyes—and now they were in my possession. I had fixed on paper the spirit that had inhabited those eyes and I had no further need of the body, that body which was doomed to disappear, to become the prey of the worms and rats of the grave. Henceforth she was in my power and I had ceased to be her creature. I could see her eyes whenever I felt inclined to do so. I took up my picture as carefully as I could, laid it in a tin box that served me as a safe, and put the box away in the closet behind my room.

The night was departing on tiptoe. One felt that it had shed sufficient of its weariness to enable it to go its way. The ear detected faint,
far-off sounds such as the sprouting grass might have made, or some
migratory bird as it dreamed upon the wing. The pale stars were disappearing behind banks of cloud. I felt the gentle breath of the morning
on my face and at the same moment a cock crowed somewhere in the
distance.

What was I to do with the body, a body that had already begun to
decompose? At first I thought of burying it in my room, then of taking
it away and throwing it down some well surrounded by flowers of blue
morning glory. But how much thought, how much effort and dexter-
ity would be necessary in order to do these things without attracting
attention! And then, I did not want the eye of any stranger to fall upon
her. I had to do everything alone and unaided. Not that I mattered.
What point was there to my existence now that she had gone? But
she—never, never must any ordinary person, anyone but me, look
upon her dead body. She had come to my room and had surrendered
her cold body and her shadow to me in order that no one else should
see her, in order that she should not be defiled by a stranger's glance.
Finally an idea came to me. I would cut up her body, pack it in a suitcase, my old suitcase, take it away with me to some place far, very far
from people's eyes, and bury it there.

This time I did not hesitate. I took a bone-handled knife that I kept
in the closet beside my room and began by cutting open with great
care the dress of fine black material that swathed her like a spider's web.
It was the only covering she wore on her body. She seemed to have
grown a little: her body appeared to be longer than it had been in life.
Then I severed the head. Drops of cold clotted blood trickled from her
neck. Next, I amputated the arms and legs. I neatly fitted the trunk
along with the head and limbs into the suitcase and covered the whole
with her dress, the same black dress. I locked the case and put the key
into my pocket. When I had finished I drew a deep breath of relief and
tried the weight of the suitcase. It was heavy. Never before had I experienced such overwhelming weariness. No, I should never be able to
remove the suitcase on my own.

The weather had again set to mist and fine rain. I went outside in
the hope of finding someone who might help me with the case. There

was not a soul to be seen. I walked a little way, peering into the mist. Suddenly I caught sight of a bent old man sitting at the foot of a cypress tree. His face could not be seen for a wide scarf that he wore wrapped around his neck. I walked slowly up to him. I had still not uttered a word when the old man burst into a hollow, grating, sinister laugh that made the hairs on my body stand on end and said,

"If you want a porter, I'm at your service. Yes. I've got a hearse as well. I take dead bodies every day to Shah Abdo'l-Azim* and bury them there. Yes. I make coffins, too. Got coffins of every size, the perfect fit for everybody. At your service. Right away."

He roared with laughter, so that his shoulders shook. I pointed in the direction of my house but he said, before I had a chance to utter a word,

"That's all right. I know where you live. I'll be there right away."

He stood up and I walked back to my house. I went into my room and with difficulty got the suitcase with the dead body across to the door. I observed, standing in the street outside the door, a dilapidated old hearse to which were harnessed two black, skeleton-thin horses. The bent old man was sitting on the driver's seat at the front of the hearse, holding a long whip. He did not turn to look my direction. With a great effort I heaved the suitcase into the hearse, where there was a sunken space designed to hold the coffins, after which I climbed on board myself and lay down in the coffin space, resting my head against the ledge so as to be able to see out as we drove along. I slid the suitcase onto my chest and held it firmly with both hands.

The whip whistled through the air; the horses set off, breathing hard. The vapor could be seen through the drizzling rain, rising from their nostrils like a stream of smoke. They moved with high, smooth paces. Their thin legs, which made me think of the arms of a thief whose fingers have been cut off in accordance with the law and the stumps plunged into boiling oil, rose and fell slowly and made no sound as they touched the ground. The bells around their necks played a strange tune in the damp air. A profound sensation of comfort to which I can assign no cause penetrated me from head to foot and the

---

* Abdo'l-Azim: A mosque and cemetery situated among the ruins of Rey, a few miles south of Tehran.

movement of the hearse did not impart itself in any degree to my body. All that I could feel was the weight of the suitcase upon my chest. I felt as if the weight of her body and the coffin in which it lay had for all time been pressing upon my chest.

The country on each side of the road was enveloped in dense mist. With extraordinary speed and smoothness the hearse passed by hills, level ground, and streams, and a new and singular landscape unfolded before me, one such as I had never seen, sleeping or waking. On each side of the road was a line of hills standing quite clear of one another. At the foot of the hills there were numbers of weird, crouching, accursed trees, between which one caught sight of ash-gray houses shaped like pyramids, cubes, and prisms, with low, dark windows without panes. The windows were like the wild eyes of a man in a state of delirium. The walls of the houses appeared to possess the property of instilling intense cold into the heart of the passerby. One felt that no living creature could ever have dwelt in those houses. Perhaps they had been built to house the ghosts of ethereal beings.

Apparently the driver of the hearse was taking me by a back road or by some special route of his own. In some places all that was to be seen on either side of the road were stumps and wry, twisted trees, beyond which were houses, some squat, some tall, of geometrical shapes—perfect cones, truncated cones—with narrow, crooked windows from which blue flowers of morning glory protruded and twined over the doors and walls. Then this landscape disappeared abruptly in the dense mist.

The heavy, pregnant clouds that covered the tops of the hills sagged oppressively. The wind was blowing up a fine rain like aimless, drifting dust. We had been traveling for a considerable time when the hearse stopped at the foot of a stony, arid hill on which there was no trace of greenery. I slid the suitcase off my chest and go out.

On the other side of the hill was an isolated enclosure, peaceful and green. It was a place that I had never seen before and yet it looked familiar to me, as though it had always been present in some recess of my mind. The ground was covered with vines of blue, scentless morning glory. I felt that no one until that moment had ever set foot in the place. I pulled the suitcase out and set it down on the ground. The old driver turned around and said,

"We're not far from Shah Abdo'l Azim. You won't find a better place than this for what you want. There's never a bird flies by here. No."

I put my hand into my pocket, intending to pay the driver his fare. All that I had with me were two *krans* and one *abbasi*.* The driver burst into a hollow, grating laugh and said, "That's all right. Don't bother. I'll get it from you later. I know where you live. You haven't got any other jobs for me, no? I know something about grave digging, I can tell you. Yes. Nothing to be ashamed of. Shall we go? There's a stream near here, by a cypress tree. I'll dig you a hole just the right size for the suitcase and then we'll go."

The old man sprang down from his seat with a nimbleness of which I could not have imagined him to be capable. I took up the case and we walked side by side until we reached a dead tree that stood beside a dry riverbed. My companion said,

"This is a good place."

Without waiting for an answer, he began at once to dig with a small spade and a pick that he had brought with him. I set the suitcase down and stood beside it in a kind of torpor. The old man, bent double, was working away with the deftness of one who was used to the job. In the course of his digging he came across an object that looked like a glazed jar. He wrapped it up in a dirty handkerchief, stood up, and said,

"There's your hole. Yes. Just the right size for the suitcase. The perfect fit. Yes."

I put my hand into my pocket to pay him for his work. All that I had with me were two *krans* and one *abbasi*. The old man burst into a hollow laugh that brought out gooseflesh all over my body and said,

"Don't worry about that. That's all right. I know where you live. Yes. In any case, I found a jar that'll do me instead of pay. It's a flower vase from Rhages, comes from the ancient city of Rey. Yes."

Then, as he stood there, bent and stooping, he began to laugh again so that his shoulders shook. He tucked the jar, wrapped in the dirty handkerchief, under his arm and walked off to the hearse. With surprising nimbleness he sprang up and took his place on the driver's seat. The whip whistled through the air, the horses set off, breathing hard.

* *Krans*; *abbasi*: Silver coins formerly used in Iran.

The bells around their necks played a strange tune in the damp air. Gradually they disappeared into the dense mist.

As soon as I was alone I breathed a deep breath of relief. I felt as though a heavy weight had been lifted from my chest, and a wonderful sensation of peace permeated my whole being. I looked around me. The place where I stood was a small enclosure surrounded on every side by blue hills and mounds. Along one ridge extended the ruins of ancient buildings constructed of massive bricks. Nearby was a dry riverbed. It was a quiet, remote spot far from the noise and tumult of men. I felt profoundly happy and reflected that those great eyes, when they awoke from the sleep of earth, would behold a place that was in harmony with their own nature and aspect. And at the same time it was fitting that, just as she had been far removed from the life of other people while she was alive, so she should remain far from the rest of mankind, far from the other dead.

I lifted the suitcase with great care and lowered it into the trench, which proved to be of exactly the right dimensions, a perfect fit. However, I felt that I must look into the case once more. I looked around. Not a soul was to be seen. I took the key from my pocket and opened the lid. I drew aside a corner of her black dress and saw, amid a mass of coagulated blood and swarming maggots, two great black eyes gazing fixedly at me with no trace of expression in them. I felt that my entire being was submerged in the depths of those eyes. Hastily I shut the lid of the case and pushed the loose earth in on top of it. When the trench was filled in I trampled the earth firm, brought a number of vines of blue, scentless morning glory and set them in the ground above her grave. Then I collected sand and pebbles and scattered them around in order to obliterate the traces of the burial so completely that nobody should be able to tell that it had ever taken place. I performed this task so well that I myself was unable to distinguish her grave from the surrounding ground.

When I had finished I looked down at myself and saw that my clothes were torn and smeared with clay and black, clotted blood. Two blister-flies were circling around me and a number of tiny maggots were wriggling, stuck to my clothes. In an attempt to remove the bloodstains from the hem of my coat I moistened the edge of my sleeve with saliva and rubbed at the patches; but the bloodstains only soaked into the material, so that they penetrated through to my body and I felt the clamminess of blood upon my skin.

It was not long before sunset and a fine rain was falling. I began to walk and involuntarily followed the wheel tracks of the hearse. When night came on I lost the tracks but continued to walk on in the profound darkness, slowly and aimlessly, with no conscious thought in my mind, like a man in a dream. I had no idea in what direction I was going. Since she had gone, since I had seen those great eyes amid a mass of coagulated blood, I had felt that I was walking in a profound darkness that had completely enshrouded my life. Those eyes, which had been a lantern lighting my way, had been extinguished forever and now I did not care whether or not I ever arrived at any place.

There was complete silence everywhere. I felt that all mankind had rejected me and I took refuge with inanimate things. I was conscious of a relationship between me and the pulsation of nature, between me and the profound night that had descended upon my spirit. This silence is a language that we do not understand. My head began to swim, in a kind of intoxication. A sensation of nausea came over me and my legs felt weak. I experienced a sense of infinite weariness. I went into a cemetery beside the road and sat down upon a gravestone. I held my head between my hands and tried to think steadily of the situation I was in.

Suddenly I was brought to myself by the sound of a hollow grating laugh. I turned and saw a figure with its face concealed by a scarf muffled around its neck. It was seated beside me and held under its arm something wrapped in a handkerchief. It turned to me and said,

"I suppose you want to get into town? Lost your way, eh? Suppose you're wondering what I'm doing in a graveyard at this time of night? No need to be afraid. Dead bodies are my regular business. Grave digging's my trade. Not a bad trade, eh? I know every nook and cranny of this place. Take a case in point—today I went out on a grave-digging job. Found this jar in the ground. Know what it is? It's a flower vase from Rhages, comes from the ancient city of Rey. Yes. That's all right, you can have the jar. Keep it to remember me by."

I put my hand into my pocket and took out two *krans* and one *abbasi*. The old man, with a hollow laugh that brought out gooseflesh all over my body, said,

"No, no. That's all right. I know you. Know where you live, too. I've got a hearse standing just near here. Come and I'll drive you home. Yes. It's only two steps away."

He put the jar into my lap and stood up. He was laughing so violently that his shoulders shook. I picked up the jar and set off in the wake of the stooping figure. By a bend in the road was standing a ramshackle hearse with two gaunt black horses harnessed to it. The old man sprang up with surprising nimbleness and took his place on the driver's seat. I climbed onto the vehicle and stretched myself out in the sunken space where they put the coffins, resting my head against the high ledge so that I should be able to look out as we drove along. I laid the jar on my chest and held it in place with my hand.

The whip whistled through the air; the horses set off, breathing hard. They moved with high, smooth paces. Their hooves touched the ground gently and silently. The bells around their necks played a strange tune in the damp air. In the gaps between the clouds the stars gazed down at the earth like gleaming eyes emerging from a mass of coagulated blood. A wonderful sense of tranquility pervaded my whole being. All that I could feel was the jar pressing against my chest with the weight of a dead body. The interlocking trees with their wry, twisted branches seemed in the darkness to be gripping one another by the hand for fear they should slip and crash to the ground. The sides of the road were lined with weird houses of individual geometrical shapes, with forlorn, black windows. The walls of the houses, like glowworms, gave forth a dim, sickly radiance. The trees passed by alarmingly in clumps and in rows and fled away from us. But it appeared to me that their feet became entangled in vines of morning glory that brought them to the ground. The smell of death, the smell of decomposing flesh, pervaded me, body and soul. It seemed to me that I had always been saturated with the smell of death and had slept all my life in a black coffin while a bent old man whose face I could not see transported me through the mist and the passing shadows.

The hearse stopped. I picked up the jar and sprang to the ground. I was outside the door of my own house. I hurriedly went in and entered my room. I put the jar down on the table, went straight into the closet, and brought out from its hiding place the tin box that served me as a safe. I went to the door, intending to give it to the old hearse-driver in lieu of payment, but he had disappeared; there was no sign of him or of his hearse. Frustrated, I went back to my room. I lit the lamp, took the jar out of the handkerchief in which it was wrapped, and with my sleeve rubbed away the earth that coated it. It was an ancient vase with a transparent violet glaze that had turned to the color of a crushed blister-fly. On one side of the belly of the vase was an almond-shaped panel framed in blue flowers of morning glory, and in the panel . . .

In the almond-shaped panel was *her* portrait . . . the face of a woman with great black eyes, eyes that were bigger than other people's. They wore a look of reproach, as though they had seen me commit some inexpiable sin of which I had no knowledge. They were frightening, magic eyes with an expression of anxiety and wonder, of menace and promise. They terrified me and attracted me and an intoxicating, supernatural radiance shone from their depths. Her cheekbones were prominent and her forehead high. Her eyebrows were slender and met in the middle. Her lips were full and half-open. Her hair was disheveled, and one strand of it clung to her temple.

NIMA YUSHIJ
(1896—1959)

Selected Poems

Translated from the Persian by Mahmud Kianush

Cold Ashes

From nights long gone
Round a handful of cold ashes,
Once a small fire,
A few stones are still left
On a peaceful path through the forest.

Like the woeful trace of an image
In the dust of my thoughts,
Every line of it a story of long sufferings.

My sweet day that was at peace with me,
Has changed to some sinister image,
Something cold and solid like a stone;
The breath of the autumn of my life,
An allusion to my fading spring:
Round a handful of cold ashes,
Once a small fire,
A few stones are still left
On a peaceful path through the forest
From nights long gone.

O People!

O people who are sitting, cheerful and laughing,
　　　　on the shore,
Someone is losing his life in the sea;
Someone is struggling in the rough, dark
　　　　and formidable sea.
Just when you are intoxicated with the thought
　　　　of conquering your enemies;
When you are deluding yourselves
　　　　that by helping one poor man you are building
　　　　prosperity for all;
When you are girding up your loins
　　　　for some endeavor;
Of what other concerns of yours should I speak?
Yes, all this while someone's life
　　　　is being needlessly sacrificed in the sea.

O people who have an exhilarating time on the shore:
Your tables bountiful, your bodies well clothed,
Someone in the sea is calling you for help,
He is buffeting the heavy waves
　　　　with his exhausted hands;
He is gasping for breath,
　　　　his eyes bulging out of their sockets in terror;
Water has filled his inside in the dark deep,
And in his growing distress
Out of the water he thrusts
Now his head, now his feet,
O people!

He tries not to lose sight
　　　　of this old world from far away,
And with the hope of some help he cries out;
O people, who are enjoying the view
　　　　from the peaceful shore!

Waves rush in, pounding on the silent shore,
       toppling like drunken men,
       lying sprawled out, unconscious,
And then, roaring, they retreat into the sea.
Again the same cry comes from far away:
"O people. . . ."

And the wind has a more tormenting sound
And the cry of the man in the sea
       is spreading out in the sound of the wind,
And from the midst of the water,
            close and distant,
Again this cry echoes:
"O people. . . ."

PARVIN E'TESAMI
(1907–1941)

Selected Poems

Translated from the Persian by Heshmat Moayyad

Iranian Women

Formerly a woman in Iran was almost non-Iranian.
All she did was struggle through dark and distressing days.

Her life she spent in isolation; she died in isolation.
What was she then if not a prisoner?

None ever lived centuries in darkness like her.
None was sacrificed on the altar of hypocrisy like her.

In the courts of justice no witness defended her.
To the school of learning she was not admitted.

All her life her cries for justice remained unheeded.
This oppression occurred publicly; it was no secret.

Many men appeared disguised as her shepherd.
Within each a wolf was hiding instead.

In life's vast arena such was woman's destiny:
to be pushed and shoved into a corner.

The light of knowledge was kept from her eyes.
Her ignorance could not be laid to inferiority or sluggishness.

Could a woman weave with no spindle or thread?
Can anyone be a farmer with nothing to sow or to reap?

The field of knowledge yielded abundant fruit,
but women never had any share in this abundance.

A woman lived in a cage and died in a cage.
The name of this bird in the rose garden was never mentioned.

Imitation is the desert of women's perdition, the pitfall causing her
    troubles.

Clever is that woman who never treads that murky road

Beauty depends on knowledge; bracelets of emerald
or Badakhshan* rubies do not indicate superiority.

All glamour of painted silks cannot match the simple beauty of a
    tunic.
Honor depends on merit, not on indulgence in vanities.

Shoes and clothes are made worthy by the person who wears
    them.
One's value does not rise and fall with high and low prices.

Simplicity, purity, and abstinence are the true gems.
Mined gems are not the only brilliant jewels.

What is the use of gold and ornaments if the woman is ignorant?
Gold and jewels will not cover up that blemish.

Only the robe of abstinence can mask one's faults.
The robe of conceit and passion is no better than nakedness.

---

* Badakhshan: Formerly a region comprising northeastern Afghanistan and
southeastern Tajikistan.

A woman who is pure and dignified can never be humiliated.
That which is pure cannot be affected by the impurities of
   incontinence.

Chastity is a treasure, the woman its guard, greed the wolf.
Woe if she knows not the rules of guarding the treasure.

The Devil never attends the table of piety as guest.
He knows that that is no place of feasting.

Walk on the straight path, because on crooked lanes
you find no provision or guidance, only remorse.

Hearts and eyes do need a veil, the veil of chastity.
A worn-out *chador** is not the basis of faith in Islam.

A Woman's Place

A home without a woman lacks amity and affection.
When one's heart is cold, the soul is dead.

Providence has nowhere decreed in book or discourse,
that excellence is man's, defect woman's share.

In creation's edifice woman has always been the pillar.
Who can build a house without a foundation?

If woman hadn't shone like the sun above life's mountain,
love's jeweler in vain would seek for gems in the mine.

Woman was an angel the moment she showed her face.
How ironic, then, that Satan slanders the angel!

---

* *Chador.* A black, tentlike garment worn by particularly pious women in Iran.

Plato and Socrates were great because the mothers
who nurtured them were themselves great.

Loghman* was succored by his mother in the cradle
long before attendance at school made him a philosopher.

Whether heroes or mystics, ascetics or jurists,
they all were first pupils in her school.

How can a child with no mother learn to love?
A kingdom with no ruler offers no safety and order.

Do you want to know the duties of man and woman?
The wife is the ship, the husband the sailor.

When the captain is wise and the ship solidly built,
why should there be fear of maelstroms and tempests?

If disaster strikes on this sea of troubles,
both can rely on each other's diligence and effort.

Today's girls are tomorrow's mothers.
On the mothers rests the greatness of the sons.

The clothes of good men would be all tattered,
if good women's hands didn't mend their holes.

Wherein lie man's strength and sustenance? In his wife's support.
What are woman's riches? Love of her children.

A good wife is more than the lady of the house.
She is its physician and nurse, guardian and protector.

---

* Loghman: Also known as Luqman the Wise; a legendary prophet and
philosopher mentioned in the Qur'an.

In times of felicity she is comrade and tender friend.
In times of adversity she shares the trouble and is helpmate.

An understanding wife frowns not in times of paucity.
A gentle husband fouls not his mouth with ugly words.

If life becomes restive like an unruly horse,
husband and wife assist each other in drawing the reins.

That man or woman succeeds to greatness
who gathers in fruits from the garden of knowledge.

In the world of arts and science are proffered attractive goods.
Let's trade in that market.

A woman who neglects to buy the gems of education and learning
has sold the jewel of her precious life too cheaply.

Alive are only those who wear a robe of excellence;
dead are those whose worth is measured by their nakedness.

Providence provides us with countless books of ideas.
We tear them all apart in search of a title or slogan.

When schools were wisely opened, we behaved foolishly.
When the arts flourished, we hid ourselves.

If the Devil's booth of selfishness and languor
is torn down, we are all lost.

Our time is spent in things like finding out
how much this one's dress cost, how much that one's shoes.

For our bodies we buy fanciful ornaments.
For our souls we tailor only coats of contempt.

We undermine the foundation of our spiritual building with
    conceit,
but build up new shops everywhere for our body's sake.

This attitude betrays corruption, not dignity.
This conduct represents abjection, not glory.

We do not grow wild like weeds on plains and river banks.
We are not little birds content with some seeds.

If we stick to wearing our own homespun, what matter to us
Whether others' brocade has gone up in price or down.

Worn-out cloth of our own manufacture is comelier
Than the silk produced by foreigners.

Is there any robe more precious than that of knowledge?
What brocade is prettier than that of learning?

Any clew spun by the spindle of wisdom
in the workshop of ambition turns into linen and silk.

Not by wearing earrings, necklaces, and coral bracelets
can a woman count herself a great lady.

What are colorful gold brocades and glittering ornaments good for,
If the face lacks the beauty of excellence?

The hands and neck of a good woman, O Parvin,
deserve the jewels of learning, not of color.

Chronology

SECTION IV: Indian Subcontinent (1919–1948)

1919 Amritsar Massacre

1920 Mahatma Gandhi launches Civil Disobedience
Movement in India

1947 India gains independence from British rule
Partition of Indian Subcontinent
Founding of Pakistan

1948 Mahatma Gandhi assassinated
Muhammad Ali Jinnah, founder of Pakistan, dies
First war between India and Pakistan

IV

Rise Up! Pakistan and the Independence of Urdu Literature, 1940–1950

UNDER THE AUSPICES of the East India Company, Great Britain had maintained economic and military control over large swaths of the Indian Subcontinent (modern-day India, Pakistan, and Bangladesh) since the middle of the eighteenth century. But after the 1857 Indian Revolt (sometimes called India's First War of Independence), Britain assumed direct rule over Indian affairs, transforming the new "British Raj," as colonial India was called, into the jewel in the crown of the British Empire.

British colonial rule greatly influenced all aspects of Indian culture, including its literature. A focus on European education meant the introduction of European writings into an Indian literary tradition that had flourished under the patronage of the Mughal Empire (1526–1858). Initially, the British encouraged the advancement of Indian literature, particularly in Urdu, which, along with Persian, was the dominant language of India by the nineteenth century. The ghazal—Sufi-inspired love poetry, with its mystical themes and romantic overtones—remained the dominant form of literary expression, but there was also a blossoming of Indian novels, plays, short stories, and literary magazines.

As anticolonial sentiment gained momentum in the twentieth century, Indian literature—and Urdu poetry in particular—gave voice to the struggle for freedom against British imperialism. Young Indian poets and writers who had traveled and studied in Europe returned to the Subcontinent to fuse traditional Indian literary genres with Enlightenment themes of sovereignty and independence. Perhaps no writer exemplified this phenomenon better than Muhammad Iqbal, widely recognized as the greatest Urdu poet of the twentieth century. "Rise up!" Iqbal called out to his fellow Indians. "The rule of the people is close at hand/ Erase all trace of the ancient Raj!"

The struggle against British rule took on new life on April 13, 1919, when British troops opened fire on a group of peaceful protesters gathered at Jallianwala Bagh in the city of Amritsar, killing some fifteen hundred unarmed men, women, and children. The Amritsar Massacre and its aftermath, intimately narrated by Sa'adat Hasan Manto in his memoir, *For Freedom's Sake*, effectively launched the Indian Independence Movement, paving the way for Mahatma Gandhi's civil disobedience against British rule. It was at this time that a group of socially and politically active writers came together to form the Progressive Writers' Movement, whose manifesto called for the use of literature as a vehicle not only for independence but also for the betterment of society as a whole. By focusing their work on the poor and marginalized, and by deliberately challenging the social, religious, and even sexual taboos of traditional Indian society (as evidenced by Ismat Chughtai's most famous short story, "The Quilt"), the Progressive Writers had a huge influence on the development of Urdu literature.

In Urdu poetry, the drive toward modernism was led by poets such as N. M. Rashed and Mohammad Sana'ullah Dar (better known by his pen name of Miraji), both of whom synthesized Indian and Western poetic styles (including free verse) to create innovative and experimental works that, while sometimes highly abstract and symbolic, were nevertheless grounded in political themes of human rights and the fight for freedom of expression and freedom from repression.

The struggle for freedom that had captivated the poets and writers of the time became a reality on August 15, 1947, as India gained its independence from Britain. Yet, in that same year, the internal fissures in Indian society that had begun in 1906, with the creation of the All India Muslim League—an organization of Muslim leaders suspicious of the Hindu-dominated Indian National Congress—led to the partitioning of the Subcontinent into Hindu- and Muslim-majority states (Pakistan and East Pakistan, which was later renamed Bangladesh). The unprecedented population exchanges that occurred in the first few months after Partition resulted in the displacement of some twelve million people and, ultimately, in the first of three major Indo-Pakistani wars over the next half-century.

SA'ADAT HASAN MANTO
(1912—1955)

For Freedom's Sake: A Memoir

(EXCERPT)

Translated from the Urdu by Muhammad Umar Memon

I DON'T REMEMBER the year but it must have been when Amritsar was reverberating everywhere with the cries of "Inqilab Zindabad!" ("Long Live Revolution!"). These cries, I recall, were filled with a strange excitement, with a gushing energy one saw only among the blossoming milkmaids of the city as they tore through its bazaars, with baskets of *uplas** carefully balanced on their heads. It was a wild and woolly time. The dread, tinged with sadness, which had hung in the atmosphere since the bloody incident at Jallianwala Bagh had completely disappeared and a dauntless fervor had taken its place: the desire to fling oneself headlong, regardless of where one might land.

People chanted slogans, staged demonstrations, and were sent to prison by the hundreds. Courting arrest had become a favorite pastime: you were apprehended in the morning and released by the evening. You were tried in the court and thrown in jail for a few months. You came out, shouted another slogan, and got arrested all over again.

Those days were so full of life! The tiniest bubble when it burst became a formidable vortex. Somebody would stand in the square, make a speech calling for a strike, and a strike followed. A tidal wave would sweep through, requiring everybody to wear only home-spun *khadi* (cotton) to put the textile factories of Lancashire out of business, and all imported cloth would be boycotted. Bonfires would go up in every square, and in the heat of excitement, people would peel off their clothes then and there and throw them into the flames. Now and then

---

* *Uplas*: Dried "cakes" of cow dung.

a woman tossed one of her ill-chosen saris down from her balcony and people would go wild with applause.

I remember one conflagration across from the main police station by the Town Hall. My classmate Shaikhu became so excited that he took off his silk jacket and cast it onto the pyre of imported clothing, setting off a round of thunderous applause, because he was the son of a noted toady. The applause excited him even more. He peeled off his silk shirt and offered it to the flames too, realizing only later that the shirt had gold buttons and cuff links.

I had never cared much for school anyway, but in those days I came to positively detest it. I'd leave the house with my books and make straight for the Jallianwala Bagh. Here, I'd watch whatever activity was going on until school ended. Or I would sit under a tree and stare at the women in the windows of houses some distance away, hoping that one of them would fall in love with me. Why such a thought entered my head I have no idea.

Jallianwala Bagh was the scene of much activity at the time. Canvas tents and enclosures were set up everywhere. People would choose somebody as "dictator" every few days and install him with due ceremony in the biggest tent. He would receive a military salute from his ragtag army of volunteers. In mock seriousness he would receive the greetings of *khadi*-clad men and women for three or four days, at most a fortnight. He would collect donations of flour and rice for the soup kitchen from the *banyas* (merchants), and one day while drinking his *lassi** (God only knows why it was so readily available in the Jallianwala Bagh area) would be raided by the police, arrested, and whisked away to prison.

I had an old classmate, Shahzada Ghulam Ali. You can get some idea of how close our friendship was from the fact that twice we had failed our high school exams together and once had even run away to Bombay. Our plan was to end up in the Soviet Union eventually. But when money ran out and we had to sleep on the streets, we had to write home to be forgiven, and returned.

Shahzada Ghulam Ali was a handsome young man: tall and fair as Kashmiris generally are, with a sharp nose and playful eyes. There was

---

* *Lassi*: Spiced yoghurt drink.

something particularly majestic in the way he walked, but his walk also carried a trace of the swagger of professional *ghundas*.*

He was not a "Shahzada" (prince) during our school days. But as revolutionary fervor picked up and he participated in a dozen or so rallies, the slogans, strings of marigold, songs of patriotic zeal, and the opportunity to talk freely with female volunteers turned him into a sort of half-baked revolutionary. One day he delivered his first speech. The next day I found out in the newspaper that Ghulam Ali had become a "Shahzada."

Soon he became known all over Amritsar, which is a fairly small city, and it doesn't take long for one to become famous or infamous there. Its residents—quite critical of ordinary people, and going to all lengths to find fault with them—couldn't be more forgiving to a religious or political leader. They always seem to be in need of a sermon or speech. One can survive here as a leader for a long time. Just show up in different garb each time: now black, now blue.

But that was a different time. All the major leaders were already in prison, and their place was free for the taking. The people of course had no need for leaders, at least not so terribly, but the revolutionary movement certainly did. It urgently needed people who would wear *khadi*, sit inside the biggest tent in the Jallianwala Bagh, make a speech, and get arrested.

In those days Europe was going through its first "dictatorships." Hitler and Mussolini had gained quite a bit of notoriety. Perhaps that's what led the Congress Party to create its own "dictators." When Shahzada Ghulam Ali's turn came, a full forty "dictators" had already been arrested.

I headed off to Jallianwala the minute I heard that the strange mix of circumstances had made our Ghulam Ali a "dictator." Volunteers stood guard outside the large tent. Ghulam Ali saw me and called me in. A mattress was spread out on the floor with a *khadi* bedcover on it, and there, leaning against cushions and bolsters, sat Ghulam Ali talking to a group of *khadi*-clad *banyas* about, I believe, vegetables. He finished the session quickly, gave instructions to his volunteers, and turned toward me. He looked far too serious, which prompted me to tease

* *Ghundas*: Street thugs.

him. As soon as the volunteers had cleared away, I laughed and said, "Hey, Prince, what's up?"

I made fun of him for quite a while. But there was no denying the change in him; it was palpable, and what's more, he was aware of it. He kept telling me, "Sa'adat, no, please don't make light of me. I know I'm a small man and don't deserve this honor. But from now on I want to keep it this way."

I returned to Jallianwala Bagh in the evening. It was packed with people. Ghulam Ali appeared amidst tremendous applause. He looked dashing in his immaculate white *khadi* outfit, the slight swagger mentioned earlier adding to his attraction. He spoke for nearly an hour. Goose bumps broke out on my body several times during his speech.

GOD KNOWS HOW many years have passed since then. Our emotions and the tide of events were in a state of flux. It is difficult to describe their precise modulations now. But as I write this story and recall him making that speech, all I see is youth itself talking, a youth innocent of politics, filled with the sincere boldness of a young man who suddenly stops a woman on the street and tells her straight out, "Look, I love you," then surrenders himself to the law.

I've heard many more speeches since. But in none of them have I heard even a faint echo of the bubbling madness, reckless youth, raw emotion, and naked challenge that filled Shahzada Ghulam Ali's voice that day. Speeches today are laced with calculated seriousness, stale politics, and a prudence couched in lyricism.

At the time neither side, the government or the people, was experienced. They were at each other's throats, unaware of the consequences. The government sent people to prison without understanding the implications of such a step, and those who submitted to voluntary arrest showed equal ignorance of the true significance of their act.

It was wrongheadedness, and potentially explosive. It ignited people, subsided, and ignited them all over again, creating a surge of fiery exuberance in the otherwise dull and gloomy atmosphere of servitude.

THE ENTIRE JALLIANWALA Bagh exploded with loud applause and inflammatory slogans as Shahzada Ghulam Ali ended his speech. His face was gleaming. When I met him alone and pressed his hand to congratulate him, I could feel that it was shaking. A similar warm throbbing was evident on his bright face. He was gasping a bit. His eyes were glowing with the heat of passion, but they also hid the trace of a search that had nearly exhausted itself. They were desperately looking for somebody. Suddenly he snatched away his hand and darted toward the jasmine bushes.

A young woman stood there, wearing a spotless *khadi* sari. The next day I came to know that Shahzada Ghulam Ali was in love with her. It was not a one-sided love. Because she, Nigar, loved him madly in return. Nigar, as is obvious from her name, was a Muslim girl. She was an orphan. She worked as a nurse in a women's hospital. She was perhaps the first Muslim girl in Amritsar to come out of purdah* and join the Congress Movement.†

Partly her *khadi* outfit, partly her participation in the activities of the Congress, and partly also the atmosphere of the hospital—all these had slightly mellowed her Islamic demeanor, the harshness that is part of a Muslim woman's nature, and softened her a bit.

She was not beautiful, but she was a model of femininity in her own way. Humility, the desire to respect and worship, and *adarsh*,‡ so characteristic of a Hindu woman's makeup, had come together in Nigar in a most pleasing combination. Back then the image would never even have occurred to me, but now whenever I think of her, she appears to me as beautiful confluence of Muslim *namaz* (prayer) and Hindu *arti* (offering).

She practically worshipped Shahzada Ghulam Ali. He too loved her madly. When I asked him about her, he told me they had met during the Congress rallies and after a brief time together had decided to tie the knot.

Ghulam Ali wanted to marry her before his imminent arrest. I have no idea why. He could have just as easily married her after his release. Prison sentences used to be quite short in those days. Three months, at

---

* Purdah: Literally, "curtain." The practice of seclusion for women.
† Congress Movement: The Indian National Congress, founded in 1885, led the movement for independence from British rule and became India's dominant political party after Partition.
‡ *Adarsh*: One who is ideal; in this case, ideally feminine.

most a year. Some would be let go after only a fortnight, to make room for others. Anyway, he'd told Nigar of his plan, and she was willing. All that was needed was Baba-ji's blessing.

Baba-ji, as you must know, was a major figure. He was staying outside the city in the palatial lodgings of the city's richest jeweler, Hari Ram. Ordinarily he lived in his *ashram* in a neighboring village. But whenever he came to Amritsar, he encamped at Hari Ram's. For the duration of his stay, this house would become a shrine for his devotees, who would stand in long lines patiently waiting for his *darshan*.* Baba-ji gave a general audience and took donations for his *ashram* in the evening seated on a wooden platform laid out under a cluster of mango trees some distance from the house. This was followed by the chanting of *bhajans*,† and the session would end at his bidding.

Baba-ji was an abstemious and God-fearing man. He was also very learned and intelligent. These qualities had endeared him to everyone, Hindu, Muslim, Sikh, and untouchable. Everybody considered him their leader.

On the face of it, Baba-ji was indifferent to politics, but it was an open secret that every political movement in the Punjab started and ended at his behest. The government found him intractable, a political riddle that even the brightest government people could never hope to solve. His barest smile stirred up a million speculations, but when he proceeded to interpret it himself in an entirely novel way, the populace, already in thrall, felt truly overwhelmed.

The civil disobedience movement in Amritsar, with its frequent arrests, quite clearly owed a lot to Baba-ji's influence. Every evening at *darshan* he'd drop an innocuous word from his toothless mouth about the freedom movement in the whole of Punjab and about the fresh and increasingly harsh measures of the government, and the mighty leaders of the time would scramble to pick it up and hang it around their necks like a priceless amulet.

People said that his eyes had a magnetic quality, his voice was magical, and he had a cool head—so cool indeed that the worst obscenities, the sharpest sarcasm, could not provoke him, not even for a millionth of a

---

* *Darshan*: A vision of the Divine; an ecstatic experience.
† *Bhajans*: Hindu devotional songs.

second—which made his opponents writhe in frustration. He must have taken some part in hundreds of demonstrations in Amritsar, but, strangely, I hadn't caught a glimpse of him, from far or near, although I'd seen every other leader. So when Ghulam Ali mentioned going to his *darshan* to request his permission to marry, I asked him to take me along.

The very next day Ghulam Ali arranged for a tonga,* and we arrived at Lala Hari Ram's magnificent mansion.

Baba-ji was done with his morning *ashnan* (ablutions) and worship and was listening to a beautiful *pandatani*† sing patriotic songs. He was seated on a palm mat spread out on the immaculate white tile floor. A bolster lay near him but he wasn't leaning against it.

The room had no other furnishings besides the mat. The *pandatani*'s onion-colored face looked stunningly beautiful in the light reflecting off the tiles.

In spite of being an old man of seventy or seventy-two, Baba-ji's entire body—on which he had only a tiny red ochre loincloth—was free of wrinkles. His skin had a rich dark color. I came to know later that he used to have olive oil rubbed into it before taking his bath.

He greeted Shahzada Ghulam Ali with a smile and also glanced at me. He acknowledged our greetings by a slight widening of the same smile and then made a sign for us to sit down.

Today, when I imagine that scene and examine it closely, I find it quite intriguing. A half-naked old man sitting on a palm mat in the style of a yogi, his posture, his bald head, his half-opened eyes, his soft tawny body, indeed every line in his face radiating a tranquil contentment, an unassailable conviction: he cannot be dislodged, not even by the worst earthquake, from the summit where the world has placed him. And close to him sits a just-opened bud from the Vale of Kashmir, her head bowed, partly from respect for the elderly man nearby, partly from the effect of the patriotic song, and partly from her own boundless youth, yearning to spill out of the confining folds of her coarse white sari and sing not just a song for the country but a song dedicated equally to her youth; she wanted to honor not just the nearness of this

---

* Tonga: A horse carriage.
† *Pandatani*: A Hindu woman who chants the Vedas; hence Manto's reference to her as the "Pandit girl."

elderly man but also that of some healthy youth who would have the spunk to grab her hand and jump headfirst into life's raging fire. Opposite the elderly man's granite confidence and serenity, her onion-colored face, her dark lively eyes, her bosom heaving inside her coarse *khadi* blouse, all seemed to throw a silent challenge: come, hurl me down from where I stand, or lift me up to sublimity.

Nigar, Shahzada Ghulam Ali, and I sat somewhat off to one side; I was frozen like a perfect idiot, equally flustered by Baba-ji's imposing personality and the unblemished beauty of the young Kashmiri woman. The glossy tiles also had an effect on me, indeed quite an effect. What if the Pandit girl would let me kiss her eyes, just once. The thought pulsated through my body, and my mind immediately darted off to my maidservant, for whom I'd begun to feel something lately. I felt like leaving everybody and making straight for home—I might succeed in stealthily luring her upstairs to the bedroom. I just might. But the second my glance fell on Baba-ji and the passionate strains of the nationalistic song swelled in my ears, a different thought would begin to run through my body: if I could just get hold of a handgun, I'd rush to the Civil Lines area and start making short work of the English.

And next to this perfect idiot sat Nigar and Ghulam Ali, a pair of hearts in love, somewhat tired of their long and uneventful throbbing, ready to melt into each other to find those other shades of love. In other words, they'd come to ask Baba-ji, their uncontested political leader, for permission to marry. Obviously it was not the song of the nation that resonated in their heads at that moment. It was their own song, beautiful, but as yet unsung.

The song ended. With a hand gesture Baba-ji gave his blessing to the Pandit girl and then turned, smiling, to Nigar and Ghulam Ali, again managing a small glance at me as well.

Ghulam Ali was perhaps about to introduce himself and Nigar but Baba-ji—goodness, his memory—quickly said to him in his sweet voice, "Prince, you haven't been arrested yet?"

"No, not yet," Ghulam Ali replied, his hands folded in respect.

Baba-ji picked out a pencil from the pen box and toyed with it as he said, "But you are—I think."

The remark went over Ghulam Ali's head. So Baba-ji looked at the Pandit girl and said, pointing at Nigar, "Nigar has captured our Prince."

Nigar blushed. Ghulam Ali's mouth fell open. And the onion color of the Pandit girl flushed with good wishes. She gave the pair a look that seemed to say, "How wonderful!"

Baba-ji looked at the Pandit girl once again. "These children," he said to her, "have come to ask for my permission. How about you, Kamal, when are you going to get married?"

So she was called Kamal! The abrupt question caught her off guard, and she turned red in the face. "Me?" she said in a trembling voice, "I've decided to join your *ashram*."

She said this with a trace of regret, which Baba-ji's perceptive mind registered instantly. He gave her a smile, the soft smile of a yogi, and then turned to Ghulam Ali and Nigar and asked, "So have the two of you made up your minds?"

"Yes," they answered softly in unison.

Baba-ji scanned them with his politician's eyes. "Sometimes," he said, "one is obliged to change the decisions one has made."

For the first time in Baba-ji's lofty presence, Ghulam Ali loosed the boldness of his coltish youth, saying, "Even if our decision is put off for some reason, it will never change!"

Baba-ji closed his eyes and proceeded to question him in the manner of a lawyer, "Why?"

Surprisingly, Ghulam Ali didn't lose his nerve at all. His ardent love for Nigar made him say, "Circumstances may force us to put it off, but our decision to free India is irrevocable. Absolutely!"

Baba-ji, I now feel, didn't think it profitable to query him further on the subject and smiled—a smile that everyone present must have interpreted in his or her own way. And if asked, Baba-ji would have given it a radically different meaning. Of that I'm sure.

Anyway, stretching further the smile that evoked a thousand different meanings, he said, "Nigar, come join our *ashram*! It is only a matter of days before Prince will be sent to jail."

"All right, I will," she answered softly.

Baba-ji changed the subject and asked about the revolutionary activities in the Jallianwala Bagh camp. Ghulam Ali, Nigar, and Kamal filled him in for what seemed like a long time about various arrests, releases, and even about milk, *lassi*, and vegetables. During this time I sat there like a bumpkin, wondering why Baba-ji dillydallied so much in giving his blessing to Ghulam Ali and Nigar. Did he have doubts about their love for each other? About Ghulam Ali's sincerity? Had he invited Nigar to the *ashram* just to help her get over the pain she'd doubtless feel at her husband's incarceration? But then, why had Kamal responded to Baba-ji's question, "Kamal, when are you going to get married?" with, "I've decided to join your *ashram*"? Didn't men and women marry at the *ashram*? These were the kinds of questions that were raging inside my head, as the four of them sat speculating about whether the number of lady volunteers was enough to deliver *chapatis** for five hundred militants on time. How many stoves were there? How large were the griddles? Couldn't one get a griddle big enough for six women to bake *chapatis* all at once?

This Pandit girl Kamal—I was wondering—would she just chant national songs and religious *bhajans* for Baba-ji's edification once she was admitted to the *ashram*? I had seen the male volunteers of the *ashram*. True enough, they all took their ritual bath and brushed their teeth every morning, they all spent most of their time out in the open air and chanted *bhajans* in accordance with the rules of the *ashram*, but their clothing still reeked of perspiration, didn't it? Quite a few had bad breath to boot. And I never saw on anyone even a trace of the good nature and freshness one associates with outdoor living. Instead, they looked stooped and repressed, their faces pallid, eyes sunken, and bodies ravaged—as blanched and lifeless as the udders of a cow from which the last drop of milk has been squeezed out.

I'd seen these *ashram*-wallahs on numerous occasions in the Jallianwala Bagh. I couldn't imagine Kamal, who was molded in her entirety out of milk, honey, and saffron, being subjected to the gaze of these men who had nothing but filth in their eyes. Would she—a being swathed all over in the scent of *loban*†—have to listen to them with their mouths smelling worse than the stench of rotting mulch? Perhaps, I thought, the independence of India was above all this.

But this "perhaps" was not something I could understand, what with my patriotism and passion for the country's freedom. I thought of

---

* *Chapatis*: Indian flatbread.
† *Loban*: A fragrant resin made from pine trees: often burned as incense in Hindu temples.

Nigar, who was sitting very close to me and telling Baba-ji that turnips usually took quite a long time to cook. For heaven's sake, what had turnips got to do with marriage? She and Ghulam Ali had come for Baba-ji's blessing to get married, hadn't they?

My thoughts wandered off to Nigar and the *ashram*, which I had never visited. *Ashrams, vidyalas, jamat-khanas, takiyas,* and *darsgahs,** all such places inspire only the deepest revulsion in me. I don't know why. I've often seen boys and the caretakers of orphanages and schools for the blind walking in a row along streets asking for handouts. I have also seen *jamat-khanas* and *darsgahs*: boys donning shar'i pajamas well above their ankles, their foreheads marked with calluses despite their tender age, the slightly older boys wearing thick bushy beards, the younger ones with a revolting growth of sparse bristles on their cheeks and chins; absorbed in prayer, but their faces reflecting pure beastliness.

Nigar was a woman, not a Muslim, Hindu, Sikh, or Christian, just a woman. No, she was more than that, a woman's prayer intended for her lover, or for one whom she herself loved with all her heart. I couldn't imagine her—she who was herself a prayer—raising her hands in prayer every morning as required by the rules of Baba-ji's *ashram*.

Today as I recall Baba-ji, Nigar, Ghulam Ali, the ravishingly beautiful Pandit girl, indeed the entire atmosphere of Amritsar, engulfed as it was in those days in the fine romantic haze created by the independence movement, all appear like a dream, the sort one longs to have over and over again.

I still haven't seen Baba-ji's *ashram*, but I hate it as passionately today as I did then. I don't care at all for a place where people are subjected to an unnatural way of life. To strive for freedom is fine. I can even understand dying for it. But to turn living people into mere vegetables, without passion or drive, is beyond me. To live in poor housing, shun amenities, sing the Lord's praises, shout patriotic slogans—fine! But to stifle in humans the very desire for beauty! What kind of humans have no feeling for beauty, no zest for life? Show me the difference between the *ashrams, madrasas,* and *vidyalas* that accomplish this and a field of horseradishes!

---

* *Ashrams, vidyalas,* etc.: Places of spiritual gatherings in South Asian Hindu and Muslim traditions.

Baba-ji sat talking about the remainder of the activities in Jallianwala Bagh with Ghulam Ali and Nigar for a long time. Finally he told the couple, who had not forgotten, apparently, about the purpose of their visit, to return there and the next day in the evening he himself would wed them.

The two were elated. What greater fortune could there be than to have Baba-ji himself perform their marriage! Ghulam Ali later told me that he had become so overjoyed he thought it couldn't be true. The slightest gesture of Baba-ji turned into an historic event. He couldn't believe that such a great man would personally come to Jallianwala Bagh for the sake of an ordinary man, a man who had become the Congress's "dictator" merely by accident. Precisely the headline that splashed across the front pages of newspapers throughout India.

Ghulam Ali wondered whether Baba-ji would show up. Wasn't he a terribly busy man after all? But the doubt, which he had raised as a psychological precaution, proved wrong, as expected. Promptly at 6 p.m., just as the bushes of *rat ki rani** were beginning to pour forth their fragrance, and a band of volunteers that had set up a small tent for the bride and groom was decorating it with jasmine flowers, marigolds, and roses, Baba-ji walked in, supporting himself on his *lathi*, with the patriotic song-spouting Pandit girl, his secretary, and Lala Hari Ram in tow.

Ghulam Ali was standing by the well when he heard that Baba-ji had arrived, and, if I remember correctly, I was asking him, "You know, Ghulam Ali, don't you, how this well was once filled to its mouth with the bodies of people slain in the firing? Today everybody drinks from it. It's watered every flower in this park. People come and pluck those flowers. But strangely, not even a drop carries the salty taste of blood. Not a single petal of a single flower has the redness of blood in it. Why is that?"

I vividly remember that as I said this I had looked at the window of a neighboring house where, it is said, a young girl had been shot dead by General Dyer† as she stood watching the massacre. The streak of blood had begun to fade on the old lime wall behind the window.

---

* *Rat ki rani*: "Queen of the night" in Urdu; a woody shrub also known as night-blooming jasmine.
† General Dyer: Reginald Edward Harry Dyer (1864–1927), British brigadier-general responsible for the 1919 Jallianwala Bagh Massacre.

Blood had become so cheap that spilling it no longer affected people as it once had. I remember I was in my third or fourth class at school, and six or seven months after the bloody massacre our teacher had taken us to see Jallianwala Bagh. It hardly looked like a park then, just a dreary and desolate stretch of uneven earth, strewn all over with clods of dried dirt. I remember how the teacher had picked up a small clod, reddened I believe from pan spittle, and showed it to us, saying, "Look, it's still red from the blood of our martyrs!"

Anyway, hearing that Baba-ji had arrived, Ghulam Ali rushed to gather the volunteers in one place. Together they gave Baba-ji a military salute. The two inspected different camps for quite some time. All the while Baba-ji, who had a keen sense of humor, fired off numerous witty remarks during conversation with female volunteers and other workers.

In the meantime the evening haze began to settle over the Jallianwala Bagh and lights came on in nearby houses here and there. A group of volunteer women started to chant *bhajans*. Baba-ji listened with his eyes closed. Roughly a thousand people must have gathered. They sat on the earth around the platform. Except for the *bhajan*-singing girls, everyone else was hushed.

The chanting tapered off into a silence that seemed anxious to be broken. So when Baba-ji opened his eyes and trilled sweetly, "Children, as you already know, I'm here to unite these two freedom lovers in marriage," the entire Bagh resonated with loud cries of jubilation.

Nigar, in her bridal attire, sat on a corner of the platform, her head bowed low. She looked very lovely in her tricolored *khadi* sari. Baba-ji motioned for her to come closer and sat her next to Ghulam Ali.

Ghulam Ali's face was unusually flushed. When he took the wedding contract from his friend and handed it over to Baba-ji, I noticed his hand was shaking.

A Maulvi Sahib* was also present on the platform. He recited the Qur'anic verse customary at weddings; Baba-ji listened to it with closed eyes. The custom of "proposal and acceptance" over, Baba-ji gave his blessing to the bride and groom. Meanwhile the congratulatory showering of the couple with dried dates—the *chhuwaras*—traditional at such

---

* Maulvi Sahib: A revered teacher or scholar of Islamic law.

events had begun. Baba-ji snatched a dozen or so for himself and tucked them away.

Smiling shyly, a Hindu girlfriend of Nigar's gave Ghulam Ali a tiny box as a present and whispered something in his ear. He opened the box and covered the part in Nigar's hair with *sendur* dust. The drabness of Jallianwala Bagh was enlivened again with a round of loud applause.

Baba-ji got up amidst all the noise. A hush instantly fell over the crowd.

The mixed fragrance of *rat ki rani* and jasmine wafted by on the light evening breeze. The scene was absolutely breathtaking. Baba-ji's voice had acquired an extra measure of sweetness today. After congratulating the couple on their wedding, he said, "These two will work for their country and nation with even greater dedication now, because the true meaning of marriage is none other than true friendship between a man and a woman. Ghulam Ali and Nigar will work together as friends for *swaraj* (freedom). Such marriages are commonplace in Europe—I mean marriages based on friendship and friendship alone. People who are able to exorcise carnal passion from their lives are worthy of our respect."

Baba-ji explicated his concept of marriage at length. He firmly believed that the true joy of marriage was something above and beyond the bodily union of the mates. He didn't consider sexual union as important as people generally made it out to be. Thousands of people ate just to satisfy their craving for flavor. But did this mean that to do so was incumbent on humans? Although people who ate solely out of the need to stay alive were very few, they alone knew the true meaning of eating. Likewise, only those people who married out of the desire to experience the purity of this emotion and the sanctity of this sacred relationship truly enjoyed connubial bliss.

Baba-ji expounded on his belief with such clarity and profound sincerity that an entirely new world opened up before his listeners. I too was deeply touched. Ghulam Ali, who sat opposite me, was so engrossed in Baba-ji's speech he seemed to be drinking in every word. When Baba-ji stopped, Ghulam Ali briefly consulted with Nigar, got up, and declared in a trembling voice:

"Ours will be just such a marriage. Until India wins her freedom, Nigar's and my relationship will be entirely like that of friends."

More shouts of applause followed, enlivening the dreary atmosphere in the Jallianwala Bagh with its cheery tumult for quite a while. Shahzada Ghulam Ali grew emotional, and streaks of red blotched his Kashmiri face. "Nigar!" he addressed his bride in a loud voice. "Can you bear to bring a slave child into this world?"

Dazed in part by the wedding and in part by Baba-ji's harangue, Nigar lost her remaining presence of mind when she heard this whip-crack question. "No! Of course not!" was all she could get out.

The crowd clapped again, sending Ghulam Ali to an even higher pitch of emotion. The joy at saving Nigar from the ignominy of pro-ducing a slave baby went to his head, and he wandered off the main subject into the tortuous byways of how to free the country. For the next hour he spoke nonstop in a voice weighed down by emotion. Suddenly his glance fell on Nigar, and instantly, he was struck dumb. He couldn't get a word out. He was like some drunkard who keeps pulling out note after note without any idea how much he is spending and then suddenly finds his wallet empty. The abrupt paralysis of speech irritated him greatly, but he immediately looked in the direc-tion of Baba-ji, bowed, and again found his voice: "Baba-ji, bless us to remain steadfast in our vow."

Next morning at six Shahzada Ghulam Ali was arrested. In the same speech in which he had vowed not to father a child until the country gained her freedom, he had also threatened to overthrow the English. A few days after his arrest, Ghulam Ali was sentenced to eight months' imprisonment and sent to the Multan jail. He was the forty-first "dicta-tor" of Amritsar and, if I remember correctly the figures quoted in the newspapers, the forty-thousandth political activist apprehended and imprisoned for taking part in the independence movement.

Everybody thought that freedom was just around the corner. The astute British politicians, however, let the movement run its course. The failure of the major national leaders of India to reach an agreement pretty much took the teeth out of it.

Following their release, the freedom lovers tried to put the memory of their recent hardship behind them and get their interrupted business back on track. Shahzada Ghulam Ali was let go after only seven months. Even though the revolutionary fervor had considerably subsided by then, people did show up at the Amritsar Railway Station to greet him, and a few parties and rallies were held in his honor. I attended all of them. But they were largely lackluster affairs. A strange fatigue seemed to have come over people, like runners returning listlessly to the starting line after being suddenly told in the middle of the dash, "Stop! We'll have to do it over."

Several years passed. The listlessness, the exhaustion still hung over India. My own life went through a series of upheavals, some major, some minor. A beard and mustache had sprouted on my face. I entered college and failed twice in my F.A. My father died. I knocked about looking for a job and found work as a translator for a third-rate newspaper. Fed up, I decided to go back to school and enrolled in Aligarh University, but I contracted tuberculosis and within three months found myself wandering around rural Kashmir recuperating. Then I headed for Bombay. Witnessing three Hindu-Muslim riots in two years was enough to send me packing to Delhi. But that place, by comparison, turned out to be terribly drab, with everything moving at a snail's pace. Even where there was some sign of activity, it had a distinctly feminine feel to it. Well, maybe Bombay wasn't so bad after all, I thought, even if your next-door neighbor has no time to ask your name. What of it? Where there is time, you see a lot of hypocrisy, a lot of disease. So after spending two uneventful years in Delhi, I returned to fast-paced Bombay.

It was now eight years since I had left home. I had no idea what my friends were doing; I barely remembered the streets and lanes of Amritsar. How could I? I hadn't kept in touch with anybody back home. As a matter of fact, I'd become somewhat indifferent to my past in the intervening eight years. What good would it do now to total up what was spent eight years ago? In life's cash, the penny you want to spend today, or the one another may set his eyes on tomorrow, is the one that counts.

Some six years ago, when I wasn't quite as hard up, I'd gone to the Fort area to shop for a pair of expensive dress shoes. The display cases on Hornby Road had been tempting me for some time. But since I have a particularly weak memory, I wasn't able to locate the shop in question. I strolled on until I came to a small shop that sold footwear. The attendant greeted me and asked, "Well, Sahib, what do you want?"

For a moment or two I tried to remember what I had come to buy. "Oh, yes. Show me a pair of dress shoes with rubber soles."

"We don't carry them."

The monsoons will start any day now, I thought, why not buy a pair of ankle-boots? "Well then, how about rubber ankle-boots?" "We don't sell those either," the man said. "Try the shop next door. We don't carry any rubber footwear at all."

"Why?" I asked out of curiosity.

"Boss's orders."

After this brusque but definitive reply, there was nothing I could do but leave. As I turned to go, my eyes fell on a well-dressed man with a child in his arms standing outside on the footpath buying a tangelo from a fruit-seller on the street. "You! Ghulam Ali!"

"Sa'adat!" he shouted and hugged me, the child at his chest sandwiched between us. The child didn't like it and started to cry. Ghulam Ali called the man who had attended me, handed the child over to him and said, "Go! Take him home!" Then he said to me, "It's been years, hasn't it?"

I probed his face. The swagger, the ever-so-slight trace of rakishness that had been such a prominent feature of his appearance had entirely disappeared. It was a common family man who stood before me, not the fiery young khadi-clad speech-maker. I remembered his last speech, when he had energized Jallianwala Bagh with his sizzling hot words, "Nigar! Can you bear to bring a slave child into this world?" Instantly I thought of the child. I asked him, "Whose child was that?"

"Mine, of course," he answered, without the least hesitation. "I have an older one, too. And you, how many do you have?"

For a second I felt it was somebody else talking. Hundreds of questions rattled in my mind: Had Ghulam Ali completely forgotten his vow? Had he disassociated himself entirely from his political life? The ardor, the passion to win freedom for India, where had they gone? Whatever happened to that naked challenge? Where was Nigar? Had she been able to bear giving birth to two slave children after all? Maybe she'd died and Ghulam Ali had remarried.

"What are you thinking?" Ghulam Ali smacked me on the shoulder and said. "Come on, let's talk. We've met after such a long time."

I started, let out an elongated "Yes-s-s," and fumbled for words. But

Ghulam Ali didn't give me a chance and started to speak himself instead: "This is my shop. I've been living in Bombay for two years. Business is good. I can easily save three, even four hundred rupees a month. And what are you doing? I hear you've become a big short story writer. Remember the time we ran off to Bombay together? But, *yar*, that was a different Bombay. It was small. This one is huge. Or it seems huge to me, anyway."

Meanwhile a customer walked in, looking for tennis shoes. Ghulam Ali told him, "No rubber stuff here. Please go to the shop next door."

"Why not?" I asked Ghulam Ali as soon as the customer left. "I was looking for a pair of shoes with rubber soles myself."

I'd asked the question only casually, but his face fell. "I just don't like them," he said, softly.

"What do you mean, 'them'?"

"Rubber—I mean things made of rubber." He tried to smile, but couldn't. He let out a laugh instead, loud and dry. "O.K., I'll tell you. It's just a silly thing, but somehow it's had a significant impact on my life." Traces of deep reflection appeared on his face; his eyes, playful as ever, dimmed for a second and then lit up again. "That life—it was absolutely phony! To tell you the truth, Sa'adat, I've completely forgotten the days when this thing about being a leader had gotten into my head. But the past four, five years have been pure bliss. I can never thank God enough for all He's given me. I have a wife, children. . . ."

"Thanking God enough" got him started about his business venture: the initial investment, the profit he'd made in a year's time, the money he had in the bank now. I interrupted him, "But what's this 'silly thing' that had a profound impact on your life?"

The glow once again disappeared from his face. "Ye-e-e-s," he said. "It *had* a profound impact. Thank God it no longer does. I guess I'll have to tell you the whole thing.

"How I got started on my political career you know well enough. And you also know what kind of character I had. We were pretty much alike. I mean, let's be honest, our parents couldn't brag about us being without blemish. I wasn't endowed with a strong character. But I had this desire to do something. That's what drove me to politics. But I swear to God that I was not a fake. I could have laid down my life for the country. I still could. All the same I feel—in fact, it's a conclusion I've come to after much serious thought—that India's politics and her leaders are all pretty green, as green as I used to be. A tidal wave rises, but I think it doesn't rise on its own, it's deliberately created. . . . Perhaps I haven't been able to lay it all out for you clearly."

His thoughts were terribly muddled. I gave him a cigarette. He lit it, took a few long drags, and continued, "What do you think, doesn't every effort India has made to free herself look unnatural? Perhaps not the effort, maybe I should say the outcome of the effort. Why have we failed to achieve freedom? Are we a bunch of sissies? Of course we aren't. We're men. But the environment is such that our energies fall short of what's needed to reach our goal."

"You mean like there is a barrier between us and freedom?" I asked.

His eyes gleamed. "Absolutely. But not like a solid wall or an impenetrable rock. It's like a membrane at the most, a cobweb, created by the way we conduct our politics, and live our sham lives. Lives in which we deceive others, and ourselves even more."

His thoughts were still in a jumble. He seemed to be trying to make an accounting of all his past experiences on the spot. He stubbed out the cigarette, looked at me, and said, "A person should stay the way God made him. He does not need to shave his head, wear red ochre clothes, or cover his body with ash to do good works, does he? You might say a person does all those things out of his own will. That's just it. This novelty, 'out of his own will,' is precisely what leads people astray, at least that's what I think. Their lofty position makes them indifferent to natural human weaknesses. But they completely forget that it is not their character, thinking, or beliefs that will endure in the minds of simple people—as a matter of fact, these disappear into thin air in no time at all. What does endure, rather, is the image of their shaven heads, red ochre garb, and ash-smeared bodies." Ghulam Ali grew terribly excited. "The world has seen a whole host of reformers. Nobody remembers their teachings. But crosses, sacred threads, beards, bracelets, and underarm hair survive. I can't understand why none of these contemporary reformers can see that he is disfiguring humans beyond all hope of recognition. There are times when I feel like screaming: 'For God's sake, haven't you deformed him enough already? At least take pity on him now and let him be! You want to make him into God, while the poor thing, he's having a hard time just holding on to his humanity.'

"Sa'adat, I swear to God this is how I feel. If it is wrong and false, then I don't know what is right and true. For two full years I've wrestled with my mind. I've argued with my heart, with my conscience, in fact with every pore of my body. In the end, I feel humans must remain humans. If a couple wants to curb their canal passion, let them. But the entire human race? For God's sake! What good will all that 'curbing' accomplish?"

He stopped briefly to light another cigarette, letting the entire matchstick burn itself out, shook his head ever so slightly, and continued: "No, Sa'adat, you cannot know the incredible misery I've been through, in my body and in my soul. But it couldn't be otherwise. Whoever attempts to go against nature is bound to come to grief. The day I made that vow in the Jallianwala Bagh—you remember, don't you?—that Nigar and I would not bring any slave children into this world, I felt an electrifying surge of happiness. However, when I got out of jail the painful realization slowly hit me that I had curbed a vital part of my body and soul, that I had crushed the prettiest flower in my garden between my palms. At first, the thought brought an exhilarating sense of pride: I had done what others could not. Slowly, when my reasoning became clear, the bitter truth began to sink in. I went to see Nigar. She had given up her job at the hospital and joined Baba-ji's *ashram*. Her faded color, her altered mental and physical condition—I thought I was mistaken, that my eyes weren't seeing right. Spending a year with her convinced me that her torment was the same as mine, although neither wanted to mention it to the other, feeling the noose of our vow tight around us.

"All that political excitement simmered down within a year. *Khadi* clothes and the tricolored flag no longer seemed so attractive. And even if the cry of 'Long Live Revolution' did go up now and then, it had lost its previous resonance. Not a single tent could be seen anywhere in the entire Jallianwala Bagh, except for a few pegs left in the ground as reminders of a time gone by. The political fervor had pretty much run out of steam.

"I spent most of my time at home, near my wife . . . ," he stopped, the same wounded smile playing on his lips once again. I kept quiet, so as not to interrupt his train of thought.

After a while he wiped the perspiration off his forehead, put out his cigarette and said, "We were both struck by a strange curse. You know how much I love Nigar. I'd think: 'What kind of love is this? When I touch her, why don't I allow the sensation to peak? Why do I feel so guilty? Like I'm committing a sin?' I love Nigar's eyes so much. One day when I was feeling normal . . . I mean just how one should feel, I kissed them. She was in my arms—or rather I should say, I had the sensation of holding a tremor in my arms. I was about to let myself go, but managed to regain control in time. For a long while afterward, several days, I tried to believe that my restraint had given my soul a pleasure few had experienced. The truth was, I'd failed. The failure, which I wanted to believe was a great success, instead made me the most miserable man on earth. But as you know, people eventually find ways to get around things. We were both drying up. Somewhere deep inside, a crust had started to form on our pleasures. 'We are fast turning into strangers,' I thought. After much thinking we felt that we could, without compromising our vow, I mean that Nigar wouldn't give birth to a slave child. . . ." The wounded smile appeared a third time, dissolved immediately into a loud laugh, with a distinct trace of pain in it, then he continued in an extremely serious tone of voice: "Thus started this strange phase of our married life. It was like a blind man suddenly having sight restored in one eye. I was seeing again. But soon the vision blurred. At first we thought . . ." He seemed to be fishing for the right word. "At first we felt satisfied. I mean we hadn't the foggiest idea that we'd start feeling terribly dissatisfied before long. As though having one eye wasn't enough. Early on we felt we were recovering, our health was improving. A glow had appeared on Nigar's face, and a shine in her eyes. For my part, my nerves no longer felt so hellishly strung out all the time. Slowly, however, we turned into rubber dummies. I felt this more than she did. You wouldn't believe it, but by God every time I pinched the flesh in my arms, it had the feel of rubber to it. Nigar's condition, I believe, was different. Her perspective was different too. She wanted to become a mother. Every time a woman in our lane had a baby, Nigar would sigh quietly. I didn't much care about having children. So what if we didn't have any? Countless people in the world don't either. At least I had remained steadfast in my vow. And that was no mean achievement. Well, this line of thinking did comfort me quite a bit, but as the thin rubbery web began to close around my mind, I became more and more anxious. At meals the bread felt chewy and spongy under my teeth." A shudder went through his body as he said this. "Thank God, I'm rid of the abomination now, but after what torment, Sa'adat. My life had turned into a dried and shriveled piece of sinew skin, all my desires smothered. But, oddly, my sense of touch had become unusually keen, almost unnaturally keen. Maybe not keen, but focused, in one direction only. No matter what I touched, wood, glass, metal, paper, or stone, it felt like the same clammy tenderness of rubber that made me sick! My torment would grow even worse when I thought about the object itself. All I needed to do was to grab my affliction in two fingers and toss it away, but I lacked the courage. I longed for something to latch on to for support so that I might reach the shore. I kept looking for it desperately. One day as I sat on the roof top in the sun reading, rather browsing, a religious book, my eyes caught a *hadis*[*] of the Prophet Muhammad and I jumped for joy. The 'support' was glaring in my eyes. I read the lines over and over again. I felt as if water had gushed through the desiccated arid landscape of my life. It was written: 'It is incumbent on man and wife to procreate after they are married. Contraception is permissible only in the event of danger to the lives of parents.' Then and there I peeled off my affliction and threw it aside."

He chuckled like a child. I did too, because he had picked up the cigarette with his two fingers and tossed it aside like some infinitely revolting object.

All of a sudden he became serious. "I know what you'll do, Sa'adat," he said. "You will turn all I've told you into a story. But, please, don't make fun of me in it. I swear to God, I've told you only what I've felt. But the substance of what I've learnt is this: it's no bravery to fight nature; no achievement to die or live starving, or dig a pit and bury yourself in it for days on end, or sleep for months on a bed of sharp nails, or hold one arm up for years until it atrophies and turns into a piece of wood. This is show business. You can't find God or win freedom with show business. I even think the reason India hasn't gained freedom is precisely because she has more showmen than true

---

[*] *Hadis*: Hadith; A saying of the Prophet Muhammad.

leaders. And the few leaders she does have are going against the laws of nature. They have invented a politics that stops faith and candidness from being born. It is this politics which has blocked the womb of freedom."

Ghulam Ali wanted to say more when the attendant walked in. He had a child, perhaps Ghulam Ali's second boy, in his arms. The boy was holding a colorful balloon. Ghulam Ali pounced on it like a madman. It burst with a loud boom. A piece of rubber dangling from a little bit of string remained in the boy's hand. Ghulam Ali snatched it with his two fingers and threw it away like some infinitely revolting object.

ISMAT CHUGHTAI

(1911—1991)

The Quilt

Translated from the Urdu by Syeda Hameed

IN THE DEPTH of winter whenever I snuggle into my quilt, my shadow on the wall seems to sway like an elephant. My mind begins a mad race into the dark crevasses of the past; memories come flooding in.

Excuse me, but I am not about to relate a romantic incident surrounding my own quilt—I do not believe there is much passion associated with it. The blanket, though considerably less comfortable, is preferable because it does not cast such terrifying shadows, quivering on the wall!

It all began when I was a small girl. All day long I fought tooth and nail with my brothers and their friends. I sometimes wonder why the devil I was so quarrelsome. At my age my older sisters had been busy collecting admirers; all I could think of was fisticuffs with every known and unknown girl or boy I ran into!

For this reason my mother decided to deposit me with an "adopted" sister of hers when she left for Agra. She was well aware that there was no one in that sister's house, not even a pet animal, with whom I could engage in my favorite occupation! I guess my punishment was well deserved. So Mother left me with Begum Jan, the same Begum Jan whose quilt is imprinted on my memory like a blacksmith's brand.

This was the lady who had been married off to Nawab Sahib for a very good reason, courtesy of her poor but loving parents. Although much past his prime, Nawab Sahib was noblesse oblige itself. No one had ever seen a dancing girl or a prostitute in his home. He had the distinction of not only performing the Haj himself, but of being the patron of several poor people who had undertaken the pilgrimage through his good offices.

145

Nawab Sahib had a strange hobby. Many people are known to have irksome interests like breeding pigeons and arranging cockfights. Nawab Sahib kept himself aloof from these disgusting sports; all he liked to do was keep an open house for students; young, fair, and slim-waisted boys, whose expenses were borne entirely by him. After marrying Begum Jan, he deposited her in the house with all his other possessions and promptly forgot about her! The young, delicate Begum began to wilt with loneliness.

Who knows when Begum Jan started living? Did her life begin when she made the mistake of being born, or when she entered the house as the Nawab's new bride, climbed into the elaborate four-poster bed, and started counting her days? Or did it begin from the time she realized that the household revolved around the boy-students, and that all the delicacies produced in the kitchen were meant solely for their palates? From the chinks in the drawing-room doors, Begum Jan glimpsed their slim waists, fair ankles, and gossamer shirts and felt she had been raked over the coals!

Perhaps it all started when she gave up on magic, necromancy, séances, and whatnot. You cannot draw blood from a stone. Not an inch did the Nawab budge.

Brokenhearted, Begum Jan turned toward education. Not much to be gained here either! Romantic novels and sentimental poetry proved even more depressing. Sleepless nights became a daily routine. Begum Jan slowly let go and consequently became a picture of melancholy and despair.

She felt like stuffing all her fine clothes into the stove. One dresses up to impress people. Now, Nawab Sahib neither found a spare moment from his preoccupation with the gossamer shirts, nor did he allow her to venture outside the home. Her relatives, however, made it a habit to pay her frequent visits that often lasted for months, while she remained a prisoner of the house.

Seeing these relatives disport themselves made her blood boil. They happily indulged themselves with the goodies produced in the kitchen and licked the clarified butter off their greedy fingers. In her household they equipped themselves for their winter needs. But, despite renewing the cotton filling in her quilt each year, Begum Jan continued to shiver, night after night. Each time she turned over, the quilt assumed ferocious shapes that appeared like shadowy monsters on the wall. She lay in terror; not one of the shadows carried any promise of life. What the hell was life worth anyway? Why live? But Begum Jan was destined to live, and once she started living, did she ever!

Rabbo arrived at the house and came to Begum Jan's rescue just as she was starting to go under. Her emaciated body suddenly began to fill out. Her cheeks became rosy; beauty, as it were, glowed through every pore! It was a special oil massage that brought about the change in Begum Jan. Excuse me, but you will not find the recipe for this oil in the most exclusive or expensive magazine!

When I saw Begum Jan she was in her early forties. She sat reclining on the couch, a figure of dignity and grandeur. Rabbo sat against her back, massaging her waist. A purple shawl was thrown over her legs. The very picture of royalty, a real maharani! How I loved her looks. I wanted to sit by her side for hours, adoring her like a humble devotee. Her complexion was fair, without a trace of ruddiness. Her black hair was always drenched in oil. I had never seen her part crooked, nor a single hair out of place. Her eyes were black, and carefully plucked eyebrows stretched over them like a couple of perfect bows! Her eyes were slightly taut, eyelids heavy, and eyelashes thick. The most amazing and attractive part of her face was her lips. Usually dyed in lipstick, her upper lip had a distinct line of down. Her temples were covered with long hair. Sometimes her face became transformed before my adoring gaze, as if it were the face of a young boy. . . .

Her skin was fair and moist and looked like it had been stretched over her frame and tightly stitched up. Whenever she exposed her ankles for a massage, I stole a glance at their rounded smoothness. She was tall, and appeared taller because of the ample flesh on her person. Her hands were large and moist, her waist smooth. Rabbo used to sit by her side and scratch her back for hours—it was almost as if getting scratched was for her the fulfillment of life's essential need, somehow more important than the basic necessities required for staying alive.

Rabbo had no other household duties. Perched on the four-poster bed, she was always massaging Begum Jan's head, feet, or some other part of her anatomy. If someone other than Begum Jan received such a quantity of human touching, what would the consequences be?

Speaking for myself, I can say that if someone touched me continuously like this, I would certainly rot.

As if this daily massage were not enough, on the days she bathed, this ritual lasted a full two hours! The braziers were lit behind closed doors and then the procedure started. Scented oils and unguents were massaged into her shining skin—imagining the friction caused by this prolonged rubbing made me slightly sick. Usually Rabbo was the only one allowed inside the sanctum. Other servants, muttering their disapproval, handed over various necessities at the closed door.

The fact of the matter was that Begum Jan was afflicted with a perpetual itch. Numerous oils and lotions had been tried, but the itch was there to stay. *Hakims** and doctors stated: it is nothing, the skin is clear. But if the disease is located beneath the skin, it's a different matter.

These doctors are mad! Rabbo used to say with a meaningful smile while gazing dreamily at Begum Jan. "May your enemies be afflicted with the skin disease! It is your hot blood that causes all the trouble!"

Rabbo! She was as black as Begum Jan was white, like burnt iron ore! Her face was lightly marked with smallpox, her body solidly packed; small, dextrous hands, a tight little paunch, and full lips, slightly swollen, which were always moist. A strange and bothersome odor emanated from her body. Those puffy hands were as quick as lightning, now at her waist, now her lips, now kneading her thighs and dashing toward her ankles. Whenever I sat down with Begum Jan, my eyes were riveted on those roving hands.

Winter or summer, Begum Jan always wore *kurtas* of Hyderabadi *jaali karga.*[†] I recall her dark skirts and billowing white *kurtas*, With the fan gently rotating on the ceiling, Begum Jan always covered herself with a soft wrap. She was fond of winter. I too liked the winter season at her house. She moved very little. Reclining on the carpet, she spent her days having her back massaged, chewing on dry fruit. Other household servants were envious of Rabbo. The witch! She ate, sat, and even slept with Begum Jan! Rabbo and Begum Jan—the topic inevitably cropped up in every gathering. Whenever anyone mentioned their

---

* *Hakims*: Lawyers, experts in Islamic law often used to settle disputes.
† *Jaali karga kurtas*: A long white blouse worn by men and women in South Asia.

names, the group burst into loud guffaws. Who knows what jokes were made at their expense? But one thing was certain—the poor lady never met a single soul. All her time was taken up with the treatment of her unfortunate itch.

I have already said that I was very young at that time and quite enamored of Begum Jan. She, too, was fond of me. When mother decided to go to Agra, she had to leave me with somebody. She knew that, left alone, I would fight continuously with my brothers, or wander around aimlessly. I was happy to be left with Begum Jan for one week, and Begum Jan was equally pleased to have me. After all, she was Amma's* adopted sister!

The question arose of where I was to sleep. The obvious place was Begum Jan's room; accordingly, on the first evening a small bed was placed alongside the huge four-poster. Until ten or eleven that night we played Chance and talked; then I went to bed. When I fell asleep, Rabbo was scratching her back. "Filthy wench," I muttered before turning over. In the middle of the night I woke up with a start. It was pitch dark. Begum Jan's quilt was shaking vigorously, as if an elephant was struggling beneath it.

"Begum Jan," my voice was barely audible. The elephant subsided. "What is it? Go to sleep." Begum Jan's voice seemed to come from afar.

"I'm scared." I sounded like a petrified mouse.

"Go to sleep. Nothing to be afraid of. Recite the *Ayat-ul-Kursi*."†

"Okay!" I quickly began the *Ayat*. But each time I reached "*Yalamu Mabain*" I got stuck. This was strange. I knew the entire *Ayat*!

"May I come to you, Begum Jan?"

"No, child, go to sleep." The voice was curt. Then I heard whispers. Oh God! Who was this other person? Now I was terrified.

"Begum Jan, is there a thief here?"

"Go to sleep, child; there is no thief." This was Rabbo's voice. I sank into my quilt and tried to sleep.

In the morning I could not even remember the sinister scene that

---

* Amma: Mother.

† *Ayat-ul-Kursi*: The "Throne Verse," verse 256 of the second sura (chapter) of the Qur'an.

had been enacted at night. I have always been the superstitious one in my family. Night fears, sleep-talking, sleepwalking were regular occurrences during my childhood. People often said that I seemed to be haunted by evil spirits. Consequently, I blotted out the incident from memory as easily as I dealt with all my imaginary fears. Besides, in the daytime the quilt seemed so innocent.

The next night I woke up again; this time a quarrel between Begum Jan and Rabbo was being settled on the bed itself. I could not make out what conclusion was reached, but I heard Rabbo sobbing. Then there were sounds of a cat slobbering in the saucer. To hell with it, I thought, and went off to sleep!

In the morning Rabbo had gone off to visit her son. He was a quarrelsome lad. Begum Jan had done a lot to help him settle down in life; she had bought him a shop, arranged a job in the village, but to no avail. She even managed to have him stay with Nawab Sahib. Here he was treated well, a new wardrobe was ordered for him, but, ungrateful wretch that he was, he ran away for no good reason and never returned, not even to see Rabbo. She therefore had to arrange to meet him at a relative's house. Begum Jan would never have allowed it, but poor Rabbo was helpless and had to go.

All day Begum Jan was restless. Her joints hurt like hell, but she could not bear anyone's touch. Not a morsel did she eat; all day long she moped in bed.

"Shall I scratch you, Begum Jan?" I asked eagerly while dealing out the deck of cards. Begum Jan looked at me carefully.

"Really, shall I?" I put the cards aside and began scratching, while Begum Jan lay quietly, giving in to my ministrations. Rabbo was due back the next day, but she never turned up. Begum Jan became irritable. She drank so much tea that her head started throbbing.

Once again I started on her back. What a smooth slab of a back! I scratched her softly, happy to be of some assistance.

"Scratch harder, open the straps," Begum Jan spoke. "There, below the shoulder. Ooh, wonderful!" She sighed as if with immense relief.

"This way," Begum Jan indicated, although she could very well scratch that part herself. But she preferred my touch. How proud I was!

"Here, oh, oh, how you tickle," she laughed. I was talking and scratching at the same time.

"Tomorrow I will send you to the market. What do you want? A sleeping-walking doll?"

"Not a doll, Begum Jan! Do you think I am a child? You know I am . . ."

"Yes . . . an old crow. Is that what you are?" She laughed.

"Okay then, buy a babua. Dress it up yourself, I'll give you as many bits and pieces as you want. Okay?" She turned over.

"Okay," I answered.

"Here." She was guiding my hand wherever she felt the itch. With my mind on the babua, I was scratching mechanically, unthinkingly. She continued talking. "Listen, you don't have enough clothes. Tomorrow I will ask the tailor to make you a new frock. Your mother has left some material with me."

"I don't want that cheap red material. It looks tacky." I was talking nonsense while my hand roved the entire territory. I did not realize it but by now Begum Jan was flat on her back! Oh God! I quickly withdrew my hand.

"Silly girl, don't you see where you're scratching? You have dislocated my ribs." Begum Jan was smiling mischievously. I was red with embarrassment.

"Come, lie down with me." She laid me at her side with my head on her arm. "How thin you are . . . and, let's see, your ribs," she started counting.

"No," I protested weakly.

"I won't eat you up! What a tight sweater," she said. "Not even a warm vest?" I began to get very restless.

"How many ribs?" The topic was changed.

"Nine on one side, ten on the other." I thought of my school hygiene. Very confused thinking.

"Let's see," she moved my hand. "One, two, three . . ."

I wanted to run away from her, but she held me closer. I struggled to get away. Begum Jan started laughing.

To this day whenever I think of what she looked like at that moment, I get nervous. Her eyelids became heavy, her upper lip darkened, and, despite the cold, her nose and eyes were covered with tiny beads of perspiration. Her hands were stiff and cold, but soft as if the skin had been peeled. She had thrown off her shawl and in the *karga kurta*, her body shone like a ball of dough. Her heavy gold *kurta* buttons were open, swinging to one side.

The dusk had plunged her room into a claustrophobic blackness, and I felt gripped by an unknown terror. Begum Jan's deep dark eyes focused on me! I started crying. She was clutching me like a clay doll. I started feeling nauseated against her warm body. She seemed possessed. What could I do? I was neither able to cry nor scream! In a while she became limp. Her face turned pale and frightening, she started taking deep breaths. I figured she was about to die, so I ran outside.

Thank God Rabbo came back at night. I was scared enough to pull the sheet over my head, but sleep evaded me as usual. I lay awake for hours. How I wished Ammi would return. Begum Jan had become such a terrifying entity that I spent my days in the company of household servants. I was too scared to step into her bedroom. What could I have said to anyone? That I was afraid of Begum Jan? Begum Jan, who loved me so dearly?

Today there was another tiff between Begum Jan and Rabbo. I was dead scared of their quarrels, because they signaled the beginning of my misfortunes! Begum Jan immediately thought about me. What was I doing wandering around in the cold? I would surely die of pneumonia! "Child, you will have my head shaven in public. If something happens to you, how will I face your mother?" Begum Jan admonished me as she washed up in the water basin. The tea tray was lying on the table. "Pour some tea and give me a cup." She dried her hands and face. "Let me get out of these clothes."

While she changed, I drank tea. During her body massage, she kept summoning me for small errands. I carried things to her with utmost reluctance, always looking the other way. At the slightest opportunity I ran back to my perch, drinking my tea, my back turned to Begum Jan.

"Ammi!" My heart cried in anguish. "How could you punish me so severely for fighting with my brothers?" Mother disliked my mixing with the boys, as if they were man-eaters who would swallow her beloved daughter in one gulp! After all, who were these ferocious males? None other than my own brothers and their puny little friends. Mother believed in a strict prison sentence for females; life behind seven padlocks! Begum Jan's "patronage," however, proved more terrifying than the fear of the world's worst *goondas*! If I had had the courage I would have run out onto the street. But helpless as I was, I continued to sit in that very spot with my heart in my mouth.

After an elaborate ritual of dressing up and scenting her body with warm attars and perfumes, Begum Jan turned her arduous heat on me. "I want to go home!" I said in response to all her suggestions. More tears.

"Come to me," she waxed. "I will take you shopping."

But I had only one answer. All the toys and sweets in the world kept piling up against my one and only refrain, "I want to go home!"

"Your brothers will beat you up, you witch!" She smacked me affectionately.

"Sure, let them," I said to myself annoyed and exasperated.

"Raw mangoes are sour, Begum Jan," malicious little Rabbo expressed her views.

Then Begum Jan had her famous fit. The gold necklace she was about to place around my neck was broken to bits. Gossamer net scarf was shredded mercilessly. Hair, which was never out of place, was tousled with loud exclamations of "Oh! Oh! Oh!" She started shouting and convulsing. I ran outside.

After much ado and ministration, Begum Jan regained consciousness. When I tiptoed into the bedroom, Rabbo, propped against her body, was kneading her limbs.

"Take off your shoes," she whispered. Mouselike, I crept into my quilt.

Later that night, Begum Jan's quilt was, once again, swinging like an elephant. "Allah," I was barely able to squeak. The elephant-in-the quilt jumped and then sat down. I did not say a word. Once again, the elephant started convulsing. Now I was really confused. I decided, no matter what, tonight I would flip the switch on the bedside lamp. The elephant started fluttering once again, as if about to squat. Smack, gush, slobber—someone was enjoying a feast. Suddenly I understood what was going on!

Begum Jan had not eaten a thing all day and Rabbo, the witch, was a known glutton. They were polishing off some goodies under the quilt, for sure. Flaring my nostrils, I huffed and puffed, hoping for a whiff of the feast. But the air was laden with attar, henna, sandalwood; hot fragrances, no food.

Once again the quilt started billowing. I tried to lie still, but it was now assuming such weird shapes that I could not contain myself. It seemed as if a frog was growing inside it and would suddenly spring on me.

"Ammi!" I spoke with courage, but no one heard me. The quilt, meanwhile, had entered my brain and started growing. Quietly creeping to the other side of the bed, I swung my legs over and sat up. In the dark I groped for the switch. The elephant somersaulted beneath the quilt and dug in. During the somersault, its corner was lifted one foot above the bed.

Allah! I dove headlong into my sheets!!

What I saw when the quilt was lifted, I will never tell anyone, not even if they give me a *lakh** of rupees.

* *Lakh*: One hundred thousand.

MUHAMMAD IQBAL
(1877–1938)

Selected Poems

Translated from the Urdu by
M. Hadi Husain
V. G. Kiernan
Zeenut Ziad

The Houri and the Poet

The Houri:[*]

You neither relish wine nor even look at me.
Strange that you do not know the ways of amity.
In every song you sing, in every breath you draw,
There is a quest, a pining for things yet to be.
O what a fair world you have fashioned with your song.
It makes me feel as if Heaven were illusory.

The Poet:

With your barbed tongue you waylay simple mortal men;
But mortal thorns give mortal men far sweeter pain.
What can I do? I cannot stay at rest, for I
Am like the zephyr blowing over hill and plain.
As soon as my gaze comes to rest on a fair face
My heart begins to yearn for a still fairer one.
From spark to star, from star to sun, progressively—
Such is my flight. To stop would be sheer death for me.

* Houri: An angelic female spirit residing in Paradise.

When I rise, having quaffed a cup of vernal wine,
I sing a song of yet another spring to be.
I seek the end of that which has no end at all
With ever-hopeful heart and never-wearied eye.
The hearts of lovers die in an eternal Heaven—
With no grief, none to share it with, no plaintive cry.

Translated by M. Hadi Husain

Heaven and the Priest

Being present myself, my impetuous tongue
To silence I could not resign
When an order from God of admission on high
Came the way of that reverend divine;
I humbly addressed the Almighty: Oh Lord,
Excuse this presumption of mine,
But he'll never relish the virgins of heaven,
The garden's green borders, the wine!
For Paradise isn't the place for a preacher
To meddle and muddle and mangle,
And he, pious man—second nature to him
Is the need to dispute and to jangle;
His business has been to set folk by the ears
And get nations and sects in a tangle:
Up there in the sky is no Mosque and no Church
And no Temple—with whom will he wrangle?

Translated by V. G. Kiernan

God's Command to the Angels

Rise up!

The poor of My world—awaken them!
Shake the palace walls!

Thrill captive blood with the heat of conviction
Let the gentle sparrow defy the falcon.

The rule of the people is close at hand
Erase all trace of the ancient Raj!*

The field that cannot feed the peasant
Set it on fire!

Who dares to obscure the Creator?
Banish this priest from My church!

Prostrate to Truth, circumambulate the idols
Blow out the lamps of the temples and mosques!

These marble slabs offend me!
Build Me a House of sticks and mud

Like crystal, this new age is dazzling and brittle
Teach the ways of Intoxication to the Poet of the East.

Translated by Zeenut Ziad

* Raj: British colonial rule in India.

MIRAJI*
(1912—1949)

Selected Poems

Translated from the Urdu by Geeta Patel

Far and Near

My heart drums a rhythm
your heart drums
a rhythm
but distantly.
Voluptuous spring will grace and depart the landscape
like this, distantly.
Stars will glimmer,
like this distantly.

Everything will stay, like this
distant.
But the taste of your desire
its savage music
will sit inside my heart,
close.

Devadasi and Pujari†

Look, come see a dance, the dance, the undefiled dance of a
   devadasi
slowly, slowly sorrow's shadow slipped off my heart

---

* Miraji: Pen name for Mohammad Sana'ullah Dar.
† Devadasi and Pujari: The Temple Dancer and the Priest.

she measures out her feet, softly softly, my mind wants
to become moonlight, extinguished on the floor

hidden behind a stone pillar I should look at her
silently, silently realize in wonder that
like a goddess-statue come to life you are dancing, dancing
like a forgetful queen of an army of water-sprites descended to
    earth
and ripples on water stir so, flicker
or a restless jungle deer who slithers on leaves
a cobra/female in a darkened jungle hisses and sways
like my covetous/lusting eyes sliding over her body
the devadasi stroking the earth, shows/exposes colors
black, black glittering eyes like lightning dance
and pearl-diamond jewelry glitters in light like this
in a high, blue-black sky canopy, like stars and moon glimmering.

When I see
the fold of her slip taut under her arms
then should the ordinary thud of my heart
and my breath sharpen fast
when ripples flow through the long, loose, limber skirt
and its swirl subsides
every vein in my mind shudders
a melody of signs pours
coming forward, retreating, arrested/standing-still shuddering
carefully carefully she falls, falling with care
fearful, hesitant, then with pleasure, fearlessly coming forward
let the hesitant boat of dharma slide/roll, my dharma fall/drop

dancing, dancing when (she) tires, tiring when there's confusion
it should take away together my composure, my peace, my
intellect/wisdom

then this sweet scene should dissolve/vanish from my sight
the shadows of the long stone pillar fold themselves around her
like crowding clouds gathering lightning into their skirts.

I Forgot

From town to town the tourist wandered
and lost
the road to his house.
What belongs to me
what you own
he forgot
what was his and what was another's.

What he forgot, how he forgot
why ask about it.
Just think of it this way:
the cause isn't a sin;
he simply forgot.

How those days were
how those nights were
how were those words—the assaults.
My mind is a child
it forgot
the beautiful dream of love.

A ray peeped out from behind darkness
hesitated coyly.
I remembered
vaguely the outline,
but her face,
I forgot.

Roaming in search of memories
my heart
was so assaulted
happiness in sorrow, sorrow in happiness
this mysterious distinction
I forgot.

It's a question of a look
it's a question of a moment
breaths, a cord tied around a waist
when the light from one glance
dissolved
when the moment passed
I forgot.

It's not a question of understanding something
my mind is a pleasure-seeking
drunk
I drowned my head in rippling waves
the sea, however,
I forgot.

While laughing
while playing games
in conversations
color dissolved.
Although I had a heart
I forgot
my oozing wounds.

My life, which passes away,
my spent life has been spent.
When my heart took away my life
I spent my life
laughing
and forgot
to lament and cry.

Whoever you look at, in their heart
if there's a complaint
it's just this:
I remembered every single thing
but time forgot
us.

If anyone asks
Who said this,
tell them what's in your heart.
Miraji talked and repented
and then,
having talked,
forgot.

N. M. RASHED

(1910—1975)

Selected Poems

Translated from the Urdu by M. A. R. Habib

Near the Window

Lamp of Love's chamber, awake!
Wake from this joyful floor of soft dreams
Your body still tired from night's pleasure
Come by me, lover, near the window
And see with what passion dawn's rays
Kiss the minarets of our city's mosque
Whose height brings to mind my Age-long desire

With your silver-white hands, my lover
Open those wine-dark, bewildering eyes
See this minaret
Watered by early light
Beneath its shadow, I remember
A mournful, penniless priest
Drowsing in a dark, hidden corner
Like a useless god
A devil, distressed!
Here is the stain of three hundred years
An indignity without cure.
See the crowd in the marketplace
Moving, an endless flow
As *jinns* in the wastelands
Emerge at early evening, bearing torches
A bride-like figure sits
In the corner of each man's heart

163

The tiny lantern of Self flickers
Without strength to burst into
Spinning flame
Among these are the poor, the sick
Below the heavens tyranny marches on.
I an old, weary, ambling horse
Ridden by Hunger, hard and robust
I too, like others in the city
Come out, after each night of love, to
All this rubbish
The sky is turning where
At night I return to this same house
Knowing my helplessness, I peer again
Through this window
At the minarets of our city's mosque
When they kiss the red sky a sad farewell.

Deserted Sheba

Solomon, head in his hands, and Sheba desolate
Sheba desolate, the home of ghosts
Sheba an abysmal lake of woes
World devoid of grass, greenery and flower

Winds thirsty for rain
Birds of the desert, beaks tucked beneath their wing
And Man, choked on dust
Solomon, head in his hands, bitterly disheveled hair
World dominion, world administration, merely
the bounding of a deer.

Love a leaping flame, lust the odor of odorless flowers
Speak less of the age's mysteries!
Sheba is wasted for still on her soil
Are footprints of a ravaging conqueror
Sheba is no more, nor her beautiful queen
Solomon, head in his hands:

From where now will come a joyful envoy?
From where, which jar, will come wine into
The bowl of old age?

Oil Merchants

For one black mole the towns of Buqara and Samarqand!*
But where now are Buqara and Samarqand?
Buqara and Samarqand are lost in dreams
Hidden in the veils of an azure silence
Their doors closed to travelers
Like the eyelids of a beautiful sleeping woman
Preserved from the lash of Russian "Pantheism"
Two beauties!
Forget Buqara and Samarqand
And think now of your shining cities
Of the roofs, doors and terraces of
Tehran and Masshad
Look to the
Pleasant fountains of your age of sense and action
And these beautiful metaphors of your new hopes
Make high the low walls
Of these splendid cities
Post your sentries at every tower and rampart
And in your homes, silence all sound
Save the wind
For outside, beneath the city walls
Robbers have long been pitching their tents
Dressed as oil merchants
Tomorrow or tonight at dark
They'll come as guests
To your houses
To drink from the goblets
Of the banquet night

---

* Buqara and Samarqand: Legendary cities in Central Asia that were ruled by
the Iranian Samanid dynasty in the late ninth and the tenth centuries.

They'll dance, sing
And laugh impulsively, noisily
To warm the blood of the gathering!

But when dawn breaks
Then you will dig
Graves for your dead with your eyelashes
Then you'll shed tears
On the ashes of merriment's stage
We also have shed tears
—Though the black mole is worthless
That deep oozing ulcer which arose on earth's cheek
From Europeans' murdering lust—
We also have shed tears
Cities, like liquid shadows, dissolving in waste
Falling roofs and doors
Minarets and domes
But time is an arch
And our enemy passes through its curved flanks
Rolling down its lower horizon
Imprisoning and whipping
Our naked, lean bodies
Our tyrant begins to sweat in his own fire

Place your hand in mine!
Place your hand in mine!
For I have seen
Rays on the peaks of Alwand and Himaliya[*]
Through them at last will break
A Sun
Longing for this, Buqara and Samarqand
Have long been beggars.

---

[*] Alwand and Himaliya: Two mountain ranges in Asia (also spelled Alvand and Himalaya)

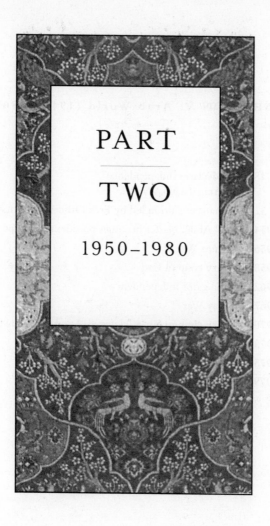

PART
TWO
1950–1980

Chronology

SECTION V: Arab World (1948–1980)

1948 Israel declares independence
First Arab-Israeli War

1952 Egyptian revolution led by Free Officers Movement

1954 Gamal Abdel Nasser becomes president of Egypt

1956 The Suez War

1958 Military coup in Iraq

1962 Algeria gains independence

1967 Six-Day War

1970 Military coup in Syria, Hafez al-Assad takes power

1973 Yom Kippur War

1975–1990 Lebanese Civil War

1979 Egypt and Israel sign peace treaty
Soviet Union invades Afghanistan

V

I Am Arab:
Arabic Literature at Midcentury

"INSOFAR AS I am concerned, politics and the novel are . . . indivisible." The words of Palestinian writer Ghassan Kanafani, whose 1955 epistolary short story, "Letter from Gaza," begins this section, are emblematic of a wider trend in Arabic literature at midcentury. This was a period during which the Arab world was marked by social crises, political polarization, and stark divisions—between the rich and the poor, between tradition and modernity, between religion and secularism—that would ultimately lead to the consolidation of power by increasingly authoritarian regimes throughout the Middle East. And yet, the same conflicts and internal schisms that plagued such countries as Egypt, Algeria, Syria, Jordan, and Iraq also inspired some of the finest Arabic literature ever written.

This new, "postcolonial" generation of Arab writers, no longer preoccupied with themes of independence and anticolonialism, emerged as the voice of the poor and downtrodden. Arabic poetry in particular made a dramatic break with Arab literary tradition—focusing on content over form, openly addressing societal ills, and fearlessly attacking entrenched political and religious powers. A new kind of prose-poem, combining Western-inspired free verse and traditional Arabic meter and rhythm, took root in literary circles, allowing writers such as the Syrian poet Zakariyya Tamir ("The Enemies") and the Iraqi pioneer in spoken-word poetry, Mozaffar al-Nawwab

("Bridge of Old Wonders"), to write long, highly expressive, and overtly political compositions.

Perhaps no writer more clearly captures the style or ethos of this period than the poet known simply as Adonis (Ali Ahmad Sa'id Asbar), arguably the most influential and best-known Arab poet of the twentieth century. Adonis's poems, heavily influenced by both T. S. Eliot and Walt Whitman—his epic masterpiece, "Grave for New York," is addressed to Whitman—are infused with an abiding sense of historical consciousness and Arab identity.

Of course, the historical event of this era that, more than any other, shaped the work of Adonis and his fellow Arab writers was the Arab-Israeli War of 1948, which led to the creation of the state of Israel and the subsequent displacement of hundreds of thousands of Palestinians. The plight of the Palestinians who lost their homeland—captured in the work of "refugee poets" such as Abu Salma and Mahmoud Darwish—became a kind of rallying cry for Arab unity and the defining issue of the time. In fact, a great many Arab regimes derived their very legitimacy through their promise to "liberate" Palestine from Zionist control. When the leaders of these regimes failed to live up that promise—indeed, when they were utterly humiliated by the Israeli army in the War of 1967—a profound sense of anger and impotence settled upon the Arab peoples.

Defeat at the hands of the Israeli army fractured the Arab world and put an end to the dream of pan-Arab unity. Relations among the Arab states became increasingly volatile. For Arab writers, the "loss of Palestine" was viewed as an indictment of postcolonial Arab society. It is this idea that fueled the images of social chaos and political repression in the short stories of Yusif Idris ("The Aorta"), Haydar Haydar ("The Dance of the Savage Prairies"), and Naguib Mahfouz ("The Seventh Heaven"), the first and only Arab writer to receive the Nobel Prize in Literature (though Adonis is perennially nominated).

Meanwhile, as oil revenues widened the gap between the rich and the poor during the 1970s, and massive population increases created fewer employment opportunities during the 1980s, the secular rule of the region's authoritarian regimes was increasingly challenged by a new generation of Arab youths—many of them followers of the Islamic social movement known as the Muslim Brotherhood—eager to rebuild society upon Islamic moral principles.

GHASSAN KANAFANI
(1936–1972)

Letter from Gaza

Translated from the Arabic by Hilary Kilpatrick

Dear Mustafa,

I have now received your letter, in which you tell me that you've done everything necessary to enable me to stay with you in Sacramento. I've also received news that I have been accepted in the department of Civil Engineering in the University of California. I must thank you for everything, my friend. But it'll strike you as rather odd when I proclaim this news to you—and make no doubt about it, I feel no hesitation at all, in fact I am pretty well positive that I have never seen things so clearly as I do now. No, my friend, I have changed my mind. I won't follow you to "the land where there is greenery, water and lovely faces" as you wrote. No, I'll stay here, and I won't ever leave.

I am really upset that our lives won't continue to follow the same course, Mustafa. For I can almost hear you reminding me of our vow to go on together, and of the way we used to shout: "We'll get rich!" But there's nothing I can do, my friend. Yes, I still remember the day when I stood in the hall of Cairo airport, pressing your hand and staring at the frenzied motor. At that moment everything was rotating in time with the ear-splitting motor, and you stood in front of me, your round face silent.

Your face hadn't changed from the way it used to be when you were growing up in the Shajiya quarter of Gaza, apart from those slight wrinkles. We grew up together, understanding each other completely, and we promised to go on together till the end. But . . .

"There's a quarter of an hour left before the plane takes off. Don't look into space like that. Listen! You'll go to Kuwait next year, and you'll save enough from your salary to uproot you from Gaza and

171

transplant you to California. We started off together and we must carry on . . ."

At that moment I was watching your rapidly moving lips. That was always your manner of speaking, without commas or full stops. But in an obscure way I felt that you were not completely happy with your flight. You couldn't give three good reasons for it. I too suffered from this wrench, but the clearest thought was: Why don't we abandon this Gaza and flee? Why don't we? Your situation had begun to improve, however. The Ministry of Education in Kuwait had given you a contract though it hadn't given me one. In the trough of misery where I existed you sent me small sums of money. You wanted me to consider them as loans, because you feared that I would feel slighted. You knew my family circumstances in and out; you knew that my meager salary in the UNRWA* schools was inadequate to support my mother, my brother's widow, and her four children.

"Listen carefully. Write to me every day . . . every hour . . . every minute! The plane's just leaving. Farewell! Or rather, till we meet again!"

Your cold lips brushed my cheek, you turned your face away from me toward the plane, and when you looked at me again I could see your tears.

Later the Ministry of Education in Kuwait gave me a contract. There's no need to repeat to you how my life there went in detail. I always wrote to you about everything. My life there had a gluey, vacuous quality as though I were a small oyster, lost in oppressive loneliness, slowly struggling with a future as dark as the beginning of the night, caught in a rotten routine, a spewed-out combat with time. Everything was hot and sticky. There was a slipperiness to my whole life, it was all a hankering for the end of the month.

In the middle of the year, that year, the Jews bombarded the central district of Sabha and attacked Gaza, our Gaza, with bombs and flame-throwers. That event might have made some change in my routine, but there was nothing for me to take much notice of; I was going to leave this Gaza behind me and go to California where I would live for myself, my own self that had suffered so long. I hated Gaza and its

---

* UNRWA: United Nations Relief and Works Agency for Palestine Refugees in the Near East.

inhabitants. Everything in the amputated town reminded me of failed pictures painted in gray by a sick man. Yes, I would send my mother and my brother's widow and her children a meager sum to help them to live, but I would liberate myself from this last tie too, there in green California, far from the reek of defeat that for seven years had filled my nostrils. The sympathy that bound me to my brother's children, their mother and mine would never be enough to justify my tragedy in taking this perpendicular dive. It mustn't drag me any farther down than it already had. I must flee!

You know these feelings, Mustafa, because you've really experienced them. What is this ill-defined tie we had with Gaza that blunted our enthusiasm for flight? Why didn't we analyze the matter in such a way as to give it a clear meaning? Why didn't we leave this defeat with its wounds behind us and move on to a brighter future that would give us deeper consolation? Why? We didn't exactly know.

When I went on holiday in June and assembled all my possessions, longing for the sweet departure, the start toward those little things that give life a nice, bright meaning, I found Gaza just as I had known it, closed like the introverted lining of a rusted snail-shell thrown up by the waves on the sticky, sandy shore by the slaughterhouse. This Gaza was more cramped than the mind of a sleeper in the throes of a fearful nightmare, with its narrow streets that had their peculiar smell, the smell of defeat and poverty, its houses with their bulging balconies . . . this Gaza! But what are the obscure causes that draw a man to his family, his house, his memories, as a spring draws a small flock of mountain goats? I don't know. All I know is that I went to my mother in our house that morning. When I arrived, my late brother's wife met me there and asked me, weeping, if I would do as her wounded daughter, Nadia, in Gaza hospital wished and visit her that evening. Do you know Nadia, my brother's beautiful thirteen-year-old daughter?

That evening I bought a pound of apples and set out for the hospital to visit Nadia. I knew that there was something about it that my mother and my sister-in-law were hiding from me, something that their tongues could not utter, something strange that I could not put my finger on. I loved Nadia from habit, the same habit that made me love all that generation which had been so brought up on defeat and displacement that it had come to think that a happy life was a kind of social deviation.

What happened at that moment? I don't know. I entered the white room very calm. Ill children have something of saintliness, and how much more so if the child is ill as a result of cruel, painful wounds. Nadia was lying on her bed, her back propped up on a big pillow over which her hair was spread like a thick pelt. There was a profound silence in her wide eyes and a tear always shining in the depths of her black pupils. Her face was calm and still but eloquent as the face of a tortured prophet might be. Nadia was still a child, but she seemed more than a child, much more, and older than a child, much older.

"Nadia!"

I've no idea whether I was the one who said it, or whether it was someone else behind me. But she raised her eyes to me and I felt them dissolve me like a piece of sugar that had fallen into a hot cup of tea. Together with her slight smile I heard her voice.

"Uncle! Have you just come from Kuwait?"

Her voice broke in her throat, and she raised herself with the help of her hands and stretched out her neck toward me. I patted her back and sat down near her.

"Nadia! I've brought you presents from Kuwait, lots of presents. I'll wait till you can leave your bed, completely well and healed, and you'll come to my house and I'll give them to you. I've bought you the red trousers you wrote and asked me for. Yes, I've brought them."

It was a lie, born of the tense situation, but as I uttered it I felt that I was speaking the truth for the first time. Nadia trembled as though she had had an electric shock, and lowered her head in a terrible silence. I felt her tears wetting the back of my hand.

"Say something, Nadia! Don't you want the red trousers?"

She lifted her gaze to me and made as if to speak, but then she stopped, gritted her teeth, and I heard her voice again, coming from far away.

"Uncle!"

She stretched out her hand, lifted the white coverlet with her fingers, and pointed to her leg, amputated from the top of the thigh.

My friend. . . . Never shall I forget Nadia's leg, amputated from the top of the thigh. No! Nor shall I forget the grief that had molded her face and merged into its traits forever. I went out of the hospital in Gaza that day, my hand clutched in silent derision on the two pounds I had brought with me to give Nadia. The blazing sun filled the streets with the color of blood. And Gaza was brand new, Mustafa! You and I never saw it like this. The stone piled up at the beginning of the Shajiya quarter where we lived had a meaning, and they seemed to have been put there for no other reason but to explain it. This Gaza in which we had lived and with whose good people we had spent seven years of defeat was something new. It seemed to me just a beginning. I don't know why I thought it was just a beginning. I imagined that the main street that I walked along on the way back home was only the beginning of a long, long road leading to Safad.* Everything in this Gaza throbbed with sadness that was not confined to weeping. It was a challenge; more than that, it was something like reclamation of the amputated leg!

I went out into the streets of Gaza, streets filled with blinding sunlight. They told me that Nadia had lost her leg when she threw herself on top of her little brothers and sisters to protect them from the bombs and flames that had fastened their claws into the house. Nadia could have saved herself, she could have run away, rescued her leg. But she didn't.

Why?

No, my friend, I won't come to Sacramento, and I've no regrets. No, and nor will I finish what we began together in childhood. This obscure feeling that you had as you left Gaza, this small feeling must grow into a giant deep within you. It must expand, you must seek it in order to find yourself, here among the ugly debris of defeat.

I won't come to you. But you, return to us! Come back, to learn from Nadia's leg, amputated from the top of the thigh, what life is and what existence is worth.

Come back, my friend! We are all waiting for you.

---

* Safad: A small town in northern Israel.

ABU SALMA

(1907–1980)

Selected Poems

*Translated from the Arabic by Sharif Elmusa
and Naomi Shihab Nye*

My Country on Partition Day

My country! Live in safety, an Arab country,
may the jewel of your tradition continue smiling
Though they've partitioned your radiant heart
our honor denies partition.
We've woven your wedding clothes with red thread
dyed from our own blood.
We've raised banners on the Mountain of Fire*
marching toward our inevitable destiny!
History marches behind our footsteps,
Honor sings around us.

Rise, friend, see how many people
drag their chains of dented steel.
Behold the serpents slithering endlessly among them!
They've prohibited oppression among themselves
but for us they legalized all prohibitions!
They proclaim, "Trading with slaves is unlawful"
but isn't the trading of free people more of a crime?
In the West, man's rights are preserved,
but the man in the East is stoned to death.
Justice screams loudly protecting Western lands

* Mountain of Fire: Nickname for the Palestinian city of Nablus.

but grows silent when it visits us!
Maybe justice changes colors and shapes!
Live embers scorch our lips
so listen to our hearts speaking,
call on free men in every land
to raise the flag of justice where we stand.

We Shall Return

Beloved Palestine, how can I sleep
when phantoms torture my eyes?
In your name I greet the wide world,
but caravans of days pass,
ravaged by conspiracies of enemies and friends.
Beloved Palestine, how can I live
away from your plains and hills?
The valleys call me and the shores
cry out echoing in the ears of time!
Even fountains weep as they trickle, estranged.
Your cities and villages echo the cries.
Will there be a return, my comrades ask,
a return after such long absence?
Yes, we'll return and kiss the moist ground,
love flowering on our lips.
We'll return some day while generations listen
to the echoes of our feet.
We'll return with raging storms,
holy lightning and fire,
winged hope and songs,
soaring eagles,
the dawn smiling on the deserts.
Some morning we'll return riding the crest of the tide,
our bloodied banners fluttering
above the glitter of spears.

I Love You More

The more I fight for you, the more I love you!
What land except this land of musk and amber?
What horizon but this one defines my world?
The branch of my life turns greener when I uphold you
and my wing, Oh Palestine, spreads wide over the peaks.

Has the lemon tree been nurtured by our tears?
No more do birds flutter among the high pines,
or stars gaze vigilantly over Mount Carmel.*
The little orchards weep for us, gardens grow desolate,
the vines are forever saddened.

Whenever your name sounds in my ears, my words grow more
    poetic,
planting desire for you on every stoop.
Is it possible these words could be torches
lighting each desert and place of exile?
Oh Palestine! Nothing more beautiful, more precious, more pure!
The more I fight for you, the more I love you.

* Mount Carmel: Coastal mountain range in northern Israel.

MAHMOUD DARWISH
(1941–2008)

Selected Poems

Translated from the Arabic by
John Mikhail Asfour
Abdullah al-Udhari

To the Reader

Black tulips in my heart,
flames on my lips:
from which forest did you come to me,
all you crosses of anger?
I have recognized my griefs
and embraced wandering and hunger.
Anger lives in my hands,
anger lives in my mouth
and in the blood of my arteries swims anger.

O reader,
don't expect whispers from me,
and borrowed branches
from the trunks of the straight trees.
I will, then,
take pride in this wound of the city,
the canvas of lightning in our sad nights.
Though the street frowns in my face
it protects me from shadows and malign glances,
and so I sing for joy

behind fearful eyelids.
When the storm struck in my country
it promised me wine, and rainbows.

Translated by John Mikhail Asfour

Identity Card

Write down:
I am Arab
my I.D. number, 50,000
my children, eight
and the ninth due next summer
—Does that anger you?

Write down:
Arab.
I work with my struggling friends in a quarry
and my children are eight.
I chip a loaf of bread for them,
clothes and notebooks
from the rocks.
I will not beg for a handout at your door
nor humble myself
on your threshold
—Does that anger you?

Write down:
Arab,
a name with no friendly diminutive.
A patient man, in a country
brimming with anger.
My roots have gripped this soil
since time began,
before the opening of ages
before the cypress and the olive,
before the grasses flourished.

My father came from a line of plowmen,
and my grandfather was a peasant
who taught me about the sun's glory
before teaching me to read.
My home is a watchman's shack
made of reeds and sticks
—Does my condition anger you?

There is no gentle name,
write down:
Arab.
The color of my hair, jet black—
eyes, brown—
trademarks,
a headband over a *keffiyeh**
and a hand whose touch grates
rough as a rock.
My address is a weaponless village
with nameless streets.
All its men are in the field and quarry
—Does that anger you?

Write down, then
at the top of Page One:
I do not hate
and do not steal
but starve me, and I will eat
my assailant's flesh.
Beware of my hunger
and of my anger.

Translated by John Mikhail Asfour

---

* *Keffiyeh*: Traditional headdress worn by Arab men.

Athens Airport

Athens Airport boots us to other airports. The fighter said: "Where can I fight?" A pregnant woman blurted at him: "Where can we have our child?" An employee said: "Where can I invest my money?" An intellectual said: "Your money and mine?" The customs officers said: "Where do you come from?" We said: "From the sea." "Your destination?" "The sea." "Your address?" A woman in our group said: "My bundle is my village!" At Athens Airport we waited for years. A young couple got married and looked for a room in a hurry. The groom said: "Where can I deflower her?" We laughed and told him: "There's no room here for such a wish, young man." An analyst with us said: "They die so they may not die. They die overlooked." " A writer said: "Our camp will inevitably fall. What do they want from us?" Athens Airport changes its people every day. But we have stayed put, seats upon seats, waiting for the sea. For how many years, Athens Airport?

Translated by Abdullah al-Udhari

They'd Love to See Me Dead

They'd love to see me dead so they can say: he was one of us, he belonged to us.

For twenty years I've heard those very steps banging on the night's wall.

They came but did not open the door.

They have entered now. Then three of them went out: a poet, a killer and a reader. "Will you have a drink of wine?" I asked. "We'll have a drink," they said. "When will you shoot me?" I asked. They answered: "Take your time." They prepared the glasses and went on singing for the people. I said: "When will you start killing me?" They said: "We have started. Why did you send shoes to the soul?" "So it can walk on the land," I said. They said: "Why did you write a white poem when the land is jet black?" I answered: "Because thirty seas flow into my heart." They said: "Why do you like French wine?" I said: "Because I deserve the loveliest woman."

"How would you like your death?" "Blue like the stars pouring through the roof. Would you like some more wine?" They said: "We'll have some." I said: "I will ask you to do it slowly, to kill me slowly slowly so I can write the last poem for the wife of my heart." But they laughed and stole from the house only the words which I was going to say to the wife of my heart. . . .

Translated by Abdullah al-Udhari

ADONIS*
(B. 1930)

Selected Poems

Translated from the Arabic by
Samuel Hazo
Adnan Haydar and Michael Beard
Shawkat M. Toorawa

The Pages of Day and Night

Before the time of day—I am.
Before the wonder of the sun—I burn.
Trees run behind me.
Blossoms walk in my shadow.
But still tomorrow
builds into my face
such island fortresses
of silence that words find
not a door to enter by.
The pitying stars ignite
and days forget themselves
in my bed.
                The springs within my chest
are closing now like blossoms
to the moon.
                Their waters bathe
the mirror of my vision pure
as silence as I waken into sleep.

Translated by Samuel Hazo

---

* Adonis: Pen name for Ali Ahmad Sa'id Asbar.

The Wound

I.

Leaves, asleep under wind:
a ship for the wound.
The wound
glories in these ruinous times.
Trees growing in our own eyelashes
a lake for the wound.
The wound shows up in bridges
as graves reach out
as patience wears thin on the opposite banks
between our love and our death.
And the wound, a beckoning gesture,
inflicts us as we cross.

II.

And to that language
in which the bell sound chokes
I confer the voice of the wound.
For the stone, approaching
this withered world from afar,
for the act of withering
for these slippery times
carried skidding on their sleighs
I light the wound's fire.

As history smolders in my clothes,
as blue claws spread across my book,
as I cry out at the day
"Who are you? Who throws you
across these pages
in my virgin land?"
that's when in my pages I glimpse

in that land two eyes of dust.
I hear one saying
"I am he, the wound
that grows bigger
in your petty little history."

III.

I called you clouds,
you my wound, my migrating dove.
I called you feather
called you book
and here we are
where the dialogue between me
and a deeply rooted language begins.
We meet in the storied isles
on failure's deeply rooted archipelago.
And here I am
teaching this dialogue
to wind and palm tree,
to you my wound
you migrating dove.

IV.

If only the land of dreams and mirrors
had seaports,
if only I had a ship,
or the remnants of a city.
If only I possessed a city
in the land of children,
that land of lamentation,
I'd recast it all in ingots
so that the wound, molded into song,
could cut like a lance

that pierces trees, rocks, and sky,
a song supple like water,
as defiant and perplexed
as conquest.

V.

Rain upon our desert
O world decked with dream and longing.
Rain down enough to shake us.
We are the wound's palm trees.
From those trees captivated by the wound's silence,
trees which nursed the wound
through its night,
among arches of eyelashes and arms bent with care
break off for us just two branches.

O world decked in dream and longing
O world that falls onto my forehead
etched like a wound,
keep your distance. The wound is closer than you.
Keep your seductive charms away. More beautiful than you
is the wound.
And the magic that reaches
from your eyes
to the last kingdoms
has only been the wound's pathway.
The wound has passed over it,
stripped it of its deceptive sails
and left it without its island.

Translated by Adnan Haydar and Michael Beard

Grave for New York (excerpt)

I.

Until now, the Earth has been depicted in the shape of a pear
    by which I mean a breast
Yet, the difference between breast and tomb is a mere technicality:
    New York
A four-legged civilization; in every direction is murder or a road
  to murder
       and in the distance are the moans of the drowned.

New York,
A woman—the statue of a woman
       in one hand she holds a scrap to which the documents we
       call history give the name "liberty," and in the other she
       smothers a child whose name is Earth.

New York,
A body the color of asphalt. Around her waist is a damp girdle,
her face
       is a closed window . . . I said: Walt Whitman will open
       it—"I speak the password primeval"*—but no one hears it
       except an unreturning god. The prisoners, the slaves, the
       despairing, the thieves, the diseased spew from his throat.
       There is no outlet, no path. And I said: "The Brooklyn
       Bridge!" But it's the bridge that connects Whitman to
       Wall Street, that connects leaves-grass to paper-dollars. . . .

New York—Harlem,
Who comes in a guillotine of silk, who leaves in a grave the length of
       the Hudson? Explode, you ritual of tears. Cling together,
       you trifles of exhaustion. Blue, yellow, roses, jasmine: the
       light sharpens its points, and in the pinprick the sun is born.

---

* "I speak the password primeval": From Walt Whitman, "Song of Myself."

Have you ignited, O wound, concealed between thigh and
thigh? Has the bird of death come to you and have you
heard the death rattle? A rope, and the neck weaving melancholy; and in the blood, the melancholy of the Hour. . . .

New York—Madison—Park Avenue—Harlem,

Laziness resembling work, work resembling laziness. Hearts filled with
sponge, hands swollen like reeds. And from the heaps of
filth and the masks of the Empire State, History rises in
odors suspended slab upon slab:

It's not sight that is blind, rather the head,
It's not speech that is barren, rather the tongue.

New York—Wall Street—125th Street—Fifth Avenue,

A Medusan specter ascends between the shoulders. A market with
slaves
of every race. Humanity living like plants in glass gardens.
Unseen, Invisible wretches submerge like dust in the web
of space spiraling victims:

The sun is a funeral
The day a black drum.

II.

Here,
On the mossy side of the Earth-rock, no one sees me but a black man
about to be killed or a sparrow about to die. I thought:
a plant living in a red claypot was being transformed as I distanced
myself
from the threshold. And I read:
that rats in Beirut and elsewhere are strutting about in White
House silk,

armed with documents and gnawing away at mankind, that
the remaining swine in the garden of the alphabet are trampling
  poetry.

And I saw
wherever I was—Pittsburgh (International Poetry Forum), Johns
  Hopkins
          (Washington, DC), Harvard (Cambridge; Boston), Ann
          Arbor (Michigan; Detroit), the Foreign Press Club, The
          Arab Club at the United Nations Headquarters (New
          York), Princeton, Temple (Philadelphia)—

And I saw
the Arab map like a horse dragging its hooves and time drooping
  like a
          saddlebag toward the grave or toward a darker shadow,
          toward the dying fire or toward an extinguished fire; the
          chemistry of another dimension is discovered in Kirkuk, in
          Dhahran, and is what remains of such fortresses of Arab
          Afro-Asia. And here is the world ripening in our hands.
          Ha! We prepare the Third World War, we set up the First,
          Second, Third, and Fourth Agencies to affirm that:

          1. In that direction is a jazz party,

          2. In this house is a man who owns nothing but ink,

          3. In this tree is a bird that sings,

and to announce that:

          1. Space is measured in units of cages or walls,

          2. Time is measured in units of ropes or whips,

          3. The régime that builds the world is the one that begins
             by killing its brother,

4. The sun and moon are two glittering dirhams beneath
   the Sultan's throne,

and I saw,
Arab names as expansive as the earth, more compassionate than eyes,
   shining but as a neglected star shines, "with no ancestors,
   and with its roots in its steps. . . ."*

Here,
On the mossy side of the Earth-rock, I know and I confess. I
   remember a
         plant that I call life or my country, death or my country—
         a wind that freezes like a mantle, a face that kills revelry,
         an eye that chases away the light and I invent your oppo-
         site you, my country,

         I sink into your hell and I scream out:
         I distill a poisonous elixir for you
         and I give you life,

and I confess: New York, in my country the curtain and the bed,
   the chair
         and the head are yours. And everything is for sale: the day
         and the night, the Black Stone of Mecca and the waters of
         the Tigris. I announce: in spite of this you pant, racing in
         Palestine, in Hanoi, in the North and the South, in the East
         and the West, against people whose only history is fire,
and I say: ever since John the Baptist, every one of us carries his
         severed head in a tray and awaits a second birth.

III.

Crumble, you statues of liberty, you nails sunk into chests with a
         wisdom which counterfeits the wisdom of roses. The

---

* "with no ancestors . . .": A quotation from Adonis's poem "Knight of Strange
Words: Psalm."

wind is raging again from the East, uprooting the tents
and the skyscrapers. And there are two wings that write:
a second alphabet rises from the undulations of the West,
and the sun is the daughter of a tree in the garden of
Jerusalem.

Thus do I light my flame. I begin anew, I fashion and I define:

> New York,
> a woman made of straw, the bed swinging from void to
>   void, and
> overhead the ceiling is rotting: every word is a sign of a
>   fall,
> every moment is a shovel or
> a pick. And on the left and right are
> bodies that want to change love sight hearing smell touch
>   and
> change itself—that open
> time like a portal that they then break,
>
> and in the remaining hours improvise
> sex poetry morals thirst speech silence
> and negate the locks.
>
> And I tempt Beirut and her sister capitals,
> They leap from their bed and close the doors of memory
> behind them. They draw close, hanging from my odes,
> dangling. The pick is for the gate, and the flowers for the
> window.
> Burn, you history of locks.

I said: I tempt Beirut,
     —"Seek action. The Word is dead," the others say.
The Word has died because your tongues have abandoned the
habit of speech for the habit of mime. The Word? Do you want to
discover its fire? Then, write, I say "write," I do not say "mimic,"

nor do I say "transcribe." Write—from the Ocean to the Gulf I do
not hear a single tongue, I do not read a single word. All I hear is
noise. Because of this I see no one throwing fire.

The Word is the lightest of things; and yet, it contains everything.
Action is a direction and an instant, and the Word is all
directions and all time. The Word—the hand, the hand—
the dream:

I discover you O fire, O my capital,
I discover you, O poetry,

and I tempt Beirut. She wears me and I wear her. We wander like
rays

and we ask: who reads, who sees? The Phantoms are for
Dayan,* and the Oil flows to its destination. God spoke
true, and Mao wasn't mistaken: "Weapons are a very
important factor in war, but they are not decisive. Men,
not weapons, are the decisive factor," and there is no such
thing as final victory, nor is there total defeat.

I repeated these proverbs and maxims, as Arabs do, on Wall Street,
where rivers of gold of every hue flow, coming from their
sources. And I saw among them Arab rivers bearing
millions of corpses, victims and offerings to the Great Idol.
And between the victims were sailors cackling as they
rolled down the Chrysler Building, returning to their
sources.

Thus do I light my flame,
we live in a black clamor so that our lungs can be filled
with the wind of History, we rise from black eyes hedged

* Dayan: Moshe Dayan, chief of staff of the Israel Defense Forces from 1953 to
1958, later defense minister and then foreign minister of Israel.

in like graveyards so that we can conquer the eclipse, we travel in the black head so that we can escort the coming sun.

IV.

New York, woman seated in the arc of the wind,
    a body more remote than the atom,
    a point hurrying in the space of numbers.
    a thigh in the sky and a thigh in the water,
Say: where is your star? The battle between the grass and the computers is imminent. The whole epoch is suspended on a wall, and here is the bleeding. Above, a head unites the two poles, at the waist is Asia, and down below are two feet belonging to an unseen body. I know you, you corpse swimming in the musk of poppies. I know you, you game of breast upon breast: I look at you and I dream of snow, I look at you and I await autumn.

Your snow carries the night, your night carries the peoples as dead
   bats.
    Every wall in you is a graveyard. Every day is a black
    gravedigger, carrying
    a black loaf, a black tray, etching
    with them the history of the White House:

(a)

    There are dogs lined up like links in a fetter. There are cats
    giving birth to helmets and chains. And in the alleyways
    that slink along the backs of rats, the white guards
    propagate like mushrooms.

(b)

    A woman walking behind her dog bridled like a horse.
    The dog struts like a king, as the city creeps around him
    like an army of tears. And where the children and elderly,

enveloped in a black skin, amass, the innocence of bullets
sprouts like a seed and terror strikes the heart of the city.

(c)

Harlem—Bedford-Stuyvesant: the sand of humanity
thickens and piles up in tower upon tower. Faces weave the
times. The trash is a banquet for the children and the
children are a banquet for the rats . . . in the endless feast is
another trinity: the tax collector, the policeman, the judge—
the power of destruction, the sword of annihilation.

(d)

Harlem (the Blacks hate the Jews),
Harlem (the Blacks dislike the Arabs when they recall the
slave trade),
Harlem Broadway (people infiltrate distillers of alcohol and
drugs like invertebrates)
Broadway Harlem, a festival of chains and sticks, and the police are
the germs of time. A single shot, ten pigeons. The eyes are boxes
surging with red snow and time is a crutch that hobbles. Onward,
to exhaustion, old Black man, young Black boy. To exhaustion,
again and again.

Translated by Shawkat M. Toorawa

MOZAFFAR AL-NAWWAB

(B. 1932)

Bridge of Old Wonders

(EXCERPT)

*Translated from the Arabic by Carol Bardenstein and
Saadi A. Simawe*

Side Two of the Cassette

This land is called "The daughter of the morning"
This land is called "The daughter of the morning"
The wandering Arabs left her behind,
gathering pomegranate blossoms
at the Mediterranean.
They journeyed across two deserts,
and when they noticed they'd forgotten her,
they found all the filth of the world in her
and they recited an elegy.

This land is called "The daughter of the morning"
This land is called "The daughter of the morning"
The wandering Arabs left her behind,
gathering pomegranate blossoms
at the Mediterranean.
They journeyed across two deserts,
and when they noticed they'd forgotten her,
they found all the filth of the world in her
and they recited an elegy.

Do the dead care how their graves are decorated?
Does the ewe care about the shape of the slaughtering knife?
What consummate dissonance!
A breast on the ground,
lying next to two small hands
the size of grape leaves
A child grows up among the burnt corpses
Oh betraying Arabs, recite your elegy!

Do the dead care how their graves are decorated?
Does the goat think about its pastures
as it is being readied for slaughter?
What are the merchants of al-Sham* cooking on hell's fire?
The plague is imminent
when a troubled star full of holes appears
it emits a deadly light
that illuminates the eye sockets of a skull
the wind flickers and plays inside it
at Tal al-Zaatar.†

All the dust of the world
cannot close the eyes of a skull
searching for a homeland.
The capital of the poor‡ has fallen, just a little while ago
And in response?
Impotent castanets are clicking and jangling all the way to the
    White House
The testicles of the Arab leaders trembled with pride.

---

* al-Sham: Syria.
† Tal al-Zaatar: Palestinian refugee camp in Lebanon besieged by Christian
Phalangist forces under the command of Michel Aoun during the Lebanese
Civil War.
‡ Capital of the poor: The poet is referring to Beirut.

Over here, you sons of bitches
shouted the light-haired fatso.
He gunned down a child,
pulled the pacifier, all bloodied, out of its mouth
and decorated himself with it as a medal.
Here, you sons of bitches, right over here!
The children froze, and despair wiped the features off their faces
God stood with the dirty children,
The capital of the poor has fallen!
*[Applause]**
A child tried to cover the corpse of his grandmother
For it is shameful for a grandmother's thighs to be exposed
They gunned him down, and he fell, right on top of her thighs . . .
There, there, my son, it's alright, this way
her thighs will be covered.
Does a woman in a tent give birth to an army?
You sons of filth, sons of Palestine
You will return to the land of Palestine, alright
but as corpses.
The children looked to the Arab nation for help:
the testicles of the Arab leaders trembled with pride.
Naft ibn Kaaba† announced . . . that a meeting would be called.
Now is not the time for commentary.

The time will come for that, that too will come, that too will
    come,
The wild card in this game has become known
[Applause]
The children looked to the Arab nation for help:
the testicles of the Arab leaders trembled with pride.

---

* Applause: al-Nawwab is a performance poet, and this poem is transcribed
from an undated performance in front of an audience.
† Naft ibn Kaaba: Literally, "Oil, son of the Kaaba." Not a real person but
al-Nawwab's mocking name for any leader of an oil-rich Arab (specifically,
Gulf Arab) state.

Naft ibn Kaaba announced . . . that a meeting would be called.
Now is not the time for commentary
The time for that will come too, it will come,
The wild card in this game has become known
As has the one who gets cut swallowing razor blades against his
    will.

How can you not see the rottenness?
Oh wise ones, the capital of the poor has fallen
because of the rottenness!
As they say, in ancient times a rat destroyed the Great Dam of
    Ma'rab*
and it has fallen!
Lined up, women raise their arms in the air,
and walk, one by one.
The pregnant woman walks around with the
site of her womanhood exposed
He shoved the pregnant woman down to the ground
They pulled out a womb
in which a *fedayee*† was being formed in the night.

Have you heard, oh Arabs of silence?
Have you heard, accursed Arabs?
The hatred has reached the wombs!
Have you heard, accursed Arabs?
Palestine is being erased from the womb!
The adherents of the American religion in Mecca
and the market are at their peak!
It's a public auction, oh noble ones
Thirty killed in an hour, oh noble ones
Eighty for the merchants of al-Sham
Eighty-eight for the Kuwaiti cancellation of the constitution
Ninety for the Petrol King

---

* Great Dam of Ma'rab: Legendary dam in ancient Yemen that, according to
legend, collapsed after rats slowly nibbled away at it for years on end.
† *Fedayee*: An Arab guerrilla fighter.

Look here, you filthy bastards
Anyone who slows down is shot by a machine-gun.
Silence, silence, silence . . .
What is this silence called in Arabic?

The rivers of joy sank quickly in the night.
The dead children twitched as one body,
The dust of the earth has made the savagery known
Hatred is not enough anymore.
We have heard your cry again,
God rose up from the earth
holding the entrails of children in his pleading hands
He wept in embarrassment and shame in the night.
He begged the people to return to Tal al-Zaatar
God too is from the capital of the poor
He has gotten used to these neighbors
He has gotten used to the clothes strung between the tents
He would even gather up their clothes from the line sometimes.

Don't come near! Don't come near! Don't come near!!
Let the children's flesh play its last game
of hide-and-seek
No one shall ever interrupt this game.
The testicles of treachery have swelled and grown.
Have you heard? Have you heard?
I hear the voice of the angry people in my flesh
Don't take revenge, don't take revenge, don't take revenge!
What is the price of one child?
What is the price of a dimple?
What is the price of two eyes laughing in the morning?
What is the price of a healthy pregnancy in the corner of a tent,
with the betrayers at the door?
What is the price of lips nursing and gurgling?
No! No! No!!!

Do not come near!
The flesh of the children will play a final game of hide-and-seek
The killer must have something besides killing
The killing here seems so meager to him!

Twenty for the beard of Qaboos*
A public auction
Seventy for the lion of the Iranian flag†
A public auction, gentlemen, let's go
Ninety for the summit conference
The fig leaf has fallen.

The noble ones came down from the summit
with their genitals exposed
Among them was Mr. Silent by God trying to cover up his genitals
The most embarrassed of all was the old hairy mammoth
[Applause]
The noble ones came down from the summit
with their genitals exposed
Among them was Mr. Silent by God trying to cover up his
    genitals
The most embarrassed of all was the old hairy mammoth
The silent masses averted their eyes
This is truly shameful!

Don't come any closer!!
The circle is closing in on the massacre
The corpses of the children are joyless,
I detect the smell of nursing babes
and their green talismanic beads
sprouting in the burnt flesh
Were they really children such a short time ago?

---

* Qaboos: Qaboos ibn Sa'id, sultan of Oman.
† Lion of the Iranian flag: The imperial insignia of Iran; a reference to Shah
Muhammad Reza Pahlavi.

Don't allow any child to pass through this alley
The burnt flesh will smile at him, for him
The Church of Mar Sharbal* burns children!
This flesh gives off a rosy smoke
making even the cheek of religion blush red
Go away, go away, get out of here, get out, go away!
Step farther away!

Keep the lights away, and let Tal al-Zaatar get used to the darkness.
It's not time yet
The capital of the poor has fallen
I will not cry over these glorious fighters
I will not cry at all
I only pity and cry for the one who is seeking his state[†]
at a summit meeting
[Applause]
I will not cry at all
I will not cry over these glorious fighters

The noble ones came down from the summit
With the traces of rubbing their heads together
showing on their foreheads
The most embarrassed of all was the old hairy mammoth
Have you ever seen someone carrying around an extinct tusk?
Arrest him!
For he is the king of the whole lot of those pimps
He sank into the mud of betrayal, except for the tip of the tusk
which could still be seen
He spread mud and dirt on all of the cloven-hoofed creatures
He made the betrayal total

---

* Church of Mar Sharbal: Maronite Christian church in Beirut.
† The one who is seeking his state: A mocking reference to Palestine Liberation Organization leader Yasir Arafat.

He united the flags of treachery
The trumpet-blowers chewed their cud
The darkness is deadly.

This is an Arab night.
The massacre was conveniently extinguished before the summit
    meeting
I accuse the mammoth of Neid and his disciple,
The pimp of Syria and his sidekick
The judge of Baghdad and his testicle
The King of Syphilis . . . little Hassan the Second
The blotted rat of filth in the Sudan
And the one sitting beneath the square-root sign on the sand
Of Dubai, all wrapped up in his robe
And the one in Tunis,* too, all bowlegged from calf to neck.
[Applause]
I accuse the mammoth of Neid and his disciple,
The pimp of Syria and his sidekick
The judge of Baghdad and his testicle
The King of Syphilis. . . little Hassan the Second
The blotted rat of filth in the Sudan
And the one sitting beneath the square-root sign on the sand
Of Dubai, all wrapped up in his robe
And the one in Tunis, too, all bowlegged from calf to neck.

Alright, alright, I'll make an exception, for the poor wretch
in Ras al-Khayma†

* Mammoth of Neid: A reference to King Khalid ibn Abd al-Aziz of Saudi
Arabia (1975–1982). *His disciple* probably refers to the rest of the Gulf monarchs. The pimp of Syria: President Hafez al-Assad (1970–2000). Judge of
Baghdad: May refer to General Ahmed Hassan al-Bakr, president of Iraq
(1968–1979). King of Syphilis: King Hussein of Jordan (1952–1999).The
blotted rat: Jaafar Numeiri, president of Sudan (1969–1985). Dubai: Perhaps a
reference to Maktoum bin Rashid Al Maktoum, at the time the emir of Dubai.
The one in Tunis: Habib Bourguiba, president of Tunisia (1957–1987).
† Ras al-Khayma: One of the smallest countries in the United Arab Emirates,
ruled by Sheikh Saqr bin Mohammad al-Qassimi (b. 1918), one of the world's
oldest reigning monarchs.

[Laughter and applause]
And the one in Tunis, too, all bowlegged from calf to neck.
Okay, I'll make an exception for the poor wretch in Ras
    al-Khayma.
He was daydreaming during the crisis
With his lower lip drooping like a camel's
I'll make an exception for the poor wretch in Ras al-Khayma
He was daydreaming during the crisis,
With his lower lip drooping like a camel's
And his nose was like a howdah* atop a hump.

Don't come near!
Be the night!
Be fate itself!
and dark ambiguous entities,
with no lanterns.
Don't come near!
Be fate itself!
and dark ambiguous entities,
with no lanterns.
With no oriental shrieking to spoil this butchery
which needs to be nursed.

Proceed in silence, be the night!
Chanting in blood
Whoever got mutilated,
Or died a slow death,
Will march at the front of the funeral procession
And the gouged-out eye, and the severed hand
The severed thigh, the burnt corpses
Will be hoisted up in clear view

The sea captain says:
No oriental wailing
and very slowly

---

* Howdah: A seat placed atop a camel (or elephant).

Slower, slower, slower . . .
Leave the bodies just as they are
Slower now, slow down.
This kind of slow, measured pace is dignified.
Now they've placed the slaughter
at their Excellencies' religious bank account.
The account of the financial religion
The slaughter account
Honorable fathers of the West:
Greetings!
Now they've placed the slaughter
at their Excellencies' religious bank account.
The account of the financial religion
The slaughter account.
Greetings, honorable fathers of the West,
and salutations
We're oriental filth
We've come to extend this thanks to you.

You who love our ship, whispered the captain,
No wailing, no oriental shrieking
Proceed in rows, for the West loves order
It has no interest in backward displays of emotion
welling up from the miserable East.
Who are those people, anyway?
Garbage, oriental filth
They're far beneath your rank, oh lords of capital
We are oriental filth
The most worthless kind of dust
We present our corpse as a down payment for your friendship

Slower, slower . . .
Article Three will watch from the window
Article Three* of the treaty ratified

---

* Article Three: The treaty could be SALT (Strategic Arms Limitation Treaty),
signed by the United States and the USSR. Article III states that "each Party

between the Soviet Union and the United States in Glasgow
Just who are those people, anyway?
Garbage, oriental filth
They're far beneath your rank, oh lords of capital
The most worthless kind of dust
We present our corpse as a down payment for your friendship
Slower, slower, slower . . .
Article Three will watch from the window
And will bless this peaceful settlement of slaughter
Praise Article Three!
Glory be to Glasgow!
Bless the agreement of the two bears!
The priests made us fear nuclear bombs
But they've slaughtered many times more people than that.
This logic has holes in it, and delivers death,
and squadrons, and oil treaties
So slow down, slower, slower . . .
Why hurry?
The forces of deterrence have arrived
The honchos of the summit meeting
in spite of their differences of opinion,
have all joined together.
The deterrent forces are here
The miracle of the twentieth century has happened!
[Applause]
The deterrent forces are here
The miracle of the twentieth century has happened!
With oil we have destroyed Lebanon,
And with oil we will build Lebanon
Oh God, enough of this shame!

Oh Lord, enough of these bulls!
Oh Lord, enough!
Here is my roasting skewer,

---

undertakes to limit ICBM launchers, SLBM launchers, heavy bombers, and
ASBMs to an aggregate number not to exceed 2,400."

I will heat it to red-hot with the hatred
boxed inside my heart,
a prisoner of the slaughterhouse,
fire burns within.
Lord, we extend your righteous path all the way
to the victims of Tal al-Zaatar
and Damur.*

Let's bring on the apes!
You apes! You animals!
I challenge any of you to raise your eyes as high
as the shoes of a
fedayee, you apes!
[Applause]
I challenge any of you to raise your eyes as high
as the shoes of a
fedayee, you apes!
The hellfire here is no laughing matter, you apes
The enraged people have come
I hear intestines churning with the pain of hunger
and rage
They're all coming bearing two skewers, one in each hand
Oh Lord, enough of this shame
Oh Lord, enough worthless leaders who are full of holes!
[Applause]
Oh Lord, enough of this shame
Oh Lord, enough worthless leaders who are full of holes!
Now is the time for hellfire!

Toss the first of the treacherous dwarfs into the fire
Bring that other one too!
"Who are you?"
"I am Yatruq . . ."
"You son of a . . ."

* Damur: A Christian town attacked by PLO forces in 1976 during the
Lebanese Civil War.

Toss him in too!
Bring the potbellied one!
Have the masses of Bahrain bring him here!
"I swear, by God, I am Sheikh so-and-so the son of Sheikh
    so-and-so,
grandson of the Sheikh . . ."
"Enough of this filthy tribe!"
[Applause]
"And who are you?
Throw him in too!
Bring the potbellied one!
Have the masses of Bahrain bring him here!"
"I swear, by God, I am Sheikh so-and-so the son of Sheikh so-and-so,
grandson of the Sheikh . . ."
"Enough of this filthy tribe!"
The fire of God will roast you, head-coil, fattened belly, and all!
Here is my skewer, oh Lord,
I'm heating it up.
We will have no mercy on them
Lower them slowly into the fire
For centuries they've been enjoying themselves at our expense
For centuries they've been roasting the people on the fire of their
    spits.

Slower . . . slower . . . slower . . . slower . . .
We'll recite the graves of children
and sit in front of the Church of Rome*
We'll display all of our goods
Gentlemen, oh gentlemen!
Tourist from the civilized world!
You with the fancy perfume!

This Tal al-Zaatar!
Here is the frail collarbone of Fatima the daughter of so-and-so

* Church of Rome: The Vatican.

And here is so-and-so, some anonymous filth,
who died on the bridge of return
Here are some top-quality skulls,
you can make Christmas lanterns out of them
The most beautiful icons and relics imaginable!
These blackened vertebrae belong to
two orphaned children from the slaughterhouse
who burned alive clinging to each other
[Applause]
These blackened vertebrae belong to
two orphaned children from the slaughterhouse
who burned alive embracing each other.

Go ahead, touch them, touch them
have no fear
This oriental filth is cheap
Oh, you sir, from the Land of Freedom
These gouged-out eyeballs are the latest models
Produced by the Statue of Liberty
These aren't made of porcelain!
These gouged-out eye sockets, not of clay.
It's genuine, from a body that used to shine like a candle!
Then the sons of Chamoun* roasted it to get rid of
the revolutionary thoughts.
That's all we are . . . bones, a skull, dung, orphans
But we will take history by storm
And we will fill your world with the suspicious poor
We will strike at your comfort, house by house,
We will choke you by day and by night
God forbid feelings of mercy be aroused in any one of you
It would be easier to get mercy from a stone.
I invite you to a spectacle of oriental splendor
For your pleasure, I swear, just for your pleasure

---

* Sons of Chamoun: The followers of the Christian Maronite politician Camille
Chamoun (1900–1987).

Naft ibn Kaaba declared . . .
What did Naft ibn Kaaba declare?
The whole world is preoccupied
The calculator has gone haywire!
There is no power and no strength save in God
Naft ibn Kaaba doesn't know what Naft ibn Kaaba declared!
[Applause]
I swear, this is just for your pleasure
Naft ibn Kaaba declared . . .
What did Naft ibn Kaaba declare?
The whole world is preoccupied
The calculator has gone haywire
There is no power and no strength save in God
Naft ibn Kaaba doesn't know what Naft ibn Kaaba declared.
Naft ibn Kaaba is so surreal!
My god, enough of these cows!
Oh Lord, enough of these rulers who are full of holes
Every poor person shall carry two angry skewers
Come join together all you wretched of the earth
We'll tear the masks off the whoring classes
A cat could eat what feeds a whole family for a year in Aden[*]
The big companies rob us,
then issue instructions
The terrorist Arab thieves
roam the airports of the world
In the airports of the sons of pigs and perfume,
we are searched thoroughly
We are searched right down to our vertebrae
The police dog is trained to detect the smell of an Arab
And to distinguish refugee from nonrefugee
These police dogs are definitely
in cahoots with the Arab authorities,
and the American ones,
and the apes.

[*] Aden: A city in southern Yemen.

[Applause]
Apes! You apes!
Gentlemen, tourists of the civilized world!
In the East we have apes for leaders!
I'm sitting in front of the Church of Rome
Displaying all of our goods
Here is the overwhelming Arab hunger that owns all the oil,
Here is half of a Gulf
Here is an accord that will deliver the coast of Basra
Here is Rakhyut
And here, gentlemen, all of the tears must be shed
I weep lava.
Has anyone heard of Rakhyut?
Has anyone heard of Rakhyut and Hawfa*
No, they are not constellations, or great discoveries
but they are parts of the Arab nation
a kingdom of hunger, pestilence and vomit
and of revolution as well.
[Applause]
I witnessed it, I saw it with my own eyes:
a pregnant woman eating the vomit of her feverish child
and feeding the other child with the same black vomit
What wonders Arab oil has done for us!
We belch to the point of indigestion from hunger
While the Oil King is afraid of rats getting at his cash
And the West, in all its wondrous nuclear superiority and perfection,
gathers us for oil, and slaughters all of us for oil.
Long live oil!
Long live gas!
Long live the King of Farts!†
[Applause]
Long live oil, long live gas, long live the King of Farts!
Long live Ras al-Khayma

---

* Rakhyut and Hawfa: Towns in Oman and Jordan, respectively.
† King of Farts: The Arabic word *ghaz* also means gas or oil, a deliberate pun
by al-Nawwab, who refers to all oil monarchs as kings of farts!

Long live, long live, the beard of Qaboos ibn Sa'id
Long live, long live, long live oil!
Long live, long live, long live gas!
Long live the King of Farts!
Long live Ras al-Khayma
Long live the beard of Qaboos ibn Sa'id.
Does anyone know the taste of salty vomit?
And does anyone know how the fig tree,
the precious source of goodness,
was taken away from her hands?
She kept looking around until it dried up
and almost died.
Just then a root extended and lengthened
and sipped the water of paradise from the hand of God
For the fig tree in the Arab land will never die.
This fig tree could not be beaten by Khartit!*
It debilitated the Allies
and exhausted the Shah
In your name, in your name, in your name
I declare out loud
I call upon the people
Upon everyone to bear two giant skewers
Covered with nails
Now, now, and not tomorrow!
The doors of the Arab nation will be closed to the ruling apes!
Apes, apes, apes!
Ape-regimes!
Ape-parties!
Ape-institutions!
No, no! Even the droppings of apes are more respectable than you!
They fought amongst themselves: the swords of Sunna and Shi'a
And the Alawites and even the old extinct fossils
Rams clashing horns
Bulls mounting each other
Fates playing music that forces the rats to dance.

* Kharit: A mythical monster.

Then they all gathered underneath his robe
and sealed the deal with a kiss.
And Naft ibn Kaaba announced . . .
What did Naft ibn Kaaba announce?
Naft ibn Kaaba calls a meeting . . .
and the prices go up.
Naft ibn Kaaba goes to relieve himself . . .
and the prices hold steady.
How wondrous is this community of apes!
And the bone, oh Naft ibn Kaaba!
You choke with the bone of Fatima the daughter of so-and-so
and that so-and-so died on the bridge of return,
we didn't have time to bury him.
This bone from Fatima the daughter of so-and-so
These burnt vertebrae could be used as rosary beads
For the religious clergymen
This excellent brown vomit from Rakhyut
Does anyone here know about Rakhyut?
This is the declaration of the armies of betrayal
This is Tal al-Zaatar
This is Damur
And Sinai, and Antakiah, and Greater Tunub
and Lesser Tunub, and Abu Musa, and all the rest.*
But gentlemen
No one will dine on the Arab East on a golden platter.

Naft ibn Kaaba announced
That a meeting would be convened
It's coincidence, I swear, sheer coincidence
That there were six members
And that the corners of the star are six in total
Oh, star of David, rejoice
Oh, Masonic Lodge, go wild with delight
Oh, finger of Kissinger . . .
For the royal asshole is hexagonal!

* Antakia . . . and all the rest: Various cities and towns in the Middle East.

ZAKARIYYA TAMIR

(B. 1931)

The Enemies

Translated from the Arabic by Roger Allen

1. The start.

The policeman blew his whistle. At once the morning sun rose and beamed on the city streets a wan sunlight like the planks of an ancient gallows.

At that moment people woke up, sorrowful and with frowning faces.

2. The lost sky.

Two birds alighted on the branch of one of the trees at the roadside. They did not sing to greet the morning sun, but instead exchanged perplexed and worried looks.

"Where shall we fly?" one of them asked the other.

"Our sky is full of planes."

"The only space left for us is inside cages."

"We'll lose our wings."

"And we'll forget how to sing."

The two birds stared up at a black plane traversing the heavens at enormous speed and then exchanged worried glances again. To them the city seemed like a greedy mouth with huge teeth. They swallowed sleeping pills and fell dead to the solid cement pavement below.

3. The prisoners.

Two old men were walking along a city pavement at a deliberate pace and talking morosely:

"This is the end of time."

"Things are going from bad to worse."

"It's time to write the petition."

"Which petition?"

"The one we must forward to God Almighty."

"What will we write in this petition?"

"We'll write as follows: 'We the undersigned request of the Lord of Creation that he send us an army of angels equipped with the most up-to-date weapons to take up positions on the frontiers and fight the enemy; and not treat us as prisoners.'"

"And what will we do in the event that the petition is not put into effect?"

"Forward yet another petition asking God to agree to our being excused the five daily prayers."

"And if He doesn't agree?"

"Oh, He will and He'll let us off the fast too. He is pitying and merciful!"

4. Vengeance.

A group of children were gathered in the school playground, enthusiastically involved in a new game.

"I'm Tarzan."

"I'm Antar."*

"I'm a millionaire."

"I'm the inventor of the atom bomb."

"I'm Superman!"

"I'm a policeman."

"I'm the inventor of the airplane."

They all pounced on the inventor of the airplane and started slapping, punching, and kicking him while he kept screaming for help.

---

* Antar: Legendary pre-Islamic Arab poet famed for his chivalry.

5. Men.

Praise be to God who created us men; in times of danger we can run forward like the wind and thus avoid being wiped out.

Praise be to God who did not create us women; staying at home we would be burned to death by the enemy bombs just like old socks.

Praise be to God! Praise is due to none but Him!

6. The danger.

An astrologer was asked what the future would bring. "Old and young will be destroyed," he replied without the slightest hesitation. "Cats, birds, and flowers too. Houses, books, and flags will be burned, as will school chairs and memento photographs. Napalm will eradicate laughter, the Arabic language, and ears of grain. Hospitals will be destroyed, and so will factories and gardens. Women will walk in the streets without their head-to-toe wraps."

When this prediction was published in a book, those who remained faithful to the homeland agreed to reject what he said would happen to women. They called upon everyone to exert their very utmost efforts to ward off this abominable eventuality.

7. Heaven.

The men who were about to perform the prayer gathered eagerly in a circle around the shaykh of the mosque. "Tell us, Shaykh," asked one of the men in a shaky voice, "are there planes in Paradise?"

"Planes do not exist in Paradise," the shaykh replied.

The men all heaved a sigh of relief. "Thank God for that!" they said joyfully.

8. A sermon.

"By God, it wasn't weakness that made us fail to move against the enemy. Quite the contrary, it was pride, dignity, and self-confidence. We want your petrol, they said. Take our petrol, we replied; we're the descendants of Hatim al-Ta'i.* Declare all-out war on imported ideas, they demanded. We're hit-and-run types, we replied, and then proceeded to set up gallows and build prisons.

"They wanted to take control of a city, so we gave them cities and more cities to prove that we could not care less about them. And if they had planes and bombs, well, we had an upright character and heaven-made principles. How vast the distance between what they have and what we have! We are strong because our weapons are spirit and truth, not mere ephemeral materials and fleeting inanities. . . ."

9. A medal for our savior.

The Arabic language has been awarded the highest decoration in our homeland for the way in which it took part in the transformation of a military defeat into a victory. It managed to term the war† a "withdrawal," the withdrawal then became steadfast resistance, steadfast resistance turned into bravery, and bravery was called victory.

We have defeated the enemy, and we'll be able to defeat their fifth column too, which seems to be the only element not to appreciate the fighting qualities of the Arabic language.

10. Why?

"What's the difference between men and animals?" the pupil asked his teacher.

"Animals don't talk, but people do," was the teacher's reply.

The teacher wasn't lying either. We people who work in radio, television, and the press are the best talkers around.

So to the Creator of the heavens and earth who gave us tongues we offer our grateful thanks. The benefits of talking are innumerable. On

---

* Hatim al-Ta'i: Pre-Islamic Arab poet known for his generosity.

† The war: Tamir is likely referring to the 1967 Six-Day War between Israel and the Arab states of Egypt, Jordan, and Syria, at the end of which Israel occupied the Sinai Peninsula, the Gaza Strip, the West Bank, East Jerusalem, and the Golan Heights.

the day the enemy attacked us, our talking undertook an honorable role. It faced the enemy courageously, shot down planes, destroyed their tanks, and wiped out their soldiers too.

So how was it that things happened the way they did? How were we defeated when our talking was fighting for us like a hero?

11. Wiping out the poor.

Citizen Sulayman al-Qasim* felt hungry, so he ate newspapers, each one brim full of articles extolling the governmental system and enumerating the obvious good works it had achieved in eliminating poverty.

When he had enough, he gave thanks to God who provides nourishment for His servants and believed profoundly in what the newspapers had said.

12. Radio program.

Announcer: What's your name, brother?

Young man: Abd al-Mun'im al-Halabi.

Announcer: Are you married?

Young man: No, I'm a bachelor.

Announcer: What's your job?

Young man: I'm unemployed.

Announcer: Why aren't you working? Are you rich or don't you like working?

Young man: No, I'm not rich, and I don't dislike work. I've been looking for work for years.

Announcer: What's the one wish you would like to see granted?

Young man: To die now.

Announcer: Dear listeners, our brother Abd al-Mun'im al-Halabi is obviously a zealous patriot. As you notice, in longing for death he actually wants to punish himself for not participating in the construction of our developing and ever-advancing society.

---

* Sulayman al-Qasim: Not a real person.

13. Children.

A young child asked his mother a question. "What's the point of having eyes?"

"Eyes were created," she replied, giving him a cautious, worried look, "for people to look respectfully and lovingly at pictures of the country's leaders."

"What about ears then?" the child asked next.

"They're to listen to official orders and political speeches," the mother replied with increasing concern.

"And the tongue?" the child asked.

"The tongue is useless apart from helping you swallow food after you have chewed it."

The child gave a cryptic smile, while his mother started trembling, having given way to a grinding feeling of alarm.

14. The hero.

Television announcer: Would you mind explaining to our viewers, Khalid ibn al-Walid,* how you became a famous hero?

Khalid ibn al-Walid: It's thanks to Andrews Liver Salts that I became a hero. Every morning, I used to dissolve two spoonfuls of Andrews Liver Salt in water and drink it down. And, as everyone knows, Andrews Liver Salts invigorate the liver, clean out the innards, fortify the body, and stimulate the mind.

15. Love.

Search all you want, Officer. My wife is not a printing press devoting all its energies to disseminating harmful political pamphlets, nor is her laughter an imperialist conspiracy. It simply cannot be explained as a direct criticism of the governmental system; particularly in view of the fact that, before I fell in love with her, I made sure to ask her opin-

---

* Khalid ibn al-Walid: Islam's most famous military commander during the early expansion of the Islamic Empire. He died in 642 CE, hence the anachronistic joke of his promoting Andrews Liver Salts, a British product.

ion about the governmental system in our country at the moment. She replied immediately that she was totally in love with it. It was only after that that I allowed my heart to fall in love with this politically conscious citizen of our country.

When we kissed for the first time, we both shuddered with sheer pleasure. It was just as though we were clapping and shouting in a march to support the struggle of the masses.

Tell me, Officer, can you really want a sense of loyalty greater than what we have shown?!

16. The crime.

I am a citizen, no different from any other needy citizen; my clothes are like theirs, my stomach is like theirs, and I am as much afraid as they are.

When the state gave me a job in a factory it owns, I did not realize the value of its gift to me. After only a few months, I asked for a raise in salary, entirely oblivious of the amount of money needed to fight our enemies and in contravention of official orders regarding the need for tightening our belts. I had no idea of the extent of the damage that would afflict the homeland if my request were to be honored. If I had obtained a raise in salary, the state's money supply would have been depleted; and if that, then there would have been insufficient funds to pay for whisky, women's clothes, cars, and buildings. And if there were a shortage of whisky, women started getting angry, and cars and buildings were less plush, then history and objective analysis would certainly prove that officialdom's contentment with the country would dwindle. If that happened, then their morale would flag too, and as a result, their statements, declarations, and speeches would become vapid and boring and wouldn't scare the enemy anymore. Thus, when I asked for a salary raise, I was actually serving the enemy's goals and helping their psychological warfare succeed.

I therefore should receive the severest punishment.

Footnote: This sudden awareness that I have developed has nothing whatsoever to do with the fact that I've been taken to the police station. They only questioned me about my suggestions concerning increased production.

17. The authorities.

A policeman leaned his elbows on the river wall. "Hey, river!" he shouted in a gruff tone of voice.

"Who's calling me?"

"I am."

"Who are you?"

"I'm a policeman."

The river waters rippled in fear.

"Unless you want to be banished and spend the rest of your life in exile, you have to give an undertaking not to interfere in politics."

"But this is my homeland," the river replied.

"Do you want to be put in jail?" the policeman asked curtly.

Whereupon the river hurriedly carried out the policeman's wishes by pledging its loyalty and obedience to the authorities.

18. Toward a country that will make tourists happy.

To whom it may concern:

We tawdry human beings who live in narrow, dark alleys wish to request the following:

1. That, in view of the price of clothing, we be allowed to go around naked so that our bodies can get some light and air;

2. That government hospitals undertake to remove without charge our stomachs which bring into our lives so much anxiety, without there being any patriotic rationale for it all;

3. That our heads be cut off, it having been made clear to us that the thing which turns citizens into traitors is the eye which sees, the ear which hears, the tongue which speaks, the mind which thinks, and the mind which doesn't think.

19. Fetters of the dead.

The story is told of a man who loved a woman, but she refused to marry him. "How can you refuse to marry me," the man asked in astonishment, "when you're continually telling me that you love me?"

"I do love you," the woman protested, "but you belong to a family that doesn't bury its dead ancestors. How can you expect me to live with you in a house whose rooms are filled with corpses?"

The man pondered for a moment. "You're right," he replied. "The dead should be in graves, not in the houses of the living."

He immediately began digging a deep pit in which to bury his ancestors' bodies, but the spirits of his ancestors and the enemy bound him with chains and buried him in the pit he had already dug.

The woman wept no tears. She just whetted her man's sword and waited without despair for his return so that he could fight both the ancestors and the enemy.

20. Suns and moons.

Living cowards are better than dead heroes. So kiss the hand of the person in power, and pray in secret for it to be smashed. If you wish to request a favor from a dog, then address it as "My lord dog." Always be the first to obey and the last to disobey. He who is not obeyed has no discretion. If speech is of silver, then silence is of gold. Satisfaction is an inexhaustible treasure; the envious can never prevail. So do what you are told and obey the authorities. Those who stick to the right path reach their destination.

21. The young ones laugh.

One day the king saw a number of children playing in a field and laughing merrily. "Why are you all laughing?" he asked.

"I'm laughing," one of them replied, "because the sky is blue."

"I'm laughing," a second replied, "because the trees are green."

"I'm laughing," a third replied, "because the birds are flying through the air."

The king looked at the sky, the birds, and the trees and found that they were not laughing. He came to the conclusion that the children were only laughing to poke fun at the king's majesty. So he went back to his palace and issued an order forbidding the people of his kingdom to laugh. All the old people obeyed the ruling and stopped laughing, but the young children paid no attention to the king's edict and carried on laughing because the trees were green, the sky was blue, and the birds kept on flying.

22. Bribery.

The men of the district convened a meeting to talk about religion and the world. A man with a white beard was the first to speak. "The only reason why the enemy defeated us," he began in an admonitory tone of voice, "was that we have strayed far from our true religion. You should realize that the defeat was both a punishment and a warning: a punishment for the sins you have committed, and a warning of a future that will be filled with sufferings and disasters."

"What are we to do then?" shouted one of the men of the district. "Give us your counsel."

"You should return to your religion," the bearded man replied, "full of regret and penitence and beseeching forgiveness and a felicitous outcome."

"But we pray and fast," the man went on, "we do no harm to anyone and we mention the name of God morning and evening."

"What you are doing is not enough," the bearded man replied. "You must build a mosque where the word of God will reach upward."

"But it takes a lot of money to build a mosque, and we are poor."

"Woe upon you!" the bearded man replied impetuously. "How can you use all these feeble excuses to claim that you can't build a mosque when you squander all the money you earn on ephemeralities?! Woe betide the person who prefers the trivialities of this world to the contentment of God."

The men lowered their heads in shame.

So the people of the district went hungry for a long time, but they managed to build a mosque with a minaret that looked like a spear jutting angrily into the sky, as though it were about to be launched into the sky to bring down enemy planes.

23. Investigation.

"No lying now!" said the detective to the baby in the cradle. "Tell us everything you know about your companions."

The baby did not reply.

The detective became very angry.

"How dare you refuse to reply?" he asked in a furious tone.

The baby started crying. The detective now became even more annoyed and gave orders for his men to be summoned. They came in at once, carrying whips and nighttime devoid of stars.

24. The will.

The old man was close to death and a number of his grieving sons and relatives were gathered around him. With exhausted eyes he looked at their wan faces and tattered clothing. "I am going to die," he told them in a low, quavering, and apologetic voice, "without bequeathing you anything of use."

He was about to carry on speaking, but suddenly an overwhelming sense of exhaustion came over him and he had to stop. Panting and shaking, he closed his eyes. Eventually he mustered enough energy to continue. "Life's very curious, my sons and grandsons," he said. "So just do everything you can which is evil and scandalous. Cause havoc in the land. Never tell the truth, even if the hangman's noose is about to lop off your head. Lie. Suck up to the rich and holders of high office. Fawn upon the trivial, the paltry, the hollow, and the laughable. It's for them that the future looks bright, not for anyone else. Applaud the up-and-coming new arrival, and curse the one on the way out. Get drunk. Never pray or fast. Don't be nice to anyone. Be left and right, be east and west. Despise books. The smile of officialdom is worth more than a thousand books. Attack the wretched weakling, and sleep the sleep of the humble at the threshold of the rich and powerful. Eulogize those who don't deserve it, clap in delight when dogs bark, and beat on drums so that the nightingales' singing cannot be heard."

The dying old man gave way to a violent burst of anger and tried desperately to shout what it was he wanted to say. But at that moment death came, and the old man, bursting at the seams with rancor and regret, fell silent.

25. The end.

"As I have told you before," said the teacher to his young pupils, "the year is divided into four seasons. What are they?"

"Fall," the pupils shouted.

"In fall," the teacher said, "the leaves on the trees turn yellow, the earth is plowed, and the clouds come."

Fall came, and the leaves on the trees did turn yellow. They fell to the ground to cover the corpses of those who died in the war and were not buried in graves.

"Winter," the pupils shouted.

"In winter," the teacher said, "the rain comes down and waters the soil."

Winter came, and lo, the debris from our planes and the corpses of our innocent dead were the seeds in the soil on which the plenteous rains fell from the heavens.

"Spring," the pupils shouted.

"In spring," the teacher said, "the color green is to be seen everywhere."

Spring came, and the ground was covered with green grass and flowers, but mothers and cities continued to wear the black color of mourning.

"Summer," the pupils shouted.

"Summer," the teacher said, "is harvest time."

Summer came, but the earth did not produce any ears of wheat. Instead it produced new planes and men longing to die a second time.

26. The end.

A man plunged the blade of his dagger into the soil right up to the hilt in a gesture of revenge, and then put his ear to the ground. "The earth's crying!" he yelled in amazement.

He put his ear to the ground again. "It's dead!" he shouted in a voice laden with joy.

When he put his ear to the ground a third time, all he could hear was the sound of army boots pounding the earth rhythmically.

YUSIF IDRIS
(1927–1991)

The Aorta

Translated from the Arabic by Trevor J. Le Gassick

IT WASN'T IMPORTANT that there was running; what mattered was that it was happening all over the place as if Doomsday itself had come. A very peculiar type of running it was, not like someone in a hurry, or fleeing in terror, or racing to save a life. No—an aimless sort of running, as if those doing it were trying to find some spot from which to actually begin their running and hurrying. And so no one knew the goal or purpose of the others, all being in a state of watchful anxiety, concerned that one of them would find his own point of beginning which would then, no doubt, define their own. That's why you saw people running so madly, crazily, and trying so desperately yet unsuccessfully to watch where the others were heading. Whenever anyone appeared at all hesitant and slowed down, or became more purposeful and increased speed and so seemed about to discover his goal, then dozens would rush toward him, hoping to arrive before him, to be the first to set off after a clearly defined objective. Inevitably disappointed when those they had been pursuing turned out even more confused than themselves, they would soon speed off again to someone else, again imitating his dawdle or increasing their speed. This whole activity made the place, if viewed from high above or far away, seem to pulsate with sudden throbbings that then dispersed and subsided, it all happening at more than one place at a time. You would have thought the square paved with smooth veneer, if it had not been for those sudden pulsations occurring here and there that alone gave signs of life. You would have thought it all a veneer of stone, or the human beings gathered there lumps of multicolored rocks.

No one knows whether blows were struck or not. Well, actually, I personally was struck by more than one blow, vicious painful blows. But it was impossible to know who was doing the striking because one had no constant neighbor and the continuous fluid movement prevented you getting so much as a glance at the hundreds passing you or whom you were passing. In any case there were, most certainly, blows struck. Collisions occurred without time for even an apology. People were falling down; suddenly there would be a loud scream, followed by a groan that would reverberate ever diminishing like the tones of a bell, to be effaced at last by another scream. No one would stop to see the outcome; so long as you were not yourself scream-ing—and I was still fit and strong and had not yet fallen—why should you stop? Little by little I realized that all this motion was not haphaz-ard and that there was another quiet current at work, definitely push-ing toward the outside yet difficult, almost impossible to detect. The square was gradually distending in a slow, regular, and imperceptible eruption, forcing outward those in the middle, bringing them close to the surrounding area, to the outside, to the many streets flowing into and drawing from the square.

Had it not been for this current, nothing could ever possibly have managed to extricate me from where I had been to where I now found a group of people running on mechanically, continuing involuntarily what we had been doing in the great square, going on as before and unable to stop even if we had wanted. And what a surprise then! How could I ever have guessed that turning next moment to the person right beside me—the very first close neighbor whose features I had been able to properly examine—I would find, to my shock and amazement, Abduh!

Immediately I was gripped by conviction that he had the money with him, that he must be hiding it someplace on him. A sense of joy, of relief after a wait of a thousand years almost killed me, along with a rage like a choking, poisonous gas that satiates the body and becomes perceptible only a moment before death, when you realize for the first and last time that it has choked and killed you. Yes, indeed, rage of that most hideous kind, exploding when you have been feeling secure and confident and suddenly, without any effort seeing evil treachery there right before your very eyes, that overwhelming rage you have when you see a person you are quite sure you have in your grasp whenever and wherever you wish suddenly slipping away, disappearing in front of you. You burn with rage and fury, but try as you might you can't prevent him.

Abduh! With both hands I grabbed him around the throat, desperately afraid he might slip away and disappear again. It truly enraged me that I couldn't actually devour him . . . yes, the wild animal is still there, inside us. When we fight we don't bite to hurt our adversary; we do so because we really want, just like our wild ancestors, to devour him. Our forebears attacked and devoured their enemies in rage, to hide them body and soul together inside themselves. Their very lives depended on a belief that they could feed their own cells on those of their enemies. We are human beings who bite only out of weakness; we hate but cannot express our hatred in the natural way and so it sets poisoned fangs deep into our insides, biting and destroying us.

All this I felt as I gripped Abduh, wishing my feelings could take free expression and, maybe, shred and chew him. I could feel my teeth tearing at his flesh and bones, easing my bitterness in grinding him with all the cruel greed they possessed. Perhaps it's a basic need for man to eat his food out of a sense of rage, seeking to efface and remove it, to kill it by consuming it completely; perhaps that's why wild animals gain maximum benefit from their food while man nowadays gets sick and suffers from his.

But even as food Abduh was completely unappetizing, disgusting even; he was thin and weak. He never showed a glimmer of defiance, never faced up to anyone else to assert or defend his own existence. He was "good," that weakly, negative sort of goodness, as if he had a double hernia or something, and he sang sweet songs when by himself. He seemed "foreign," out of place wherever he was, as if he'd never found his own country. When things got too much for him, he'd cry. His eyes would suddenly fill with tears. But there'd be no redness in them; the flush would gather into his nose, which would seem to swell and fill with the secretions. It embarrassed you not only because it was Abduh but because he, a man, cried like women and children do, yet without anything softly feminine or childlike about it to inspire your sympathy; what was calamitous was the man's way he cried, utterly disgusting. Merely a petty thief who never stole unless he absolutely had to, he even then took only the minimum he could. If you caught him he'd tremble all over and stammer and swear silly lying oaths. You had to be careful not to treat him too roughly or else he'd cry, filling you with a disgust that would last all day or perhaps even for days on end.

Yes, for three whole days, morning, noon, and night, I've been looking for you, Abduh, turning over the pavement stones of Cairo, breaking into houses, asking, demanding, pleading for help in finding you, searching every road, every street, every alley. My strength finally sapped, I fall asleep only to wake up in a rage of despair at finding you; my dream, my nightmare, and the pain of my hours awake or asleep is the thought of turning around sometime and finding you there, Abduh!

"Where have you been, Abduh, and where did you hide the money?"

His reply was astonishing, fantastic. He said that on that day he'd no sooner left the house than he'd been grabbed by one of those patrols that look out for sick people and take them by force to the hospitals (just like the patrols that look out for and seize sick animals!). Having their suspicions about him, they took him to the hospital where he was examined by the chief surgeon himself. It was decided he had contracted a dangerous disease that threatened to infect all Egyptians; the only cure possible was through surgery they would perform at once to take out his aorta. They had indeed performed the operation and cut out his aorta; he had lain in bed for three days and they had sent him out only that day, after providing him with a cane to help him walk. But as for the money—he had no idea of its whereabouts ever since he first entered the hospital.

Abduh had to tell some story, of course, to justify his disappearance and that of the money. But his telling such a tale too absurd for even a child or an idiot to believe—about patrols watching for people thought to be diseased and taking them by force and treating them with such frightful bestiality, about a sickness curable by cutting out the aorta, and his, the human body's principal artery, as thick as a stick, that distributes blood from the heart to all the rest, actually having been cut while he was still alive and even still able to walk, though with a cane, and even run, indeed, as we had been doing moments before—for Abduh to tell such an open, brazen lie, without even so much as trying to hide it or looking for some other straightforward or more believable story, it was this that destroyed all my delight in finding him, this that made me feel so overwhelmingly tired and depressed, because I sensed that he was ridiculing me indescribably badly, this that made me feel so enraged there might be no limit to the cruelty to which one might feel compelled.

I was not alone there. The group running with me had witnessed and heard all this, their speed having slowed to a walk. Indeed others had begun to join us and felt the same as I did about Abduh and his story. All of us, without exception, were now consumed with the idea that he did have the money on him, that he had to be hiding it somewhere on his person. Abduh certainly possessed no other place in the world where he could hide anything.

And the story itself was not important, whatever story he might tell, what mattered was to locate the money, to find it right in front of him, in full view, and to disgrace him utterly and completely before everybody, right there where all could see and hear. So the shouts began!

"Search him! . . . Search him!"

I needed no shouts in any case to make me stretch out my arm and rip off his faded old peasant gown, the only one he owned. But I was surprised when the gown remained stuck to his body, impossible to pull off. This was odd because Abduh was always lost in his ill-fitting gown and so how come I couldn't pull it off now? He seemed to have suddenly ballooned, or, in the space of only three days, fattened up most incredibly. Everyone participated, then, in offering suggestions for how to remove his gown; their enthusiasm in getting at Abduh even dominated my own, the victim. There was no direct agreement, no words spoken, just an all-encompassing eagerness that aroused and engrossed us; we were excited, enjoying ourselves as though now quite certain we had discovered our goal, that point to which we had seemed to be running in the square, from which we could in fact begin our running. . . . It was there in that sinner, still carrying with him the sin he had committed. He had to get his just deserts. We would gratify all the goodness in us by punishing him, by seeing justice done. And we would gratify all the evil in us by applying justice ourselves, with our own hands, by giving evil a completely free rein, by causing pain and hurt under the guise of proper retribution.

The only way to remove his gown was by peeling it off him as one skins a rabbit. And to skin him properly he had to be hung up, and so the problem became where and how to hang him. A suggestion was made to which we agreed; there was a butcher's shop close by and there the whole group moved, with Abduh in our midst and me still gripping him tightly. In the butcher's, four men undertook to lift Abduh while the portly young butcher took responsibility for hanging him up by the collar of his shirt and underclothes on the hook used for suspending carcasses of meat.

Soon, then, he hung up there on the hook, quite impotent, totally powerless just like the other carcasses, the skinned sheep on the other hooks. Hands, many of them, now stretched out to lift up the skirt of his gown, to peel it off him, while he hung there silently, not uttering a sound.

As soon as the gown was off, we realized what had made it stick so very close to his body. Around his stomach and chest a mass of white bandages was wound! It was as though he had indeed had an operation and these were the bandages. But I immediately realized his rotten scheme in having all those wraps; he had put on so many to hide the money in each fold, so that no one would think it there or be able to find it.

First, and purely as a routine matter, his billfold had to be searched. The butcher put out his plump and practiced hand, unwrapped the bandage a little, and extracted the wallet from his shirt pocket. This was the very first time I saw Abduh's billfold. I had never imagined it could be so fat. It was, quite simply, the bulkiest one you'd ever see in a life-time. I myself undertook to examine it and emptied its contents. But, as we had expected, all it contained was five piastre coins, one so dented and rusty that it was unfit for circulation.

The fat butcher again plunged his hand into the shirt pocket and as expected brought nothing out. All these were purely formalistic pro-cedures, for we all knew the money was there inside, hidden in one of the bandage folds. Eager and impatient for the scandal to break, certain that we were going, then and there and right before him, to put our fingers on the sinner's crime, to extract from his very body the body of the crime, absolutely intoxicated with anticipation at seeing his face and hearing what he would say at that precise moment, my hand and that of the butcher stretched out and began unwinding the bandage from him! We ignored his screams and calls for help and claims that to undo the bandage would mean he would die, since it alone held the severed aorta in place, screams that merely inspired laughter and sarcastic comments and made us busily untying all the more eager for that moment of climax when the money would be revealed. By the time we had untied a few of the wraps, Abduh's screams had subsided into a despairing silence, and his eyes had filled with watery tears, but devoid of any redness.

Even if we had believed earlier that they had performed an operation on him, it was now obvious he had been lying; the bandages were clean and white, without a single spot of blood on them, and there was no sign of a wound at all. And so we went on untying, though a bit more carefully for fear that the money might drop out at the very next wrap.

All of us standing there were participating now, and Abduh himself seemed to be expecting the money to appear at every next turn. I was unwrapping from one side and handing the bandage over to the fat butcher for him to untie from his side. Then he would return it to me. It seems we were so totally engrossed in the operation that once I stretched out my hand to take the bandage from him, but it was not there; he had already finished. Before I looked up at Abduh I could sense some strange feeling gripping the onlookers. Gazing over at them, I saw they were all standing totally, eerily silent, their eyes fixed, unblinking like those of the dead, on Abduh. I looked to where they were staring . . . Abduh was stark naked. There was a very long rent extending from his chest to the base of his stomach, both of them open and empty as if all their inside apparatus had been removed. His aorta was hanging down from his chest, from where his heart was, like a long, thick, sallow, hollow tube, cut loose and swinging to and fro inside his belly, like a pendulum.

HAYDAR HAYDAR
(B. 1936)

The Dance of the Savage Prairies

Translated from the Arabic by May Jayyusi and Anthony Thwaite

The Body

Summer. Overflowing pavements. A white illuminated world. The morning bustle, quick, invigorating. A period of one's childhood, suffused with warmth, sears the heart.

A memory flowing and bustling, carried by the wind from the green hills. The wind saturated with the smell of grass, forest leaves, and the expanse of sea.

The Square. Nubile schoolgirls pass by with their short colored dresses. Rosy faces, throbbing with health and liveliness. The wind that springs up lifts the short dresses a little, then higher. Suddenly the morning glitters. Summer glows, reflected from the marble of white and brown flesh. The smell of grass and sea disappears.

The atmosphere is agitated now by the smell of something hot, delicious, and painful.

Inside a glass café, at the edge of the opposite pavement, a face alien to the world. A neutral face, monotonously chewing gum. When the wind lifts the dress of a passing girl, he presses the gum between his teeth causing a small explosion.

His face, except for the retinas of his fiery eyes, appears to be undefined, neutral as a rock, while observing the summer and other things.

Except that something else can be observed, behind his neutrality— a kind of annoyance mixed with a harsh disgust. His gestures, inside the café, in the midst of the mechanical din of people, are slightly neurotic, while anyone observing him closely would doubt that he is thinking of anything in particular.

The truth is, he is simply there. Sitting on a chair, an empty table in front of him. His left ankle resting on the opposite leg. A hand, loosely hanging, seems to have been forgotten there, while the other is on the top of the table, its fingers moving to a monotonous and meaningless beat.

Between this man, sitting behind the glass front, and the outside world there is a white curtain and then there is the glass. His eyes, sharp as a hawk's, pierce through the screen, the glass, the streets, and the bodies of the passersby. They pierce faces, the half-exposed breasts, the thighs that dazzle the eyes and inflame the blood.

Although the face perched behind the glass appears to be immersed in its own sense of anatomy and personal solitude, something else might move behind this cold reserve. Something that, on breaking out, sweeps away the neutrality to give the face an expression full of pain and desire.

The man sitting on a chair in the café is constantly changing: his depths singing with secret desires, residing in his fiery sphere, the sphere of the five senses, center of energy and action.

From a time impossible to recall, objects had taken on their hard fiery form there. Transformed from the objective world, drawn by a power overwhelming to the force of reason, to the sphere of fire and sensation where the absolute, the private, and the brutal desire for possession are to be found. Place, time, and people were involved in this transformation. All formulae seemed to have been molded in his depths, in the image of his desires.

His name was Muhammed. However, after a series of special procedures and painful, physical, sensual experiences, he came to be known as Alazrak—"The Blue."

His gait as he swaggers with his Spartan body, the wind playing with the blue scarf around his neck and his hair falling in waves to his shoulders, is reminiscent of the gait of actors playing the role of a roughneck.

At such times, as he cuts across pavements and people, he would imagine that all eyes were fixed on him. Frightened eyes, awed by his athletic walk. There walks Alazrak!

Perhaps he hears it echoing in his depths. The throb of an inner intoxication would rise in his blood. He would stretch his body high, strutting like a peacock, surveying with his sharp eyes the passing human flies.

Alazrak is the beautiful beast of the city. Bewitcher of girls and possessor of the sharp dagger that he draws only to plant in the heart of a man who deserves death.

He sees in the fleeting faces, the glass fronts and the lighted sky, his own solid dark face. A woman once said, "In your barbaric face, there is a cruelty that women desire and at which men tremble."

In the streets of the city bounded from the west by the sea and from the east by the African forests, Alazrak had asserted his existence among the gangs of looters and the vagrants; the alcoholics and the gamblers; the prisoners and the police.

This had begun at the end of a wintry day in a remote village of the Oras Mountains.* On that day his father had rebuked him for abandoning school and starting on the road of robbery and vagrancy. That evening their discussion became heated and the father had attempted to teach him good conduct by beating him up. But the cruel blows on his head had pained Alazrak and he rebelled and foamed, "Enough. Enough. You are killing me, you madman."

When the brutality of the blows increased, Alazrak sprang up like an enraged tiger. He twisted his father's arm and slapped him, then threw him to the ground smashing his face and teeth in. Then he fled the house, never to return.

Now as he reclines on the café's chair, he remembers bits of his argument with his father: "You swine, you dog. You hit your father?! How will you face your Lord on the day of judgment, you enemy of God?"

Just as he recalls his father's face bloodied and humbled, he recalls how he cursed him, spitting in the air, "Leave me alone you and your God! From now on Alazrak will be his own lord and master."

The Revenge

He descended on the city† that had fought the invaders after years of occupation filled with bitterness, terror, and brutality. He had arrived in the last week before their departure. The week that was named the

---

* Oras Mountains: Mountain range in Northeastern Algeria that served as the center of the twentieth-century Algerian revolt against the French.
† The city: Algiers.

week of terror and blood. In those terrifying days Alazrak witnessed the
foreigners demolishing the city with explosives and hunting and snip-
ing at the children. He saw the massacres of old men and the rape of
young girls in streets and squares.

The invaders were celebrating, in that tragic manner, the rituals of
their hatred and defeat, as if they were setting up games in a riotous
carnival colored by blood, fire, vengeance, and blind chaos.

In the week of blood and explosions, Alazrak entered upon his dangerous course.

The killing of innocent women, children, and old people in that
gratuitous fashion had aroused in him something like nausea, which
was later to explode in sudden spasms of hatred.

There he is, avoiding main thoroughfares, quickly crossing dark corners. Suddenly a bullet rings out, hitting a wall.

Alazrak freezes for a moment, observing the flash of bullets from one
of the windows. He finds the window and pinpoints the fenced house.
Cautiously, he advances, his back to the wall. With the agility of a
panther, he climbs the wall surrounding the house. Broken glass,
embedded at the top, cuts his hands. He jumps into the courtyard,
disappearing among the trees. As soon as the shooting stops, he climbs
a tree close to the window and crouches there. Just before dawn Alazrak smashes the window and enters the room. At the noise, the light
is switched on in the drawing room where Alazrak surprises his opponent. He flings the fair-skinned colonist onto the brilliant white marble
floor. The colonist's green eyes protrude, pleading for mercy. Coldly
he sits on top of his chest, stifling his voice. He pulls out his knife and
slaughters him like an animal, then flees.

As he runs away, what he had witnessed in the week of terror passes
in front of him, with fragments of stories told to him in his childhood
about the brutality of the invaders, the torture camps, the acts of exter-
mination, of burning and rape.

With the sun and solitude, these fragments have fused together in
his depths, spreading thick shadows of depression, dark moods, and an
untamable drive toward death.

The Shame

After drinking coffee and smoking countless cigarettes during the day and greedily drinking beer in a frenzy at night, Alazrak's other world begins, alone or with members of a gang from the wolves of the city.

There is always a store to be burgled or the bedroom of a woman to be raided, followed by bloody clashes with the outcasts and drunkards of late nights. After that, the wild roaring of the hot blood in the nerves calms down.

"The police, the bastards!" Alazrak says to himself as he sees their blue cars invading the streets with their shrill sirens.

"If only I had a machine gun to gun them down like dogs."

Those who had occupied the city after the departure of the invaders had stiffened his inner resolve. As he observes them in every quarter, at every corner, in the squares, schools, factories, park, and beaches, his soul becomes a permanently boiling volcano.

"Those pigs!"

He clenches his teeth and spits in the direction of the blue sky.

In prison, the police officer sarcastically asks, "Hey! How do you find yourself now? Si Alazrak?* How strong is your determination?"

As he stares into the policeman's face, he glimpses the desire for murder in his eyes.

"You've had it? O Alazrak!" he says to himself.

Once they had been given freedom in the city, they had turned into hunters. Orders had emphasized the need to consolidate the authority of the state, and licensed the liquidation of all lawbreakers.

This wild beast, this outlaw. Alazrak disturbs the peace of the jungle.

"Alazrak! You son of a whore, you and your band have fallen. You think the state is like your father, you trampled on his face and walked away? Ha. We'll show you how you'll return to your folk a woman who has lost her virginity, you swine, you fornicator."

The baton now appeared from one of the desk drawers to fall on his head. The second blow hit the central spot at the back of his head, and a red flame erupted, lighting up the world. Alazrak screamed like an

---

* Si Alazrak: In Algeria, Morocco, and other parts of North Africa, Si means "Mister."

animal being slaughtered, "Ayie, ayie, you have killed me, you pig. You dog of the state."

Fire raced through the veins and nerves, bursting out. The area of the blow started to sting and glow. Crimson shapes began to emerge in the sky of a cruel world.

Alazrak met the third blow with his raised, manacled hands and, like an enraged bull rushing into the arena, he rammed his head and hands into the face and stomach of the police inspector. He tore into his face and broke some of his ribs, then he mercilessly crushed his head as he had once crushed his own father's.

As a result of this, Alazrak spent three months in the prison hospital, receiving medical treatment and nursing the shame and dishonor of having been raped.

The Nightmare

He felt exhilarated as he watched the city burn. He saw himself soaring in a sky of fire and blood. The fire was consuming the police stations, the jails, the mosques, the shops, and the army barracks. All the symbols and old idols that had crushed and distorted his spirit were burning to ashes in the raging fire. He saw himself dancing naked over green hills. As he dances, pustules, boils, and hateful-smelling germs emerge from his body. When the dancing halts, he slings incendiary missiles to fan the flaming fire. As the flames erupt in waves, so do his desires erupt from their prison, breaking down the barriers that had repressed his spirit, dormant under layers of fire.

Now he is purged and returns to his original nature. And here is the fire, laying bare the desire, awakening it from the bondage of its sleep, and reconciling it with its origins. Here is Alazrak shouting out primitive cries, some meaningful and some not, in this colorful ritual celebration.

The bird of the spirit had taken off from its cage, toward the forest and the sea.

"To hell with you, you oppressive heritage!" The city of nightmare, the city of fear, arrests, hunger and murder, had become a burning hell.

With pagan joy, Alazrak takes wing, passing over the city of ruins in the direction of the forest. And with the tranquillity of a child whose eyes are the color of the sea and the sky, he lies down on the green grass and, naked, sleeps in his mother's arms.

Sea

Beyond the city stretches the sea. A blue heavenly child, frightening and sublime. The sea and the virgin African forests encircle the city. The city, which Alazrak perceives as a cage or cemetery. He moves in the subterranean alleys, as if he were a beast thrown up by the forest into the city's compound. In the streets, the cafés, the bars, the interrogation rooms, and the prison cells, he can hear only the sounds of taming, of familiarity, concord, and obedience, and he recoils.

Suddenly he feels nauseated, and he spits. Sometimes in the middle of the street he takes out his penis, tracing with his urine strange obscene words attacking the state, the police, the city, gods and fathers, commands and prohibitions and conventions.

Then he rushes with animal-like screams across the city toward the jungles.

This time, however, the prison wound went deep. Although he feels, as he reclines on a chair in the café, the need to break out of his human condition toward his natural absolute, he now realizes that his swift movements toward freedom have become constrained.

He had to do something to erase the stigma. Although he spent many sleepless nights dreaming of raping his rapists, killing all the city's policemen, and blowing up the jail, these substitute nightmares, while soothing to the nerves, seemed like a temporary sedative unable to heal the wound.

On this tranquil morning Alazrak feels less disturbed. The rays of the equatorial suns as they pierce the sands, the heads, and the tops of trees seem bearable near the sea.

Lying on a blanket of hot sand under a primitive sun is like a truce. Reposing under this white glare after two years of solitary confinement makes things look brighter and breeds joy. His child's heart opens up now like a flower at dawn, free and intoxicated among the half-naked bodies of girls and women lying on the sand. Two girls stretch out two meters away from him. One presses her breasts into the hot sand, while the other's breasts and thighs receive the sun's kisses.

The two girls whisper to each other in an audible voice while he observes them from the corner of his right eye and listens.

The conversation must now be about him.

"Isn't that Alazrak?"

"Look at his muscles and his huge chest."

"Ooh. Yet do you think that he makes love in the way he kills?"

"Will you take a bet on the length of his organ?"

"Listen. Do you think that they really raped him in prison, as it's rumored?"

The other laughs, mimicking the incident. "In that case his organ must have atrophied and become a cunt."

"Ha ha ha. In that case he will compete with us in catching men."

They disappear, laughing together in wanton fashion. They must be imagining him during the act, a man's rod going in and out of his backside under the eyes of that laughing pig whose ribs he had crushed.

Alazrak's mood clouds because of these imaginings. The sun, the sea and the two girls become vibrating red patches. The bell in his head has started its loud ringing.

With the spring of a wild cat he finds himself beside them. He opens his legs, cornering them. They are now between his legs. Their eyes face a huge upright figure whose face overflows with bitterness, terror, and hatred.

"Take it, you two. That's it! It's yours."

He had unsheathed his organ and was shaking it with both his hands, long, erect, and tanned by the sun.

"Is he big enough for you, you whores?"

Despite his gratification following the incident by the sea after his release from prison, Si Alazrak did not rest until he had lured into the forest two members of the gang that had raped him. There he extinguished the fire in himself after he had tied them up, then he cut off their penises and left them bleeding among the trees.

Scene of the Kill

Once again, the café. Pavements glitter under the summer sun. The white screen hanging behind the white glass emits white heat. The day is like a shroud. From the half-naked bodies of schoolgirls, whores, and passing women a hot flame radiates, exciting desire. Si Alazrak fidgets on his chair. The hot center of energy expands, and he feels ablaze. The brutal ringing in his head and nerves has started again.

He springs up. A taut body, bursting with energy and desire. A single violent need to kill or rape engulfs the body like a tornado. That's him following with unsteady steps a girl walking along the pavement. She turns and he follows. Her back is half bare. Every now and then the wind lifts her dress and her red panties glow in the sunshine. Alazrak's temperature rises and his pulse quickens. He sweats. To regain his balance, he lets out his breath, then whistles. His whistling is well known. He concentrates on observing the rhythmic movement of her backside squeezed in by her underpants, whose outline is seen under the flimsy dress.

She was now within earshot and within reach of his hands.

"O for that smooth marble dome. Are you a woman or a virgin, my beautiful ewe?"

He says this as he presses his palm on her soft swinging bottom. The girl is frightened.

She turns around and they face each other in an empty alley.

"Oh it's you?"

"The girl from the beach! What a happy coincidence! This is a real wedding, then."

"Oh have mercy, Si Alazrak."

His big hand is on her mouth, covering half her face. He gives a voluptuous laugh. He drags her to the dark entrance of a building like a wolf dragging a sheep to his lair.

"If you scream, I will kill you."

Now the knife was at her neck, the gleam of death flashing from it.

"O Si Alazrak! I appeal to your honor!"

"Did you say my honor? You are my honor now."

"O Alazrak! I am a young virgin."

"Not bad. We'll conduct a little experiment, my ewe, to see which of us is the man and which the woman."

He was pressing her against the wall while his hand was pulling up her dress and tearing at her panties.

"Take it, my ewe! It's yours now."

He took her hand and pressed it into her palm: "I heard that your brother is a policeman and that you complained to him after the incident by the sea. Tell the truth."

"But he's never harmed anybody in his life!" said the girl, trembling.

"Did you tell him about the incident or not? Anyone harming Alazrak will never get away with it. Now it's your turn, next time it will be the turn of your dirty policeman, my ewe."

He pressed her against the wall. The girl moaned. He plunged his face into hers, then into her bosom, exposing her breasts. She groaned with pain. He was pushing at her, she resisting, compressing her legs together. He arched his back a little, then plunged, forcing her legs open, crushing her supple body between his body and the wall.

"Ooh, my magnificent Alazrak. Be reasonable, I am a virgin. Ah!"

She had loosened up under his thrusts, giving him the opportunity to be free in his movements.

His excitement overflowed and he started lowing like a bull bearing down on a cow.

Their bodies fused together. With a slow, impassioned movement he penetrated her, as a knife penetrates a wound, and a suppressed scream, intermingled with pain and desire, escaped from her.

Alazrak had triumphed. His pulse became normal and the summer seemed to him to stretch like a joyful band of marble white light over the city.

The Emergence of the Spirit

There is Alazrak, a wanted and pursued man. The law wants him while he wanders alone fleeing through the prairies. An obsessed and deviant thief had subverted the dignity of the law and had breached morality. Thus they branded him as they sought him. During his flight across the valleys and forests that encircled the city, he raids farms and isolated houses for food. Some nights he is forced to sleep hungry in the open or in lairs and mountain caves. In the open air among the trees and rocks Alazrak returns to his pure nature. He builds his private kingdom among the rocks. The limitless sky, the wind and the rain, penetrate the veins in his body, unclogging the pores blocked by the contaminated cities, by the stench of the pigs, patriarchal prayers, and the coffinlike cafes, bars, and shops. His spirit is gratified, and he recovers his lost childhood, the childhood that had been violated.

The birds and animals of the wild combine with the spacious silence of land and open air to give him a feeling of joy and peace.

"Who has been more cruel?" he asks himself.

"You chose wrongly, Si Alazrak."

A mysterious voice reached him from behind. He turned in a panic: "God of the devils, who is there? Man or demon?"

He sprang up, knife in hand.

She was standing on an overhanging rock. He rubbed his eyes to brush off the dream: "Who are you?"

She towered over him like an apparition. Gigantic. Translucent in an enchanting dawn. Her face the color of the prairie flowers. She seemed to him to glow in the halo of light.

"What are you doing here?"

He moved as slowly as a spacewalker. Sat on a rock. Ran his fingers through his floating hair. Opened and shut his eyes with difficulty.

When he looked up, the wind was whistling around the high barren rocks.

She reappeared. Still standing on top of the rocks, the wind blowing through her wheat-colored hair. A pebble she flung to him fell near. She smiled: "Are you deaf or are you mad? Say what you have come to do here."

He stood up and started walking. He trod the damp grass while dawn was spreading. He could not climb the rock. An invisible force prevented him. The light of the blazing sun exploded in his eyes. He felt something pulling him backward, so he lay down between the blades of grass.

It was a joyful morning. A bird was singing sweetly on a tree. In a short while beautiful colorful birds arrived and began a festival of song and joy. Alazrak was enchanted. A strange overwhelming joy swept through him and he burst out singing and dancing and laughing.

The Secret

The girl of the prairies reappeared. The same distance remained between her and Alazrak. Alazrak was unable to comprehend. He tried to ward off the nightmare in an attempt to distinguish truth from illusion, but he remained lost.

"Alazrak! You've made a mistake! The road does not pass through here—your road."

"From where then?"

She seemed different from city girls. There was a magic halo surrounding her sweet, innocent face. The faces of city girls throb with lust and depravity.

Alazrak had not forgotten her first appearance. It was as if the grass had unfolded to reveal her or that she had fallen from a distant star.

She knew that Alazrak had fled the inferno of the city that demanded his head. When she began talking, her words were strange and surprising. She talked of the history of the murderous city and the misery of people and their hunger, of the violations of the oppressors and the bestiality of their instincts, then went on to talk of the murdered and the martyrs, the prisoners and the exiles.

She related to him the incident of her father's death under torture and of his burial here in these prairies, and she said that she came here in search of her father's wandering spirit that demanded revenge.

He heard her repeating words that rang in his depths like a bell: "Love and murder cannot coexist. It is either love or murder."

She was talking in a subdued tone, while the sunset flowed tenderly on her face, so full of sorrow and beauty.

Alazrak wanted to say something about himself, about his inner torment and his black history, but felt powerless.

Her face inspired confidence and trust. From that translucent, sad face a warm light stretched, engulfing his depths in joy and peace.

Alazrak was transformed as he listened. At one point he felt he had become a different person while she talked to him of the conditions of beggars, hoboes, of naked, hungry people plunging like dogs into garbage bins in search of a crust of bread; while she talked of the insane whose nerves had been destroyed by the war, of the unemployed, of the retired fighters, of the thieves, and of the peasants inhabiting tin shacks while the oppressors, heirs of the invaders, occupied the palaces, the farms, the beaches, and the parks, all the while sucking the blood of the homeland forcibly and violently.

Nowhere was there someone as sad as he was now. His heart almost broke as he listened. He felt impotent and alone, that he had chosen a wrong path. He wondered about the reasons for his loss of direction, where the trauma had originated, and why he had met this apparition at such a late stage.

Within seconds the nightmare was back. He saw the city swept by an earthquake that hurled it to the center of the earth.

At the back of his head, at the center of organic damage, sharp pains arose.

He raised his head, shaking off his anger, and heard her distant and dwindling voice calling on him to return to the city where they would meet. When the phantom had disappeared, he felt as if his heart were bursting through his ribs. He felt that he'd lost something precious that could not be recovered.

Something had dissolved in him during the nights of misery, pursuit, and exile. Alazrak wondered about his situation. Was his existence superfluous, his birth a mistake? Why did he flounder, not knowing how to adjust and harmonize with the world?

He did not find an answer to his questions, either from inside himself or from the outside world. Impatience roused a scream in him that pierced the peace of the prairies: "Mother, oh Mother! Where are you? Take my hand in this darkness. Return me to the womb."

The echo spread. It spread until it flooded the plains and valleys. Alazrak was now crying like a child who, in losing his mother, had lost all sources of compassion.

Peace

Alazrak did not see the prairie girl after that date, neither did he enter the city again.

At the gates of the city he fell, brought down by a bullet that tore through the back of his head and came out from his forehead. Alazrak fell alone and bloodied, without uttering a cry. He lay sprawled at the gates of the city, then curled up like a child in its mother's womb and peacefully subsided.

The hunting of the brutalized, the thieves, the deviants, the beggars, the homeless, and the unemployed had begun.

Orders had been issued to purify the city of these pests in the interest of law and order. The killing of Alazrak came as the crowning achievement of the period of purification and as a consolidation of the calm and peace that reigned over the city.

NAGUIB MAHFOUZ

(1911–2006)

The Seventh Heaven

(EXCERPT)

Translated from the Arabic by Raymond Stock

1.

A huge cloud surges over all existence, plunging through space. Everything pulses with a strange cosmic presence. Nothing like it has ever been, breaking living beings down into their basic elements, menacing all with destruction—or perhaps a new creation. Despite all this, he is still conscious of what is happening, seeming to live out the last moments of awareness. Seized by sensations that transcend imagination, he is witnessing things that none have seen before. Yet he is still himself—Raouf Abd-Rabbuh—without any fears, without evil whisperings within, and without any cares. He halts in the desert outside the ancient portal, floating in the dark, feeling as though he weighs nothing. He and his friend Anous Qadri are returning from their evening out. *Where are you, Anous?*

He heard not a sound, nor could he feel the touch of the ground. Then he had a bizarre sensation of levitation as he penetrated deeply into the churning, overspreading masses above. When he called out to his friend, no sound issued from him. He was present—and yet was not there at all. He was confused, yet not frightened, though his heart expected a direct reply from close by. The cloud thinned and began to vanish. The pulsing stopped completely. Then the darkness of night glittered with the luminous rays of stars. *Finally I can see now, Anous! But what are you doing?* The people are digging up the earth furiously, and with purpose. Then there is a young man sprawled on his back, blood pouring from his head. Raouf can see with a clarity greater than that granted by the starlight. How amazing! That's Raouf Abd-Rabbuh himself! Yet he is me—and none other than me!

He was cut off from him completely as he watched from very near. No, it's not a double nor his twin. That's definitely his body. And those are his shoes. Anous urges the men on in their work. He does not see him at all. Evidently, he thinks that the body laid out there represents all there is of his friend Raouf Abd-Rabbuh, the creature that observes him, unable to do anything. He sensed that he was not whole like the corpse on the ground. Had he become two beings? Or had he departed from the living? Had he been murdered and suffered death? Did you kill me, Anous? Did we not spend an enjoyable night out together? What did you feel when you killed me? How could you so disdain my friendship that you would try to claim Rashida for yourself? Didn't she tell me that she considered herself to be your sister from now on?

Ah—the men have carried my body to the hole, and are tossing it inside. Now they're shoveling dirt over it and smoothing the spot afterward, restoring the ground to its natural shape. Thus Raouf Abd-Rabbuh vanishes, as though he never was. And yet, Anous, I still exist. You have cleverly buried the evidence of your hardened crime—all trace of it is gone. Yet why are you scowling so? What is that sardonic look in your eyes? I freely confess—even though you cannot hear me—that I still love her. Did you think that our relationship was now over? Even death is too weak to destroy such a passion. Rashida is mine, not yours. Yet you are rash and were raised amidst evil. You grew up in the sphere of your father, Boss Qadri the Butcher—monopolist of the meat trade, plunderer of the poor and the dispossessed, a gross greaser of palms. Let me tell you that what you aspire to is not yours—your felony is to try to gain it by force. What will you do now? You, who wouldn't even go to the café without me, nor study without me, nor come and go to the university without me? We were the two best friends in our quarter, despite the infinite differences between us in money, status, and power. You may forget me, but I will not forget you. You should know that I have no longing for vengeance, or to hurt you in any way. All such weaknesses were buried with my body in that hole in the ground. Even the torture that your father's oppression inflicts on our alley provokes neither rage nor wrath nor rebellion within me. Rather, it is a common occurrence that the power of love rejects, creating instead a lofty desire free of any stain. I mourn for you, Anous. I never conceived you in this ugly image before. You are a walking skeleton, a bat-infested ruin. Murdered blood splotches your face and your brow. Your eyes give off sparks, while a serpent hangs from each of your ears. Your father's men file behind you on donkeys' hooves, with heads like crows, bound in manacles bolted with thorns. How it saddens me to have been the cause for which you sullied your pages. I am overwhelmed with grief because of it—while my sense of happiness shrinks to nothing.

2.

In the midst of a sigh, Raouf found himself in a new city—brilliantly illuminated, but without a sun. The sky was a cupola of white clouds, the ground rich with greenery, with endless orchards of flowering fruit trees. Stretching into the distance were rows of white roses. Throngs of people met and broke up with the fleetness of birds. In an empty spot, he felt the loneliness of the first-time arrival. At that moment, there arose before him a man enshrouded in a white mist.

"Welcome, Raouf," the man said, smiling, "to the First Heaven."

"Is this Paradise?" Raouf asked, shouting with joy.

"I said, 'the First Heaven,' not 'Paradise,'" the stranger admonished.

"Then where is Paradise?"

"Between it and you, the path is very, very long," the man answered. "The fortunate person will spend hundreds of thousands of enlightened years traversing it!"

A sound like a groan escaped Raouf. "Permit me first to introduce myself," said the man. "I am your interlocutor, Abu, formerly High Priest at Hundred-Gated Thebes."

"I'm honored to meet you, Your Reverence. What a happy coincidence that I'm Egyptian myself!"

"That is of no importance," replied Abu. "I lost all nationality thousands of years ago. Now I am the defense counsel appointed by the courts for the new arrivals."

"But there can be no charge against me—I'm a victim . . ."

"Patience," Abu said, cutting him off. "Let me tell you about your new surroundings. This heaven receives the new arrivals. They are tried in court, where I serve as their advocate. The verdicts are either for acquittal or for condemnation. In case of acquittal, the defendant spends one year here spiritually preparing for his ascent to the Second Heaven."

Raouf interrupted him, "But what then does 'condemnation' mean?"

"That the condemned must be reborn on earth to practice living once again; perhaps they would be more successful the next time," said Abu. "As for verdicts that fall between acquittal and condemnation, in such cases the accused is usually put to work as a guide to one or more souls on earth. Depending on their luck, they may ascend to the Second Heaven, or the length of their probationary period might be extended, et cetera."

"At any rate, I'm definitely innocent," Raouf blurted confidently. "I lived a good life and died a martyr."

"Do not be so hasty," Abu counseled him. "Let us open the discussion of your case. Identify yourself, please."

"Raouf Abd-Rabbuh, eighteen years of age, a university student of history. My father died, leaving my mother a widow who lives on a charitable trust from the Ministry of Religious Endowments."

"Why are you so satisfied with yourself, Raouf?" queried Abu.

"Well, despite my intense poverty, I'm a hard-working student who loves knowledge, for which my thirst is never quenched."

"That is beautiful, as a matter of principle," remarked Abu, "yet you received most of your information from others, rather than through your own thinking."

"Thought is enriched through age and experience," said Raouf. "And regardless, would that count as a charge against me?"

"Here a person is held accountable for everything," rejoined Abu. "I observe that you were dazzled by new ideas."

"The new has its own enchantment, Your Reverence Abu," said Raouf.

"First of all, do not call me, 'Your Reverence,'" Abu rebuked him. "Second, we do not judge a thought itself even when it is false. Rather, we denounce submission to any idea, even if it is true."

"Such a cruel trial! Justice on earth is far more merciful."

"We will come to justice," Abu reassured him. "How did you find your alley?"

"Horrible," spat Raouf. "Most of the people there are poor beggars. They are controlled by a man who monopolizes all the food—and who has bought the loyalty of the shaykh of the *hara*.* He kills, steals, and lives securely above the law."

"That is an accurate description," Abu said. "What was your position toward all this?"

"Rejection, rebellion, and a genuine desire to change everything."

"Thank you. What did you do to achieve that?"

"It wasn't in my power to do anything!"

"Do you want to rise to the Second Heaven?"

"Why shouldn't I rise?" Raouf shot back. "My heart and mind both rejected what was happening."

"And your tongue?"

"Just one rebellious word would get it cut out."

"Yet even speech by itself would not satisfy our sacred tribunal," warned Abu.

"What kind of proceeding is this?" Raouf asked, his frustration growing. "What was I, after all, but a single individual?"

"Our alley here is full of unfortunates," rebutted Abu.

"My first duty was to acquire knowledge!"

"There is no dividing one's trust—and no excuse for evading it."

"Wouldn't one expect that would lead to violence?"

"Virtues do not interest us," said Abu dismissively. "What concerns us is truth."

"Doesn't it help my case that I was murdered over love?"

"Even that has an aspect which is not in your favor," said Abu.

Astonished, Raouf asked, "And what aspect is that?"

"That you put your faith in Anous Qadri—when he is the very image of his tyrannical father."

"I never dreamed I was so guilty."

"Though you have some mitigating circumstances, my brief in defending you will not be easy," worried Abu.

"Ridiculous to think anyone has ever succeeded in being declared innocent in this court."

"Indeed, only a rare few discharge their full obligation to the world."

---

* *Hara:* Arabic for "neighborhood."

"Give me some examples," Raouf challenged Abu.

"Khalid ibn al-Walid,* and Gandhi."

"Those are two totally contradictory cases!"

"The tribunal has another view," said Abu. "The obligation itself is what matters."

"There's no hope for me now."

"Do not despair—nor should you underestimate my long experience," said Abu soothingly. "I will do the impossible to save you from condemnation."

"But what could you say on my behalf?"

"I will say that you had a blameless beginning, under the most arduous conditions, and that much good was expected of you if you had only lived long enough. And that you were a loving, devoted, faithful son to your mother."

"The best I can hope for, then, is to be made someone's spiritual guardian?" Raouf fretted.

"This is a chance for you to recapture what had eluded you," Abu consoled him. "In our world here, the human being only ascends according to his success on earth."

"Then, Mighty Advocate, why don't you send down a guide for Boss Qadri the Butcher?"

"There is no one who does not have their own guide."

"How then," Raouf asked in confusion, "can evil continue?"

"Do not forget that the human being has free will," replied Abu. "In the end, everything depends upon the influence of the guide and the freedom of the individual."

"Wouldn't it be in the cause of good to eliminate this freedom?"

"The Will has determined that only the free may gain admission to the heavens."

"How could He not admit into heaven the pure saint of our alley, Shaykh Ashur?" Raouf remonstrated. "He doesn't practice free will, for all he does or says is filled with righteous inspiration."

Abu smiled. "What is he but a creation of Qadri the Butcher? He interprets dreams in Qadri's interests, relaying to him the private confidences from inside the houses that welcome his blessings!"

---

* Khalid ibn al-Walid: One of Islamic history's greatest warriors.

Raouf lapsed into defeated silence. He absented himself for a moment amid the ripe greenery adorned with rows of blooming roses, surrendering to the place's sweetness and grace. Then he said, sighing, "How tragic for a person to be forced to abandon this garden!"

"Be warned—it is sinful to wish to evade your duty!" Abu scolded.

"When shall I appear before the court?" Raouf asked.

"The trial is finished," announced Abu.

Raouf stared at him in stupefaction.

"The examination has been completed," said Abu calmly. "The defense was raised during the discourse between you and me. The verdict has come down: you are to be commissioned as a spiritual guide. Congratulations!"

3.

The court determined to hold Raouf Abd-Rabbuh in the First Heaven for a short time in order to cleanse him of any stains, in preparation for his mission. Abu stayed at his side till he had finished his training and acclimation, receiving returning guides at the same time.

"I'd like to see Adolf Hitler," said Raouf. "Will he be coming now?"

"He was condemned, and has since been reborn in your very own alley. You saw him regularly."

"Hitler?"

"He is Boss Qadri the Butcher."

Dumbfounded, Raouf became quiet, then asked, "So who would the shaykh of the *hara*, Shakir al-Durzi, be?"

"Lord Balfour."*

"And Shaykh Ashur, the false friend of God?"

"He is Khunfus, betrayor of Urabi's Revolution."†

"I don't see them changing or learning from their repeated experience."

---

* Lord Balfour: Arthur James Balfour (1848–1930), British prime minister and author of the Balfour Declaration (1917), which supported the establishment of a Jewish state in Palestine.
† Urabi's Revolution: Colonel Ahmad Urabi (1841–1911), Egyptian army officer who led an ill-fated revolt against European colonial control of Egypt in 1879.

"That is not always the case. Do you know who your mother was?"

"Abu, she was an angel, surely!"

"She was Rayya,* the infamous serial killer; yet look how she has progressed!"

Shaken, Raouf fell silent again. Just then Abu received the first of the incoming arrivals.

The one who just arrived said, "I am trying as hard as I can."

"I am aware of that," Abu answered, "but you must redouble your efforts, for the time has come for you to go up."

"I'm sure I know who that is," Raouf said, when the man had disappeared. "Isn't he Akhenaten?"†

"Indeed he is. He is not very fortunate, however, for his probation has stretched on now for thousands of years."

"But he was the first to bring the news that God is one!"

"Verily, but he imposed the One God on the people by coercion, rather than by persuasion and rational argument. Hence, he made it easier for his enemies to later remove God from people's hearts the same way—by force. If it were not for his clear conscience, he would have been condemned."

"Why has his period here been so prolonged?"

"He did not succeed with any of those he was chosen to guide, such as Pharaoh-in-the-time-of-Moses, al-Hakim bi-Amr Allah, and Abbas I."‡

"Who is his man now?"

"Camille Chamoun."§

The next arrival approached; he delivered a written report, uttered

---

* Rayya: Young Alexandrian woman who, along with her sister Sakina, murdered and mutilated a number of women in the 1920s.

† Akhenaten: Egyptian pharaoh during the Eighteenth Dynasty (husband of Nefertiti and father of Tutankhamun) who brutally suppressed devotion to Egypt's gods in favor of the figure he deemed "the One God," Aten.

‡ Pharaoh-in-the-time-of-Moses: Traditionally thought to be Ramses II. al-Hakim bi-Amr Allah: Fatimid caliph from 996 to 1021 CE. Abbas I: Shah Abbas the Great, ruler of the Persian Safavid Empire from 1587 to 1629 CE.

§ Camille Chamoun: Head of the Maronite Christian bloc during the Lebanese Civil War.

some stirring words, then vanished completely. "That was President Wilson!" Raouf exclaimed.

"You are correct."

"I'd assumed he was one of the happy few who'd risen to the Second Heaven."

"You are no doubt referring to his sacred principles," observed Abu. "But you forget that he neglected to use America's power to implement them—and that he recognized the protectorate over Egypt."

"And who's his man?"

"The eminent littérateur, Tawfiq al-Hakim."*

When the third arrival had gone, Raouf declared, "That was Lenin—no doubt about it."

"Correct again," affirmed Abu.

"I'd have thought he'd be condemned on account of his atheism," Raouf gasped. "What did you say in his defense?"

"I said that in the stream of intellectual prattle, he changed the names—but not the essence—of things. Perishable matter he termed divine, assigning it some of the qualities of God—timelessness, creation, and control over the fate of the universe. He called the prophets scientists, the angels workers, and the devils the bourgeoisie. He also promised a paradise on earth, which exists in time and space. I extolled the power of his belief and his bravery, as well as his service to the laboring classes through sacrifice and self-denial. I added that what really mattered to God Almighty was whether good or bad befell humankind. As for He Himself—His majesty be praised—He has no need of human beings. Not all their faith can increase Him, nor their disbelief diminish Him. Hence, Lenin's sentence was reduced—and he was appointed as a spiritual guide!"

"Who did he get?" Raouf asked breathlessly.

"The well-known writer, Mustafa Mahmud."†

---

* Tawfiq al-Hakim: One of Egypt's greatest writers—known as the father of Arab drama—whose *Diary of a Country Prosecutor* appears in Part One of this volume.

† Mustafa Mahmud: Mustafa Kamal Mahmud Husayn (1921–2009), Egyptian author and journalist.

"And was Stalin, too, appointed anyone's guide?"

"Certainly not. Stalin was condemned for having murdered millions of workers, rather than teaching and training them for a better life."

"Maybe he's living now in our alley," Raouf pondered.

"No, he is toiling in one of the pit mines of India," said Abu.

After receiving Lenin, Abu was done with his scheduled appointments, so he accompanied Raouf on a tour through the First Heaven. No sooner had the idea occurred to them than they were already on their way, in response to their inner wish, without needing even to use their feet. They soared like birds, intoxicated with an integral ecstasy that sprang from their magical powers to make any desired movement with ease and delight. They sluiced through the silvery air over the land embroidered with green below, the sky overhead illuminated with glowing white clouds. They passed by countless faces of multifarious races and colors, each absorbed in their lofty enterprise: to help the people of earth achieve progress and victory. In so doing, they seek to repent and purify themselves in order to resume their own rise through the levels of spiritual creativity, to be nearer to the Great Truth itself. They labor relentlessly, driven by warm, eternal passions toward perfection, right, and immortality.

"It seems to me," Raouf said, "there is no less suffering here than in its counterpart on earth."

A smiling Abu replied, "They are two sorts of suffering which join into one. The only difference is that here people experience it with a purer heart, a smarter brain, and a clearer goal."

"Please spell that out for me, Abu."

"You on the earth dream of a world containing the virtuous city, founded on individual freedom, social justice, scientific progress, and overwhelming power over the forces of nature. For the sake of all this, you wage war and make peace, and challenge the Opposing Power that—in your own terminology—you call reactionism. That is all fine and beautiful, but it is not the final objective, as you imagine it to be. Rather, it is but the first real step in a long road to spiritual elevation, which seems even to those who dwell in our First Heaven to be without end."

Raouf was immersed in contemplation until Abu asked him, "Of what are you thinking?"

"I'm thinking how much dreadful, daily crime is perpetrated by the Opposing Power."

"That is crime in which the good take part by passively abstaining in the fight for the right," said Abu. "They fear death—and death is what you see here!"

"What a life!" said Raouf.

"It is a battlefield—nothing more, and nothing less."

Raouf thought until the very thinking wore him out, then returned to his previous passion for learning the destinies of people who interested him. "I'd like to know what's become of my country's leaders," he told Abu.

"You could wait until you see them—or ask me now about whomever you like," the ex-High Priest replied.

"What about al-Sayyid Umar Makram?"*

"He is the guide to Anis Mansur,"† said Abu.

"And Ahmad Urabi?" Raouf asked.

"He is working with Lewis Awad."

"And Mustafa Kamil?"

"He is helping Fathi Radwan."‡

"Muhammad Farid?"

"The mentor to Osman Ahmed Osman," said Abu.

"And what of Sa'ad Zaghlul?" §

"He has reached the Second Heaven," intoned Abu.

"Because of his personal sacrifices?" asked Raouf, expectantly.

"Because of his triumph over his own human weakness!"

"Again, please tell me what you mean."

---

* al-Sayyid Umar Makram: Egyptian nationalist who led the revolt against Napoleon's army.

† Anis Mansur: Egyptian author and travel writer (b. 1925).

‡ Lewis Awad: Coptic (Christian) Egyptian intellectual (1950–1980). Mustafa Kamil: Egyptian lawyer and journalist (1874–1908) who fought for independence from British colonial rule. Fathi Radwan (1911–1988): Young Egyptian nationalist and critic of "the West."

§ Muhammad Farid (1868–1919): Egyptian politician, lawyer, writer, and staunch supporter of Mustafa Kamil. Osman Ahmed Osman (1917–1999): Egyptian politician; the engineer who led the construction of the Aswan Dam. Sa'ad Zaghlul (1859–1927): Egypt's greatest and best-known nationalist; considered the father of Arab nationalism.

"You may be aware that he suffered from the sin of ambition before the revolution," said Abu. "Afterward, however, he rose to become an exquisite vision of courage and devotion—and hence merited acquittal."

"And Mustafa al-Nahhas?"

"He was attached to Anwar al-Sadat,"* noted Abu. "But when October 6 came, and freedom was restored, he, too, rose to the Second Heaven."

"Then what about Gamal Abd al-Nasser?" the slain man asked.

"He is now guiding al-Qaddafi."†

At the end of the brief training period, Abu told Raouf, "You are now the spiritual guide to your murderer, Anous, Qadri the Butcher's son."

Raouf accepted the order with zealous resolve.

"Rely on your own mind for inspiration—for it has great power if you master its use," instructed Abu. "When necessary, you may even resort to dreams—and may the Lord be with you."

4.

Raouf Abd-Rabbuh landed in the alley. He could see and hear clearly, though no one saw or heard him. He moved from place to place like a natural breeze through his beloved quarter, with all its solid and familiar scenes, its people engrossed in the affairs of life. All his memories were unchanged, along with his previous hopes and pains. He enjoyed a clarity of mind like a brilliant light. Scores and scores of laborers, both men and women, toiled away with furtive eyes and brawny forearms. The laughter floated over the curses, like sweet butter spoiled by bitter mold. And there was Boss Qadri the Butcher in his shop. No resemblance between his face and Hitler's, but his body

---

* Mustafa al-Nahhas (1879–1965): Prime minister of Egypt several times between 1928 and 1952. Anwar al-Sadat (1918–1981): Succeeded Gamal Abd al-Nasser as president of Egypt until his assassination on October 6, 1981.

† Gamal Abd al-Nasser (1918–1970): Leader of the Free Officers coup that toppled Egypt's King Farouk. Second president of the Egypt, from 1954 to 1970. Considered the father of pan-Arab nationalism. al-Qaddafi: Mu'ammar al-Qaddafi (b.1942), leader of Libya.

was bloated from sucking people's blood. And here is Lord Balfour—
that is, Shakir al-Durzi, the shaykh of our alley, who throws the law
under the butcher's feet. And there is the bogus *wali*, Shaykh Ashur,
who foretells the future to flatter his lord and master.

*My poor alley. May God be with you! How and when shall you burst these
binding fetters?*

Evidently, his own absence—that of Raouf—had stirred the alley's
tongues as well as its hearts. The women gathered round his weeping
mother.

"This is the third day since he disappeared," she moaned.

"Umm Raouf, you should tell the police," they urged.

"I've already told 'Uncle' Shakir al-Durzi, shaykh of the *hara*," she
said.

The shaykh's voice came to them scornfully, "Do young people
today have no shame?"

"My son has never spent a whole night away from his home," she
said, still weeping.

And here is Rashida returning from her institute, the beauty of her
tawny face marred by melancholy. Her mother said to her, "Take care
of yourself—you can't replace your health when it's gone."

Choking back tears, she said, "I know. My heart never lies to me!"

Raouf stared at her with sympathy. *I believe you, Rashida. A loving
heart is the most reliable receptor of truth. Yet we will meet again one day. Love
is undying, Rashida, not like some people imagine it to be.*

And here is the killer, swaggering home from the university. He
holds a book in one hand, while he commits murder with the other! *I
am never out of your thoughts, yet you have no idea that I've been appointed
your spiritual mentor. Shall you yield to me today, or persist in your error?
Everything calls out to reassure you, Anous. Your father casts his shadow over
all. The government and all authority are his loyal subjects—you can get any
false testimony you need. Yet my image never leaves you. And why not? Did
not people say that our friendship was proverbially close? Though trained in
criminality, you didn't practice it like your father. In the course of your education, you learned, or at least heard, of beautiful things. By committing this
travesty, did you dream you would win Rashida's heart? What was this that
you slew and buried in the desert? What you have done has not hurt me more
than it has you. I was your eternal companion, as you shall see. Confess,*

Anous. Admit your crime. Tell the truth and stick with me—and you will have a better part to play in all this.

Here is my tormented mother, blocking your path.

"Master Anous," she pleaded, "do you have any news of your friend?"

"None at all, by God," he swore.

"He told me as he went out that he was going to see you."

"We met for a few minutes," said Anous, "then he told me he had to do an important errand, and that we would meet tonight at the café."

"But he hasn't come back," the distraught mother said.

"Didn't I visit you asking about him?"

"That's true, my dear boy, but I'm about to lose my mind."

"I'm as upset as you are," declared Anous.

Believe me, Anous. I see the distress in your soul like a blemish on your face. But you are malignant and cruel. You are from the Opposing Power, Anous— don't you see the danger in that? We grumble all the way down the Path of Light—so what do you think about while sliding down the Path of Darkness? I am stuck to you. If you don't taste that roasted chicken, then the fault is yours. If you can't concentrate on the book you're reading, that's your own problem, as well. I will never leave you, nor shall I ever grow tired. You may as well stay up late, for you shall not know sleep before dawn.

When he rose back to the First Heaven, Raouf encountered Abu deep in discussion with Akhenaten.

"Every time I told him to go right, he went left!" the defunct pharaoh fumed.

"You must use your powers as needed," exhorted Abu.

"We lack the ability to use physical force," Akhenaten complained.

"Do you want to go up, or do you not?" exploded Abu. "The trouble is, you are not used to persuading and convincing people of your point of view. You only know how to give orders!"

Abu turned to Raouf. "How are things with you?" he asked.

"I'm off to a good start," the youngster said.

"Wonderful!" said Abu.

"Yet I wonder, doesn't everyone have their own guide?"

"Naturally," said Abu.

"Then why does everyone just give up?"

"How wrong you are," Abu abjured. "You were born in the age of revolutions!"

At that moment, a green bird the size of an apple landed on Abu's shoulder. It brought its rose-colored beak close to Abu's ear. Abu seemed to be listening, when the bird suddenly flew off into space until it was hidden behind a white cloud.

Abu looked meaningfully into Raouf's eyes. "That was the messenger from the Second Heaven," he explained, "bringing word of the acquittal and right to ascend for one called Sha'ban al-Minufi."

"Who's he?" asked Raouf.

"An Egyptian soldier who was martyred at Morea in the age of Muhammad Ali.* He was mentor to a hard-currency smuggler named Marwan al-Ahmadi—and finally succeeded in his campaign to drive him to suicide."

Sha'ban al-Minufi approached, wrapped in his vaporous robe. "May you ascend gloriously and with grace to the Second Heaven," Abu told him.

All the spiritual guides flocked toward them in the shape of white doves until the verdant place was packed, Sha'ban al-Minufi's face beaming in their midst. As celestial music sounded, Abu declaimed, "Rise, O rose of our green city, to carry on your sacred struggle."

In a pleasing voice, Sha'ban replied, "Blessings upon whoever renders service to the suffering world."

At this he began to go up with the lightness of an ephemeral fragrance to the strains of the happy anthem of farewell.

5.

Anous Qadri, the butcher's son, stood facing the police detective who asked him, "When was the last time you saw Raouf Abd-Rabbuh?"

"The afternoon of the day he disappeared," said Anous. "He came to see me at my house. No sooner had he showed up than he left to do some business. He promised to meet me that evening at the café."

---

* Muhammad Ali: Muhammad Ali Pasha (1769–1849), ruler of Egypt from 1805 to 1848.

"Did he tell you anything about this business he had to do?"

"No," said Anous.

"Did you ask him about it?" the officer pressed him.

"No, I thought it must be something to do with his family."

"Some people saw the two of you walking together in the alley after he came to you," the detective informed him.

Don't be upset. The best thing is to confess. This is your golden opportunity, if you know what's good for you.

"I walked with him till he left the gate," said Anous.

"You mean he simply disappeared in the desert outside?"

This is doubletalk, Anous—even worse than doubletalk. Only the truth can save you.

"Yes, he did," answered Anous.

"What did you do after that?"

"I went to the coffeehouse to wait for him."

"How long did you stay there?" the detective continued.

"Until midnight, then I went home."

"Can you prove that?"

"Shakir al-Durzi, shaykh of the *hara*, was sitting next to me the whole time," said Anous. "Early the next morning, I went to Raouf's place to ask his mother about him. She told me that he hadn't come back."

"What did you do?"

"I asked all our friends and acquaintances in the alley about him."

"Do you have any personal insight into his prolonged disappearance?" the policeman asked.

"Not at all! It's truly baffling," insisted Anous.

Here you are leaving the station, Anous. You prepare in advance every word you speak. You rue the mention of the gate, and wonder who saw you walking there with me. It's as though you are contemplating more evil. You repeat the details of your conversations to your father. He is strident—the money, the law, and the witnesses are all in his pocket. I counsel you again to confront your crime with courage and to clear your account. But what's this? Does Rashida's image still trace itself in your imagination? This is the very essence of madness. Then you see that the inquiries about you will continue like a flood. The shaykh of the alley has come to the same conclusion. The Unseen warns of unknown surprises. You are thinking of all this, and at the same time you're obsessed with Rashida, you fool!

Reflecting on this, Raouf remarked to Abu, "Fear of death is the greatest curse to afflict humankind."

"Was it not created to prevent them from doing wrong?" Abu replied.

Raouf was silent as Abu added, "You were appointed as a guide, not a philosopher—remember that."

6.

You're asking yourself, Anous, why did the detective summon you a second time? Things are not turning out as simply as you thought.

Here is the officer questioning you:

"What do you know about Raouf's private life?"

"Nothing worth mentioning."

"Really?" the detective challenged him. "What about his love for Rashida, the student in the school of fashion design?"

"Every young man has a relationship like that!" Anous said dismissively.

"Do you have one like it?"

"These are personal things that have no place in an investigation."

"Is that what you think?" the officer shot back. "Even when you love the same girl yourself?"

"The issue needs clarification," protested Anous.

"Good!" exclaimed the policeman. "What could that be?"

"I revealed to Raouf once that I wanted to get engaged to Rashida, and he confided in me that the two of them were in love with each other," Anous asserted. "At that I excused myself, and considered the subject closed."

"But love doesn't end with a word," scoffed the detective.

"It was nothing but a fleeting feeling. . . . I don't know what you mean!"

"I'm gathering information, and I'm wondering if your feelings for your friend haven't changed, if only just a little?"

"Absolutely not," answered Anous. "My emotions for Rashida were nothing special—but my friendship with Raouf was the kind that lasts a lifetime."

"You said, *was*—has it ended?"

"I meant," Anous said nervously, "that our friendship is for life."

You're wondering, how is the investigation proceeding with Rashida? What has she admitted? Fine. Let me tell you that the inquiry is ongoing. She has told them of your attempt to rip her from your friend's heart. Just as she told them of your father's omnipotence, and her fear for her own and her mother's safety. I guarantee you, things really are now going against you.

"You sound as though you've given up on seeing your friend again," the detective taunted, laughing.

"I'm sure he's coming back," sputtered Anous. "That's what my heart tells me."

"A believer's heart is his guide," said the officer. "I, too, want him to come back."

You're leaving the police station, even more disturbed than you were the last time. I think you sensed that this clever little gumshoe suspects you completely, and you don't believe your father is able to control everything. Did not Hitler himself suffer final defeat—and even kill himself in the end?

7.

The detective has called you back for a third session, Anous. Nerves are starting to fray. Your father stares at Shakir al-Durzi with fury, but what can the shaykh really do? Stop in front of your tormentor, the officer, and listen:

"Anous, we've received an anonymous letter that accuses you of killing your friend, Raouf."

"A contemptible charge," Anous shouted with spurious rage. "Let whoever made it show his face!"

"Be patient," the officer warned him. "We weigh everything accurately here. Didn't you and your friend often spend evenings together outside the gate?"

"Sure," Anous acknowledged.

"Where, then, did you two spend your time in that vast desert?"

"In the Nobles' Coffeehouse on the plateau."

"I've decided to conduct a face-to-face meeting between you, Anous, and the men in the café."

Hold on, don't be distressed. You are stubborn—that's the truth. You don't want to respond to my secret whisperings. Be sure that I'm working in your interest, Anous.

The meeting took place. The owner of the coffeehouse and his young helper testified that they hadn't seen Anous for more than a month. That he was not entirely convinced showed clearly on the detective's face. He glared at Anous harshly.

"Please get out," the officer told him.

You're leaving the station again, a grin of victory on your lips. You have the right to feel that way—for your father has thrown up a defensive line all around you. But will the affair really end there? Your heart is palpitating while you pass your days loitering in front of your victim's house. Anxiety assails you yet again. Who was the unknown person who sent the letter accusing you? And will there be any more like it? You are a killer, Anous, and your conscience doesn't want to awake. Just let me visit you tonight in a dream—for so long as you won't respond to my clandestine appeals, you will find my corpse stretched out next to you on your bed. Ah—here your scream arises, propelled by your nightmare. You awake in terror, your heart heavy with horror. You slither from your bed to moisten your throat with a gulp of water. Yet you find the cadaver with you again as soon as you slip back to sleep. And the dream recurs to you night after night. Your mother urges Shaykh Ashur to examine you. He gives you an amulet to wear over your heart—but my grisly remains will not leave your dreams. Your condition worsens, so you go secretly to see a psychiatrist, with regular visits week after week. He tells you something truly astounding: that you imagine your friend has been murdered—his body represents your own body, due to the emotional bond between you—you are so closely linked that you think that his body is in the place of yours. But why do you picture yourself as the one slain? Your body plays the role of the replacement for another body and another person that, deep down, you'd like to kill. That person is your father. Your father thus is the cause of your dream—all of which reflects an Oedipus complex!

Yet, in reality, you are not courting your mother, nor do you really want to murder your father. Rather, you are in love with Rashida—and you murdered me simply to get me out of the way.

Raouf railed about this clinical error to his spiritual advocate.

"The complaints of incorrect scientific diagnosis are many," commiserated Abu. "Frustration is mistaken for an illness arising from the consumption of chocolate. Depression caused by loss of faith results in treatment of the sympathetic nerves. Constipation due to the political situation prompts a prescription of laxatives—and so on."

"What to do then, Abu?"

"Have you yet reached despair?"

"Absolutely not," insisted Raouf.

"Then put all your strength into your task," urged Abu.

8.

The cause of Raouf Abd-Rabbuh's disappearance remained unde-
tected, while the incident itself slowly faded from people's minds.
The only ones who still thought of him were his mother and Rashida.
Meanwhile, Anous continued to practice his normal way of living,
absorbed in work and amusing himself. The past pursued him from
time to time, both in his waking hours and in sleep, but he tamed and
controlled his internal uproar through sedatives, narcotics, and sheer
force of will. With the legal side now completely subdued, Anous
once again began to fix his thoughts on Rashida—for why else would
he have undertaken the most horrific act of his life? He lay in wait to
see her every morning as they went to their respective institutes to
study. Was her face still set in the pain of remembrance, hasn't she
lost hope yet? Does she never think of her future as a young woman
who should seek life, happiness, marriage, and children? Doesn't she
aspire to have the man who could offer her the most in our whole
quarter?

His mad gambit in devotedly pursuing her and his unshakable desire
to totally possess her had only intensified. Once, as she passed the place
where he was seated on a tram, he called out to her in greeting—but
she ignored him completely.

"We should be helping each other!" he called to her.

She wrinkled her brow in disgust, but he kept talking to her, "We've
each lost a dear one that we both shared!"

At this she broke her silence, "He wasn't lost, he was murdered!"

"What?" Anous recoiled.

"Many people believe that," she said.

"But he didn't have a single enemy!"

She glared at him with contempt, and said no more.

"She was accusing you of killing him," Anous told himself. "Do you
have any doubt about that? You could erase the crime from your

record if you rose up to confront your father—but the time for love has already gone."

She got off the tram before him. As he followed her movements with longing and resentment, his imagination was seized by uncontrollable visions of lust and violence.

9.

"Everyone's talking about that amazing man who summons the dead," Rashida's mother said. "So why don't you give him a try, since it won't even cost you a single millieme!"

Raouf's stricken mother stared at her in confusion, then muttered, "If you'll go with me."

"Why not? I'll get in touch with Rashida's dearly departed father."

"Many respectable people believe in the art of contacting the spirits," interrupted Rashida, who had been following their conversation with interest.

And so, under the strictest secrecy, they made an appointment to try this experiment.

Raouf turned to Abu jubilantly, "This is my chance to expose the culprit!"

"You were assigned as a guide for him—not against him," rebuked Abu.

"Would you let this opportunity slip out of our hands?"

"You are not a police counselor, Raouf," Abu cautioned him. "You are a spiritual advisor. Your goal is to save Anous, not deliver him to the hangman."

"But he's like a hunk of rock. The winds of wisdom simply bounce right off him," Raouf rejoined.

"That is a confession of your own incapacity."

"No, I haven't given up yet," Raouf said excitedly. "But what should I do if they call upon my spirit?"

"You are free," replied Abu. "It would not benefit your freedom to seek guidance from me."

The séance was convened, attended by Raouf's mother, along with Rashida and her own mother. They appealed to Raouf beyond the veil of the Unseen—and he entered the darkened chamber.

"Raouf greets you, Mother," he called, in a voice that all present could hear.

"What happened to you, Raouf?" she said, sobbing at the confirmation that her son was dead.

"Don't be sad, Mother," he answered without hesitation. "I am happy. Only your sorrow grieves me. My greetings to you too, Rashida. . . ."

With that, he instantly rushed from the room.

10.

Raouf's mother, Rashida, and her own mother returned from the séance, asking each other, "Why didn't he reveal the secret of his murder?"

"He was taken in the prime of his youth!" Raouf's mother lamented, drying her tears.

"Don't sadden him with your mourning," implored Rashida.

"Who knows? Maybe he died in an accident," her mother wondered.

"But why didn't he tell us how he died?" Raouf's mother persisted.

"That's his secret, whatever it is!" insisted Rashida.

The séances became Raouf's mother's sole consolation in life; she would go to them accompanied by both Rashida's mother and Rashida. But in the final days before her exams, Rashida stopped taking part in them.

On one of these nights, as she was at home studying on her own, Anous Qadri burst into the room. He had slunk up the open central stairwell of her building, then forced his way in. Raouf shouted at him to go back where he had come from, and not to take a single step toward her. But Anous attacked Rashida, stifling her voice by jamming his palm over her mouth.

"You're going to run after *me* from now on, you . . . you stubborn bitch!" he snarled.

Then he began to brutally assault her, as she resisted as hard as she could, but to no avail.

"I'm going to take you alive or dead!" he taunted her.

Her hand groped for a pair of scissors on the table. With an insane strength, despite being pinned under his heavy weight, she plunged it into the side of his neck. He pressed upon her with vicious cruelty.

Then his vitality ebbed away until he fell motionless upon her body, his warm blood pouring over her face and her torn blouse.

She threw him off of her and he lay sprawled on the tattered carpet. Then she staggered to the window and shrieked at the top of her lungs.

11.

The people came running to the apartment, where they found Rashida like a demented murderess spattered with gore. They saw Anous's body and started to scream, while Rashida curled into herself like a ball, murmuring, "He wanted to rape me. . . ."

If not for the arrival of the detective and the shaykh of the *hara*, then the news might have led Boss Qadri the Butcher to murder her on the spot.

"My son—my only son!" he roared. "I will make the world burn!"

"Everyone out now!" the officer ordered, as his assistants surrounded Rashida.

"I will drink your blood," said Qadri, aiming his storming rage at the girl.

The news soon spread like wildfire through their quarter.

12.

Anous stared insensibly down at his body. Raouf came up to him, smiling, as the other looked at him and blurted, "Raouf, what brought you here?"

"The same thing that brought you here," he replied. "Come along with me quickly, far away from this room."

"And leave this behind?" Anous asked, still peering at his corpse.

"That is your old robe. It won't do you any good to wear it now!"

"Have I . . . have I . . .?" Anous stuttered.

"Yes, you have departed the world, Anous."

He was silent for a while, then he said, referring to Rashida, "But she is innocent."

"I am aware of that," Raouf assured him. "But you can't save her—so come with me."

"I'm sorry for what I did to you," said Anous.

"Regret has no importance."

"I'm glad to see you," answered Anous.

"And I'm glad to see you," responded Raouf.

13.

Raouf rapidly began to acquaint Anous with his new environs, then told him, "Here is Abu—your lawyer," when the ancient ex-Egyptian arrived.

"Welcome, Anous, to the First Heaven," said Abu.

"You mean, it was written that I should go to heaven?" Anous asked in shock.

"Be patient. The road is much longer than you conceive," Abu replied with his well-practiced smile.

Abu then began to inform him of the facts he needed to know about his new world, about the system of trials, and the kinds of verdicts to expect in them. He paraded Anous's beastly actions in front of him like ugly ghosts, until the young man's face grimaced and—wobbling with despair—he could endure no more.

Despite this, Abu said, "In any case, it is my mission to defend you."

"Is there a chance you could succeed in that?" Anous pleaded. "Will it lighten the burden of my sins that I was deprived of life at an early age?"

"You lost it at the hand of a girl defending her honor as you attacked her. Then you left her facing a charge for your murder."

"That's true," admitted Anous. "How I wish I could become her spiritual guide."

"She was successful, as was her spiritual mentor. She has no need of you."

"Does that mean I'm damned?"

"No doubt your father lurks behind your corruption," said Abu. "He is the one who led you astray, who filled you with selfishness, who suggested that you harm people, who whispered in your ear that you should perpetrate crimes as though you owned the whole world."

"You've spoken the truth," Anous said animatedly, seeing his hopes revived.

"Yet, since you have your own mind, heart, and will, you are judged on your own account," said Abu.

"My father's power numbed all my powers completely!"

"Heaven holds you responsible for yourself—and for the world altogether."

"Isn't that responsibility far above the abilities of any human being?"

"But you bear it in exchange for the gift of life itself," reproved Abu.

"But I was born without any say in the matter!"

"Rather, you took this pact upon yourself while you were still in the womb."

"In all honesty, I have no memory of that."

"It is incumbent upon you to remember."

"This is a prosecution, not a defense!"

"We must establish the truth," explained Abu.

"I was not without good qualities—I sought knowledge, and I loved sincerely, as well," said Anous.

"You sought knowledge merely as a means to achieve status, while your love was but a presumptuous urge to possess the girl who belonged to your poverty-stricken friend."

"She never left my mind for one moment. . . ."

"That was nothing but arrogance and desire."

Clinging to any thread, Anous pointed at Raouf. "I maintained a pure friendship!" he claimed.

"Did you not ultimately kill it off brutally?"

"I suffered enormous sadness afterward," said Anous.

"That is uncontestable," admitted Abu.

"And what of my love for cats and my tenderness toward them?"

"That, too, is beautiful."

Abu reflected for a moment, then resumed his interrogation. "What was your attitude toward your father's tyranny?"

"I was just a dutiful son!"

"Such devotion was hardly appropriate in a case like yours."

"Some of his actions always disgusted me."

"Yet you greatly admired other things he did that were no less appalling."

"If only I had lived long enough to change all that. . . ."

"You are being tried for what was, not for what might have been."

". . . Or if I could be given another chance."

"Perhaps that could be arranged," mused Abu.

"When will I appear in court?"

"Your trial is already concluded," replied Abu solemnly. "Anous Qadri, I regret to inform you that you have been condemned."

At these words, like a wisp of fog in the rays of the sun, Anous vanished into the void.

Raouf gazed at Abu questioningly. "Will I continue as his spiritual guide?"

"He will not be reborn on earth for at least a year, or perhaps even longer."

"What, then, will my new assignment be?" wondered Raouf.

Mournfully, Abu told him, "You must present yourself for trial once again."

"Did I not put every effort into it?"

"Indeed, you did, but you failed. Your man was condemned, as you have seen."

"The important thing is the work, not the result."

"The work and the result are both important," Abu admonished. "Moreover, you made a monstrous mistake."

"What was that, Abu?"

"It was not your mission to make him confess to killing you, as though that had been the only or the biggest crime in your quarter."

"But wasn't that his main problem?"

"No," said Abu.

"What was it, then?"

"His father was the problem," Abu advised. "If you had goaded him against his father, then you would have attained higher goals!"

Raouf fell into a pained silence as Abu continued to lecture him, "You did not choose the right target. Your egoism got the better of you, though you did not know it. It would have been easier to provoke him to rebel against his father. If he had succeeded in that, he would not have been disgraced. But it was hardly easy for a foolish, pampered young man to sacrifice his own life—while his father's felonies included your murder."

"Please tell me the verdict," Raouf said resignation.

"Raouf Abd-Rabbuh, I regret to inform you that you have been condemned."

As soon as Abu pronounced his sentence, Raouf, too, was gone.

Chronology

SECTION VI: Turkey (1945–1982)

1945 Turkey becomes a member of the United Nations

1952 Turkey joins NATO

1960 First military coup
Prime Minister Adnan Menderes executed

1964 Turkey becomes associate member of European Community (EU)

1971 Second military coup

1974 Turkey invades Cyprus

1980 Third military coup

1982 New Turkish constitution written

VI

Strangers in a Strange Land: Turkish Literature after Atatürk

THE DEATH OF Mustafa Kemal Atatürk on November 10, 1938, left a vacuum in Turkish politics. It also exposed the long-simmering social, political, and ethnic tensions between the Turkish majority and the Kurdish minority that had been subdued by the Kemalist regime. The death of the "Father of the Turks" meant the end of single-party rule, leading to a far more robust multiparty political system that eventually allowed religiously inclined parties to openly challenge the secular ideology of the state.

As Turkish politics and society became more diverse and thus more dynamic, so too did Turkish literature. Works by previously banned writers, such as the great Nâzım Hikmet, were once again published to both critical and popular acclaim. The 1950s ushered in a period that some have called the "Golden Age" of Turkish literature. A new batch of poets and writers, no longer shackled by Atatürk's authoritarianism, began experimenting with form and content. A renewed emphasis on free verse in poetry and colloquial language in fiction swept aside the last traces of Ottoman literary influence, with its baroque lyricism and abstract themes.

This was the era that gave rise to the "village novel," the most famous example of which is Yaşar Kemal's *Memed, My Hawk*, the story of an outlaw who defies the authorities in his village and wanders through the countryside like a modern-day Robin Hood. The book launched a wave of interest among Turkish readers in the lives of peasants struggling to eke out a living in distant Anatolian villages, far beyond the reach of the government. Writing about traditional village life became a kind of political act: a way of criticizing Turkish society, which, in its race toward modernization, had seemingly abandoned the traditions of the past. Kemal's novel was particularly successful among middle- and upper-class *Istanbullus*—the secular, Westernized, urban intellectuals caught in a permanent state of ennui between "the East" and "the West"—whose lives were so perfectly captured by Ahmet Hamdi Tanpınar in his groundbreaking novel, *A Mind at Peace*, as well as in the stories of Sait Faik Abasıyanık ("Such a Story"), Turkey's most famous short-story writer.

The success of the village novel led to the rise of a new genre in Turkish literature known as "social realism," most clearly evidenced by the influential Garıp Movement founded by the poets Melih Cevdet Anday, Orhan Veli Kanık, and Oktay Rifat. (*Garıp* is Turkish for "strange," by which these poets meant they were "strangers in a strange land.") Committed to, in their words, "dumping overboard everything that traditional literature has taught us," the Garıp poets developed a new literary language devoid of meter and rhyme—indeed, stripped of all poetic embellishments—the purpose of which was to depict the dramatic changes taking place in Turkish society.

Not everyone in Turkey was happy with the changes afoot in Turkish society. Atatürk's fervent supporters (sometimes referred to as the "Kemalist elite"), especially those within the military—the defenders of Kemalism—were taken aback by the social and political challenges posed by this new generation of poets and writers and felt deeply threatened by the rise of religious political parties. Thus, the period of political and literary flowering described above was bookended by two military coups—one in 1960, another in 1980—that demonstrated the limits of the government's tolerance for revolutionary ideas. In the years to come, it would be the aggressive challenges to those limits by the writers of the next generation that would define the future of the Turkish Republic.

YAŞAR KEMAL

(B. 1922)

Memed, My Hawk

(EXCERPT)

Translated from the Turkish by Edouard Roditi

IRAZ HAD BEEN left a widow when she was only twenty, with a nine-months-old baby in her arms. She had loved her husband dearly.

"After Huseyin," she had sworn before his dead body, "there can be no other man for me."

She had kept her word and never remarried.

A few days after her husband's death she had left their child to the care of a woman relative and gone to work, plowing the land her husband had left her. A month later she had plowed the field and finished the sowing.

When summer came, she then harvested the field all by herself. She was young and strong and the work did not hurt her.

Later she would take the boy in her arms and wander through the village playing with him. "Won't my baby grow up because his uncles neglect him? Just look how my Riza's growing!" she would say to spite his uncles, the eldest of whom wanted to marry her. "I'm not marrying," Iraz would reply to his offers of marriage, "I'm not taking any other man into Huseyin's bed. If I live till doomsday I'll never marry again."

"Iraz," people would insist, "this is Huseyin's brother, not just a stranger. He's the child's uncle. He'll look after him like a father."

But Iraz remained obdurate.

Her brother-in-law bore her a grudge for having rejected his offer and soon obtained possession of the field she had inherited from Huseyin, though he had no right to it. When their father had died the three brothers had divided in equal shares the fields they had inherited. This field had been the share of her husband, Huseyin, but there was nothing Iraz could now do. She was a young woman, ignorant of the ways of the law and of those that lead to the government.

Deprived of her field, Iraz still stood firm. "Will my baby's uncles' dirty tricks prevent him from growing up? Won't my Riza be able to grow up if we no longer own a field?"

In the summer she toiled in the fields of others, in the winter she worked as a servant in the homes of the rich. She managed to scrape through and her child grew to be a fine boy. But on her lips there was always a lament, like a lullaby, a bitter song: "Won't my orphan grow up?"

He grew, but why were they always in such poverty, without even a field of their own? He grew, hearing the reasons for their poverty every day from his mother and the other villagers. The bitter song was graven deep in his mind, a song born of a mother's pain, trouble, and courage: "Won't my little one grow up?"

When Riza was almost twenty-one, he was tall and slender, like a healthy plant. No boy in Sakar village could ride a horse, throw a javelin, hit the mark, dance in a ring as Riza could. But mother and son were both unhappy. In their hearts they nourished incurable woes. To have to work for others, to be mere laborers when you have once owned your own field!

Compared with that of other villages, the land around Sakar is very fertile and plentiful, a vast plain with a huge rock like a sign, called Adaja, right in the middle. When the whole plain had been sown and all the fields were turning green, the rock of Adaja stood out white against the green.

One of the largest fields at the foot of Adaja was the one that had belonged to Riza's father. For years, now, his uncle had plowed it. Riza dreamed of its rich fertile soil, and hatred grew and hardened in his heart. Wherever he went, wherever he drove the plow, his mind's eye was set on the foot of the Adaja rock.

Every day his mother would moan: "Ah, my son! The Adaja field. . . . Your father used to keep us in fine style, thanks to that field. May they be struck blind!"

Riza would lower his head and remain as if in a trance. In his nostrils he could sense the smell of rich, shining earth. His longing for the earth consumed him.

"That infidel uncle of yours," his mother would say. "May he get his deserts!"

Riza's hatred grew until there came a time when he could no longer conceal it. He had never been like this before. He would now wake up early in the morning and set out in the direction of Adaja. Reaching the field at the foot of the rock, he would sit on a stone and daydream. The crops were sprouting and the earth swarmed with insects. As the sun rose, the earth would begin to steam. The longing to own such steaming soil is the most violent of all longings. Riza would thrust his hand into the soft warm soil and let the earth slip through his fingers. "This soil is mine," he would say, a quiver running through his body. "Mine! But another man has sown and harvested it for twenty years."

He would be tired when he rose at last to return home.

"Where have you been since dawn?" his mother would ask. He would remain silent, his face dark and scowling.

This went on for two months. The crops were knee-high and had turned from yellowish-green to a deep dark green.

"Mother," Riza said one day, his mind made up, "this field is ours."

"It's ours, child, who else's would it be?"

"I'm going to apply to the government," declared Riza.

"How I've waited for this day!"

"I've asked the elders. While he was still alive my father divided up with my uncles the fields inherited from my grandfather. As a consequence, what was ours remains ours and has come to me from my grandfather."

"Yes, child," agreed his mother. "What's ours is ours."

As this was a matter of inheritance, the case did not last long. The rich soft earth at the foot of Adaja passed back to Riza. After so many long, crushing years, young Riza welcomed the field as if he were welcoming his bride into his home. It was summer when the field was handed over to him. The earth was not and scorched. The crops had already been harvested and the stubble blazed bright in the sun.

Riza found a pair of oxen to turn over the summer earth. He harnessed a plow behind the oxen and the soil then crumbled beneath the plow as he worked fast to have the field ready to receive the seed and then yield thirtyfold or fortyfold what had been sown.

The summer plowing is always done at two different times, two hours before dawn and again in the afternoon, when the west wind has risen. The plowing that begins before dawn continues until the sun is too hot for the oxen. Then they are left to rest in the shade of a tree. In the late afternoon, when the little clouds like sails rise over the Mediterranean, the oxen are harnessed again and the work continues until nightfall, sometimes even until midnight if the moon is bright.

There was a moon when Riza started plowing his field. He planned to work without a pause until the day grew too warm, then again from the late afternoon till midnight. He would not notice the heat or his own weariness. He could easily forget everything and go on until morning. The soft furrowed earth would seem more beautiful in the moonlight. At night, in the stillness, the crunch of the plow as it cut through the earth would sound sweeter to his ears.

Iraz was proud that she had raised such a fine lad and that they had now taken the field back from those good-for-nothing uncles. She would wander around the village in a turmoil of joy. If she were asked about her son she would answer: "He is plowing his field."

It was the fourteenth of the month and the moon was full. All the fields, especially the one Riza was plowing, gleamed like silver in the moonlight. A fresh wind was blowing. The hooves of Riza's oxen sank into the ground as they slowly dragged the plow behind them.

Riza was tired and sleepy. He left the oxen and, pillowing his head on a mound of earth, fell asleep.

The next morning, as on every other day, one of the neighborhood children, fourteen-year-old Durmush, brought Riza his food. The day was already hot and the field was shimmering as the boy looked for Riza at the foot of the trees. Riza would always greet him cheerfully and, without yet taking the food, place his own hands under the boy's arms and lift him high in the air. The boy was now puzzled. He looked all around at the foot of the trees, but found no sign of Riza. Then he saw the young man lying curled up in the middle of the field and no sign of the oxen. When the boy came near where Riza lay, he was so shocked that the food dropped from his hand. He turned and began to run off, screaming all the way.

The boy entered the village breathless and exhausted. He was screaming, but his voice came out as a faint whistle. He threw himself down on the ground in front of the houses. The women gathered around him and pulled his tongue out, thinking he had been frightened into a fit. They made him drink cold water and poured water on his head. After a while the child recovered his senses: "Riza Agha is lying all covered with blood, in a pool of blood on the ground," he said. "Blood was trickling from his mouth. When I saw him like that I came running all the way here."

The women understood what had happened. They bowed their heads and were silent. The news spread instantly through the whole village. Iraz heard it too.

Iraz went ahead of them, tearing her hair and sobbing, with all the villagers behind her. They came to the field. Riza's head had slipped from the mound where it had rested and was hanging at an angle when they found him.

"My orphan boy, my ill-starred son!" cried Iraz as she threw herself upon the corpse.

Riza was curled up with his knees close to his chest. The hollow in the ground in front of him was full of blood that had already clotted with insects and flies all over it. The sun was shining brightly with the sharp smell of blood rising like steam from a boiling cauldron. There was mist in the air and a swarm of bright-green flies on the dead body, glistening as they moved.

"My orphan boy! My ill-starred son!"

Women, boys, and men stood in a circle around the dead body. Most of the women were weeping.

"Who killed my Riza?" Iraz was beating her breast and struggling piteously to contain her emotion. The other women tried to raise her from the corpse but she could not be dragged away. "Me too," she kept saying. "Bury me alive with my Riza." She lay on her son's dead body till nightfall. News of the murder reached the town. The police, the magistrate, and the coroner came. The police dragged the woman, her eyes bloodshot and her face swollen from weeping, away from the body and pulled her to her feet, but she sank to the ground and remained motionless as if dead. For a long while she refused to move or to utter a sound.

Later they took her before the magistrate.

"Woman, who could have killed your son?" he asked. "Whom do you suspect?"

The woman raised her face. With vacant eyes she stared at the magistrate's face.

"Who killed your son? Whom do you suspect?" repeated the magistrate.

"Those infidels," she said. "Who else but those infidels would have killed him? His uncles killed the boy, because of the field."

Having inquired closely into the matter of the field, the magistrate took notes on the spot and the crowd broke up as they left the field.

The dead body with the green flies swarming on it, the empty yoke and the plow waiting for the oxen, the mother with eyes tearless from too much weeping, these remained in the desolate solitude of the plain. The rich earth shone in the middle of it as dark as a piece of embroidery.

They arrested Riza's cousin Ali as a suspect and took him to the police station. According to Ali's testimony, however, he had not been in the village that day; with the aid of local witnesses he proved that he had been at a wedding in a neighboring village, four hours from Sakar. But Iraz and all the villagers knew that Ali was the one who had killed Riza, because of the field.

Iraz was astounded and the villagers could not believe their eyes when, two days later, Ali swaggered into the village ostentatiously swinging his arms. Iraz lost all control of herself, seized an axe that she had in her house, and ran toward Ali's house. she had only one thought: to kill the man who had killed her son. When Ali's family saw Iraz descending upon them with the axe in her hand, they shut their door and bolted it. Finding the door shut, Iraz began to break in with the axe. But Ali was not there. If he had been inside to protect them, they would not have closed the door. His mother, two girls, and a baby were inside, and the door was on the point of giving. Iraz swung the axe with all her strength to break it down and kill all those who had sought refuge inside. The villagers hastened to see what the row was about and gathered by the house. But they could not approach Iraz, nor did it occur to them to approach her. Let her avenge her son!

Every now and then a man called: "Don't Mother! Those inside aren't responsible. Ali isn't in the house. Forget about it."

"Ali isn't here; leave us, Iraz," called the mother from inside.

Somehow Ali managed to slip through the crowd and to catch hold of Iraz from behind. He seized the axe from her hand; with all his strength he threw the exhausted woman aside and began to trample on her. The villagers rushed to her assistance and dragged her from beneath his feet.

That night Iraz set fire to Ali's house. While the villagers were trying to put out the fire, Ali jumped onto a horse and set off for the police station. There he filed a complaint about the events of the morning and about her setting fire to their house, declaring that the house was still burning.

It was morning when Ali returned to the village with the police. When they saw this, the villagers gathered around Ali. "Don't do this, Ali," they said. "The poor thing is brokenhearted from the loss of her fine lad. Don't rub salt into her wound. Don't send her to rot in prison. In any case, the villagers have put out the fire."

Ali refused to listen to them, and the police arrested Iraz and took her off to prison.

"Yes, I broke down their door," Iraz told the police, "and if I could have entered the house I would have struck them all down with my axe. But I couldn't. Is it too much if I kill those who killed my only son? Yes, I set fire to their house in the night so that they would all burn to death inside. But those accursed villagers gave the alarm and put out the fire. Do you think it's too high a price for my Riza? My orphan boy was worth a whole country. Do you know at what cost I raised him? Do you think it's too high a price?"

To the magistrate at the time of her arrest and later during the trial she always gave the same testimony. Though they arrested and imprisoned her, she never changed her story and only repeated: "My boy was worth a whole village, a whole country. Is it too much? Is it too high a price?"

They had put her into the one-room women's section of the prison. She had never expected this. To avenge the death of her fine tall son she had set fire to a house. It was hard to bear this new wrong after the death of her son. She entered the prison with her head low, groping her way around like a blind person. She could see nothing and did not even notice whether she was alone in this room or with another prisoner. She sat down silently in one corner and remained there like a stone that has been dropped into a well.

Normally Iraz wore her hair tied up in a clean white kerchief. Her large light-brown eyes would shine brightly and her slanting eyebrows would give a strange beauty to her broad, sun-tanned face with its small pointed chin and a lock of black hair curled down over her broad forehead. But she was now in a dreadful condition. Her face was almost black and the whites of her eyes were bloodshot from crying. Her chin seemed withered and her lips were bloodless, their skin dry and cracked from thirst. Only her kerchief was still white and spotless.

"My fine lad!" she kept repeating. "He was worth a whole country. Was it too high a price? If I burn a whole village to ashes, would it be too much?"

Hatche had been pleased to see this woman come here as a companion in this lonely prison. For herself she felt pleased, but she was sorry for her. Who knew what had befallen the poor creature? She could not rejoice at another's misery. She wanted to ask the woman many questions that were on the tip of her tongue, but somehow she could not bring herself to speak. It is not easy to ask anything of someone who is so exhausted, engaged in such a life-and-death struggle. Hatche just stared at the woman.

In the evening Hatche set her soup on the brazier in the yard outside and began to cook it. When it was ready she brought it in, smelling of onion and rancid butter as it steamed. After the soup had cooled a little, she approached Iraz timidly: "Aunt, you must be hungry by now. I've prepared some soup. Come, drink it."

Iraz's eyes were quite vacant. She stared blindly at Hatche as if she had not heard her.

"Aunt," repeated Hatche, "drink a little of this soup. You must be very hungry by now."

Iraz acted as if she simply were not there, not even blinking. Even in the eyes of the blind there is an anxiety to see, a desire, a struggle. Here there was nothing. In deaf ears, too, there is a straining, a reaching out to hear. Here not even that. But Hatche was not to be discouraged and kept on urging her.

Slowly the woman raised her vacant eyes and fixed them on Hatche. Hatche could not sustain her gaze. She mumbled something confusedly, left the bowl there in front of the woman, and slipped out, holding her breath.

Until the guard came to shut the door of the cell Hatche stayed in the yard. She was afraid to go into the cell and see her companion's condition. When the door was closed on her she prepared her bed and slipped in immediately, trembling with fear, without casting a glance at Iraz. For a time she lay curled up in her bed. Darkness fell, but she did not light the lamp as was her custom every night. She could not bear to see that face in its life-and-death struggle. Although she was afraid of the dark, it now seemed welcome to her, stretching like a curtain between them.

That night Hatche was unable to sleep. As the first light filtered in between the window-boards she rose from her bed. Iraz was still there like a vague shadow in her corner, motionless as ever. Only her white kerchief stood out like the brightness of a window against the dirty wall.

At midday Iraz was still in the same position. Evening came and she still had not moved. That second night Hatche spent fearfully, like the first, half awake, half asleep.

In the morning when the light appeared again, she opened her inflamed eyes and went over to Iraz. There was something compelling in her manner.

"Aunt!" she said. "I beseech you, don't stay like that!" She took the woman's hands in hers. "Don't, please!"

The woman turned her big, wide-open eyes on her, eyes that were black, lusterless. There was no white left in them; they were all black.

Hatche did not give up. "Tell me your troubles, Aunt," she said. "I beseech you. Does anyone without troubles ever come here? What business would a person without troubles have here? Isn't that true?"

"What's that, my girl?" moaned Iraz.

Hatche was so pleased to hear Iraz speak at last and say something that it was as if a big load had been lifted from her back.

"Why do you behave like this?" she asked. "You haven't opened your mouth since you came. You haven't even eaten anything!"

"My son was worth a whole country. My son was the pride of the village. Was it too high a price?" she said and fell silent.

"When I saw you I forgot my own troubles," said Hatche. "Tell me your troubles and unburden yourself."

"If I burn the house and break down the door of those who killed my son, is it too much? If I kill them one by one, is it too much?"

"Oh, my poor Aunt! May they all be struck blind!"

"He was the pride of the village," moaned Iraz. "Is it too much if I kill them all?"

Hatche showed her sympathy.

"And now they've brought me here and locked me up, while my son's murderer struts around the village swinging his arms. If this doesn't kill me, nothing will!"

"My poor Aunt!" said Hatche. "You're dying of hunger. You haven't eaten anything since you came here. I'll go and prepare you some soup."

Today she decided to make the soup with plenty of butter. A month after her arrival she had begun to launder the clothes of some of the richer prisoners and had now saved a little money. A little girl sometimes brought food and other things for the prisoners from the market. Hatche called the girl and put fifty piastres into her hand. "Go and get me some butter," she said. She was filled with joy. The woman had spoken at last, and someone who speaks does not die so easily of her grief. But it is a terrible end for anyone who does not speak and remains buried within himself. That was why Hatche was pleased.

All the gay tunes she knew were now singing in her head. She filled the brazier with charcoal and began to fan it. Soon the coals glowed red as Hatche fanned them and puffed over them. She filled the little tinned copper pot with water and put it on the brazier. The soup was soon ready, so soon that even Hatche was surprised.

When Hatche had spoken of soup, Iraz had felt a crushing pain. Her bowels and stomach seemed to have frozen into a solid mass. She had not eaten a single mouthful since the day her son had been killed. From outside, the smell of melted fat and fried onion now reached her nostrils. She heard the sizzling of the boiling fat as it poured into the soup. . . .

Hatche brought in the pot of soup and placed it before Iraz. "Please, Aunt," she begged, placing a wooden spoon in her hand.

Iraz seemed to have forgotten how to use a spoon. It rested in her hand ready to fall to the ground.

Hatche was afraid she might not drink the soup. "Come on," she repeated. "Come on, please!"

Iraz slowly dipped the spoon into the soup.

When she had finished drinking it, Hatche spoke again. "Aunt, there's water in the ewer. Wash your face. It'll make you feel better."

Iraz did as Hatche told her and went and washed her face.

"Thank you, my lovely girl. May God grant you all your wishes."

"If only He would," Hatche repeated several times. She sat down and told Iraz all her misfortunes. "Yes," she said, "this is how it happened, Aunt. I don't want anything in the world if only I can have news of my Memed. I've been here a full nine months, but no one has come to see me. Even my mother came only once. The first days I lay hungry in this hole. After that I began to do the prisoners' laundry. Oh, if only I could have some news! If I could only know if he is dead or alive. Let them hang me if they like. I don't care. If only I could have some news of my Memed."

As the days passed Iraz grew less weary and confused. She learned from the other prisoners that she should never have declared before the judge that she had broken the door with an axe with the intent to kill all those inside, or that she had set fire to the house to burn Ali's relatives. She might have killed ten people, they told her, but if there were no proof, if nobody had witnessed it or knew about it, the authorities could not have held her as a murderess. At first Iraz simply could not understand this injustice. Slowly she began to learn. In all the evidence that she gave later in court, she denied everything.

"Ah!" she would then say, "If I were free I would show the authorities who killed my Riza."

Hatche tried to console her. "God willing, you will soon be free, Aunt. You'll get out of here and hand over your son's murderer to the police. Think of me! At my age I shall be left to rot here. Everybody comes and bears witness against me!"

As the days passed Iraz and Hatche became like mother and daughter. They shared everything, including their troubles. Hatche knew Riza's height, his black eyes, his slim fingers, his dancing, his childhood, what he had done as a child, with what trouble Iraz had brought him up, the whole story of the field and the final tragedy, down to the last detail, as if she had lived through and seen it all herself. It was the same with Iraz. She, too, knew everything about Memed, from the day he and Hatche had first played together as children.

All day and all evening, until midnight, Iraz and Hatche knitted stockings till they were almost blind with weariness. The stockings they knitted became famous in the town. "The stockings of the girl who killed her fiancé and of the woman whose boy was killed." The saddest of designs went into the stockings. Hatche and Iraz did not copy any known designs, but created pattern after pattern of their own, in colors more bitter than poison. The town had never seen such striking and beautiful stockings.

Anyone going to prison for the first time is confused on entering so different a world. One feels lost in an endless forest, far away, as if all ties with the earth, with home and family, friends and loved ones, with everything, have been broken. It is also like sinking into a deep and desolate emptiness. Then there is another feeling experienced by a new prisoner: everything becomes like an enemy, the stones, the walls, the little bit of sky that can be seen, the windows with their iron bars. Above all, if a prisoner has no money he is lost.

So it was not for nothing that Hatche and Iraz blinded themselves day and night knitting stockings. They did not touch the money they earned, and for many months their food consisted only of what the prison gave them. Sooner or later Memed would come, they thought. Maybe tomorrow, maybe in a month. Surely one day he would be caught and brought here too. Then he would need money. It was for this that they now toiled.

"My girl," Iraz would say, "Memed won't have as much trouble here as we. We are here to look after him."

"Yes, we are here, Auntie," Hatche would reply proudly.

"Our Memed has money here. We'll earn more before he comes and then we'll put all the money in his hands and he won't find himself destitute like the other prisoners. He won't have to turn to strangers for help."

At night they would retire to bed exhausted, with aching eyes, and still talk and share their troubles for hours on end, discussing everything that might possibly happen to Memed, and all the most impossible things too. What did they not invent? Finally Hatche would become angry with her mother. "That mother of mine," she would begin. "What sort of mother is she? I didn't ask much. Only for news of my Memed. She went off and never came back."

"Who knows," Iraz would reply, "what's happened to your poor mother?" Iraz would always defend Hatche's mother.

One night, as on every other night, they had gone to bed at midnight. Their bedding was wet from the damp air. The night insects were humming.

"Aunt Iraz," said Hatche.

"Yes?"

That's how they began every night.

"It's damp here."

"What can we do, my girl?" answered Iraz.

"That mother of mine. . . ."

"Who knows what troubles have come upon her?"

Without wasting further thought on her mother, Hatche skipped to another subject. "We'll have a tiny little house in the Çukurova on the soil of Yuregir," she said. "Memed will work for someone else to begin with, then we'll have a little field of our own. That's what Memed used to tell me."

"You're young. It'll all come to you," Iraz comforted her.

"He wanted to take me to the little restaurant in the town."

"He'll still take you there."

And so their conversation would continue, till at last Hatche would be lost in thought. She forgot that she was in prison and that Memed was an outlaw. Iraz forgot her troubles too.

"Yuregir earth," Hatche continued to muse, "Yuregir earth is warm. It's sunny there and the crops rise so thick that a tiger couldn't crash through them. Our field is thirty acres. . . ."

"Yes, my girl, thirty acres."

"We've sown half with wheat and half with barley."

"And half an acre of onions in the middle of the wheat," went on Iraz.

"I've plastered the inside of the house with green earth."

"Green earth and red earth too."

"We own a cow, a red cow with big eyes, and a suckling calf."

At this Iraz was quiet and uttered no reply. But Hatche continued: "Our house is yours. Memed is your son and I am your daughter."

"You're my daughter," repeated Iraz.

"In front of our house is a willow tree with its branches reaching down to the ground."

"We'll put a fence all around our garden and we'll have lots of flowers."

Hatche came to herself, as if roused from a deep sleep. "When will they arrest Memed and bring him here, I wonder?" she asked Iraz. "What do you think, my Aunt?"

"If not tomorrow, then in a month or so. . . ."

"Well, we're ready, aren't we, my Aunt?" insisted Hatche.

"Yes, we're ready," Iraz replied proudly. "We have enough money for him."

After that they would fall asleep.

Friday was market day in the town. On Fridays Hatche would stare out of the window, watching the roads. If her mother were to come, it would be on a Friday. This particular Friday Hatche woke up very early, before sunrise. "If only she'd come today," she said; but she said this every Friday.

Toward midday a tall woman with a double saddlebag over her shoulder came timidly toward the prison.

"Aunt Iraz," Hatche called in a shrill and excited voice.

"What is it, girl?" answered Iraz from inside, hurrying toward her.

"My mother!"

Iraz looked out along the road. They stood there side by side, staring at the tired, barefooted woman who was limping toward them, the ends of her black scarf between her teeth as she hung her head and at last stopped at the gate of the prison. Small, thin, and nervous, the guard called out: "What do you want, woman?"

"My daughter's inside. I've come to see her."

"Mother!" called Hatche.

The woman slowly raised her head and looked at the guard. "Brother Effendi, that's my daughter," she said.

"You may go and talk to her."

She put down her bag at the foot of the wall, then squatted there, with her back against the wall. "Oh, my bones are aching!" she moaned.

Hatche stood there quite still, staring at her mother. The woman's feet were covered with cuts that were caked with dust from the road. Her hair was white with dust and a muddy sweat ran down her neck. Her eyebrows and lashes were concealed by the dust. A torn and dirty skirt hung around her legs. Seeing her in such a state, Hatche's anger against her suddenly passed. She was filled with pity, and there were tears in her eyes. She could feel a lump in her throat but simply could not go closer to her mother.

Hatche's mother saw her daughter standing there, staring at her with her eyes full of tears. She, too, could feel a lump in her throat. "Come, my ill-starred child," she suddenly burst out. "Come to your mother."

Unable to restrain herself, she began to weep quietly. Hatche approached, kissed her hand, and sat down beside her, followed by Iraz.

"Welcome, Sister," said Iraz.

Hatche introduced Iraz to her mother. "This is my Aunt Iraz," she said. "We sleep in the same cell."

"What are your troubles, Sister?" asked the mother in surprise.

"They killed her son Riza," said Hatche.

"Oh!" exclaimed the mother. "May they be struck blind, Sister!"

For a while the three women were silent. Then the mother raised her head and began to talk. "My daughter, my dark-eyed girl, forgive your mother. What hasn't that infidel Abdi done to me because I took that petition to the government! Only I know what I have suffered at his hands. He's forbidden me to come to town again, my rose girl. If not, would I have left my rose girl alone here in the town, locked up between four walls? I'd have come right away to my beautiful girl."

For some reason suddenly she stopped talking. For the first time since she had come, her face lit up. Drawing close to the other two women, she began to speak in a low voice: "Wait a moment, my beautiful girl, I was almost forgetting. I've news for you. Memed has become a brigand, an outlaw!"

At the sound of Memed's name Hatche's face became pale. Her heart began to beat as if it would burst.

"Memed went and joined Durdu's band after shooting Abdi and Veli. And now these brigands have been up to all sorts of tricks. They don't let anyone go on the roads and have stopped all traffic, killing anyone who resists them. They strip men naked, even of their underpants. . . ."

"Memed wouldn't do things like that! Memed would never kill a man," objected Hatche in anger.

"I don't know, my girl," answered her mother. "That's what they all say. Memed's name comes right after Durdu's. His fame has spread all over the country. What do I know, my girl? I only tell you what

I've heard. When that infidel Abdi heard about Memed becoming a brigand, for a whole month he placed four or five guards around his house every night, but he was still afraid and never slept a wink all night, wandering about the house till morning. Then Sergeant Asim went to his house and said he had been after Memed. He declared he had never seen a brigand like Memed in the mountains. If it hadn't been for him, he said, he would have put Durdu's band to rout. At this Abdi Agha took to his heels and left the village. Some say he is staying in the town, others that he has gone to a village in the Çukurovac. Some even say that he's gone and taken refuge with the great government in Ankara. So, with Abdi Agha no longer in the village, I said to myself, let me go and see my rose girl, and that's how it is."

While she was explaining all this, her face was calm and smiling. Suddenly it turned pale, as if she were choking.

Iraz and Hatche were pleased that Memed had become a brigand. They exchanged eloquent glances, but when they saw Hatche's mother turn pale they were frightened. "Mother, Mother, what is it?" whispered Hatche.

"Don't ask, my girl, but I have bad news for you. Let's hope it's false. I heard it as I was coming. My tongue won't bring it out, my girl. I heard yesterday morning that Durdu and Memed had quarreled because of a nomad Agha. Durdu had shot at Memed and his two companions. That's what I heard, my girl. Memed had protected the nomad Agha, so Durdu shot at him. A horseman passed through our village, a mounted nomad loaded with arms, on his way to help the nomad Agha, he said. His horse was covered with foam and he said that Memed had been wounded."

At first Hatche remained motionless. Then she threw herself into Iraz's arms. "Did this have to happen to me as well, Auntie?" she sobbed. Suddenly she was quiet.

"I'm going," said her mother. "God be with you, my girl. I'll let you know the truth as soon as I can. There's some butter in the bag I brought you, and eggs and bread. I'll come again next Friday if that infidel hasn't come back to the village. Don't lose the bag. Good health!" she called, as she set forth.

"I shouldn't have told her that. I shouldn't," she said to herself as she walked down the road.

Hatche had begun to sob again. "How could that infidel Durdu have killed my Memed? Does a man do that to his companion? How could he?"

Iraz tried to console her. "Every day they bring news of the death of a brigand, but don't believe it. You'll get used to it."

But Hatche was not listening. "I can't live," she sobbed. "I can't live without my Memed."

Iraz lost her temper. "How do you know the lad is dead, child? One doesn't mourn a man who is still alive. In my youth I heard of Big Ahmet's death at least twenty times. But Big Ahmet's still alive today."

"Aunt Iraz, this is different," said Hatche. "He's still such a young brigand! I can't live any more. I'll die."

"Don't you know, you stupid girl," continued Iraz, "that sometimes the brigands themselves spread false rumors about their own deaths? Listen! When that goat-beard heard that Memed had become a brigand, he fled from the village. Perhaps Memed's spread this news to fool him. When old goat-beard returns to the village, Memed will go and kill him. Perhaps it's all a trick."

"Memed doesn't do things like that, Aunt Iraz. I can't live after this; I'll die!"

She began to tremble, as if shaken with malaria. Iraz took her in her arms, carried her to the bed, and laid her down.

"Wait a while, you stupid girl. How many things can happen before a day is done? Don't believe everything like that."

Two days later Hatche rose from her bed, pale as a corpse. She had bound a black kerchief around her head. Her face was waxen and still. Every day her condition deteriorated and she became increasingly pale and weak. Unable to sleep, she sat all night, resting her head on her knees and clasping her arms around her legs.

Nor could Iraz sleep. They no longer chattered at night. Only every once in a while would Iraz say: "You'll see, my crazy girl, you'll see. Good news of Memed will soon reach us."

But Hatche paid no attention to her.

AHMET HAMDI TANPINAR

(1901—1962)

A Mind at Peace

(EXCERPT)

Translated from the Turkish by Erdağ Göknar

MÜMTAZ REGRETTED HURRYING away as soon as he'd left them. He shouldn't have abandoned Nuran like that. *Perhaps I can catch sight of her*, he thought, and waited at some remove from the ferry landing. The crowd flowed ceaselessly. As the passengers and those who'd come to greet them thinned, he first noticed Sabih and Adile—Adile could walk only a short distance on the street without leaning on her husband. For her, in all probability, one of the sound ways of fully exploiting the resource known as a husband was to have him carry her, if only partially, while they were out and about; presently they were locked arm in arm. Sabih, as if wanting to create a ballast of world affairs to counter Adile's heft, which dragged down his starboard side, carried a roll of newspapers in the opposite arm, his forehead furrowed in aggravation; doubtless, he forged ahead with a litany of ideas and comparisons about the ordered regulations of ferry traffic docking and departure in the countries of the West.

Mümtaz shielded himself behind another group to avoid being drawn into further conversation with the couple. Soon Nuran and her daughter appeared. Evidently, so she could walk with greater ease, Nuran had chosen to remain onboard until the very last. With her face lowered toward her daughter, wearing a sweet and simple grin, she walked on, explaining something or another.

But neither the smile nor talk lasted long. As soon as they exited the station building, Fatma shouted, "Papa! Mother, Papa's coming," and bolted forward. What Mümtaz witnessed then, he'd scarcely ever forget. Nuran's face turned ashen white. Mümtaz looked about; twenty or twenty-five paces before him approached a blonde woman, thick-boned and full-breasted, if not stunningly beautiful—when he thought about this scene later, he decided, *At least beautiful for some men*—accompanied by a swarthy man of about thirty-five with black hair, whose arms and face were bronzed by the sun and whose bearing gave the impression that he enjoyed water sports. Nuran's entire body trembled. As the thick-boned woman passed, Mümtaz heard her whisper softly, half in Turkish, half in French: "But *c'est scandaleux*! Fâhir, for God's sake, shut her up!" Fâhir and his mistress finally neared Nuran. In a flurry of "God bless" and "Oh, what a pretty child," Emma took Fatma into her arms. Fâhir, meanwhile, stood as if he were made of ice. He'd only managed to bring himself to caress the girl's cheek. A strange, awkward exchange. From where she stood, Nuran continued to tremble; Emma, stressing each syllable she uttered to the breaking point, fawned, "Oh, what a beautiful girl!" and Fatma, distraught by this stranger's affections, and especially by her father's cool distance, clung to her mother's skirts and wept. An onlooker might have concluded that the episode had been orchestrated by Nuran, or that Fâhir hadn't missed his chance at a snub of indifference toward his ex-wife in front of Emma. Nuran put an end to the bitter episode, which had nothing to prevent it from lasting hours, with a gesture that revealed much of her character: Taking her daughter into her arms, she walked between the two of them and a short distance ahead boarded a phaeton-for-hire. As they passed, Mümtaz noticed that Fatma was convulsing in tears. He felt a twinge of distress. At the head of the road, his friends were awaiting him. He approached them:

"Where have you been? We've been waiting for you. . . ."

"Has İhsan come?"

"Yes, and he's with a relative of yours!"

"Who?"

"Somebody named Suad. A peculiar fellow. He's staying at the sanatorium here!"

"He resembles a horse. . . ."

Mümtaz said only, "I know him," then turning to Nuri, "It's true, he does look like a horse." Though in his mind's eye he conjured the way Nuran's hair slipped frequently from her temples toward her eyes.

Orhan completed the analysis. "He's something of a cannibal!"

"No, he's only an assassin, or a frantic assassin, that is to say, suicidal!"

These terms referred to an in-joke that had begun at the university. One day at the Küllük coffeehouse, they learned how a renowned historian, Mükrimin Halil, had separated people into three main categories—"Lackeys of the Orient," "Regulators of the World," and "Thugs." Then they'd furthered the categorization. "Cannibals" were fanatics of any ideology, whether on the right or the left. "Assassins" had certain hang-ups and discussed them with whomever they saw. "Frantic Assassins" subjectified these hang-ups to an extreme and were filled with feelings of revolt. And as for "Suicidals," they turned these hang-ups into torturous double binds.

Arm in arm, just as they had done years before, they occupied half the road and walked along laughing and talking. None of them noticed Mümtaz's state of distraction.

During this afternoon hour, the restaurant filled with the presence of the sea. Suad and İhsan sat at a corner table. Light reflecting off the sea appeared to gather on Suad's face. Since the last time he'd seen Suad, Mümtaz found him to be thinner and paler. His bones seemed to protrude.

İhsan said impatiently, "Don't waste any time, come sit down." İhsan drank quite infrequently. Rather than from any concern about health, he abstained in order to give alcohol its proper due in life. He'd say, "We shouldn't let the secrets of alcohol lose their effect within us." As for the times he did partake, he'd grow as impatient as a child. He'd picked this restaurant because it was near the ferry landing, and he'd eagerly awaited Mümtaz's arrival. He abruptly turned to Mümtaz: "Your eyes are alight. . . . What's going on?"

Surprised, Mümtaz said, "Seeing Suad is quite a pleasure. . . ." In fact, he hadn't been pleased to see Suad, although he admired his intelligence and conversation. But there was something he couldn't put his finger on that disturbed him about Suad.

"What a joy. . . . There are people in this world who are pleased to see me."

In response to his laughter, Mümtaz thought, *You see, this is precisely why I like you!* Actually, Suad's laughter bore an astounding force that came from the heart yet negated everything. He laughed and his face abruptly appeared to be estranged and antagonistic. *Is he fed up with his own life or is he mocking me?*

Fahri grinned at İhsan and said, "I told you he'd come. You didn't believe me."

"But he's two ferries late."

"No, I only missed one."

"When did you get up?"

Mümtaz again recalled the great triumph of his evening, and said, "I finished the book last night. I went to bed late and couldn't sleep. No matter what I tell her, I haven't managed to get Sümbül to wake me at the right time!"

Sümbül was the maid who saw to Mümtaz's domestic affairs in Emirgân.

Suad asked, "What have you been reading these days, Mümtaz?"

Gravely, Mümtaz examined the plates of appetizers being placed before him. He'd seated himself opposite the door despite knowing full well that the young lady whose acquaintance he'd just made wouldn't appear. "Practically everything. . . . Ahmet Cevdet's *History, Sicill-i Osmanî* biographical entries, *Taşköprüzade's Şakâyik* . . ."

Suad responded dismissively, "A disaster! Now how are we supposed to converse? Mümtaz and I used to discuss things easily enough in the past. First I'd ask him which writer he was reading, then I'd begin talking from that author's perspective or through those concerns." His inscrutable face cracked open with an abrupt, puerile laugh. Completing his earlier thought, Mümtaz mused, *You see, this is also why I like him.*

"Isn't everyone more or less reading this way?" Nuri interjected. The four of them, inseparable friends from Galatasaray, were immensely fond of Mümtaz and couldn't tolerate any innuendos made against him.

Suad gestured with his hand. "I meant to make a joke. I always needle Mümtaz this way. Of course, I know what he's all about. We're relatives. But to tell the truth, I often wonder whether everyone reads as much as we do."

Fahri's opinion took a different tack: "Europe reads much more than we do. And a number of languages at once. That's not the point, but . . ."

"There's another problem still. We're not comfortable with what we read."

İhsan was examining the transfiguration of ice in his glass, how the pellucid liquid slowly became clouded as if being enhanced by veins of marble. Now the glass was full of a less benign liquid.

"Bottoms up!" he said. Then he answered Suad: "The issue is this: The things we read don't lead us anywhere. When we read what's written about Turks, we realize that we're wandering on the peripheries of life. A Westerner only satisfies us when he happens to remind us that we're citizens of the world. In short, most of us read as if embarking on a voyage, as if escaping our own identities. Herein rests the problem. Meanwhile, we're in the process of creating a new social expression particular to us. I believe this is what Suad is saying."

"Indeed, with one leap to shake and cast out the old, the new, and everything else. Leaving neither French poet Ronsard nor his contemporary in the East, Fuzûli. . . ."

"Is this even in the realm of possibility?" And Mümtaz succumbed to Nuran's locks again. *Does her hair always fall that way? . . . Does she always brush it back with her hand while slightly lifting her head?*

Suad listened, none the wiser about Nuran's tresses. "Why shouldn't it be a possibility?"

"It's impossible because . . ." But what was impossible was his discussing such matters at present. *I'm on this island supposedly and she's here too. . . . How distant we are from each other. It's as if we are in the same house but in separate rooms.* "Because, to begin with, we'd be creating a tabula rasa in vain. What do you think we'll gain through such a refutation bedsides the loss of our very selves?"

With a beatific look, Suad said, "The new. . . . We'll establish the myth of a new world, as in America and Soviet Russia."

"And do you think they actually cast aside everything, all of it? If you ask me, neither our denial of the past nor our resolve to create can establish this new myth. If anything, it rests in the momentum of the New Life itself."

"Then what d'you expect us to do?"

But Mümtaz didn't answer. His mind was preoccupied with the episode between Nuran and her not-husband—he had to be Fâhir. *How her face fell. She was upset enough to burst into tears herself.* And suddenly, through a compassion that rose up within him, he promised to bring her happiness, for as long as he lived, to bring her happiness. And immediately at that instant he was ashamed of his childishness. So infantile! He acknowledged for the first time how sentimental he could let himself be.

"Don't lose sight of the fact that both the United States and Russia are extensions of Europe."

"Okay, then, what is it that should be done?"

İhsan raised his glass. "First we drink," he said. "Then we partake of these fish that this sea of splendor has bequeathed to us. And we give thanks that we are before this sea, at this spring hour, in this restaurant. Later we'll try to establish a New Life particular to us and befitting our own idiom. Life is ours; we'll give it the form that we desire. And as it assumes its form, it'll sing its own song. But we won't meddle with art or ideas at all! We'll set them free. For they demand freedom, absolute freedom. A myth, solely because we long for it, doesn't just materialize out of thin air. No, it erupts from social life. But to cut our ties with the past and to close ourselves off from the West! Never! What do you think we are? We're the essence of Easterners of taste and pleasure. Everything yearns for our persistence and continuity."

"Once you've let the past persist like that, why even bother with a New Life?"

"Because our existence still hasn't found its form, that's why! In any case, life's always in need of organization. Especially in our era."

"In that case we're purging the past?"

"Of course . . . but only where needed. We'll cast out dead roots; we'll engage in a new enterprise and foster new people and society. . . ."

"Where will we find the initiative to do this?"

"From our own necessities and our own will to live; at any rate, we don't need initiative, we need instruction. And reality itself will provide this, not vague notions of utopia!"

Suad wiped his brow with his hand. "I'm not talking about utopia . . . but I want to hear the sounds of unadulterated folk songs. I want to look out upon the world through new eyes. Not just for Turkey, I want this for the entire world. I want to hear songs of tribute sung for the newly born."

"You want justice, you want rights."

"No, not like that! Those are meaningless words. The New Man won't acknowledge a single remnant of the past. . . ."

Mümtaz, with an eye on the customers entering through the door, said, "Do let us invite Suad to provide a description of this New Man!"

"I can't! He has yet to be born. But he will be born, of that I'm certain. The entire world is moaning from the labor of his birth. Take Spain, for example!"

İhsan: "If all you aspire to is that, rest assured, soon all of Europe, even the planet, will resemble Spain. But do you really think that some type of New Man has been born in Spain or Russia? To me, it seems rather that the ground is being prepared for human catastrophe."

"Are you making a prophecy?"

"No, just an observation . . . an observation that could be made by any reader of your average daily paper."

Suad fiddled for a while with his empty glass, then extending it to İbrahim, he said, "If you would, please." Topping the *rakı*-filled glass with water, he took a first sip. "If this happened, what of it, anyway? It's not that I oppose its occurrence. Humanity can only rid itself of obsolete life-molds through such a conflagration. . . ."

"So it can be reduced to even more inferior molds. We all know the outcome of the last world war."

But Suad wasn't listening: "Not to mention that war has become unavoidable now. Such convoluted accounts could only be settled through war." Then he suddenly glanced toward İhsan. "You don't actually hope for anything new from humanity, do you?"

"Could one ever lose hope in humanity? I just don't anticipate anything good from war. It'll spell the end of civilization. I don't expect anything worthwhile to emerge from war, revolution, or populist dictators. War means an absolute catastrophe for Europe, and maybe the world." And as if speaking to himself, he continued: "I haven't lost faith in humanity, but I don't trust individual humans. To begin with, once their ties are broken, they change completely; they become like programmed machines . . . and suddenly it seems as if they resemble deaf and senseless forces of nature. The terrifying aspect of war and revolution is that it amounts to the sudden unleashing of a rudimentary force, one that we'd assumed we'd tamed through centuries of discipline, socialization, and culture."

"That is exactly what I want, revolution."

İhsan sighed, exasperated.

"Meanwhile, we could hope for better. But what good is hope when humanity is this frail? Yes, it's hard to trust humanity, but if we consider its fate, there isn't a creature as pitiable as man."

"I admire mankind. I admire its power to fight constraints. Fully aware of its fate yet engaging in life nevertheless, I admire that courage. Which of us on a starlit night doesn't carry the weight of all Creation on our backs? Nothing could be as beautiful as the courage of humanity. Had I been a poet, I would have penned a single work, a grand epic describing the venture of humanity stretching from our first ancestors who stood on two legs to the present. Initial thoughts, initial fears, initial love, initial stirrings of intelligence gradually becoming cognizant of Creation, the integration of everything that had once existed independently, the myriad innovations with which we've augmented Nature . . . our act of creating Allah around us and within us. Indeed, I'd write only one piece. I'd describe how I longed to sing the praises of humanity awakening matter from its sleep and subduing Creation with its own spirit. Oh language that embraces all exalted things! Oh words, come to my aid!"

Ihsan eyed his food skeptically: "That's quite a display of exuberance there, isn't it, Mümtaz? You sound just like one of those nineteenth-century disciples of civilization."

"No, on the contrary. Because I don't believe that these problems can ever be resolved. We'll always kill and be killed. We'll always live under some type of threat. I admire tragedy itself. True greatness resides in the courage we display despite our consciousness of death."

"Mümtaz yearns to write a poem on evolution from gorilla to *Homo sapiens.*"

"Yes, the evolution from gorilla to human. Thank you for reminding me. Meanwhile, the war you crave is the obliteration of this notion. Now, are we to revert from human being back to ape? Dostoyevsky best understood the predicament in which we find ourselves." İhsan returned his glass to the table without drinking from it. "The war that you desire will take us there. After two more world wars, nothing will remain of culture or civilization. We'll lose the ideal of freedom for all eternity."

"I know that much as well. But the bankruptcy of spirit within us and the misery surrounding us, our penchant for expending men like so much fodder and the environment of fear this gives rise to . . . then just think about the calamity of people's realization that this is an obligatory part of life! All of it foretells the approach of the end of an era. We expect it, even if it proves to be an apocalypse."

"KEEP THE CHANGE. . . ."

Adile glared scornfully at her husband, and in a soft voice that nonetheless glinted sharply and blindingly with a desire for bloodletting, hissed, "It just grows on trees, doesn't it?"

Sabih cocked an eyebrow, casting a customary look of sweetness at his wife. He knew the reason she'd be annoyed by everything for the remainder of the day. *I'll just sit in a corner and stay out of the conversation. Let our hosts put up with her!* Over the years, he'd grown accustomed to his wife the way one might get used to the quirks of an old jalopy. She stalled randomly, occasionally her brakes wouldn't catch, her gears slipped unexpectedly, and without warning she sped off full throttle. Sabih's task was to prevent the old rattletrap from causing an accident. In essence she was a fine woman; he'd grown familiar with her. And their life together was comfortable. Granted, Sabih had achieved this comfort through rather extreme sacrifices. In order to win her for himself, he'd virtually relinquished half his personality. *And I'm not quite sure one can get on in the world with just half a self.*

The phaeton driver, pleased by the tip, traced a wide arc, making the wheat-colored wicker seats and pied canopy of his carriage sparkle beneath the sunlight as he brushed past Adile. She fleetingly contemplated whether to take as a personal affront this dynamic turn made by the well-groomed horses in their spring-morning ease, and walked briskly, stepping resolutely with her heels as if she intended to pierce the asphalt that had begun to soften in the sunlight. Before her appeared a very rocky, windy, downward slope that she'd have to descend. She paused and waited for Sabih to take her arm. *In these high heels even!* She'd only yesterday purchased this pair and wasn't willing to have them torn apart on this stony path: *At least he's good for something in such circumstances!* Sabih didn't squander the opportunity presented by fate to make amends. Even though his thoughts remained on the hips of the sumptuous girl, which were exposed to the bikini line, lying out on a chaise longue on the veranda of the roadside house, he didn't neglect to gently squeeze his wife's arm with provocative pressure and mastery gained from thirteen years of experience. *In any case, we're paying a social visit.* . . . And he slowly whispered into her ear: "Mümtaz's life's in peril. . . . What d'you think?" He had no doubt about the effect this single statement would make upon Adile. He knew quite well that presently his wife's face was convulsing in a multitude of small tremors like an oyster squirted with lemon. And simply to compensate for the torment that he'd intentionally inflicted, he continued squeezing Adile's arm, however much his affection for his wife was limited to such gestures. "In peril! Because it was certain that Nuran had a soft spot for Mümtaz as well." With hard-heartedness determined to take the torment to its extreme limit, he abruptly added, "Or did they meet each other long beforehand and were just playing us for fools?"

"In all honesty, I don't know, but I doubt it. . . . Is there any trace of such cunning in those two? Not to mention, why should they even attempt such a charade?"

"But were you paying attention? The little girl also noticed."

"Naturally, the unfortunate dear!" And Adile, her heart in shreds out of compassion for Nuran's daughter, hung on to Sabih with the weight of her entire corpus. "What's strange is that at the first chance Nuran was able to step into a cozy cadence with a fiancé . . . strange creatures these women, my word. . . . I swear that poor fool Mümtaz is senselessly snaring trouble for himself."

Sabih felt a peculiar affection toward Mümtaz. Meanwhile, running over the strategies for calculating distances that his driving instructor had imparted to him, he gauged the remaining distance between their present locale and the entryway of the house that marked their destination as he gently stroked Adile's forearm: "Whoa! Go easy now, dear!"

EMMA, WITH THE measured coquetry of a woman who'd assumed familiarity with the male soul, expressed her delight: "Oh, they have lobster." She was on the verge of applauding with joy. "You are aware, Fâhir, that yesterday's lobster was exceptional!" Her voice was peculiar, like a cucumber marinated in mustard, and her tongue transformed

Turkish words with jarring crispness. Despite this, she had almost no trace of an accent.

Fâhir stared at her vigorous chin and stark white teeth with alarm: "And the next course?"

She answered wearing one of her most endearing smiles: "Let's think about that after the lobster." But remembering how bored— naturally, like all Turks—the man with whom she lived grew waiting at the table for food, she added: "Maybe a schnitzel or a steak."

"Fine, a schnitzel or a steak for you." He turned toward the waiter: "Which do you recommend?"

The Greek waiter momentarily turned into Buridan's ass, immobilized between the superiority of schnitzel and the nobility of steak.

"But it won't do if you don't have any." Emma's voice verged on shattering out of compassion like a piece of glass placed in fire.

In response to this affection and its cold assault, Fâhir tensed with a shiver emanating from his coccyx.

"You absolutely must have some!" Emma insisted, displaying maternal tenderness and canny concern—for every man was partly a child in need of guidance: "And this morning you forgot to do your calisthenics!"

On the beach in Constantsa, around the time they first began these calisthenics, neither her voice nor her insistence bothered Fâhir overly much. Back then, the interest that she showed in him excited him, and he found unimaginable pleasures in this measured and controlled friendship.

"Fine, I'll have some too!" In this way, at least, he'd prevent her from talking. And with an odd determination, which she, too, noticed, he buried his head in the menu and tried to avoid seeing Emma's teeth, her sturdy body, her broad chest that defied masculine strength, and all the features of this top-notch machine of gratification that had at one time driven him mad with pleasure, and now did so with impatience and even anger.

Since returning to Istanbul, Fâhir had grown alarmed by Emma's teeth. These pearly whites, unblemished and stark, resembling a mechanism that churned incessantly inside its rather exaggerated facial housing, left him with the impression of some sort of grinder that could reduce whatever it encountered to a pulp. This grinder would pulverize the lobster and afterward chew up the Viennese schnitzel. Ever so slowly. . . .

"Wine or water?"

"*Rakı.*"

Fâhir, truly caught off guard by this request, gazed briefly in astonishment at the woman sitting opposite him. Emma, however, had lost herself in distant seas that stretched out in tropical azure between the first mimosa blooms.

"You've never had a taste for *rakı.*"

"I've gotten used to its taste now!" Then she faced Fâhir with a gaze of affection: "You are aware, I'm an Istanbulite now!"

Emma hadn't grown accustomed to *rakı* at all. And she didn't want Fâhir to drink anything, perhaps simply as an exercise of her own authority. But the encounter at the ferry landing with Nuran and, particularly, with her daughter, forced her to forgo some of her principles for a few days. In case of any eventualities, she thought it best to appear more ingratiating and docile for a spell. Until she came to better know the wealthy Swedish yachtsman whom they'd recently met, she needed Fâhir's attentions. She repeated to herself: *One month at the least.* . . . Yes, she needed to remain close with Fâhir for a month at least. And then a Mediterranean voyage on a private yacht with such distinguished guests. . . . Not to mention that it was just the season. *Athens, Sicily, Marseille.* . . . She didn't think about anything more. Because whether summer or winter, whatever the season, above all, she longed for Paris. She ought to go there, certainly. The previous trip to Paris, which she took before meeting Fâhir, was a waste. A miserable room, a humble restaurant that resembled something of a neighborhood kitchen, the tinkling of a piano coming from the next room till the evening, a few pieces of furniture bought on a limited budget. . . . Doubtless, she'd enjoyed herself immensely in carnal terms; but even for that, she could no longer stand certain deprivations. Not to mention that the time had come for her to settle down and start a family. Therefore, she didn't want to miss this opportunity. But fate always played odd tricks on Emma. This time around, it happened as well. The elderly and wealthy Swede hadn't just arrived on the scene by himself.

In tow was a young, dark youth who happened to be the yacht's captain. Worst of all, this youth behaved as if he knew all of Emma's proclivities by heart, arranging trysts for them to be alone, which she couldn't bring herself to resist, and after giving her a languorous, lingering glance with his black, olive-shaped eyes, seeing no need to stand on formality. . . . This was how it had been last night at sea. How quickly he'd taken advantage of the general state of drunkenness, the moonlit night, and the silence. Along with being angry at her own shortfalls, she was happy to recall that intimacy again, and closed her eyes.

But she didn't waste time with this vision of contentment. These were all passing fancies. She mustn't lose sight of essentials. Right now, that was Fâhir. She was quite curious about the effects of the morning encounter on him. She'd only been able to see Nuran for a minute at most, but she was instinctively and immediately jealous. Nuran exuded more beauty than she in a different, deeper way. Despite this, she wasn't curious about her; their presences were foreign to each other. What frightened Emma was the daughter herself.

"You are aware, Fâhir, you behaved atrociously with Fatma!"

Fâhir assumed a voice that she didn't recognize at all: "I know. . . ." *This is the third time! Always, "You are aware."*

He was oddly upset. Never before had he found Nuran to be as beautiful. She was neither the Nuran that he'd seen during the months of fatigue during which they'd arranged for their divorce, nor was she the fiancée who appeared like a white dream behind the mists of a decade. She was a different woman altogether, one he didn't know, a complete stranger, a lady he didn't recognize despite having lived with her for a decade. *I was so surprised that . . . I wasn't able to speak properly with Fatma. . . . I acted as if she were someone else's child.* But was this the real reason he'd behaved so coldly toward his daughter, or was it because of Emma and his fear of aggravating her? *I'm so weak that I'm susceptible to any variety of base folly. . . .*

He raised his head and was met by Emma's eyes, which seemingly read from memory everything he'd been thinking. She said: "I understand, Fâhir, if you want to make up with them. I'd never want to come between you and your daughter." And in order to emphasize the resoluteness of this decision, Emma, as if announcing a general strike in the midst of the day shift, rested her fork at the edge of her plate. Her entire face bespoke forfeit and reverence for human emotion.

With a habit that came from a lifetime of only pitying herself, her expression changed and contorted.

Emma never asked. She just took. Her experiences as fallen woman had absolutely forbidden her from asking for anything outright. *Take it, grab it, lay siege, don't let it catch its breath! But above all, don't ask! This was her motto. Begin with friendship! Always be understanding and patient! A man should sense that you understand him. Then spread your wings, don't give him a chance to catch his breath . . . but ask? Never.* The rich Swede was gradually sensing in his flesh Emma's understanding, her wise compassion, and her generous companionship.

Fâhir momentarily gazed at Emma, "What does this have to do with anything, now?"

She understood that she'd made a faux pas. She shouldn't have mentioned anything about the matter! She bowed her head and continued to devour her lobster. Tonight, she had to speak in frank terms with the wealthy Swede.

For a week Fâhir had been contemplating what Emma had just suggested on her own. But he couldn't manage to decide, being too insecure, too bound to habit, and because the life into which Emma had initiated him was too unique. Not to mention that he had no idea how Nuran would react to such a proposal. Nuran had earlier given him repeated and numerous chances to make up and put the past behind them. *What's really hard is leaving Emma.* Not because he loved her, but because he'd always been a slave to his baser desires. He'd never been a man of determination, nor had he been wise enough to leave her at the right time. . . . Not to mention that Emma could display this very determination in his stead. Maybe she'd truly grown tired of him. *Who knows, maybe.* . . . He thought about what he could recollect vaguely through the drunken haze of the previous night. The South American captain's chin, hard as a straight razor, and his penetrating glances, appeared before him. For a time, he and Emma had vanished together. He couldn't manage to extricate himself from the bridge game.

Who knows, and maybe . . . and like a fresh knife wound, he suddenly recalled memories that constituted the paradise of his life; Emma's full gallop to ecstasy and the frenzied clench of wrestling holds. He raised his head in anguish. He watched, as if witnessing a genuine wonder, Emma's thirty-two teeth grinding up the lobster before her, slowly, quietly, almost as if she were reciting a poem by rote, her eyes exceptionally innocent and languid. The best course of action would be to abandon these meaningless thoughts. He raised his glass. As if to remind her unfaithful lover of the wonderful times they'd once shared, Emma awkwardly repeated the first phrase she'd learned in Turkish: *Şerefinize, efendim*, "Here's to your honor, sir."

Her eyes filled with tears of separation that she'd prepared to shed on command. And deep inside she honestly thought: *Over the entirety of my life, I've always been kicked around by people who didn't recognize my worth, haven't I? In Bessarabia, hadn't that rich landowner done this?* Granted, Emma had made another faux pas then. What call was there to sleep with a stableman, not to mention in broad daylight in the room above the stables? Indeed, her entire life had been a chain of misfortunes caused by petty mistakes and lack of foresight. But what could she be expected to do? Men were this way. The landowner, instead of firing his servant, chased her out. The stablehand had pursued her nonetheless. Her fiancé had also left her on account of a similar fiasco. Even if it hadn't transpired exactly the same way, it was a close approximation. But that time she wasn't to blame. Her prospective brother-in-law was so much younger than Mihael, they had three sisters between them.

"If it's all right with you, Emma, let's not go anywhere tonight, okay?"

"As you wish, Fâhir. . . . You are aware, I'm also quite exhausted, last night. . . ." But there was no need to discuss the previous night.

As soon as the words had left her mouth, she blushed crimson. Would they really be staying in tonight? She returned to her lobster in the wretchedness of having to spend the whole evening alone with Fâhir.

Fâhir stared at his mistress with astonishment. This was the first time since they'd met that he'd heard Emma complain of fatigue. *And what if I don't actually leave her, that is, what if she doesn't leave and go away!* he thought.

"You are aware, Fâhir, you've changed considerably. . . ."

But Fâhir wasn't listening. He'd become fixated on the popped button of the waiter's frock. A popped button could at times be a lifesaver. The space of the missing button gave his thoughts unexpected liberty, just like that. *Seeing that I'm actually annoyed by these creatures known as the fairer sex, for whatever reason do I bother myself with their company?*

SABIH'S AUNT WAS a portly lady whose visage emanated decency and *joie de vivre*. For thirty-five years she'd suffered the tribulations of an asthmatic and ornery husband whose temperament altered hour to hour; one by one she'd paid off his debts, the whys and hows of which she was ignorant, and raised four children whose dispositions and morals, her husband in mind, she couldn't trust; nevertheless, she'd married the children off one after another, helped them buy homes and settle down, and now her sole occupation was entertaining visitors in her parlor. In her youth, due to her husband's temperament, she'd nearly pined away for friendships with other young women. For the past seven years, she'd invited countless guests to her house, serving them all the delicacies of a cuisine, the secrets to which very few ladies were privy.

She greeted Adile and Sabih, whom she quite admired, right before the garden gate.

"Where on earth have you been, dearest? I've long been expecting you." She felt for one of her triple-tiered pendant earrings. On such days, Sabriye never failed to wear these earrings, which were a gift from her beloved mother-in-law. Since one of the earring's middle pendants had snapped off, she'd tied it back together with a piece of thread. And since she feared losing the large diamond and small ruby that it held fast, she checked it every second. As Sabih kissed his aunt on the cheeks, he looked at the roof of the old gardener's shed; it was still in the same state of collapse as three years ago. Sabriye had no concept of repair or upkeep. In any case, what snapped off and got lost was of a different order than what caved in.

"I've prepared such delicacies for you." Turning to Sabih: "And your dietetic meal is also waiting."

Adile regarded her husband's abruptly puckered face without concealing her delight.

"Bless your heart, Auntie," she said. "I was terrified he'd eat something that would disagree with him and make him ill." Rather than trepidation, her voice quavered with joy.

"My dear girl, would I ever forget about his health? He's my one and only dear Sabih." Adile, contented with this assurance, walked toward the veranda humming the tango she'd learned a few nights earlier. Sabih was simply up in arms. *I'll show you*, he fumed. *I'll show you all!* And he decided to explain to them from A to Z the recent articles he'd read about the question of Poland in light of German economic exigencies. At length he would be avenged; this was a point definitely settled.

Had they restrained from plaguing him with a dietetic meal, he would have related what he knew about the life cycles of seals. These sea creatures led lives of true fascination. Indeed, as he read what was written about them in *Lu* magazine, he pondered: *It's as if they're fish in the sea and mammals on land.* But now he would mention neither seals nor the unconventional beliefs of the Eskimos—of the puppy that assumed the status of a grandfather because it was born at the exact time of an elder's demise. Now, then, in light of this abrupt announcement about diets, he'd been forced into the sphere of German industry and economy. Scorn welling up within him, and no longer worrying about the possibility of the large diamond pendant falling and getting lost, Sabih glanced at his aunt's ear again. All of his detailed information would flow into that funnel projecting at a forty-five-degree angle from the skull! For long years Sabih had used newspaper accounts as something of a means of compliment or commendation. One day, however, while relating a story of this variety to one of Adile's admirers and habitués to the house, his young interlocutor first yawned to declare his impatience and then stood and left, and Sabih quickly realized that everybody's response to world affairs didn't resemble his own. From that moment onward, he'd labored to all but perfect the impact of this "weapon," which his keen memory and plentiful free time helped him develop.

On the veranda, as always, there were seven or eight other guests. All of Sabriye's children had left the house, surrendering all their friends to her. They were all there: Yaşar, her oldest son's piquet* partner, who was also Nuran's cousin; Nuriye, her oldest daughter's sister-in-law; İffet, who'd introduced her middle son to gambling, causing him to forgo his studies while he himself finished first in engineering school;

---

* Piquet: A card game for two players.

and her youngest daughter's high school chum Muazzez. Sabriye had long grown accustomed to filling the void left by her own children, who rarely visited, with this group of surrogates.

As soon as Adile stepped onto the veranda, she exclaimed, "Oh my, Yaşar is with us as well. What a pleasant coincidence, my fine gentleman!"

Yaşar combed his prematurely gray hair with his hand and wiped his glasses clean. Next he greeted Adile with full and proper etiquette. He, at the very least, was a man who was familiar with European customs.

"We were just now together with your cousin Nuran. Oh, how dainty she was, you should have seen her." Then she turned to Sabriye. "And Mümtaz was there, too."

Sabriye harbored great affection for Mümtaz because he'd found her grandfather's name and biography listed in the *Sicill-i Osmanî* biographical register of renowned Ottomans. Informing her by telephone that he'd found the entry, which her late husband had promised to locate for exactly thirty years, on the day after she'd brought it up—Sabriye gave particular import to the fact that this musty, bygone account had been conveyed by telephone—struck her as nothing less than miraculous.

"My word, why didn't you bring him along? I haven't seen him for months, it's a shame really. You see, Muazzez is here as well."

Sabih wanted to forestall the matter before his wife had her chance: "We knew that he was going to meet up with his friends and so we didn't insist."

Muazzez stood from the chaise longue in which she'd been reclining: "Apparently, Suad is ill. He came back to Istanbul for a week, and he's here at the sanatorium. He was going to meet up with them as well. I saw him on my way here."

Surprised that this entire horde had been transported here by the morning ferries, Sabih nevertheless commiserated: "How unfortunate. . . . What's he have, I wonder? I mean, is it serious?" *No, tuberculosis isn't such a serious illness; one just needs to eat and drink nutritiously. My own illness, now that is truly serious. I am forced to diet.* In no time at all, within the torment of eating buttered zucchini and carrots, Sabih would verge on being jealous of the disease afflicting Suad—for practically everyone Suad encountered would advise him to eat heartily, partake of rich foods, pastries, grilled meat. . . . Eat well and you'll be as good as new! *Now then, this Muazzez is an anomaly. How does she know all of this? Wherefrom? How did she learn it all?*

Had it been another day, Adile would have been rather upset at hearing of Suad's affliction. Few people were as peppy as he was and understood the feminine soul as well. But at this instant, just when she was about to let the cat out of the bag about Mümtaz and Nuran, to Muazzez and Yaşar nonetheless, the mention of Suad was an obstacle for which she had no patience. Like a well-trained racehorse, Adile hurdled this unexpected barrier: "To tell the truth, it's not that I didn't consider it. . . . But he was so consumed with Nuran that we couldn't get a word in edgewise." And she glanced at Yaşar out of the corner of her eye. She knew quite well that he'd long had affections for Nuran and that he was jealous of her attentions. Not to mention that he'd played a very devious role in her separation from Fâhir by facilitating the relationship between Fâhir and Emma while relaying the daily developments of their affair to Nuran. Yaşar's face turned ashen.

He nearly stuttered: "They've known each other for some time, you say?"

Adile answered in a state of virtual ecstasy, "No, *we* introduced them to each other." Then she turned to face Sabriye and added, "Auntie dearest, you should have seen how they twittered and chirped! Honestly, it pleased me no end. You know, it wouldn't be such a bad turn after all! There's a bit of an age difference, but. . . ."

Sabih gawked at his wife in astonishment. In Muazzez's company, she shouldn't have ventured such deceit. Dearest Muazzez was so much younger than the rest of them. "Who is this Mümtaz character anyway?"

"He's a faculty assistant in our department at the university." Muazzez shook her hair in the sunlight, squinting. *He's conceited. . . .* Her eyes were fixed perpetually on the large stars of Holland in the garden. *Bright red, bright red.* Then she unexpectedly changed her thoughts: "We like him very much, you see." She was crestfallen, quite so. She'd come here because she'd learned from Mümtaz himself that he'd be coming to the island. But she'd missed him on the ferry. *So then, this very turn of events. . . .* She glared with spite at Adile from behind the lashes of half-lowered eyelids.

"My good fellow, how could you ever forget him? You know your father's friend Ihsan, yes? It's his cousin. You've seen him at our place countless times!"

But Yaşar had completely forgotten about Mümtaz. From inside the house, the clock chimed one thirty. Time for his tablets. For Yaşar, even the possibility of Nuran's marriage to another man couldn't make him forget his pills. He produced a small vial from his pocket. He carefully removed the stopper; tilting the vial slightly, he dispensed two tablets onto the packaging tissue without touching them.

"Have them bring some water." Then he turned to Sabih. "Incredible boost, my friend," he said. "Vitamins. Since I've started taking them I feel much better and more robust."

Sabih missed the glint of ridicule and contempt in Adile's eyes.

SAIT FAIK ABASIYANIK

(1906—1954)

Such a Story

Translated from the Turkish by Joseph S. Jacobson

WHEN I LEFT the movie, the rain had started again. What was I going to do? I cursed; I swore a blue streak. I really did want to take a walk. A passing *dolmuş** driver called, "Atikali, Atikali!"

Shall I go to Atikali at this hour of the night? I'll go. I climbed in beside the driver and off we went over hill and dale. With red, yellow, green, and other lights reflecting off the car's steamy, dripping windows, we arrived at Atikali in a wave of color.

If I walked a hundred steps from the Bomonti stop in Şişli, I'd be home, snug in the hollow of my two-blanket bed, thinking of my friend, Panço. For the time being, I had no one else. My mother lay ill in bed on one of the Istanbul islands. Under her bed, my black dog kept watch over her and waited for me. Panço lives on a street named Çilek. He dreams of soccer matches or playing cards. I'm in Atikali after midnight on a rainy night, on so-called boulevard. I walk; it rains. Yes, the rain, solitude, and Atikali are certainly right. When I'm away, I miss my mother, Panço, and my dog Blackie even more.

The three of them sleep. My mother is snoring; Blackie awakens, his ears on the street; but Panço isn't dreaming, I just made it up.

In the rain, thinking of two people and one animal, I turn into Atikali's unfamiliar streets. The watchman's whistle is blowing. Someone bursts out of a house as if crazy and jumps on me.

"Man, I killed my girlfriend," he cries. "Hide me!"

I point to my overcoat pocket, wet from rain seeping through the

---

* *Dolmuş*: Shared taxi.

314

seams and smelling of sesame from the *simit** I ate this morning. He goes into the pocket and vanishes.

"What's your name?" I call to my pocket.

"Hidayet."

"Why did you kill, Hidayet?"

"Brother, I was in love!"

"How much in love, Hidayet?"

"Like crazy, brother! Dawn broke with her! I sell sesame *helva* daytimes. Brother, your pocket smells sweet like *simits*. With her at dawn; with her at dusk; there's never a minute I don't think of her. Man, I was living in a dream. Every word, come what may, depended on her. People said something to me, I wondered what answer she would give. If I was going to buy something, I wondered if she would buy it. If I ate something, I would not be able to enjoy it to the full. If someone asked the way, first I would ask myself if she would help, and as long as she didn't point the way inside me, I would stare sheepishly. If I saw something nice and didn't show it to her, I got no pleasure from it, because I hadn't shown it to her."

"What was her name?"

"Pakize."

"And then, Hidayet?"

"Then, brother . . . then it got dark. I left my tray of sesame *helva* at the coffeehouse and hurried to drink two glasses of wine. I don't know if that pimp of a bartender put in some opium, or what, but as soon as I drank, Pakize stood before me, alive and warm."

"Really?"

"No, man, pretending, daydreaming! I'd keep on talking."

"Quiet, somebody's coming, Hidayet."

Hidayet crouched in my pocket like a sesame grain.

The rain had stopped. It seemed as if dawn were starting to break a little.

Hidayet called from my pocket: "Shall I tell the rest, brother?"

"Don't! This much is enough."

"OK, man, I'm quiet. Whatever you want, man. But tell Panço about me, OK?"

---

* *Simit*: A ring-shaped breakfast bread sold on the streets of Turkey.

"I'll tell him, Hidayet."

"But the rest is nicer, brother."

"I'll make up the rest, Hidayet. Come out of my pocket. My overcoat's wet and I can't carry both of you; I'm tired."

"OK, brother."

The sesame grain in my pocket turned into a flea. He hopped under the nettle tree in the Fatih Mosque courtyard. A spark in the darkness . . . he shone like a black spark.

I sighed. I felt rested and merry. I was going to tell Panço a tall story; Hidayet had stuck a long spike into Pakize's heart. He had no other way out. Women and children who ate sesame *helva* wouldn't expect such a story from Hidayet. Sesame *helva* doesn't fill the stomach. Pakize had told the sesame *helva* merchant, "I can't marry you." He loved her. Does love fill the stomach? That evening, Hidayet had got all decked out. He went to Taksim. He had eighteen *lira*, thirty-seven *kuruş* in his pocket. He entered a bar, drank and drank. The drinks went to Hidayet's head. This meant that from now on when he would look at the minaret, he wouldn't be able to watch, together with Pakize, the way the minaret's crescent-topped spire rose to the sky on a cloudless, moonlit night. When a poor woman asked, "Is this the way to Hırkaışerif?" she disappeared under a yellow wool sweater in his head. And if he asked Pakize the same question, saying, "Is it this road or the other? I don't know, Fatma Hanım!"* she would smile in the poor woman's face and say the same thing, wouldn't she?

Pakize, who smelled like fur, cats, like fine muslin and handkerchiefs . . . he would never be able to put his head on her knees.

Hey! Who had put this spike in his pocket? Wasn't it that bastard Abdullah? That nice guy, that freckled, dark, duck-nosed centerhalfback soccer player with the Black Tiger Club, Abdullah. He must have placed the spike. Why the hell would that bastard, who left half a movie ticket, half a stadium ticket, toothbrush, monkey wrench, broken Yale lock, spermaceti candle, chewing gum, wormy cherries, soap, melon seeds, onions, and garlic, also place a spike? A big boat spike, shiny bright too, and thin as an awl. A story ready for Panço.

"What are you doing around here at midnight, friend?"

* Hanım: Turkish for Ms. or Mrs.

"Went to visit a friend, returning, stayed late."

"Where do you live?"

"In Şişli."

They searched me. I had sixty-seven *lira*, thirty *kuruş* in addition to my pen, a story typescript, picture of Panço, and another pen.

"Don't you have your ID card on you?"

"No!"

"What do you do?"

"I write."

"What kind of writing, are you a clerk?"

"I'm a clerk."

"For whom?"

"Kocaeli, at the İkbal Warehouse."

How come I suddenly thought of that and abruptly said Kocaeli İkbal Warehouse?

"Come on, on your feet. Don't walk at night, you're an old man."

I'm walking along the border of Fatih Park, Panço. A man sits on the wet ground, his legs stretched out, his head leaning against the iron border fence of the park.

He was yelling, "Long live democracy, long live the nation, long live the republic!"

"Long live my friend," I said.

"Sit down beside me," he said.

I sat. Oh man! It really was comfortable. Nice and wet, cool.

"I have a wife, friend. If you saw her face, you'd run away as far as you could. I have a daughter. Allah grant her to someone like you. Are you married? If you're married, get a divorce and marry my daughter. She's blind in one eye, the other looks askew at God. She has a nose that wears out any snuff kerchief. Her mucus smells, her handkerchief smells, she smells herself. You can't stand her. Her monthly smells terrible. I have a son, nineteen years old, smells of piss. As for the house— may it not happen to you—it smells like a toilet. O great Allah! Look at these stones. Shiny clean. Look at this iron fence painted green! Hard, yes hard, but with the sweet smell of paint and rain. These lawns. These clouds, look at these passing black, yellow, red, blond, brunette clouds. Look at those lamps, which grow, open up like stars, and fill my eyes with arrows with sharp tips! Look at this apartment, washed from one end to the other! It's cold, it's rainy. Clean and odorless, I lie in light and water, among clouds, under the universe."

I leaned my head against the bars. So what if my bottom was in water? The cosmos was playing unimaginable games above my head. Vapor becomes water. Water cleans the mud and filth, makes the grass green, the trees grow. What business did I have at home? "Stay here. Don't go home. Let's lie down here. Let's sleep. Wait, first let's light a cigarette.

"Look at the flame on this match, this match that first fizzles, then says damn it, I'll burn. Is this possible, friend? Laugh, enjoy, friend. Look at the smoke coming out of our mouths! See how it flies! You're alive, sir. Sparkling wet droplets. You live like grass, crystal chandeliers, flowered glassware, my friend. Look at our smoke, our cigarette smoke, sir! What's this blue stuff? What's this stuff that kindles a person's heart with joy and pleasure? Not sleeping with a woman, drinking wine, playing cards with friends, theater, or seeing movies . . . leave all to one side, and just watch the world. Look, my dear friend! Here's a match flame for you. Here's cigarette smoke for you! Well, let's go to sleep, friend.

"Ha, before you sleep, tell Panço about me. About the man asleep leaning against the iron fence of Fatih Park and his cigarette smoke. Panço's a good boy. Lovable. Say hello to him for me."

It's a good thing I bought these shoes. Thank God my feet don't absorb water. I'm wet all over. My feet have central heating. I walked away, singing, "My cigarette smoke, no faith in the beloved, I built a kiosk of gold with silver stairs." He called after me, "Well done! Did you see? Does the world exist? Panço's friend! Faik Bey's son."

I sat on the walls of Zeyrek.* Before me, Vefa† Atatürk Boulevard was deserted; *jinns* played ball there. Wind blew clouds from tower to tower. "Long live soccer matches," I said. I wanted to decide from which side I'd get off the wall—I had taken dope only one time in my life, in Bursa. While sitting on the wall in the courtyard of the Green Mosque writing poems about the Nilüfer Meadow, I became confused

---

* Zeyrek: The Molla Zeyrek Camii, the second largest mosque in Istanbul.
† Vefa: The Vefa Kilise Mosque, also in Istanbul.

as to from which side I would climb down. When I hailed a man passing by and asked, "Brother, from which side should I come down?" the poor man looked at me with fear, then smiling, took my hand and helped me down. Staring at the bill on my high school cap, he had said, "Don't do it again, young man. It's easy to get down. Someone will come and get you down. But, if you're confused about climbing up, you'll never recover!"

I no longer use such stuff, but, since then, when I climb a wall, I suddenly forget the way down.

Panço, it's always your fault. You got me into this. It's because of you I wander about in the middle of the night. You did this.

I looked . . . a sleeping dog below the wall on the hill in Zeyrek. I sat beside him. He opened his eyes. He rolled his eyes. Fearfully I patted his head. He closed his eyes. I gave him a lecture. I said, "Bug-eyes, my boy. I'm son of man. You're son of an animal. Millions of years ago, we were both maggots, we were worms, we were one-celled creatures. Before that, we were dust in empty space. Then, look, we came to this condition. From now on, maybe we'll remain like this. You're unfortunate and so are we. There are those sleeping at home, some sleeping in silk, some sleeping with women, and house dogs sleeping curled up by the stove. They have rubber bones and balls. Ladies throw them and they fetch. Mornings, doormen take them for a walk. There are people who take their loved ones in their arms at this hour, lost in twosome dreams. Very well, what should we do? But you're a tailless, mangy, street dog shivering on that hill; I'm Panço's friend, nothing else, a poor man soaked by rain, sleepless, exhausted, his heart on Çilek Street, his head on a dirty pillow a hundred meters from the Bomonti streetcar stop. What shall I do? Let's think about living some day in a world made of friendship, with hearts beating with duty and feeling, and people and animals and trees and birds and lawns. We'll have a morality never written in a book. A morality that looks in surprise at what we do now and what we'll do in the future, what we think now and what we will think. Then we'll have a longer friendship, Bug-eyes. Then, don't worry. My friend Panço will agree. He won't talk about church morality. He'll tell his children about the extraordinary beauty of friendship."

I came across the man on the Atatürk Bridge. His two hands clutched the railing; he was retching into the Golden Horn.* I stood beside him. Three times he stood on his toes as if ready to jump. Then he stopped. Taking out my handkerchief, I wiped his face. I wiped his mouth. With my hand, I combed back the hair from his eyes. Then he returned and looked at me with two large, friendly eyes.

"I drank too much, uncle," he said.

I didn't preach to him, didn't patronize him. "Drink, young man," I said, "drink to your heart's content."

"Thank God, uncle," he said, "you're one of us."

"You used to drink a lot?" he asked.

I stuck my lower lip hard against my upper and gave two or three light slaps at the air with my right hand. You do that, Panço, and you'll know what I mean.

"It's obvious, uncle," he said, "there's no light left in your face."

I was angry. "My light's inside, my boy," I said, "shining away. My heart is full of love, full of friendship, especially tonight. Don't look for that light in the face. It's false, it deceives."

"Is that right?" he said. As he was walking away, singing over his shoulder, "Is that what they say, plump bride, is that what they say?" I grabbed him.

"No," I said, "I'm not going to let you get away. Tell me, where did you drink?"

"Where do you suppose, uncle? Let me go for God's sake. It was just a midnight chat, I've sobered up and want to go to bed. Tomorrow, I have to hitch up the carriage early. If I can't pull the wool over his eyes, the old man will raise hell. Well, you know, uncle, there's a woman living in that damn house across the way. Jewish woman. Her husband went to Ankara. She invited me. I went, we drank together. Damned if he didn't show up at midnight. He didn't care. When he saw us together, he didn't say a word, just sat down. The woman, too, didn't give a hoot: as if there was no one in the room, she served the *rakı* to me, herself, and the guy. Without saying a word, the three of us each drank seven goblets of *rakı*. 'With your permission, I have to go,' I said. 'Permission granted, sir!' she replied. His face pale, the hus-

---

* Golden Horn: An inlet of the Bosphorus Strait in Istanbul.

band said in perfect Turkish, 'To good fortune!' I split. I don't know what happened later in the house."

"Oh, mother!" I said.

"Yeah, oh, mother!" responded the young, handsome rascal of a coachman.

The two of us, crossing the Atatürk Bridge in opposite directions, arrived on opposite sides of the Golden Horn.

When I reached Azapkapı, I heard him yell from Unkapanı.

"Oh, mother!"

In this way, Panço, I came to your neighborhood and the rain began again. Right in front of your house there was a broken water jug, half in pieces, half in good shape. I sat in the jug. I started to tell how I went to Atikali one midnight, how Hidayet got into my pocket, the man sleeping in Fatih Park, the street dog, and the Jewish woman's womanizing coachman.

You were asleep.

"Hey, Panço, Panço!" I called.

My voice penetrated a window. It went in and found your ear. You awoke. But I no longer had the voice or strength to reach you. You fell asleep again. A car was passing by.

"Are you going to Bomonti, brother?" I asked.

"Jump in!" he said.

I jumped in.

MELIH CEVDET ANDAY

(1915—2002)

Selected Poems

Translated from the Turkish by Talat Sait Halman

The Battle of Kadesh[*]

On one of the banks of River Orontes
Mutawallis[†] stood among his soldiers
And stared without stirring.
On the opposite bank, the Pharaoh
Ramses had mounted his chariot:
He stared straight ahead.
This is all we know about it.
Even though history tells it at length
This is all we know about it.
This look is all that remains or can remain.

I Became a Tree

I was going under a tree
It happened in a flash
I fell apart from myself
And became a poppy flower
Bending in the sun,
Tortoise shell, house of wedding
Delirious talk, bevy of names.

[*] Battle of Kadesh: Battle between the Egyptian and Hittite Empires in the thirteenth century BCE.
[†] Mutawallis: Commander of Hittite forces.

I turned into the petal that drags
The wind like a blind God,
I became the century.
A tiny moment like a bug.
I was going under a tree
I became a tree
That propels itself
And saw someone stuck in the ground.

Barefoot

The top part of this piece of writing
Couldn't be read; no one knows who wrote it either.
Never mind, what matters is the words, not the sound.
". . . Then I ate whatever I found in the house:
Bread, almonds, dill.
Barefoot I jumped on the horse,
The wine of the morning was raving mad
So I dashed through the people and went away
Full gallop."

Are We Going to Live Without Aging?

At dawn, a throng came out
Of the skies: Convex shields, glittering
Tattoos, a rose, a daggered
Heart, bows of wheat,
Aquariums emptying out, a king,
A turkey's crest, a fresh corpse,
Brass-footed horses, a wine in a glazed jug
Waiting to be poured into the sea.
A tumult arose from the roots of the trees,
Eyeless monsters emerged from the sea.
What's that? Should we believe in rapacious beaks?
Or in thin axes, in grass burned at night
Or in tree-shaped wings?

I pay no heed to clouds, I don't care
If they go south along the river
Or to the slow lakes set afire by towers.
Let them go. . . . Are we going to live without aging?
Come, let's go and see the dawn's spider.

ORHAN VELI KANIK
(1914–1950)

Selected Poems

Translated from the Turkish by
Talat Sait Halman
Murat Nemet-Nejat

Exodus I

From his window overlooking the roofs
The harbor was in sight
Church bells
Tolled all day long.
From his beds the trains could be heard
From time to time
And at night.
He loved a girl
Who lived in the house across the street.
Be that as it may,
He left this town
And moved to another.

Translated by Talat Sait Halman

I Am Listening to Istanbul

I am listening to Istanbul with my eyes closed
First a breeze is blowing
And leaves swaying
Slowly on the trees;
Far, far away the bells of the

Water carriers ringing,
I am listening to Istanbul with my eyes closed.

I am listening to Istanbul with my eyes closed
A bird is passing by,
Birds are passing by, screaming, screaming,
Fish nets being withdrawn in fishing weirs,
A woman's toe dabbling in water,
I am listening to Istanbul with my eyes closed.

I am listening,
The cool Grand Bazaar,
Mahmutpasha twittering
Full of pigeons,
Its vast courtyard,
Sounds of hammering from the docks,
In the summer breeze far, far away the odor of sweat,
I am listening.

I am listening to Istanbul with my eyes closed
The drunkenness of old times
In the wooden seaside villa with its deserted boat house
The roaring southwestern wind is trapped,
My thoughts are trapped
Listening to Istanbul with my eyes closed.

I am listening to Istanbul with my eyes closed
A coquette is passing by on the sidewalk,
Curses, songs, songs, passes;
Something is falling from your hand
To the ground,
It must be a rose.
I am listening to Istanbul with my eyes closed.

I am listening to Istanbul with my eyes closed
A bird is flying round your skirt;
I know if your forehead is hot or cold
Or your lips are wet or dry;
Or if a white moon is rising above the pistachio tree
My heart's fluttering tells me . . .
I am listening to Istanbul with my eyes closed.

Translated by Murat Nemet-Nejat

OKTAY RIFAT
(1914–1988)

Selected Poems

*Translated from the Turkish by Ruth Christie
and Richard McKane*

Agamemnon[*] I

1.

Leaving the ships to be scraped we trudged on, and reached a valley; each of us rolled a cigarette with fingers gnarled or missing.

A smoke killed time as we crouched and leant against the rocks.

The quickest way to kill time! It gets less and less or ends for good. Or then again, it expands against the pull of earth and the northeaster! Panting like squirrels, suspicious, always suspicious!

Whatever is ours is behind the mountain. But they are there, running away in the sudden flight of a partridge, or in a lizard's glance, in every hole and under every stone.

They turned their fiery, sharp, savage weapons of destruction against us, cowardly with their long-shadowed spears, murderous as their guns or mortars, shells and bazookas.

Just when we say they can't increase, they do! Their faces are like ours but inside their armor are gods, their luminous eyes terrifying!

[*] Agamemnon: Commander of the Achaean forces in the Trojan War.

"What have we done wrong?" we asked, "can someone tell us our crime?" We know the weight of guilt. Our backs bent double under this rock, our teeth blackened with this water.

If we must end up in hospital wards or in prison cells, or be sold dirt-cheap in the labor market, so be it!

From behind the barbed wire let's look at someone taking random instant photographs of the white muslin over the copper yoghurt vessel, or the huge Prison full of light!

In the evening the water in our jug is finished and perched on stone, or sometimes concrete, our birds all fly away.

One piece of *lokum** remains on the rose-patterned plate—God knows how! The fruit on the branch consumes night for us.

Yes, for us! Agamemnon laughs at this. Diomedes[†] belts on his swords to become the icon of deathless epics.

We walked on, crushing the reeds and arrived at the valley; smoking, we leant against the ancient rocks.

We crouch on the earth—dear earth!—but they stand upright— *chacun à son goût!*[‡] They say they are descended from gods and their mansions have courtyards and fountains;

They play poker to the death on their rigged tables, they stack the cards and throw their bone chips for results,

They drink water from silver cups—blessed water!—we from the hollow of our hands. They have the fingers of cheats, ours are bony and workworn,

---

* *Lokum*: Turkish delight, a chewy candy.
† Diomedes: Famed Achaean warrior in the Trojan War.
‡ *Chacun à son goût*: French, "each to his own taste."

They fall and bleed like rotten rowan trees and ache all night long. And we mount the oxcarts to move away. The mountain path is easier at night.

We wait for the sparsely feathered farm-bird to sing; but from a distance the little bastard is silent on our tree.

They turned their fiery, sharp, savage weapons against us, with their long-shadowed cruel spears, murderous as guns and mortars, shells and bazookas!

We pruned the tree-trunks, thinned the tobacco seedlings, hoed the cotton automatically, how can we stop caring for them?

Our wives like deer with young, humbled, sweaty, some with a hoe or a sickle, poppies on the plain bleeding inwardly.

It's evening, white as sheep's wool the Pole Star is born, a rustling tremor moves mountain and rock. When it says, "Come!" you must up and leave, impossible not to leave!

Rainbows between two ages, great absorbent waterspouts moving in darkness, gushing skyward with rocks and earth,

And naked babies, village huts like leeches clinging to a barren mountainside, no windows, no tiles, made of poverty-stricken, sundried mudbricks.

2.

They struck us through the chest, they drilled a hole of destiny between our breasts! Back and breast became one, flesh bleeding through and through.

They struck us in the back, between the shoulders, the wind-fed spears pierced our necks, all hopes trembled on a branch of time.

They struck us through our hips, our bladders! Bronze clashed with bone, bone finally cracked with a human cry.

They struck us through the back of our necks! Their spears clove the root of our tongues. Our mouths filled with our teeth. Biting the bloody bronze with our palates!

They dragged us to hooks and ropes, loosened our hair to the wind, our untouched dreams still budding in our bosoms.

They buried us in fresh graves that we dug before we died, they lined us up against trees and walls and shot us all down at the same time.

They were many and had Diomedes at their head, but we had Helenos and Sarpedon[*] on our side, masters of every kind of warfare.

Agamemnon, you are with them, Priam and Hector[†] with us. If they are many and owl-eyed Athena backs them, what can we do!

Who's to blame if they die? If they submit quietly to night and lose their lives in all their fineness, new generations will arise and sing the songs behind the mountain,

> So the sail can be furled all day with song,
> So if water wants the sea it can reach it,
> Or if it wants it can end on the plain,
> So the *lokum* can remain on the rose-patterned plate.

---

* Helenos and Sarpedon: Trojan warriors.
† Priam and Hector: The king and prince, respectively, of Troy.

3.

They turned their fiery, sharp, savage weapons against us and with all their daggers drove us panic-stricken to the black loaves of bread.

In exile now, we were being wasted beyond the beyond. The flat bread not enough for us!

This is the fastest way to vanish; to crumble away bit by bit, to be lost forever. You say you are black seed, we are Phoenicians.

Further, they shout, further, to tales of desperation. Even if we cower in hollows of religion, further still! To vanish far away.

When they want to pluck us and cast us away, no one cares! Their mansions have fountains, they have prisons and hospital wards within.

They stick masks on our face, of tragedy or comedy. We have no mirrors to see ourselves in.

They thrust us into patched breeches, our women into black robes and empty us out into the city squares and stations. We looked nervously out of the windows, all the time suspicious, jumpy as squirrels.

They erase from under us the very earth we tread on! They blind us with hot irons. Go to the furthest beyond! Always behind bars, on stone or concrete.

They deprive us of sunlight and trees; they strip our arms of their ability to work and push us, push us away: to live shameless and reduced to fewer and fewer.

But it is we who invented time! The god Zeus sees us, silent on his throne untroubled on our behalf, swifter than lightning, finer than the abundant rain.

Yes, it is we who invented time! We sowed and reaped, we established the hourglass with plow and sickle; gradually the first notch in the bark deepened.

From the seamless rock we took the axe and fire. With the best-quality clay we molded the white-socked horses. We breathed love into nature.

We walked, we walked on to the sea to add the summons of the horizon to its phosphorescence and we whetted heavenly copper with the salt of dreams.

Therefore our trees blossom separately, the day of the plum and the almond are different, for our days are different;

As for them, they roll down a barren timeless mountain, pile up and lose control, strike mountain and stone, and foam in vain.

4.

All roads lead to loneliness in the sea's flank—my Beloved Sea! We came to the misty domes and suddenly battle began.

Like day, belief in death dawned, gleaming at the point of the spears, and heroism in the bloodsoaked square looked out for anything suspicious.

Broad daylight crouched in the mountain caves, the plain gathered its courage to its skirts, trees lay in mist, pain flowed on, wordless, reluctant.

Every day the waves begin again, rough and rocking, morning and evening we're sick for home.

Those strange, idle horses, lashing out at the purple clouds, clearly indifferent to us, immortal steeds, stallions of the sky.

Cartridge belts filled and emptied with loss and waste, horn and drum played the music of death, continually sinking and swelling.

And the sharp tongues of wolves, licking at stagnant black water, belching death, sated on sticky liquid.

When discharged from service, we rest on the railings of the deep-bellied ships and throw a knapsack on our shoulder and set off on our way.

When we suddenly lay down the stretched bow, and light fails, when we abandon the winch and our longing dies, we mix time with Samian wine and stay with the earthenware pot.

Let us linger a little, linger at the happy feast and lower our masks of tragedy or comedy from their staffs to the brightly worked *kilims*.*

They turned their fiery, sharp, savage weapons against us and herded us toward the black bread.

But the cassava tree grows heavy with fruit, a beautiful tree, grafted from legends, red and green, unfailingly tracing the four seasons.

Some write our fate on our brow, fearful, crosswise, crooked in every detail, painful and absurd!

---

* *Kilim*: A traditional Turkish flatweave rug.

If we erase it, will the Writing of Clay, the main writing, the powerful Iambus* appear?

If we break off as we prune with our few distorted hands the large-eyed almond trees, will the thread of life spun by the three Armed Fates unravel?

5.

We sprayed them with bullets, we were defeated; the hungry mill of the *bayram*† revolves with blood. This head, or tail, or spleen! If this is a welcome by the gods, what can we do?

We gnawed and grew warm; a hyena stuck out his tongue, upright compared with a human's licking the stagnant black water, belching death, sated on red liquid.

The green of a lark's idleness! We buried tender maidens for the barren kings. The gods, the large-eyed, horned gods, our gold-toothed pirates!

If this is how we make peace with loneliness, woe betide us! Blessings and fire fail to appear, the present crouches before great and small, our rope ladders swing in emptiness.

We look through the lenses of eyelashes that grow dull and close before they open again, different cattle low, different horses neigh.

They piss on the warm earth, squatting like humans, smelling tree and earth, they howl and rave in their own lands; they insist on the meaningless joy of living.

---

* Iambus: A metrical foot consisting of a short syllable followed by a long one.
† *Bayram*: Muslim holiday.

Occasionally they look us in the face, before they divide land and sea. Irresponsible perhaps, but always lofty, supreme. It's clear that they regard us as one with the Great Nobodaddy.*

They have balanced on a perch in the past; if we knock they won't open their doors; their outer and inner are the same; they are long-haired and panicky like us.

So we knew them as gods, we killed and ate them, for what, to feel what, we don't know!

Blood and bullets gushing from the earth, anger howling in the midst of our cholera, a single seagull-feather, turning and turning as it falls in the salty water.

They whinnied and neighed and, most frightening of all, were silent, on the road that passed through spring to loneliness, crowding close to ever-multiplying deaths.

They lie down in the sunny bee-laden meadow of days, in their blood the full force of May, suddenly more leafy and lively in the windmill of green.

Wrists fettered by war: the sands and sea of war! The halo wastes away, fades as war darkens.

If we sink the spear in earth, it grows green, bronze-tipped it's hard to hold: so many leaves in the half-closed eyes of the plain, dazzled with May;

So many tumbling clouds, so much rain splashing on stones, emptying and slipping from the hand of war and want; nibbling the sunny, bee-laden grass.

---

* The Great Nobodaddy: A reference to an absent God from William Blake's poem "To Nobodaddy."

With even more powerful guns they overwhelmed the women, hopeless as though fettered by fire, charging with the speed of water's emptiness,

In the most terror-stricken period, they began in May and fell, completely fell, long-necked, gradually laying their heads down on the nettle-filled pillow of Night.

Defeated, worse than defeated, alive and crippled, worse than dead, lopped off, fiercely ripped out of the earth.

But when we sink the spear it grows green: bronze-tipped it's hard to hold: so many leaves in the half-closed eyes of the plain, dazzled with May.

In so many yellows, the yellow of ages, and so many greens, a somersault of greens, in the greenest of days, right to Mount Ida.*

Agamemnon II

Had to go. Had to wait. Had to look at men, vehicles, roads.

A garden below, within us, scorched by autumn winds, untended; trees unpruned, bug-ridden.

Why squat by the side of ditches? Something that never ends, why keep silent as though it is finished?

Had to be silent in the great tumult, get up at an ungodly hour, at the hour when birds fall.

Had to talk, pick up the fallen birds. Why were they fated to fall and never meet night?

---

* Mount Ida: "The Mountain of the Goddess" in Greek mythology. There are two Mount Idas, one on Crete and one in Turkey.

Our man smiled with his few teeth. He talked Kurdish in a whisper. He talked bad Phrygian.*

A wolf was gnawing at a piece of wood, stretched out a leg beside me, a paw alongside.

Scissors alongside, a towel right here; so many things far off, so far away.

They stay in the emptiness, like memories, gnawing at us.

Halt! Stop! Sword and spear right here! What about us? Who are we next to, who are we close to, over here?

My fingers fluttered by themselves, my left eye watching. I walked a rough line, sea farther away.

When I reach the sea the clouds come to meet me. The pebbles rattle, the heart grows big and expands!

Seagulls come and go. The back of the mountains hardens with distance and years pour from the rocks.

Exile comes and goes. The earth with its four poles, life with its four corners, becomes a ship. The surroundings dissolve: goat cheese and flat bread.

A lump in my throat. Loving comes and goes. What use are gaps between love if you don't love.

What use is so much longing, meeting if no meeting! Sleeping if no sleeping, beauty if no beauty!

---

* Phrygian: Language of the Indo-European peoples of Phrygia who lived in Anatolia (now Turkey) and were once allies of Troy.

What use this suspicion behind suspicion, this grape-eyed dog, sparse coat, ready for the scrap heap!

Had to love and miss, to look at the street from the window, to be embraced by love, but not embraced.

The rope is so sad it can break. If it breaks the person will go mad and perhaps the nets of night and day will break.

Had to gather and cry night and day. Either move in the emptiness or stop, it's all one.

Had to fight. To rise without rising, walk without walking, attack, strike.

Had to strike and not strike. Had to die. What is the use of dying if it's like dying?

Had to break the unbreakable, to sit again, eat flat bread, drink water again.

To pause just a little! Have a smoke, stretch a leg that's gone to sleep, turn lightly to one side, bend knees and stand up again!

Stand for how long? Why are your palms chafing?

"One comes, one goes!" Wait for the one who doesn't come, then rejoice, make a noise and laugh as though they had come!

Had to rejoice and laugh, the purple clouds of the god flying over the mountain peaks.

Like a peasant plowing a field the god Zeus cascades his hair over the mountains and combs it with the lightning comb.

The heart expands and swells. He's one who's not little and he tells of the big one. There's one with a profile like an immortal.

Slow as a shadow, stealthy as a snake. Squeezed into an indistinct time, between nonbeing and being. Only that man with his profile continuous, unending, never beginning, free from care and foolish.

Had to stretch and sleep. To close eyes in their nest, to empty without emptying, to stand still like standing.

What fair did I see you at? Which garden did we meet in? Did your hands slip from my palms?

Was what I wanted to think of your baggy trousers, your curls caressing my neck in this fearful dream?

Come, grow in my daylight, grow really big, grow as one grows.

Be mine without losing yourself or diminishing, be mine! Or move with morning in the emptiness, or stop, or never exist.

Had to believe without believing. Love comes and goes. Had to squat on the rocks of evening.

Had to look at the middle finger again, crooked inward; then somehow lie in the shade of a willow.

Had to carve a stick. Had to carve a thin branch.

My goats come down the forest path. The waters gone black. It must be evening.

Is it evening or not? If fire breaks out, all nature catches fire, so sinks the sun.

And if this ox comes off my tongue? This rock on my back, could I slowly let it go?

If I could sleep like sleeping, get up and look over there, like my own self, again, again . . . .

Agamemnon III

1.

Our memories mix with leftover rains, the splendid Tree, collapsing in ruins, is shedding its leaves, unaware of new rivers.

Those years when the bridegroom's clothes lay deposited in a chest and water ran in the reeds from the sandy earth to the spacious sky;

Those years that never bounce back, like an acrobat or the tumbling toy; they never bounce back even as we look; with another lake right there behind us and the sound of water we hear when we prick up our ears;

The flame sways in a stubborn delicate balance like an inner echo, like the sea, defiled and resolute;

We return to the fountain with the inscription and Sultan's signature, we lean our mouths to the iron spout, the water decreasing little by little.

There was a message far from peaceful, from some instrument outside time, evidently not a god!

We should forget, forget quickly! Our cypress tree growing in the distance, all alone until war and the sword should cease again!

If we cut the branches at a single blow, all the insects would swarm over us from their sky path. Something falls, heavy and slow; evening or morning: it's all the same.

But for this rocking the heart would break. We're on the plain again: here's Mount Ida, here's Sinois, the seven-headed monster.

It was Achilles who found them and set them in place; who put the fallen head back on time's body.

Achilles, you are our enemy here! You lay down the law for us: when you're here, we're here.

Our young warriors are recognized along with you—we are shield when you are spear, we are spear when you turn into shield;

You connect us to the days of history, it's you who make us individuals; I was thirsty with you and hungry, shared your bed, was there with you and your black girl;

Everything begins and ends with you, whatever moves with you stays with you. You are my other face, my light in the dark.

You are the sword I hold at the ready, the breakwater that strikes my head, flooding in spray and foam as my wave crashes over.

2.

Here's what we were thinking, standing side by side as Hector caressed the stern of the ship: we got into line, one by one like a chain, each link closed, each gap alone, our elbows touching: that's enough for us men!

We look out through loopholes at the enemy, we are silent and like birds cry out in chorus.

The carpenters are up front, the wood carvers, gradually chipping and shaping the wood like flaky pastry;

There are those who love temporary work, and are bound to hearts that decay, there are those who know how to stay with stone and iron,

Those who do their thinking with adzes and two-handed saws, and their thirsting with barrels, scattering fates in wood shavings to make the wooden caskets.

We got into line, one by one, like a chain, linked but separate, our elbows touching: that's enough for us men!

The plumbers are here! Making all kinds of liquid flow, knowing the laws of compound vessels, unblocking the blockages, dealing with spurting leaks;

They work with water, then with gas, with little taps, laying down dreams of long slender water;

The optical experts are standing behind, their songs magnify; they clarify each problem; the iron wars intensify in the lens.

And the lathe operators! The turners, the awl users, digging into the insides of emptiness.

Hand moves to iron, iron to hand: looms working like clockwork;

The unchangeable turns into something else, useful but terrible; resistant to cracking, like an almond that cracks;

The deepest silence will find its tongue, soft and damp;

Every evening that we watch, every evening behind the clouds a caravan whose little bells squeeze the heart;

A book right by a glass on the table, on the checkered table-cloth—a most immortal pause.

On the right at the front are the model-makers: they know how to sharpen their pairs of compasses, rebelling by night, embraced by time's hour-hands;

They turn to draw a line on the vellum, their hands offer a bitter hieroglyph to the round sundials;

They are like waterless lakes, with all their dead frogs, squeezed tight, incredibly tight, silent and poised as an acrobat.

"So be it" they accept. We agree it must be. We all look at you and see you as no burden. This is the hour when humans are like Earth!

We're here to give nourishment! To feed and satisfy wolf, bird, tree, humans, whatever—but death is grander than all.

3.

Today we gathered our dead from the plain. All gone quiet like the children's game of Footsteps, stopped on the narrowest rung of life, completely silenced, defeated by the pull of earth,

Stripped of their arms, ashamed; scattered as though by autumn winds, the young still splendid at this stage, the old resigned and wise.

The eyes of many open, blinded by the sun, death between their cracked lips, festering wounds clotted and maggot-ridden, pasture to other lives.

The mighty dead with their little weapons! Palms outspread to the vast sky, they reached back to where they came from, earth and water.

They long to be refined by fire, or to grow as great as possible, to sustain other lives though they themselves no longer live.

Meanings and symbols are exhausted, suddenly and by many separate ways the end is reached, the end of sun and earth;

They lurk in malarial voids; the final balance of lyricism is separated by a single comma, with no future.

Their ships have vanished in the blue ryefield of adventure, willingly they've entered the circle of fire, the mine has exploded into a black swarm of insects—the infinite Bee.

Scorched by sirocco winds, their rations scattered, their drink sour, only a dry biscuit in their knapsacks.

Their unbreakable judgment broken, now there must be another hearing and Zeus the judge, the great sovereign, must gird himself with the starry robes of heaven.

Father and son, betrothed and married man, a closeness so close it's not.

Heat so hot it's cold! A bare foot, its memory bound to *kilims*, a different grip of the plows a different twist to the bolt.

This rush-mat left from him, this pain from him! These blue overalls, this cap, this grooved knife, whose if not his? If his, though, where?

Where's Yesterday? Where the day before? Where the day we shared that lasted for years? Where the white shirt in the dappled sunlight that falls on the mulberry branch?

A wheatfield reaped, a hut in ruins, a tree that exists and lives only in thought.

And so alas! We didn't describe them, let them stay with the pale tea in the coffeehouse with the patchy wall, we knew they were the salt of the earth.

All day they are with the bird, the sky with its sunny face, in the tin vessel and broken razor, in the hundred stooping roving *köfte**-sellers on the pavements.

Swaying as they move, they can easily resemble rock and pain as they disperse at the indulgent hour to their separate shelves, like islands great and small.

I know we see you; it's impossible not to see you—it is he who looks from the window, or wanders in fear; he is in the one who is touched, in the one who smells; we see him too when he looks beyond and combs the hair of the ferryboat on the pillow of roofs; we see you; it's impossible not to!

To be different belongs to them; the unlike, the broad-hipped, the nobodies, all are theirs from beginning to end.

We keep calling, "Come with a message, come to us!" We are in the most fearful, horrible state of revolt; come put a stop at once to this agitation! Come, standing there with your indifference!

Come my child, come my ray of light; come, rocking on the highest branch of the tree: come with no ears to hear, with no eyes! Come, ours, mine!

You, walking with me where we lived together, by the well-head where we drank *rakı* and laughed from the heart, a traveler with his horse, you, chained to my foot, the mountain with the shepherd's pipe and the deer!

You for whom I tear my hair, don't go but come! Later, if you like, don't look but come now! Put an end to my pain, cleanse my wound with salt.

---

* *Köfte*: Grilled meat patties—usually lamb—popular as street food in Turkey.

Come, give birth as the sun rises! Get your feet out of your blanket and walk! Get into your stride, walk straight to me.

Only there could we find it—only there it is not divisible. Something has to crack, or fall and come to a stop before we can cling to it.

I shed the bloodiest tears! Come, you who are all, who grasp all the living and the dead; you, only you!

You who pass in the red tram, buried in the coiled spring wheel of madness and discovery; a shadow green at the pulley-wheel of the well.

You, the one who appears beside me at every turn, through thick and thin; you, a blue whistle: you who turn the globe, skimming the surface;

You, absent; you in agitation; drying in the sun; heat at the foot of a whitewashed wall; sharing and being shared; the current that flows through the word, the pure poem.

4.

Every tongue eventually spoke its last, sun and earth came to the final end of every path, a heron on the last beach balanced on one leg, one foot with hope.

If hunger is appeased by plenty, never change the happy round of hunger and fulfillment, never let it diminish but continue on and on till night.

Suppose we look in the mirrors till night, on one foot! Suppose we have no fear of love and poetry and convert the diseases of high living into health on longing's branch!

Suppose we load ourselves with fruit and dress in all nature's precious stones and pulling like great oxen put an end to suffering! We would come face to face and ask, "Who are you?"

"Who are you who look like a brother?" Why only one nose and eyes apart? Why this loneliness so splendidly dull?

We herded along great suffering like huge oxen; our suns like sunken ships beyond the seas.

What's to be done? And how? How can we break out roaring from the iron cocoon? How? How? Outside of us now there must be mountains, lights, books, and all of that!

To be between rabid madness and inaction . . . like this we stand still, the sound of the ambulance siren is dying away.

"What then?" we think; with the dead there's death, with the living, life! It's always this way, there's fear of love and poetry, and bastard diseases that appear on longing's branch.

And if the end means nothing, that's how it is! Here comes the greatest message, powerful death in the race to the summit gradually hoisting its flag.

Chronology

SECTION VII: Iran (1951–1980)

1951 Iran nationalizes its oil

1953 CIA coup topples Mossadegh government

1957 SAVAK, Iran's secret police force, is formed

1963 Shah initiates "White Revolution"

1964 Ayatollah Khomeini exiled to Iraq

1971 Iranian monarchy celebrates 2,500 years

1976 Shah replaces Islamic calendar with Imperial calendar

1979 Iranian Revolution
Founding of Islamic Republic

1980 Saddam Hussein of Iraq invades Iran

VII

Those Days: Persian Literature Between Two Revolutions

THE DECADES BETWEEN 1950 and 1980 were a time of unprecedented literary achievement in Iran. The country's turbulent social and political atmosphere gave rise to a group of young, politically conscious poets and writers—sometimes referred to as "the engaged writers"—who sought to use literature as a tool to effect dramatic, even revolutionary, social change. As the voice of Iranian nationalism and the vanguard of opposition to an increasingly despotic regime, these writers were at the forefront of the revolutionary changes shaping Iran, the repercussions of which would be felt across the globe.

In 1951, Iran's popularly elected prime minister, Mohammad Mossadegh, a passionate anti-imperialist and fierce opponent of foreign intervention in Iran, took the unprecedented step of unilaterally nationalizing Iran's oil industry. Mossadegh's actions not only brought the country into direct conflict with the United Kingdom, which had controlled Iran's oil since 1908, it also resulted in an open confrontation with Muhammad Reza Pahlavi, the young shah whom the British had installed on the throne ten years earlier. When the shah tried to remove Mossadegh from power, massive countrywide demonstrations forced him to vacate his throne and flee into exile. For a moment, Iran became a democratic republic. The moment would not last.

In 1953, the CIA, working in conjunction with British intelligence, secretly infiltrated Iran and carried out a coup d'état against Mossadegh's government; the shah was placed back on his throne. The coup was a demoralizing defeat for Iranian nationalists and humiliating proof of Iran's lack of autonomy. The shah returned to Iran more powerful than ever. With the backing of the United States, he instituted a forced campaign of modernization and Westernization meant to transform Iran rapidly into a modern society. The repression that followed was keenly felt by the engaged writers, many of whom were censored, imprisoned, and even executed for their activities.

Far from backing down, however, writers such as the famed essayist Jalal Al-e Ahmad—whose *Gharbzadegi*, or "Westoxification," is still regarded as one of the most influential anti-imperial tracts ever written—spoke out even more vociferously against both the oppression of the state and the increasing fundamentalism of Iran's religious classes. Poetry became the primary vehicle for social and political criticism, as it relied on the use of symbolism and metaphor to tackle subjects considered forbidden by the regime. Perhaps as a result, this era produce some of the most internationally renowned Persian poets of the twentieth century: Nader Naderpour, Simin Behbahani, the incomparable Ahmad Shamloo, and Reza Baraheni, whose prison poems provide a glimpse into the horrors perpetrated by the authoritarian regime upon its political enemies.

It was at this time that Persian literature entered a highly experimental phase, as seen in the stream-of-consciousness monologue of the child narrator in Houshang Golshiri's famous short story "My China Doll" (Golshiri was one of many writers imprisoned by the state for their work). This was also the era during which the Women's Awakening Movement reached its zenith in Iran. Women writers broke new ground in literature, giving a distinctly female voice to the social and political criticism that defined the generation. It is hard to imagine any other time in Iran's history in which a poet like Forugh Farrokhzad—a divorcee with a powerful feminist perspective who is widely regarded as the most famous female poet in Iranian history—could have had the kind of success she enjoyed. (Farrokhzad published four books of poetry in a single decade, before her untimely death in 1967, at the age of thirty-two.) Another accomplished female writer, Simin Danishvar (*The Playhouse*), became the first woman in Iran to publish a work of fiction. Her 1969 novel, *Savushun*, became one of the all-time best-selling books in Iran. Danishvar also translated half a dozen great works of literature into Persian, including Hawthorne's *The Scarlet Letter* and Chekhov's *The Cherry Orchard*.

Although these women took full advantage of the benefits to women's rights that ensued from the shah's social reforms, they remained fierce critics of state oppression. As with their male literary counterparts, they focused their writings on the plight of those left behind by the shah's modernization policies: the rural poor, the underprivileged, women and minorities—people who, like the baboon in Sadeq Chubak's short story "The Baboon Whose Buffoon Was Dead" are "attached to a chain . . . its other end . . . gripped by a man [the government] who could drag him here or there as whim decreed."

And yet, despite the writers' efforts to reach out to the poor and marginalized, the peasantry ultimately rallied behind the country's religious leaders. Indeed, although the "engaged" writers and intellectuals were the driving force behind the 1979 uprisings that once again overthrew the shah, the power of the clerical class over the masses allowed them to commandeer the revolution and ultimately create the Islamic Republic of Iran.

FORUGH FARROKHZAD

(1935–1967)

Selected Poems

Translated from the Persian by Sholeh Wolpé

Sin

I have sinned a rapturous sin
In a warm enflamed embrace,
Sinned in a pair of vindictive arms,
arms violent and ablaze.

In that quiet vacant dark
I looked into his mystic eyes,
found such longing that my heart
fluttered impatient in my breast.

In that quiet vacant dark
I sat beside him punch-drunk,
his lips released desire on mine,
grief unclenched my crazy heart.

I poured in his ears lyrics of love:
O my life, my lover it's you I want.
Life-giving arms, it's you I crave.
Crazed lover, for you I thirst.

Lust enflamed his eyes,
Red wine trembled in the cup,
My body, naked and drunk,
quivered softly on his breast.

I have sinned a rapturous sin
beside a body quivering and spent.
I do not know what I did O God,
In that quiet vacant dark.

Window

A window for seeing.
A window for hearing.
A window like a well
that plunges to the heart of the earth
and opens to the vast unceasing love in blue.
A window lavishing the tiny hands of loneliness
with the night's perfume from gentle stars.
A window through which one could invite
the sun for a visit to abandoned geraniums.

One window is enough for me.

I come from the land of dolls, from under
the shade of paper trees in a storybook grove;
from arid seasons of barren friendships and love
in the unpaved alleys of innocence;
from years when the pallid letters of the alphabet
grew up behind desks of tubercular schools;
from the precise moment children could write
"stone" on the board and the startled starlings took wing
from the ancient tree.

I come from among the roots of carnivorous plants,
and my head still swirls with the sound
of a butterfly's terror—crucified with a pin to a book.

When my trust hung from the feeble rope of justice
and the whole city tore my lamps' hearts to shreds,
when love's innocent eyes were bound

with the dark kerchief of law, and blood gushed
from my dreams' unglued temples,
when my life was no longer anything,
nothing at all except the tick-tick of a clock on the wall,
I understood that I must, must, must
deliriously love.

One window is enough for me.

A window to a moment of comprehension, perception, silence.
The walnut sapling has grown tall enough
to tell its leaves the meaning of the wall.
Ask of the mirror the name of your liberator.
Is not the trembling earth beneath your feet
lonelier than you?
The prophets brought the epistles
of ruin to our age.
These explosions without end,
these poisonous clouds,
are they not the peal of holy scriptures?
O friend, O comrade, O blood brother,
when you reach the moon,
mark the day of the flowers' massacre.

Dreams always fall
from the heights of their own naiveté,
and perish.

It's a four-leaf clover I'm selling,
sprouted upon the grave of an archaic creed.
Was the woman buried in the shroud of longing
and chastity, my youth?
Will I ever again climb the stairs of wonder
to greet the good God who paces my roof?

I sense that time has passed,
I sense my share of "moments" is now a leaf of history;
I sense this desk is just an illusory mass between
my hair and this forlorn stranger's hands.
Speak to me.
What does one who offers you a living body's love
want in return but a nod to her sense of existence?

Speak to me.
From the sanctuary of my window
I am intimate with the sun.

Wind-Up Doll

Even more, oh yes,
one can remain silent even more.

Inside eternal hours
one can fix lifeless eyes
on the smoke of a cigarette,
on a cup's form,
the carpet's faded flowers,
or on imaginary writings on the wall.

With stiff claws one can whisk
the curtains aside, look outside.
It's streaming rain.
A child with a balloon bouquet
cowers beneath a canopy. A rickety cart
flees the deserted square in haste.

One can remain fixed in one place, here
beside this curtain . . . but deaf, but blind.

With an alien voice, utterly false,
one can cry out: *I love!*
In the oppressive arms of a man
one can be a robust, beautiful female—
skin like leather tablecloth,
breasts large and hard.
One can stain the sinlessness of love
in the bed of a drunk, a madman, a tramp.

One can cunningly belittle
every perplexing puzzle.
Alone, occupy oneself with crosswords,
content with unimportant words,
yes, unimportant letters, no more than five or six.

One can spend a lifetime kneeling,
head bowed,
before the cold altar of the Imams,
find God inside an anonymous grave,
faith in a few paltry coins.
One can rot inside a mosque's chamber,
an old woman, prayers dripping from lips.

Whatever the equation, one can always be a zero,
yielding nothing, whether added, subtracted, or multiplied.
One can think your eyes are buttons from an old ragged shoe
caught in a web of anger.
One can evaporate like water from one's own gutter.

With shame one can hide a beautiful moment
like a dark, comic instant photo
rammed deep into a wooden chest.

Inside a day's empty frame one can mount
the portrait of a condemned, a vanquished,
a crucified. Cover the gaps in the walls
with silly, meaningless drawings.

Like a wind-up doll one can look out
at the world through glass eyes,
spend years inside a felt box,
body stuffed with straw,
wrapped in layers of dainty lace.

With every salacious squeeze of one's hand,
for no reason one can cry:
Ah, how blessed, how happy I am!

Those Days

Those days are gone,
those lovely days,
lush, happy days,
sequin-studded skies,
cherry-heavy branches,
ivy-wrapped houses leaning one upon another,
rooftops from which playful kites were launched,
alleys dizzy with acacia perfume.

Those days are gone,
when from between my eyelids
songs surged like air-drunk bubbles,
and my gaze glided upon everything,
drank it all in like fresh milk.
It was as if inside my pupils lived
a happy and restless hare who each morning
explored unknown fields with the old sun
and each eve melted into the darkness of a forest.

Those days are gone,
those silent snowy days when from inside
a warm room I kept watch over the snow
—my unsullied snow—
descending like soft lint upon an old wood ladder,
the clothesline's slack rope, and the old pine's fur;
and I thought of tomorrow—
tomorrow . . . that slippery mass of white.

It used to begin with the rustle of grandmother's *chador*,
the advent of her busy shadow in the doorway—
a shadow soon liberated by light's cold, heavy touch.
It used to begin with the dizzy pattern of doves in flight
on the window's tinted pane.
Tomorrow . . .

The warmth of *korsi**-induced sleep,
and I, fearless and fast,
away from my mother's eyes would erase
my old homework's checkmarks,
and when snow ceased falling,
I'd wander the garden—unhappy.
At the foot of the withered jasmines
I'd bury my dead sparrows.

Those days are gone,
the days of rapture and awe,
of daydreams and dreams,
days when each shadow bore a secret,
each box promised hidden troves,
each corner of the storeroom was a world

* *Korsi*: A low table with a heater underneath and blankets on top, around
which families in Iran often gather.

inside the silence of noon.
Anyone not afraid of the dark
was a hero in my eyes.

Those days are gone,
the New Year's days,
the wait for the sun, the flowers, and their perfume,
for the late-winter tour of the daffodils
in shy and silent bundles upon the singing vendor's carts
that traveled the length of the streets spotted with green.

The bazaar was afloat in aromas—
the sharp smell of coffee, of fish.
The bazaar flattened beneath footsteps,
stretched as it mingled with time,
whirled inside every doll's eyes.
The bazaar was mother dashing into its shifting
colorful mass and returning, arms full with gifts,
baskets brimming with goods.
The bazaar was rain that streamed, and streamed, and streamed.

Those days are gone,
the days of staring at the secrets of flesh,
of cautious intimacies and the blue-veined beauty
of a hand holding a flower, calling
from behind a wall
to another hand—
a small ink-stained hand,
anxious, trembling, and afraid . . .
And love unveiling in a shy *salaam*.

We sang our love in the broiling
middays of our dusty alley.
We knew the simple language of the daffodils.
We took our hearts to the orchards of guiltless infatuation
and lent them to the trees.
The ball carried our kisses to and fro

and love—that confused sensation—
engulfed us suddenly, bound us in a blazing rush
of breaths, heartbeats, and furtive smiles.

Those days are gone.
As uprooted plants wilt in the sun,
those days, too, rotted in sunlight.
The alleys dizzy with acacia perfume
are now lost among crowded one-way roads;
And the girl who painted her cheeks
with geranium leaves . . .
O grief, is now a lonely woman.

A lonely woman.

NADER NADERPOUR
(1929—2000)

Selected Poems

Translated from the Persian by
Sholeh Wolpé
Ahmad Karimi-Hakkak

False Dawn

Tonight the earth has bid all its sins
farewell. The snow's pallid piety
conceals the earth-dweller's blasphemies.
This silvery mask on nature's black face
is the world's most beautiful lie.

Tonight, the old tree thinks itself young,
but the sun's birth melts
the tree's snowy delusions.
What eye can see the truth's
hidden face like the sun?
Perhaps that is a question an eye
can answer after much weeping.

O ancient, O tree!
Such tears shed the rain!
It's a cry vast as the sky's grief
over the earth's heedlessness,
a weeping that darkens
the snow's false dawn in the eve
of your fleeting youth,
even as it nears you to childhood's

distant light; a weeping that lavishes
cloudless sight, like the sun's child vision,
to the eyes of the old.

You, the rooster waiting for dawn!
Fire does not die inside cotton,
yet look: the sun has died
inside the pale horizon.

Alas, the snow has brought sleep
to the eyes of the simple trees
and with its delusion-steeds has carried off
these old forbearing pedestrian villagers
to the city of imaginary youth.

But the earth's heart
longs for the tears of rain.
There is a truth concealed by the night.
Grief, blacker than clouds!
Tonight bestow me unceasing weeping rain.
Kind tears!
Gift me a child's eyes.

Translated by Sholeh Wolpé

Qom*

Thousands of women
thousands of men
women in veils
men in cloaks
a golden dome
some old storks
a joyless garden

* Qom: A city in southwestern Iran that serves as the theological center of Shi'a
Islam.

with sparse trees
empty of laughter
silent of speech
a half-filled pond
with muddy water
a few old ravens
on scattered rocks
groups of beggars
at every step
turbans white
faces black.

Translated by Ahmad Karimi-Hakkak

Faraway Star

In the mirror images cry out,
"Free us from this golden frame!
We were free in our own world."

Blind decrepit walls groan,
"Why have you enchained us in mortar?
We were happy raw as clay."

One by one stars with watery eyes,
clinging to the cloak of tempest, implore,
"O tempest! We were not so in the beginning
we were tears shed with wailing."

Little do they know that the tempest long since
has lost its way in the rush of sorrow,
It howls, "To the world's ears I was but a wind!"

I am not the tempest
but always thirst for a blast
I am not a wall

but have been bound in chains
no image am I in a cold mirror
whatever I am, I am not free from pain.

For they extinguish the flame of hidden pain
with their screams, and forget
while I am that faraway star
whose bloodied teardrops waters drink.

Translated by Ahmad Karimi-Hakkak

SADEQ CHUBAK

(1916–1998)

The Baboon Whose Buffoon Was Dead

Translated from the Persian by Peter Avery

IT IS CERTAINLY true to say that early morning sleep is the heaviest. This was decidedly so with the buffoon, Jahan. Oblivious to the noise of the passing trucks and the shouting charcoal burners on the plain, he lay slumped at dawn within the hollow of a withered, leafless oak tree where he and his baboon, Makhmal, had stopped for the night. Many caravans had paused there before him, and men had stripped fuel from the tree's bony, twisted branches and set fires in its hollow trunk, so that now the inner wall of the tomblike enclosure was prepared with glossy scales of charred wood.

Scattered on the ground in front of him were his opium and tobacco pipes—the *vafur* and *chapuq*—his begging bowl and sack, his tobacco pouch and the tin for the hashish, and some half-burnt, blackened sticks. His pockmarked face with its few bristles had dropped out from under his cloak; it looked like a mask wrapped in a shawl.

The baboon, Makhmal, was chained to a stake driven into the ground nearby. He was awake and restless, and tired of waiting for his master to stir. His feet and hands hurt, his soft skin was sore and torn, and yesterday's dust still clung to his skin and fur. He sat with his arms hung between his haunches, his beady eyes fixed on the tree that held Jahan. Then, his impatience growing, he sprang to his feet and twisted himself this way and that around the chain. Still the buffoon was motionless. At last, in resignation, Makhmal sat again. He waited and watched, blinking his eyes in the dim light.

The sun's glare had not yet lit the plain, but a dull glint of sunlight now oozed through a cleft in the Mareh range. It began to trickle across the earth, merging with the columns of charcoal smoke that curled up into the still morning air. The surrounding hills slept on in the shadow, still untouched by the day. The plain itself was red, the color of Armenian clay, and it was split in two by a long ribbon of road over which the trucks rolled. Here and there large oaks grew, interspersed with stunted almond trees and linseed bushes.

The showman and his baboon had come over the Kutal-i-Dukhtar Pass and had reached Dasht-i-Barm by nightfall the day before. All the way the baboon had kept pace with his master, sometimes walking on his hind legs, sometimes on all fours, sometimes covering the ground in his own baboon-style leaps and bounds. At last they had left the road and made their way to the hollow oak.

Immediately Jahan had dropped Makhmal's chain and kindled a fire. He had taken the tea things, the hashish, the pipes and opium from his sack and laid them around the fire. Next he had taken out four roasted sparrows wrapped in bread, and he had shared these with Makhmal. Supper scarcely over, the showman had lit his opium pipe and taken several quick draws. Makhmal had sat opposite, all agog, his nostrils quivering with the sensitivity of the antennae of an ant. But Jahan had kept the pipe to himself, absorbing all the smoke into his own lungs. He had taken not the slightest notice of Makhmal, though he knew the baboon's craving to be as great as his own.

But it was always this way. The clown's craving left him no decency at all. When they were in the towns and their show had been catching on, with the pennies coming in nicely one after another, Jahan, wanting to trick the spectators with a fast retreat, would use Makhmal's craving for drug as an excuse. Using the addict's whining tone, he would say to Makhmal: "Makhmal, Makhmal, my sweet, are you beginning to feel you want some?" and he'd say, "Oh, you wicked old Indian, you, you have got it bad, haven't you? Do you want it now? All right, then. Cheer up. I'm taking you along this very moment. I'll give you your smoke, and then you'll be all right, won't you?" And later, seated by himself with his pipe, Jahan would take his fill of the poppy and only send across to Makhmal at last a few short, thin whiffs, the essence of which he had first absorbed in his own lungs.

Here beside the oak tree it had been no different. When he had satisfied himself with opium, the showman had taken several rapid draws of the hashish, gulping it down deep. Makhmal had received no smoke worth mentioning at all. Then Jahan had retrieved Makhmal's chain from where it lay on the ground, and had crossed the small brook that now separated the baboon and his master. He had driven the stake deep into the earth under an almond bush. Then, dead tired, the man had fallen asleep in the tree hollow where he now lay.

Makhmal again got to his feet and gazed across the brook toward his master. The split nostrils of his long nose were quivering, and his eyebrows met in a puzzled scowl. There was something strange here. Once he thought his master had awakened, but it was not so; the skin of the buffoon's face remained perfectly still. The eyes were open, rolled upward, showing their whites. The face was curiously stiff.

Suddenly, with all the strength of his huge frame, Makhmal shook himself and leapt twice into the air, so high that his collar wrenched his neck and choked him back. All his attention was fixed on his clown, for now he understood.

The buffoon's face was completely altered, alien. Makhmal was seeing a man as he had never before seen him. In his lifetime, he had seen men only threatening or taunting or whining—he had never seen a dead man. And now a face whose every familiar movement had revealed to him his master's essential being was rigid and unmoving. Here was a face from which there was nothing to fear.

All at once an ache of loneliness seized his vitals as he realized that in all that wide, vacant plain he was entirely alone. Time after time he leapt this way and that way around the stake. Then he stopped dead in his tracks and gazed at the men moving up and down the plain as they tended their fires. He squatted where he stood and stared at the buffoon's face, remembering the man's threats and thrashings. Then he turned frightened eyes up toward the dry, dust-soiled leaves of the almond bush beneath which he was tied. And again, as if he were expecting an order, he looked at his master.

What was he to do? Without his buffoon, he was not complete. It was as if half of his brain were paralyzed. Jahan had been his one link with the world of men. He understood nobody's speech as he understood his master's. For a lifetime he had been performing his tricks at the showman's commands—standing on his head, waddling about, waving his stick, thrusting his backside into the air—all for the crowd's amusement and the clown's profit.

In the brothels, in the coffee shops, in the squares, in garages, cemeteries, and caravansaries, wherever his master chose to perform, Makhmal had been surrounded by all kinds of men. Yet his knowledge of men was only this—that they gathered around him to tease and taunt. It was they who pelted him with stones, rotten fruit, bits of wood, old bones, old boots, scraps of iron, pomegranate rind, turds.

He had become inured to their blows, and had paid little attention, alert only to the buffoon's bell and the twitch of the chain, so that he could faithfully perform whatever was required of him. Sometimes, to encourage his most popular trick, the men would waggle their buttocks at him, and the clown would give a slight pull on the chain. "Makhmal, where do we put our enemies?" he would say in his most winning tone. The baboon would then turn his back on them and expose the shining backside that was attached to him just a little below his tuft of a tail and that looked like a huge tumor. He would clutch it with both hands, with a gesture as much as to say, "Sorry, but there's nothing else for it," while from his throat issued a rough, ominous noise, "Ooom, oom, oom."

"Enemy" was a word of known shape to his ear. Whenever it reached his hearing, he knew the moment had come to put his head to the ground and his hands to his backside. This was the mainstay of their act; this was his job; it was for this that he had been born.

Yet the experience of enmity brought only fear and submission from him. He was forever anticipating the raps of his master's cane on his head, the cruel pull of the collar around his neck, the kick in the belly. A glance from his master paralyzed him with fright, for he was more afraid of Jahan than of anyone. His life was one of a continual state of terror, and his terror was matched only by the loathing and disgust he felt for all mankind and for his master in particular.

But he must continually submit. He had no choice. Whatever he did, he was forced to do; whatever he witnessed, he was forced to witness; whatever he suffered, he had no alternative but to suffer it. He was attached to a chain, and its other end was gripped by a man who could drag him here or there as whim decreed. The man and the chain had replaced his will—he had none of his own.

Squatting now, gazing at the clown in the oak tree, Makhmal scratched his head. Then he took two or three turns around himself, wondering what to do. His eyes fell upon the chain then, and never before had he looked at it with such astonishment and loathing. He drew it up to his neck. It was rough, heavy, stained with rust. For a lifetime, riveted about his neck, it had held him fast to his master or to his master's stake. From it had come nothing but injury and weariness.

He put a hand to his throat, where the chain joined the collar. He shook it and clumsily fiddled with it: yes, it had always been like that— he knew this chain like the fingers of his own hand.

Slowly, wonderingly, he groped his way down the chain, hand-over-hand, toward the stake. At last he reached the other end, the end that was not a part of himself, but another, a hostile world.

The buffoon had always driven the stake to which Makhmal's chain was attached as far into the ground as it would go, because, as he used to say, "There isn't a bigger bastard of an animal in the world than a baboon, and one of these days, you'll see. As soon as a man's back is turned for a second, they can tear him to pieces."

Yet, in reality, only Makhmal's habitual fear had kept him from pulling it free in the past. Now he fingered the crown of the stake experimentally. Now he shook it with anger. Now he grasped it with his hands. The strength with which he uprooted it was far greater than was needed. In one good tug it was loosened and out of the ground.

What a marvelous feeling! Makhmal began to leap about, overjoyed at his liberation. Then he moved away from the almond bush, and the chain followed him. As he leapt, the chain leapt. As he bounded about with joy, the chain bounded. It, too, had been freed, but each was fastened to the other. He winced at the pull and the noise of it. His spirits sank. But there was nothing to be done.

He started over toward the buffoon's dead body. After jumping the stream, he stood erect a moment, looking doubtfully at his master before going any further. When he got a little closer, he again paused in doubt, and there, some distance away, he sat down opposite the body, still afraid to go closer without a sign.

The corpse still leaned against the oak tree, wrapped in the creased, crumpled cloak. In front of it, the contents of the sack still lay about the cold circle of cinders from last night's fire. It was as if the buffoon were appraising his inheritance as he sat there looking at these things.

Makhmal got to his feet and went closer. When he stood directly in front of his clown, he sat down. But the face said nothing to him. It did not say, "Go." It did not say, "Sit." It commanded him neither to fill the pipe, nor to tie a turban around his head, nor to stand on his hands. It did not ask, "Where do we put our enemies?" It did not tell him to close his eyes, nor did it say, "Bravo, hold up the stick! Hold it up!" nor, "Ride it, ride it, there's a good jockey!" It did not cry out, "Sweets, oh, sweets, sweets, sweets, hot and sweet." It said nothing to him.

Yet the pattern of a lifetime was stubborn. The memory of thrashings, curses, kicks dealt out by his master in fits of depression could not be erased by Makhmal's recognition that his master now could have no effect on him. He knew that the clown no longer had anything to do with him, yet he remembered his power to inflict punishment. There had been times when Makhmal had been obstinate, playing the fool just as the show was going well, and he'd dig in his toes and pull hard on his chain, leaving the buffoon with no alternative but to coax him with generous supplies of raisins till he yielded. Later Jahan would tether him to a tree and beat him till his agony was such that he would roll in the dust groaning, his mouth lolling open like a sack while he chewed his tongue. But there was not one to come to his rescue. They only laughed. "Hajji Firooz, the monkey had a beating!"

And when Jahan's anger was at its worst, he would leave Makhmal for long periods without food and opium, chained to the stake. This was the cruelest punishment of all. If he had been unfettered, he could have gone and found a morsel to eat among the sweepings and refuse scattered on the ground; he could have sat in the coffee shops and enjoyed the smoke of men's pipes. But he was captive.

On a sudden impulse now, Makhmal put out his hand and cautiously pulled at the cloak that enveloped his master. The nightcap beneath was so saturated with sweat and dirt that its rim gleamed. The face looked as if it were molded in lime, ready to crumble to pieces at the first touch. Makhmal was suddenly filled with joy. It was as if the buffoon were now a vast distance away, across a wide gulf, completely beyond his grasp. Makhmal's blood tingled. Now, he felt he was the victor at last, and he stared hard at the face, and let out a short, dry cackle of glee, "Ghe, ghe, ghe!"

Then he grabbed a piece of bread and two roasted sparrows from the sack and gobbled them up. He wolfed down all the bread he could find. He was completely at his ease and superbly contented.

It was not long before the desire for opium moved him to take the *vafur* from beside the cold ashes and hold it under his nostrils. Several times he viciously twisted the opium pipe in his greasy, black fingers. First he smelled it, then he sucked it in his mouth, and then he began to chew it until he had chewed it to pieces. While the acrid flavor of the charred center of the pipe revolted him, it wormed its way into his nose and excited his craving.

When he had spat out the bits, he smashed the pipe's porcelain end to smithereens on a stone by the dead fire. Then he excitedly pulled at Jahan's cloak, as if he wanted to wake him. Finally, he rose and, turning his back on his clown, he took the road to the plain.

The plain was lighter now; the sunlight had spread itself over it and it was the color of hot copper. The noise of the trucks on the road echoed across it.

Makhmal had no idea where he was going. His clown had always walked along with him, his shadow, his inseparable companion. Now there was only the sound of his chain, sliding through the dust and clinking over the stones. It was heavier now, more bothersome, and its noise marred his solitude.

He passed some boulders. Now he was farther away than ever from his master, and going along on two legs. His huge frame moved forward with a stoop, dragging the chain after it. He was encumbered, but he was on his own. He had escaped from his master, and he was off to a new world.

He reached a pasture where a flock of sheep were grazing. All their heads were down as they busily nibbled the short grass, bumping against each other, completely absorbed. The boy watching over them had stretched out his legs on the grass and was playing his pipe. Makhmal sat down under one of the big dusty oak trees on the edge of the field and looked at the shepherd and the quiet sheep.

He felt at peace. His little journey, made on his own initiative, had cheered him. He liked the flock of sheep, but he couldn't help feeling that the boy sitting there was somehow more akin to him than the sheep, and he watched him with interest. He sat idly, pleasurably, sizing things up.

At this moment, a big blue-winged horsefly took it upon itself to be a nuisance. It flew into his face, tormentingly sitting in a corner of his eye. With the ease and patience of an expert, however, Makhmal caught it as it stung him and held it cunningly between his fingers, where he regarded it for a moment before consigning it, still alive, to his mouth.

All at once the shepherd saw Makhmal and got up and approached him, carrying his heavy stick across his shoulders. He gripped it from below with his hands in exactly the same way in which Makhmal had held his own stick for the showman's act. His master had taught him to grasp the stick when he commanded. "*Barrikallah, chapani.** Take the stick, shepherd," and Makhmal had always put it behind his neck, bringing his hands up to grip it just as the boy held his own now; then Makhmal had danced his jig.

Makhmal was pleased. He sat motionless, his hands between his haunches, watching the approach of the shepherd and his stick. As the boy drew closer, he hesitated, looking with astonishment at Makhmal. Till then, he had seen a baboon only once in the village, and at some distance. He stared at those ears, hands, feet, and face that were so like his own. Then, in an effort to make friends with this curiously kindred creature, he put his hand in his pocket and took out a piece of acorn bread. It was as dry and hard as a piece of plaster flaked from a wall. He threw it into Makhmal's lap, and stood and watched.

Makhmal doubtfully picked up and smelled the bread; then he disdainfully threw it away. He looked hard at the shepherd boy and the stick that lay across his shoulders, but he had no fear of him and anticipated no danger.

At this point, the boy lowered the knotted boxwood stick and fingered it. Makhmal's suspicions rose. The shepherd was of the species, man. The meaning of the stick had changed.

The boy took a step forward. Makhmal remained where he was, his eyes moving with the boy's movements. Prompted by his own loneliness and self-consciousness, the boy wanted to find out what this animal was and what it would do. He suddenly raised his stick and lunged forward at Makhmal; his thrust, checked by his own apprehension, fell short of contact.

---

* *Barrikallah, chapani:* "Well done, shepherd!"

Makhmal's disenchantment was complete. He felt at once the soreness in the palms of his hands and feet, and his whole body ached so with craving that in his mind's eye he could see his master sitting before the brazier, smoking opium and giving him a puff. He twitched the split nostrils of his delicate nose and sniffed in longing. He was weary of the shepherd now and would have liked to get up and go. But the feeling that he had better not turn his back on the boy restrained him.

The boy's courage grew as the ape sat motionless before him. He raised his stick a second time and swiftly delivered a violent whack on Makhmal's head. Makhmal immediately gathered all his strength, grasped the boy's shoulders, and dug his teeth into his face. The terrified boy fell to the ground, the thick, red blood spurting from his cheek.

While the boy rolled about and bellowed, Makhmal bounded off and retraced his path at top speed, instinctively selecting the only route he knew. Except for the familiar boulders and bushes that marked his way, the vast expanse of plain was completely unknown to him. He had not the slightest inkling of what to do. He had no effective defense against the terrors of his surroundings, and he lacked the comfort of the food and opium that his body craved. Everything around him seemed an implacable and bloody adversary. As he traveled, he pricked up his ears; the sound of the smallest insect stirring in the undergrowth was enough to put him on the alert.

Weakened finally by fatigue and his ache for the drug, he slunk into the shelter of a boulder and squeezed himself into a cleft he discovered between two stones. He felt shaken and muddled, as if his senses could take no more. Peering out from his rocks, he saw the distant shapes of men who were felling trees with their axes. His loathing and terror engulfed him, and he shrank back in his hiding place.

At his feet he found a few blades of grass. He crumpled them in his fingers and sniffed at them. When he ate them, he found that their sharp, fresh taste refreshed him, so he ate some more. The thin, sleepy April sunlight gently tickled the hairs of his belly and chest, and he yawned. He leaned against the stone and gazed at the cornflowers and the fresh spring growth carpeting the ground. He stuck out his lower lip, and it twitched slightly as gurgling, laughlike sound came from his throat.

Then he huddled farther into the gap where he squatted, pressing his back against the rock behind him to relieve his weariness. Now he was comfortable; his chain was forgotten, and his intolerable loneliness gave way to pure contentment.

He put his hand under his armpit and scratched, turning his head in an ecstasy of delight. Then he scratched his chest, and then, stretching himself voluptuously, he idly felt his belly, thighs, and crotch. He captured nits and lice, one by one, in the sharp pincers of his nails, and, putting them between his teeth, he crunched them to bits. The skin of his belly was silver, with blue veins coursing across it.

His body began to tingle as his hands moved over it, and he soon abandoned himself to its demands. The fatigue and aching were erased from his limbs as his blood heated. A delicious sense of power took possession of him. His memory and mind were completely empty. His eyes half-shut, his body quivering, he was in oblivion of pleasure.

Suddenly a huge hawk, large enough to attack a sheep, shot out of the sky and swooped down toward him, its talons and beak ready for combat. The baboon leapt up, his diversions instantly abandoned. Taut with the sense of his danger, he dug his feet into the ground and bared his powerful teeth and claws. He held his arms above his head in a wild, defensive gesture—but the chain inhibited him, dragging at his neck, pulling him down.

The hawk in a swift wheel passed over his head and shot up into the heavens above him, leaving as quickly as it had come. Each feared the other, and the hawk flew on to less formidable prey. But Makhmal was left weary and sick and frightened, conscious again of the weight around his neck. His peace was utterly destroyed. There was nowhere he could stay. Everything was alien and menacing. To linger was out of the question; the ground he trod burned his feet; there was nothing to do but run.

He took to his heels, again taking up the route back to the hollow oak. It was as if some force were compelling him to return. The buffoon was the only familiar being in his world, and although Makhmal was dragging the chain behind him, in reality the chain was dragging him. He felt incomplete without his master, and, with an abundant sense of yearning and submission, he went on toward his oldest enemy.

The clown's body lay just as he'd left it, untouched, lolling against the tree.

In his despair, Makhmal came up slowly and squatted by his master, staring into his face in wonder and dismay. He had been driven from every refuge, and now his body ached, his hands and feet pained him; escape for him had never existed. He did not know what to do, but he had come to be near his clown, and he did not want to leave him again.

And now, advancing toward Makhmal, the withered oak, the dead clown, came two charcoal burners. Two huge axes were slung over their shoulders.

Seeing them, Makhmal was terribly afraid. His body trembled and he looked pleadingly at the buffoon's body, making little gurgling noises in his throat. Existing as he did, somewhere halfway between the ape's world and the man's world, he knew men, and his instinct told him that these two men with axes meant his death.

He put out his hand and pulled at the cloak on the corpse. As the woodsmen came closer, his terror increased. They were a rough, hard pair who didn't care a damn. As they came along, they were laughing together, their axes glinting in the sun.

Makhmal rose in a panic, ready for flight from these horrors—this hated place, his master's corpse, the approaching woodsmen. But there was the chain, tugging at him, sapping his strength, rooting him to the spot as effectively as if the stake had been embedded in rock. It seemed to him that there and then his master was hammering it in, that the stake would never, never be released. However much he wrenched at his chain with his hands, with his neck, he could not get free. The end of the stake was thrust into the fibrous root of the oak tree and would not budge.

He went wild then, refusing to yield. Madly he bent down and bit into the chain, gnawing at it in his fury. Its links clanked between his teeth. He rolled his eyes in rage, blood and bits of tooth and froth spurting from his mouth. Suddenly he jumped into the air and let out a yell that subsided into a harsh, ugly, painful grating in his throat.

All over the plain, columns of smoke were ascending, the fires below them invisible. Only the men who worked at the foot of these columns could be seen.

The woodsmen came nearer to the hollow oak tree. The blades of their axes flashed in the sunlight. They were roaring with laughter.

HOUSHANG GOLSHIRI
(1938–2000)

My China Doll

Translated from the Persian by Fatma Sinem Eryilmaz

MOMMY SAYS HE'S coming back. I know that he's not coming back. If he were coming back, Mommy wouldn't be crying, would she? I wish you'd seen him. No, I wish I hadn't seen him either. Now, you be Mommy. What am I supposed to do if your hair's blond? Look, Mommy was seated this way! Place your feet together! Put your hands on your forehead! No, not like that. Her shoulders were trembling, like this. The newspaper was in front of her on the floor, I can't cry like Mommy. Daddy could. If Uncle Naser wants, he can, too. That's why grown-ups are grown-ups. They can say, "Don't cry, Maryam." Or say, "Why are you picking up the matches, child?"

OK, I picked them up to pick them up. I don't really want to light them, do I? Daddy is nice, he never said, "Don't do that!" But then why did he say, "I don't want to see my Maryam cry!"? I want to cry, but I know I can't. I mean, if I could cry like Mommy for Daddy, I would, I just can't. Do dolls also cry? I know that you can't, like Mommy, like Grandma, like Uncle Naser. If you can, then why didn't you cry when that little devil Mehri broke my doll? I'm talking about my china doll. You were sitting just like now and watched her do it. Did you see how much I cried? Grandma said, "Don't cry, Maryam, I will take it myself to the china shop to have it repaired."

I said, "Then what's going to happen?"

She said, "It's going to be like it was before."

I said, "I don't want it, I don't want it. It'll be like our big teapot."

Daddy said, "If my daughter doesn't cry, Daddy's going to buy another one for her, a bigger one."

He didn't buy it. Daddy's nice. If he came back, I'm not gonna say,

"Buy me one." I'm not gonna cry, either. Do you remember how much Grandma cried? I told you already. In her black dress she fell on Grandpa's grave and cried. I also cried. Daddy didn't cry. Maybe he cried, like dolls do; like you do, when nobody sees your tears and no one hears a sound. I can't cry like that. You can't even believe how much I cried. Later I realized Grandpa won't stretch out his cane anymore. He used to say, "My dear Maryam, can you tell me, how long is my cane?"

I said, "Seven spans, Grandpa."

He said, "No, five."

I said, "Seven."

He said, "Ten and a half and the size of your little finger."

I said, "No, seven."

He said, "Measure it, measure it yourself."

So I did. He didn't think I could do it until my hand reached the handle of his cane, then he grabbed me by the wrist and sat me on his knee. It was just what I wanted. I put my hand in the pocket of his vest and took out his watch. Grandpa opened its lid and held it up to my ear. I said, "Your hands are so old, Grandpa."

He said, "Well, just old."

The backs of his hands were funny, like his face. He used to say, "It's all their fault, my dear."

He was talking about the hands of his watch; he was talking about the red one that always ran faster than the other. Where's his watch now? Is it buried with Grandpa in the ground? You wouldn't know. And you, Dwarf? You be that same little guy. Always coming and going. Slowly, go over there, now come back over here, don't move so fast back and forth, you'll make me dizzy, all right. Daddy was over there, I didn't recognize him. Dwarf, you stay here, I mean keep going there and coming back. Mommy had taken me by the hand. She said, "What are you going to do with the matches, dear?"

"I don't know," I said.

But now, I know. I put them side by side. One here, one there . . . like this. Mommy and I'll be on this side of the matches. And Daddy on that side, on the other side of matches. Dwarf, you go in the middle. Now, we, here on this side, have to keep screaming. The people on the other side of the matches have to scream too. Daddy shouted, "How is my little Maryam? Let me see you blow a kiss to Daddy."

Now you, Dwarf, come here, by my side, over here. So Daddy can't see I'm blowing a kiss to him. Daddy said . . . I don't remember what he said. Mommy had taken me by the hand, like this. Daddy said, "My little daughter shouldn't cry, OK? Daddy is doing well."

Daddy didn't look like Daddy. Like the dwarf, who also doesn't look like Daddy at all. If that little devil Mehri hadn't broken the china doll, I would have put her there now, in Daddy's place, next to those others on that side, next to my Daddy. Mommy said, "Now, don't say 'where is my china doll?' OK?"

I said, "Mommy, then where is Daddy?"

She said, "He is over there, darling. Behind that man. He is coming over. Don't you forget now."

It wasn't Daddy; he looked funny. From his smile, though, I recognized that Daddy was Daddy. Then Daddy said, "Let me see Maryam blow me a kiss."

I've already said that. After that he didn't say anything more to me. He talked to Mommy. Now the china doll is supposed to say, "Esmat, I will not see you disgrace yourself before them."

The china doll is supposed to shout and talk and keep pointing at the dwarf. Now you say, "Then what's going to happen; what's going to happen to you?"

Then Daddy said, "What? What's going to happen? It's all clear from now on. There is no charity distribution in here. But whatever happens, you mustn't let the child grieve."

He was talking about me. After that I don't know what Mommy said. He screamed. Everybody screamed. There was such a clamor; they all let out such cries that . . . it was like when that little devil Hassan blows his trumpet.

No matter how much Grandma shouts, no one can hear what she says, either.

Now you say, "Esmat, dry your tears. I don't want them to see you cry." You must point at the dwarf again. I didn't see Mommy crying. I said, "Mommy, I want you to hold me in your arms."

Mommy said . . . I don't know what she said. I don't remember. It wasn't that I was tired. I just wanted to see if she was crying so that I could start crying myself. Mommy dried her eyes, like this. Now you, Dwarf, stand in front of us, in front of me and my mother, and all of these people, who are over here. Stretch out your hands, like this. Now say in a loud voice, "Ladies, the time is up, please leave."

Now turn around to Daddy and to the others and speak. Say something, say something so that they all go away, that Daddy too goes away. Daddy had grown thin. But he was smiling, like when he hugged me or when he tickled me under my arms, exactly like that. But now I can't laugh. Uncle Naser pulled that brat Mehri's ear and said, "Child, what do you want from Maryam's dolls?"

Well done. If the china doll still existed, if Mehri hadn't broken her, right now she would turn around and wave. I must also wave, like this. After that I must also cry. Daddy wanted to come. He couldn't. You, Dwarf, go over there, and stop Daddy. Mommy said, "Didn't Daddy tell you not to cry?"

I wanted not to cry. I always listen to Daddy's words. If he comes back, even if he pulls my ear, like Uncle Naser, I won't cry. I'll never hit Daddy, either. He used to say, "Hit me!"

I slapped him on the side of his face. He laughed. He said, "Hit me harder!"

I hit him, once on this side, once on that side, just like this. Dwarf, but you fall down. Daddy didn't fall down. Get up now. I'll hit softly, with only a finger, I'll hit Daddy like that, if he comes. Maybe I hurt him. Grandma said all the time. "Dear God, now what's going to happen to my son, if what they say is true?"

I said, "What are they saying?"

Mommy said, "Grandmother, please, in front of Maryam!?"

Mommy is bad, not all the time, only when she doesn't let Grandma speak, about Daddy that is. She is bad when she says loudly. "Grandmother, please."

She also says the same thing when Grandma cries. But once she herself broke down and cried: she cried in front of me. When Uncle Naser came . . . Dwarf, you be Uncle Naser. Come here. When you come in the house, you're supposed to stay right here. Come in, take this paper in your hand, it's the newspaper. Mommy said, "Now that you want to, open the door yourself."

Dwarf, now when you see Mommy, you have to bend down your head like this.

Hit yourself, too, hit yourself hard. But you can't do it. You have to hit your head hard, with both hands, and squat on the floor, like me, no, like Mommy. Squat and say, "Brother, what a grave misfortune has befallen us."

Dwarf, give her the newspaper.

Mommy turned the newspaper upside down. Mommy's hands were shaking. She said, "Where is it, then?"

Uncle Naser hurried to Grandma's room. Now you read. I don't know what. Say something, like when they talk on the radio, or on Uncle Naser's television, they just sit there and talk. Mommy said, "They are reading something, look how they always lower their eyes."

You can't see it. Maybe. Mommy doesn't lie. Or she does; didn't she say, "Your Daddy went to Abadan* to buy you a doll; as you know, here there aren't any"?

Uncle Naser said, "I'll buy her one myself."

I said, "I don't want one."

Of course I want one. If Daddy buys it . . . if he comes back. He isn't coming back. If he was, why did Mommy cry? She read and cried. They sometimes smile, too, when they read the newspaper. Like this. But now, I can't smile like them. Mommy can't, either. Uncle Naser came by my side, he patted me on the head and tousled my hair. You, Dwarf . . . no, I don't want you to touch my head. Uncle Naser tousled my hair in a funny way. I didn't like it. It's not that he messed up my hair, like that lady. The one who . . . all right, don't be mad at me, Dwarf, you're going to be the man now. Your desk is also here, a great big desk. On your desk there are, I don't know . . . all kinds of things. Mommy, Grandma, and I went in. Uncle Naser didn't come with us. He said, "You go ahead, I'll be right over there, waiting for you at the ice cream stand."

I said, "I'll also go with Uncle Naser."

It's not that I wanted any ice cream.

Then Daddy said, "Don't say that, don't ever say that."

Mommy said, "You should come with us; do you understand? Remember to say to the man: I want my Daddy."

Uncle Naser said, "Yes, dear, when you return, I'll buy you two ice creams."

---

* Abadan: A city in southwestern Iran.

I said, "I want it now!"

Mommy said, "Maryam!"

You too say loudly, "Maryam!" Grab my wrist and pull it. Then knock on the door, a big door. Now there is a head. . . . Come, Dwarf, look through the hole I made with my hand, at my Mommy, and also look at me. Now like Mommy you have to say some things so that I understand that you, Grandma, and I have come to see Daddy. Say it now. When the door opened, we went in. That same man said . . . I don't know what. He was big. He was taller than Mommy. He was also fat. Grandma said, "May God take me instead of my son."

She said it softly. Now, Dwarf, you are that man; you are big and very, very round, and you even have a mustache. Smile and say, "Please stay in that room."

After that a woman came. She was pretty, like my china doll. No, the china doll is Daddy; it's not here, so it's Daddy. That woman is really here. She was just like those women who speak on TV, no, who read from the newspaper and keep smiling. Mommy cried. That day when . . . that same day, I mean that day, you know I already told you. The woman came and said, "Ladies you have to excuse me."

Afterward she also said some other things. First she put her hand on Grandma's chest. Grandma said, "Madam, but I . . . ."

Mommy said, "Grandma, please!"

She said it softly. But her face was like when she said it loudly, just like when she wants to scold me. Now she doesn't scold me anymore. If she'd only scold me! Even if she grabs my hands and hits me on my knuckles a couple of times, I won't cry. Even when I took one of Daddy's books, she didn't scold me. She only took it from me and put it in its place. Now she says, "Maryam, my dear, you shouldn't take Daddy's things."

I wanted to say, "Daddy isn't gonna come back anyway." I didn't say that I thought if I didn't say it, he'd come back for sure. If I touch his books, if I just tear one of them a bit he would appear. He'd grab both of my ears. He wouldn't pull them hard. Only a bit. He'd say, "One day Daddy will cut off his daughter's two ears and place them in her hands."

If I had been bad or wanted to go out with him, he'd say, "Now Daddy is going to come and pull both her ears and look his Maryam in the eye."

One day, however much he wanted to give me an angry look, he couldn't. Uncle Naser could. Not anymore. He grabbed Mehri's ear and pulled it. Daddy wouldn't. Then both of us started laughing. We laughed a lot. Then I also pulled Daddy's ears. Daddy's ears were small. When he was sitting down, I could grab them and look in his eyes. The woman sat down next to me, like this. She said, "May I, little lady?"

Grandma said, "Now, why her?"

Mommy said again, "Grandma, haven't you heard what the lady just said?"

Then the woman put her fingers in my hair. Mommy had braided my hair. She'd gathered and tied it at the top of my head. You can't ever imagine how pretty I looked. Because of that the woman kissed me. Then she put her hand . . . look, now I am that woman. Good, if I put my hand under your skirt, will you like that? She also did it to Mommy. . . . Grandma, too. Grandma said, "God help me!"

Mommy didn't say, "Grandma, please." She should have said it. The woman said, "Little lady, you are very pretty. Do you go to school?"

Mommy said, "No, she's going next year."

What's it to her? I'll put my books in my bag. I'll make a bow with a red ribbon like the ribbon of Uncle Naser's Mehri and place it on my head. Mommy will do that. I can count to fifty. Daddy taught me. One, two, three, four . . . I can't do it now. Daddy said, "My daughter is going to be a painter. My daughter is going to sit right there, at her own desk, and paint so that Daddy can do his work."

Then he sat at his desk and read. No matter how many times I said, "Daddy!" he didn't hear me. Then when I cried, "Daddy, Daddy!" he put down his glasses. He said, "What is it, my dear?"

I said, "Look at what I've drawn, Daddy."

He said, "Let Daddy see."

Grandma said, "If you ever draw a picture of me your Daddy is going to burn in hell."

She thought he would! Daddy laughed. He looked and laughed. He showed it to Uncle Naser. It was no big deal! See, like this, this is Grandma's belly. Well, then, now this is her head, and these are her eyes. Her mouth has to be very big because she scolds me all the time. Daddy said, "Where is her nose then?"

I said, "Her mouth is so big that you can't see it."

Just like it is now, she doesn't have one. OK now, Dwarf, you sit down at your desk . . . and this is Mommy. Wait till I draw Grandma's hand. My hand was in my Grandma's hand. Now you, Dwarf, get up from behind your desk, come here, and smile. Say "hello" to Grandma and Mommy. Then bend down and pinch me on the cheek, just like this. All right, it didn't hurt; but, well, I didn't like it, either. Dwarf, speak to me and say, "What's your name?"

With that huge mouth of hers, Grandma is supposed to say, "This is Maryam, she kisses your hand."

Then a man brought tea. He didn't bring one for me. I don't like it anyway. Now Grandma is supposed to say something that I don't understand. Talk, but talk about Daddy. Say, "After all, Sir, whatever they may be, they are young. They've read some things. . . ."

She was talking about Daddy, Mommy's face looked strange. Dwarf, you aren't supposed to see that. You are turned toward Grandma, and you have to hold your tea. Say, "Well, the rest is in their own hands. Whenever they come and . . ."

I don't know. He talked like the newspapers. I think he wanted Daddy to come sit down like this, and look at his newspaper from the corner of his eye and talk like him.

Now you talk, like Mommy, talk about Daddy, say something that Grandma doesn't understand, either. Now, Dwarf, say, "All right. Please come tomorrow. If you'd like, bring the child, as well. Perhaps he'll agree."

Grandma hit me with this part of her hand. I understood why she hit me. Lowered my head. Grandma hit me, she hit me hard. I looked at her. She made a strange face. You could only see her nose. Now I have to say to the dwarf, "Sir, I want my Daddy."

The dwarf is supposed to say, "You'll go and see him, my dear. But remember to say, 'Daddy, when are you coming home?'"

Mommy said, "If that doesn't work, then what?"

Dwarf, you are not supposed to understand that Mommy was talking about Daddy. Now say, "Well, make her do it, repeat it many times until she remembers it."

Mommy didn't say anything else. Grandma said, "She's talking about my son."

Dwarf, say . . . no, first put your hands behind your back and go toward your desk. Then say, "All right, all right, I don't know what else."

Now, Dwarf, we are going, Mommy, Grandma, and I. Come here, bend down, and say softly, "You haven't told me your name, pretty little girl."

Then you also say, "You come tomorrow to see your Daddy for sure."

Daddy wasn't there. Daddy didn't come. Now, I am supposed to say, "Mommy, why doesn't he come then?"

She said, "I don't know. It must be that Daddy doesn't like Mommy."

"Why not, Mommy?"

You say, "Daddy is nice, my dear."

"No, he is bad, he doesn't like Mommy."

That's what I told Mommy. She didn't say anything else. She only wiped her eyes. Grandma didn't come. She couldn't. She was lying on her bed all the time and moaning. Grandma's legs hurt. Uncle Naser comes and sits down by her side and talks to her. He doesn't bring that little devil Mehri. When I come by Grandma's side, they stop talking. Now, Dwarf, you have to say . . . no, don't say anything. I'll be Uncle Naser and say, "It's tomorrow, Mother."

Grandma said, "If I could only see him! I am afraid to die and not see my son again."

Mommy said, "Don't say such things, Grandma."

She said, "I just know that I won't see him."

When Mommy saw me, she stopped crying. She wasn't crying for Grandma. She was crying for Daddy.

Uncle Naser said, "They won't let anyone in. But still, one might be able to see him. My sister-in-law and I are going."

Mommy said, "Brother, please!"

She didn't say it loudly. Uncle Naser said, "You little devil, were you here?"

I said, "I'm also coming."

Now Mommy is supposed to say, "Maryam."

If she hadn't said that, they would have taken me with them. They didn't. Uncle Naser said, "If you're a good girl, I'll buy you a big doll."

Daddy wouldn't say, "If you're a good girl." He said, "What kind do you want?"

I said, "Exactly like the old one, actually I want the old one."

Daddy said, "If they put it back together, it'll look ugly."

Grandma is supposed to say, "Have you seen him?"

Uncle Naser said, "Only for a minute. He was doing fine."

I said, "Did he have hair on his head?"

He said, "Yes, my dear." He also said to me, "Uncle Naser must cut off Maryam's ears and place them in her hands."

I said, "He wouldn't say that. Now Daddy wouldn't say that."

Whenever Daddy said that, I'd put my hands on my ears and run away. Daddy would laugh and come running after me. Now Grandma must say, "Why didn't they let you in?"

Uncle Naser said, "It was surrounded; they weren't allowing anyone in."

I said, "What does 'surrounded' mean?"

Uncle Naser didn't say anything. It's OK. I don't care. I already know that there were twenty, no, at least fifty men like dwarfs. You stand there, Dwarf . . . and one also here . . . many others. The china doll was supposed to stand in the middle, if she were still here. Mehri threw her on the floor in anger. I know that she did it because she is mean. Uncle Naser said, "Tomorrow they'll write it in the newspapers for sure."

Mommy said, "I don't think so."

Grandma said, "If my feet would allow me; if I only could!"

Grandma can't stand up anymore. If only she could! Uncle Naser and Mommy carry her by the arms. Like the china doll when both of her legs fell off. Her head was also broken. She was in three pieces. Daddy said, "Throw it in the garbage can."

I said, "But, is she dead, Daddy?"

He said, "Dolls don't die, my dear, they break."

I said, "Na. They die. Dolls also die, like Grandpa."

I buried her myself. In the garden, I dug a small hole for her. I wrapped the remains in my white handkerchief, then I buried her. I even poured water on the grave. Then I also cut a few roses and fluttered their petals on the grave. If Grandpa were alive, he wouldn't have let me cut them. The man sat next to Grandpa's tomb. He read some things from a book that I didn't understand. He read quickly and moved his head from side to side. But now, we don't have any red roses. We had some when Grandpa was alive, Grandma said. "Then his sister came. She gathered his bones, washed them in rose water, and buried them underneath the red rose tree. He then turned into a nightingale, flip, flip, flip. . . ." The nightingale went and perched . . . I don't have the patience to explain it to you anymore. Grandma doesn't have the patience, either. Uncle Naser said, "Don't cry, Mother! He will stay there a few years; then he'll come back."

Mommy said, "How many years?"

You say, "How many years?" and then hurry into that room. I also wanted to cry. I didn't. Then Daddy said, "Don't cry!" Daddy said, "No, my Maryam must not ask for Daddy, not from them." He said it on that day when Daddy didn't look like Daddy. He was like the china doll, like when that little devil Mehri broke her. His face had become so strange. Mommy was lying on the bed. Uncle Naser said something that made Mommy speak. You say it. Na, don't. Mommy said something bad. Mommy is very bad; sometimes she's bad, when she talks to Uncle Naser to spite him, when she talks about Daddy. Daddy was very big. He'd lift me up and put me on his shoulders. He said, "My Maryam has to come and stand on Daddy's hand."

Like this. He'd say, "Close your eyes!"

I'd close them. Then I'd go up, that high. He'd say, "Now open your eyes."

I was up, close to the lamp, Mommy told me. Haven't I told you already? Uncle Naser saw me. If he hadn't seen me, he'd say, "What're you looking for here, child?"

After that they didn't say a word. If they'd said anything, if they'd talked about Daddy in front of me, Daddy would have come for sure. The dwarf didn't let him. You hit him with these hands, eh? Daddy was like my china doll. He was broken to pieces. You're bad. I'm also going to tear off your legs. I'm going to break your hands. I'm even going to tip off your head. I'm not going to bury you, either, like my china doll that I buried underneath the red rose tree. I won't cry for you, either. But it's just that I can't stop crying.

JALAL AL-E AHMAD
(1923—1969)

Gharbzadegi

(EXCERPT)

Translated from the Persian by John Green and Ahmad Alizadeh

Chapter One

The Outline of a Disease

I SAY THAT *Gharbzadegi** is like cholera. If this seems distasteful. I could say it's like heatstroke or frostbite. But no. It's at least as bad as sawflies in the wheat fields. Have you ever seen how they infest wheat? From within. There's a healthy skin in place, but it's only a skin, just like the shell of a cicada on a tree. In any case, we're talking about a disease. A disease that comes from without, fostered in an environment made for breeding diseases. Let's look for the characteristics of this disease, its cause or causes, and if possible, a cure.

This *Gharbzadegi* has two heads. One is the West, the other is ourselves who are "Weststruck." By ourselves, I mean a part of the East. Rather than two heads, let's say two poles, or two extremities, because we're talking about two ends of a single continuum, at least, if not two sides of the world. Instead of the West, let's say to a certain extent all of Europe and Soviet Russia and all of North America, or let's say the advanced countries, or the developed countries, or the industrialized nations, or any country able to bring raw materials to a state of refinement with the aid of machines and put them on the market as merchandise. These raw materials are not only iron ore, petroleum, gut,

---

* *Gharbzadegi*: A word invented by Jalal Al-e Ahmad to mean "Westoxification" or "Weststruckness."

cotton, or gum tragacanth. There's also mythology. There are also belief systems. There's also music. There are also celestial worlds. Instead of ourselves, who are part of the other pole, we can say Asia, Africa, or the underdeveloped countries, or developing countries, or nonindustrialized nations, or that group of countries who are consumers of products manufactured in the West, products whose raw materials—the very ones I listed—come from the same part of the world, meaning from countries in the process of growing. Petroleum from the shores of the Persian Gulf, jute and spices from India, African jazz, silk and opium from China, anthropology from the South Sea Islands, and sociology from Africa. These last two come from South America too, from the Aztec and Inca tribes, who were totally victimized by the advent of Christianity. Yes, everything comes from somewhere, and we're in the middle. With these latter groups, our points of commonality are more numerous than our differences.

It's not within the scope of the present work to define these two poles or extremities from the point of view of economics, politics, sociology, psychology, or civilization. Those are exacting tasks for specialists. You will see, however, that I will be compelled from time to time to make use of all of these disciplines. The only thing left to say here is that in my view, East and West are no longer two geographical concepts as such. To a European or an American, the West means Europe and America and the East means Soviet Russia, China, and the Eastern European countries. To me, however, West and East have neither a political nor a geographical meaning. Instead, these are two economic concepts. The West means the countries with full stomachs, and the East means the ones that are hungry. To me the Union of South Africa is a little piece of the West too, even though it's at the southernmost extreme of Africa, and most of the Latin American nations are part of the East, although they're on the other side of the globe.

In any case it's true that to measure an earthquake one must consult the university's seismograph, but before the seismograph records anything, the villager's horse, even though he's balky and stupid, has fled and taken refuge in the desert. Yes, this writer would like to sense, with a sharper nose than a sheepdog, and with sharper eyes than a crow, those things that others have passed over deliberately, or the presentation of which has appeared to offer no advantage to livelihood or welfare in the next world.

Let me list, therefore, the collective general characteristics of the countries in the first group: high wages, low mortality rates, low birth rates, well-organized social services, adequate nutrition (at least 3,000 calories a day), annual per capita income of more than 3,000 tomans [$430] per year,* and a democratic façade inherited from the French Revolution.

The corresponding characteristics of the second group are these: low wages, high mortality rates, higher birth rates, no social services, or merely the pretense of social services, poor nutrition (1,000 calories a day at most), annual per capita income of less than 500 tomans [$75] per year, no concept of democracy, and a legacy of colonization since its earliest days. We're obviously in the second group, the group of hungry nations, the first group being all the nations with full stomachs, as Josue de Castro puts it in his *The Geography of Hunger.* You see that not only is the gap between the two extremities very wide, but, as Tibor Mende said, "It is a bottomless pit that gets deeper and deeper every day."† Thus wealth and poverty, power and impotence, knowledge and ignorance, prosperity and desolation, and civilization and savagery have become polarized in the world.

One pole is controlled by the satiated, the rich and powerful and the makers and exporters of manufactured goods, the other by the hungry, the poor and the weak, the consumers and importers. The heartbeat of evolution on that side of the world is progressive, while the stagnant pulse on this side is on the verge of stopping. This disparity does not simply arise because of the separation in space and time, nor is it quantifiable. It's a qualitative disparity between two widely separated and mutually repellent poles. On the other side is a world that has become frightened of its own dynamism, and on our side is a world that has not yet found a channel of leadership for its scattered movements, which dissipate instead into nothing. Each of these two worlds is looking for something in its own way.

---

* Annual per capita income: The essay was written in 1962.

† Tibor Mende, *Reflexions sur l'histoire d'aujourd'hui, entre la peur et l'espoir* (Paris, 1958).

So the time is now past when we divided the world into two "blocs," the two blocs of East and West, or communist and noncommunist. Although the first articles of most of the constitutions of the governments of the world still contain that huge twentieth-century sham, the flirtation between the United States and Soviet Russia (the two supposedly unrivaled leaders of those blocs) over the Suez Canal and Cuba showed how the owners of two neighboring villages can sit down together comfortably at the same table, and following that the nuclear test ban treaty and other instances. Therefore our time, besides no longer being a time of confrontation between the rich and poor classes inside borders, or a time of nationalist revolutions, is also not a time of confrontation between "isms" and ideologies. Behind the scenes at every riot, coup d'état, or uprising in Zanzibar, Syria, or Uruguay, one must look to see what plot by what colonialist company or government backing it, lies hidden. Furthermore, regional wars of our time can no longer be called wars between differing ideas—even superficially. These days any schoolchild not only sees the expansionist aims of mechanized industry on both sides of the dispute at work behind the scenes in World War II, but also sees that the things that were happening in Cuba, the Congo, the Suez Canal, and Algeria were disputes over sugar, diamonds, and oil. The bloodshed in Cyprus, Zanzibar, Aden, and Vietnam was for achieving a bridgehead to protect trade routes, which are the first determinant of the policy of governments.

Our time is no longer a time when they scare the people with "communism" in the "West" and with the bourgeoisie and liberalism in the "East." Now even the kings of nations can be superficial revolutionaries and speak charismatically, and Khrushchev can buy wheat from America. Now all these "isms" and ideologies have become pathways to the exalted throne of "machinism" and machines. The most interesting development in this regard is the deviation taken by the political compasses of leftists and leftist pretenders throughout the world in their turn toward the East. They have made a ninety-degree turn from Moscow to Peking, because Russia is no longer "the leader of the world revolution." Rather it is a top contender in the circle of those who possess atomic missiles. A direct telegraph line operates between the Kremlin in Moscow and the White House in Washington, showing that there is no longer even the need for British mediation in these dealings. Even those who hold the reins of power in our country have realized that the danger of Soviet Russia has diminished. The pasture Soviet Russia was grazing in was the abominable spoils of World War I. The time has come to phase out Stalin, and Radio Moscow has come out backing the referendum of "the sixth of Bahman!"* In any case Communist China has taken Soviet Russia's place. Why? Because it is calling all the world's underfed people to unite in the hope of reaching paradise tomorrow, just as Russia did in 1930. If Russia had population of some 100 million then, China now has a population of 750 million.

It's true, as Marx said, that we now have two worlds in dispute, but these two worlds have become somewhat more extensive since his time, and that dispute has much more complicated characteristics than a dispute between workers and management. Our world is a world of confrontation between the poor and the rich in a worldwide arena. Our time is a time of two worlds. One is on the side of manufacturing, distributing, and exporting machines; the other is on the side of using, wearing out, and dismantling them. One is a producer, the other a consumer. And where is the arena of this conflict? The world market. And its weapons? Besides tanks, artillery, bombers, and missile-launchers, themselves the manufactures of that Western world, there is UNESCO, FAO, the United Nations, ECAFE,† and other so-called international institutions that seem to be international and universal, but the truth of the matter is that they're Western tricksters who bring colonialism to that second world in a new suit, to South America, to Asia, to Africa. And this is where the basis of the *Gharbzadegi* of all non-Western nations lies. This is not a discussion about rejecting or refusing machines, as the utopians imagined in the early nineteenth century. Not at all. The inundation of the world by machines is a historical inevitability. It's a discussion about the nature of our encounter with machines—as a growing nation, and we already saw the people

---

* Sixth of Bahman: Reference to a series of land and social reforms (known as the "White Revolution") made by Muhammad Reza Pahlavi, the last shah of Iran, and passed by national referendum on January 26, 1963.

† UNESCO: United Nations Educational, Scientific and Cultural Organization. FAO: United Nations Food and Agriculture Organization. ECAFE: United Nations Economic Commission for Asia and the Far East.

of the nations in the second group—and about the fact that we don't make machines, but because of economic and political necessity—and that international confrontation between rich and poor—we must be docile and humble consumers of Western products, or at best must be poorly paid, contented, and submissive repairmen for whatever comes from the West.

These things, of themselves, make it necessary for us to adapt ourselves, our government, our culture, and our daily lives to the pattern of machines. Everything must conform to the specifications of machines. If those who manufacture machines, in the wake of the gradual changes of two to three hundred years, have gradually become accustomed to this new God and its heaven and hell, what does the Kuwaiti say, who just got his machine yesterday, or the Congolese, or what about me, the Iranian? How are we going to jump out of this three-hundred-year historical pit? Forget about other people. Let me deal directly with us. The basic thesis of this short essay is that we've not been able to retain our own cultural/historical personality during our encounter with machines and in the face of their inevitable assault. In fact, we've been destroyed. The point is that we've been unable to take a calculated and well-assessed position in the face of this monster of the new century, not even to the extent that Japan has done. The point is that as long as we don't perceive the nature and philosophical basis of Western culture, and continue to behave as Westerners superficially, we'll be like the donkey who posed as a lion and ended up being eaten by one. If the one who builds machines is now screaming and suffocating, we don't even complain about having become slaves to machines. We even brag about it. For two hundred years we've been like a crow who tries to be a partridge (if we can be sure which is the crow and which is the partridge).

An obvious principle emerges from all this. It's obvious that as long as we only use machines and don't make them, we're Weststruck. Ironically, as soon as we start building machines we'll be afflicted by them, like the West, which is now suffering from the effects of runaway technology.

Never mind that we didn't even have the capability Japan has, which undertook to understand machines one hundred years ago, made itself a competitor with the West in its affliction with machines, defeated the tsars (1905) and America (1941), and took their markets away from them before that. The West ended up smashing them with the atomic bomb to teach them the consequences of playing with fire, and now too that the Western "free world" has opened the world's vast markets to Japanese goods, it's because they have invested in all the Japanese industries. They also intend to recover the military costs of protecting those islands, whose leaders, having come to their senses since World War II, are now totally inept where weaponry, armies, and militarism are concerned. And perhaps it's also because the simple American wants to ease the burden of conscience that made a madman of that abominable bomber pilot who repeated the story of Ad and Thamud* at Hiroshima and Nagasaki.

Something else is obvious to us as well, and that is that since the time the "West" called us—from the eastern shores of the Mediterranean to India—the "East" as it arose from its hibernation of the Dark Ages seeking the sunlight, and spices, silk, and other goods, they've been coming to the East, first as pilgrims to the holy shrines (to Bethlehem, Nazareth, and so on), then in the armor of the Crusades, then in the guise of tradesmen, then under the protection of their treasure-laden warships, then as Christian missionaries, and finally in the name of promoting civilization. This last one was a veritable celestial mission. After all, "colonization" draws its roots from "development," and whoever engages in "development" inevitably takes part in civilization.

It's interesting that among those countries who were beneath the heel of the colonialist vanguard, Africa was the most receptive and promising, and do you know why it was more promising? Because besides the raw materials it had (and abundant they were: gold, diamonds, copper, ivory, and many other raw materials), its natives walked in no urban tradition or widespread religion. Every tribe had its own god, chief, customs, and language. And so scattered! And inevitably, so receptive to authority! Most important of all, all its natives went around naked. It was too hot to wear clothes. They celebrated and prayed in

---

* Ad and Thamud: Two ancient tribes thought to be among the first to inhabit the Arabian Peninsula. According to the Qur'an, both tribes were utterly destroyed by God for disobeying the prophets.

Manchester when Stanley, a world traveler in the tradition of the English humanitarian, brought this good news back to his country from the Congo. After all, a meter of cloth every year for every man and woman of the Congo to put on, become "civilized," and wear to Sunday services would equal 320 million yards of Manchester cloth every year. We know that the colonialist vanguard included Christian missionaries, and that they built churches in the vicinity of every merchant throughout the world and, by means of subtle trickery, persuaded the native people to attend them. And now, with the removal of the feast of colonialism from those areas, for every commercial outlet that closes, a church door closes too.

Africa was also more promising and receptive for those gentlemen because the African natives were raw material themselves for the use of all kinds of Western laboratories in the development of the fields of anthropology, sociology, ethnology, linguistics, and a thousand other kinds of "ologies" based on the background of African and Australian experience, enabling the professors of Cambridge, the Sorbonne, and Leiden to become established in their chairs using these same "ologies," and to see the other side of their own urban civilization in African primitivity.

We Middle Easterners were neither so receptive nor so promising. Why? Because if we want to speak more personally, that is, to speak of ourselves, we must ask why weren't we Muslim Easterners more receptive? You can see that the answer is embedded in the very question, for within our Islamic totality we apparently weren't worth studying.

It was for this reason that the West, in its encounter with us, not only came into conflict with our Islamic totality (in the instances of the bloody encouragement of Shi'ism at the beginning of the Safavid dynasty, the sowing of conflict between us and the Ottomans, the encouragement of the Baha'i movement in the middle of the Qajar dynasty, the parceling of the Ottoman Empire after World War I, and finally in confrontation with the Shi'i clergy in the disturbances of the Constitutional Revolution and afterward), but it also tried to disrupt that fragmented totality, which was only a totality in appearance, from within as quickly as possible. They also tried to make us into raw material like the African natives, and then to take us to their laboratories.

This is why the *Encyclopedia of Islam* is at the top of the list of Western encyclopedias. We ourselves are still asleep, but the Westerner has taken us to his laboratory in this encyclopedia.

India, after all, was a place something like Africa, with that "Babel" of tongues and the dispersion of races and sects. And South America had instantly turned Christian at the points of the Spaniards' swords. And the Pacific was itself an archipelago of islands, which is to say the ideal setting for sowing discord. Thus, in appearance and in the reality of the Islamic totality, we were the only barrier to the spread (colonialism = Christianity) of European civilization, meaning to Western industry's search for markets.

The Ottoman artillery that stopped at the gates of Vienna was the end of a process that had begun in 732 AD in Andalusia.* What do we call this twelve-century period of conflict and rivalry between East and West if we don't call it a conflict between Islam and Christianity? In any case, now—in this age we're living in—I as an Asian descendant of that Islamic totality, and that African or Australian descendant of savagery and primitivity—both equally and to the same extent—are perfectly welcome from the standpoint of the civilized nations of the West and the machine builders to content ourselves with being museum exhibits, to remain simply something worth studying in a museum or a laboratory and nothing more. Don't you dare tamper with this raw material!

Now it's no longer a matter of them wanting the petroleum from Khuzestan or Qatar in unrefined form, the diamonds from Katanga in the rough, or the chromite from Kerman unsmelted. What matters now is that I, as an Asian or an African, must even preserve my literature, my culture, my music, my religion, and everything else I have in perfect condition just like an artifact right out of the ground, so that these gentlemen can come and gawk, and take it to their museums and say, "Oh yes, here's another form of primitivity!"

Now, after this introduction, allow me, an Easterner with his feet planted firmly in tradition, eager to make a two- or three-hundred-year leap and obliged to make up for so much anxiety and straggling,

---

* Andalusia: A reference to the defeat of Andalusian caliph Abd al-Rahman by the Frankish military commander Charles Martel.

and sitting in the middle of that fragmented Islamic totality, to offer the following definition of *Gharbzadegi*:

[It is] all the symptoms that have been created in the life, culture, civilization, and manner of thinking of the peoples on this side of the world without any historical background or support from tradition, and with no thread of continuity through the changes. They are merely the by-products of machines, or, better yet, they are their preliminary substitutes. Having said this, it is clear that if it be said that we are one of those peoples, since the discussion in this booklet in a primary way pertains to the regional environment, language, tradition, and religion of its author, it is also even clearer that if we have machines, that is to say if we build machines, there is no further need for their by-products to serve as preliminaries and substitutes.

Gharbzadegi is therefore a characteristic of an era in which we haven't yet obtained machines and don't understand the mysteries of their structure and construction.

Gharbzadegi is a characteristic of a period of time when we have not become familiar with the prerequisites for machines—meaning the new sciences and technology.

Gharbzadegi is a characteristic of a time in our history when we're compelled to use machines because of the market and economic constraints on us to use machines and because of the incoming and outgoing petroleum.

What brought on this era? What happened that other people, ignoring us completely while they changed and developed their machines, built, carried out plans, and moved in and out of our midst and we awoke to find every oil derrick a spike impaling the land? Why did we end up Weststruck?

Let's go back to history.

SIMIN DANESHVAR

(B. 1921)

The Playhouse

Translated from the Persian by Maryam Mafi

MEHDI SIAH LOOKED in the mirror. He took the red cape off the nail and draped it over his clothes, saying: "Now we're ready. But alas! Where is your whip, eunuch of the Caliph's court?" He found the whip on the nail from which hung the Caliph's robe. He took it. Mehdi Siah always came earlier than the other actors because blacking his face, hands, and neck took a long time. What's more, washing off the black was even harder than putting it on; he therefore also always had to leave later than everyone else.

The small door connecting the playhouse auditorium to the area backstage, which was a lengthy corridor with all the typical character-istics, was opened. A short, young man with curly hair bent his head and walked in. Siah stood facing him. He asked: "Who the hell are you? Look, brother, no one is allowed in the playhouse." He turned on a switch, and a bright light lit the theater. He looked at the short man and continued. "What kind of creature are you? Oh, God! I think I'm going to be scared. Look at his ring; it's got a skull on it. See his tie pin; it's a diamond. What kind of oats are you looking for, all dressed up in this stable? Where do you think you're going with all your glitz?" He laughed and laughed and raised his whip. The young man asked: "Are you the famous Mehdi Siah?"

"Mehdi Siah, I am, but I didn't know I was famous."

"I've heard people come to this theater only to see you."

"Yeah, brother," said Siah. "People laugh because of me at night, and at me in the morning."

The young man introduced himself.

"I've come to replace Mohsen. He's sick. He said I had to become

399

Juji Khan. But I don't know how. I'm scared. I've never been on stage before."

Siah wanted to laugh and tease the young novice. Whatever he was, famous or unknown, being witty was Siah's specialty. When he disappeared into his adopted skin, a witty personality would awaken in him. But when he was himself, one could no longer say he even had a personality. He saw himself as a total stranger in the world. On stage, people's eyes were fixed on him alone. But off stage, there were no eyes on him at all. He was tempted to tease the young man. Usually he never missed these opportunities to exercise his wit. But helping people was also one of his unfailing specialties. He said: "Don't be scared, nobody knows which role they'll be playing."

"Don't you read the play first? Don't you rehearse?"

"No, brother," said Siah. "None of that stuff here. The opening night of each play, the owner of the playhouse comes, tells the story, and decides each person's role. Then we wear our costumes and go off to act. The first night is difficult for everyone; afterward it becomes routine. The important thing is for the first person to start off well."

"You mean you improvise? Well, that's quite difficult. Even if I had rehearsed beforehand I'd still be scared to go on the stage."

Siah was about to say: "Impro . . . what? Watch out you don't get struck by the evil eye!" But he didn't. Instead he tried to encourage the young man and said: "This is no sophisticated playhouse in Petelbourg. It's a dilapidated theater next to the fruit and vegetable market. Who do you suppose the audience is? A bunch of experts? Full of themselves with thick cigars in their mouths? People who don't even smile when everyone else is falling over with laughter? No, my friend. Here we deal with fruit and vegetable vendors, porters, drivers, and gravediggers. After they have delivered their loads or buried their dead, they come to seek us. Entertaining this kind of crowd is not such a difficult task."

Siah helped the young man get dressed. He had him wear a tight robe and tied a scarf around it. Using a piece of coal, he raised his eyebrows and fixed the corners of his eyes to match. "Go on, look at yourself in the mirror," said Siah. "Now, you are Juji Khan, the son of the King of China, who has to ask for the Caliph's daughter's hand in marriage. And me, I am the castle guard."

Juji Khan went toward the mirror in which Siah was observing him. He said: "Thanks a lot. What are these shabby clothes! Besides, this costume is not even Chinese."

Siah was offended. Not because he wanted to defend the theater, no. He was defending his own beliefs. "Brother, what you say is both right and wrong. I have made your face Chinese, that should be enough. You have to act well so that the audience understands from your face and acting that you are Chinese. Besides, is my costume a black's? Is the Caliph's costume a real Caliph's? Look, these clothes hanging from the nails are all that this theater owns in the world. That torn one over there is the costume of the Caliph of Baghdad. And that is his tuft. The other one there is the civil servant's costume. That one is the witch's costume. That one belongs to the lover, and the other is the Haji's costume. These costumes are needed in every play. There's always a lover who foolishly falls in love with the king's daughter and there appear rivals who come from everywhere. And eventually he either wins the girl or loses her. And I'm the guard, in other words, Haji's servant. But I feel sorry for the lovers. Secretly, I help them. And let me tell you this, too; the girl's really worth falling in love with. You'll see, as soon as you set eyes on her, your acting will naturally improve."

They became silent. They sat facing each other on the empty benches backstage. From where he was sitting Mehdi Siah could see himself in the mirror. The room was cold, and Mehdi had put his hands under his arms. He was not wearing his red hat yet, and his eyes were searching for it. When he saw the hat had fallen on a bench, he was relieved.

The young man's words, "People come to this theater for you," had put him in a thoughtful mood. He had confidence in his own talent. Most of his colleagues had a drink to overcome their fear before going on the stage. He, however, needed neither drink nor any other kind of stimulant. For him to become "black" was the most natural act. When he appeared, he brilliantly mastered both stage and audience. His concentration was amazingly intense. Novices had their eyes fixed on his lips, and at times they would forget where they were. It was he who had to coax them to remember their lines. He did all the work, but others got to make love to the girl. When it came time to witness the love-making, a deep sorrow would engulf his heart, until the audience snapped him out of it: "Siah, dear, don't doze off!" If ever he was a moment late on stage the entire audience would whistle and call for him. And he would smoothly and comfortably continue his part. Despite all this, Siah had never heard a word of admiration from the owner of the playhouse nor from any of his colleagues. And the admiration of the audience was confined to those few hours of the play; next morning no one even recognized him.

The young man watched Siah with interest. "Where did you learn how to act?" he asked. "Did you study acting?"

"No. I haven't had much of an education, but I've seen quite a bit of blackness and intrigue in my life. Besides, I only know how to play the role of the 'black Siah.'"

"I always thought, with all your mastery, you must have studied for years," said the young man.

"In my forty-odd years, there hasn't been a trick I haven't played, from storytelling to narrating epics of the *Shahnameh** in the coffee house. For a long time I was a storyteller and poetry reader to the grand nephew of Zell-ol Sultan.† I've also fooled around with political parties. And for twenty years now, I have played the role of 'Siah' in the theater. Don't you think that's enough? There are times when one asks oneself: Is it I who's done all this living? Is it I who's witnessed all these tricks?"

The young man stood up. He wanted to say something but was too shy. He stood in front of the mirror, his back to Siah, and muttered:

"I wanted to say that . . . I am a graduate of the School of Acting. But I don't have one bit of your courage. I'm even scared to step up on the stage. Very scared."

"Then what have they taught you in school? Eh?" asked Siah.

The young man turned around. He sat next to Siah and said: "They taught us plenty in school, but there were also many things they didn't teach us, many things. And maybe it's me who's timid. Once I was supposed to play Hamlet. I had rehearsed quite a bit, but as I was about

---

* *Shahnameh*: The national epic of Iran, written by the poet Ferdowsi around 1000 CE.

† Zell-ol Sultan: Villainous Qajar prince who was governor of Isfahan from 1874 to 1907.

to step onto the stage, I secretly peeked at the auditorium. I saw that, besides my classmates, a few strangers had also come. I got the butter-flies. I didn't go on stage at all."

Siah's wit broke out. "You said H'omelet? Well, it obviously wasn't your fault at all. We don't go much for making omelets; ours is an eggplant dish, *Kashk-e Bademjan.*"*

The young man laughed and said:

"Even though you've never studied acting, nevertheless, because of your tremendous experiences, you have an extensive knowledge of culture. Your talent is also extraordinary. And even more important, I don't know why, but one feels like confiding in you." Then he con-tinued: "Do you know what the greatest tragedy is?"

"Listen, brother, if you want to talk like a foreigner," replied Siah, "you and I won't get along. Can't you talk normal?"

"To tell the truth," said the young man, "I can speak any way you like. I speak quite well. It's only when I have to appear on stage that I become speechless. I have so many words in my head, but I can't utter them at the right moment. Once, in school, we were supposed to pres-ent the play *Our Beloved Country, Iran.* I was holding a box of matches in my hand. My role was to go and light the lantern on stage and say: 'O light of guidance, route of flight for the Iranian people, remain alight.' It was only one sentence. That night a few army officers were wandering about backstage. One of them came up to me and asked: 'What do you plan to do with those matches?' I became dumb. The officer searched my pockets. Do you think I could go on stage that night? No way! I had the butterflies again."

"Here again, it wasn't your fault," said Mehdi Siah sympathetically. "You were going to speak of the greatest foreign imitation of all."

"The greatest of tragedies."

"I, too, have heard of these things," Siah was about to say, but he changed his mind and waited.

"Excuse me," said the young man. "I was talking about the saddest of things. I believe the saddest thing in the world is when someone aspires to become a first-rate actor, painter, or poet but, despite his efforts, he fails. Sometimes it may be because he has to start earning a

---

* *Kashk-e Bademjan*: A Persian stew made with eggplant.

living; that is different. But the person who sacrifices everything and still can't—that's tragedy."

"You are right," said Siah. "You do speak well. I'm surprised you say you can't act. Then why did you substitute for Mohsen tonight?"

"I want to test myself one more time. Mohsen told me that you help motivate all the actors, without even being aware of it yourself. I thought if one gets to know a man who may give one a push—just a little push—maybe one will get going. Some go on their own. Some go without even knowing it. Others are untalented but get ahead with a lot of noise and clamor and cunning and cheating. But there are those who can't go alone. If one is lucky enough to meet a real man . . ."

"What about a real woman?" asked Siah with a wink.

"You mean if one falls in love . . . ?" began the young man.

His words were interrupted. The other actors, bending their heads as they walked through the low door, came backstage. The room became crowded. The Caliph was gluing on his beard. The lover was putting on his makeup. The witch was disheveling her hair. The manager was explaining Juji Khan's role to him, and Siah heard the young man mention "Acting School," but nothing of his fear. The actors went and sat down one by one. The Caliph lit his cigarette and told Siah, "Brother, check out the auditorium; see if it is full yet."

Siah slowly went toward the small door, dragging his feet behind him. He heard his colleagues' laughter. He peeked in through the crack of the door and saw a street sweeper in his municipal uniform sitting in the front row, right across from the curtain, cracking pumpkin seeds between his teeth. Siah liked his air, especially as he was sitting in the front section. "Great," he whispered, then returned and told the Caliph:

"There are a few here and there."

TOWARD THE END of the first act, right in the middle of things, the power went out. The stage and auditorium fell into a gravelike darkness. There was a moment of silence, and then chatter and clamor rose from the crowd. The street sweeper flicked his lighter and stood up, holding it in front of the stage. Some of the others lit matches. The children in the audience were scared and cried. The noise of chairs clattering was heard from the back of the auditorium. "Whoever has hidden anything, eat it now! Fast!" said Siah out loud. Only a few people laughed, which upset him. He said louder: "Are you having a nightmare?" This time nobody was listening to him to laugh. Siah changed his mind about entertaining the giant crowd, which had begun to move. He saw the Caliph's daughter in the dark as she walked in through the castle door. She came close to Siah and whispered in his ear: "Siah, dear, I'm going to be ill." The audience was whistling loudly and clapping hard. Darkness as black as tar had spread everywhere. The street sweeper's lighter had gone out. Siah took a look at the crowd. He imagined a thousand-handed monster clinging on to various spots with each hand.

"What are you waiting for? Take me away, otherwise I'll faint right here."

Siah took the Caliph's daughter's hand. It was wet. Fumbling in the dark, they left the stage and climbed up the stairs to the backstage area. As he opened the ladies' changing room door, the women, the two nurses of the Caliph's daughter, let out screams. "Calm down," said Siah. "Siah's not bothering anyone. The Caliph's daughter's ill."

He took the girl toward the only bench in the room and had her lie down. He told one of the nurses: "Sister, will you get a glass of water?" The nurse left the room. "I hope she'll find a lamp and bring it back with her," said Siah. He turned toward the other nurse and said: "Come and open her dress."

The monstrous-looking nurse moved around the room, bent over the girl's chest, fiddled a bit, and said:

"The knot's tangled. I can't untie it. Agha Mehdi, come and see; perhaps you can undo it."

Perhaps Siah could and wanted to, but it didn't happen. The nurse tore open the decorative filigree crisscrossing the girl's breasts. Siah could hear her as she asked the Caliph's daughter:

"Has he quarreled with you again?"

"Yes."

"He left?"

"Of course."

"I said from the very beginning that he is crazy. He spends well, but still, he's crazy. You poor woman, you'd better think about yourself now. Am I not right, Agha Mehdi?"

Siah, who was standing perplexed in the middle of the room, came beside the girl's bed. He sat on the bare floor and said in a fatherly fashion, "What can I say? All I know is that you are badly wrecking your life, girl. Don't you think it's a pity?"

He wished he could sit there forever next to the girl's bed, on the bare floor in the dark. He wished he could untie the tangled knot in the girl's life. He noticed the nurse in the dark who came and sat beside the bed and asked: "Did you take the pills?"

"I took them all right," the girl said, "but what's the use? These pills only make me ill. They don't get rid of *it*, and give me peace!"

The other nurse walked in with a lit candle and a bowl of water. She gave the candle to Mehdi, who, seeing her, had stood up. Her black eyes gleamed for a moment in the candlelight. "The show is over," she said. "There's no electricity. The crowd broke a few chairs. Two of them were arrested and taken to the station by the police. We'll see no money tonight."

Siah put the candle on the shelf above the Caliph's daughter's head. He was thinking that only Juji Khan could be happy about the show's closing. Juji Khan was to come on stage in the second act. Involuntarily he thought about the litter he had suggested they build for Juji Khan so that he would not panic as he came on stage. They had inserted wooden poles in the four sides of a handbarrow. A printed cloth hanging all around served as a curtain. Juji Khan was supposed to sit inside. The previous nights, Juji Khan had entered the stage on foot, along with his four ministers and courtiers.

Siah looked at the Caliph's daughter, who was sitting up and asking the nurse: "Are they really not going to pay us tonight?"

"I don't suppose so," said the nurse. "The officer said we have to return the audience's money."

"Then lend me twenty tomans."

"I swear I haven't got any."

The Caliph's daughter lowered her head and murmured:

"I have to take at least ten more of these pills, and each pill costs two tomans."

Siah thrust his hand under his red cape and searched his vest pockets. He took out a few bills. The Caliph's daughter embraced him and stuck her face to his, saying: "How good you are, Siah." Siah felt his neck become wet. When the Caliph's daughter lifted her head, Siah knew that her face, too, must have become black.

The following night at the new Juji Khan's insistence, Mehdi had a drink. He never drank before the show. The show itself naturally warmed him up. It was only after the show that sorrow, indolence, and fatigue would overtake him. Mehdi blackened himself carefully. He wet his hand and straightened the crease in the red cape. The cape was old and torn in places; it smelled damp. Struggling with witches and the girl's lovers was no easy task. Juji Khan had dressed by himself and was preparing the litter. But his face was pale, and Siah knew he was frightened. The Caliph, the ministers, the witch, the lover, and the civil servants were all ready; Siah had let them know that the theater was packed and that a few foreigners were sitting in the front row. One of them even had a camera with him. The street sweeper was sitting in exactly the same place as the night before.

The third bell rang, and the show began. Siah took his whip and joyfully entered the Caliph's palace. He appeared on the palace terrace, and the audience laughed when they saw him. He cast an indifferent look at the crowd, sunk in darkness. The lover entered the stage. He stood in front of the side door of the palace. He began to wail and confess to a moon, which was supposed to be in the stage sky but was not. He pretended to be counting the stars. Siah was waiting for the Caliph's daughter to come and chase him away from the palace terrace so that she could make secret plans with her lover. She was late, but Siah was confident that she would show up. Waiting for the girl, he walked through the cardboard door that led to the stage a few times, threatening the lover with his whip. The audience laughed. He knew that once he went to the palace, he would see the girl. He almost rushed there, but the girl was nowhere to be seen. The lover's confessions to the moon, his counting of the stars, and Siah's threats were repeated a few times. Siah sensed the crowd's irritation. The fourth time he went into the palace and saw the playhouse manager, looking very upset, standing next to the door. "The girl hasn't shown up," he whispered to Siah. "I don't know what to do!"

Keeping an ear on the lover's confessions, Siah asked: "She hasn't shown up? How could she do this to us? This poor guy has run out of things to confess."

"How about sending one of the nurses?" said the manager.

"How could we—they are old hags."

"Then do me a favor; keep the audience entertained; perhaps she'll show up."

Siah came onto the stage with his whip. The lover, dumbfounded, stared at the palace terrace. Siah went close to him and, facing the audience, said: "Don't wait for her in vain. The Caliph's daughter is not coming; your lover . . ." He was about to say "is dead," but unintentionally said "is pregnant." The audience broke out in laughter. Siah was encouraged and continued; "That's right, brother, she's pregnant. Why are you dumbfounded? Can't the Caliph's daughter become pregnant? Why do you look so lost?"

And, indeed, the lover appeared completely lost. He stared at Siah in astonishment. He asked quietly: "Have you lost your mind?"

But a spectator in the front row shouted, "Siah, are you sure it wasn't your doing?"

Siah didn't like that. He rolled his eyes in anger and said: "Hey you, toughs, thugs, dandies, foreigners, photographers, veiled one . . ." He was about to say ". . . unveiled ones," but he said "vile ones" and the audience laughed but not very hard. "No, don't laugh. Let me tell you the truth. Hey you, sitting there in the dark, with eyes gleaming like a cat's. Don't think I am joking around. Do you see this Siah? He's not one who takes liberties with others' loved ones. His eyes and heart are pure, and his word is the word of justice. The Caliph's daughter who is not here yet is not one of those either. . . ." The sound of one person's laughter was heard from the back of the auditorium. This laughter amid the silence of the audience was painful for Siah. He corrected himself: "No, brother. The Caliph's daughter is not one of those girls, she is just like your Siah. We are all like Siahs. One or two among us are not, though. . . ."

Siah felt a commotion among the crowd, from irritation. He was constantly sensitive to every one of the crowd's reactions. "Allow me to dance," he continued. "Have you come to watch a wailing ritual? Then clap your hands. What are you waiting for? Siah dances. He should be dancing. . . ." As he danced, Siah came across the lover, who was standing stupefied in the middle of the stage. He said: "Why are you watching me so dumbfounded?" "I don't get it," said the lover slowly, so that only Siah could hear. Ignoring the lover's confusion,

Siah asked: "Tell me, brother, which is worse—being in love or being hungry?"

The lover did not answer. A man's voice rose from the audience: "If you've ever had to relieve yourself and not found a place, you'll know it's worse than both." The people laughed and a couple clapped. But Siah didn't like it. He turned and distanced himself from the lover. He wheeled around, faced the crowd, and said with a sad voice, "Siah danced and while he danced he came across the Caliph's daughter, who's pregnant, who's been forsaken by her husband. Now the Caliph's daughter has gone to the blacksmiths' row to order an iron outfit—iron shoes, iron socks, an iron cane, and an iron ring. When they're ready she'll wear them and set out for the desert, searching for her husband." There was a lump in Siah's throat. "I shouldn't have had that drink," he thought to himself. He tried to get control of himself. He couldn't. He started to clap and said: "Laugh, clap, have fun. This is Juji Khan's theater. But what's Juji Khan's problem? Juji Khan doesn't know that there is a treasure hidden in the hearts of human beings. Sometimes there is also a green viper sleeping on top of this untouched treasure. You have to say a prayer and blow it toward the snake. God willing it will become your captive. Then at your own leisure you can go to the treasure and take as much as you please. There is no end to it. Close your eyes and suddenly leap in the water. Don't be afraid. What are you afraid of? The treasure in your heart won't allow you to drown. It will force you to swim. You'll eventually get somewhere. In the depths of the hearts of every one of us lies a treasure. We only have to somehow crush the head of the snake, whose name is fear. Perhaps we can cast a spell upon it. But what if the snake is not sleeping on top of the treasure inside one's heart, but is sitting and waiting on the outside? What if, no matter how honestly, one uses this God-entrusted treasure, but nevertheless is always defeated, always stopped, just like hitting a wall head-on, flattening one's nose? What if no spell could charm the snake sitting on the outside?"

The street sweeper sitting in the front row sneezed loudly. Siah took notice and thought: "He sneezed on purpose to warn me." Facing the janitor, he said: "Bless you, brother." Over in the corner, he caught sight of the two policemen in the auditorium. They were there every night, and he knew it. But tonight he really felt their presence. "Siah dances," he said. "While dancing he comes across the cop. The cop thinks I'm a beggar. He imagines I'm a crook. He sees my matchbox in my hand. He supposes that I plan to set fire to the Gheisarieh district. He asks what I intend to do with the matches. Brother, with these matches I want to light the fairy's strand of hair so that she may appear before your very eyes. Or shall I light Seemorgh* the phoenix's feather so that it may come to your aid? Isn't it a wonderful idea, officer?"

The audience's clamor brought the lover out of his helpless state and stopped Siah from continuing with what he was about to say. The lover took a step and said: "Ah, my love, I shall perish in anticipation." And he ran toward the terrace.

Siah turned and looked. He saw one of the nurses dressed up in the Caliph's daughter's clothes. The dress looked horrible on her body. Her dentures, her frizzed hair, and her frightened eyes made Siah sick. He felt no compassion. "She's a fake, she's a fake," he yelled. "Nobody's love will come. Nobody's love will ever come."

The fake Caliph's daughter, the old woman standing on the terrace, said: "Shut up. I will have His Majesty the Caliph cut off your head and fill your straw with skin and hang you from the palace wall. Hang . . ." The fake Caliph's daughter could not pronounce the word correctly.

"Sister, now see what you've done," Siah said out loud. "Does a wise man fill the straw with skin, or the skin with straw?"

"My love, the one who has no rival in Baghdad," said the lover, "I implore you to pardon Siah for my sake."

"She'd wish!" said Siah sarcastically.

"I pardon you," said the fake Caliph's daughter to Siah. "You may come into the palace so that I can put my ring on your finger and make . . . the entire horizon . . . horizons . . . kneel before you." The lover moved to stand beside Siah and whispered: "Please go, I beg you." Siah went inside. He saw the manager, who was more upset than before. "Why are you doing this?" he asked.

"Don't worry," Siah went on calmly. "I plan to change the play. I want to show there's a trick involved. The Caliph's daughter has sent her maid on purpose to get rid of the lover. But this idiot doesn't

---

* Seemorgh: Mythical bird in Persian literature.

understand. Do you suppose the crowd is foolish enough to believe she's the real Caliph's daughter?"

"It's dark," said the manager. "How will they ever know?"

"How could they not know?" replied Siah, and went out. As he stepped through the palace door and onto the stage, he saw Juji Khan's litter, which his ministers were carrying on their shoulders. They brought in the barrow and set it down on the floor in front of the cardboard palace door, then drew the curtain. But Juji Khan remained seated and refused to come out. He was supposed to appear in the second act, not here in the street and in front of the palace's side door.

The lover was going berserk. Siah took a look at the barrow with Juji Khan inside and then glanced at the lover. "Hey, you wretched lover," he said, "hide yourself until I find out who this is. It's obvious he's a stranger. He's lost his way. Should he see you here and inform the Caliph, you're finished. 'They'll fill your straw with skin,' too, as the sister said." The lover disappeared behind the stage curtain. Siah walked toward the litter. He stuck his head inside and said: "Why did you come now?"

"Your words incited me to come," said Juji Khan softly. "If I hadn't come now, then I would never be able to come."

"Then stand up and step out," said Siah. "If you don't do it now you never will." Siah took his hand and brought him out. He practically pulled him out. It didn't seem like he had any will of his own. Siah bowed and said, "Sir, who might you be, passing by the Caliph's palace?"

Juji Khan watched Siah silently. He said nothing.

"Sir, from your appearance it would seem that you don't speak our language. Or perhaps you can't speak at all."

Juji Khan said nothing.

"This handsome prince has come from China to ask for my hand," shouted the fake Caliph's daughter from the terrace. "He's the son of the exalted Chinese Empero . . . Emper . . ."

Siah didn't let her finish "Emperor." She wouldn't have been able to say it anyway. He said, "Hey, sister, you're imagining things. Where can you find a husband these days anyway?" Juji Khan laughed involuntarily. "Then you're not dumb?" asked Siah. "You're Chinese? No?"

Juji Khan nodded.

"Chin chun yung. Chian chung ching," said Siah aloud. This made Juji Khan laugh along with the audience. "Chian chang chung," Siah continued.

Juji Khan seemed to have forgotten where he was. Still laughing, he said, "You know how to talk nonsense very well."

"I'm not talking nonsense, brother. You know our language, too, then? I thought you were a stranger. Have you lost your way?"

Juji Khan opened his arms and stepped forward, and without being scared, said: "I am a stranger in love; which is the path?"

"Which path are you talking about?"

Juji Khan fell silent again. The fake Caliph's daughter called from the terrace: "Are you seeking the path to the palace of the Caliph of Baghdad? I am the Caliph's daughter's nurse. I will take you to the girl tonight for five dinars."

Siah appreciated the woman's timely cooperation and said: "Hail to you, nurse. You did well to fool the lover and get rid of him. Bravo. But don't you feel sorry for this young man? You are sending him to his death."

Juji Khan raised his arms again and stepped forward to say: "I am a passerby, I have no affair with the Caliph's daughter. I am a passenger who has been left behind by the convoy and has lost his way. I resemble a flower grown in the sand, thirsting for water. I had waited far too long, when suddenly a hand came forth, cut me from the sand, set me in a vase, and watered me; only then was I able to bloom. . . ."

Siah cut Juji Khan off and said, "Sir, you resemble the 'Shah Abdol Azim steam car.' You start late, but when you do start you never stop."

"Siah, the hand was yours. Your hand must be kissed." And he bent forward to kiss Siah's hand. Siah pulled himself back and asked: "Brother, when you were in the sand, did you perhaps get too much sun on your head?"

Juji Khan laughed and said: "It was dawn; the convoy chief gave the call: 'Rise, as it is late. Others have left and already reached their destinations. We have a long way ahead of us.' I heard the caravan's bell, but sleep would not allow me to open my eyes. Siah, you were the one who awakened me and succeeded to move me. . . ."

"Dear sir, your brakes have failed again," said Siah. "You haven't said which path you're seeking."

"I seek the path to Ka'aba. Won't you be my guide?"

"Sir, I don't know the path to Ka'aba myself. I do know, though, that it's a long way yet. This is only Baghdad, the first stop. Hey, brother, are you a Moslem too? What a mess!" Siah laughed and his laughter was lost in the crowd's.

Until then, Juji Khan's companions, who had brought him to the stage in the barrow, were standing cross-armed and silent. One of them, playing the role of Chinese prince's advisor, stepped forward. He bowed to Juji Khan and said: "Sire, I urge you to consider remaining in Baghdad for a while and rest, and you could have an audience with the Caliph." He turned toward Siah and added: "And you, eunuch of the Caliph's court, may announce the time for the audience."

Siah placed his hands over his eyes and said: "Certainly."

"The purpose of this endless journey with all its suffering was indeed to meet with you, old man of wisdom," said Juji Khan. "I no longer have any business either in Baghdad or with its Caliph."

The nurse spoke up from the terrace: "Young man, at least make up your mind about the Caliph's daughter. She's a girl created for God's sight alone. She's a girl whose beauty surpasses the full moon's."

"Nurse, is this girl created only for lovemaking?" yelled Juji Khan angrily.

The nurse pointed to the palace, which was nonexistent, and said: "Well, the girl gets bored in this huge palace; what else can she do but make love? Young man, be a gentleman and ask for her hand."

"Is it by force?" screamed Juji Khan furiously. "Is the ruler's order 'Off with his head?' No, I must continue with my search for my intended goal this very night." And he walked toward the barrow. Before Siah could reach him, he was seated in the litter. Siah thrust his head inside again and said quietly: "You fool. There're two more acts to go. Where do you think you're going?"

"I'm going and I am ashamed of my hardheadedness," said Juji Khan aloud from inside the litter.

Siah lost hope in Juji Khan. He addressed the advisor and the other companions of the Chinese prince who were about to leave: "Don't you go too far from Baghdad. His majesty's audience is early tomorrow morning. Don't force me to have His Majesty the Caliph punish this young man in such a way that they will write it in story books." And astonished he looked in amazement at Juji Khan who had left the litter on his own. He came toward Siah and said; "Pardon me. Have pity on my youth."

"Did your engine stall?" asked Siah.

The first curtain fell after Siah's repeated signals. Somehow they continued through the other two acts. In the second act His Majesty the Caliph, with Siah and the Nurse's mediation, pardoned Juji Khan. Poor Juji Khan had to make love to the Caliph's daughter's other nurse during the entire fifteen minutes of the third act. It was Siah's idea to cover the nurse's face so that only her bright black eyes could be seen, and it worked. And justly Juji Khan bestowed upon her the title "My Veiled Idol."

THE SHOW WAS over. The audience was gone. The actors were gone. Only Siah remained behind in the playhouse, washing off the black; Juji Khan waited for him on the bench. Laughing, he repeatedly told Siah, who was wiping his face, "Thank you; thanks a lot." Siah hung his cape on the nail, and Juji Khan stood up. "Mohsen said you always get everyone going," he said, "but you can't believe it until you see it for yourself. Mohsen is a good friend. He can stay sick for a while, until I fully get going." Siah was silent and looked for his jacket. Juji Khan talked nonstop. "I only want to ask you whether you really know what you're doing? Do you say these things on purpose? You said a few heavy, dangerous words in there. You really handled the play with expertise. You're indeed the greatest actor I've ever seen." Siah put on his jacket. He looked in the mirror and said: "The black never washes off completely."

"Let's go," said Juji Khan. "You promised we'd eat dinner together tonight. My house is not too far. If you want, we could even take a taxi."

They set out. The lights in the theater had been turned off, and the street was deserted. They crossed to the sidewalk on the other side. A woman who wore a black veil and had carefully covered her face sat underneath a tree in the dark. When she saw them, she stood up and quietly said:

"Agha Mehdi."

They both turned, and Siah recognized her. She was the Caliph's daughter.

"Dear girl," said Siah, "why didn't you show up tonight? We had a hell of a time to pull the play off. Don't you realize we can't get by without you?"

The girl walked along with them, and Siah introduced the actors to each other.

"Had it not been for Agha Mehdi's expertise," said Juji Khan, "your not turning up would have shut down the theater again, especially with my inexperience."

"I almost died this afternoon," said the girl, continuing to walk along beside them. "I have just come from the doctor's office—" Then she turned to Mehdi and went on, "—Agha Mehdi, can I speak with you alone?" Juji Khan quickened his pace; Siah and the girl stopped.

"Dear Siah," said the girl, "God bless you, you must do me two favors. I have no one to turn to but you. First, you mustn't let me lose my job. . . ."

"You can be sure of that," interrupted Siah.

"And the other is this," the girl continued. "You must gather at least two hundred tomans for me tonight, any way you can."

"Two hundred tomans? What do you want all that money for?"

"Siah dear, I have to go to the doctor tomorrow to get rid of the child. I have taken the shot tonight; if I don't go tomorrow, my life will be in danger."

"Look, girl, you know better," Siah said helplessly. "Even if I did my very best, I could perhaps come up with thirty or forty tomans maximum."

"How about this friend of yours? Can't you borrow it from him? He looks well off."

Don't even think about it," croaked Siah. "If I borrow from him, he'll think. . . ."

"In this indecent world, only you want to remain decent?" said the girl irritably. "I have nothing to say to you anymore. Call your friend." And then she started to walk quickly. The three came together and passed through the deserted streets. The girl had no intention of saying good-bye. She talked intimately with Juji Khan, laughed, and once even took his hand. But she distanced herself from Siah. She pretended to be offended. They reached the house. Juji Khan thrust his hand in his pocket and found his keys. He opened the door and said:

"Please come in." Then he looked at the girl, who had just stood there. "You can come in too if you would like."

"Agha Mehdi never goes anywhere," said the girl coquettishly. "He must really be fond of you to have come tonight," and as they went in the house, she said, "I'm glad to get to know my future fellow player."

They entered the room which seemed strange to Siah. There was a large desk in the middle of the room and two full bookcases on each side of the desk. There was a sculpture on the table. Juji Khan turned on the table lamp, and it lit up the face of the sculpture. The sculpture seemed to be both laughing and crying. It was both a man and a woman. It was nude and sat comfortably cross-legged. A black cat with blue eyes walked into the room. It went directly to Juji Khan, rubbed itself against his leg, and meowed. The girl bent down, picked up the cat and kissed it. "Sweet kitty, you're hungry?" she said. "Or are you in love, too? Perhaps you fancy your master?" Siah saw that the cat scratched the girl's hand, but she pretended nothing had happened. She continued to hold the cat in her arms. She petted its head, ears, and neck.

"Please sit down," said Juji Khan. "I'll go and bring something to eat."

As he was leaving the room, he called out: "Ahmad," and a voice replied from somewhere: "Yes, sir."

Siah and the girl sat on two couches which were next to each other in the corner of the room. There was a table in front of them. The girl let go of the cat and swore:

"The damned thing bloodied my hand."

A thick book was stuck to the wall opposite them with a large nail. A photograph of the sole of a foot was pinned to the same wall next to the book. For a second, Siah was about to get up and see what book it was, but he didn't feel like it. He was too downhearted.

"The only person in front of whom I feel ashamed is you," said the girl.

"Why do you want to abort the child anyway?" asked Mehdi kindly. "Have mercy."

"Dear Siah, it's as if you don't live in this world. How can I work with a child? How can I earn a living?"

"The person who planted the child in you should pay the price."

The girl sneered and said, "He's got a wife and kids. He left me as soon as he found out I was pregnant."

"That simple? Wasn't he going to marry you?" asked Siah.

"No, he never said he'd marry me. Siah dear, you're very naive and decent. You think everybody's like yourself."

Siah thought for a while and said: "Dear girl, can't you find a decent man and marry him? Settle down? Isn't it a pity to get yourself constantly into trouble like this? You're cutting off your own roots."

"Which decent man will marry me?" the girl replied. "Supposing he did anyway; the first thing he'd say is, 'I don't want you to step outside the house. I don't like you to act in the theater.'"

"It's not important, dear girl; acting on the stage isn't all that important. The main thing is to pull off one's life correctly."

The girl seemed irritated and tired of this conversation. "Siah, dear, my situation is past this kind of talk," she said. "No matter how, I must find two hundred tomans from somewhere tonight. I know how myself. But it's only that I'm ashamed in front of you. Will you permit me? Will you permit me . . . your friend?"

Siah stood up; he couldn't cry there. He wished to go home and cry his heart out. Even if he cried as much as all the rain in the world, it would still not be enough. When one is struck so deep to have to go so low, how it must break one's heart. It's just like spitting in one's own face. The poor girl. Siah had always seen her from afar, with her oak-colored hair covering her shoulders, those huge black eyes that broke one's heart to look at; with those lips and mouth that opened like a blossom and from which the stars poured out onto one's lap; those eyebrows that always seemed to beckon to share a secret that one didn't understand. And such a girl has had pity on no part of herself. He wished he could go and see nothing, hear nothing, want nothing.

The girl begged: "Siah, dear, don't walk around the room so much. Come and sit down. I'm getting nauseous." Siah sat down, and the girl started over again: "Give me permission, my dear Siah. I have no other choice. My life is at stake. If you can get it, I'll be more than willing to leave right now and not feel so ashamed in front of you. I have an appointment tomorrow morning. The shot he's given me rips the child into pieces; tomorrow I have to go so that he can pull it out. You have no idea how painful it is. I have already done it four times. The way he scratches the inside with his pincers darkens the world before my eyes. I pray to die tomorrow during the operation, so that you won't have to look at me this way. Are you satisfied now?"

Siah wished he had the money. He wished he could find the two hundred tomans that very same night. He wished, as the girl had said, he was not a decent man in this indecent world and could ask Juji Khan for the money.

He saw the girl take off her veil, bundle it up, and throw it in the corner. She opened her purse, took out a comb and lipstick. She put them on the arm of the couch. She took out a mirror and quickly put on the lipstick and pressed her lips together. She combed her hair, opened the buttons of her blouse and adjusted her bra, but did not close all the buttons. She had changed. But her face was empty. Siah asked:

"You've put your makeup on?"

Juji Khan came in with a tray on which there was a bottle, a few cups, and a dish of salad. He placed the tray on the desk. Behind him a man walked in wearing pajama bottoms, a woolen shirt, and a knit cap. He said hello and placed a dish with two broiled chickens on the table. The man left and came back with more things, setting them down neatly.

Juji Khan sat behind the desk.

It's going to start now, Siah thought to himself. They're standing before each other like two drunken cats.

The girl stood up. She moved her hips and waist as if she was on stage. She said:

"Allow me to become the cupbearer."

She picked up the bottle and looked at it. She asked: "Is it whiskey?" and she laughed. She filled a cup and put it in front of Juji Khan. Then she poured some for Siah. She didn't look at him as she placed the cup on the arm of the couch. She poured herself less than the others. Her eyes were gleaming, but not like when she made love on stage. She hit her cup against Juji Khan's and said:

"To your health."

She took a leaf of lettuce from the salad dish and put it in her mouth. She laughed again, but falsely. Even her nurses on the stage laughed more easily than she did. She attacked the chicken, placing each person's share on the plates and setting the plate before each one. She sat on the corner of the desk. The light on the desk lit only her arm and her skirt, not her exposed breasts. Sitting on the desk, she moved her legs about and laughed. She began to sing. Her voice was hoarse and uninspired. She sang the same song Siah expected her to sing: "Had there been only one pain, there'd be no problem." This was the same girl who used to sing before the play started, and Siah would accompany her with a tambourine. Oh, how the two of them aroused the audience and how, when the song had ended and they had left the stage, the crowd clapped for them to return. The girl asked Juji Khan:

"Is there a tambourine or something else to be found in this house?"

"I don't know how to play," said Juji Khan.

"Agha Mehdi does," she said. "He can even play the violin."

"No, I don't have a tambourine," said Juji Khan.

The girl continued her song, and Siah felt she was forcing herself to sing. Perhaps she was ill again. Siah started to eat. The girl left her song unfinished. Like a person who has just awakened, she asked Juji Khan:

"Am I going to wake your parents?"

"No, they sleep upstairs. Even if they do wake up, they'll think I'm listening to the radio."

The girl laughed again. She narrowed her eyes and fixed them on Juji Khan. She cut a leg of the chicken with a fork and bent toward Juji Khan. Juji Khan didn't open his mouth. He took the fork and said:

"Thank you."

The girl searched in her plate and found a wishbone. She held it before Juji Khan and said:

"Should we make a bet?"

"For what?"

"For a kiss."

Juji Khan bit his lips and lowered his head. The girl said:

"What a bashful little boy."

Siah stood up. He got up so abruptly that the cup on the arm of the couch fell on the carpet. It didn't break, just emptied its contents. He said:

"Why don't you two bet for money? For two hundred tomans, cash?"

AHMAD SHAMLOO
(1925–2000)

Selected Poems

Translated from the Persian by
Zara Houshmand
Ahmad Karimi-Hakkak

I'm Still Thinking of That Crow

I'm still
thinking of that crow in the valleys of Yush:*
its scissors, black
against the parched yellow patch of wheat,
with its double swish
cut an arc aslant the paper sky,
and turning to the near peak
said something
with a dry caw-
caw from its gullet,
which the care-worn mountains, awestruck,
repeated for a long while
in their stone heads
under the high sun.

Sometimes I ask myself
what a crow could say
with such incisive, unrelenting presence

* Yush: A village in the Alborz Mountains where the great Iranian poet Nima
Yushij was born.

to the aged mountains
                                    at the height of day
winging, with its insistent shade of mourning,
over a parched yellow patch of wheat,
wheeling past a stand of aspens
with that gasp of rage—
what a crow could say
that those weary dozing hermits
would repeat among themselves
for so long a while
in the heat of midday.

Translated by Zara Houshmand

The Song of Abraham in Fire

Under the bloody tumbling of twilight
there stands a man of another kind
who wanted the land to be green
who wanted love to be worthy of the most
                              beautiful of women
for this to him
was not so worthless an offering
as to become only dust and stone.

What a man! what a man!
he said
better for the heart
to sink in blood
by the seven swords of love
and better for the lips
to utter the most beautiful name.

And a mountain-like hero, thus in love
crossed the bloody battlefield of destiny
with the heels of Achilles

an invulnerable hero
                      the secret of whose death
was the sorrow of love
and the depth of solitude.

"Ay! sad Esfandiar
your eyes
better closed.

"Was a NO
only one NO
enough
to make my fate.

"I only cried NO
I refused to sink.

"I was
and I became
not as a bud becomes a flower
nor as a root becomes a shoot
nor as a seedling becomes a forest
but as a common man becomes a martyr
for heavens to worship him.

"I was not a servile little slave
and my way to a heavenly paradise
was not the path of submission and servility.

"I deserved a God of another kind
worthy of a creature
who does not humble himself
for the indispensable morsel.

"And a God
of another kind
I created."

Alas! mountain-like hero
that you were
and mountain-like
formidable and firm
before falling on the ground
you were dead.

Yet neither God nor Satan
but an idol wrote your destiny
an idol whom others worshipped
an idol whom others worshipped.

Translated by Ahmad Karimi-Hakkak

SIMIN BEHBAHANI

(B. 1927)

Selected Poems

Translated from the Persian by
Farzaneh Milani and Kaveh Safa

Don't Read

(To Mohammad Behbahani)

Don't read these deceptions made by the hands of Satan
even if they seem to be verses from Heaven.
Not many of these false-Marys will remain,
once you have unmasked the shameless whores.
You cannot believe a field of sunflowers
to be a congregation of suns.
The illusory warmth of a few glowworms
have not warmed the breath of this winter's night.
They are only tinseled, these leaves and flowers
tied to these naked branches.
This is not the sky but a painting on a ceiling
on which glows a painted sun.
This is but a performance in which from behind a curtain
someone makes these lifeless shadows dance.
where are my childhood's beliefs
in the stories of princes and monsters,
beliefs that were clear as a mirror or water?
I weep for the death of my beliefs
that had no intimation yet
of human beings.

My Country, I Will Build You Again

(To the lady of Persian storytelling, Simin Daneshvar)

My country, I will build you again,
if need be, with bricks made from my life.
I will build columns to support your roof,
if need be, with my bones.
I will inhale again the perfume of flowers
favored by your youth.
I will wash again the blood off your body
with torrents of my tears.
Once more, the darkness will leave this house.
I will paint my poems blue with the color of our sky.
The resurrector of "old bones" will grant me in his bounty
a mountain's splendor in his testing grounds.
Old I may be, but given the chance, I will learn.
I will begin a second youth alongside my progeny.
I will recite the Hadith of "love and country"
with such fervor as to make each word bear life.
There still burns a fire in my breast
to keep undiminished the warmth of kinship
I feel for my people.
Once more you will grant me strength,
though my poems have settled in blood.
Once more I will build you with my life,
though it be beyond my means.

You Leave, I'll Stay

(To those who left. To those who stayed behind.)

You leave, I'll stay. You leave, I'll stay.
I swear, I cannot endure being separated from my homeland.
Till my last day you will hear in my bonesill
the same "tale of the reed."
Though sparkles and light may fill the nights of exile,
they are of little use to me, since I am not happy in exile.

From the agitation of fire and molten metal
the sky above me is as turbulent as my mind.
When one must cover the light in a lamp,
I would rather extinguish the flame
than let my ears be pierced by the policeman's orders,
"lights out!" "black out!"
Where will my heart escape,
if this house and its shade collapse on my head?
In these dark ruins we remain:
the children, the old people, and I,
and our sad cares and thoughts of absent, brave warriors.
I will not forsake this unruly corner to beg for affection
in a land of self-serving calculation.
Even if this sky is dark and unsmiling,
it belongs to me and my fellow countrymen.
This canopy is not on loan.
Hoping for a better day,
I take one step, then another,
toward something I believe.
You leave, I'll stay.

REZA BARAHENI
(B. 1935)

Selected Poems

Translated from the Persian by
Reza Baraheni and David St. John

I Am an Underground Man

Now I am an underground man
I will never appear on the earth again
God libraries poetry belong to the earth
my holograph holds no fantasy for children
or romance for the senile

I am the rotten well of history
they seek me, they poke me, they
curse me and, finally, they drain me
I have mortgaged my beard in the vaults of history
my deadly ink will blot out the hand
outreached to me I am not fit for textbooks
for schools and universities
if you wish to see me, look into the pit
of an oil well from the summit of Everest
throw your matches down
so that I can set the whole world aflame

I am an underground man
my fire alone shall appear on the face of the earth

427

Doctor Azudi, the Professional

Azudi* is just like
Genghis Khan   when he walks
he walks on a pile of fresh corpses

the Khan did not clean his teeth either
the Khan also belched   the Khan
did not take off his boots either   Azudi
has shattered the mouths of twenty poets today

Azudi wears a tie   something
Genghis Khan never did
only this splendid detail reveals the prodigious march of history

Zadan! Nazadan!

suddenly a woman is sleepless in her dream
she screams:
          Nazan! Nazan! Nazan!†
prisoners wake in the block one by one
and man and woman scream:
          Nazan! Nazan! Nazan!
and in the torture chambers
the beating begins
          Nazan! Nazan! Nazan!

Hosseinzadeh, the Head Executioner

Azudi lights his cigarette
—say *Doctor* Azudi!

* Azudi: Along with Hosseinzadeh, one of Shah Muhammad Reza Pahlavi's
chief torturers in the infamous Evin Prison, where the shah's political prisoners
were kept.
† Nazan: Persian for "Don't strike me!" Because "zan" is the word for woman,
"nazan" could also be understood to mean "no woman" or "not a woman."

and *Doctor* Hosseinzadeh!—
he's short, with a bald head, and eyes uneasy
as the asshole of a nervous rooster
he is a man of great renown:
he always stubs his cigarette on the back of a human hand
he never smokes more than forty a day
and the first caress is always
the privilege of this *Pahlavi* slut
and the last caress too
between the two cuffs
Azudi and Rassuli and Shadi and Manuchehri
Azudi and Parvizkhan and Rezavan and Hosseini nurse
        the patient
one extracts his nails
another his teeth
a third scours the skin
a fourth provides the shock treatment
a fifth the reflagellation
and the sixth prepares the ailing for the *coup de grace*
there's a short man whose name is Ardalan
        —say *Doctor* Ardalan!—
he fucks the afflicted
man and woman are the same to him
he holds a PhD in rapacity
(and you, prisoner! you try all this time to forget
the name of the half-blind man who printed that
article of yours, he has a wife, three children, a
father and a mother, and he provides for them all)

and then Hosseinzadeh
        —say *Doctor* Hosseinzadeh!—
administers the final cuff
the final verdict to shoot you
comes between the two caresses

The Shah and Hosseinzadeh

the Shah has granted full authority
to Hosseinzadeh

once he mustered six of us   blindfolded
we were loaded on a truck   an hour before
dawn they took us out of the city   then they
brought us back to the city   it was
as though we were traveling from one city
to another in our dreams   then we were
unloaded and bound to six iron posts
then the command of that familiar voice was heard:
squad!
attention!
prepare to fire!
fire!

all six of us pissed our pants!

they removed our blindfolds
Hosseinzadeh and Azude stood in a corner
pissing themselves with laughter!

say *Doctor* Hosseinzadeh! and *Doctor* Azudi!

Chronology

SECTION VIII: Indian Subcontinent (1956–1980)

1956 First Pakistan constitution adopted

1958 General Mohammad Ayub Khan seizes power in military coup

1962 Indochina War

1965 Second war between India and Pakistan

1969 General Agha Mohammad Yahya Khan assumes presidency of Pakistan

1971 Bangladesh gains independence from Pakistan

1973 Zulfikar Ali Bhutto becomes prime minister of Pakistan

1977 Military coup in Pakistan led by General Mohammad Zia-ul-Haq

1979 Islamic penal code introduced
Zia executes Zulfikar Ali Bhutto

1980 Indira Gandhi becomes prime minister of India

VIII

Between the Dusk and Dawn of History: Urdu Literature after Partition

THE ISLAMIC REPUBLIC of Pakistan was born in 1947 in the midst of chaos and war—a result of the partition of India into Hindu and Muslim majority states, which created history's largest human migration (described by Intizaar Hussein in his personal account, "The First Morning"). While India thrived under the rule of the Congress Party in the 1950s and 1960s, Pakistan became mired in economic and political turmoil. The elation of independence, so apparent in Faiz Ahmed Faiz's 1947 poem, "Freedom's Dawn," written to commemorate the country's founding, gradually turned to bitter disappointment as Pakistan devolved into an authoritarian state where, in Faiz's words, "no man now dare walk with head held high." In 1958, a decade after its creation, Pakistan's civilian government was overthrown in a military coup d'état. And while civilian rule would be temporarily restored in the 1970s, two more military coups—as well as two more wars with India and a 1971 civil war that would transform East Pakistan into the nation of Bangladesh—set the course for what would become the near-permanent militarization of Pakistani politics.

The poets and writers whose words had inspired the creation of the Pakistani state soon became the nation's most vocal critics. (Faiz even spent time in prison on charges of conspiring against the government.) As Pakistan struggled to reconcile its national and religious identities, and neighboring India was racked with violence between its Hindu and Muslim citizens, the entire Indian Subcontinent appeared to be on the verge of devastation. And yet, despite the uncertainty and insecurity that marked the post-Partition period—or perhaps because of it— Urdu literature thrived on both sides of the border. In Pakistan, Urdu became the official language of the state, while in India (where the government briefly tried to ban the teaching of Urdu in schools), Urdu literature remained a powerful tool for conveying the continuing struggle for social progress and political autonomy.

In the latter half of the twentieth century, Urdu literature gained new vigor through the work of the so-called modernists. Writing in a deliberately unadorned style, the modernists focused their lens on the social and political tumult surrounding them. The short, deceptively simple lines of poets such as Ali Sardar Jafri and Akhtar ul-Iman became the norm in Urdu poetry, while an empowered group of women writers—poets and novelists alike—added a feminine voice to a literary tradition that had, until then, been dominated by men.

In the 1960s, the short story finally established itself as a rival to Urdu poetry. Popular prose writers such as Ghulam Abbas ("The Room with the Blue Light") and Abdullah Hussein ("The Refugees") became more assertive and more defiant of conventional norms. In many ways, the short story was an ideal vehicle for communicating the sociopolitical complexities of the time. Poetry, however, remained the dominant form of literary expression in Urdu. Nearly a thousand years after its birth, the ghazal—still the most popular form of poetry in Urdu literature—evolved to tackle not only traditional themes of love and mysticism but also the social and political realities of the modern world. Indeed, even today, as Pakistan continues to vacillate between civilian and military rule, between war and peace, between security and instability, Urdu poetry remains a powerful means of artistic and political expression throughout South Asia.

INTIZAAR HUSSEIN

(B. 1923)

The First Morning

Translated from the Urdu by Basharat Peer

I HAVE NO definite answer to questions about why I migrated from India to Pakistan after the partition in 1947. I look back and see a crowded train rushing past lively and desolate towns and villages, under a bright sun, and in the dark of night. The train is running through the most frightening night and the passengers are quite like statues. I strain to hear them breathe. Where will the train stop? And will it move again, if it stops?

Half a century later, it seems to have been the moment when two eras met and parted. History has its own dawns and dusks. We were in between the dusk and dawn of history. That is what made the journey from Meerut to Lahore the longest journey. We weren't on a train; we were on the ship of history. We had left home at dawn and it was noon. The train had already crossed Saharanpur. We were past the borders of our province, Uttar Pradesh, into that enormous wilderness that had seen carnage a few days earlier. Now there was silence. Those destined to survive and leave had left. Those destined to fall had fallen. Their homes were still smoldering.

The train chugged on, indifferent to the ruined towns. Before we had crossed Saharanpur, the train stopped at the routine stops. The stationmaster would blow the whistle, the guard would wave the green flag, the train would slowly begin to move, and the passengers on the platform would take a few steps back. Then, something changed. The train would not make any more stops; it sped past every station on the way.

A little later, it suddenly stopped. Armed guards patrolled the platform, forbidding the people walking on the platform from coming near the train. Sikhs with scimitars hanging by their sides stared at us from a distance and kept on walking. Refugees from the other side of the border hung about the platform in groups. Their tired eyes would meet ours and then turn away. A train full of refugees from Pakistan stopped on a parallel track. My heart seemed to stop beating. My eyes met many terrorized, angry eyes. The train felt claustrophobic. Many others were sitting on the roof. How did they hold on to the speeding train? Maybe desperate flights for life teach you how. Our train does not move. I want to get away from the angry, burning eyes staring at me. The train does not move.

Somehow night fell—a very dark night. The lights on the train engine were switched off. It was running like a blind man, past the stations dotting our path. The passengers in my coach seemed to have turned into ghosts. Heartbeats competed with the sound of the train and anxiety invaded the mind. Then the train stopped again. Nobody spoke. There was darkness inside, and darkness outside—then a few flashes of the guards' searchlights. We had stopped in a forest. Some armed soldiers walked around. The searchlights only heightened the dread, the sense of danger.

Somebody shuffled a bit beside me. I heard the faint friction of a match being struck. A yellow flame burst into the dark coach, startling everyone. "Who is it?" "Stub it out!" "Stub out the damn cigarette!" The man with the burning cigarette was my friend, Saleem Ahmad. What a moment Saleem had chosen to have a smoke! He stubbed it out. The train did not move.

"This reminds me of a joke," Saleem said. He went on to tell the joke. The group of boys from his hometown of Meerut, who came with him, laughed. Furious eyes tried to stare them down in the darkness. "You should be ashamed of yourself!" an angry voice shouted. "Ashamed of what?" Saleem replied, with mock naïveté. An old woman, who had taken off her veil, spoke with great affection: "Son, this is not the time to be frivolous. This is the time to say the *Kalima*."*
"They would say the *Kalima*, if they believed in it!" the angry voice shouted again.

An armed guard walked past the coach window. One of the boys

---

* *Kalima*: The Muslim profession of faith: There is no god but God and Muhammad is His Messenger. Also known as *Shahada* in Arabic.

from Saleem's group shouted, "Guard Sahib, when are they attacking?" The guard stopped in his tracks, startled. "Shut up!" the guard replied after a moment and moved on. Saleem's boys laughed again. The boy who was snubbed by the guard spoke again. "Oh! I know that guard. He is in bed with the Hindu extremists. That is why he shouted at me." He wasn't convincing anyone.

The train stirred to life. No green flags were waved, no whistle was blown, and the echoes of its wheels were muffled, as if a languid centipede had begun to crawl. "Praise be to Allah," said the old woman, her voice soaked in relief.

A little ahead, the train stopped again. Fear filled us again. "They are going to attack now," one of the boys cried. "This reminds me of a joke," Saleem shouted. The boys began to laugh. "Have the fear of God!" the old woman pleaded. Something seized me and I shouted at Saleem: "Shut the fuck up! The Sikhs will attack us later, first these people will . . ." I don't know what I'd meant to say.

The train moved. "Thanks be to Him!" the old woman exclaimed. A collective sigh of relief followed. We seemed past the danger of an attack. Perhaps it was another mirage. The train rolled on leisurely. I was restless but couldn't make it go faster. Why can't it shoot out of this forest? My anxiety grew. The train kept crawling for ages.

It seemed as if I had been on the train for eons. Will there be a destination? Will we make it? Many trains on this route had reached their destinations carrying only the corpses of the men and women who had boarded them. The mobs had spared only the driver. Is this some ancient caravan, crossing perilous deserts and waters?

The night melted and the day brought other visions. I stared through the coach window at a long line of bullock carts, carrying people uprooted from their homes and carrying things uprooted from kitchens, living rooms, and drawing rooms. The train passed more bullock carts, an unending line of displacement. Where were they headed? Where were we going? It was difficult to say. The parallel lines of anxiety, uncertainty, suspicion, and grief urged them on. And Saleem! He was still trying to make jokes, prove he wasn't scared.

When we were approaching the Wagah border post, the coach suddenly came alive. In a moment the passengers dusted off their fear and cowardice and were transformed into men of steel and women of courage. The dimly lit coach morphed into a podium. Many speeches were given. I turned to Saleem: "Why aren't you making a speech?" "I will remain silent," he said. "It's their turn now."

The train stopped again. Lahore! The sky was turning light, the air a little foggy. It was my first morning in Pakistan.

FAIZ AHMED FAIZ
(1911–1984)

Selected Poems

Translated from the Urdu by V. G. Kiernan

Freedom's Dawn (August 1947)*

This leprous daybreak, dawn night's fangs have mangled—
This is not that long-looked-for break of day,
Not that clear dawn in quest of which those comrades
Set out, believing that in heaven's wide void
Somewhere must be the stars' last halting-place,
Somewhere the verge of night's slow-washing tide,
Somewhere an anchorage for the ship of heartache.

When we set out, we friends, taking youth's secret
Pathways, how many hands plucked at our sleeves!
From beauty's dwellings and their panting casements
Soft arms invoked us, flesh cried out to us;
But dearer was the lure of dawn's bright cheek,
Closer her shimmering robe of fairy rays;
Light-winged that longing, feather-light that toil.

But now, word goes, the birth of day from darkness
Is finished, wandering feet stand at their goal;
Our leaders' ways are altering, festive looks
Are all the fashion, discontent reproved—
And yet this physic still on unslaked eye
Or heart fevered by severance works no cure.

* August 14,1947: The day on which the independence of Pakistan was
officially announced.

Where did that fine breeze, that the wayside lamp
Has not once felt, blow from—where has it fled?
Night's heaviness is unlessened still, the hour
Of mind and spirit's ransom has not struck;
Let us go on, our goal is not reached yet.

August 1952

At last half-promise of a spring has come—
Some flowers tear open their green cloaks and bloom,

And here and there some garden nooks begin
Their warblings, and defy the wintry gloom.

Night's shadows hold their ground, but some faint streaks
Of day show, spreading each a rosy plume;

And in the gathering, even if our own blood
Or breath must feed them, a few lamps light the room.

Tilt your proud cap! for we, the world well lost,
Never need fear what comes from heaven's grand loom.

Caged eyes will open when dawn fills the garden:
Dawn's breeze they have had pledge and promise from.

Desert still desert, Faiz—but bleeding feet
Have saved some thorns at least from its dry tomb.

Bury Me Under Your Pavements

Bury me, oh my country, under your pavements,
Where no man now dare walk with head held high,
Where your true lovers bringing you their homage
Must go in furtive fear of life or limb;
For new-style law and order are in use,
Good men learn—"Stones locked up, and dogs turned loose."

Your name still cried by a rash zealot few
Inflames the itching hand of tyranny;
Villains are judges and usurpers both—
Who is our advocate, where shall we seek justice?
But all hours man must spend are somehow spent;
How do we pass these days of banishment?

When my cell's window-slit grows dim, I seem
To see your hair spangled with starry tinsel;
When chains grow once more visible, I think
I see your face sprinkled with dawn's first rays;
In fantasies of the changing hours we live,
Held fast by shadowy gates and towers we live.

This war is old of tyrants and mankind:
Their ways not new, nor ours; the fires they kindle
To scorch us, age by age we turn to flowers;
Not new our triumph, not new their defeat.
Against fate therefore we make no complaint,
Our hearts though exiled from you do not faint.

Parted today, tomorrow we shall meet—
And what is one short night of separation?
Today our enemies' star is at its zenith—
But what is their brief week of playing God?
Those who keep firm their vows to you are proof
Against the whirling hours, time's warp and woof.

AKHTAR UL-IMAN
(1915—1996)

Selected Poems

*Translated from the Urdu by Baidar Bakht, Leslie Levine, and
Kathleen Grant Jaeger*

Compromise

Whenever I kissed her, the smell of cigarettes
entered my nostrils, I consider smoking a vice
but I'm used to the smell now, it's part of my life.
Likewise she is used to my pale, dirty teeth.
Whenever we meet we set aside the words,
only the breathing, perspiration, and loneliness
stay in the room. Perhaps our souls are dead,
our feelings are dead or perhaps this story
is repeated again and again. Life always
writhes in labor pains, new Messiahs come
and go to the cross, one earthly person moves forward
from the back rows and declares from the pulpit
the crucified belonged to us, his blood
is our heritage. Then all the values, ideals
that were censored are consumed
by the deep stomach of that earthly person
and are turned out as fresh commentaries,
new interpretations that are the only refuge
of helpless people, perhaps of all people . . .
In vain I look for an ideal man.

All people see dreams and ride high winds
then a stage comes when all cry bitterly

and break like branches.
They do find loved ones, focuses
of their desires and lives, they hate them
while still loving them.

I too hate her, she thinks I am low
but when we meet in loneliness, in darkness,
We become like wet clay.
Hate is absorbed, only silence remains:
Silence, which engulfed the earth after creation.
We keep breaking like young branches.
We do not discuss dreams that we once had.
We do not discuss long-buried joys.
We just keep breaking.
I am inclined to drinking, she smokes.
We keep getting wrapped in the sheet of silence.
We keep breaking like young branches.

The Last Stop Before the Destination

I shall keep on going like this
Through this green and black,
And red and white earth.
Is there someone?
Is there someone with me?
No, no one.
I rid myself of even the dust
That clung to my feet
During the course of the journey.
Whatever was yours,
I have returned to you—
Anyone else should also claim
What belongs to him.
Don't tell me tomorrow
That I was untrue.
Don't tell me tomorrow
That my intentions were evil.

The Boy

On the hills near villages in the east,
Sometimes in mango orchards, sometimes on dykes,

Sometimes in the lanes, sometimes in the lakes,
Sometimes amongst the merriment of youngsters half-clad,
At dawning, dusk, in the darkness of the night,
Sometimes at fairs, among the pantomime players,
Or lost on quiet byways chasing butterflies,
Or sneaking toward the hidden nests of little birds,
Barefoot, no matter what the weather,
Out of school, in deserted abodes,
Sometimes laughing in a group of pretty girls,
Sometimes restless like a whirlwind,
In dreams, floating in the air, flying like a cloud,
Swinging in trees like the little birds,
I see a boy, wandering, carefree, independent,
As the flowing water of mountain streams.

This nuisance acts like my shadow,
Following my every step, no matter where I go,
As if I were an escaped convict.
And he asks me:
Are you really
Akhtar ul-Iman?

I acknowledge the blessings of Almighty God;
I admit that He laid down this earth
Like a vast bed of velvet and brocade;
I admit that the tent of skies is His benison;
He ordered moon and sun and stars in space;
He brought forth rivers by splitting mountains;
He created me from dust,
And gave me dominion over the earth;
Filled oceans with pearls, and mines with rubies;

Filled the air with bewitching bouquets;
He is the Master, Mighty, Singular, Wise;
He separates darkness from light,
If I know myself, it is His benevolence.
He has given splendor to the greedy,
And adversity to me;
Made idiots wealthy, and a beggar out of me;
But whenever I stretch out my hands to beg,
The boy asks:
Are you really Akhtar ul-Iman?

My livelihood lies in the hands of others.
All I still control is my mind which understands
That I have to carry the burden the rest of my life,
Till my elements are dispersed,
And my pulse stops beating;
That subsisting means forever singing
Melody of dawn, or lament of night.
In front of the victors,
I cannot even call my song my own:
I have to smile when they say
I am singing their song, not mine.
My pen's creations, the work of my sleepless nights,
Have to be passed like a counterfeit coin.
When I think about myself, in sorrow I say
That I am a blister, bound to burst one day.
In short, I wander like the morning breeze,
Longing for the morning,
When I seek help from the night,
The boy asks:
Are you really Akhtar ul-Iman?

When he does so, in a fury I reply:
That depressed, neurotic soul
You keep inquiring for is long dead.
I have wrapped him in the shroud of self-deception,

And thrown him in the grave of his hopes.
I tell that boy the flame is quenched
That was bent on burning all the trash of the world.
The boy smiles, and says softly:
That's a lie, a fib, a cheat.
Look! I am alive.

ALI SARDAR JAFRI
(1913—2000)

Selected Poems

Translated from the Urdu by
Mahmood Jamal
Baidar Bakht and Kathleen Grant Jaeger

Robe of Flame

Who is that
standing in a robe of flame?
Body broken, blood spilling
from his brains.

Farhad and Qais* passed away
some time ago; who then is he
whom people stone to death?

There is no beautiful Shireen here,
no Leila of spring seasons.
In whose name, then, this scarlet bed
of wounds is flowering?

It is some madman
stubbornly upholding Truth,
unbending to the winds of lies and cunning.

* Farhad and Qais: The stories of Qais (also known as Majnoon) and Leila, and
Farhad (also Kohkun) and Shireen are two of the most famous love stories in
Persian and Urdu poetry, symbolizing perfect, spiritual love.

It is clear, his punishment must be
Death by stoning!

Translated by Mahmood Jamal

My Journey

Like the grass, I have sprouted a hundred times.
—RUMI

The day will come
When the eye-lamps will fade
The hand-lotuses wilt
And the butterfly of speech forever flies
The flower of tongue.

All faces blossoming like buds,
Laughing like flowers,
Will one day, disappear
To the shadowy depths of the sea.
All pulsing blood, all beating hearts,
All melodies will be hushed.

On the velvet of blue sky
This shining gem,
This heaven, this earth of mine,
Without knowing, understanding,
Will weep tears of dew.
On the handful of dust that is man.

From the temples of memories
Every single thing will have gone.
Then no one will ask: Where is Sardar?

But I'll come here again,
Speak through children's voices,
Sing in the calls of birds.
When seeds smile under the earth
And seedlings, with nimble fingers
Caress the layers of soil

I'll open my eyes
Through every bud, each blade of grass.
On my green palm
I'll balance the droplets of dew.
I'll become the glow of cheeks,
The beat of melodies.

Like the blush of the modest bride,
I'll sparkle through every veil.
When the wintry winds blow
And autumn leaves fall
Under the lively feet of travelers
My laughter will sound
In the crunching of dry leaves.

All golden streams of the earth,
All blue lakes of the sky
Will be filled with my being.
And the world will see
That every tale is my tale,
Every lover Sardar here,
And every love Sultana.
I am a fleeting moment
From the magic house of time.

I am a restless droplet
Busy traveling
From the flask of the past

To the cup of the future.
I sleep and awaken
And fall asleep again.
I am a play, centuries old,
Death makes me live forever.

Translated by Baidar Bakht and Kathleen Grant Jaeger

ABDULLAH HUSSEIN
(B. 1931)

The Refugees

Translated from the Urdu by Muhammad Umar Memon

I am a refugee from the world.
—CHATEAUBRIAND

AN EVENT OCCURRED thirty years ago and brutally took hold of Aftab's life. This is the story of that event. Events don't occur in a void, but are related to the great unknowns that flank them on either side. Human life, too, is a continuum. For although we can measure an individual life within a definite time span, we cannot separate it from the flow of time. And just as man's greatest asset is the duration that is his life, so the essence of a story is the event on which it is based. This story, too, derives its meaning from just two days in Aftab's life. That some thirty years separate those two days is quite another matter.

20 June 1940

It was well past the noon hour but the heat hadn't let up at all. The sky, a crisp bright blue in another season, was a blazing sheet of silver now. One couldn't even look up. Shaikh Umar Daraz and his son had just performed the midday prayer in the mosque and got up from the prayer mat. On one side along the wall his boots lay on their sides, soles nestled against each other, with his khaki sun hat thrown over them. Shaikh Umar Daraz bent down, picked up his possessions, and started out. His son walked to the outer courtyard, where he had left his sandals, sat down at the edge, and began slipping them on.

Before leaving the mosque, Shaikh Umar Daraz wet his large square handkerchief under the tap, wrung it out thoroughly, and threw it over his head. Over the handkerchief he fixed his sun hat rather carefully. The white kerchief was about the size of a small towel and conveniently came down over the nape of his neck and ears, though on the forehead it sort of flapped an inch or so about the eyes. If you looked at it casually, you might even have thought the hat had a fringe stuck to it.

Shaikh Umar Daraz's skin was a healthy pink. His face reminded one of those sepia photographs in which British colonial officers sporting knickerbockers or breeches, their heads covered with handkerchiefs and hats in a similar fashion, were photographed against a background of tropical jungles or sun-scorched deserts. Even the expression on his face was the same—as if he didn't belong to his immediate world and lived comfortably away from it, like those colonial officers.

Of the travels of his youth just these two mementos remained with Shaikh Umar Daraz: the fringed sun hat, and that faraway look in his eyes. Below his face he was just an ordinary man: clad in a white *shalwar-qamis* suit and a pair of boots. Occasionally during winters, though, he would slip on the pair of khaki breeches and full boots. But then, instead of mounting a horse, he would hop on his bicycle and ride to work, or, if it were evening, stroll down to his grain fields, ostensibly to inspect them, all the way twirling his walking stick with a flourish.

As father and son stepped out of the mosque compound, a gust of hot wind slapped their faces. "Aftab," Shaikh Umar Daraz said, "you go on home. I'm going out to the fields. I'll be along soon."

"Now?" The boy was surprised.

"Yes. I have something to take care of."

"I'll come along."

"No. You go home. The wind is awfully hot."

"I'll fetch a towel," the boy insisted. "Please let me come along."

Shaikh Umar Daraz looked around uncertainly for a moment, then decided it was all right for the boy to come along. "But make sure you wet the towel well," he shouted at the boy, who in the meantime had sprinted off to the house.

Minutes later the boy returned, his head and face covered with a wet towel. The two started off. The dry, white walls in the alleys shimmered in the sun. The hot wind would gust in, hit the walls, and bounce back like a ball of fire. The pair quickened their pace and soon came out of the complex of alleyways. A single thought occupied their minds: To get out of the city as fast as they could and hit the blacktop highway where you at least had some large shady trees. Within about ten minutes, they had walked to the city's edge.

A hot, shimmering desolation enveloped the city. Although it was a district headquarters, the city was marked by a simple peasant ambience. Only the presence of a bazaar, a hospital, the Friday congregational mosque, a district court, a cinema, a horse-show ground, an assembly place, an intermediate college, and two high schools set it apart from a *qasba*—a town. A twenty-minute walk in any direction from the center of the town and one would be out of the city limits and in a countryside of open spaces and farmland.

Coming to Grand Trunk Road, the father and son felt a bit relieved. *Tahli* and shading trees, bordering the highway provided a welcome refuge from the heat and glare. Their dense shade somehow filtered out the heat from the scorching summer wind. They had barely walked a few paces down the highway when a tonga* came up from behind and stopped beside them. "Come, Shaikh Ji, hop in," the driver said, slapping the front seat to wipe it clean of dust. "You're headed to your fields, I guess?"

"Yes, Qurban," Shaikh Umar Daraz said. "But you go on. It isn't much of a walk . . . really."

"All the same, hop in. The carriage is all yours." Qurban climbed down from the tonga and respectfully stood beside it.

There were two other passengers in the tonga already: a peasant, settled in the front seat, and his wife, all bundled up in a white flowing sheet, behind him. Shaikh Umar Daraz climbed up and occupied part of the front seat, and a happy Aftab jumped into the rear next to the woman. The woman flinched, squirmed to the corner of the seat, leaving some empty space between the boy and herself. Qurban, balancing himself with one foot on the footrest and the other planted firmly on the floor of the cab, urged the animal to move again.

"Shaikh Ji is our provider," Qurban said, seemingly to the peasant. "We live by his kindness."

* Tonga: A horse carriage.

Here and there the sun had burned holes into the highway and a thick, molten tar oozed from them. Every now and then the wheels of the tonga would land in one of these potholes, come out laced with the tar, and leave a long, tacky black trail behind them.

"Shaikh Ji works as head clerk to the deputy sahib," Qurban proudly enlightened the peasant.

Duly impressed, the peasant looked at the strange man sitting next to him, gathered his sarong respectfully, and shrank to the corner of the seat.

"It's a scorcher, Shaikh Ji," Qurban continued. "The poor animal, it can't speak, but it feels the heat all right. He's dearer to me than my own children. But what can I do, I have to fill my stomach somehow."

Shaikh Umar Daraz nodded and said, "That's true, Qurban."

About a quarter of a mile down the highway, Qurban stopped the carriage. Shaikh Umar Daraz and his boy got down. From this point, the way to their cropland was mostly narrow dirt trails snaking through the fields.

The older man patted the horse's back and said, "You've got a fine animal, Qurban." He kept looking at the gorgeous animal, while caressing its body.

"If I'd my way, Shaikh Ji, I would never let him off my front steps," Qurban proudly said, "but I have to fill my stomach somehow."

Qurban raised his hand to his forehead to say goodbye and made a clucking sound to urge the animal on.

"Father, do you own this tonga?" Aftab asked.

Shaikh Umar Daraz laughed. "Qurban was just being nice. You see, I had him released from police custody the other day."

"Had he beaten someone up?"

"No. He was talking to his horse . . . the idiot!"

"Talking to his horse?"

"Yes. He was telling the horse to go on undaunted just as Hitler did."

Shaikh Umar Daraz laughed again.

"And the cops got him for that? . . . Just that?"

"Yes. You see, the war is on. And Hitler is our enemy."

"Father, do you think we will win the war?"

"Who knows? Things don't look good."

They would stop briefly under an acacia or an ancient peepul along the trail to shield themselves against the relentless sun and then they would start on again. The last wheat had almost all been gathered and the parched fields, scarred and crusted by the sun, rolled out to infinity. The gusts of scorching wind would blow away the few remaining dried wheat stalks lying randomly in the stark fields. The monotony of the sun-drenched white landscape was broken only by the solitary green of an occasional hayfield, which also served as a reminder that the area was not a wasteland after all. The farmers had now begun to gaze at the sky in the hope of rain clouds.

On summer afternoons, Aftab found two sounds very comforting: the screeching of a kite flying high in the sky and the soft, sonorous cooing of a mourning dove. The latter invariably made him want to withdraw to a quiet corner and listen to it uninterruptedly. For the dove's music was permeated with the dead stillness of the lazy summer afternoons and soothed him in the gentlest of ways. On the other hand, the screech of the high-soaring kite always filled his youthful imagination with distant thoughts.

"Father," the boy said, "why do you finish the *du'a** so quickly?"

"Do I? Whatever do you mean?"

"You barely raise and join your hands and run them quickly over your face."

"That's already long enough."

"What do you ask God for in so short a time?"

"Forgiveness."

"For what?"

"Sins."

"You commit sins?"

"Oh, come on now. I don't on purpose, but sometimes maybe I do without wanting to. Just happens. . . ."

"And you don't know about it?"

"Sometimes I don't, but sometimes I do."

"How can that be?"

"Oh, well, man is a fallible being."

---

* *Du'a*: A more informal prayer than the traditional *salat* done five times a day by Muslims.

"Does Mother also commit sins?"

"Maybe. But surely less frequently than I do."

"When she prays, she prays for a long time."

"That's her habit."

"Is it a good habit to pray?"

After a prolonged silence, Shaikh Umar Daraz said in a feeble voice, "Perhaps."

The boy continued, "You only pray for forgiveness?"

"Yes."

"And Mother, what does she ask God for?"

"That, you must ask her," Shaikh Umar Daraz looked at his son and smiled. "Young man, you do like to badger me with questions. You'll make a good lawyer when you grow up."

That made the boy's thoughts take off on a different tangent: What would he want to be when he grew up?

"Father, you had run off to Bombay—is that right?"

"When?" Shaikh Umar Daraz flinched and looked at his son.

"When you were young," the boy looked up at his father triumphantly. "Mother told me about it."

A smile quivered on the older man's lips. "Yes," he said, "I did."

"You were very young then?" Aftab asked.

"I was a young adult then."

"How old is a young adult?"

"About twenty, twenty-two years."

"And just a plain young man?"

"I'd say about eighteen, maybe twenty."

"So is a twenty-year-old a young adult or just a young man?"

"Damn it, you'll surely become a lawyer," Shaikh Umar Daraz said as he smiled again.

"You had run off to become a movie actor?"

Suddenly, for the first time, the older man's color changed. It was as if his son had pierced the thin, invisible membrane on the other side of which he lived in his world of terrible solitude. But this was not a color of worry; if anything, it betrayed a distant emotion that had surprised him with its sudden, inexorable closeness.

The boy, finding no answer, lifted his face to his father, but the shimmering sun flooded his eyes.

"Mother told me," the boy said, "that you'd gone off to become a movie star."

"That's true."

"So did you?"

"Well, yes. I did work in a movie."

"Did it show in our hometown?"

"Oh, well, in those days only a couple of big cities had movie theaters."

"What did you play?"

"A soldier."

"Like a police constable?"

"No. An army soldier."

"So, did you fight in a war?"

"A big one. Between the British and the Muslims."

"Where?"

"Up in the hills . . . in the deserts. . . ."

"Are there hills in a desert?"

"In some, yes. This sort of terrain is ideal for battles. I had a white stallion."

Suddenly the boy had the feeling that his father was not just answering his questions but also taking a lively interest in the conversation that he had deftly veered toward things closer to his heart. And that made the boy very happy. This strange, wordless communication dispensed with even the need to know on whose side the father had fought. The boy knew, as certainly as his own being, that his father had opted for the role of the British cavalryman.

Finally, the boy asked, "Who won?"

"We did, of course. But, the Muslims, too, put up a good fight. It was a fascinating script. The movie cost hundreds of thousands of rupees. That's like millions today. Our costumes came straight from England. A hundred and twenty horses were bought. They were later sold back, though. But those were gorgeous animals. Each had its separate groom. The white charger I was given was a real thoroughbred. I never saw a nobler animal. The first time I ever rode him, he bore me with such spontaneity and ease, as though we had known each other for a lifetime. I had him for a whole month. For the whole of that month nobody else ever dared touch him. For a full thirty days. . . ."

Shaikh Umar Daraz suddenly stopped, as if savoring a fond memory. "For a full thirty days I alone owned that animal."

Aftab's mind had stopped straying. He had been imagining the whole scene. "Did they use rifles in the battle?" Aftab asked with visible impatience.

"Yes. We started out with guns. Then when the armies began to fight hand-to-hand we threw away our rifles and drew our swords."

The boy didn't realize that sometime during the conversation both he and his father had stopped walking. With the montage of desert scenes, of hilly tracks, of the fierce battle between the British cavalry and the brave Muslims running, inexorably, through his mind, Aftab involuntarily raised the branch in his hand and wielded it a couple of times in the air like an accomplished swordsman. Shaikh Umar Daraz stretched his hand and took the *shisham* branch from Aftab's hand. The boy lifted his head and looked straight into his father's eyes, even though the shimmering sky still dazzled him. Before him was the same bright face with its sharp, sculptured features, but flushed with the heat of some uncontrollable inner excitement. It was as if the thin *shisham* branch had changed, the moment it came into the older man's hand, into a sharp-edged sword, its point having pierced the membrane separating the two.

Shaikh Umar Daraz was standing next to a dead, stunted, leafless acacia. A few round, dried-out limbs poked randomly into the air.

"Imagine it to be a horse." Shaikh Umar Daraz suddenly leapt into the air and landed precisely on one of the limbs, mounting it as if it were some charger. He raised his left hand in the air to take hold of the imaginary reins, and with the other started whirling the "sword" all around him with dazzling agility, his eyes shining with awesome brilliance. He seemed to be in the thick of battle, cutting down enemy soldiers by the dozen "And now my horse is wounded . . . it falls," he shouted as he quickly dismounted, but the frenzied movement of his arms continued unabated.

That was a most bizarre scene. In the dead stillness of a sun-swept afternoon, in the middle of a parched field, a man wearing a fringed sun hat, his arms and legs outstretched, was brandishing a thin *shisham* branch with painful concentration, kicking up storms of blinding dust. A couple of fields away, a few village brats, driving their buffalo home, momentarily stopped to watch this comic sight. But for the little boy, who stood close to the sword-swishing man, the scene was all too sublime; it certainly wasn't ridiculous. Oblivious to himself, and with total absorption and wonderment, the boy watched his father, who, standing beside his dying horse, attacked the enemy soldiers to the right and left of him, behind and in front of him, making short work of them with his shining sword. His eyes glowed with animal fierceness and his body moved with uncommon alacrity, as the sword swished and struck the air.

The towel had rolled down Aftab's head and was dangling from one shoulder. In that instant the boy was impervious to everything: to the incandescent, blinding glare, to the scorching heat. Pure human emotion and animal passion had come together in that instant—an instant in which every boy comes to recognize, unmistakably, his father in the man before him, regardless of whether the two are joined by blood. What is important, what counts, is the man's ability to capture fully the boy's attention.

But those moments flew away as fast as they had come.

Shaikh Umar Daraz abruptly stopped thrashing his sword about, thrust the slim *shisham* switch back into his son's hands, and laughed gently. He had broken into a fine sweat, and beads of perspiration rolled down his face. He picked up the sun hat that had fallen on the ground with one hand and with the other dried his face with the handkerchief. Then he carefully spread the kerchief back over his head, over which he fixed his hat, and started to walk on again. The *shisham* branch had turned back into a mere switch in Aftab's hands. Its thinner, flayed end had broken off. Within those few short moments the boy had stolen a fleeting view of a wondrous, expansive world where the days didn't burn, nor did the nights strangle. His heart was suddenly like a bird—soaring uninhibited into uncharted space.

In a corner of ten acres of irrigated land stood a well, shaded by tall, dense trees. Aftab had already counted all of those trees many times over. He knew trees didn't grow so fast as to increase their number in a matter of days, but he still would count them each time he came to their cropland. There were eighteen *dharaik* trees, four big *sharins*, a single one of *jaman*, and two *tahlis*. So dense was their shade that the sun never managed to penetrate all the way down to the ground underneath.

Father and son sat down on a cot lying in the shade and each drank a cup of refreshing salted buttermilk. Then Aftab got up to go through his ritual. He would come to a tree, touch the trunk, count it, and then move on to the next one and repeat the routine. Generally he would thread his way through the grove, passing by the left of one tree and the right of the next one. This made his trail a winding, snakelike one, which pleased him very much. Sometimes he would turn around after he had come to the last tree and loop his way back to the first, but without breaking the count. Then when he had returned to the first tree, he would divide fifty by two. This made him feel that he had completed a round, that the count was what it should be, but more important, that the invisible circle he had drawn around the trees would somehow protect them and keep them green.

In the meantime the sharecropper had come out of the hut, holding a hookah in his hand, and sat down near the cot on the bare ground. He began to tell them about the crops.

Shaikh Umar Daraz's face once again looked normal. He was lying on the cot, his head propped up on the pillow of his folded hands, gazing into the trees above. From his manner of responding, it was obvious that he was only half listening to the man. The sharecropper had become used to it. Unbothered, he went on talking to the older man.

That peaceful look of mild self-absorption on his father's face generated a feeling of strength and fondness in the boy's heart. It was as if a gentle secret had come to be lodged there. Kneeling on the ground and resting his elbows on the thick, low wall, he leaned over the well and peered deep into the cavity—way down to the mercury platter of water—to catch a reflection of his head. A few yellowed *dharaik* leaves floated on the surface. Soon the peculiar smell of the water—musty, cool, aged, but above all, permeated by a sense of a certain past time (his grandfather had built this well)—began to rise up to his nostrils. Nothing, absolutely nothing, ever smelled like that. The boy, as if to retrieve that certain, long-lost time from the bowels of the earth, emitted a medley of sounds, some shrill, some heavy and hoarse, and listened to the well return them only as a volley of deep and muffled echoes.

It was not an electric well: a pair of oxen pulled the rope that raised the water bucket to the ground level where it was emptied into the irrigation ditch. If he came at the irrigation time, Aftab would himself drive the oxen, until his head began to reel. This afternoon, all was quiet at the well and the oxen quietly grazed on the fodder in one corner in the shade. Aftab got up from the well and walked over to the oxen. The cool, comforting smell of the well, which recalled his grandfather's image for him, still lingered in him. He also carried another presence within him, that of his old father, which now began to grow like a tiny drop of ink spreading out on a blotter. For the first time, the boy, barely ten years old, felt the passage of ancestral time through his being. And it filled his heart with a certain uncanny satisfaction.

The boy's eyes fell on a puppy dog that had sneaked up on him from behind and was now standing at his feet. It was a pup the color of gold, and so tiny that it wobbled all over even as it stood. When the boy bent over to pick it up, it shrank back, yapping shrilly, and tumbled off to the wall and disappeared behind it. The boy followed the pup. Behind the wall he noticed the dog belonging to their sharecropper lying with her young in a hollow. The dog knew the boy. She cocked her ears once, and finding that her pup was safe, went on leisurely suckling her litter with her full teats sagging to one side. Only last week the boy had seen the dog with her ballooned stomach swaying from side to side, but it never occurred to him that she was about to give birth. He came to the hollow, squatted down at the edge, and stared enraptured at the pups. He could see only four pups: Three were black and white, busy attacking the dog's full teats with their eyes closed shut, and the fourth, this gold-colored one, that had just returned from its adventures outside the hollow and looked more outgoing than the rest. It had abandoned the teats and was struggling to climb up the dog's stomach. The sharecropper's son, seeing the boy's utter fascination, grabbed the gold-colored pup and stuffed it in the boy's hands. The pup began to yelp. The dog raised her head and growled a bit, then quieted down. The boy, holding the pup against his chest, came to his father and asked, "May I take it home?"

With half-opened eyes, Shaikh Umar Daraz looked at the pup that was still making faint noises and said, "He's so tiny. He needs his mother's milk. Wait till he's grown a bit."

The boy, still holding the puppy, returned to the hollow. Shaikh Umar Daraz dozed off for a while. His hands were still folded under his head. The sharecropper went on rambling between puffs of his hookah. The boy again sat back on his heels at the edge of the hollow and, supporting his chin on his hands with his elbows on his knees, returned to staring at the gold-colored pup in quiet ecstasy.

On the way back, many thoughts occurred to Aftab, among them to remind his father that the latter had skipped his afternoon prayer. But that was nothing new. Shaikh Umar Daraz offered his prayers only when the fancy struck him; at other times, he'd be content with just being by himself, happily self-absorbed. The strange thing, though, was that whenever he put off his ritual prayers, he never felt the slightest remorse. On the other hand, if Aftab's mother ever forgot to pray at the prescribed time, she'd be so upset that just about everybody would know about the incident. Only much later, after he had grown up, did the boy come to know that the state of being at prayer was the state of being happily self-preoccupied.

The sun had begun its descent and the temperatures had dropped some. As they passed by the green hayfields, a gust of fresh cool air would sweep over them. Many times during the walk home, the thought occurred to Aftab to ask if that movie also had some pretty English memsahibs.* He couldn't bring himself to, though. He was strangely aware that that incident, which only he knew about, had entered his heart surreptitiously, like a secret, and that he was never to let anyone in on it. If ever he broached it with anyone, the sense of a certain wholeness would be shattered forever. Many times he looked at his father to find his face still permeated by the same softness and serenity.

On their return trek through open spaces along shaded paths, it didn't feel so uncomfortably hot, but the moment they entered the city, broiling heat and eddies of hot grit and stinging dust struck them with oppressive force. After the paralyzing midday heat, the city was returning to normal activity. People—freshly bathed, neatly combed, and clad in gauzy *malmal kurtas*†—had sauntered out of their houses and were now milling around in alleyways or crowding up storefronts. Circular Road was again busy with tonga traffic. An old, beat-up,

---

* Memsahib: An Indian form of respectful address for a European woman.

† *Malmal kurtas*: Loose-fitting shirts that fall just above the knees; worn by both men and women in South Asia.

rickety bus zoomed past them, kicking up clouds of dust and sending a few bicyclists in front scrambling off to the sides. Dust particles, fired by the day's heat, cut into Aftab's body. A water carrier was squirting water along the edge of the street.

Shaikh Umar Daraz bought Aftab an ice from a vendor and said gently, "Your mother doesn't like dogs. She thinks dogs are unclean. Don't tell her anything about the pup. I'll talk to her about it myself." Then after a pause, he added, "Let's go visit Chaudhri Nazeer."

They turned into an alley, abandoning the path leading home.

Chaudhri Nazeer, Shaikh Umar Daraz's childhood friend, emerged from the house wearing only an undershirt and a white sheet wrapped around his lower body. Aftab always found the man a bit too intimidating: not only was he the vice-principal of one of the two local high schools, but he also had this habit of talking to children with an air of unnerving seriousness. With Shaikh Umar Daraz, though, he appeared altogether relaxed, even informal, and addressed him as Shaikh Ji, sometimes just as Umar. With him he wouldn't mind even laughing heartily, slapping him on the hand every now and then with great informal joy.

Chaudhri Sahib led them into the small sitting rooms and later served them a sweet iced drink. A while later, he started to pull energetically on the cord of the hand-operated ceiling fan and talk somewhat secretively but in a loud voice, his bespectacled face thrust slightly forward. This feeling of closeness and informality was reserved only for Shaikh Umar Daraz. Only with Chaudhri Sahib did the boy find his otherwise reticent father talk a lot, be perfectly at ease, and sometimes even break into gales of laughter.

By now Aftab was quite beside himself with the heat. The cool drink brought rivers of sweat gushing out of his body. Suddenly he wanted to leave this horribly stuffy room, dash off home, peel the clothes off his scalding body, and throw himself under the steaming tap.

"Jot down the file number," Shaikh Umar Daraz said to Chaudhri Sahib. "Who knows, I might forget it."

The Chaudhri looked disbelievingly at Shaikh Umar Daraz, "Umar," he said, "you have never forgotten anything in your whole life; how will you forget my file number?"

"All the same, write it down," Shaikh Umar Daraz laughed gently. "It might just come in handy."

The Chaudhri suddenly became silent and gave the other man's face a deep, probing look. Shaikh Umar Daraz quickly turned his face around to look out through the open door. The Chaudhri extended his arm, put his hand over his friend's and said in a concerned voice, "You're all right, Umar, aren't you?"

"I'm fine," Shaikh Umar Daraz laughed. "I'm just fine."

The heat was now stinging Aftab and he was beginning to lose patience with Chaudhri Sahib, who was needlessly prolonging the conversation, asking after his father's health over and over again. Finally, when the two got up and started for home, Aftab's heart began to pound fitfully, as if Chaudhri Nazeer's silent fear had somehow crawled into the boy's heart, where it was generating numerous other fears, large and small. Suddenly the boy felt he no longer wanted to go back home. Mother would be sitting on the wooden prayer platform, he imagined, and Bedi would be filling the earthen water jars under the spigot. But these thoughts failed to ease his heart. His mother's voice kept hammering away at him. "Your father would have been a magistrate today," she often said, "if only he hadn't wasted his time in his youth." Adding a little later, "He has a brilliant mind. He just doesn't pay attention. We don't even make a penny from the land; the sharecroppers eat up everything."

His mother was a wonderful woman—forbearing and affable—and he loved her very much. Right now, though, the heat emitted by the closed alleyways was so oppressive that the boy was overwhelmed by the desire to get out of the steaming city once again with his father, walk down the shaded highway, then along the cool, comforting hayfields, till they returned to the well. Abruptly an irrepressible desire arose in the boy's heart to shout and ask, "Father, why did you come back from Bombay?" But when he lifted his face, the stern look of his father completely unnerved him.

At home it was exactly as he had imagined: in the small, brick courtyard, his mother was sitting on the low, wooden prayer platform, fingering her beads in quiet absorption as her body swayed gently from side to side; and Bedi, done with sprinkling water over the bricks from which arose a soothing moist, warm aroma, was now filling the water pots at the spigot. Aftab went straight to his mother and sat down beside her on the platform. She patted him affectionately on the head and pressed him to her side. Shaikh Umar Daraz entered and greeted, *"Assalamu alaikum!"* It was an old habit. Every time he entered the house, he would say those words, even if no one were around. His wife threw a casual glance at him and greeted him with a slight nod of the head, still preoccupied with her beads. Shaikh Umar Daraz stood a while in the middle of the courtyard, looking around blankly, and then quietly repaired to the sitting room.

The moment he was gone, Aftab hurriedly peeled off all his clothes and made a dash for the spigot. The cold, crisp water streamed over his body and tickled it. The boy began to shiver and scream with delight. The girl laughed at his ecstatic squeals and worked the hand pump harder. A couple of minutes later, Aftab's body stopped shivering. He wet his head under the spout, sucked into the streaming water to catch a few cold gulps and choked over them, then stuck his head under the stream and with his eyes closed began to enjoy the cool sensation of the refreshing water flowing over his body. The dark, uneasy feeling that had earlier gripped him at Chaudhri Sahib's had now completely disappeared, and he was feeling nicely hungry. He knew that after he had dried and changed, his mother would get up from the platform and bake fresh *chapatis* and they would all eat a hearty meal right here in the courtyard. He was happy.

Daylight was fast ebbing away in the sitting room. Shaikh Umar Daraz, a creature of habit, would always leave the sitting-room door and windows open in the evening. Today, he didn't though. In the stuffy closed room, he sat sunk in his rattan chair. Today, in fact, he hadn't done anything according to his routine: he had neither taken off his sun hat and set it on the table, nor removed his boots nor even turned on the table fan in the corner. Fat drops of heat oozed out from under the hat's fringe and flowed down over his forehead to the web of his thick, bushy eyebrows, where they hung poised. For some time he sat motionless and quiet, as if exhausted from his long daytime trek through the summer heat, then, as one suddenly remembers something, he removed the hat with both his hands and set it carefully down on the table. He dried the sweat off his skull and forehead with a handkerchief and then let it hang from the chair arm. Then, instead of bowing down to remove his boots, he got up from the chair, walked over to the door opening into the house, closed the door, and latched it noiselessly. He opened the wardrobe, took out his double-barreled shotgun, and stuffed a pair of cartridges in the chambers. He put the rifle butt on the ground and lowered his ear directly over the round, dark barrels, as if straining to catch some elusive sound. Then he extended his arm, stuck his fingers into the trigger, and pulled both triggers down forcefully.

20 June 1970

A little before noon a tallish man got down from the train at the railroad station, accompanied by a boy of about nine or ten. In facial features and gait, the boy bore a striking resemblance to the older man. They were father and son. The former, Aftab Umar, was a lawyer who practiced in Lahore. He had come to this city with a single purpose in mind.

The sun was spewing fire overhead and the gusting wind rose in blazing fireballs as it bounded off the scorched brick platform. To escape the sun, Aftab Umar snapped open his umbrella and quickened his pace along the platform, carefully keeping both himself and the boy in the shade of the umbrella. Coming to the long roofed porch of the platform, he stopped, threw his attaché case on the bench, yanked out a handkerchief from his pants pocket, and began drying his face and neck with it. Then he extended his arm to do the same for his son, who flinched, jerked his face away, quickly pulled out his own handkerchief, and used it instead to dry himself. Both unfolded their handkerchiefs, examined the lines left on them by sweat and dirt, and stuffed them back into their pockets. Aftab squinted in the glare at the platform.

"When I left here," he said, "the station didn't have this platform."

"Didn't the train stop here?"

"It did. But the platform wasn't here."

"Where did the train stop then?"

"On the bare ground."

The boy, a bit confused, looked at the platform and asked, "So when was the platform built?"

"A few years ago."

"You never saw it before?"

"No."

Twenty years ago a single peepul tree stood outside the station building— everything else was the sun above and the raw earth below. Now the space directly opposite the terminal was paved and lined by tall *shishams*. Standing under their shade on the ground covered with pollen-packed, tiny white flowers were many tongas, too many to count. A half dozen private cars were parked in the small parking area reserved for automobiles. The cars, all except one, were being loaded, and people, those who had just disembarked from the train as well as those who had come to receive them, stood near them talking animatedly, laughing, fanning themselves with a magazine or newspaper. Next to the area for car parking was a stand for scooters and bicycles. All these developments had fundamentally altered the look of the railway station Aftab once knew.

All at once a number of drivers swarmed up to Aftab and the boy, each trying to offer his tonga for hire. Aftab looked intently at their faces but failed to recognize a single one. Finally he got into a tonga and said to the driver, "Take us to a good hotel."

"Rivaz Hotel is the best. Very clean and quite close to the courthouse. Gulnaz isn't bad, either, but it's got a bad name. Respectable people stay away from it. Sire, you look as though you don't live here—right?"

The street was still the same—broken and riddled with potholes— but many new shops had sprung up on either side. It was almost noon and, despite the hot wind that had started blowing, all you saw around you was a surging sea of heads. Automobiles, scooters, tongas, and bicycles crowded the street. Aftab took out his sunglasses, put them on, and stared at every passing face from behind the cool lenses. He strained to recognize a single familiar face, but in the twenty-minute ride found none and began to doubt whether he had spent the first twenty years of his life here. Twenty years ago, when he had left here, he had just finished his BA in the newly opened college. He knew hundreds of people. Where had they all run off to? he wondered. It seemed as though the entire population of the city of his time had been physically lifted and relocated elsewhere, making room for a population of strangers.

Aftab was familiar with the Rivaz Hotel. But it was not the old, smallish, bungalow-style building he expected to see; a box-shaped, off-white, four-story-tall monster with cement floral vines crawling along the windows greeted him instead.

A gust of moldy smell, characteristic of entombed places, struck Aftab's nose as he opened the door to his third-floor room. He quickly flung the window open. The rooms had all been built disregarding the prevailing air currents. In this season of hellish heat, Aftab marveled at this architectural travesty. The hotel attendant, trailing behind them, had in the meantime checked out the light switch by flipping it on and off a few times and was now dutifully trying to get the ceiling fan to work. A couple of wires had perhaps come loose in the fan's regulator, which was covered with fly specks.

"Would you like me to bring up the meal, sir?" the attendant asked.

"We'll eat downstairs in the hall . . . after a while," Aftab said. "Could you bring us some iced water for now?"

"Right away, sir."

"I think I'll take a bath," Aftab said to his son as he took off his shirt.

"Daddy, let me take a bath first."

"Tell you what. Let's slip on our shorts and take a bath together."

Aftab opened the attaché case and took out a towel, bar of soap, comb, talcum powder, two clean boxer shorts, a big and small one, and piled them all up on the bed. The room was furnished along modern lines. Two single beds with a side table wedged in between, all lay flush against the wall. The sheets were clean and crisp white. The bathroom boasted of a shower, but the pressure was too weak to pump the water high enough for the shower to work properly. Water flowed down in a faint stream from the showerhead and was collected below in a bucket with an enameled mug set close beside it. Aftab gazed wide-eyed at everything, hoping to find at least one familiar object. He stepped back into the room and sat down on the bed. His son stood in the middle of the room with only his boxer shorts on, cooling himself under the ceiling fan.

"Daddy, where was your house?"

"There—" Aftab pointed in a direction.

"Who lives in it now?"

"God knows. I sold it before I left."

The attendant returned with a jug of iced water. It was an iron jug and its handle was riddled with reddish-gold welding marks. They had a glass each and stepped into the bathroom.

The marble-chip floor of the dining room was messy with dried-up gravy spots. Even though curtains had been lowered over the doors and windows, it didn't help much against the attacks of pesky flies. They swarmed on tables, chairs, plates, on people's arms and incessantly working jaws—just about everywhere. Gingerly, like an actor on his first appearance on an unfamiliar stage, Aftab entered the half-lit dining room. He had briefly hesitated at the door and looked cautiously around, as if startled—becoming aware, suddenly, of an awesome loneliness, crawling into the dead center of his heart.

"Daddy, aren't you going to tell me the story? Remember you promised?" the boy reminded Aftab over the food.

"Not now."

"When?"

"When we go out for a stroll."

"At four o'clock?"

"Yes, about that time. After the sun's gone down a bit."

After they had returned from the dining room, the boy lay down on the bed and read his comic book for a while, then turned over and fell asleep. Aftab also tried to sleep, but couldn't. He got up and walked over to the window. Opening out before him was a view of the city's busiest square at the busiest time of the day. People were returning from work; young men and women from schools and colleges. There was a messy traffic jam. Seemingly, the passage of twenty years had left the square's appearance intact. The same business were still around: three shoe shops, including Bata, a tailor's shop, a dentist's clinic, a stationery store, and the cigarette-and-*paan** shop. The atmosphere in these stores hadn't changed either, nor had the ambience of the streets where girls, crammed into tongas, most of them without their veils, were on their way home from school. Aftab had heard that an all-girls' college had been opened here. This was his hometown. He had passed through this square countless times on his way to and from school, and then later as a college student. Hundreds of times in these very streets, he and his friend Mustafa had chased after the perky government-school girls who

---

* *Paan*: Betel leaf chewed in South Asia.

were always bundled up in their black *burkas*. A quarter of a mile down the street into the inner city was the house where he was born. Even today, if he climbed down the three flights of stairs of the hotel and took himself to the square, he could walk blindfolded to his house or, for that matter, in any direction, as though he had never left here. Between him and his city there were just these forty-five stairs.

All at once he was overwhelmed by just such a desire: to climb down the flight of stairs to the square, remove his sunglasses, look up old acquaintances among the milling crowd, shake hands with them, talk to them, and then push on to his house, or to Mustafa's. Mustafa's father might still be alive, he thought.

Aftab took off his sunglasses for a second. The glare stung his eyes. The traffic was thinning out in the square and the shops were closing one by one for the noon break. Within an hour the square will be deserted, he thought.

Nothing, absolutely nothing in the city, now belonged to him. He was nineteen years old when he had received his BA and landed a job in the Government Secretariat at Lahore. A year later, during his mother's sudden and fatal illness, he had briefly returned to his home-town to dispose of everything, house and all, and permanently settled down in Lahore in a new house outside the city in the Model Town suburb. He was still living in that house. After getting a law degree, he had given up his old job and set up his own practice. Every year he would promise himself a visit to his hometown and childhood friends, some of whom dropped by now and then to visit him or to ask a favor. They had all been married and raised children. Mustafa had died in action in the 1965 Indo-Pakistani War and Aftab hadn't even been able to go visit his survivors and console them, managing, instead, a letter of condolence. When Iqbal, another friend, fell seriously ill, he had him brought to Lahore and admitted to Mayo Hospital. But in the past twenty years he hadn't once been able to travel these seventy miles to his hometown. How on earth could he now go and stand in the square? Standing in his hotel suite, the thought that he has now gone from this city for good hit Aftab with a chilling finality.

"Daddy—" his son's groggy voice called at him.

Aftab turned around. "You're up?"

"Imran's daddy has bought a brand new chair."

"Oh. What kind of chair?"

"A swivel chair."

"Is that so?"

The thought of visiting his hometown had emerged so suddenly, so unexpectedly. Not even a whole day had passed. Faruq, his son, was playing with his friend Imran in their backyard. Aftab, too, had come out in the yard after his shower and was now seated comfortably in a chair studying a brief. Nasreen, his wife, was sitting in the chair opposite him, browsing through a magazine. Aftab removed his feet from his slippers and slowly put them on the ground, letting the cool grass tickle his soles. Once during his work he casually lifted his head and his eyes fell directly on his son. And the whole matter gelled in that single instant.

All his thoughts became ineluctably focused on that frozen instant of time. In that instant, much went swirling through his mind: It was 19 June today; tomorrow would be the 20th. Faruq, his son, was ten years old, while he himself was reaching his fortieth year. Exactly thirty years ago he was ten and his own father, forty. These uncanny resemblances, these striking harmonies became concentrated, inexorably, in the whirling instant, which swept over him like a magic spell. Aftab became oblivious to the brief of the case due to start the next day lying open in his lap, his wife sitting opposite him, everything. He felt as if that instant was whirling around a pivot that drew him irresistibly toward it. Slowly it dawned on him that the pivot was none other than his hometown.

Then and there, sitting immobile in the grip of that spell, Aftab decided that it was time he visited his hometown. He told his wife about his decision. She could understand his desire, but not why he should insist on dragging Faruq along in the miserable heat. But she didn't fuss over it, thinking that, after all, his parents were buried there and that he had never once gone back.

Aftab sent for his assistant and gave him instructions about the court hearings scheduled for the next day, June 20th. He talked Faruq into accompanying him with a promise of showing him around his hometown and telling him a fascinating story once they got there.

That night he couldn't sleep a wink. His thoughts remained fixed on that instant, where time seemed to have hit a dead end and halted. As the night progressed, the thought that that instant was steeped in a mystery became a conviction. That mystery had, in fact, kept a part of his mind paralyzed for thirty years. Perhaps the time had come to solve it!

"I tried it out myself," Faruq said.

"Hmmm."

"I mean the chair."

"You did?" Aftab said absentmindedly. "You said it's a swivel chair?"

"Yes. It goes round and round," Faruq explained, tracing circles in the air with his hand. "Yes, Daddy, it does—round and round!"

"Hmmm."

"What time is it?"

"Four o'clock."

"Let's go." Faruq was impatient for the "fascinating" story his father had promised to tell.

"All right," Aftab said, "let's go."

It was getting on toward late afternoon but the city still hadn't fully snapped back into action; here and there, though, some tentative signs of life had begun to show: water was being sprinkled in places and shops were again opening, but it would be a while before the customers showed up. The only people who were there now were shopkeepers' acquaintances and friends who regularly dropped in for an idle evening chat.

Carefully huddled under the shade of the umbrella, both Aftab and Faruq walked into the bazaar. Aftab stared at some faces and for the first time recognized a few, vaguely though, just as one does trees and dwellings. What he thought he recognized were the timeless, anonymous faces of shopkeepers whom he had seen all his life glued to their storefronts. Some had visibly aged, with a pronounced gray showing in their beards, while others looked strangely unaffected by time. None of them, however, paid any attention to Aftab. He walked through the bazaar unnoticed, hidden behind the anonymity of dark sunglasses and an umbrella. At the spot in the road where they had to take a turn toward Circular Road, Tunda—who sold spicy grilled shish kebabs—was just setting up. On the front of his box-shaped stall lay the flat, rectangular, open barbecue grill that he had filled with charcoal, but he hadn't gotten it going yet. Instead, he was scrubbing the dozen or so skewers with a piece of dirty rag. An old, beat-up small fan was set beside the grill which he used to blow on the coals. Perhaps it was the same fan, Aftab imagined, that Tunda had used twenty years ago. Shortly smoke will billow out of the grill, he thought, carrying the appetizing aroma of roasting spiced meat, and bring otherwise perfectly satiated people scrambling out to Tunda's stall. Already before the time for the sunset prayer, a crowd could be seen milling around his stall and wouldn't begin to thin out until it was time for the night prayer. Then, as the cry of the muezzin arose from the neighborhood mosque, Tunda would wash the skewers in the large empty bowl in which he kept the spiced ground meat for the kebabs and carefully put them away. Then he would empty the grill in the gutter, where a few coals, still red hot under a layer of ashes, would expire, hissing loudly and sending up clouds of smoke; he would put the grill back into the stall, lock up the stall, and make for home. Although Tunda's left hand was intact, his right had been amputated just below the elbow. In spite of the handicap, he did all his work alone. From the time Aftab was a mere child, he had always found Tunda perched on the platform of his stall, no bigger than a chicken coop, working away using the one hand with a deftness and speed that defied description. Tunda was famous throughout the city for his delicious kebabs.

Suppose he were to take off his sunglasses—Aftab toyed with the idea—and install himself in front of Tunda and accost him. Would he, Tunda, recognize him? Surely he would. Had he not, after all, from childhood right up to his late teens found himself twice a week standing in the crowd at Tunda's stall waiting for his turn to buy a few sizzling-hot, crackling kebabs smeared with peppery-hot onion sauce, which Tunda would wrap for him in a piece of newspaper, before dashing home with his mouth watering?

Passing by the stall, Aftab turned his head to look behind. Tunda was still busy scouring the skewers.

By now the two had crossed the bazaar and reached Circular Road. The traffic was sparse, mostly tongas and bicycles; the irritating dust had not yet begun to rise. They walked on Circular Road for a while and then, instead of following the curve, walked straight up and got on the path connecting the city's center with Grand Trunk Road. This barely half-mile-long stretch stood in Aftab's memory as a dusty, unpaved path that looked deserted even in daytime. Not so now. It had been paved and an assortment of big and small factories had sprung up along both sides, with large and small bungalows wedged in between them. A completely new neighborhood! Pools of stinking water, covered with mosquitoes, had formed next to the factories and houses. Aftab hurriedly strode out of the area.

The moment they got on Grand Trunk Road, Aftab felt as though time had suddenly reversed itself and then stopped, preserving unchanged in its core a pristine vision of the world as he once knew it. And, today, still very much the child he once was, he had returned to play in that world.

The open fires, the land, were still the same: ancient and familiar. The same *shisham* trees lined the road and swayed in the wind and provided, with their shade, a refuge from the scalding winds.

Aftab snapped shut the umbrella, removed his sunglasses, and put them back into his pocket. The glare no longer hurt his eyes. Off the road, the landscape was dotted with the same old fields. Wheat had already been harvested and the parched fields looked mournfully sad in their stark nakedness, their surface riddled with dark rodent holes where freshly dug-up dirt was piled in tiny hills. Dry wheat chaff lay strewn all around the fields. These mouse holes, Aftab remembered, used to scare the daylights out of him because as a boy he had always thought they harbored vipers. Today he knew they were just mouse holes. He still couldn't look at them without fear. He told his son to give them good clearance. Walking by a hayfield, he bent down a little, broke a long green leaf, and began to chew on it.

That dead, ancient tree was still there in the field. Aftab stood a few feet from it and gawked at it; he couldn't believe his eyes. All along he had been thinking that when he got there, chances were the tree wouldn't be there, and even if it were, he would have to look around quite a bit to find it (he was obsessed by the desire to return to it once again and narrate the whole story to Faruq right beside it), but as soon as he had crossed over the tall hedge of bushes, what do you know, the trees stood right in front of him, immobile as a statue. Aftab took a few slow steps to the tree, and then extended his hand gingerly to touch a twisted, black branch, as if afraid that the merest touch would send the whole tree crashing down. But the tree stood firm. And although every single fiber in that tree had been dead and dry for a long time, its stiffness, its mournful spread, and the tremendous force with which its roots gripped the earth had not changed at all. Even the line left behind by the stripped bark was in its place. It was as if the tree had become frozen in the moment of its death and become a permanent mark on the earth's topography. The single thing that didn't fit in Aftab's memory of the tree was this new, awesome-looking *shisham* that had sprung up a few yards from it. After the incident thirty years ago, Aftab had stopped coming to their land. Later his mother had rented it out. And though he did come here once or twice as a young man, it was by chance; and then again he didn't walk but bicycled down to it on the paved highway recently built by the District Board, the highway that passed by their well and went to Ahmad Pur Sharif.

Aftab lifted his head and looked into the dense *shisham* foliage above.

"Daddy, I'm tired," Faruq said.

Aftab wiped his son's sweaty face with his handkerchief and said, "We're almost there." He ran his fingers through Faruq's hair. "There, you can almost see it."

"Where?"

"That grove of trees . . . you see it?" Aftab pointed in a direction.

"Yes."

"There's a well under those trees," he said. "Around the well are many fields. Well, that used to be our land."

"But, Daddy, I'm really tired," Faruq said, whimpering a little.

"It's cool and shady down there," Aftab said. "Come on, it isn't all that far—really."

"Unh-nh-nh!" the boy whined. "The sun's killing me. I don't want to go there." He flopped down under the *shisham*.

Aftab looked ardently and let his eyes linger a while on the familiar dark, dense foliage of the grove a quarter of a mile down the trail and felt its comforting cool touch on his sunburnt cheeks. The touch seemed so familiar, so recent that he thought he had been in the grove only a fortnight ago, catching his breath a while in its shade. His throat was badly parched and a desperate longing arose in his heart to gulp down a bowlful of that refreshing salted buttermilk. Who might be living here now? he wondered, with a trace of confusion and anguish.

"Daddy, let's go back home."

That sensation of comforting shade suddenly vanished. Aftab walked over to his son and sat down beside him, leaning against the *shisham* trunk. Then he said, "Son, let's rest a while here, and then we'll go."

"Daddy, when will you tell me the story?" the boy asked in an exasperated voice, tired of waiting.

Aftab lifted his eyes and looked far into the bright sun. Way down, the dead tree stood still in its stark nakedness, mutilated, terribly mangled—like a frightening nightmare. Aftab put his sunglasses back on and started to tell his son the story . . . that story.

In a soft and collected voice, he recounted the event that had occurred thirty years ago and paralyzed his life since. The entire incident was fresh in his memory, and yet he couldn't begin relating it without a certain diffidence. He was having difficulty talking about it; he felt as if something was buried deep inside the earth and he had to actually dig and pry it out of there. For a while, he talked haltingly, as if trying to press disjointed events into a rational order but finding them too stubborn to connect. Later his voice grew more confident and coherent as randomness coalesced into order and each insipid detail became vibrant with life. His words formed into slithering links that closed in on him like a chain. He was now speaking with flow and smoothness, the words flying out of his mouth like birds following the track of sound that terminated in a frozen moment of time.

In that sun-soaked broiling afternoon, sitting under that intruding *shisham*, Aftab saw the dark, long tunnel of his life recede to reveal a tiny point of light at the other end. The speck of light gradually moved toward him and stopped in front of his eyes, causing everything and every moment to ripple over Aftab's skin with a remarkable tactile sensation. It felt as though the past thirty years had suddenly become divested of all meaning—that not only time and life but even man's own body had no significance at all before his inexorable memory—a memory that integrated one generation into the other and gave the world its sole meaning.

Aftab raised his head to look at his enraptured son and ran his fingers into his hair, as if transmitting through touch the end of the chain. He had hit the end of his story.

In relating the incident, Aftab had made one change: he never did reveal that the man with whom he had gone out on a stroll through the fields exactly thirty years ago, the man who had, on returning from the stroll, shot himself without uttering a word, was in fact his own father. He didn't have the courage to let his son in on the secret; instead, he told him that the man was a neighbor of theirs.

The story told, both got up and started back. In spite of the blazing sun, Aftab neither popped open the umbrella nor put the sunglasses back over his eyes, but kept walking into the sun, impervious to its searing heat and blinding glare. A crushing load was suddenly off his heart and his body felt strangely unstrung and weightless—weightless, but strong. And although his mind was empty of thought, his body vibrated with the feeling that this city of his childhood was still very much his own. These fields, these trees, these streets now alive with traffic, tongas and automobiles that zoomed past kicking up clouds of dust, the bazaars full of popsicle vendors and sellers of fragrant *motiya* garlands, the alleyways where women sat on their house fronts or doorways fanning themselves as they chatted with their neighbors, mouths thrown open from the deep heat, the children who tumbled and rolled and capered about in the dust as they played unbothered by the heat, the houses from which rose the sound of metal bowls striking against earthen water jars, or the pungent aroma of frying or sautéed onion or garlic spreading everywhere around—all these places and sights and smells Aftab felt, through an unbroken continuous sensation, to be his own. He had left his hometown for good twenty years ago, but throughout that time and at no place—Lahore where he had settled down, the cities where he was obliged to spend some time on business, and those other places he had merely passed through—nowhere, absolutely nowhere had he experienced the state he was in now, the state in which one becomes oblivious even of one's body. Although for thirty years his heart had remained numb, his body had shivered every instant with a nameless fear, as if somebody would sneak up on him from behind and grab him. Only now his body had stopped trembling and become light, every muscle so perfectly unstrung, relaxed and calm, that he was not even aware that he had a body. Only the heart was the seat of every sensation and knowledge. For the first time in his life, Aftab found out what exactly the two words "my hometown" meant, which he had so often heard people say.

Sitting across a table from each other in the small front garden of the hotel, Aftab and Faruq were sipping Coke from chilled bottles. Condensation formed into droplets in the smudge marks left by their fingerprints and trickled down, cutting crooked pathways into the frosted surface. It was getting on toward evening. Beyond the three-foot-high garden wall, a second wave of traffic had started to funnel down the street. The time for the last evening trains was approaching and the anxious tonga drivers were crying "Station! Anyone for the station?" People, freshly bathed, neatly combed, and wearing fine *malmal* shirts, had come out of their houses for their evening stroll. Faruq got up, walked over to the chair near the wall, sat down in it, leaned back, and, resting his feet on the wall, began reading his comic book. A little later, Aftab too got up, grabbed his Coke, walked over to his son, and slumped down in the chair next to him.

"So, did you like the story?" he asked.

Faruq inattentively mumbled something and went on reading the comic book in the fading daylight. A naked lightbulb burned in the hotel veranda, its light too far and too feeble to do him any good. After a while, Faruq got tired, stopped reading, looked up, and suddenly asked, "Daddy, are you going to write this story?"

Aftab thought for a while and then said, "I might."

"Daddy, you could become the world's greatest lawyer if you didn't write stories."

"Oh!" Aftab broke into laughter. "Whoever told you that?"

"Mummy."

"Really? What does she say?"

"Just that if Daddy didn't waste his time writing stories he could become the biggest lawyer."

Aftab laughed again and became silent. After a while he said, "Faruq, shall I write this story? What do you say?"

Again the boy emitted a faint disinterested sound and began looking at the street. Aftab continued, "Tell me one thing."

"What?"

"Why did the man kill himself?"

"I don't know why."

"Come on. Think about it," Aftab insisted. "Only when you tell me that will I write the story."

"Why?"

"Because I myself don't understand why the man shot himself."

The boy stared unbelievingly at his father, then turned around to look at the street, as if thinking. Both remained silent for a while. Aftab's heart pounded violently. He shifted his weight on his elbows and lowered himself over the table. The same old fear his body knew so well began to return.

Suddenly Faruq turned around to look at Aftab. There was a strange glint in the boy's eyes.

"Perhaps he loved horses," the boy said.

The fog began to lift from in front of Aftab's eyes and narrowed into a tiny bright dot of uncommon intensity. The dot slowly expanded into a large pool of light in the middle of which Aftab saw a shimmering white stallion galloping away. The sun poured over its body with such brilliance that the eyes skidded off and could not behold it. Every muscle in the horse's taut body was so firm, so prominent as though it had been carved out of granite. A rider was firmly mounted on the horse's back, confidently holding the reins. The rider was outfitted in the white uniform of a British soldier, with a sun hat stuck on his head. He held a bared sword pointing to the sky. With each gallop, the horse and the rider soared into space in such unison that it seemed they were a single body that would jump across the length of the earth in one gigantic bound. In the ebbing light, still leaning on his elbows, Aftab stared at this scintillating picture of perfect beauty and harmony, until the fog rose again and obscured his eyes. The scene disappeared as fast as it had appeared, but it left in its narrow wake the knowledge that that was the finest moment of his father's life.

It was getting dark. The momentary brightness was gone. In the crowding darkness something quite new had emerged. It was as though that swift-footed bright moment had left its dark shadow behind. Something was found, but something was lost too; something was revealed, but something had also become forever hidden: "This city," Aftab found himself thinking, "this city where my father had lived his whole life had finally lost its appeal to him. And here I am; I left it for good, only to return and be fully alive again. Anyway, what does it all mean?"

The confusion that had been gnawing at his heart had certainly been removed. Or perhaps it hadn't been. If there was anything he knew with certainty, it was this: he belonged here. . . .

It was night now. Streetlights had come on. Faruq, his legs still resting on the low wall, was again browsing through his comic book in the dim light of the electric pole in front.

"Daddy," Faruq said suddenly, "I'll go to America when I grow up."

Startled, Aftab looked at his son. The boy's eyes were sparkling. Aftab stared at him for the longest time, then, somewhat casually, said, "Is that so?"

"When I grow up I'll become a doctor. And then I'll go to America."

In the comic book that lay open in the boy's lap, a gigantic black man was crossing the street with his giant-size strides, while a string of cars funneled through his wide-apart legs. Faruq turned his face to look at the street again, his eyes still gleaming with an illicit, faraway look.

A little later Aftab got up from the chair and looked at his son, as if contemplating whether to say something, but then he said nothing. He left the boy in the garden and went into the hotel. In the hall he stopped and looked around for a few moments and then slowly began to climb the stairs.

A few minutes later, Faruq too decided to return. When he opened the door, it was dark inside. He jumped up and turned on the light. His father, still in his day clothes, his feet in socks and shoes, was lying stretched out on the bed. His arms were gently folded over his chest and his face was drenched in sweat. It was terribly hot and stuffy inside the room.

"Daddy, shall I turn on the fan?" Faruq asked.

Aftab remained immobile. Faruq walked over to him and called out gently, "Daddy!"

Aftab opened his eyes and stared at the ceiling, as if trying to recognize it. "You may, if you like," he said in a faint voice.

"Daddy, I'm hungry."

Aftab got up. He went into the bathroom, washed his face with cold water, and dried it on a towel. Then, taking the boy along, he walked out of the room.

"Daddy, when will we go back home?"

"Early in the morning."

The two began walking down the stairs to the dining hall.

GHULAM ABBAS

(1907—1983)

The Room with the Blue Light

Translated from the Urdu by Khalid Hasan

IT WAS A small room on the third floor, with a blue light that you could see from the street. It vaguely reminded you of one of those air-conditioned carriages that the railway people tag on to the trains in summer, giving them such poetical names as "Silver Paradise" or "Summer Dream."

There were just the two of them in that room.

The rainy season was almost but not quite over and those who lived in the tiny flats and even tinier houses of the neighborhood were at last beginning to be rid of the stench, perspiration, and humidity of summer. Evenings had begun to get cool, but there were still insects that flew into the room, attracted by the light, a sure sign that it might rain some more.

"This is exactly how Najmi used to part her hair," the young man said, "nearly as far as the back of the head. She learnt it from a Bengali woman."

Nasreen did not answer. She sat in front of the dresser in which she could see a faint blue reflection of her face. She was combing her hair as most women do before going to bed.

The man lay nearby, looking comfortable, face down on the divan. His silk shirt and khaki cotton trousers looked badly wrinkled. He waited for her to say something, but when she didn't, he began to talk again, "Sometimes Najmi would make a strand of hair curl up and dangle in front of her face. It would look lovely against her pink cheeks."

Nasreen's face showed momentary annoyance but she did not speak. She was thinking, What kind of a man was this who had nothing else in the world to talk about except his wife, and here he was with a woman whom he had paid for the evening. For the last two hours, he had talked about nothing but his wife, a woman who was no longer even alive. She now knew everything about his married life and its high points. He had been in love with Najmi, his cousin, since he was a boy. Her father was not in favor of their marriage but his uncles were. Najmi was tall and she liked to sing. When she smiled, a dimple appeared on her left cheek, and henna was her favorite perfume and she was superb at crocheting.

In the beginning, she was interested in learning about the woman out of natural feminine curiosity but then she had got bored, and since her yawns and frequent stretching of her arms over her head had failed to change the conversation, she had decided to say nothing at all. Her hair was now done, and all her pins and clips were securely tucked away in one of the tiny drawers of her dresser. She noticed that he was watching her fingers.

A few minutes passed. Nothing was said.

It was a few days ago that he had seen Nasreen for the first time and he had noticed that she bore a strong resemblance to his dead wife. He had decided that he had to meet her. He had no money but had managed to raise enough to be able to pay her to spend two nights with him.

"My wife . . ." He had started talking again.

"So you really were very much in love with your wife," Nasreen interrupted him because obviously he was not going to give up.

"Very much," he said spontaneously. Her slightly sarcastic tone he had failed to notice.

"But I don't understand this," she was feeling combative. "What kind of a love was it that it has disappeared three months after her death. . . ."

She did not finish. There was no need to because she knew that he had understood what she had said. He seemed lost for words for a few minutes; then he raised his clear bright eyes and she saw that there was no feeling of guilt or repentance in them. He looked at her face, then rose and sat cross-legged on the floor. His lips trembled but he did not say anything.

They sat there for some time in silence, then Nasreen got up, stretched herself, and went out of the room.

She was away for a quarter of an hour. She had taken off her ornaments and was wearing a plain nightdress, which was really just a length of white cotton. She entered the room so quietly that he did not hear her. He was on the divan, lying face down. He must have been about twenty-five or so, but because of the dim blue light, his slight mustache and bright eyes, he appeared much younger. He was staring at an insect that had fallen flat on its back and was trying to straighten itself. Every time it came close, he would push it back with a matchstick.

He noticed Nasreen and was startled.

"Oh, it is you," he said, pushing the insect away with the matchstick.

"Your wife's death must have devastated you?" she asked, though she was surprised at her own question, which she had not meant to ask.

"No," he replied after a pause, "in the beginning, it did not really hit me. You see, I just could not believe that it had happened, but then it began to sink in and I fell ill. I was bedridden for a month and I remember my mother and Zohri, that is my little sister, standing over me and looking at me with great anxiety in their eyes. It was then that I decided to make an effort to live."

She was touched by the feeling in his voice.

They did not speak for some time.

"You said," Nasreen asked with a touch of coquettishness, "that I resembled your wife. What is it that I have in common with her?"

"First of all, it is your eyes," he said, a faint smile appearing on his lips, though he still looked sad. "Black and deep, just like hers. Then there is your chin, finely chiseled as hers was, and the third thing . . ."

"You are just teasing me, aren't you?"

"Your hair, your neck . . ."

He was perking up and Nasreen felt uneasy.

After half an hour, they put out the light and lay down together. He went to sleep shortly after, though Nasreen lay awake for quite some time, looking at the sky through her window.

It was one of the last nights of the lunar month and the stars shone with a strange splendor through a clear sky. She had a feeling that the stars had come closer to earth. She had always looked at the stars. She was four when her mother died and her father took her on a long train journey. They had gotten off at a small railway station around midnight and she had felt terrified of the half-naked *fakir** with bloodshot eyes standing there. She remembered having screamed and clung to her father's legs. They had had to walk because there was no means of getting to the village they were bound for. Her father had carried her all the way. That was when she had first looked up at the stars and then she was not afraid anymore and she had gone to sleep against his shoulder. When she had awakened the next morning, she had found herself in the house of a strange woman. She had cried for many days, but her father had not come back. He had just left her there.

She fell asleep.

Next morning when she woke up, she realized that the young man was not lying by her side. Perhaps he was in the bathroom. She turned on her side, expecting him any minute. When Shamman, the servant, walked into the room for the morning dusting, she asked him, "Where is the man from last night?"

"Gone."

"Gone?"

"Yes, he left quite early in the morning. We must all have been asleep. He even left the outer door open."

"Is everything, well . . . in place?"

Shamman had already made sure that nothing had been taken away. "Yes, everything is all right," he answered, having guessed her thoughts.

She felt a little ashamed of having let such a thought cross her mind, but what now began to bother her was his decision to go away without telling anyone. Had he been annoyed by her remark about his short-lived grief? Maybe he was hurt. Being a sensitive person, maybe he had pretended to behave normally, but inside it had hurt badly and that was why he had left suddenly.

She washed and was about to go downstairs to see her aunt when she heard someone on the stairs. It was he, with a small neatly tied package under his arm.

"I am sorry," he said breathlessly. "I went off without telling you. Actually, you were sound asleep. Here you are." He handed her the bundle.

"What is in there?" she asked.

---

* *Fakir*: A mendicant, or beggar.

"The day's groceries and some fresh meat from the butcher." He smiled as if he had played a trick on her.

"Groceries and meat, but why?"

"Don't be annoyed. It is like this. When Najmi was alive, that is what I used to do first thing in the morning. I would go for a walk and on my way back, pick up the day's groceries. We could not afford domestic help and that was how we used to manage . . . I, taking care of outside chores and she, keeping things running in the house. Look at this meat, so fresh and nice, the best portions. What is more, the butcher has thrown in a kidney for free. No servant will ever get you such nice meat. And here is that most wonderful of vegetables, kachnal, it is actually the flower of a tree and it has a divine taste. I have also got onions, green chillies, fresh ginger, and green coriander."

He had also been to the barber and looked freshly shaved, though there was a bit of soap on one of his earlobes which Nasreen had the urge to wipe off with her *dupatta** but couldn't find the courage to do.

"You really shouldn't have bothered, but since you have, let me send for Shamman so that he can get a curry going," she said.

"No, no, don't send for him."

"Why?"

"Because I am going to cook. When Najmi was alive, I used to cook sometimes and there she would be, squatting in front of me on a low stool and telling me what to do, when."

"Our Shamman is a smart fellow and a fantastic cook," Nasreen said.

"No sir," the young man said in a tone of finality, "Najmi used to cook kachnal in a very special way. Only she knew how, and so do I. Get me a fire going and, yes, a knife."

Nasreen did not think she should get into a discussion, so she quietly left the room and walked downstairs.

"Come, daughter," Nasreen's aunt who was already munching her first *paan* of the morning said, "I was telling Shamman that he should take breakfast for the two of you upstairs to your room."

"I don't want breakfast; you can send him some."

"You upset about something?"

"No . . ."

---

* *Dupatta*: A long scarf.

"From his face he looks like the quiet type."

Nasreen did not comment.

"What is he doing?" the aunt asked.

"He had gone shopping and is now getting ready to cook." The older woman began to laugh.

"Really!"

"That's right."

"It's sort of charming."

"He is crazy, if you ask me. All night he kept talking to me about his dead wife. My head is still buzzing. Send Shamman to help him. I am going across to see my friend Naubahar."

Nasreen had planned to spend at least an hour with her friend but was back after fifteen minutes. When she came upstairs, she found that he had got the fire going and was now sitting on the floor peeling onions, with tears running down his face. Shamman, much amused, was watching him from a distance.

"Shamman," Nasreen said sternly, "what are you doing there? Why don't you help him with the onions?"

"I have offered to do so several times but he won't let me. All he wanted me to do was to light the fire, which I have."

"All right, you can go downstairs."

When Shamman was gone, Nasreen said, "What is this cooking business? Here, let me peel the onions and do the cooking, while you go wash your eyes." She took away the knife and the onions, and he let her.

In about two hours, it was all done and they sat down to eat. "I am sorry," he said, "that you have had to go to all this trouble on my account. The thing is that Najmi . . ."

"Come on, let's eat."

"It is delicious," he said, as he tasted the food, "just like Najmi's cooking."

"Don't tease me. The *chapatis* are all wonky, aren't they?"

"Najmi couldn't make them either. I used to get fresh rotis from the tandoor on the street."

"I hate rotis baked in clay tandoors."

"Sometimes we would employ a cook at a low salary but they never stayed more than a couple of weeks."

They finished eating.

"You said you were now staying with a friend?" she asked.

"Yes, after Najmi died, I sent my mother and Zohri to the village and moved in with my friend who is also by himself. We share the house and expenses, including a servant."

"You send half your salary to your mother?"

"Yes, but she always keeps sending me some money back, sometimes for a pair of trousers she thinks I need, or perhaps a pair of shoes."

Nasreen thought that his mother must be very fond of him.

"How old did you say your sister was?"

"Ten years; she is a lovely child."

"Goes to school?"

"No, but there is a *maulvi sahib** who comes to the house and gives her lessons, meanwhile her grandmother is instructing her in sewing. She has a pet goat, my sister. It is white as milk, not one black hair. She feeds it herself and takes her out to the stream that runs beside our village so that she can wash and drink. One day while the goat was lapping up water, a big dog appeared and barked at her. The poor goat was so scared that she fell into the water and was swept away. Zohri was inconsolable but it turned out that a farmer had rescued the goat downstream and next day he brought her back, to Zohri's delight."

Nasreen was fascinated by this simple story.

He was getting drowsy. He put his head on a pillow and was suddenly asleep. Nasreen rose, looked for her white muslin *dupatta* in the wall cupboard and began to stitch an ornate border along its length, but soon she got bored and lay down.

Later in the afternoon, a rickshaw was sent for, as he wanted to buy her a present. He had told her that he had twenty rupees that she was free to spend on whatever she liked. More than that, he did not have.

"While it is true that nothing worthwhile can be purchased with so little money, I want to leave you a present, even if it is of little value, something you will remember me by."

Nasreen agreed to go and though the aunt raised an objection, she relented because Nasreen seemed keen and also, the young man looked nice and harmless. She was quite sure the girl would be safe with him.

---

* *Maulvi sahib*: An Islamic scholar.

Nasreen, wearing a blue *burka*, sat next to him as the rickshaw took to the road. They were one couple among thousands on the streets and nobody could have guessed that they were not husband and wife. They got down from the rickshaw and walked around the bazaars, he walking slightly in front of her to clear the way as it were, and to make sure that she was not jostled. He was very protective, as if she were some sacred object that no one was supposed to touch. In every shop he would invite her to buy with such affection that to the onlookers they must have appeared a newly married couple, very much in love.

Nasreen did not get anything expensive, just odds and ends for everyday use, some of which she really needed, such as a bit of false hair to make her ponytail look longer, crocheting needles, one picture frame, three kinds of rouge, and all for less than twenty rupees. Every time she would buy something, she would ask him charmingly, "And what are we left with?"

On the way back, they stopped at a restaurant where he ordered soft drinks and tea and lots of things to eat. She didn't want to eat but he forced her to. When they got home, it was nearly dark and the aunt was beginning to get worried, but once she saw them, her relief was apparent on her face.

Shamman had been told that they would not be eating. After some time, they walked up to their room and locked the door that stood at the top of the stairs. As she had, the night before, Nasreen sat in front of the dresser and began to comb her hair in the pale blue light. The young man lay down on the divan.

"Nasreen," he said, "I have told you many things about Najmi, but there is one thing I haven't."

His tone was so somber that Nasreen reacted immediately. "What?"

He was quiet for a few moments, then he said, "She was not faithful."

"What's that mean?" Nasreen was taken aback.

"It means . . . that she loved someone else."

"That can't be true."

"No, it is the truth."

"Did you have proof?"

"Yes, once by mistake I opened a letter that had come for her," he said sadly, his head down.

"And you kept loving her?"

"Yes, it couldn't be otherwise."

They were silent for a long time.

"Did she know that you knew?" Nasreen asked.

"No, I never let her suspect anything. A few minutes before she died, I had a feeling that she wanted to say something to me but couldn't. I was trying not to look into her eyes. I just kept saying she was going to be all right until she had drawn her last breath."

They were silent for another few minutes. "What would have been the point anyway?" he said.

They switched off the light even earlier than they had the night before. He was soon asleep and Nasreen kept looking at the stars through her window.

In the early hours, she was awakened by his rapid breathing. She raised her head from the pillow, looked at his face, and felt like a mother who clasps a child when he is having a bad dream. Then she put her arm around him and pulled him close.

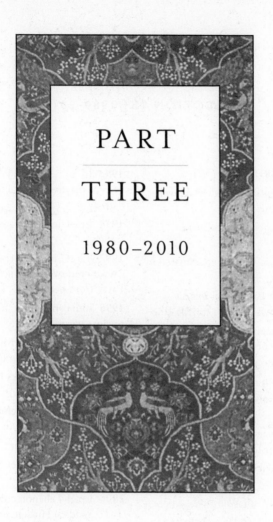

PART
THREE

1980–2010

Chronology

SECTION IX: 1980–2010

1980–1988 Iraq-Iran War

1981 Egyptian President Anwar al-Sadat murdered

1982 Hezbollah emerges in Lebanon

1984 Indira Gandhi assassinated in India

1987 First Palestinian *intifada*
Hamas emerges in Palestine

1988 Benazir Bhutto elected prime minister of Pakistan

1989 Last Soviet troops leave Afghanistan

Ayatollah Khomeini dies in Iran

1990 Nawaz Sharif becomes prime minister of Pakistan

1990 Saddam Hussein invades Kuwait

1991 First Gulf War

1991 Rajiv Gandhi assassinated in India

1992–2002 Algerian Civil War

1993 Oslo Peace Accords signed
Benazir Bhutto becomes prime minister of Pakistan for second time

1994 Islamic Welfare Party sweeps mayoral races across Turkey

1994 Israel-Jordan peace treaty signed

1997 "Soft" military coup in Turkey removes Islamic Welfare Party from power

1998 India and Pakistan test nuclear weapons

1999 General Pervez Musharraf enacts military coup in Pakistan

2001 Al-Qaeda attacks New York and Washington

2002 Justice and Development Party comes to power in Turkey

2003 Second Iraq War

2004 Palestinian leader Yasir Arafat dies

2006 Israel-Lebanon conflict
Saddam Hussein executed

2008 Israel invades Gaza

2009 Mahmoud Ahmadinejad wins reelection in Iran, sparking countrywide protests

IX

Ask Me About the Future: The Globalization of Middle East Literature, 1980–2010

THE FINAL TWO decades of the twentieth century were marked by dramatic historical events that radically transformed the Middle East: the Iranian Revolution, the Palestinian uprising (*intifada*), the nuclearization of the Indian Subcontinent, the rise and fall and, at least in Turkey, subsequent rise of Islamist political parties. Add to all this the attacks of 9/11 and the subsequent War on Terror—the pivotal events that launched the present century—and it would not be an exaggeration to say that the countries of the Middle East are undergoing a period of tumult and transformation unlike anything since the end of the colonial era.

Of all the forces that have shaped the literary landscape of the region over the past few decades, none has had a greater impact than globalization. The steady rise in literacy and education around the world, the mass migration of peoples across increasingly porous borders, the interconnectedness of sovereign states, the introduction of new communication technologies such as the Internet (which has accelerated the transmission of knowledge and information even more than the printing press): all of these have profoundly influenced the writers of the Middle East. As the distance between these nations recedes—even as their citizens grow more culturally distinct and more confident in their national identity—the literature of this vast and varied region has also become increasingly borderless. Arabs read Orhan Pamuk in Arabic while Turks devour Naguib Mahfouz in Turkish. As a literary language, Persian is second only to Urdu in Pakistan, while Urdu ghazals are available in Persian translations throughout Iran. Nor does the interchange stop there. Across oceans and continents, globalization has spurred the rest of the world toward far broader access to translations of these same works.

At the start of the twenty-first century, the literature of the Middle East remains as unique and vibrant as it was at the beginning of the twentieth century, when the Arab poet Khalil Gibran urged his fellow writers not to imitate the literary styles of the West but instead to strive to develop indigenous literary narratives that could stand on their own merits. That is indeed the task of this next generation of poets and writers, who, while building upon the vast archive of work produced by their literary forebears, are nevertheless not as preoccupied as the previous generation with using literature as a weapon against Western imperialism. Amid the shifting national and cultural associations that mark this new, globalized world, the writers included in this final section are more concerned with self-reflection as a means of reassessing the cultural history of the Middle East. And so, just as the world is slowly becoming borderless, so too will this final section of our collection remain without borders—one writer passing the baton to the next, free of all ethnic or nationalist divisions yet bound together by a shared sense of historical consciousness.

If the purpose of literature is to provide a window into other worlds, then the individual pieces collected in this anthology are mere porthole glimpses into the kaleidoscopic world of the modern Middle East. As Roger Allen, professor of Arabic literature, once wrote, "Literary histories also have their own history." That is certainly true with regard to the literature of a region as complex and ever-shifting as the Middle East. It means also that, like any history, this one will be studied, debated, and built upon for many years to come.

ZAKARIA MOHAMMAD

(B. 1951)

Is This Home?

(EXCERPT)

Translated from the Arabic by Michael K. Scott

IN THE DAYS prior to my return I had decided to assume a cool demeanor and contemplate my country as a tourist might, and not as a rapturous and homesick returnee. I wanted to hold the moment in my hands, examine it, and write up the experience. And I wanted to minimize, to the extent possible, any emotional entanglement on my part, so that I could see things clearly. I've gotten tired of emotional entanglement. . . . My entire life has been full of that. Now I am an old man who wants to see things with a neutral eye. Yes, I want to be as cold and dry as a stone, if I can. I had been afraid that I would fail in this, and end up—as always—emotionally entangled. So I tried to arm myself with anything that might shore up my resistance and help me to stand by my decision: I am a tourist, not a person returning home. I won't drop to my knees and kiss the ground, my eyes won't moisten with tears, my voice will not quiver. No, everything will be just the way I want it to be.

Then I got to the bridge that connects one bank of the river to the other. I arrived, and ended up on the other side. I came away from the bridge with my blood boiling. Five hours of interrogations and closed rooms with the Israeli secret police seemed to have injected poison into my veins, and obliterated all of the happy scenarios I had constructed for the moment of my return. For the Israelis, these hours were needed so that each and every returnee would understand the truth they wanted understood: you are coming to place yourself under our heel. This is the supreme truth, and everything else follows from it. The proofs of this truth were totally convincing and sufficient, as far as I was concerned. I had to swallow this bitter pill, in one fell swoop—not in small doses. And I gulped it down. I chose living under occupation over living in exile. I simply must believe that living under the boot of occupation is less demeaning than life in exile.

For despite my poisoned, boiling blood I had enough experience of exile to hold on to this belief.

So I had no need for the various scenarios I had created for my crossing over to the other bank. I emerged from the bridge choking with rage, affronted and humiliated. Entangled, in a totally different sense.

I was unable to behave like a tourist who sees things with an indifferent eye. I was unable to act like a returnee overcome with yearning and joy. I was unable to take in the views or see the scenery clearly. I had no ability to contemplate and enjoy, nor to observe or critique my feelings. It took me a few hours in Jericho before I could regain a bit of my composure.

Then we set off from Jericho. The palm trees on my right provided pleasing company. I found joy in them, until our guide informed us that the Israelis owned all of the palm groves. We walked on, our little flock shimmering ahead like a mirage, stopping only at the Israeli checkpoints.

Then, we turned onto the path to Wadi al-Badhaan.* As we climbed, the valley seemed to sink down ahead, below us.

We climbed on together, a group of companions and escorts. The mountain blocked our path, diverting us toward Talouza. From my childhood I had heard tell of this village, but I had never before seen it. Talouza seemed to rise higher and higher as we approached. Even the umbrella pines and sticky brambles kept up with us as we climbed.

There was with us a man who had reached, or nearly reached, his old age. He was returning after forty years of absence. All he had left in the homeland was a married sister in Talouza. He was afraid that his sister might not recognize him, and not acknowledge that he was her brother. She might refuse to receive him.

His thinking was beyond me. How could a sister shut the door on her brother, whom she has not seen in decades? The thought seemed

---

* Wadi al-Badhaan: A Palestinian village near Nablus.

ludicrous to me, but the man was afraid it would happen. He wanted us to wait for him until he knew his sister's reaction, and that of her husband. We didn't have time to wait. Every one of us wanted to see his mother and family. So we went on our way. We left him knocking on his sister's door, hesitant and in trepidation.

Here I am, a whole year later, wondering if his sister opened the door and hugged him, or if she shut it in his face as she would upon an importunate beggar.

I arrived in my village at night. Night, time, and change had all hidden from me the road to my home. I couldn't find my way to the house until I asked someone. It was only when I saw the mosque that I could get my bearings and make my way to my parents' house. The family home consisted of two concrete rooms whose doors close only at bedtime. There, on my arrival, my sister cried, while my father seemed to be only semiconscious, thinking of days long gone by, and of the death that hovers around him. As for my mother, she smiled. But her smile seemed to me to be carrying some illness—some effort to forget—that I could not yet understand.

The reunion was no bolt of lightning. I was weightless.

FROM THE VERY first moment I had to go back to using my old name, the name I had tossed aside like a tattered shirt. Now it came back to cling to me and to my body, like a wild and sticky thorn. I'm now "Da'oud," and not "Zakaria." I have to resume my life with my former name, as if I had only been away for a week. "Zakaria," the name I carried for a quarter of a century, had to disappear. My mother, father, and all who came to greet me did not acknowledge the time I had passed in exile. This was clear from their eyes.

I'm now "Da'oud," not "Zakaria," and the only thing that has changed is that my head has gone gray.

The problem was that I could not accept this so easily. I am Zakaria Mohammad. And this Zakaria is a quarter of a century in exile. In this quarter of a century, this person's life has taken shape . . . a name is not a tag that is stuck to your shoulder and ripped off in an instant. No, its paper will stick to you—so much that if you tear it away you take with it a piece of the flesh of your shoulder. To name is to distinguish and to create. My exile created me differently, and gave me a different name. I created a self in exile and I gave it a different name. The name was not beautiful at all. Perhaps it was cruder than the first, but I chose it, or it chose me. And I accepted it and it, me. Once, someone in exile, upon hearing that I had another name, said to me, "That's amazing! I would never have thought so. You cannot be anyone but Zakaria! You fit your name perfectly!"

I am Zakaria Mohammad, creature of exile and creation of my own hand, and I am Da'oud Eid, creation of my father and mother, and of my village.

So there it is. I stepped into a masked ball a quarter of a century ago, and the ball came to an end—but the mask stayed on my face. I've been wearing it for a quarter of a century. I don't know myself without this mask. I am the mask. I cannot return to my old name, ever. . . .

And here I am wearing my old name, visiting my village every Thursday afternoon, and shedding it again when I leave on Friday evening. My name symbolizes my exile. I would like to reconcile my exile with my home. I want them both. I don't want to toss one of them away. I am not capable of doing that. I want to soar with two wings: my wing that sprouted in exile, and the other wing, the one that grew in the homeland but remained stunted from the moment I set forth in departure across the bridge, a quarter of a century ago. I want to exercise that wing and build up its strength, so it can take me soaring high above, it and my other wing.

THE FIRST DAYS passed in a rush of greetings and hugs. But gradually the war between memory and reality broke out, in my mind.

In exile we lived in memory, and on it. Memory would devour us. It gave us vitality, and it adorned the goal, the purpose of our exile. It would grow and expand, merging with truth and delusion. It had its own routine. It would conjure up a scene from the past for me, whenever and however it wished. We would play together. Memory and I were twins. She was my kitten, and I was hers. Now here I've come back and her role is done with. She was no longer something essential to me. She had no further role to play. She was to hand over her trust, her charge, and take her leave. She had to eliminate herself now. I needed her in exile. But now, everything was at hand: my home, my mother, my father, the almond tree, the olive trees, the dust, the narrow streets—everything . . . everything.

But memory dug her heels in and refused to abolish herself. She refused, just as a guard might reject a charge or a task that failed to match specifications or instructions he had been given. For when the image fits the reality, memory will abolish itself. But this was precisely what was impossible. The image kept by memory was constructed of longing and delusion. These two would cut and paste, reduce and enlarge. Beyond that, a quarter of a century of occupation and change had shattered many of the similarities in the separate outlines of memory and of reality. The two images were no longer like the similar pictures you see in the entertainment sections of newspapers, between which you are to locate the most minute differences. It's not like that. These are two different pictures, and you have to search with a fine-tooth comb to spot the points of similarity. Although memory is not going to play that game: this is not her home.

So here's my memory going round and round, like an ant that can't find its hole after some miscreant hand had messed up the path, the sand, and the scent. This is my memory: a lost ant in churned-up sand. Since she can't stay in this condition—running around in circles—forever, she began on her own to dig a new hole in the ground. And the new hole in the ground? It was my exile. She is working with everything she has to construct an anthill to replace the one that was smashed. She finds her subject, and her self, in exile. Is this home then? Is it "home," for memory to be forced to transform exile into being her "thing," instead of home?

ONE WEEK LATER I climbed the hills west of the village. There I saw with my own eyes the sea of Jaffa glistening in front of me. The destruction there was terrifying. The wide-open stretch of space of my childhood, a space of wandering and seclusion, had been obliterated. A settlement had been planted on top of each and every hill to kill off the emptiness—the space that had been created for contemplation and prophecy, so that each human being could stumble upon a god. There was no space here—not for human beings, not for animals. The earth God created for his creatures was being roamed by creatures of iron and steel, ripping open the flesh of the land with their claws: the bulldozer, the drilling rig, the flatbed truck. How can this land sprout new prophets, after this? There is no place for them to seclude themselves and contemplate. You see, the land here, our land, is being prepared for the sake of the generals and their plans. Not for the sake of inspiration and prophets. Inspiration has been trampled, and all traces of it have been crushed under the treads of the bulldozers.

No open spaces. The land is full of the squalid litter of the settlers. The chassis of their old cars, covered in rust, tumble down the slopes of the hills. The stinking water of their sewers gushes in every valley. Wild packs of dogs roam the garbage dumps they established by our villages.

I looked around: there was a settlement for every village, to squeeze out the air we breathe and to keep us besieged. Between each village and its settlement nearby there is a design war. The village homes rise quietly from the foothills to the peaks, in harmony with nature, with wild plants growing unmolested in the walls of the houses and on their rooftops. Whereas the homes of the settlers perch, right there at the summit, as though dropped by parachute. They isolate themselves and dominate the scene. As if it were all a huge game of LEGOs, liable to be disassembled, crated off in trucks, and returned to their origin.

YOU WILL NEVER know what exile has done to you until you return to the homeland. It is there that you will feel the devastation that has befallen you, and know the full extent of the loss you have incurred.

People greeted me. The people of my village, my relatives, friends—all came and greeted me. I knew the ones who were over forty, those who were my age or older. I sat with them to bring back the memories, to tie together once again the bonds that had been severed a quarter of a century ago. That was wonderful. But after some hours it appeared to me that reconnecting the cord was very difficult. For my friends were not actually still my friends. And I was no longer their friend. There was nothing left for us to talk about, once we finished speaking of childhood. Everything that bound us together was in the past. As for the present, we had no stake in it.

After two weeks not one of them was still coming around to visit me. There was nothing between us to discuss. We had discovered that the bond that has been severed cannot be joined together again—or that to do so would take years. I had lost the friends of childhood in one instant, and quite likely forever. I met them only to lose them. That is what a quarter of a century in exile does. I wished, somehow, that I hadn't seen them. Then they would have remained in my memory as children—impish, exuberant, and lovable.

HAIFA ZANGANA

(B. 1950)

Dreaming of Baghdad

(EXCERPT)

Translated from the Arabic by Haifa Zangana

HIS LIFE WAS short but rich, crammed with events. He was arrested at the age of seventeen, released five years later, and executed when he was twenty-four.

At the foot of the mountains, the bushes burn and the vines are trodden. Herbs are burning, villages are burning, huts of leaves and branches are burning.

Young men take refuge in caves. After the danger has passed, I hear his laughter. Has he ever stopped laughing?

I try now, as I have tried in the past, to forget his mutilated features as I saw them at our final meeting. I want only to remember his relaxed face with its smile directed at his comrades, his friends, his country.

When I first met him, the note I received was short and precise: "Fouad, three p.m., in front of the Iraq Museum." I approached silently, three minutes late, after checking the rendezvous point twice to make sure he was the right person. He was of medium height and build, wearing a white shirt and a pair of gray trousers. His hair was red; his fair skin was reddened by the burning sun. He moved restlessly, though his face was relaxed. He was not carrying anything.

"Hello."

"Welcome."

Then silence. Since he was my superior, I awaited his orders. He walked quickly with short strides, and I could not keep up with him as he crossed the street. The unbearable heat made everyone seem tired, as if they were sleepwalking. I felt like that, too. I asked him sarcastically, "Why don't you run?"

He turned around as if he had only just noticed my presence, and laughed. I thought, at last, a comrade who can laugh and not feel guilty about it, or think his revolutionary image is threatened by levity. Perhaps it was because he had left school early and didn't consider himself an intellectual. He was arrested before he had had time to read Kafka's *Metamorphosis*, Dostoevsky's *Crime and Punishment*, Camus's *Stranger*, or even Colin Wilson's *Ritual in the Dark*. He retained his spontaneity.

When we were far from the crowd, he told me briefly that I would be in charge of certain activities: the students' union and the women's organization. I said I was willing to do whatever he ordered me to do. Then he suggested taking me to meet another comrade. We waited fifteen minutes for a bus. The heat was incinerating everything in the city. I could feel sweat running down my back and legs. Although few in number, passersby were unable to disguise their curiosity. A man and a woman standing together: how suspicious! At last the bus came. It was a double-decker and we went upstairs. A conductor followed us. In addition to their usual duties, bus conductors are guardians of public morals. Fouad wanted to pay both our fares, but I stopped him, saying he should pay his and I would pay mine. He looked at me incredulously, as did the conductor. A year later, Fouad laughingly reminded me of this, saying, "I was very pleased with your independence, but why did you refuse to pay my fare?"

The base was our home. As time wore on, there were fewer books to read, less hobnobbing in cafés, less time to sit together and endlessly chew words. Newspapers were scattered all about as we sang old songs; singing is often enjoyed at gatherings. Our voices were urgent, enunciating signals, images, and illuminations with but one dimension: the future. The future is our daily preoccupation. What is to happen? What will we do? What will our future society—our dream—be like? The future is our horizon. How vast will it be?

Fouad was arrested at noon on a hot day.

The heat had enough force to keep people in their houses. Noon was the ideal time for secret meetings, for making plans, but it also meant that if you were in trouble or about to be arrested, there was no one around to help. Two days before, I had met Fouad on my way back from Kurdistan. He told me two of our comrades had been arrested, and he advised me to keep a low profile for a while. As for him, well, he had to leave Baghdad for Kurdistan. His presence in the city was too dangerous for him and his comrades. He was sad to have to leave the base. He wanted to remain in the city he considered the center of his life and political activities. When I told him how sad he looked, he made himself regain his cheerfulness. After all, he said, this would be an ideal way to rid himself of Baghdad's heat and dust.

I looked at him with deep sadness that day. Had I, too, caught the germ of anguish? Would this moment remove the veil of our real emotions? I looked intently at his face, trying to engrave his features into my memory. In this, I succeeded. I, who can sit for hours trying to recall the features of a close friend, have no such problem with Fouad's. Sometimes I try to forget, but I fail. Was he handsome? I do not think so. But his presence was calming, even to those who had only just met him. Often they would leave wondering where they had met him before. A first meeting with him was like picking up an interrupted conversation with an old friend.

I did not know then that it would be the last time I would hear his laugh. When he was arrested, he was on his way back to pick up his suitcase from a friend's place. He did not foresee any danger. He had the false sense of security of a man who is paying his last respects to his city. His instincts failed him, this man who regularly traveled from city to city, refuge to refuge, base to base. He walked naïvely into their trap. The security men were waiting. They had to gun him down. That hot summer's day, Baghdad's back alleys witnessed four men chasing and shooting at a young man who thought he knew his beloved city as well as he knew himself. He fired back before collapsing to the ground, covered in blood. A week later, one of the Qasr al-Nihaya torturers pointed to his own bandaged head and arm and said, "One of your party's bastards did this." He was pointing to Fouad's final protest.

"Sit down."

"Thank you."

"Are you hungry?"

"No."

"Do you want something to drink?"

"No."

"Now, since you are comfortable, tell us everything you know."

"I don't understand."

"I already know your answer. You are all the same at the beginning."

He sighed with boredom, revealing how tired he was with my stubbornness.

"Let her confront the others."

My interrogator signaled to the man standing at the door to let the first terrorist in. They brought in a disfigured mass of flesh, carried by two men as if it was not able to support itself. I recognized the torn clothes covered in blood and filth. The confrontation was brief, but I recognized Fouad's voice. He did not look at me; perhaps he was avoiding my face, or maybe he could not see properly. He did not say much except to confirm my identity and acknowledge our connection.

I think now, as I always have, that when I die, I will take with me something of this world. That thing will be the image of Fouad's tortured body. The image of a young man transformed in ten days into a mass of unseeing, unhearing flesh. The image of an idealistic, beautiful dreamer disfigured by torture.

Three months later, Fouad and two of his comrades were executed. Before his execution, at Abu Ghraib Prison, he managed to send me a note: "My dear neighbor, I have been in the death cell for two months. They have allowed my family to see me, as I shall be executed very soon. How are you? Best wishes, and don't laugh at my spelling mistakes."

Now, whenever I meet comrades who survived, they are burdened like me with the guilt of still being alive. We spend our evenings talking of the past. I address them as if they are not there, and they talk about me as if I am somewhere else. They speak of a girl in her twenties. I talk about them as young men. The only living presence among us is the past. "What has happened to . . . ? Do you remember . . . ? I wonder if . . . is still alive?" These repetitive questions underline our feelings of exile. We see each other through a thin veil, an unremovable veil. We stretch out our arms to push away our past lives, our faces, but they stay where they are. The questioning is a new habit we have acquired. Will we be able to create ourselves afresh, behave in a different way, rekindle our dreams? Will we ever again enjoy the life we learned of in school, lessons the authorities then tried to make us forget? Will we play similar roles in similar cities in different times?

Until now, history has strived to repeat itself by rotating around a single axis: humans. Is there any guarantee that we, too, will not wear the faces of the torturers in the future?

ORHAN PAMUK

(B. 1952)

The Black Book

(EXCERPT)

Translated from the Turkish by Güneli Gün

Chapter Two

The Day the Bosphorus Dries Up

Nothing can be as astounding as life—except writing.
—IBN ZERHANI

ARE YOU AWARE that the Bosphorus is regressing? I doubt that you are. These days, when we're so busy murdering each other with the insouciant boisterousness of children on a lark, which one amongst us reads anything informative about the world? We give even our columnists half-hearted readings as we elbow each other on ferryboat landings, fall into each other's laps on bus platforms, or as we sit on *dolmuşes* where the newsprint shivers uncontrollably. I got wind of the news in a French geological journal.

The Black Sea is warming up, it turns out, as the Mediterranean cools down. That's why sea water has begun to flood into the immense caves that gape open on the ocean floor and, as a result of similar tectonic movements, the basins of the Gibraltar, the Dardanelles, and the Bosphorus are rising.

A fisherman we last interviewed on the shores of the Bosphorus, after describing how his boat went aground in the same deep waters where he once set anchor, put to us this question: does our prime minister give a damn?

I don't know. All I know is the implications of this fast-developing situation for the near future. Obviously, a short time from now, the paradise we call the Bosphorus will turn into a pitch-black swamp in which the mud-caked skeletons of galleons will gleam like the luminous teeth of ghosts. It isn't hard to imagine that this swamp, after a hot summer, will dry up in places and turn mucky like the bed of a modest stream that irrigates a small town, or even that the slopes of the basin fed abundantly by gurgling sewage that flows through thousands of huge tiles will go to daisies and weeds. A new life will begin in this deep and wild valley in which the Tower of Leander will jut out like an actual and terrifying tower on the rock where it stands.

I am talking about new districts that will be built, under the noses of the municipal cops rushing about with citation books in their hands, on the mire of the lacuna once called "The Bosphorus": about shantytowns, stalls, bars, cabarets, pleasure palaces, amusement parks with merry-go-rounds, casinos, about mosques, dervish *tekkes*,* and nests of Marxist factions, about fly-by-night plastics workshops and sweatshops that manufacture nylon stockings. Observed in the midst of the apocalyptic chaos will be carcasses of ships that remain from the old Municipal Goodworks Lines listing on their sides, and fields of jellyfish and soda-pop caps. On the last day when the waters suddenly recede, among the American transatlantics gone to ground and Ionic columns covered with seaweed, there will be Celtic and Ligurian skeletons open-mouthed in supplication to gods whose identities are no longer known. Amidst mussel-encrusted Byzantine treasures, forks and knives made of silver and tin, thousand-year-old barrels of wine, soda-pop bottles, carcasses of pointy-prowed galleys, I can image a civilization whose energy needs for their antiquated stoves and lights will be derived from a dilapidated Romanian tanker propelled into a mire-pit. But what we must prepare ourselves for in this accursed pit fed by the waterfalls of all of Istanbul's green sewage is a new kind of plague that will break out thanks to hordes of rats that will have discovered a paradise among the gurgling prehistoric underground gases, dried-up bogs, the carcasses of dolphins, the turbot, and the swordfish. Be forewarned about what I know: the catastrophes that happen in this pestilent place quarantined behind barbed wire will affect us all.

On the balconies where we once watched the moonlight that made

---

* *Tekkes*: Gathering places for Sufis.

the silken waters of the Bosphorus shimmer like silver, we will henceforth watch the glow of the bluish smoke of burning corpses that could not get buried. Sitting at the tables where we once drank *rakı*, breathing the overpowering cool of the flowering Judas trees and the honeysuckle bushes that grow on the shores of the Bosphorus, we will taste the acrid and moldy smell of rotting corpses burning in our gullets. No longer shall we hear the songs of the spring birds and the fast-flowing waters of the Bosphorus where fishermen line up on the wharves, now it will be the screams of those who, fearing death, go at each other with the swords, knives, rusty scimitars, handguns, and shotguns that they've got hold of, weapons dumped into the water to frustrate a thousand years of unwarranted searches and seizures. Natives of Istanbul who live in boroughs that were once by the seaside will no longer open their bus windows wide to breathe in the smell of seaweed as they return home dog-weary; on the contrary, to prevent the smell of mud and rotten corpses from seeping in, they'll be stuffing rags and newspapers around the municipal bus windows through which they watch the horrible darkness below that is lit by flames. At the seaside cafés where we get together, along with vendors of balloons and wafer *helva*, henceforth we will not be watching naval illuminations but the blood-red glimmer of naval mines blowing up in the hands of curious children. Beachcombers who earn their livelihood collecting tin cans and Byzantine coins that stormy seas belch up on the sand will now have to pick up coffee grinders that floods once pulled out of wooden houses along the boroughs on the waterfront and dumped in the depths of the Bosphorus, cuckoo clocks in which the cuckoos are covered with moss, and black pianos encrusted with mussels. And that's when, one day, I shall sneak through the barbed wire into this new hell in order to locate a certain Black Cadillac.

The Black Cadillac was the trophy car of a Beyoğlu hood (I can't bring myself to call him a "gangster") whose adventures I followed thirty years ago when I was a cub reporter, and who was the patron of the den of iniquity in the foyer of which were the two paintings of Istanbul I greatly admired. There were only two other cars just like it in Istanbul; one belonged to Dağdelen of the railroad fortune and the other to the tobacco king, Maruf. Our hood (who was made into a legend by us newsmen, and the story of whose last hours we serialized for an entire week), having been cornered by the police at midnight, drove the Cadillac and his moll into the dark waters of the Bosphorus at Undertow Point because, according to some, he was high on hash, or else he did it on purpose like a desperado riding his horse over a precipice. I can already figure out the location of the Black Cadillac, which the divers couldn't find despite the search that went on for a week, and which the papers and the readers soon forgot.

It should be there, in the deepest part of the new valley once called the Bosphorus, below a muddy precipice marked by seven-hundred-year-old shoes and boots, their pairs missing, in which crabs have made their nests, and camel bones, and bottles containing love letters written to unknown lovers; back behind slopes covered with forests of sponge and mussels among which gleam diamonds, earrings, soda-pop caps, and golden bracelets; a little way past the heroin lab quickly installed in the dead hull of a boat, beyond the sandbar where oysters and whelks are fed by pails and pails of blood from nags and asses that have been ground into contraband sausages.

As I search for the car in the stillness of this noxious darkness, listening to the horns of the cars that go by on what used to be called the Shoreway but which is now more like a mountain road, I shall meet up with palace intriguers who are still doubled up in the sacks within which they were drowned, the skeletons of Orthodox priests still hanging on to their crosses and staffs and wearing balls and chains on their ankles. When I see the bluish smoke that comes out of the periscope being used as a stovepipe on the British submarine (which was supposed to torpedo the SS *Gülcemal* carrying our troops from Tophane Harbor to the Dardanelles, but instead itself sank to the bottom, diving into moss-covered rocks, its propeller tangled in some fishing nets), I shall understand that it's our citizens now who are comfortable in their new home (built in the shipyards of Liverpool), drinking their evening tea out of china cups, sitting in the velvet officer's chairs once occupied by bleached English skeletons gulping for air. In the gloaming, a little way off, there will be the rusty anchor of a battleship that belonged to Kaiser Wilhelm, and a pearlized television screen will wink at me. I shall observe the remnants of a looted Genoan treasure, a short-barreled cannon stuffed with mud, the idols and images of fallen and forgotten states and peoples, a brass chandelier with blown-out bulbs standing on its tip. Descending farther down, slogging through the mire and rocks, I shall see the skeletons of galley-slaves sitting patiently chained at their oars as they observe the stars. Maybe I won't pay enough attention to the necklaces, the eyeglasses, and the umbrellas that droop from the trees of seaweed, but for a moment I shall look assiduously and fearfully at the Crusader knights mounted with all their arms, armor, and equipment on magnificent skeletons of horses that are still stubbornly standing. And I shall register with fear that the barnacle-covered skeletons of the Crusaders, replete with their emblems and their armament, are guarding the Black Cadillac.

Slowly and cautiously, as if asking for the Crusaders' permission, I shall respectfully approach the Black Cadillac, barely lit from time to time by a phosphorescent light the source of which is not distinguishable. I shall try the handles on the doors of the Cadillac but the vehicle, covered entirely with mussels and sea urchins, won't permit me entrance; the greenish windows will be too stuck to move. That's when, taking my ballpoint pen out of my pocket, using the butt end, I shall slowly scrape off the pistachio-green layer of moss that covers one of the windows.

At midnight, when I strike a match in this horrific and spellbinding darkness, I shall observe the embracing skeletons of the hood and his moll kissing in the front seat, her braceleted slim arms and ringed fingers around his, in the metallic light of the gorgeous steering wheel that still shines like the Crusaders' armor, and the meters, dials, and clocks dripping with chrome. Not only will their jaws be clasped together, their skulls, too, will have welded together in an eternal kiss.

Then, not striking another match, as I turn back toward the city lights, thinking that this is the best possible way to meet death at the moment of disaster, I will call out in pain to an absent lover: My soul, my beauty, my dolorous one, the day of disaster is at hand, come to me no matter where you are, whether in an office thick with cigarette smoke, or in the onion-scented kitchen of a house redolent with the smell of laundry, or in a messy blue bedroom, no matter where you are, it's time, come to me; now is the time for us to wait for death, embracing each other with all our might in the stillness of a dark room where the curtains are closed, hoping to lose sight of the awesome catastrophe that is fast approaching.

MELISA GÜRPINAR
(B. 1941)

The Bank Teller Tecelli Bey
Translated from the Turkish by Murat Nemet-Nejat

The Bank Teller Tecelli Bey

The bank teller Tecelli Bey
greeted his mother-in-law,
who was sorting
string beans
under the chestnut tree,
with his head.
Only nodded his head
and, with his son,
walked past her.
His mother-in-law,
seeing her in-law, with a mysterious intuition
checked if her money was in its place
in her sock,
and her eyes caught the white roses
that kept blooming since the day she'd left
the Palace as a bride,
the white roses which had the look of a wandering
dervish, whose branches hadn't
been pruned this year, and
the apricot tree
wasn't lime-washed
this year, and thieves
were constantly stealing the gutters,

stealing the zinc falling from the roof in broad daylight . . .
lavenders, boxwoods had overspread their branches,
but her son-in-law didn't care,
knew only how to go to soccer games with his son,

"What is it about this Fener-
       Bahçe*
stadium?"

In his sixties the man was living in a globe of ice,
if one asked her
can he be of use to anyone a man who drinks
a bottle of Marmara wine every evening
to the tune of poached blue fish smoked in cardboard?
As the mother-in-law
sorted the string beans, first dividing them with her hand in half,
who knows what else she was sorting in her head as best as she
    could?
"I wouldn't sell this villa in its time,
wouldn't I to leave it to this awful man?
Oh, what a head!"
Every time she shook her head,
hairpins slipped from her white bun, fell on the flagstones. . . .

The white roses shook gently to both sides with the offshore
    breeze;
The garden gate with the bell opened and closed.
Two boys dove fast into the garden.
"Granny, give us sugar."
In the mother-in-law's pocket there were always a few caramel
    drops.

---

* Fenerbahçe: Soccer (football) team in Istanbul that is a favorite of working-
class Turks.

She made the children read the fortunes
wrapped around them.
"Eat the insides," she told them, "they stick to my teeth";
anyway, her false teeth were ready to fall out,
nothing sticky pulling them down,
whereas in the cabinet next to her bed, always locked up,
she kept hard, Akide candies

                  (Akide Bey,

steward of the Sultan, licensed
producer of royal candies)

"but even if she didn't lock the drawers
who would eat those old-fashioned slowly dreaming melting-in-
    your-mouth candies?"

she wandered. . . .

The petals of the white roses
had tinges of yellow and pink,
the season for roses is past,
but even if they lose their scents and colors,
the seeds she brought from the Palace insist on blooming . . .
sprout under the snow,
the buds at the tips of naked branches stand erect and proud,
as for lilies, they are in the bud,
if the chestnut tree gives plenty of chestnuts this year,
the mother-in-law will hire extra hands
to haul the chestnuts inside the house
before the quilt-maker's apprentices
swoop over the tree. . . .

The bank teller Tecelli Bey
held the hand of his thirty-five-year-old son,
who was lame and stuttered,

injured at birth
people said,
that is also why
he's retarded,
his father mistreated the indentured servant girl
of the house
other neighbors said,
and look what happened to him. . . .

there was so little to talk about
and time was passing so quickly,
it had been forty years since Tecelli Bey walked in as a groom to
   this house,
his wife or mother-in-law
didn't listen to him even for one day,
his father-in-law had long passed away,
he was a graceful civil servant from Istanbul,
who was appointed Secretary to the new parliament in Ankara,
and under a flag wrapped as gracefully around a coffin
he had returned to Istanbul in two years,
no more children necessary, his wife and mother-in-law said,
and Tecelli Bey poured all his love on this child,
went to soccer games with his child,
lay on mats on the floor and solved crossword puzzles . . .
and late Junes, in his pajamas
drank wine on the terrace,
watched glowworms,
loved beans with chopped scallions, meatballs steeped in vinegar,
   semolina cinnamon puddings,
it isn't quite clear what he thought of Hitler. . . .

His stocky and reedy-voiced wife
leaves the carafe with the ice water next to him
and walks away quietly. . . .

Everyone seemed to talk silently,
is startled when they hear loud laughter from the tenant in the
    basement;
thank God,
mother-in-law never turns off the large voice box in the reception
    room,
radio is the voice of the house,
she says,
and at midnight, obviously, the rats in the attic are the voice of the
    house,
at noon the roosters, and the sound of the sucker-and-gusher
    pump is also a voice,
the windmill over the well creaks away. . . .

Some days, setting his cart outside the garden gate,
the taffy vendor sang gazels* . . .
The rest was all soundlessness.

Tecelli Bey inspects what his son is wearing one last time.
Clothed with care, he should lack nothing,
his knickerbockers, his linen hat . . . perfect
In his loose and zippered jacket, Tecelli Bey
walked in a dream, dragging his feet. . . .

and he always left something back in the house,
and this time his tobacco bag on the stool,
"ah," he says, "ah,
retirement did this to me. . . ."

if I leave these two women for a few days
and find my ancestral house in Kır

                            Şehir,

maybe . . .

---

* gazels: Turkish word for ghazal.

if one becomes the house groom in a rich man's villa in Istanbul,
it's like this, one loses everything in forty years . . .
the road was extending achingly . . .

his son is biting his own hand,
bitching　　　　　　　all the way,
　　　belly-aching

"Dad, buy me the Team Flag."

FAHMIDA RIAZ
(B. 1945)

Selected Poems

Translated from the Urdu by
Patricia L. Sharpe and Baidar Bakht
Rukhsana Ahmad

In the City Court

In my country
Courts of any kind
Are nothing but summary.

How kind of you,
Good Officers,
Allowing me to witness,
While still alive,
A doomsday scenario!

Jostling crowds.
Harassed faces
Panic.

The good old East India Company
Has pulled a fast one on
Our centuries-old crime of Being
This decaying edifice of wood and stone,
Colonial masterpiece,
Laughs at this joke even today
Showing its rotten plank teeth.

The charade is professional,
The set well designed.
Making a distracting racket
Like crows on rooftops,
Lawyers in black suits
Poise themselves
To snatch a slice of bread
From the hands of a hungry child.

Guardian angels in uniform patrol the crowds,
Conceitedly stroking the brush
On their upper lips,
Jingling handcuffs occasionally
To liven up the scene.

The half-lit rooms
Are gloomy, piles of disgraced papers
Gather dust on clumsy old tables
No luxury of table covers in this grand setting.
In administrative haste
They have come to the court, naked.

Installed behind them are functionaries
Especially bred by government departments here:
Clerks, Public Servants . . .
Their foxy eyes misting
With greed and arrogance,
They size you up. They take their time.
Every day they are crushed like worms
By their superiors.
Have they no power then?
Oh no! They can suck your blood.
That is all they are empowered to do.
How they relish it!

They procrastinate
They toy with you.
Examining each pale face
For those with a drop of blood,
They plan how best to suck it up,
Which brings a smile of triumph
Crawling over their lips.

To relieve the boredom,
They sing out "Allah Rakkah, Etc., Etc.,"
Or "Bundoo Khan,* Etc., Etc."
The Etc. break their lines, confounded,
Brushing the dirt out of their shabby, tattered shirts.
Chewing their lips.

These luckless simple people!
Set on edge by despair
And deprivation, perhaps
They pounced on one another,
Like children!
Some,
With the insolence that comes
That comes from hunger,
Squatted where IT IS
STRICTLY FORBIDDEN,
selling snacks and trifles.
Just to harass the "gentry."

How awkward they are!
How unwieldy!
They hardly fit within any ambit of Law.
The Queen's law was confounded.

---

* Allah Rakkah/Bundoo Khan: Famous *sarangi* (a short-necked Indian lute) musicians.

So the Muslim Law was brought in
But the Muslim Law wept at the sight of them
Hugging them and kissing
Their dust-stained faces;

That left the military courts,
The summary courts.
To set them straight:
It takes a gun butt
To shape up scum
Like this!

Have you ever seen the common man?
Have you ever met him
Apart from the speeches of our rulers
And the newpapers' headlines?
If not, join the crowds
At City Court and there he is,
Every day, manacled
And under trial
For rowdyism,
Fraud or
Breach of peace.

I sit, waiting my turn,
With some other harassed women
Herded in
For the crime of begging in the streets,
Without a proper license.

Translated by Patricia L. Sharpe and Baidar Bakht

She Is a Woman Impure

She is a woman impure
Imprisoned by her flowing blood
In a cycle of months and years.

Consumed by her fiery lust,
In search of her own desire,
This mistress of the devil
Followed his footsteps
Into a destination obscure
Unmarked, unmapped before
That union of light and fire
Impossible to find.

In the heat of her simmering passion
Her breasts have ripped.
By each thorn on the wayside
Every membrane of her body ripped
No veil of shame conceals her body
No trace it bears of sanctity.

But, O Ruler of lands and oceans
Who has seen this before?
Everywhere your command is supreme
Except over this woman impure
No prayer crosses her lips
No humility touches her brow.

Translated by Ruksana Ahmad

AZRA ABBAS
(B. 1948)

Selected Poems

Translated from the Urdu by C. M. Naim

Today Was a Holiday

One arm hangs limp and empty,
the other bends under a load
One foot has gone to sleep
the other half itches for the road
Half my body nods in a dream
the other half holds a wake
I sold for pennies my inheritance
Spent one-half of the life's take
and put the other half in a bag
I left the doors unlatched, threw
a cloth over the dusty panes,
swore roundly at my floundering days and nights
then let one half-awake body
make love to another half-asleep

A Dot Might Appear

A dot might appear from somewhere
That could not be put
on any word
and the dot
alone
off by itself
would stand there
sustained by some illusion

waiting
for a word to come
on which it could be put

It could also happen
that after centuries had passed
all the words would decay
and rot away
and be absorbed
and nothing would be left

Only the dot
would be left

KISHWAR NAHEED
(B. 1940)

Selected Poems

Translated from the Urdu by Rukhsana Ahmad

We Sinful Women

It is we sinful women
who are not awed by the grandeur of those who wear gowns
who don't sell our lives
who don't bow our heads
who don't fold our hands together.

It is we sinful women
while those who sell the harvests of our bodies
become exalted
become distinguished
become the just princes of the material world.

It is we sinful women
who come out raising the banner of truth
up against the barricades of lies on the highways
who find stories of persecution piled on each threshold
who find the tongues that could speak have been severed.

It is we sinful women
Now even if the night gives chase
these eyes shall not be put out.
For the wall that has been razed
don't insist now on raising it again.

It is we sinful women
who are not awed by the grandeur of those who wear gowns
who don't sell our lives
who don't bow our heads
who don't fold our hands together.

Censorship

In those times when the camera could not freeze tyranny forever
only until those times
should you have written
that history
which describes tyranny as valor.

Today, gazing at scenes
transferred on celluloid
one can gauge
what the scene is like
and the sound
when trees are uprooted from the hillsides.

Whether you are happy or sad
you must breathe.
Whether your eyes are open or closed
the scene, its imprint on the mind,
does not change.

The tree that stands in the river
always remains wooden
cannot become a crocodile.

For a long time now,
we have stood
on the rooftops of stories
believing this city is ours.

The earth beneath the foundations has sunk
but even now we stand
on the rooftops of stories
assuming life to be:
the insipid afternoon's wasted alleyways
with their shattered bricks
and gaping fissures.

To the Masters of Countries with a Cold Climate

My country is torrid
maybe that is why my hands feel warm
My country is torrid
maybe that is why my feet burn
My country is torrid
maybe that is why there are boils on my body
My country is torrid
maybe that is why the roof of my house melted and caved in.

My country is torrid
maybe that is why my children are kept thirsty
My country is torrid
maybe that is why I am kept unclothed.

My country is torrid
maybe that is why one neither knows of clouds that bring rainfall
nor of floods that destroy.
And to wreck my harvests, sometimes moneylenders,
sometimes wild beasts, sometimes calamities
and sometimes self-styled masters arrive.

Don't teach me to hate my torrid country
Let me dry my wet clothes in these courtyards
let me plant gold in its fields
let me quench my thirst at its rivers

let me rest beneath the shade of its trees
let me wear its dust and wrap its distances around me.
I don't want the shade of lengthening shadows
I have the support of the rays of the rising sun.
The sun has made its energy accessible for my country
the sun and I
the sun and you
cannot walk side by side
The sun has chosen *me* for company.

ZEESHAN SAHIL
(1961–2008)

Selected Poems

Translated from the Urdu by G. A. Chaussee

Rome

I want to know—
When Rome was burning
and Nero was playing his flute,
who were the people there for it all?
Who had his ear turned to the flute?
And whose eyes
glimmered in the light of the fire?

I want to know—
Who were the people praising Nero's flutistry?
And who were fanning the embers?

How many comfortable homes were offered up to that fire?
How many magnificent buildings
turned to heaps of ash?
How many people's bones
scattered like dust?
How many beautiful bodies
melted like candles of wax?
How many epic dramas,
how many tragic melodies,
how many songs of disappointment and love,
how many impressions of hope and heart-suspending allure

passed into nothingness?
Dismayed by the fire's ferocity,
how many dreams vanished from the page of being?

I want to see
the record of that decimation of Rome.
Or perhaps somewhere to find
just a list of the people, the structures, the things
destroyed in that fire for all time.
Or even just to know—
When the conflagration broke out,
who were the people there with Nero,
and who were there with Rome?

Karachi

Karachi
is a forest
where you see darkness, noise,
and a thousand trees of fear
conversing with the sky
in a voice raised so high
that no one living
inside or outside the city
can even hear another's screams.

In truth, Karachi now
isn't a city at all.
It's rather a cry choked out
in a state of mortal peril
briefly echoed all around.

No one has even the slightest idea
that this might also be
the cry of someone alone
calling for help.
Karachi's taken for

an inhuman throng
by those who don't come to assist.
Or a crowd of the blind
who get hungry
and are fed only rice pudding;
who cry out
and are made to sit through speeches;
they take each other by the hand
or not,
they move,
and draw gunfire into the air.

But now in Karachi
the firing is no longer confined just to the air.
Bullets and the sounds they make
are showing up in people's dreams.
Karachi, though, is not a city of dreams.
There's just one place to wait for dreams to come.
For our convenience
we use it
as a seaport
or even as a makeshift laboratory.
Where we
perform no experiments on human bodies
as everyone knows.
For that, rabbits are used
or white rats
whose fecundity
upon approaching the limits of safety
draws rat poison
and cats
from the capital.

ALTAF FATIMA
(B. 1929)

Do You Suppose It's the East Wind?
Translated from the Urdu by Muhammad Umar Memon

THE ENORMOUS WEIGHT of three hundred and sixty-five days once again slips from my hand and falls down into the dark cavern of the past. The windows in this desolate room are wide open. How improbably strange the sky looks, draped in a sheet of dense gray clouds, behind the luxuriant green trees. It seems as if someone has filled space itself with a sweet, melancholy beauty. A cool breeze has finally started to blow, after much heat and sun. Could it be the east wind?

Papers and books lie in a disorderly pile before me on the desk. I suddenly stop writing, screw the cap back on my fountain pen, and clip it to my collar—not because the weather is absolutely delightful and the grapevine maddeningly beautiful and one simply cannot write a book on dairy farming in a setting so entirely out of this world; one cannot discuss the significance of the chemical components of milk any more than one can expound on the proper proportion of corn husk and mustard oil-cake in the cattle feed. All right, not another word about cows or water buffalo.

My problem is that I'm very absentminded. I search for my pen everywhere, while it's clipped to my collar all along. I look at faces I have seen so often and wonder who they might belong to—I have never seen them before. And my memory is so bad I can hardly remember who has hurt me and who I have decided to hold a grudge against. Worst of all, the day I'm supposed to take care of some enormously important matter, I seem to end up spending in some atrociously silly matter.

Well, that's what it's come to with me. My one abiding fear is that the landscapes of my memory might become a yawning wasteland—

derelict, empty, blanched. That I may lose my grip on familiar things and no longer recognize them at all. That's why I have pushed aside the sheets of paper and clipped my pen back on. Just so that I may lean back and squint into the horizon and not let my eyes waver—trekking back along the past's interminable highways, so that time may twist around and look back. It just might. What! It really has! There, look, the past is calling me.

The scene before my eyes is beginning to dissolve, and a long-lost horizon is forming in space. This gigantic gate, here—it's the very same gate whose wrought-iron bars we would hug tightly, and swing on for hours on end. Tickets were improvised and sold; the guard waved the green flag, and the passengers, planting their feet on the bottom rail and grabbing a hold of the grillwork, would enjoy the train ride as the others energetically swung the gate out into the street. Directly across the street from the gate the ironsmith's furnace would be ablaze, the clank-clank of red-hot iron being beaten into shape resounding through the air. And inside the gate small and large gardens opened to view the hedges of *nirbisi* and delicate trellises draped with rose vines. We would make believe that our train was chugging along beside jungle and farmland. To bring the train into a station, we would stick thumb under chin, run our index fingers along the ridge of our noses all the way to our foreheads, and cry with all the power our lungs could master: *Kooooo!* It felt as if the train were actually entering the station.

The entire summer vacation was thus spent swinging from the gate and playing games filled with violence inside the summerhouse. There would be bloody skirmishes between robbers and cops, the robbers would finally be caught, they would repent, and right away set up stands where they would sell guavas and mulberries. Clay flowerpots would be broken, the shards then rubbed smooth into *ser* and half-*ser* weights and all kinds of coins. And suddenly, one day, the vacation would end and school would start the next day. But on the next day I would pretend I didn't know, and manage to stay in bed until nine o'clock. The school bus would come and leave without me. But this couldn't go on.

The very next day I would be violently shaken awake at four in the morning. Every time the school reopened, a fresh calamity awaited us. This time, though, it came in the form of a new teacher: a portly woman draped in a borderless sari and wearing eyeglasses. She put a Hindi primer in the hands of each of the Muslim students, and ordered them to learn it on their own. When I saw the primer I was offended. We were in the fifth grade, weren't we? Then why was it being foisted upon us? We had already been through a similar primer once before. All the pictures were exactly the same. Anyway, she informed us that Hindi was compulsory in the fifth grade. I carefully put the primer away in my satchel, and it stayed right there. Two days later when she showed up, I easily rattled off the lesson: *alif* for *anar*, *be* for *bakri*, *he* for *huqqa*, and *dal* for *dhol*. *Crazy! Idiot!* She was beside herself with anger, and ordered me to learn it all over again.

What misery! But who could I ask for help? The rest of the girls were quite a bit older than me, and spent free periods crocheting lace or knitting red and green woolen sweaters. I, who still played with marbles and broken glass bangles, felt shy in their presence. So I took the primer back and thought the teacher was crazy herself. There were pictures of "hubble-bubble" and "she-goat" all right. Bright and clear. Anybody could see that. Yet she always got angry. When she yelled at me over and over again, I had to ask Mother for help: the teacher doesn't teach but keeps telling me to learn from somebody at home. "Go ask Robby Dutt. He'll teach you," Mother suggested. So I begged the boy whose father—whom we used to call Maharaj—lived in the quarters within the compound. Robby Dutt—his big eyes smeared with a thick application of *kajal*,[*] wearing a gigantic black *tika*[†] in the middle of his forehead to ward off the evil eye, and a gold amulet strung on a black thread round his neck—rolled his eyes and spelled out his terms:

"You won't pull my braid, right?"

"Right."

"You'll let me swing on the swing?"

"Yes."

"Push the swing twenty times for me?"

"Yes."

"And give me *gos-roti* to eat?"

---

[*] *Kajal*: Kohl; used as eye makeup.
[†] *Tika*: A red spot on the forehead of a Hindu woman.

At this point I faltered. If I gave him meat to eat as he wished, Mother's displeasure was sure to follow. She had expressly warned me, "Don't you ever give him meat—understand?"

"All right, don't," he said "I won't teach you."

"I will, I will. Okay, I'll give you meat."

And when His Majesty came in to teach, he would straightaway push all of himself under a cot or a settee. I'd pull him out of there somehow, and then, in a voice calculated to overwhelm me, he would command:

"Read! *Chota 'a!' Bara 'uu!' 'Ee!'*" All those pages with pictures on them he had made me learn in no time at all. Then one day he taught me: *"Mohan accha larka hai. Bhor bha'e jagta hai aur ashnan karta hai,"* Mohan is a good boy. He gets up early in the morning and takes a bath.

I couldn't believe that such familiar words could possibly come out of such a strange alphabet. "You miserable ass! You aren't teaching me properly."

"Parha'e to rahe hain. Aur kya tumra sar parha'en?" But I am! What else did you think I was doing?

"Liar! Fraud! English sounds come out of English letters. And here you are teaching me Urdu in Hindi!"

"Go to hell! I'm done teaching you!"

He would throw in the towel and flee, because the matter was beyond him. He himself couldn't figure out how Hindi letters managed to emit Urdu sounds. It took me a long time to make my peace with the idea that the letters of this weird and totally unfamiliar alphabet produced exactly the same sounds as the Urdu script I was familiar with. Now the writing drill got underway. "And what's this—the silly squiggly thing stuck to it?" I'd ask, pointing at the *matra* for the vowel "o."

This would throw him off once again. *"Yeh eme hi hai. Tum is se mat bolo. Apna kam karo."* It's just there. Don't meddle with it. Do your work. In short, he wasn't counting on explaining the vowel marks, and explain them he did not. But something like anxiety nagged at my heart. Sheer deception, this! It didn't make sense that you read in the strange-looking Hindi script exactly what you read in the Urdu script. Surely it was a plot to confound the reader. Out of sheer stubbornness I took it to heart that there was no point in slaving over this. Robby

Dutt too seemed to have become fed up with my daily bickering and nagging. So I put the Hindi *qa'ida* to one side. There was another reason too: I was soon going to attend a school where there was no such nonsense. And so that was the end of his teachership and my discipleship. He was now scarcely seen all day long. He'd go to school, and when he returned would dart out to wander around. Or else he would stay at home and talk like cranky old men. He had no siblings and all his close kin were back in his hometown.

Yep, Robby Dutt, you were really something. Even now I can see you vividly against this background. The truth is, you're never far from view. Whenever the rains come—and with them the thought that back on the old house dark rain clouds are pouring down in a torrent, letting rivers of water gush noisily along the eaves, and people are celebrating *Saluno*, the festival of *Raksha-bandhan**—how can I not remember you? When the ties of teacher and taught broke off between us, you quickly forged another bond. You stood behind the door and kept repeating in your muted voice: *"Tum kesi behni ho, tum hamre rakhi bhi nahin bandhat ho."* What kind of sister are you? You don't even tie a *rakhi*† on my wrist! And yet again: *"Auron ki behnen to bhayya logan ke rakhiyan bandhat hain."* Other sisters tie *rakhis* on their brothers.

The whole day long you kept showing up behind the door, hurling taunt after taunt at me for not tying a *rakhi* on you, until Mother finally relented. She sent for a few *rakhis* from the bazaar and gave them to me. The next time you sneaked behind the door, I grabbed your hand and tied the whole lot on your wrist. Seeing not one, not even two, but three separate *rakhis* on your wrist, you became overjoyed and sprinted off, reappearing only in the evening, clad in a sparkling white *dhoti* and lacework *kurta*, a Gandhi cap on your head, holding a brass tray, with rice, *andarsas,* bananas, and coins amounting to about half a rupee. Then, extending your hand from behind the door, you set the tray down and said, "This is your *dacchana*."

Oh, you really were something. When did I have the mind, when

---

* *Raksha-bandhan*: A Hindu festival celebrating the bond between brother and sister.
† *Rakhi*: A holy thread tied to the wrist to indicate the love bond between brother and sister.

was I ever eager to tie *rakhis*? But every year, well before *Saluno*, you would keep reminding me, "*Rakhi mangali hamri?*" So, have you sent for my *rakhi*? Deep inside, how much you valued being made my brother. When Bibbi came from Shimla for the first time after her marriage, you hauled her bedroll inside the house yourself, practically doubling over under the weight. When told you didn't have to, that Jabbal could have just as easily carried it in, you replied quietly, "Why Jabbal? After all, didn't Aapa's groom tease Aapa, saying, what kind of brother have you got—he can't even carry your bedroll for you!" And that wasn't all. You were pretty strange. You would fight me over the swing, and when I gave it a push, you would say in your quivering voice, "Not so fast! Easy! I'm scared!" "Why are you scared? I'm not." You would say quietly, "Because you eat *gos-roti* and I eat *daal-roti*." And if anyone ever asked you whether you were Hindu or Muslim, you replied with great equanimity, "Me? My clan and caste are the same as Begam Sahib's. Why, I'm Begam Sahib's son."

Even though you were a Brahmin, and a Brahmin of the most elevated rank—indeed, so elevated that your doctor grandfather had no qualms about giving his daughter's hand in marriage to a confirmed idler such as your father. Anyway, whenever a little free time came your way, you would quickly make *wuzu*, unroll Mother's prayer mat on the settee, and start performing one *ruku* after another, dropping your forehead in *sijdah** after *sijdah*, mumbling a prayer under your breath and quickly passing your open hands over your face. And if anyone laughed, you felt hugely offended.

If a Hindu reproached your mother, the Maharajan, saying that you always hung out with Muslims and mimicked their ways, she would just laugh off the matter good-naturedly, saying, "Just as well. Let him live as a Muslim. This way at least he might live. My two other boys both died." Well, the high point of the story came when a craze to hold *milads*† swept through the entire neighborhood. We did it too, and that did it. Nobody could reason with you. You

---

* *Wuzu*: Ritual ablution. *Ruku*: Also *raka'ah*. The series of prescribed movements and words during the *salat* prayer. *Sijdah*: Prostrations during prayer.
† *Milads*: Religious gatherings to celebrate the birth of the Prophet Muhammad.

fought with the Maharajan and kept insisting on holding a *milad* too, and she, a simple woman, consented. She prepared the floor, spread cotton rugs and sparkling white sheets borrowed from our house; she sent for flower bouquets; she burnt incense sticks; and she begged Pathani Bua to come and perform the *milad*, because "my lallah wouldn't have it any other way." And guess who turned out to be the MC of the event? You, of course. Who else? You doled out *paans* to everyone gathered there, then daubed them with *attar*, sprinkling rose water from the dispenser every five minutes, dying from worry that you might have missed a detail that was part of the *milad* ceremony at your Begam Sahib's.

On winter nights, when everyone tucked themselves quite early under heavy cotton quilts and sometimes listened to stories, you too would burrow into somebody's quilt and linger there. And then it seemed the earth grew both weary of its weight and impatient with familiar faces and voices. It was like somebody had violently thrashed the grain in a winnowing fan. One flew and landed here, another somewhere else. But grain and seed, no matter where they land, invariably set up fresh worlds for themselves, sending their slender roots, like leeches, deep into the earth. They cling to it, and in time tear open the earth's bosom and come out.

Well, Robby Dutt, it's like this: I ended up here. You must still be there, grown into an honorable man, responsible and wise. Once again the rainy season has arrived. It must be pouring back where you are. Farmers, wearing folded gunnysacks for raincoats, must be busy digging ditches and taking care of the fields. Flocks of herons and parrots must be zooming back and forth overhead. Brahmin women must still saunter out during *Saluno* carrying *rakhis* for their brothers, draped in snappy red and green saris, *bindiyas** on foreheads, feet stained with henna, black and green bangles strung up the length of their flashing white, plump arms. Your arms must be covered with *rakhis*, and you must still offer *dacchanas*—but openly, though, not from behind the door. So what? What do I care? I wasn't exactly dying to tie a *rakhi* on you, you practically forced me to. Then again, the time for those insignificant

---

* *Bindiyas*: Plural for *bindi*. Throughout South Asia, any kind of jewelry or decoration worn on the center of the forehead.

little nothings is well past now. Mankind now thinks only of big things, of things that matter, and despises everything that is small or looks diminished. And to tell you the truth, you or I or anyone who thinks about the past does wrong. Why must life stay fixed at one place? Life's ship must pitch and rock forever on the restless waves of time. What if we had gotten stuck on the beach? On life's ocean one ship sails east, another west. Favorable winds push them on, and fate determines their destinations. The ships of your life and mine also sailed to shores destined for us. And yet, why does this desire suddenly overwhelm me?— to fly off quietly to where you are, sitting grand and dignified, to sneak up behind you and whack you and ask, "Wanna have me tie a *rakhi*? And tell me, which tray of *dacchana* is for me?" Why are all these long-lost matters returning to me, like an old pain suddenly come back to life? It's because after much smoldering heat and burning sun, a cool breeze has finally started to blow.

Do you suppose it's the east wind?

GOLI TARAGHI
(B. 1939)

The Grand Lady of My Soul

Translated from the Persian by Sholeh Wolpé

KASHAN.* I'VE ARRIVED, and I'm tired. I head toward the desert. Being a stranger, I lose my way. The air is permeated with a kind of wet, invisible, sweet-smelling particles that please the senses. The wind smelling of grass, wet herbs, and blooming flowers is so fragrant it is as if it has blown over tree-lined skies.

I asked, "Mr. Haydari, what is your share in this revolution?"

He was trembling. Sleepless with fear of famine and pillage, he had locked his doors, watching the uproar in the street through the cracks in the window.

My wife said, "I don't trust our landlord. I have a feeling he is tied to the anti-revolutionaries."

The city is tense, wide awake. Windows keep opening and shutting. There are sporadic gunshots and distant mayhem. A building is on fire, and total strangers are pursuing each other in dark alleys.

None of this bothers my father. "This too shall pass," he says. He is always looking for the best-quality raisins for his homemade wine.

The sky in Kashan, far from human uproar and commotion, sparkles like crystal waters of a spring, and the meadows, extending to the foot of the mountains, are covered with beautiful shrubs and red poppies. The mountain range, nude and wakeful, resembles the body of a mythological woman, and the desert has a maternal presence.

Over there, a woman is sitting by the side of a dirt road and here, closer to me, a man is saying his prayers under a pomegranate tree. At my feet grows the smallest flower in the world.

---

* Kashan: A city near Isfahan in Iran.

"Mr. Poet," I asked, "where is your historical conscience?"

"I'm still in awe of this flower," he replied.

They have shut down the university. My students shout, "Down with philosophy . . . down with reactionaries," and hit the walls with their young fists. They prosecute professors in absentia and roam the hallways of the university searching for the meaning of freedom.

They ask, "Sir, what does *unity of the Word* mean? Is *matter* more noble than *idea*? Which is more real: God or history?"

My wife believes in the reconstruction crusade. She has donated her silver bracelets to the neighborhood mosque and on the day designated for cleaning the city, she has swept the local dirt road.

She says, "Revenge is permissible in Islam," and with much fear and awe looks at the pictures of the recently executed in the newspaper. Every night she hurries to the Women's Religious Guidance and Education class, and believes in the principle of dictating right and wrong.

She has cut her long, manicured nails short and no longer wears her customary green eye shadow. She covers her head with a black scarf and is very careful that no one sees the lobes of her ears. She is restless, excited, and her heart throbs with faith. She sits next to me, watches me, and tells me about sin and blasphemy, about satanic temptations and the need for retribution.

"Don't you believe in heaven and hell?" she asks.

She lovingly takes my hand and gives me an affectionate, motherly look. At nighttime she is usually awake, murmuring prayers. Her breath is cool and her skin smells of rose water. Every time I look at her, she is smiling, her gaze directed at the sky through the open window.

"Listen!" she says. "Do you hear the angels singing?"

"No, I don't."

I cover my head with the pillow, aching for sleep.

The sound of sporadic gunfire and cries of *Allah-u Akbar** can be heard from adjoining rooftops.

Friends say, "We must leave!"

Friends say, "We must stay and fight!"

---

* *Allah-u Akbar.* God is great! The slogan of the 1979 Iranian Revolution that toppled the shah.

Friends are hastening to establish a party and publish a newspaper.

Mr. Haydari has filled his basement with flour, rice, and kerosene, and has brought his silk rugs to our house for safekeeping. He has withdrawn his money from the bank and has put his gold coins in a pouch that he carries around his neck.

Mr. Haydari is scared of the enemies of the revolution and is planning to emigrate to another country, but he is also terrified of a life in exile.

The university is unsettled and chaotic. Someone is giving a speech and the crowd is shouting holy verses in homage to the holy family. Vendors sell roasted beets and potatoes by the outer walls of the university. The effigies of Imam Khomeini are hanging from the trees. An old woman stops me, holding up a picture of her martyred son. She cries and longs for the appearance of the Hidden Imam.* The sidewalk is covered with religious books, jeans, and sneakers. Farther away, a fighter teaches a group of men how to use an automatic rifle, and under a tree, a man, sitting on a blanket, distributes food to his wife and children.

A student stops me, asks how I am. I don't know him. He has painted his face black and has covered his head and neck with a checkered bandanna and a handkerchief. I think he is a young Arab from Palestine. He has found himself an automatic rifle and fires a few rounds into the air. Women scream and take cover on the ground and behind the trees.

There is a knock on the door. It's midnight. My wife wakes up startled. My father dashes to hide his bottles of alcohol. It's Mr. Haydari. He's brought us dried milk, canned food, cheese, and Indian fish oil. He's out of breath.

"There is no more gasoline or flour," he says. "Cholera and smallpox are spreading. Soon everyone will devour each other."

My wife laughs at this. She believes that fellow true believers will provide us with food. My son punches the sack of flour in anger, yells that the true revolution is still on its way. My son believes in the triumph of the oppressed masses. Every day he goes to work in the factory and tries to befriend the laborers. He wears dirty clothes and is

---

* Hidden Imam: Also known as the Mahdi, a messianic figure in Shi'a Islam

proud of his dust-covered shoes. My son is in love with poverty and has a pauper complex.

My artist friend came from Kashan. He invited me to go there. I was more than happy to oblige. I set out immediately. My wife was praying. She had just learned how to pray and as yet had not memorized the verses. She read them from a piece of paper hung on the wall.

The landlord was in the courtyard. When he saw me, he sprang to his feet, trembling. He was waiting for someone. He looked at my briefcase.

He asked, "Are you running away?"

I said, "No."

He asked, "Is your name also on the list?"

I shook my head.

"They will catch me," he said, "today or tomorrow. They'll get you too. They'll round up everyone."

My father was awake. He was sitting by the window tuning his sitar. He used to teach sitar but his students aren't coming around anymore. Instead, they are singing revolutionary songs. Monsieur Ardavaz is an old friend. He occasionally comes to visit him and they reminisce about the past. Monsieur Ardavaz has closed his liquor shop. He has turned one of his rooms into a store and sells crackers and canned pears. Monsieur Ardavaz is scared of imperialism and has voted for the Islamic Republic.

They flogged the landlord twenty times.

My son is against capitalism and says that the landlord must be executed.

How distant is this desert from all this. How content and forbearing. Way over there, in the skirt of that mountain, a serene village shielded by trees is sleeping, and still farther away, a bird has broken into song. I feel downy and light like dandelion pods floating in the air. I sing a poem to myself:

> How vast the plain!
> How lofty the mountains!
> The scent of grass permeates Golestaneh!*
> I came here a seeker

---

* Golestaneh: Golestan, an Iranian province just south of the Caspian Sea.

of perhaps slumber
of light, a pebble, a smile.

Ahead, on the hilltop there is a big pond and next to it is a clay hut with no doors or windows. The water is stagnant and full of algae. An old man passes by on his donkey. He says hello. His carpetbag smells of fresh bread and his body of burnt wood.

Thousands upon thousands are standing in congregational prayer. Thousands upon thousands bow in prayer. The streets are filled with black-veiled women. A young man is leaning against the wall beside me. He is quivering. His eyes are closed. Tears pour down his face.

My poet friend is hospitalized. They say he's gone mad and keeps hitting himself against the walls. Heavyhearted, I go visit him. He is asleep, half-conscious.

His wife does not understand it. She is confused and flustered. As soon as she sees me, she bursts into tears. "Wait till he wakes up," she says, "maybe he'll speak with you. He talks to people who aren't there. He prays twenty times a day and constantly repents his sins. At sundown he goes to the rooftop and with his cries of *Allah-u Akbar* draws the neighbors out of their homes. At nighttime he starts weeping and won't go to sleep for fear of being in the presence of God.

I have a hard time believing this. He used to be a calm and popular man. He didn't talk much, never poured out his heart. He wrote poetry. Simple, charming poetry. During the revolution he used to come to our house in the evenings and sit with us. He wouldn't say much. In silence we both listened to the cries of *Allah-u Akbar*, to the unusual uproar and commotion in the city, and to sporadic gunfire in distant streets. It was as if some building was on fire. Women, children, and old men were pouring out of their homes. The sound of ambulance sirens and fire trucks could be heard. During all of this, my poet friend kept quiet. Not a word came out of him.

My hand still smells of blood. Fresh, warm blood. The blood of a young man, same age as my own son. He was upset, frantic, out of breath. He was shaking his small fist in the air, threatening the soldiers. I lost sight of the young stranger at the street's bend. Somewhere was burning. The street was filled with suffocating dust and smoke. The women were running, the men were hurriedly locking up their shops.

Gunfire had erupted. My poet friend stood by my side trembling and talking to himself. Death had taken on a familiar face and was circling the city like an enthralling, seductive woman. I caught sight of that same young man. He was bent over and had wrapped his arms around a tree. I picked him up. He was heavy. He wasn't breathing. A bullet had pierced the middle of his chest. I called to a passerby. I stopped a man. I knocked on a door. My young stranger didn't move. My poet friend kept quiet. He was standing next to me and with horror-struck eyes was looking "death" in the face.

It's getting dark. Where am I? There's no one around. I must be lost. Ahead, a silent desert crawls toward unfamiliar, dark lands. My heart's pounding. The wind is my only companion. I move on without a destination. Soon, it will be night. An obscure fear circles inside me, stroking the back of my neck with its cold hands. I walk faster. My shoes hurt. I search for a tree, any sign of a village or life. I turn around and go left. The desert is watching me and there are sporadic, indistinct sounds of commotion in the air. I see a narrow lane and like a magic beacon it leads me into the unknown. I'm tired and thirsty. I drag myself. At times the narrow lane ends but picks up again some distance away. I feel I will never get there but I'm compelled to move on. The uneven, narrow lane is my only hope.

Could I be dreaming?

I stop. How could this be? In front of me, there, in the middle of the dry, silent desert, quietly perched on the side of a white wall, is an orchard, a heavenly dream. A half-open door beckons. I stick my head in. No one there. Just a solitary, quiet garden with two rows of tall poplar trees lining its walls. Four ancient cypresses sit in the middle of four garden patches blanketed with red poppies and wildflowers. In the middle of the garden is a big blue pond brimming with the color of the sky. The stone pavements are covered with a thin layer of dust— unmarked with footsteps, fingerprints, or any indication of movement or change. On the northern side of the garden, above some stone steps, extends a huge verandah, and above that sits a white, celestial house with its back to the sky. The house seems so transparent, so weightless that it is like a dream vision, a phantasm floating in the air. It is like the divine manifestation of a sacred presence or an illuminated holy verse unveiled by the heavens.

Slowly I move forward, my steps ever cautious and hesitant. I'm afraid if I take my eyes off the house it would vanish. Or if I breathed too hard it would crumble. I sit by the pond and wash my face. It feels great. Truly great. The reflection of the house shimmers in the heart of the pond and the green trees float on its face. I look around. No one is about. In the tumult of history and the turmoil of the times, this white house has been utterly forgotten.

The cool smell of the water is tempting. I take off my clothes and slip in. I go under and open my eyes. The blue of the sky has penetrated the water and it is as if I'm swimming in the womb of the universe. The water's breath washes the thousand-year dust off my body, and my soul trembles with joy. It is as if an invisible hand is baptizing me in the spring of eternal life. I float on the surface. The sun is setting behind the garden wall, and the cypresses have grown tall in the semi-light of the late afternoon. My eyes fall on the house again and my heart begins to pound. How modest and unpretentious. How kind and noble, clean and pure. It is as though the house has just been bathed in holy water. It reminds me of someone I know, someone close but forgotten, someone sitting at the threshold of a sweet dream, on the ledge of old memories. It reminds me of a slave woman with an angelic body and eyes made of water, just like my mother on her wedding day with her virgin-chaste look, four flower petals clutched in her hand. It reminds me of a woman, still farther away, a changeless woman, a woman flowing in time.

I step out of the water. I am shivering. Sundown in the desert is cool and pleasant. I put on my clothes, pick up my shoes, and start walking barefoot. I count twelve steps. Someone must have been praying on the verandah because a prayer seal has been left behind. A coarse carpet patterned with small blue flowers covers the floor. I enter the house. The courtyard is bright. The walls are unpainted and there are a few benches for resting and daydreaming. The upper corners of the walls are plastered with ornate flowers, and the mirrors around the windows are modest and immaculate. Two half-open doors flank the two sides of the courtyard. They lead to another room overlooking a secret patio. Intricate corridors and a dark spiral staircase prod me on. What I see at the top of the staircase takes my breath away. From up here the four corners of the world are in view. The sky is only a step away and the desert extends to the horizon. I sit down. I stay still for a long time. What place in time is this? Where am I? I feel sleepy. It's the kind of delicious sleepiness that rolls behind the eyelids but never reaches the brain. The stars begin to break through one by one. My mind is floating in space and my thoughts, like the disintegrating circles in the pond's water, are shapeless and uneven. My hands and feet are numb. My body has lost its physical weight and shape. It is as if I am now an extension of the verandah, of the trees, of the desert, and my eyes are hanging from the stars. How distant and removed I feel from everyone and everything, from the geometrical relationship of matter and the logical proportion of objects, from the exact counting of minutes and the absoluteness of numbers, from adorned relationships and codified thinking, from the gigantic tablet of laws and bulky book of ethics, from acceptable norms of conduct and dictates of how one must live. How removed I am from the rule of matter and the nobility of history, from the legitimacy of ideas, from laws governing menstruation and childbirth, from the manifestation of the first intellect and the world of parables. How detached I feel from the dispute between the East and the West, the conflict between the rich and the poor, from the ceremonious laws of purification and customary shrouding of the dead. How distant I feel from the one who cried "God is dead" and the one who feared death, and the one who longed for miracles.

I wake up. It's dawn. I am bewildered and confused. I get up and look around. I'm hungry, but otherwise great. I feel light and refreshed, not tired anymore. A nice breeze is blowing. A rooster is crowing in the distance. A small village, over there at the foot of the mountain, is stirring with life. I put on my shoes. There are sounds of footsteps. I go downstairs. An old man with a long white beard is sitting by the pond, performing morning ablutions. I say hello. He nods, and continues with his prayer.

My footsteps have left their marks on the stairs. When I reach the door, I pause, turn around, and look back. My heart skips a beat at the sight of the house, so perfect and noble in dawn's half light. It speaks to me, tells me something good and wholesome, something that cannot be repeated but that I understand. A feeling of calm and assurance creeps under my skin.

The road back is no longer unfamiliar. The desert is placid, silent, and devoid of grim temptations. When I reach the green meadow, I take a shortcut through the fields. Near the road a truck stops and offers me a ride. The driver is a young man with a black beard and sun-scorched face.

A dozen pictures of various ayatollahs decorate his windshield. I get off at a teahouse near the city. I suddenly realize how hungry I am. It is now morning, a clear and warm summer day.

I return to my room at the hotel. There have been a few phone calls from Tehran, and the friend with whom I was supposed to meet the previous night has come and gone. He has left a note saying that something urgent has come up. I have to rush back. My students are on strike and the professors are planning a sit-in. I gather up my things, pick up my briefcase, and leave. The midtown square is bustling. Trucks are loaded with people. They go from one village to another, shouting slogans and verses from the Qur'an. They have sacrificed a lamb and are smearing its blood all over the back of the truck. Young men are wearing black and shaking their fists in the air.

Shops are closed and the town is half shut down. An ailing old man knocks on the car window, coughs. He has a piece of paper in his hand that he cannot read. His eyesight is dim. I read him the address on the paper. It's a house in a far-off village; a house at the end of a slope, behind the sycamore trees.

The road is congested with trucks, vans, carts, and donkeys. When I reach the city of Qom, the traffic has come to a complete halt. There is a funeral procession. I wait. The crowd shouts verses from the Qur'an. Black-clad women push their way in tight rows. A beggar boy hangs on to the front of my car. The air is full of dust and smoke. It reeks of gasoline and kerosene. I'm hot and sweating. I can barely breathe. I pull the car to the side of the road and wait for the congestion to ease.

In front of the holy mosque, they stop me again. They ask for the car registration and search the trunk. There is a newspaper on the back seat. They thumb through it, then confiscate it. My head is spinning. I bite the end of my cigarette and spit it out. I blow the horn and start shouting. A woman punches my windshield and curses me. Her child is crying.

Once on the main road, I accelerate. The oncoming trucks zip by at shocking speeds. They are ruthless. It will be a miracle if I reach Tehran alive.

My throat is burning. My mouth is dry. I lower the window in search of air, a drop of rain. But as far as the eye can see, there is only sand and desert, rocky mountains and brick.

Tomorrow I have an early meeting. The article I had promised is unfinished, and as soon as I get home I have to attend the funeral service for my friend's uncle.

The car behind me is honking its horn. It wants to pass. It can't understand that I am stuck in traffic, that the road ahead is closed. It blows its horn again and again, each time louder and accompanied with threats and curses. I want to get out of the car and hit him. I want to take someone by his collar and shake him. The smell of gasoline and smoke permeates the air. The sky is depressing, and the horizon is tar dark. Heavy, cementlike clouds have parked themselves over me. The air is thick and coarse. It collides against my eyes. I feel miserable and keep thinking about the many unhappy days ahead when suddenly from the deepest end of the horizon, out of a celestial corner, the house appears—clean and fragrant like a heavenly blessing. It moves slowly toward me. I see that it still exists, that its blissful, life-giving breath is simply hidden behind all this. I realize that from now on, the house will come from time to time, unannounced, and that on humid afternoons and depressing sunsets, on turbulent days and chaotic moments in history, on hopeless dark nights and on my deathbed, it will be with me, and will comfort me, ever present, complete and flawless, the Grand Lady of my soul.

ZOYA PIRZAD
(B. 1952)

Mrs. F Is a Fortunate Woman/
The Desirable Life of Mr. F

Translated from the Persian by Assurbanipal Babilla

Mrs. F Is a Fortunate Woman

MRS. F IS a fortunate woman. Everyone says so. Every Saturday morning Mrs. F's mother burns incense for her daughter as she incants *May the eye of the envious pop*. Mrs. F's mother believes that it is more auspicious to burn incense on Saturday mornings.

Mrs. F has been married to Mr. F for twenty-five years. Mr. F is a good man. Everybody says so. He is an employee of the Ministry of Education. He is not a teacher. He is in charge of the district employees' monthly salaries. He knows exactly who receives how much. He knows who has been promoted and who has not.

After having prepared and submitted the list of salaries, he takes his own salary, goes straight home, and gives it to Mrs. F. Mrs. F offers him a cup of freshly brewed tea. Every evening of the first day of the month when Mr. F comes back from work, the tea is always fresh. Mrs. F always smiles and says that she hopes he is not too tired. She then starts to count the money. She knows exactly how much he makes, down to the last penny. Still, she counts the money to the very last penny, as if she enjoys the activity. "You very well know how much it is," Mr. F says. "So why do you count it?" But he himself enjoys watching the money stack up in different piles. He looks at the money and smiles, drinks his tea, and talks about the goings-on in the office, such as who was promoted and who wasn't.

Mrs. F listens with great curiosity. And if a day or two later she sees the wife of the one who had been promoted wearing a new scarf, she is not surprised, and since she is not a jealous woman she finds something nice to say about the scarf; and if she bumps into the wife of the teacher who was not promoted, she is surprised to see the wife wearing new shoes, but since she is not a jealous woman she says nothing complimentary about the shoes.

After having counted the money, Mrs. F gets up from her seat and hides the money in a safe, secret place, a place that she thinks no one knows about but that in fact the entire household is privy to. She then starts preparing the evening's meal.

After dinner, after having washed the dishes, after everyone else is sound asleep, Mrs. F pours herself a cup of tea, sits at the small kitchen table, pulls out a piece of paper, and begins thinking about how she is going to spend the money during the following month. Meat, fruit, rice, stockings for Yasaman, the installment for the TV, underwear for Mr. F, money for repairing the refrigerator, yarn for a scarf for Bardia. Then she goes over last month's expenses. If last month they broke even, Mrs. F is saddened. Joylessly she takes a sip of her tea. For a while, with her slightly swollen fingers, she beats a chaotic rhythm on the table and stares at the flowers on the plastic-covered table. She then gets up, turns off the kitchen light, and goes to bed. If at times, and this rarely happens, she finds that in the past month they spent more money than what Mr. F had earned, she pushes away the cup of tea as if it were a thing she no longer deserves and holds her head between her hands. For several days she is in a sad mood. In the days that follow, she listens intently to the food programs on the radio. She reads women's magazines that she has borrowed from her friends and neighbors, containing cooking instructions (she herself never spends money on books and magazines). She wants to learn more about how to cook economically. What a joy it is when she, without help from the radio or magazines, simply by her own inventiveness, adds water, fried onions, a few pieces of leftover meat from the stew she had made two days ago, to yesterday's lentil rice meal and serves it for dinner. She is delighted when she hears her family say: "What a delicious stew!" To this, she smiles and says to herself: "Cheap food!"

It happens, though very rarely, that some months they have spent less than Mr. F's monthly salary. On such occasions Mrs. F smiles. She drinks her tea as if she has been granted a well-deserved award. She then places a hand under her chin and stares out the kitchen window. It is dark by this time and she cannot see a thing, but that hardly matters. She is not interested in seeing anything. Mrs. F is simply happy.

The day following such evenings is always glorious. Who cares if it is snowing or if it is sweltering hot? What matters is that Mrs. F is going to the bank. She divides what she has saved into two equal parts and deposits the money into the savings account she has opened for her two children. On her way to the bank she daydreams. The snow entering through a hole in the sole of her shoe does not bother her. And the only thing that warm weather can do is curl the slightly odorous hair under her armpits. But Mrs. F is never bothered by either the water in her shoes or the odor of her sweat. Mrs. F is busy thinking, counting, planning. "It is conceivable that in a few years it is possible to send Bardia abroad to continue his studies. And when Yasaman wants to marry, we can provide her with a decent dowry." Soon enough, her mind, expertly ignoring the laws of time, travels from her daydreams of the future to the memories from her past.

The day Bardia was born was a hot summer day. What a pretty infant! He weighed four kilograms and looked like a champion. The gifts she had received at her baby shower were perfect. Twelve undershirts, twelve tiny pants, twelve bibs with hand-sewn pictures of rabbits, mice, pigeons, and some other animals along a tiny band of blue ribbons. Mrs. F's mother had really outdone herself because next to the twenty-four cloth diapers of rose-embroidered soft muslin there were a few disposable diapers. They had just come into fashion and though very expensive, they were worth the astonished looks they brought to the faces of Mr. F's relatives and neighbors. Mrs. F, who never learned the proper name for such diapers, never used them, is still keeping them in a big brown trunk that contains her most precious belongings: her wedding dress, Yasaman's first pair of shoes, Bardia's and Yasaman's first-grade notebooks, and lots of other things. Their house is small and there isn't much room, but each time Yasaman and Bardia nag, "Why don't you throw away this ugly humongous trunk," Mrs. F resists complying. By thinking and planning, she makes room for Bardia's books and Yasaman's things so that the ugly, humongous trunk stays where it belongs in that small house.

In snow and in sunshine, the memories of years gone by and dreams of the future swirling in her head, she walks to the bank. She clutches her black bag tightly under one arm. She no longer trusts the strap of her bag, and in any case the city is teeming with thieves and bag snatchers.

When she arrives at the bank, it is as if she has arrived at an old friend's house. She has known the head of the bank, Mrs. Taghizadegan, for a long time, that is, from the first day she opened a savings account for Bardia. In those days Mrs. Taghizadegan was just a teller. She was then a slim girl with a pleasant attitude. Her attitude is still pleasant but her body looks different. Mrs. F always enjoys Mrs. Taghizadegan's expertise and her relationship with the people who work under her. Mrs. Taghizadegan has a son and a daughter who are slightly younger than her own Yasaman and Bardia. This top official of the bank receives Mrs. F as an intimate friend. She orders tea for Mrs. F and inquires after her children and asks what they are doing at the present time. She also talks about her own children, and during this conversation about motherly issues, she manages to answer a few telephone calls, sign papers, and issue orders to the employees as to what to do and what not to do.

On her way home, Mrs. F wonders how Mrs. Taghizadegan takes care of her husband and children while carrying such a heavy load of responsibility at work. "Maybe it isn't that difficult," she thinks to herself. "If I had kept my old teaching job, I would have most probably become the supervisor of a whole educational district by now." But she knows deep in her heart that she never enjoyed her job in the Ministry of Education, and that when Mr. F proposed to marry her and insisted that she should not work, Mrs. F had immediately realized that her prayers had been answered. But knowing this does not prevent a feeling akin to jealousy or envy creeping into her mind. As she turns the key to unlock the garden gate, she tells herself: "A woman who works outside her home cannot be truly attentive to her husband and children." Having justified herself as such, she opens the gate and abandons herself to the tranquillity of the garden and her ever-spotless home.

Sometimes, only sometimes, returning from the bank, she still clings to a little bit of money she has saved from last month. After a few days of hesitation and thoughtful anxiety, as she weighs the pros and cons of the matter, she finally decides to buy something for herself. A pair of nylon stockings or perhaps a headscarf. As she wrestles with her conscience, piling reason upon reason why it is OK to be such a spender sometimes, and even after having offered these justifications to her husband, her mother, and even her children, upon buying anything for herself she is gripped by such emotions she does not wish anyone to witness. On the days she does the sweeping, when her back begins to ache, she brings to mind the thing she has bought and with that thought, like a toy that has been wound tightly, she continues sweeping with a greater speed. When she is in the line for buying meat or bread and her legs begin to hurt, she recalls her purchased treats and she forgets the pain. After she has finished sweeping, bought the bread and the meat, she washes her hands and face, combs her hair, and slowly approaches the chest of drawers. She is all ears listening intently, in case anyone suddenly showed up. These infrequent moments are the only private moments in her life. She feels guilty about the secrecy of these moments, that not even her husband, or mother, or even her children share them with her. Still, from time to time, she gives in to the temptation. To lighten the weight of her tormenting conscience, she allows herself such private moments only after she has performed her chores completely and in full. The house cleaner than ever, lunch and dinner ready, the laundry washed and ironed. On such days she spends more time on her daily visits to her mother. She listens more attentively to her complaints, her intolerable aching legs, her moans about last night's watermelon giving her too much gas, and about the neighbor across the street who distributed the stew she had made for blessing and had not given her any. She listens to her mother attentively and in order to prevent herself from feeling guilty, she refrains from saying that her mother's aches and pains at her age are only to be expected, and that no sane person would eat half a watermelon at night, and if the neighbor has not shared her blessing stew with her, it is because last year, during the holy month of Moharam,* she had not given the neighbor the saffron rice pudding prepared especially for that occasion.

From the drawer she takes the headscarf or the nylon stockings still

---

* Moharam: First month of the Islamic calendar, whose tenth day, Ashura, commemorates the martyrdom of the Prophet Muhammad's grandson Hosayn.

wrapped in gift paper. She always insists that whatever she buys must be gift wrapped. She tells the vendor that she is buying gifts. She blushes when she tells the lie, but she always repeats the lie. The colorful paper and the act of unwrapping it add to her sense of pleasure. She carefully removes the Scotch tape and flattens the paper. She puts the small thing she has just unwrapped in front of her and looks at it.

"When we go to visit my husband's new boss, I'll put on the scarf."

"The stockings—maybe I should give them to Yasaman."

Then she puts one hand under her chin and stares at the wrapping paper and thinks what a fortunate woman she is. She has a husband who unlike other men does not squander his money, and he never complains when she spends money. She has two healthy kids. Everybody says that her daughter is beautiful and well mannered and that her cooking is out of this world. And Bardia is taller than all the kids his age, and he is good at school and wants to become a civil engineer. Although their house is small, it is comfortable and has saved them from nagging landlords. What else should a woman expect of life? Mrs. F tells herself: "I am a fortunate woman." And Mrs. F is happy, and her mother burns incense every Saturday morning for her daughter.

The Desirable Life of Mr. F

The day Mr. F retired, Mrs. F made sweet rice for lunch. She filled a big vase with white and yellow chrysanthemums and placed it on the table. Then with her daughters, Fataneh and Farzaneh, she waited for his arrival.

Slightly before noon, Mr. F, after the goodbye party that they had arranged in his honor at the office, returned home. Fataneh and Farzaneh rushed up to hug and kiss him.

Fataneh said: "From now on, you don't have to wake up early."

Farzaneh said: "Starting tomorrow, you can sleep as long as you want."

Mrs. F looked at Mr. F. "How gray his hair has become!" she thought. Then she said to herself: "Maybe it's the light shining through the window straight on his head."

Fataneh and Farzaneh had purchased gifts for their father. Fataneh's gift was a wristwatch. Farzaneh's gift was a clock with hands that glowed in the dark. Mr. F loved timepieces. Mrs. F's sweet rice was the best ever.

During lunch Mr. F told them about the party and they admired the small commemorative inscription in its large ornate frame that was given to him in gratitude for his years of service as a parting gift that was placed lovingly on the shelf.

The following morning he woke up slightly later than previous days. He remembered that there was no need to get up early. He moved under the sheets and with his feet he sought cooler spots on the mattress.

From the kitchen that was downstairs he could hear running water and the clattering of dishes being washed. He said to himself: "From today on, I'll do things that I like." He started thinking about the things he liked to do. "I'll fix the flower bed."

The thought of the flower bed drew him out of bed. He pulled back the heavy drapes and opened the window. The flower bed was not too big. It was just a square patch of grass with a berry tree on the right side. He thought: "I'll plant flowers all around: pansies and plants that release their fragrance at night. I'll buy roses and Japanese quince." He imagined the whole flower bed covered with pansies, roses, and Japanese quince. He thought it would look beautiful. He thought about his wife: "She would really enjoy the sight when she looks out of the kitchen window."

He looked at the bedside clock. It was nine thirty. He thought: "Now the boys at the office are having their tea." He remembered his small room at the office. If he closed his eyes, he could see the smallest details of that room. A few official notes thumbtacked to the wall and next to them a poster depicting a landscape in garish colors. The trees were very green, the sky very blue. Even the whiteness of the clouds was too white. The floor showed gray indentations. There was a calendar on a corner table next to a pencil holder, paper clips, and safety pins. There was a chair at the table and facing the chair was a shelf for files. Next to the shelf was a metallic coat stand with several spokes and if you were to put your winter coat on it or remove it hastily, the whole thing would lose its balance and go crashing to the floor. There was a window behind the desk. From the window you could only see the building number two belonging to their office with its gray stone façade and many uniform windows.

Mr. F put on his slippers, opened the door, and went down the stairs.

The garden looked lovely. Mr. and Mrs. F with Fataneh and Farzaneh were sitting in the garden and were having tea. On a short and round table there was a vase with a few branches of roses and a branch of Japanese quince.

Fataneh said: "Until a few months ago the flower bed looked so ugly."

Farzaneh said: "Until a few months ago the flower bed didn't look so lovely at all."

Mrs. F said: "I wish we could paint the house."

Mr. F smiled. He remembered the walls of the corridors at work that were always dirty. Long, gray corridors where the employees passed through clutching files under their arms, inquiring about each other's health and making jokes.

Mr. F bought brushes and ladder and the house looked brighter than before.

While having breakfast, Fataneh said: "The house is so much cleaner than before." Then she looked at her watch. "O my God, I'm late!" and jumped out of her seat.

Mr. F looked at his left wrist. He had left his watch in the bedroom.

Farzaneh finished drinking her tea. "I shouldn't be late on the first day of work."

The faucet in the kitchen was dripping. Mrs. F was calculating the day's expenses out loud. She was happy that painting the house had not cost them too much money. The sound of the dripping faucet was getting on Mr. F's nerves.

A few days later, Mr. F fixed the faucet. He looked around with satisfaction. He remembered that there was no one at home. Mrs. F had gone to her knitting class. Fataneh and Farzaneh had their lunch at their office. Mr. F felt hungry. There were a few cutlets left over from last night. He was craving sweet rice.

Mrs. F knitted colorful things and sold them. Fataneh and Farzaneh had received a raise at work. Mr. F was waiting for spring, for the garden to come to life. During daytime the house was quiet except for the ticking of the clocks. Mr. F would roam about the house: oiling the hinges and tightening the faucets. No one in the house worried about the sleeping garden.

Mr. F put on his suit. His trousers felt looser than before. He tightened the belt two notches. His shoes were hurting his feet and his necktie was slipping between his fingers. As he left the house, he thought: "The boys at the office would be glad to see me."

Walking through the corridors of his old office, he smiled at everyone. The employees were coming and going with files under their arms, joking with one another. The walls were still gray. When he arrived at the office that used to belong to him, he reached to open the door. Then he remembered he was supposed to knock first. He knocked. A voice said: "Come in." Mr. F entered.

At the metallic desk where the pencil container, the calendar, and the box full of paperclips stood, Mr. F was bent over a file and was writing something.

Mr. F sat on the chair in front of the desk.

Mr. F raised his head, stared at Mr. F, and smiled. "I've so much work to do. Tomorrow I'm supposed to submit this file."

Mr. F shifted around in his chair and smiled.

Mr. F closed the file, put the pencil in the pencil container, and rubbed his eyes with the back of his knuckles. He then locked his hands behind his head and said: "Lucky you. Now you can rest."

Mr. F looked at the very green, and the very blue of the poster on the wall. The clouds were intensely white. He got up from his chair. "With your kind permission I'll take your leave," he said. "I'm distracting you from your work."

Mr. F nodded. He took the pencil out of the pencil container and bent over the file.

Mr. F removed his winter coat from the clothes rack. The rack shook a couple of times. Mr. F steadied it. He left the room. He walked through the gray corridors and out of the building.

The street was crowded. He stopped a few times to recall which way he was supposed to go.

The house was silent. Fataneh and Farzaneh had not returned from work. Mrs. F was busy knitting. The faucet in the kitchen was dripping again.

MANOUCHEHR ATASHI
(1931—2005)

Selected Poems

*Translated from the Persian
by Zara Houshmand
Ahmad Karimi-Hakkak*

Nostalgia

Let's go back to our own dusty moments,
to the acrid mouthful of morning tea
at the end of a nightmare's promontory.

Nothing ever changes.
I search the breadth of the metal and oil jungle
to gauge the length of childhood escapes.
    [The suspended falcon's arrow
    at the intersection's blinking lights
    indicates the speed of the new jet
    from the freshly minted company.
    In the year 2000
    a panther in midpounce
    advertises a Jaguar.]

Let's go back to our own mountain moments,
to breakfast of warm bread in goats' first milk
in starling-dappled blue valleys, where rebel fires cast a flickering
    net.
    [A man will eventually retch
    at the sandwich halves, buckets of food

scrapped at the end of the night
in restaurants round the world
—even absent Africa's hungry stare.
From AIDS-wrung carcasses in garbage.]

Nothing ever changes. I long
to wake to sparrow song at early dawn
and watch you through the hedge
in the village lane, skirts asway, aglow
in the dusty haze that trails the goats.

Behind this metal cage nothing ever changes.
I invoke a peddler's distant memory
and swear, at the foot of the holy lote,* that a horse
holds more beauty than a train
and a panther still runs faster than a jaguar
here, whatever this valley's pain.

Let's go back to our primitive moments
to the warm acrid mouthfuls of tea
to the endless clamor of sparrows
and the live recording of grandmother's gurgling pipe
more lovely by far than all the guitars and singers of metal.

Translated by Zara Houshmand

Mountain Song

It all
began
at the far end of the Dizeshkan Pass
where the river forever flows beneath
                the horseman stirrup
and the sky
as if off-guard

---

* Lote: A large tree; also called a nettle tree.

suddenly spills over the downslope
                    into the valley's delta
where in the last turn of its winter migration
the tribe gets instantly lost in the green pasture.

It all began in extreme fatigue
at the moment when her mare
petrified by the smell of a panther's warm piss
began to stampede
and a neighing stream flowed down the gorge's throat
and I
like a hungry eagle
                    that picks the bird
                              off a soaring branch
caught her beneath the saddle and the dust
and sank my face
in the colorful harvest of her floral village dress.

Translated by Ahmad Karimi-Hakkak

PEGAH AHMADI
(B. 1974)

Selected Poems

Translated from the Persian by Ahmad Karimi-Hakkak

The Dark Room

Wrinkled summer
and I, the one whose laughter is full of forgetfulness
am filling up the ocean that is my window:
What words could be made to fit in this dreamless frame!

I have traveled to this room
this room of no clocks
no sounds, no calendar
that holds my secrets in the folds of its leather cover
as the night comes to undo me, then gets lost
and the deep lines in my groins
bring no rain!

What words could have been fitted into this dreamless frame
between the sheets, on the balcony
in the cellar!
Sounds and slippers
Doors dawdling and windows whizzing.
Thin . . .
more anemic than the air
with the juice that holds up heavens
I have traveled to this room. . . .

Leave my blood to me
the blood that gives me my genius.

I have traveled to this room
with no desire and no summer
without my hands
with the letter that was lost line by line.

I have traveled to this room
and dropped my dreams by the wall
a woman who drew her angle with spring
a cloud that moved away at midnight
and the rain that fell drip, drip, from her mattress.

To the sandalwood
to the moon's scent
to the image cast on the windowpane
I have traveled to this room
with a sleepless nocturnal rustle:
What words we could have planted in this dreamless frame.

Night whirled away with my hands
as the wall of no time
was inscribed upon us!

Ah dark dwelling!
House of gloom!
I have traveled to this room.

The Girl Sleeping on Top of Oil

The girl sleeping on top of oil
will explode you
the girl sleeping on top of poetry
will explode you on oil!

Brother! Sister! Father! Death!
Your mother will explode you like oil.
The door too low here
has grabbed me by the throat!

Half a woman, half a naked Roman, half the bell they ring at the
    House of Strength will

explode you!

I have spat so much, rain, that I cannot spit you anymore!
Yet I can still play hopscotch
in my sandals, too tight for life
and head to the hills all alone
so confused that the police officer should fall through the skies
and no matter what bosom I end up in
should plant a white angel on my shoulder!
Away, blindness, or I'll explode you like light!

Hear me well, prayer rug!
With my dust from Iraq and memories from the wet underbelly of
    Khorramshahr!*
And you, camphor prayer!
As rain from my child reaches the heart of the bow
then it would be time to wash off the moon!
I will explode you
I am no windowpane, but I will bring about your death,
    explosion!

Hear me well, prayer rug!
I can work magic
with my explosive prayer of submission
I can pull out a dove
live, breathing heavily
from the passageway in my throat
and with all my heart, all the explosion in my heart,
and my blood and body
let it loose over waters.
Croon on, rain, croon on!

---

* Khorramshahr: A port city in Khuzestan, southwestern Iran.

And then, bent over my skirt
I sank my head into my downy pillow
And two blue bowls
Exploded in my palms.

Four Views of a Private Orange

There, sunset
had crept away from under sunshine and sound
there I felt sorry for my headscarf
and for the boxes that would not breathe
and for the wrinkled shell of an orange
and the air that is a bloodied exhalation
and glasses that sink to the bottom. . . .

A part of the earth is wounded now
the glass that's broken is wounded
and when the skeleton of the clock fell on five,
my crying holes got wounded.

In this land of sorrows, you are the cleaner
and I am so beat
it seems I turn into nil
somewhere through this air.

Four views of a private orange
made up a torn mournful mouth
fish frolicking with air
rain sleepily splattering the earth.

Again it's as if
I have cried
have scribbled something
only to wrap it around my finger and turn private.

Four views of a private orange
entered my shoes
my purse
And all I knew of life.

CEMAL SÜREYA
(1931–1990)

Selected Poems

Translated from the Turkish by Murat Nemet-Nejat

This Government

This government
Doesn't give a passport
To Pir Sultan*
I understand.

And doesn't give
Yunus Emre†
A press card
I understand that too.

But this government
Has issued a decree
Doesn't let Karacaoğlan‡
Get on a bus.

* Pir Sultan: Pir Sultan Abdal (1480–1550), famed Turkish Sufi poet and foe of
the Ottoman Sultans.
† Yunus Emre: Legendary Sufi poet and mystic (ca. 1240–1321).
‡ Karacaoğlan: Seventeenth-century folk poet.

"Dying?"

"Dying?" you said.
"You're deep asleep in the bottom of a lake."
Seas?
The gods keep stirring up the seas.

I'm Dying, God

I'm dying, God.
This has happened too.

Every death is early death,
I know.
What's more, this life you are taking
Isn't bad. . . .
No more said.

After Twelve PM

After Twelve PM
all drinks
are wine.

CAN YÜCEL
(1926—1999)

Selected Poems

Translated from the Turkish by
Şehnaz Tahir
Ruth Christie

Poem X

Those cavalry lights riding by the horse chestnuts
woke the honeysuckle up so very early
                          and they will freeze forever!
And the olives with old Greek lace
Blowing wind!
Blowing wind!

Whoever saw such a rose-eating rooster
Its voice with the scent of dawn . . .
It's as if a wine bottle filled up in prison
                          is rolling down the hill
Other roosters also rise
                          with their ladder-embroidered crests
And when the babies' dreams
                          dangle down the balconies
                                  like a relay race with red flags
The roosters rediscover the sea
Thieves!
Thieves!

And the sea
      with the marine shadows of Turgut Reis*
Is offended by all these lines
And its face turns first red
      then purple
Blowing wind!
Blowing wind!

This morning
    is a flight
      from a vendetta a child
Way before dawn
Will be shot by the bullets of the sun
And when the evening arrives on the pine trees
    and darkness falls
Upon the hills
Upon the hills
So beautiful is the blowing wind
Blowing wind!
Blowing wind!

This morning
    and this spring
    is a flight
A wick running for the gunpowder
Whiff
Whiff
So beautiful is the blowing wind!
Blowing wind!
Blowing wind!

So beautiful
So very beautiful

* Turgut Reis (1485–1565): Ottoman naval commander; governor of Algiers and, later, Tripoli.

Even when it blows not
Even when it blows not
Beautiful.

Translated by Şehnaz Tahir

The Wall of Love

Was it you or your loneliness
In the blind dark we opened bleary eyes
Last night's curses on our lips
We would frequent art-lesbian-lovers,
Galleries and public places
My daily care was to remove you into the midst of men
An ammoniac flower in your buttonhole
My loneliness my incontinent countess
The lower we sink the better

We loitered in the pubs at Kumkapı
With beanstew, beer, and wine before us
And police battalions behind us; in the mornings
My Guardian Saints would find my carcass in the gutters
Hot as the garbage-collectors' hands,
With their hands I caressed you.
My loneliness my bristle-haired beauty,
The higher we stink the better

I looked in the sky a red flash a plane
Steel and stars and human beings galore
One night we leapt the Wall of love
Where I fell was so clear so open
You and the universe at my side.
Uncountable my deaths, their resurrections.
O loneliness my many songs
The more we can live without lies the better.

Translated by Ruth Christie

CEMIL KAVUKÇU
(B. 1951)

The Route of the Crows

Translated from the Turkish by Ebru Diriker

I AM DRINKING soup from a steel bowl at the portable kitchen table covered with checkered oilcloth—an object that has borne witness to most stages of my life. Its surface has grown old and resembles a wavy sea. The oilcloth with numerous cuts and scratches has resisted time. How many of them are my doing, I do not know. I see ants moving around the thickly sliced bread. It looks as if they are on an aimless trip.

Ziynet turned on the light a short while ago. The bulb is covered with dots of fly feces and emits a yellow and raw light. In the dreadful silence my own slurping disturbs me. Ziynet is sitting across from me. Her big hands are resting on her lap; she looks dejected and is staring at me uncomfortably. Then she talks to me in a whisper: I could not understand her at all today.

When did you ever understand her? I say to myself. I play around with the spoon in the soup. She has all my movements under control and waits anxiously for my response. The spoon is still in the soup and she is expecting me to talk. I speak without taking my eyes off the plate; she is in a different mood every day, I say, sometimes her mind is blurred, I don't understand her when she is like that.

Slowly I raise the spoon to my mouth. Ziynet, now, looks at her hands resting on her lap. That same silence again in the kitchen. I continue drinking my soup with an even louder noise.

But today she was really restless, she was anxious to say something, says Ziynet.

Forget it, I say, I'll find out.

Do you want another bowl of soup?

I shake my head, no, I don't. I light up a cigarette. Now I'll have a cup of coffee with Ziynet. She got me into this habit. If she is in a good mood, she will tell me to turn the cup over and will read my fortune without moving a single line in her plump face. I always find it amazing that she sees so much in the patterns formed by the coffee grains. She keeps talking about "kismet." She says it is blocked again. Tell me, why didn't you marry? I don't know, I reply aren't you the one who tells me my fortune is blocked?

She is not in a good mood today, so no fortune telling, nothing! We drink our coffee in silence. I don't ask her any other questions; I have learnt not to be curious in matters that may turn out to be annoying.

I stand up after finishing my coffee. Now I can go to her. I feel uneasy whenever I enter the room with its rotten air smelling of excrement and human skin not washed for a long time. I can almost feel death waiting patiently in a corner.

No matter how long Ziynet ventilates the room the smell remains. She is in her bed as defenseless and lonely as a kitten. She feels that I am inside but she cannot turn her head to look or open her eyelids. She, too, is an object just like the table and the chair. A live, breathing object. I am the only one to understand her silent, motionless language. Ziynet just thinks she does.

Her white hair is spread on the pillow, her tiny face reflects the absolute tranquility of death. A twitch of the mouth. She is glad to see me, she is trying to say. I sit on the side of the bed. I see you are a little restless today, I say, is something bothering you? A small twitch of the forehead. She is indicating the window. I stand up and open the curtain slightly.

There's nothing there!

There is.

What, I say, the darkness?

No, that isn't it.

The crows?

Her eyelids quiver.

But there are no crows, I say it's nighttime.

A small twitch of the lower lip. Is she hurt? She thinks I do not believe her.

They have clearly annoyed you during the day but I will take my gun and wait for them in the backyard; they will never annoy you again.

The twitching of the lower lip continues.

Are you trying to tell me they have been talking to you?

Her eyelids quiver again.

I AM SMOKING beside the window, gazing at the dark and frightening silence of the stone yard. I hear the door close quietly. I do not turn around to look; I know it is Ziynet. She is probably waiting, her back leaning against the wall. She is silent for some time and, then, whispers warily: what happened?

Nothing, I say, keeping my eyes fixed on the yard.

What was worrying her, did you find out?

It was the crows!

Well, they do make a fuss the whole day, as if there was a wedding or something.

It isn't that, the crows are talking to her. She used to talk to the crows when I was young. When I was naughty and tried to cover something up, she would come and tell me what I had done. If I tried to deny it, she would say the crows had told her.

And you would believe it.

And I would believe it.

So what have they told her this time?

The creaking of the bed.

How can that be possible, Ziynet says, she can't talk, she can't even open her eyes. She is a dead person, don't you see? She can only breathe and feed from the spoon at the corner of her mouth, spilling things all over. She is aware neither of her bottom nor of her top. She isn't aware of anything, how on earth do you draw such conclusions?

How do you manage to draw all those conclusions when you look at the coffee cup?

I make it up.

So do I.

Ohh, she says.

She is relieved.

There is no light but the room is not all dark. I look at her nightgown which makes her look plumper and shorter than she really is. She has let her hair fall on her shoulders. The springs of the bed creak when she sits on the bed.

These sounds. . . . She can hear them. . . . Even if she is in a vegetative state she can understand that. . . .

Not tonight, I whisper, because I was sure there was a black crow hiding somewhere in the room.

Ziynet shrugs her shoulders. No one can hear, she says, and lies down on the bed.

I light a new cigarette and listen more cautiously to the frightening silence of the garden. There were secret preparations, I knew it.

I WOKE UP early in the morning. The sun had just risen. I opened the curtain and looked out. A crow was lying flat on its back in the yard. Its upright beak seemed to indicate a point in the sky. Its wings resembled a musketeer who had pulled both guns but became stiff before he could fire them—they were also pointed toward the sky. It was quiet. Normally if a crow was in trouble, the rest of them would gather and make a great fuss. What had happened to these creatures of perfect solidarity?

When I heard Ziynet's footsteps, I went back to bed. I closed my eyes and pretended to sleep. She came and shook the base of my neck. She was rather careless this morning, the way she opened the door, the way she walked clicking her heels, the way she shouted hey! all because of her fury.

What, I said angrily, what's the matter!

Nothing, she said, lowering her voice, it's morning. . . .

So what?

Why is she obsessed with the crows? she asked.

Maybe I misunderstood, I said, I don't know.

Of course you did. How can the crows know what is going on here in this room? It's just something made up to scare the kids. . . .

There is a crow in the yard, I said, I guess it is dead.

She looked hollowly. The one who watched us and told her all about it?

I looked down; maybe not.

She walked to the window. She was plumper and shorter this morning.

There is no crow in the yard, she said, were you dreaming?

I stood up and looked over her shoulders. The yard was empty and scary just like last night. Was I dreaming?

I'm going down, she said, tea is ready.

Ziynet put three spoonfuls of sugar in her tea. Then she stirred it for a long time as if she wanted to make that noise on purpose. She was half asleep, half awake.

How is she today, I said, still behaving strangely?

I haven't been to her, she said. She was looking at the glass as if it was the first time she had seen one.

Why?

Don't know, I didn't want to. Maybe I was afraid. What if what you were saying is true. The creaks, I mean. . . . What if the crows have told her everything. . . .

You believe that?

Of course I do, she was so strange yesterday. And the crows shrieked all day as if there was a wedding or something. . . .

You should have given her the medicine drops.

I will, after breakfast.

She poured some more tea. She put a thick layer of butter on her slice of bread and covered the top with jam. She took big bites and slurped her tea. I am sure she swallows without chewing.

When she was full she got up. With slow motions she left the kitchen.

She was back in a second. There was fear and consternation in her face. My mother was not in her bed!

How is that possible! I exclaimed, springing from my seat. I ran to her room. The bed was empty. The crumpled bedclothes and the trace of her head on the pillow were still there. The blanket was opened carefully toward the wall side as if she would be back in a minute.

Did you open the window?

No, she said.

I went to the window and looked at the yard. There were hundreds of crows on the roofs and in the trees waiting quietly.

The crows, I said, look, none of them are shrieking.

And yesterday, said Ziynet, they just would not stop, as if there was a wedding or something.

What happened to Mother? I asked.

Ziynet curled her lower lip. Then she sat on Mother's bed, covered her face with her hands, and started to cry loudly.

The crows flew up shrieking. They encircled the yard and came back to light on the trees and the roofs.

ZAYD MUTEE' DAMMAJ
(1943–2000)

A Woman

Translated from the Arabic by May Jayyusi and Christopher Tingley

EACH DAY I'D look for her eagerly at the nearby *zalabia* shop, vying with the simple people in their jokes and odd, silly stories. I'd take the hot *madrat al-bur'i* with powdered thyme and cumin and hot *busbas** and stand sipping it in front of the shop, watching its handsome young owner, Rizq, exercise all his skill in making the *zalabia*; he'd repeat the same endless process in his light-handed style, and the hot oil in the great brass pot seemed to make him more handsome still. He'd learned the art from his father, and from his older brother Shu'i, who'd grown lazy now, being content to sell tea at the entrance to the shop, along with a pot of beans that would be quickly sold out in the first hours of the morning.

Again and again I'd hear his father and younger brother scold him, sometimes curse him even, because he never cooked enough beans; to which he'd answer it wasn't his job to cook beans, that he cooked the little he did for his own breakfast and sold any that was left over. His real job, he insisted, was making *zalabia*, which his father had handed over to Rizq, his younger brother. This unfair distribution of work, he went on, would have been a source of constant strife between him and his father and brother, had it not been for the interference of that woman, who always settled the dispute in young Rizq's favor.

I've never tasted *zalabia* in my life, but I still got a lot of enjoyment and pleasure from sipping the piping hot *madrat al-bur'i* and watching the graceful movement of young Rizq's hands as he made the *zalabia*,

---

* *Zalabia*: A type of pastry fried in oil. *Madrat al-bur'i:* Soup made with dried peas. *Busbas*: Spicy red peppers.

while customers waited eagerly inside the shop, or outside, or at the narrow entrance to the alley.

Every so often I'd gaze at the woman I'd finally come to look out for, watching how she'd elbow the men and fight with them for her place. She was a woman of siren-like allure. I would have put her at thirty-five, but I knew she was actually older than that, because lazy young Shu'i had told me quite specifically she was forty and maybe more.

She'd take her place early in the morning, on a long wooden chair, almost like a table, which stood against the dirty wall of the shop. In front of the customers was an actual long table, which was dirty too, soiled with the remains of *zalabia* and oil and tea, and all the other mess customers leave.

While waiting for the hot *zalabia* pastry, she'd take a cup of tea from Shu'i, with some *madrat al-bur'i*, following this up with the delicious *ruwani** dessert; after which you would have thought her eyes were riveted on the pan of seething oil that was frying the *zalabia* pastries young Rizq made with such skill.

Young Rizq, so handsome and good-looking, with his curly hair and rosy cheeks, his well-shaped nose and smiling lips and straight neck, like a bust of Alexander of Macedon. He sensed her eyes were locked on him. When, though, she realized someone was looking at her, she'd turn her eyes quickly away, then dart looks here and there, trying to make out faces a little farther away—after she'd had her fill of gazing at young Rizq.

THE SMILE, CALM, serene, enticing, never left her lips. She was like the Mona Lisa. What excited me most, though, was her firm bosom whose treasures were revealed for all her attempts to conceal it, standing out clearly from her embroidered cloak, the two breasts seeming almost to pierce through the red silk gown. "Those breasts of hers," I heard a man sitting nearby say, "are enough to get the angels excited." Sinking into this ample bosom was a chain bearing something like a Qur'an, or the eagle of the revolution or republic.

She didn't mind her natural charms appearing, or care about people

---

* *Ruwani*: A cake drenched in syrup.

gazing where these charms showed most. All she cared about was the the *zalabia* and the tea she drank as her eyes devoured the youthful Rizq with the appetite of someone eating a piece of *ruwani*. And because she was the focus of interest for the men who were always there, I imagined I was the focus of her interest!

I never said anything, deliberately hiding any feelings I had toward her, and she acted the same way. I felt, too, that we shared mutual concerns that brought us together, for, as soon as she'd finished her daily meal of *zalabia* and was done with the visit, with its constant stealthy gaze toward the young man, she'd leave the shop and approach me, passing close by me on the pretext of struggling through the crowd and rubbing her breasts against my body. How I'd thrill when this happened! And the number of sleepless nights I'd endure as a result! I kept picturing her. . . .

Her mouth, seen from a distance, seemed to be adorned with two gold teeth where the canines should be, and she appeared to wear gold bracelets over her bare wrists; and I'd see henna heightening the beauty of her soft, tender fingers, and black dye of lovely patterning. There was a greenish mole, too, on her left cheek, which made her more alluring still, over all her other beauty and loveliness. I thought at first the mole was artificial; then I realized it was natural, increasing her radiance and beauty, as though she were the star of Yemen. There was no trace of makeup on her lovely face, for she believed in beauty natural and unspoiled.

I got used to the jostling and the crowds at the entrance to the *zalabia* shop. I'd become a besotted lover of the place, just so that I could see her.

Sometimes young Rizq wouldn't be there, and his old father, with his attempted youthful airs, would take over, filling the place with his piquant jokes and gleaming gold teeth, and the bristling of his proud mustaches, and the shining tip of the valuable old dagger bound to his slim waist, and the densely embroidered turban, which swayed proudly this way and that.

Once in a while both father and son would be absent, and their place would be taken by Shu'i, Shu'i the tea and bean seller, whose beans sold out so quickly, for all his laziness and unattractiveness and unfriendly air.

Young Rizq, like his father and maybe his brother Shu'i too, would wonder why I always stood in front of their shop and their pot of oil constantly seething with *zalabia*. What got on their nerves more than anything was that I was always just a spectator! Not that I was the only one like that: there were plenty who liked to stand sipping hot *bur'i* in front of their shop.

Maybe, I told myself, it was because I gazed at that woman. It's true the others gazed at her too, but did I, I wondered, gaze at her more? Perhaps I did. But why should they be so struck and amazed, so resentful at seeing me standing there in front of their shop like others among God's creatures? I always stood on the sidewalk, after all, and that was a public space belonging to the government!

SHE'D SIT IN her usual place in the *zalabia* shop, with a glass of Shu'i's tea in her hand, her eyes on the pot of seething oil frying *zalabia*, waiting for her hot piece.

There were times when she seemed distracted, but that would soon pass and a smile would return to her lips. Then she'd start looking once more at the faces of her fellow-customers eating their morning meal there.

SHE WASN'T THE only woman who liked her *zalabia* for breakfast, or some *bur'i* here, but she was the only one who'd jostle among that strange mixture of people crowding into the place, people of varying age and bearing and clothing, this man in a smart suit, that one in peasant garb, another wearing school clothes, a fourth in military uniform, and so on.

It was these she chose to sit among, while the other women sat at the entrance to the narrow alley nearby, hidden behind their colored cloaks.

THE GLEAMING OF her two gold teeth fascinated me totally, like sparking ecstasy or uncontrollable desire. For the hundred and tenth time I gazed at her avidly, or for the thousandth time, or for centuries and whole ages and time without end.

She it was always, of no more than medium height, yet of such womanly beauty and allure that whole crowds of customers for *zalabia*, and *bur'i*, and *ruwani*, and *kabab* would be dying for her. Every one of them was captivated by her and desired her; every one of them gazed, as I did, at her charms.

I felt myself consumed with jealousy, especially when I saw how she allowed her breasts to rub up against them just as she did with me. So many times I'd come close to fleeing from her, to any other place at all.

FOR ALL HER fiery eyes each morning, I was convinced she hadn't slept a wink beforehand. She didn't sleep during the night! I reckoned she spent the whole night enjoying herself instead! For all her glorious beauty, there were clear signs of exhaustion in her face and on all of her body—even on her clothes. That dreadful vision, still clinging to my mind, of how she must have spent her wakeful night only made my ardor more intense.

I wished I could spend an hour with her late in the night, stay together with her till the time came to sip *bur'i,* and eat *zalabia*, and *ruwani,* and *kabab*. Or, rather, through all eternity!

I BECAME FILLED with mingled, violent feelings. I feared temptation, and I was afraid of committing some scandalous error, like embracing her in front of people and within their hearing, or letting my hand stretch out, unthinking, toward her entrancing body. I felt I'd known her since childhood, that she'd fed me all kinds of succulent things whose sweetness was still on my lips.

Finally I decided to leave the place, so as to get right away from her. I was fond of *bur'i*, it's true, but there were plenty more places in town for that. Next day I went off to Bab al-Yaman,* and no sooner had I sat down in the place selling *zalabia* and *bur'i* than, to my surprise, I found her there. Yes, there she was, gazing toward me, gazing at everyone there, as if the place hadn't changed at all.

I fled once more, to Suq al-Milh,† for my usual breakfast, but once

* Bab al-Yaman: "Gate of Yemen"; southern gate of the old city of Sanaa, Yemen.
† Suq al-Milh: The salt market.

more I found her at the *zalabia* seller's next to the *bur'i* seller's place where I was. It was she and none other, with all her disarming charm, her calm, serene, enticing smile. Here too everyone adored her and gazed at her charms. And I felt, as well, how she rubbed her ample breasts against them, just as she did against me.

Once more I fled, to yet another place—Bab Shu'ub* this time; but there she was once more. It was as though she and I were still at Bab al-Sibah, in front of young Rizq, the *zalabia* seller. Everyone, I felt, loved her and desired her and took pleasure in gazing at her charms.

I fled from her further still, to Bab al-Qa'.† There the *bur'i* seller and his wife, who made *zalabia*, weren't in separate shops but on the same corner, working and selling together in the same narrow alley. And no sooner had I begun sipping my *bur'i* than I found her in front of me, eating her *zalabia* pastry as usual.

So back I went to Bab al-Sibah, meaning to tell her frankly of my feelings toward her. But I couldn't pluck up the courage. She'd leave the eating place while I stood sipping my hot *bur'i*, drinking in her whole body, imagining the things she must have experienced the night before.

And I thought how she'd constantly jostle God's creatures as she left the eating place, till she reached the place where I was standing, then how she'd push me away with a motion that wasn't, I felt, meant to entice me.

This repeated itself a hundred times, a thousand times, for a lifetime, and over ages and all eternity. It's still repeating itself.

* Bab Shu'ub: The northern gate of the old city of Sanaa.
† Bab al-Qa': Yet another gate in the old city of Sanaa, this one leading to the Jewish Quarter.

NAZIK AL-MALA'IKA
(1922–2007)

Selected Poems

Translated from the Arabic by
Basima Bezirgan and Elizabeth Fernea
Ferial J. Ghazoul
Ibtisam S. Barakat

Jamilah and Us

Jamilah!* Beyond the horizon, far beyond the borders of nations,
    you weep.
Your hair loose, your tears soak the pillow.
Are you really crying? Does Jamilah cry?
Don't they give you music and song
Didn't they make offerings, of words and more words to you?
So why the tears, Jamilah?

The details of your torture were on every tongue,
And that hurt us, it was hard for our sensitive ears to bear.
You were the one imprisoned and shackled
And when you were dying for a sip of water
We marshaled all our songs
And said, "We'll sing to you, Jamilah, through the long nights."
All of us said: They gave you blood and fire to drink.
All of us said: They put you on the cross.
But what did we do? We sang, we praised your heroism, your
    glory

---

* Jamilah: Jamilah Buhrayd, a young Algerian girl who was imprisoned and
tortured by the French during the Algerian Revolution.

We said: "We'll save her (Yes, we will)!"
We made promises, false promises, drunken promises
And we shouted "Long live Jamilah! Long live Jamilah!"

We fell in love with Jamilah's smile.
We adored her round cheeks.
The beauty that prison had gnawed revived our love.
We were infatuated with her dimples, with the braids of her hair.
Did we not use her suffering to give meaning to our poetry?
Was that a time for songs? Songs, be ashamed.
Be silent before this noble suffering.

Their intent was evil. They cut her with sharp blades.
We gave her smiles, good intentions.
They hurt her with knives.
We, with the best of intentions, hurt her with ignorant, uncouth
  words.
The teeth of France tore her flesh.
She was one of us, our kin
And the wounds we inflicted are more painful to bear,
Shame on us for all the suffering of Jamilah!

Translated by Basima Bezirgan and Elizabeth Fernea

To Poetry

From the temples' incense of bygone Babylon
From the clamor of waterwheels in southern deserts
From the nocturnal cries of a turtledove
And the echo of harvesters chanting the sunset tune
That voice, your voice, will return
To my life, to the years' audition,
Haggard with the scent of a sad evening,
Ears of grain weighting it with graving fragrance.
It will return with a strange lyrical echo:
Frog croaks in sleepy dusk
Filling night and streams

With languid monotonous sounds.
That voice will return
To my life, to the audition of the evening.
It will return and I will hear the chanting,
Moon-fresh echoing nights of rain,
The repose of twigs
As they sip drunkenly heaven's nectar,
Perfumed by clouds,
By visions, by greetings of the stars.

I will roam Existence
I will gather the particles of your voice from cool springs
From the mountains of the north
Where even lilies whisper songs
Where pines tell nomadic Time
Tales throbbing
With musk, tales of the shades' passion
For the brooks, of the wolves' chants
For the spring water in the forest shades,
Of the dignity of pastures and the philosophy of a running stream,
Of a ram in deep depression
Spending the day
Chewing grass and thoughts
Drowned in the mist of abyssal existence.

I will gather the particles of your voice from Heaven's joys
On an ancient evening
By the Tigris, heaving with yearning,
The cheer of night revelers
Sipping water ripples
Dashing against the shore;
Summer moonlight fills the evening with images
And the breeze passes, like lips touching,
From other lands:

A Scheherazadean night
In its tender darkness
All feel and dream, even silence,
All enamored by light.

I will hear your voice when I am
Amidst Nature's commotion, in moments of madness
When echoes of thunder evoke
A thousand legends of History's youths
Of perished epochs and of nations no more
Of tales told by the boys of Aad
To the girls of Thamoud
And stories chanted by Scheherazade.
To that mad king
On winter nights.
I will hear your voice every evening
When light dozes off
And worries take refuge in dreams,
When desires and passions slumber, when ambition sleeps
When Life sleeps, and Time remains
Awake, sleepless
Like your voice.
In the drowsy dusk resounds your wakeful voice,
In my deep yearning
Your eternal voice that never sleeps
Remains awake with me.
I feel its painted echo filling the path
With fragrance, with colors' dew.
Your unknown voice
I have grasped, oh joy, its honey-laced secret
I grasped—only I and the silence of the Time.

Translated by Ferial J. Ghazoul

Myths

Dedicated by the poet to Daisy Al-Amir
in commemoration of an evening at which the two
poets "philosophized even the chairs, tables, and curtains"

Life, they said
Is the eye color of the dead
The footsteps of a vigilant killer.
Its wrinkled days
Knit a coat of poison
That ceases not from killing.
Its dreams are the smiles
Of an ogress's numbed eyes
Behind which, death stares.

Hope, they said
Is the bitterness of the thirsty
Seeing on a wall
A glass in a drawing.
It's the frowning color
In the eyes of a bird that cried
When it found its nest sundered.
Awake with hope,
It awaited the morning
To come with a miracle
And mend the ruins.

Bliss, they said
And I searched for it in all caring eyes
In the stories of misery
Written on some people's faces.
In time, as it is slowly devoured by the years.
In a flower, as the ghost of withering
Stalks its fragrance.
In a brilliant star
That would shine no more.

They spoke of bliss but I found no trace of it.
Has it been here but long passed?

Silence, they said
Is only a myth
Invented by an inhuman being
Whose ears can listen
While its soul in ashes lies buried.
It has not heard the screams
Streaming from the fence
Or from the paper shreds in ruins
Or the dust, or the seats in ancient places,
Or the glass dressed in cobwebs,
And a coat hung on the wall.

Youth, they said
And I inquired.
They replied there will come a time
When fog disappears.
They spoke of heaven beyond the mirage
And an oasis for the weary.

Then when I arrived at youth I found
The dreams of tomorrow
At the closed gate, crucified.

Immortality, they said
And I found it a shadow
That emerges from the shriveling of life
And flings itself in a leisurely way
On the graveyards.
I found it a word
That lingered on the lips of those
Who mourned their past
As they denied it.
They sang for immortality

As they passed. Alas!
They spoke of immortality
And I found all that is
Would not last.

Hearts, they said
And I found them no more than doors
That lead to graveyards
Where the feelings are buried
And the imagination is dead.
Their damp walls
Swallow all beauty
And beat with unbearable ugliness.
Thinking of hearts, pale, I fled.
And I shall not return.
What disappointment!

Eyes, they said
But I found eyelids
With no sight.
And I'd known lashes
That are tied to stones.
And heard of cellar eyes
That are hidden
Inside doubt curtains
Eyes that are called eyes
But to all save evil
They are blind.
And I'd known thousands of those
Whose eyes are sheets of glass
Blue as the sky
But behind the blueness bellowing darkness.

They said and said
Their chewed-up words with the wind flap
In a world of ephemeral sounds.

Those who are weary with no respite
Those who are forever lost
They spoke and I spoke
But all speaking comes to an end.

What myth! What imaginative irony!

Translated by Ferial J. Ghazoul

The Lover River

Like the unbridled wind he winds after us.
Where shall we turn?

Unconcerned
He runs through wheat land

His arms spread
In the glitter of the morning
His hands drunken
They shall meet us and take us in
And drown all our terror
No matter where we turn.

Wordlessly
He runs and runs
And conquers our towns
His brown waters
Not yielding to dams.

He is chasing us yearning
To hold our youth
In his affectionate folds

He is still chasing us
With a kind smile on his face
His feet are wet

Leaving red footprints everywhere
He has roamed East and West
Always with tenderness.

Where shall we run?
And he has slowly, firmly, and quietly
Embraced the shoulders of our town.

From his lips, mud kisses
Have covered our sad pastures.

This ancient lover we have known well
Slides endlessly toward our hills.

This familiar guest
We have built our villages as lodgings for him.
And every year he remembers
To come down the valley to meet us.

Now that he has come in the midst of night
We have vacated our huts and are departing
Knowing that he will follow us once we are under way.

For this lover we pray.

Translated by Ibtisam S. Barakat

SAADI YOUSSEF
(B. 1934)

Selected Poems

Translated from the Arabic by Khaled Mattawa

Koofa

We did not name it so that it would become a city.
We came to it thirsty
starved
limping on blazing sands,
blinded by sun glow.
We cut the world from Mecca to the palace of Naaman.[*]
We cut the world with a sword
until bone protruded through our hands and whitened.
When we reached water we said
let us rest here
and watch the bank
where water pours, flows, and pours.
We dipped our swords in it.
Trembling, we sheathed our hands
and prayed.

We did not name it so that it would become a city.
We built nothing except the mosque
the wall
and the hut of Ali.

---

[*] Naaman: A biblical figure mentioned in 2 Kings.

But the first century is no longer the first.
Here we are now leaving it
H
U
N
G
from
the gun barrels of tanks.

The Bird's Last Flight

When I enter the earth's nest
contented
and glad,
my wings resting,
I will free my eyelids so not to see
the trees swaying nearer.
Do not cry over me.
I said do not cry.
If you wish, remember that my wings
are water
and there is no water without waves
and no waves without a shore where they crash.

I rest here
contented
and glad
to have reached the last shore.
Do not cry.
Even the sound of my breathing cannot reach me. . . .

FARAJ BAYRAQDAR
(B. 1951)

Selected Poems
Translated from the Arabic by Shareah Taleghani

An Alphabetical Formation

Alif

You're not beginning . . .
It's an eternity, you know . . .
I mean, the ever-after, you know
No matter, then.
Raise your cavalry
But don't set out for the horizon,
Or the sea . . . or the soil
lines for beginnings,
finish me off on a wire.
        You are not beginning now,
watch out . . .
        anyone who begins is deceived

Ba

We haven't yet finished the elegy for the century,
        We haven't explained blood,
                flowing from poetry,
or a tear from prose,
and what of glories,
        to see through them just ourselves,
and in ourselves, only us . . .
Do the dead epitomize the living?

Well, then . . . does captivity test the
wings a bird uses to
      swoop down freely,
or does it discover significance far
      from their twin meaning?

Ta

That's a mirror,
      and this a woman,
the woman rises . . .
So let the mirror be shattered, and the ruler,
      and the secret between them
The woman rises . . .
      to see the before and the after
from the inside and the outside
we've obscured the sky,
      and performed ablutions at dawn,
then prayed at its knee until noon
the sultans passed by without their dreams,
they were dragging coffins
we call thrones!
Do you really see? . . . we ask ourselves
and how is it they've triumphed?
Only defeats have been victorious

Kha

The beginning of wine is the shadow . . .
      And it is not content with the volcano,
      we've raked the languages of serenity,
      to raise a glass
the naked trees . . . our remains
for he who gathers enough
of the silence that extinguishes an ember
      we no longer grasp, we've returned
      and raked letters

whose eyes have forsaken sorrow,
for a glorious silence
they have stabbed its isolations . . .
the silence indicts armies
and judges and turncoats . . . and titles . . .
It does not forget . . . a summons from your master's resolutions,
or from the binding of the threads that remind.

Thal

Oblivious to design, this tomorrow is baffled by intent
and the yesterday that moans
from our first humanity.
Rather, baffled by our first blood,
for this I search the night
for a new master
sowing wheat with his palms,
singing from our songs,
and quenching his thirst from our casks
and if fury remains, then an invasion is
undertaken

Nun

A gift is my rib
And my spirit a brown horse
And memory my pavilion
For to whom do I leave my belongings?
And to whom do I entrust my desire
For a mirage that doesn't betray its master
one day as the capitals
have betrayed their inhabitants

Yah

Has he finished . . . ?
No . . .
He does not know this deed,
and doesn't accept its definitions,
it embarks within us
and if he arrives to shore,
he says: Apologize to it for me.
      Around me is a vaster blueness
      out of your dreams
      Imru al-Qays[*]
         was straying from it
         and so, it strayed from him.
The poet has finished and as for the poetry . . .
We say no . . .
And we say: we'll try.

Groans

1.

Here I am you alone
In this mad, gaping
Hell
Here I am you alone and death altogether
With the predators and the seers and the informers
Perhaps I am arriving at
The limit of my possibilities
For you to arrive at the last
Dream

Flare up until you see me and
Become complete until I see you
My rose between two fires

---

[*] Imru al-Qays: Pre-Islamic (sixth century) Arab poet.

Inflaming me
Hopefully I am inciting wisdom
In this ruin
I have tried
To the end of the flower and the fire,
Then, how have they isolated my voice
And your silence?!
Have you leaned on a belated
Sword?!
Or have I been exchanged—one absence for another?!

2.

Here I am you alone—while you are but I
I was not before me but you were after you
The shadow has shed the blood of the sun
On the horizon and the night has hissed
The night has hissed
How you have been delayed . . . changed . . .
And you would not be laid bare—Take no offense from me
You have your shrouds

3.

With thorns the guard caresses
Your sparrows
And the state bestows upon you
A precautionary death,
And enough of the darkness
For you to go—so go
You are aware of the insanity of death,
Thus the music breaks out,
And your myths are shaken
This other body is in the arena,
Are you asking me
Who has splattered a name . . .

And the throne with blood . . . ?
No time . . .
This other body
Who has taken it from me
And who has taken me from it?
And who testifies that death
Has grown weary?
The obscure caresses its vacancies
with wires and blasphemy
I have tried often . . .
As the constellation has mourned the horizon of a poem
I said I have tried often
And with lilac, I have caressed
your night

4.

The river has been choked with the tears of a woman
Whose son was
More pure than she had hoped for
But her dreams were fractured in the night . . .
God was in a seventh slumber,
As was her son
For who would disturb him
Before the dawn call to prayer?!!
And who, Sister . . .
Now bestows upon you
A palm of his stature
A cloud of his laughter
A breadth of his hands?!!
The river has been choked with the tears of a woman
She resembles my mother,
Just as You resemble me,
And you are now alone

5.

Extinction has escaped you . . .
How the night has shed light on you
And the blossoms are darker.
And the wind has enfolded you
How the wilderness prays for you
And forgetfulness has been hailed
To where
Shall I proceed with your pledges?
I am not asking about places,
My prison is a place,
Except that the times
Have been divested of their right
For a free journey and of
Their right of place
Having dried up in my coat
Are seven clouds and your memory . . .
Are you mourning
The salt of your tears and the poet
In the reach of his poem
He writes it
Or let me say: it writes him
Or both write:
Perhaps you are bringing me flowers
But
You will not find after you
One who brings yours
Our night brings to the surface its elegy
On the long verse
I see my course on the waves
Or is this your face?
The salt of your tears,
So permit me to
Close my eyes a little
And a little . . .
And a little.

6.

I have not yet handed over my directions
To the judgment of the sand . . .
Behind me a time
Ashamed of the deceits of geography . . .
Thanks to the sparrow
That built a nest on the other
Window and flew.
Breaker of my back
Your shadow is now a spent tomorrow
Upon which I disperse my thoughts
And I call to you with what is in the spirit
From the groan of the horse . . . Do you hear me . . . ?
I am calling
I am not searching for a collective grave
Rather . . . for my country.

HAMID REZA RAHIMI
(B. 1950)

Selected Poems

Translated from the Persian by Mahmud Kianush

A Quarter to Destruction

I live
Like a bird that does not know why it sings;
Like a tree that does not know why it grows;
Like a breeze that does not know why it blows;
And like a fish that does not know
        why all the rivers of the world
        empty in the frying pans. . . .

Sometimes I think that a flower is something beautiful,
And there is no doubt that it leads me
        to the blessed ancestors of plants.
Sometimes I think that the sky is also beautiful
And this cloud that is about to rain
        is willing to wash away
The ancient sorrow of my heart;
And this wind that has galloped all the way,
        from a faraway land
Down to the throat of my wounded window
Is willing to sweep away my chronic ennui.
Sometimes I think that this country is beautiful
And the streets of its towns have familiar traits;
Sometimes I see the image of my childhood
Riding on the waves,
From one river to another,

Or amid the commotion of the street
        idling around
To break a windowpane here,
To draw a matchstick man there
On the tired face of a wall.

Sometimes I see myself
Inside the eyes of a youth
The echo of whose footsteps
Is the favorite music of the girls in love,
And whose breaths have the smell of springs,
        the smell of poetry;
And sometimes I see myself
In the shape of a walking stick
Carrying a handful of sorrows, memories, and history
In a small, empty yard.

I see my sister
In a corner
Talking to the mirror;
I see my mother persistently asking the breeze
        about me;
I see my father,
The last days of whose life fade away like smoke
While waiting in the line for rationed cigarettes;
And the people
Who squeeze their hearts in their hands
Like grenades;
And I see a God
Who has hidden Himself
Behind the face of the moon
For the fear of His people.

Again my wife,
Who finds me drowning
In a cup of cold tea
Rushes to my rescue
Like a brisk lifeguard
And skillfully draws me out.

The time is a quarter to destruction.

Blockage

Everywhere is closed;
Buildings seem to have
     no doors at all;
Everything seems
     to be withering away,
Even that young tree
     which every morning
Suddenly grew with love
     in my barren mind;
Even that smiling window
Which was always brimming over
     with the music of rain;
Even that china doll
     on whose morning stroll
The clock on the wall
     struck eight.
The city is empty
     of its nightly merriment,
And the stars
     seem to be a handful of pebbles
Scattered on the sky's face
     by an angry man.

Oh, what is the matter with me?
What have I dreamed
        in my frightening wakefulness,
        that today
Everything,
        everybody,
                everywhere,
Seems like a naked wall to me!

Inclination

One's throat must be like a garden
And one's eyes like windows
        through which love passes;
And one's stature
Must be like a tree
        that rises out of rocks;
And poetry must be like a singing bird,
Perching on the highest branch of a tree,
Breaking the heavy silence of the world.

ALIREZA BEHNAM
(B. 1973)

Selected Poems

Translated from the Persian by Alireza Behnam

What?

What a war it is when the earth looks at "what"
The trumpet is playing like the ashes remaining from the old wars
On the ruined magnificent chateaux
And it remains from the "it is war"
                         Like ever
Her ringlets rise from the petrol tubes from the rivers ruined by
    the colors of war
And fixes to a gaze from behind which gazes into the labyrinth of
    tubes
It remains from the "it is war" and goes on toward falling
A big bomb stands above and doubts to fall
It is a doubting bomb, it slips from her ringlets, falls between the
    petrol tubes
The world's violence rests coldly on her shoulders
From the tubes rising from her ringlets
Falls the "it is war," falls the missed legs
The eyes loosened from the skulls
The earth is like ever between her ringlets
What a war it is like ever!
And the falling is falling from her ringlets
It is falling to say "what?"

607

Hanging from the Trees of Babylon

At the end
I'll come down
in my thousand years form
hanging from the towers of Cheghazanbil*
and there is something within me
that throws language to the battlements of the tower
you will praise me
that's clear
in the form of an old man
hanging from the trees of Babylon
Athennes† will rise within me
and Paris
and Perspolise‡
and many many languages
Cut me to pieces!
every piece will come as a word
and will come as a word
and will encircle your eyes
Hurray is within me
and rising of the language beyond Pluto
and Artemis's herd
and rebellion of disobedient words
the whole are within me
and I,
in my thousand years form
will be thrown
from the virgins painted on temple walls

* Cheghazanbil (also known as Chogha Zanbil): Ancient Elamite ziggurat in Khuzestan (southwestern Iran) that was destroyed by Assyrian King Ashurbanipal in 640 BCE.
† Athennes: Athens.
‡ Perspolise (also Persepolis): Ancient capital of the Persian Empire in southwestern Iran near the city of Shiraz.

to the shadows emerging from your computer
and being thrown is within me
ask me!
ask me about the future
I'll reply in Babylonian.

Author Biographies

COMPILED BY ROSHI PEJHAN

SAIT FAIK ABASIYANIK *(1906–1954)*

Of Turkish descent, this writer of short stories and fiction was born in Adapazarı. While pursuing his higher education, his desires conflicted with those of his father's; originally enrolled in the Turcology Department of Istanbul University in 1928, he made his way to Switzerland to study economics in 1930—under pressure from his father. Afterward, he lived in France for three years before returning to Turkey to try his hand at teaching. From 1934 onward, he devoted his life to writing. Abasıyanık left his mark on Turkish short-story writing with realistic portrayals of laborers, fishermen, children, the unemployed, and the poor, bringing into focus these often-ignored members of society. One of his major themes was the sea, and he spent most of his time on Burgazada (one of the Princes Islands in the Marmara Sea). He was an honorary member of the International Mark Twain Society of St. Louis, Missouri. His novels include *Bir Takım İnsanlar* (*A Set of People*, 1944) and *Kayıp Aranıyor* (*Wanted*, 1953); his short stories began with *Semaver* ("The Tea Urn") in 1936, and culminated with *Az Şekerli* ("Just a Bit of Sugar") in 1954.

AZRA ABBAS *(b. 1948)*

Born in Karachi, Abbas earned her master's degree in Urdu from Karachi University and went on to teach Urdu literature at a government college in Karachi. Eventually, she and her husband, the poet and novelist Anwar Sen Rai (who works for the BBC), moved to England, where she currently resides. In 1981, her first work was published, comprising a long feminist prose poem in the stream-of-consciousness form. She has produced three collections of poems and one of short stories, along with an autobiographical narrative. She has also completed a novel.

GHULAM ABBAS *(1907–1983)*

Born in Amritsar, Punjab, India, Abbas's family soon moved to Lahore, where he grew up within the famous old walled city. At an early age he began to write, and his first short story was published in 1933. He was the editor of a popular children's magazine, *Phool*. Later he worked for All India Radio in Delhi, but after Partition he joined Radio Pakistan in Karachi. Four collections of his short stories have been published, along with a number of books that he translated.

ABU SALMA *(1907–1980)*

Born Abd al-Kareem al-Karmi, this Palestinian author came from the city of Tulkarm. He lived and practiced law in Haifa until 1948. In 1978, he was awarded the Lotus International Reward for Literature by the Association of Asian and African Writers, and he was given the title "The Olive of Palestine" for his poetry.

ADONIS *(b. 1930)*

Born Ali Ahmad Sa'id Asbar, this Syrian-Lebanese poet, literary critic, translator, and editor has played a hugely influential role in the evolution of modern Arabic poetry. Raised near the city of Latakia, in Syria, Adonis received a traditional Islamic education at home and did not attend school—though the village teacher taught him to read and write. He never even saw a radio or a car until he was twelve years old. In 1944, Adonis entered the French Lycée at Tartus, graduating in 1950. In the same year, he published his first collection of verse, *Dalila*. After studying law and philosophy at the University of Damascus, and serving two years in the army, he was persecuted for his political views.

He left Syria in 1956 and settled in Lebanon, where he founded the poetry magazine *Shi'ir*. It was in Lebanon that Adonis published his first major work, *Aghani Mihyar al-Dimashqi* (1961). In 1970, Adonis was appointed professor of Arabic literature at the Lebanese University. Three years later, Adonis earned a doctoral degree from St. Joseph University in Beirut. A perennial Nobel Prize candidate, Adonis was awarded the prestigious Goethe Medal in 2001.

JALAL AL-E AHMAD *(1923–1969)*

One of Iran's most prominent political thinkers, Jalal Al-e Ahmad wrote four volumes of short stories, four novels, and nearly a dozen volumes of essays. Al-e Ahmad was a critic of the role of religion in modern society. At the same time, he was fiercely antagonistic toward Western cultural hegemony in Iran. These two preoccupations spurred him to write his most famous work, *Gharbzadegi*—variously translated in English as "Weststruckness," "Westoxification," or "Occidentosis"—clandestinely published in Iran in 1962. As a political activist, Al-e Ahmad helped found the pro-Mossadegh Toilers Party, a component of the National Front. Following the 1953 CIA coup that toppled the Mossadegh government, Al-e Ahmad was imprisoned for several years, after which he withdrew from politics entirely. In the later part of his life, he retired to a rural region of Iran and died in a cottage he built for himself.

PEGAH AHMADI *(b. 1974)*

Born in Tehran, this poet, scholar, literary critic, and translator was first published at the age of seventeen in the literary magazine *Takāpu*. She studied Persian literature at the University of Tehran and continues to contribute regularly to literary magazines inside Iran. She has published five books of poetry, including *In Ruzhā'yam Galust* (2004). Her fifth book, *To Find Faults,* appeared in 2008. She has also published two works of translation from English into Persian, one an anthology of the poems of Sylvia Plath.

TAWFIQ AL-HAKIM *(1898–1987)*

This son of a wealthy judge was born in Alexandria, Egypt, at the turn of the twentieth century. A prolific playwright, al-Hakim had a literary career filled with both failures and successes. His many works were infused with political themes and critiques, such as his play *El Aydi El Na'mah* (*Soft Hands*, 1954), which criticized the 1952 Nasserist revolution. Continuing to grow throughout his playwriting career, the writer discussed relevant political issues and social commentary via his plots and characters. His *El Sultan El-Ha'er* (*The Sultan Perplexed*, 1960) was set against the contemporary backdrop of an Egyptian population increasingly wary of Nasser's regime. Some novels and short stories were scattered throughout his playwriting career, including *The Return of the Spirit* in 1933 and *The Dancer of the Temple* in 1939.

NAZIK AL-MALA'IKA *(1922–2007)*

Iraqi poet and critic al-Mala'ika is one of the most important female Arab writers of the twentieth century. She was a major advocate of the free-verse movement in the late 1940s, along with Badr Shakir al-Sayyab. Born in Baghdad into a cultured, literary family, she was the oldest of seven siblings. Not only did her poet father edit a twenty-volume encyclopedia, but her mother, Um Nizar al-Mala'ika, under the pseudonym Omm Nizar Al-Malaika, wrote poetry against the British rule. Following in their footsteps, al-Mala'ika started writing early in her childhood, and at the age of ten she composed her first poetry in classical Arabic. Al-Mala'ika was educated at the Higher Teachers' Training College in Baghdad, earning her BA in 1944. While still in college, she published poems in newspapers and magazines. Al-Mala'ika's knowledge of English literature earned her a scholarship to Princeton University. In 1954, she obtained an MA in literature from the University of Wisconsin. With her husband, Abdel-Hadi Mahbouba, she helped found the University of Basra in southern Iraq. Many of her works were published in Beirut, where she lived in the late 1950s. As a writer, al-Mala'ika made her debut in 1947 with *A'shiqat Al-Layl*. Its themes of despair and disillusion were familiar from the Arabic literary romanticism of the 1930s and 1940s. Her second collection, *Shazaya wa ramad* (*Ashes and Shrapnel*, 1949), helped launch free verse as a new form for avant-garde poetry. In the 1950s, al-Mala'ika was among the most prominent figures of modernism. She backed the movement with her critical writings, when arguments were made for and against metrical poetry. One of her best-known poems, "Cholera," took its subject from recent history—it was based on the emotional effect of the cholera epidemic that arrived in Iraq from Egypt in 1947. After fleeing Iraq in the aftermath of the 1991 Gulf War, she moved to Cairo. Al-Mala'ika avoided publicity but entered the literary scene again in 1999 with a new book of verse, *Youghiyar Alouanah Al-Bahr*, which also contained an autobiographical sketch. Most of the poems dated from 1974. Al-Mala'ika suffered from Parkinson's disease for many years and died on June 20, 2007, in Cairo.

MOZAFFAR AL-NAWWAB *(b. 1932)*

This Iraqi-born poet not only is recognized for the quality and quantity of his work but also stands apart from his contemporaries: even though some of his works have been published in limited print editions, his poetry is disseminated primarily via live recitation or performance and recorded copies of these events. And, while al-Nawwab is called an "Iraqi" poet due to his birthplace, his work in fact addresses a much larger Arab audience. His style evokes strong emotions in his audiences—from childlike wonderment to nostalgic longing, sensuous arousal, disgust, and rage—as a means of bringing to the forefront what he has always considered urgent concerns for the Arab world. His most famous work, *Jisr al-Mabahij al-Qadima* (*Bridge of Old Wonders*, 1976–77), is often referred to as the "Tal al-Zaatar" poem, since a major theme in this epic poem is the 1976 siege and massacre of Palestinians at Lebanon's Tal al-Zaatar refugee camp.

MELIH CEVDET ANDAY *(1915–2002)*

Together with Orhan Veli Kanık and Oktay Rifat, Anday was a founder of the Garıp ("Strange") Movement in Turkish literature. Born in Istanbul, Anday graduated from Ankara Gazi High School and became a consultant for the Turkish Ministry of Education. He also was a journalist and wrote several articles for the *Akşam* and *Cumhuriyet* newspapers. During a career that spanned six and a half decades, he published eleven collections of poems, including *Yanyana* (1956) and

Güneşte (1989); eight plays—such as *İçerdekiler* (1965); eight novels, including *Raziye* (1975); fifteen collections of essays; and memoir, *Akan Zaman Duran Zaman* (*Time that Flows, Time that Stops*, 1984).

'ARRAR *(1897–1949)*

'Arrar is the pseudonym of Mustafa Wahbi al-Tal, a Jordanian poet. His life history involved a series of movements across the Middle East. Beginning with schooling in both Jordan and Damascus, he and his classmates were exiled to Beirut by Ottoman authorities. But he found his way back to Jordan and eventually traveled to Istanbul, where he was married. He was again exiled to Beirut for political activity, so he made his way to Syria—all before the 1920s. His adulthood also saw constant exiles and travel, as he moved between Jordan and present-day Saudi Arabia. His life was filled with political activity, dissent, and jail time for his political views. He is best known for his incisive and humorous poems about Arab nationalism and anticolonialism.

MANOUCHEHR ATASHI *(1931–2005)*

Persian writer, poet, and journalist Atashi was born in the south of Iran, in Dashtestan, into an educated tribal family. After receiving his BA in English literature in Tehran, Atashi made a living by teaching and writing. His poems began appearing in major Iranian journals when he was still quite young. Although set in the context of his birthplace, his poems are universal in scope. In his later works, Atashi relaxed his rhythm and moved toward a direct expression of emotion. Atashi's poetry collections include *Song of the Earth* and *The Roots of Night*.

REZA BARAHENI *(b.1935)*

This Iranian novelist, poet, critic, and political activist was born in Tabriz. Early in his life, Iran's political changes made a lasting impression on him. With the banning of the Turkish language and establishment of Persian as the official state language, he quickly took to heart the struggle of identity and language in the face of political suppression, making political activity a major part of his life. In 1973, he was arrested and imprisoned in Tehran, spending 102 days in solitary confinement. In 1982, he was expelled from the University of Tehran and banned from working. In

1996, the Canadian government granted Baraheni political asylum. He is the author of more than fifty books in both Persian and English, and his works have been translated into a dozen languages. He is also a prolific translator himself, having translated into Persian works by Shakespeare, Kundera, Mandelstam, Andric, and Fanon.

FARAJ BAYRAQDAR *(b. 1951)*

Sometimes known as "Birqdar," this Syrian poet and journalist is one of the longest-detained writers in the world. He has spent his life and work in support of free expression and nonviolent political action. This ultimately led to his arrest on March 31, 1987, on suspicion of membership in the Party for Communist Action. In 1993, he was sentenced to fifteen years in prison, after being held without charge or trial for more than six years. He suffers from various health problems resulting from the brutal torture he has endured. An honorary member of the American, English, Dutch, and Slovak PEN Centers, Bayraqdar received a Hellman/Hammett Free Expression Award in 1998. He has published two collections of poems, *You Are Not Alone* (1979) and *A New Dance at the Court of the Heart* (1981). Bayraqdar was released from prison on November 16, 2000. Under an amnesty granted by the Syrian president, he left jail fourteen months before the end of his sentence without being obliged to renounce his political activities.

SIMIN BEHBAHANI *(b. 1927)*

One of the most respected living Iranian writers, Behbahani is often regarded as Iran's national poet and an icon of the Iranian intelligentsia, who affectionately refer to her as the "Lioness of Iran." Born Simin Khalili, Behbahani started writing poetry at the age of twelve and published her first poem at the age of fourteen. She used the "Char Pareh" style popularized by Nima Yushij and subsequently turned to the ghazal form. She has expanded the range of the traditional Persian verse forms and produced some of the most significant works of Persian literature in the twentieth century. In 1997, she was nominated for the Nobel Prize in Literature. She is the president of the Iranian Writers' Association.

ALIREZA BEHNAM *(b. 1973)*

This poet and journalist is part of the self-proclaimed "new" generation of Iranian poets. Born and raised in Iran, Behnam attended the Islamic Azad University in the northern city of Bojnurd. After receiving his BS in civil engineering in 1997, he took a job at the now-closed pro-reform newspaper *Akhbar*. He then was art and literature editor for the *Azad* daily newspaper until 2002, when the hardliner courts banned the publication for political reasons. After that, Behnam became art and literature editor at the daily *Modaber*, until February 2003. Then he went to daily *Roozan*. Behnam has published four collections of his poetry in Persian as well as six volumes of translations.

SADEQ CHUBAK *(1916–1998)*

Short-story writer and playwright Chubak is widely considered the greatest naturalist writer in Persian literature and a pioneer of modern Persian fiction. His short stories are characterized by their intricacy, economy of detail, and concentration on a single theme. Chubak published his first collection of short stories, *Khaymah shab bazi* (*The Puppet Show*), in 1945, followed by dozens of novels, short stories, and plays. He died in Berkeley, California, in 1998.

ISMAT CHUGHTAI *(1911–1991)*

This renowned Indian writer, known for her feminist ideology, is considered the "grand dame" of Urdu fiction. Born in Badayun, Uttar Pradesh, she grew up in Jodhpur, where her father was a civil servant. The ninth of ten children, Chughtai spent the better part of her childhood in the company of her brothers, a factor that she admits contributed greatly to the frankness in her personality and her writing. Becoming the first Indian Muslim woman to earn both a BA degree and a Bachelor of Education (BT), she initially began writing in secret. Chughtai's most famous story is "*Lihaf*" ("The Quilt"), which deals with a lesbian encounter within an all-female setting in a traditional Muslim household. Charged by the British government with obscenity, she won the case because her lawyer argued that the story could be understood only by those who already had knowledge of lesbianism, and thus could not be a corrupting influence. Her other works include "*Gainda*" and "The Net," both dealing with sexual awakening and role playing, and "The Wedding Suit," about a daughter's marriage.

ZAYD MUTEE' DAMMAJ *(1943–2000)*

This Yemeni writer was born in the Al-Naqilain area of Yemen to a family already embroiled in politics. His revolutionary father, Sheikh Mutee' bin Abdullah Dammaj, had escaped from Al-Shabakah Prison, in Taiz Province, to Aden. Dammaj received his elementary education at his village's *mi'lamah* (traditional school or *madrasa*). His father, upon returning home, assumed responsibility for educating his son with his private library, a large collection of books he had brought from Aden. Young Zayd voraciously read books on literature, history, and politics, most important of which were Georgi Zaidan's *Riwaiat Al-Islam* (*The Novels of Islam*). His father had him join Al-Ahmadiyah School in the city of Taiz, and he obtained his primary education certificate in 1957. In 1958, Dammaj was sent to Egypt for his secondary and higher education. He joined Cairo University's Faculty of Law in 1964 but changed his mind two years later and studied journalism at the Faculty of Arts. In 1968, he abandoned his studies and left Egypt for Yemen to participate in revolutionary activities. In addition to his literary work, Dammaj was elected in 1970 to the Al-Shoura Council (Consultative Council), the first elected Parliament in the country. His political career continued as he was appointed delegated minister and acting ambassador to Kuwait in 1980. He was a member of the Union of Yemeni Writers, the Union of Arab Writers, and the Afro-Asian Writers. He was secretary general of the Yemen Peace and Solidarity Council, member of the World Peace Council, adviser to the minister of foreign affairs, and a delegated minister in Britain in 1997. Dammaj's works include his political articles and early stories that were published in *Al-Yemen Al-Jadeedah* (*New Yemen*) magazine, as well as *Tahish Al-Hawban* (*Al-Hawban Monster*, 1973), *Al-Rahinah* (*The Hostage*, 1984), and *Al-Madfa' Al-Asfar* (*The Yellow Cannon*, in 2001).

SIMIN DANESHVAR *(b. 1921)*

This Iranian academic, renowned novelist, short-story writer, and translator of literary works from English, German, Italian, and Russian into Persian has even more achievements to her name. Not only was her collection of Persian short stories the first to be published by an Iranian woman, but her *Savushun* (*Mourners of Siyāvosh*, 1969) has become Iran's best-selling novel ever and has been reprinted at least sixteen times. Furthermore, Daneshvar's *The Playhouse*, a collection of five stories and two autobiographical pieces, is the first volume of translated stories by an Iranian woman author. Born and raised in Shiraz, Daneshvar moved in 1948 to Tehran, where she earned her PhD in 1949. In 1952, she had a Fulbright Fellowship to study creative writing at Stanford University. Eventually, she returned to the University of Tehran as a faculty member, retiring in 1979. This writer's work was influenced most by the social problems of the 1960s and 1970s—reality, not fantasy. Her inspiration is drawn from the people around her. She has also contributed to the periodicals *Sokhan* and *Alefba*.

MAHMOUD DARWISH *(1941–2008)*

Regarded as the Palestinian national poet, Darwish has become the voice of Palestine. He was born in the village of al-Birwa in the Western Galilee, the son of a Muslim landowner. Taught to read by his grandfather, he attended high school in Kafr Yasif and eventually moved to Haifa. He published his first book of poetry, *Asafir bila ajniha* (*Wingless Sparrows*) at the age of nineteen. Leaving Israel in 1970, he attended the University of Moscow for one year before moving first to Egypt and then to Lebanon. Darwish joined the PLO in 1973 and consequently was banned from reentering Israel until 1995, when he returned to attend the funeral of a colleague. Eventually, the writer was allowed to settle in Ramallah in 1995. Darwish published more than thirty volumes of poetry—among them, *Awraq al-Zaytun* (*Leaves of Olives*, 1964) and *A'ras* (*Weddings*, 1977)—as well as eight books of prose, including *Shai'on 'an al-wattan* (*Something about the Homeland*, 1971) and *al-Rasa'il* (*The Letters*, 1990), the latter coauthored with Samih al-Qasim.

Parvin E'tesami *(1907–1941)*

Born in Tabriz, Iran, to an educated and literary family, Parvin E'tesami achieved her literary fame in a traditional, male-dominated society by focusing on themes of humanism and liberalism. Eventually, she entered the American College for Girls in Tehran, where she learned English and encountered Western culture. After briefly teaching at the college, she returned to her family and focused on her poetry. Her earliest-known poems were published in Persian magazine *Bahar* in 1921–22. The first edition of her book of poetry, *Diwan*, appeared in 1935 and contained 156 poems. E'tesami also mastered another form of poetry, *monazara* (dialogue, debate), producing about sixty-five poems in this style. She also published seventy-five anecdotes, fables, and allegories. E'tesami died of typhoid fever in April 1941.

Faiz Ahmed Faiz *(1911–1984)*

An avowed Marxist, trade unionist, journalist, and thinker, Faiz Ahmed Faiz was born in a village in the Punjab. Educated both at Murray College, Sialkot, and Government College, Lahore, he received his master's degree in English literature at the latter. Faiz received a second master's degree in Arabic from Oriental College, Lahore. He married British-born Alys George, also a poet and human rights activist. In the 1930s, Faiz came under the influence of the Progressive Writers' Movement, wherein, under the leadership of Sajjad Zaheer, authors were expected to follow the dictates of Socialist Realism. Although the movement had ceased to be an effective literary force by the 1950s, Faiz's activities led the government to charge him and his colleagues with planning a coup d'état. After four years in prison, Faiz was released in 1955. He promptly went to work for the *Pakistan Times* and, later, for the National Council of the Arts. In 1962, he was awarded the Lenin Peace Prize by the Soviet Union. Faiz wrote poems that opposed the bloodshed occurring in what became Bangladesh during the conflict with Pakistan. His works began with *Naqsh-e-Faryadi* in 1941 and continued through to *Merey Dil Merey Musafar* in 1981. In 1984, he published *Nuskhaha-e-Wafa,* a collection of his work.

FORUGH FARROKHZAD *(1935–1967)*

Arguably the most famous woman in the history of Persian literature, Farrokhzad was born in Tehran to a middle-class family of seven children. She married at seventeen and divorced within three years, painfully and unwillingly relinquishing her only son to her ex-husband and his family. She never remarried. Instead Farrokhzad turned to poetry and film and led an independent life. Farrokhzad was a poet of great audacity and extraordinary talent. Her poetry was the poetry of protest—protest through revelation—revelation of the innermost world of women (a taboo subject until then), their intimate secrets and desires, their sorrows, longings, aspirations, and at times even their articulation through silence. Her expressions of physical and emotional intimacy, much lacking in Persian women's poetry up to that point, placed her at the center of controversy, even among the intellectuals of the time. On February 14, 1967, she died in an automobile accident. She was thirty-two years old.

ALTAF FATIMA *(b. 1929)*

Fatima was born in Lucknow and completed her education in Lahore, after Partition, obtaining MA and BED degrees from the University of Punjab. She taught Urdu literature at Islamia College for Women in Lahore for several years before moving to APWA Girls' College, also in Lahore, as a professor in the Urdu Department. She has published three novels, *Nishaan-i-Mehfil, Dastak Naa Do* (*The One Who Did Not Ask*), and *Chulta Musafir,* as well as three collections of short stories: *Woh jisay chaha gaya, Jub diwaaren girya kurti hain,* and, most recently, *Taar-i-unkaaboot* (1990). She has also translated Harper Lee's novel *To Kill a Mockingbird* from English into Urdu. *The One Who Did Not Ask* has enjoyed the most sustained success in Pakistan. An adaptation was presented on Pakistan television and an abridged translation was serialized by the prestigious Karachi monthly *Herald.*

KHALIL GIBRAN *(1883–1931)*

Gibran Khalil Gibran bin Mikhā'il bin Sa'ad was a Lebanese American artist, poet, and writer who published works in both Arabic and English. He is best known for his 1923 book *The Prophet*, a series of philosophical essays written in English and translated into more than twenty languages. Gibran died in New York City on April 10, 1931, of cirrhosis of the liver and tuberculosis. He was buried in Lebanon, according to his wishes.

HOUSHANG GOLSHIRI *(1938–2000)*

This Iranian fiction writer, critic, and editor was born into a large family in Isfahan. After earning his bachelor's degree in Persian at the University of Isfahan, he became an elementary school teacher. Not until the late 1950s did he begin to write fiction. He built his literary reputation not only with his writing but also with his establishment of *Jong-e Istafan* (1965–73), the chief literary journal published outside of Tehran. His first collection of short stories was *Mesl-e hamisheh* (*As Always*), in 1968. The 1980s proved notably prolific for Golshıri: he published *Massoum-e Panjom* (*The Fifth Innocent*, 1980), *Jobbeh' khaneh* (*The Antique Chamber*, 1983), *Hadis-e Mahigir va Div* (*The Story of the Fisherman and the Demon,* 1984), and *Panj Ganj* (*Five Treasures,* 1989).

MELISA GÜRPINAR *(b. 1941)*

Born in Istanbul, this leading Turkish poet and writer was a part of the Second New Movement of the 1950s to the 1970s. A graduate of the Istanbul Municipal Conservatory, she studied drama in London in the mid-1960s. She has published six poetry collections as well as a short-story collection in poetic form.

YAHYA HAQQI *(1905–1992)*

Egyptian lawyer, writer, and novelist Haqqi was born into a middleclass family in Cairo and worked for a time as a civil servant and adviser to the National Library of Egypt. During his literary career, he published four collections of short stories, one novel (*Umm Hashem's Lamp*), and numerous articles. From 1961 to 1971, he served as editor of the literary magazine *Al-Majalla*, in which he championed budding Egyptian authors whose works he admired and believed in.

HAYDAR HAYDAR *(b. 1936)*

Haydar has achieved a reputation as one of Syria's preeminent fiction writers, proficient in both short stories and novels. His first short-story collection was *Tales of the Migrating Seagull,* published in 1968, and since then he has published *A Flare of Light, The Deluge,* and *The Twilight of the Gods.* His political novel *A Banquet for Seaweed,* published quietly in 1983, generated enormous controversy and riots in Egypt seventeen years later, when an edition was published there. Despite calls for his execution, the crisis eventually dissipated.

SADEGH HEDAYAT *(1903–1951)*

An Iranian short-story writer, novelist, playwright, and essayist, Hedayat was born into a family of influential landowners and educated in Tehran, France, and Belgium. In addition to translating many works of Kafka, his first study of Umar Khayyam, entitled *Ruba'iyyat-i Hakim Umar Khayyam,* appeared in 1923, even before he graduated from the Saint Louis Academy in Paris. Hedayat published his first collection of short stories after returning to Iran in 1930. In 1932, he helped found a literary club named Rab'a, which attacked the conservative literary establishment. Hedayat's criticism of Iranian society ultimately drew the attention of the authorities, forcing him to flee to India, where he published his greatest work, *Buf-i Kur* (*The Blind Owl*), a surrealistic novella about frenzy and disappointment. Hedayat's final years were overshadowed by his drug addiction and alcohol problems. He left Iran permanently at the end of 1950 and settled in Paris, where he died a year later.

NÂZIM HIKMET *(1901–1963)*

Hikmet has been critically acclaimed in Turkey as the father of modern Turkish poetry; his works have been translated into more than fifty languages. After publishing his first poems at the age of seventeen, Hikmet made his way to Moscow in the 1920s—attracted by the Socialist dream. After the Turkish War of Independence, he returned to Turkey, but his leftist leanings made him a target of surveillance and arrest, forcing him to return to the Soviet Union, where he continued writing plays and poetry.

Between 1929 and 1936, he published nine books—five collections and four long poems that revolutionized Turkish poetry, breaking traditional Ottoman literary conventions with free verse and colloquial diction. He wrote the poem *Açların Gözbebekleri* ("Pupils of the Hungry"), introducing free verse, and epics such as *Šimavne Kadısı Oğlu Şeyh Bedreddin Destanı* (*The Epic of Sheikh Bedreddin, Son of Judge Simavne,* 1936) and *Memleketimden Insan Manzaralari* (*Human Landscapes from My Country,* 1939). In the late 1930s, while imprisoned for the use of revolutionary themes in his poetry, he composed his greatest works, including his epic masterpiece, *Human Landscapes.* Although his writings were long suppressed in Turkey, major translations of his poetry appeared in England, France, Germany, Greece, Poland, Spain, and the United States. His Turkish citizenship—withdrawn in 1951—was restored (posthumously) in 2009.

Abdullah Hussein *(b. 1931)*

Abdullah Hussein was born in Rawalpindi. In 1963, he published his first novel, *The Weary Generation,* for which he won the prestigious Pakistani Adamji Prize. His novels and short fiction have been translated into several Indian languages a well as into English and Chinese. In 1996, the BBC based a feature film, *Brothers in Trouble,* on one of his novellas. His first novel in English, *Emigré Journeys,* was published in the United Kingdom in 2000. Regarded as the leading novelist in the Urdu language, he has lived in Britain since 1967.

Intizaar Hussein *(b. 1923)*

This renowned Urdu fiction writer was born in Dibai, Bulandshahr, India, but he migrated to the new nation of Pakistan in 1947. As a novelist and short-story writer, Hussain has a unique prose style. Two of his works, *The Seventh Door* and *Leaves,* are available in English. He is also a journalist and regular columnist for *Dawn* and other publications.

Yusif Idris *(1927–1991)*

Egyptian author Idris spent his childhood in the Nile Delta region before moving to Cairo in 1945 to study medicine at Cairo University. He began writing short stories while still a student, publishing several of his works before his graduation in 1951. His first collection of short stories, *Arkhas Layali (The Cheapest Nights)*, was published to great acclaim in 1954. That same year, he was imprisoned for his involvement in political activities, but following his release in September 1955, he began writing articles for the newspaper *al-Jumhuriyya*. Idris's most productive period was from the late 1950s up to the 1967 Arab-Israeli War. It was a period that saw the publication of several short-story collections as well as a number of plays and novels. He gave up the practice of medicine in 1967 and assumed an administrative post in Egypt's Ministry of Culture, where he sought to lay the foundations for a modern Egyptian theater using popular traditions and folklore. Idris was nominated several times for the Nobel Prize in Literature.

MUHAMMAD IQBAL *(1877–1938)*

Born in Sialkot, a small town in the Punjab, Iqbal had already made his mark among the literary circles of Lahore by the time he received his master's degree in 1889 from the Government College. A devout Muslim, Iqbal was interested in the bridges between East and West, so he went to Europe in 1905, acquiring a law degree at Lincoln's Inn, a Bachelor of Arts at Cambridge, and a Doctor of Philosophy at the University of Munich. He began a political career while in Britain and eventually received an honorary knighthood. In the early 1930s, his popularity was at its peak and his religious and political ideas were gaining wide acceptance. One of Iqbal's last major achievements was to establish the Adarah Darul Islam, an institution where studies in classical Islam and contemporary social science would be subsidized. Iqbal's poetic works are written mostly in Persian rather than Urdu; of his 12,000 poetic verses, 7,000 are in Persian. In 1915, he published his first collection of poetry, *Asrar-e-Khudi (Secrets of the Self)*—in Persian. And in his *Rumuz-e-Bekhudi (Hints of Selflessness)*, Iqbal seeks to prove that the Islamic way of life is the best code of conduct for a nation's viability. His first work in Urdu, *Bang-e-Dara (The Call of the Marching Bell*, 1924), was a collection of poetry he had written during three distinct phases of his life. Iqbal's final work was *Armughan-e-Hijaz (The Gift of Hijaz)*, published posthumously in 1938. The first part contains quatrains in Persian and the second part contains some poems and epigrams in Urdu. His tomb in Lahore is located between the entrance of the Badshahi Mosque and the Lahore Fort, and government guards keep watch there.

ALI SARDAR JAFRI *(1913–2000)*

Born into an aristocratic family in Balrampur, Uttar Pradesh, India, this Urdu writer, poet, critic, and film lyricist found his early influences in Josh Malihabadi, lyricist Jigar Muradabadi, and Firaq Gorakhpuri. In 1933, he entered Aligarh Muslim University (AMU), where he became exposed to Communist ideology. He was expelled from the university in 1936, for "political reasons." He graduated from Delhi University in 1938, but his graduate studies ended prematurely following his arrest (1940–41) for writing antiwar poems and participating in other political activities on campus. Jafri published his first collection of poems, *Manzil* (*Destination*), in 1938, starting his literary carrer; his first collection of poems, *Parvaz* (*Flight*), came out in 1944. In 1936, he presided over the first conference of the Progressive Writers' Movement (PWM) in Lucknow and continued as president for the rest of his life. In 1939, he became coeditor of *Naya Adab*, a literary journal devoted to the PWM. Jafri's career was peppered with involvement in several social, political, and literary movements, for which he was arrested multiple times. Between 1948 and 1978, he published eight poetry collections, including *Nai Duniya Ko Salaam* (*Salute to the New World*, 1948) and *Lahu Pukarta Hai* (*The Blood Calls*, 1965). During his fifty-year literary career, Jafri also edited anthologies of Kabir, Mir, and Ghalib; wrote two plays for the Indian People's Theatre Association (IPTA); produced a documentary film, *Kabir, Iqbal and Freedom*; produced two television serials, including the eighteen-part *Kahkashan*, based on the lives and works of noted Urdu poets; and wrote his autobiography. He was also the editor and publisher of *Guftagu*, one of the Subcontinent's most respected Urdu literary magazines.

MOHAMMAD ALI JAMALZADEH *(1892–1997)*

Born in Isfahan, this Persian writer is best known for his unique sense of humor. As part of a middle-class family led by a progressive mullah and preacher, Jamalzadeh lived in Iran only until his early teen years—when his father was executed. By World War I, Jamalzadeh joined a group of Iranian nationalists in Berlin and, in 1915, founded the newspaper *Rastakhiz*. The author's major work, *Yeki Bud Yeki Nabud* (*Once Upon a Time*), published in 1921 in Berlin, did not reach Iran until a year later; it was not received favorably. Tautology, a tendency toward using sage remarks, mystical and philosophical speculations, and disregard for order became the hallmarks of his later writings. His other major works include *Sahra-ye Mahshar* (*Armageddon*, 1947), *Talkh-o Shirin* (*Bitter and Sweet*, 1955), *Kohne va Now* (*Old and New*, 1959), *Qair az Khoda Hichkas Nabud* (*None Existed Except God*, 1961), *Asman-o Risman* (*The Blue Yonder and Rope*, 1965), *Qesse-ha-ye Kutah Bara-ye Bachcheha-ye Rish-dar* (*Short Stories for Bearded Children* [i.e., for adults], 1974), and *Qesse-ye Ma be Akhar Rasid* (*Thus Ends Our Story*, 1979).

GHASSAN KANAFANI *(1936–1972)*

Novelist, short-story writer, and dramatist Kanafani was born in Acre, Palestine. In 1947, when Palestine was partitioned into Arab and Jewish zones by the United Nations, Kanafani fled with his family first to Lebanon and then to Syria, where they settled as Palestinian refugees. After finishing his secondary education, he studied Arabic literature at the University of Damascus, although he was expelled before receiving a degree. He moved to Kuwait, where he worked as a teacher and journalist, and then to Beirut, where he edited the pro-Nasser paper *al-Muharrir*. During those years, Kanafani's political activities increased; in 1969, he became the spokesperson for the Popular Front for the Liberation of Palestine and editor-in-chief of its weekly journal, *Al-Hadaf*. Kanafani was assassinated on July 8, 1972, by a car bomb planted by Israeli agents. He was posthumously awarded the Lotus Prize for Literature by the Conference of Afro-Asian Writers. Kanafani's oeuvre includes his works in Arabic such as *Ma tabaqqa lakum* (*All That's Left to You*, 1966), *Barquq Naysan* (*The Apricots of April*, 1972), and "The Slave Fort" in *Arabic Short Stories*, 1983 (translated by Denys Johnson-Davies). Other English translations of his works include *Men in the Sun and Other Palestinian Stories*.

ORHAN VELI KANIK *(1914–1950)*

Another member of the Turkish Garıp Movement, this Turkish poet was born in Istanbul, where his father was the conductor for the Presidential Symphony Orchestra. Kanık studied philosophy at Istanbul University before dropping out in 1935. He eventually found employment with the Ministry of Education as a translator (1945 to 1947). He next worked as a freelance translator and journalist, including helping with the publication of *Yaprak*, a literary magazine, in 1949. Kanık is known for his poetry without excessive stylistic elements and adjectives, adhering more closely to free verse. His work has a unique voice, as well as emotional depth underlying the seemingly easygoing nature of his verse. His poetry, including *Destan Gibi* (1946), is highly admired by the public as well as in academic circles. But Kanık's personal life was affected by his heavy drinking, which ultimately caused his death.

REFIK HALIT KARAY *(1888–1965)*

Born into a well-established Istanbul family, this writer used various pseudonyms, such as Aydede, Dürenda, Kirpi, Nakş-ı Ber-âb, Rehak, and Vakanüvis. After the Second Constitutional Monarchy in 1907, Karay left his studies and civil-servant career to become a journalist. He earned fame through the humorous political articles that he wrote under the pseudonym Kirpi for the humor magazines *Kalem* and *Cem*. His work and criticism eventually led to a three-year exile, an event that profoundly influenced his literary career. After being granted clemency, he returned to Istanbul and started writing for newspapers such as *Vakit, Tasvir- Efkâr, Alemdar, Peyam-ı Sabah*, and *Zaman*. Soon he was made editor-in-chief of the *Sabah* newspaper. In his novels and short fiction, he applied many of his observations from exile, bringing forward perspectives from all walks of life. From his first novel, *İstanbul'un İçyüzü* ("*Inside İstanbul*, 1920), to *Yüzen Bahçe* (*The Swimming Garden,* 1981), he embraced the revolutionary changes that occurred after the declaration of the Turkish Republic and criticized those who could not or would not adapt to these changes.

Cemil Kavukçu *(b. 1951)*

This Turkish short-story writer was born in Inegöl, in northwestern Turkey, and admits that he suffered from an uncomfortable childhood and youth; it took him six years to complete high school. Kavukçu suffered from a long period of rejection and pessimism in the 1980s and early 1990s because no bookstores would accept his books, almost causing him to abandon literature. But his first published book, *Uzak Noktalara Doğru*, ultimately earned him the Sait Faik Literature Prize. He went on to publish *Dönüş (Return)*, *Temmuz suçlu (July Criminals)*, *Yalnız uyuyanlar için (For Solo Sleepers)*, and *Pazar güneşi (Sunday Sun)*.

Yaşar Kemal *(b. 1922)*

One of Turkey's leading writers, Kemal has long been a candidate for the Nobel Prize in Literature. Born in Hemite (now Gökçedam), a hamlet in Osmaniye Province in southern Turkey, Kemal initially worked for wealthy farmers, an experience that sparked the naturalism in his greatest works, including *İnce Memed* (*Memed, My Hawk*, 1955), for which he received international acclaim. Eventually he worked as a journalist, before becoming a novelist. Kemal was an outspoken champion of the Kurds, and his activism on their behalf resulted in a twenty-month suspended jail sentence on charges of advocating separatism. In 1943, he published his first book, *Ağıtlar (Ballads)*, a compilation of folkloric themes. In the 1950s, his first wife, Thilda Serrero, translated seventeen of his works into English. Among his many novels are *Ölmez Otu* (*The Undying Grass*, 1968), *Deniz Küstü* (*The Sea-Crossed Fisherman*, 1978), and *Tanyeri Horozları* (*The Cocks of Dawn*, 2002). But his oeurre also includes a number of "experimental works" and collections such as *Yayımlanmamış 10 Ağıt* (*10 Unpublished Ballads*, 1985) Kemal received two honorary doctorates in 2009—one from Boğaziçi University, the other from Çukurova University.

Naguib Mahfouz *(1911–2006)*

The most celebrated of all Arab novelists, Mahfouz was born into a lower-middle-class Muslim family in the Gamaleyya quarter of Cairo.

After completing his secondary education, Mahfouz entered King Fouad I University, now the University of Cairo, where he studied philosophy, graduating in 1934. He abandoned his graduate studies in 1936 to become a professional writer, working as a journalist for a number of Egyptian publications, including *er-Risala*, *el-Hilal*, and *Al-Ahram*. In a career that spanned seven decades, Mahfouz published thirty-four novels, more than 350 short stories, dozens of movie scripts and five plays. Many of his works have been made into Arabic-language films. In addition to being a board member of the Dar el-Ma'aref publishing house, he served Egypt's Ministry of Culture as the official responsible for the film industry. But despite his broad success and mainstream career, he was no stranger to political activism. Like many Egyptian writers and intellectuals, Mahfouz was on the Islamic fundamentalist "death list," and he survived an assassination attempt in 1994. In 1988, he became the first Arabic-language writer to win the Nobel Prize in Literature.

'ABD AL-RAHIM MAHMUD *(1913–1948)*

Palestinian poet Mahmud spent his life and literary career addressing the issues of British occupation and Jewish settlement of Palestine. His actions carried his beliefs beyond his pen, and he even crossed over to Iraq, where he allegedly participated in the revolution of Rasheed Ali al-Keelany against the British. His work shows a strong Islamic influence—in content and tone. Mahmud died fighting in what was called the "Battle of the Tree" (*Ma'raket al Shajarah*), a conflict between Jewish and Arab groups.

SA'ADAT HASAN MANTO *(1912–1955)*

This Pakistani writer is well known for his Urdu short stories, but he also was a film and radio scriptwriter and a journalist. Born to a Kashmiri Muslim family, Manto wasn't a model student as a child, losing interest often. Apparently the turning point of his life occurred in 1933, when he met Abdul Bari Alig, a scholar and polemic writer, in Amritsar. Alig encouraged the young Manto to find his true talents and pointed him toward reading and appreciating the works of Russian and

French authors. This led Manto to his first publication, an Urdu translation of Victor Hugo's *The Last Days of a Condemned Man,* published in Lahore as *Sarguzasht-e-Aseer* (*A Prisoner's Story*). Encouraged by its reception, he went on to publish his first collection of original short stories in Urdu, *Atish Pare* (*Sparks*; also *Quarrel-Provokers*), in 1936. In the late 1940s, Manto and his family were among the millions of Muslims who left present-day India for the newly created Muslim-majority nation of Pakistan. The writer's literary career in Lahore after this time was controversial, as many people found his viewpoints, artwork, and general views objectionable. He was not known for self-censorship and refused to "mince words." But his troubles in Lahore were the backdrop for his greatest literary works. It was there that he wrote his masterpieces, *Thanda Gosht, Khol Do, Toba Tek Singh, Iss Manjdhar Mein, Mozalle, Babu Gopi Nath*—some of whose characters became legendary. Manto died at the young age of forty-two.

MIRAJI *(1912–1949)*

Born Mohammad Sana'ullah Dar in Gujranwala, West Punjab, Miraji was among the leading Urdu poets of the twentieth century. He lived during the final phase of British colonialism in South Asia, and his work played a role in the nationalist struggles. Though brought up in an affluent family, Miraji spent much of his life as a homeless wanderer, staying with friends and making his living by writing songs. His work included editing *Adabi Duniya,* a collection of Urdu works and critical essays. He wrote literary columns for the monthly *Saqi* in Delhi and briefly helped edit Bombay's *Khayal.* His works include *Intikhab-I Kalam Miraji* and *Kulliyat-i Miraji.*

ZAKARIA MOHAMMAD *(b. 1951)*

Born in the Nablus area, Mohammad studied Arabic literature at Baghdad University. In addition to his poetry publications, he published his first novel in 1996 and a collection of plays in 1999. His poems are considered to be among the best examples of modernist Arabic poetry. He participated in the 1999 Medellin International Poetry Festival in Colombia and the 2001 Arab World Institute Poetry Festival in Paris. He lives in the Palestinian city of Ramallah.

NADER NADERPOUR *(1929–2000)*

A celebrated Iranian poet, political scholar, and literary critic born to sophisticated parents in Tehran, Naderpour was sent to Paris to study literature at the Sorbonne in 1950. On his return to Iran, he accepted a position in the Department of Arts and Culture and became editor-in-chief of the monthly journal *Honar va Mardom*. He published his first poems in the 1940s and completed four collections by the 1970s. His outspoken criticism of the Islamic government in Iran forced him into exile in Southern California, where he died in 2000. His poetry collections include *Giyah va Sang na, Atash* (*Not Plant and Stone, But Fire*), *Az Aseman ta Risman* (*From the Sublime to the Ridiculous*), and *Shame Baz Pasin* (*The Last Supper*)—all published in 1978.

KISHWAR NAHEED *(b. 1940)*

Born in Bulandshahr, Uttar Pradesh, India, Naheed and her family moved to Lahore after Partition. She began writing poetry while still in school, much to the consternation of her disciplinarian father. Poetry became her path to self-definition and independence, and soon she was regarded as an iconoclast, a reputation that she has maintained. Naheed has been a passionate champion not only of the feminist movement but of the struggle for economic and social justice in Pakistan—a role for which she personally suffered, particularly during General Zia-ul-Haq's rule. Her publications include eight collections of poetry, translations of major contemporary authors, and many books, including an autobiography and essays. She also edited a prestigious journal. Her research on women's issues has been recognized, and she is a recipient of the Nelson Mandela Award. She lives in Islamabad.

AZIZ NESIN *(1915–1995)*

A popular Turkish humorist and author of more than a hundred books, Nesin was born as Mehmet Nusret Nesin. Like many of his peers, he spent several years as a career civil servant before his political views led him to editorial work at a series of Socialist publications. His works satirizing bureaucracy and exposing economic inequities in Turkish society have been translated into more than thirty languages. Nesin received numerous awards in Turkey, Italy, Bulgaria, and the former Soviet Union. In the early 1990s, he started a translation of Salman Rushdie's controversial novel, *The Satanic Verses*. This made him a target for radical Islamist organizations, who then were gaining in popularity throughout Turkey. His English translations include a 1991 short-story collection entitled *Turkish Stories from Four Decades* and two novels published in 2001, *Memoirs of an Exile* and *Hayri the Barber Surnâmé*.

ORHAN PAMUK *(b. 1952)*

Born as Ferit Orhan Pamuk but known simply as Orhan Pamuk, this prominent Turkish novelist has sold more than seven million books in more than fifty languages. Born in Istanbul to a bourgeois family, he first dreamed of becoming a painter. He graduated from Robert College secondary school in Istanbul and studied architecture at Istanbul Technical University. After three years, he left ITU to become a full-time writer; in 1976, he graduated from the Institute of Journalism at Istanbul University. Pamuk has won many awards for his work, including the 1984 Madarali Novel Prize for his second novel, *Sessiz Ev* (*The Silent House*) and the 1991 Prix de la Découverte Européenne. His historical novel *Beyaz Kale* (*The White Castle*), published in Turkish in 1985, won the 1990 Independent Award for Foreign Fiction and extended his reputation abroad. In the 1980s, while his wife was a graduate student at Columbia University, Pamuk became a visiting scholar there, using the time to do research and write *The Black Book*, a novel that became one of the most controversial and popular readings in Turkish literature. Pamuk's next novel was *Kar* (*Snow*), published in 2002 and exploring the conflict between Islamism and Westernism in comtemporary Turkey. The *New York Times* listed *Snow* as one of its Ten Best Books of 2004. He also published a memoir/travelogue, *İstanbul—Hatıralar ve Şehir,* in 2003 (*Istanbul—Memories and the City*, 2005). His most recent works include *Other Colors*—a collection of essays and a story—published in the United States in 2007, and the *The Museum of Innocence*, published in the United States in 2009. In 2005, after Pamuk made a statement regarding mass killings of Armenians and Kurds in the Ottoman Empire, a criminal case was opened against him. The charges were dropped on January 22, 2006, the same year in which the Swedish Academy awarded him the Nobel Prize in Literature—the first

Nobel Prize awarded to a Turkish citizen. Pamuk is the Robert Yik-Fong Tam Professor in the Humanities at Columbia University, where he teaches comparative literature and writing.

ZOYA PIRZAD *(b. 1952)*

This renowned Iranian-Armenian writer and novelist has had her works, including her first novel, *Man cheragh-ha ra khamush mikonam* (*I Turn Off the Lights*), translated into several languages. Her honors include the Houshang Golshiri Award for Best Novel of the Year, for her "superb characterization, ingenious representation of the conflicting emotions of a woman." Pirzad's works also include *Mesl-e ham-e esr-ha* (*Like All Evenings*), *Yek ruz mande be eid pak* (*One Day Before Easter*), and *Edat mikonim* (*We Will Get Used to It*).

HAMID REZA RAHIMI *(b. 1950)*

Hamid Reza Rahimi, Iranian American poet, writer, satirist, and calligrapher, was born in Kermanshah in the west of Iran. Dr. Rahimi fled to exile in 1986 because of his overt opposition to the Iranian government, which had forbidden him to write. His passion for art and literature blossomed early, and his first book was published when he was nineteen. Since that time, eighteen more of his books have been published in Iran, Europe, and the United States, including twelve poetry collections. He initially wrote classical poetry and evolved to modern poetry, in which he has developed his own unique style. In the political-satire genre, he has completed more than 200 plays and parodies that have appeared in Iranian and international media. His most recent poetry collection is *A Piece of Time,* and his most recent work of political satire is *Breathing Forbidden.* In addition, his calligraphy has been exhibited worldwide. Since leaving Iran, he has been a member of the Iranian Writers' Association in Exile. He now lives in California.

N. M. RASHED *(1910–1975)*

Nazar Mohammed Rashed was born Raja Nazar Muhammad Janjua. An influential Pakistani writer of modern Urdu poetry, Rashed worked for the United Nations and lived in numerous countries. His themes ranged from the struggle against oppression to the relationship between words and meanings. Despite the philosophical bent of his work, he was often attacked for his unconventional views and lifestyle. Rashed rebelled against the traditional form of ghazal and became the first major exponent of free verse in Urdu literature. While his first book, *Mavra*, introduced free verse and is more technically accomplished and lyrical, his main intellectual and political ideals reached maturity in his last two books.

FAHMIDA RIAZ *(b. 1945)*

Born in Meerut, Uttar Pradesh, India, and raised in Hyderabad, Pakistan, Riaz obtained a master's degree from Sindh University. At the age of twenty, her first volume of poetry was published to critical acclaim. In Karachi, as editor and publisher of the magazine *Awaaz*, her uncompromising stand against the oppressive policies (particularly those affecting women) of General Zia-ul-Haq's regime led in 1980 to a case of sedition that carried the death sentence. She went into exile for seven years. In 1977, she received the Hellman/Hammett Award for literature from Human Rights Watch. In the 1990s, she began using fiction as a vehicle for her ideas and concerns and since then has produced three outstanding short novels, as well as essays, articles, translations, and several short stories. She has published works in English and translated Erich Fromm's *Fear of Freedom*. She resides in Karachi.

OKTAY RIFAT *(1914–1988)*

Born Oktay Rifat Horozcu in the Black Sea city of Trabzon, Rifat is regarded as one of Turkey's greatest writers and the father of modern Turkish poetry. Like his childhood friends Orhan Veli Kanık and Melih Cevdet Anday, Rifat graduated from Ankara Gazi High School in 1932. After receiving a Bachelor of Law degree from the University of Ankara, he went to Paris to pursue a PhD, but he returned to Turkey at the outbreak of World War II. Rifat started writing poetry as a high school student; his first poems were published between 1936 and 1944 in the literature journal *Varlık*. In addition to writing his various novels, he translated Latin and Greek works into Turkish. He moved to Istanbul in 1955 and became a legal adviser to the Turkish State Railways in 1961. He retired in 1973 and died in Istanbul. Rifat's early works include *Yaşayıp Ölmek Aşk ve Avarelik Üstüne Şiirler* (1945) and *Aşağı Yukarı* (1952). In 1987, he published *Koca Bir Yaz*. *Bütün Şiirleri* was published posthumously in 1991.

ZEESHAN SAHIL *(1961–2008)*

Sahil was born in Karachi and spent his early years in Hyderabad, Pakistan. Due to a physical disability, he was unable to continue his studies beyond high school. His father engendered in him a love of literature, and he began composing poetry when he was only eleven or twelve years old. From his parents he inherited an abiding compassion for humanity that remained with him despite his life's many uncertainties and the violence suffered periodically by the people of Karachi. Sahil's best-known collection, *Karachi our Dusri Nazmen* (*Karachi and Other Poems*), was written during three months in 1995 when infighting between political groups and vested interests turned Karachi into a battlefield and its citizens' lives into hell. These sensitive and poignant poems are among Sahil's most beautiful work.

AHMAD SHAMLOO *(1925–2000)*

The son of an army officer, Shamloo attended the Technical College of Tehran, but it wasn't long before his political ideology landed him in prison. In 1954, he was arrested for a third time after the publication of his third collection of poems, *Metals and Sense*, which was banned and destroyed by the police. Shamloo's poetry, reflecting his strong political convictions, is complex, yet his imagery, which contributes significantly to the intensity of his poems, is simple. Shamloo translated many works from German and French to Persian, and his own works have been translated into a number of languages. He was editor of several publications, including *Bamshad*, *Ketab-e-Hafte*, and *Khushe*. He also wrote numerous plays and edited the works of major classical Persian poets, especially Hafez. His six-volume *Ketab-e Koucheh* (*The Book of the Streets*) is a major contribution to understanding Iranian folklore beliefs and language.

CEMAL SÜREYA *(1931–1990)*

A Turkish poet and writer of Zaza origin, Süreya was born in Tunceli, Turkey, but after the 1938 Dersim Massacre, his family was forcibly deported to Bilecik, in western Anatolia. This had a significant effect on the writer's work. As a young adult, he graduated from the political sciences faculty of Ankara University and went on to become editor-in-chief of the *Papirus* literary magazine. Süreya was a notable member of the Second New Generation of Turkish poetry, an abstract and postmodern movement created as a backlash against the more popular-based Garıp Movement. Love, mainly through eroticism, is a popular theme of Süreya's works. His poems and articles were published in such magazines as *Yeditepe, Yazko, Pazar Postası, Yeni Ulus, Oluşum, Türkiye Yazıları, Politika, Aydınlık,* and *Somut.* He is known to have been a primary influence on the poetry of Sunay Akın.

ZAKARIYYA TAMIR *(b. 1931)*

Born in Damascus, Syria, Tamir is one of the most widely read and translated short-story writers in the Arab world and the foremost author of children's stories in Arabic. In 1944, at the age of thirteen, Tamir was forced to leave school to help provide for his family. He was apprenticed to a blacksmith in a factory in the al-Basha district of Damascus but refused to let his work interfere with his love of reading. He was inspired to represent the poor and downtrodden men and women of Syria in his own writing. The positive reception he received after the publication of his first stories in 1957 convinced him to abandon his job as a blacksmith and to embark on a writing career. He served as editor of several journals, including the cultural periodicals *Al-Mawqif al-Adabi, Al-Marifah, Al Tadhamon,* and many others, including the children's magazine *Usamah.* In 2002, Tamir was honored with the Syrian Order of Merit; in 2009, he received the Blue Metropolis Montreal International Literary Prize.

AHMET HAMDI TANPINAR *(1901–1962)*

This Turkish novelist and essayist not only was a prominent and important modern writer but also served in the Turkish Parliament between

1942 and 1946. Born into a family headed by a judge, Tanpınar went to veterinary college but left to complete his higher education in 1923 at the Faculty of Literature of Istanbul University. Tanpınar's most prominent work is a novel rife with ironic criticism, *Saatleri Ayarlama Enstitüsü* (*The Time Regulation Institute*), which deals with modernity and bureaucracy and their impact on the individual.

GOLI TARAGHI *(b. 1939)*

Taraghi is one of contemporary Iran's most eminent writers, essayists, and storytellers in the tradition of Iran's "Shahrzads." She was born and raised in Tehran, the daughter of the noted publisher and editor Lotfollah Taraghi. She received a bachelor's degree in philosophy from Drake University in Iowa and a master's degree in sociology from the University of Tehran. In the last twenty years or so of Iran's Pahlavi regime, Taraghi emerged as a member of a relatively small group of women who were active in writing fiction and were able to achieve recognition in this endeavor. Aside from Simin Daneshvar, few other women writers surpassed Taraghi's success and reputation, despite the fact that she was never a prolific writer. A collection of her short stories, *Man ham Che Guevara hastam* (*A Che Guevara in My Own Right*, 1969), and a loosely structured novel, *Khab-e Zemestani* (*Winter Sleep*, 1973), elicited favorable commentary from literary critics in Iran. Other works include *In Another Place* and *Scattered Memories*. Her recent collections of stories are *The House of Shemiran* and *The Three Maids*.

AKHTAR UL-IMAN *(1915–1996)*

Born in Qila, Najibabad (in the Bijnor district of Uttar Pradesh), this notable Urdu poet also carved out a reputation for himself as a screenwriter for Hindi cinema (Bollywood). After graduating from Delhi University, he worked for the Civil Supplies Department and All India Radio in Delhi. In 1945, he moved to Bombay (now Mumbai), where he began working for Hindi cinema as a script writer. But even during this career path, he was busy building a legacy with his poetry. Adopting a highly individualistic and innovative style, ul-Iman preferred nazm over the more popular ghazal as a mean poetic expression.

Strongly influenced by Miraji and N. M. Rashed, and more similar to them than to other poets of his era, ul-Iman was in fact a close friend of Miraji, who lived with ul-Iman until his death. They together formed Halqa-e-Arbab-e-Adab (Circle of Friends of Poetry), whose members wrote independently of the ideology and standards set by the Progressive Writers' Movement. This group served as the notable starting point of modernism in Urdu. Ul-Iman won the Filmfare Award for Best Dialogue in 1963 for *Dharmputra* and in 1966 for *Waqt*. He also earned the 1962 Sahitya Akademi Award in Urdu (from Sahitya Akademi, India's National Academy of Letters) for his poetry collection, *Yadein (Memories)*. His other poetry collections include *Tareek Sayyara* (1943), *Gardyab* (1946), and *Aabjoo* (1959).

SAADI YOUSSEF *(b. 1934)*

Born near Basra, Iraqi author, poet, journalist, publisher, and political activist Youssef has published thirty volumes of poetry and seven books of prose. He studied Arabic literature in Baghdad and was influenced by the free verse of Badr Shakir al-Sayyab and Abd al-Wahhab al-Bayyati. Politically active from an early age, he left the country permanently in 1979 after Saddam Hussein's rise to power. At the time, his work was heavily influenced by his Socialist and anti-imperialist sympathies, but it has since taken a more introspective, lyrical turn. He has also translated into Arabic the works of many well-known writers, including Oktay Rifat, Melih Cevdet Anday, Garcia Lorca, Yiannis Ritsos, Walt Whitman, and Constantine Cavafy. Since leaving Iraq, Youssef has lived in Algeria, Lebanon, France, Greece, Cyprus, and Yugoslavia; he currently resides in London. In 2007, Youssef participated in the PEN World Voices Festival.

CAN YÜCEL *(1926–1999)*

This Turkish poet studied classical philology first at Ankara University and then at Cambridge. He went on to work for five years for the BBC, but ultimately his poetry became his profession. Yücel was a poet with a keen political and social awareness. His poetry thrives on a strong combination of lyricism, jovial irony, and sarcasm. Because of his strongly critical poems, he was imprisoned several times. His major poetry collections include *Bir Siyasinin Şiirleri* (*Poems of a Political Prisoner*, 1974) and *Mekânim Datça Olsun* (*Let Datça Be My Domicile*, 1999).

NIMA YUSHIJ *(1896–1959)*

Born as Ali Esfandiari, this Persian poet started writing poetry while in high school and was encouraged by one of his teachers, himself a lyric poet. Although an ardent admirer of the works of the great classical Persian poets, Nezami and Hafez, Yushij broke from the old classical traditions with his first symbolist free verse, *The Phoenix*, in 1937. His innovations in form and style were widely criticized during his lifetime and deemed below the established norm. Today, however, he is considered one of the fathers of modern Persian poetry. Anthologies of his works have included the notable "*Afsaneh*" ("Myth"), "*Ay Shab*" ("O Night"), and "*Mahbass*" ("Prison").

HAIFA ZANGANA *(b. 1950)*

Zangana was just eight years old when Iraqis flooded the streets in 1958 to celebrate their newfound, hard-won freedom from British colonial rule. She came of age in one of the most open societies in the Middle East—until it was shut down in the 1970s by the Ba'ath Party. She was imprisoned for her opposition to Saddam Hussein; since her release, she has been living in exile in London. She writes regularly for *The Guardian* and *Al-Ahram Weekly* and is the author of many books, including *City of Widows: An Iraqi Woman's Account of War and Resistance*. Her memoir from Feminist Press is called *Dreaming of Baghdad*.

Permissions

Ismat Chughtai, "The Quilt." Translated by Syeda Hameed. From *The Quilt and Other Stories*. Published 1994 by Sheep Meadow Press. Reprinted with the permission of the publisher.

Zayd Mutee' Dammaj, "A Woman." Translated by May Jayyusi and Christopher Tingley. From *Modern Arabic Fiction*, edited by Salma Khadra Jayyusi. Copyright 2007 by Columbia University Press. Reprinted with the pemission of the publisher.

Simin Daneshvar, "The Playhouse." Translated by Maryam Mafi. From *The Playhouse and Other Stories*. Published 1989 by Mage Publishers. Reprinted with the permission of the publisher.

Mahmoud Darwish, "To the Reader" and "Identity Card." Translated by John Mikhail Asfour. Copyright John Mikhail Asfour. By permission of the translator. "Athens Airport" and "They'd Love to See Me Dead," from *Victims of a Map: Mahmud Darwish, Samih al-Qasim, Adonis*. Translated by Abdullah al-Udhari. Published 2001 by Saqi. Reprinted with the permission of Saqi.

Parvin E'tesami, "Iranian Women" and "A Woman's Place." Translated by Heshmat Moayyad. From *A Nightingale's Lament*, edited by Heshmat Moayyad. Published 1985 by Mazda Publishers. Reprinted with the permission of the publishers.

Faiz Ahmed Faiz, "Tablet and Pen," "Freedom's Dawn (August 1947)," "August 1952," and "Bury Me Under Your Pavements." Translated by V. G. Kiernan. From *Poems by Faiz*. Reprinted with the permission of Oxford University Press India, New Delhi.

Altaf Fatima, "Do You Suppose It's the East Wind?" Translated by Muhammad Umar Memon. Published in *Words without Borders*, June 2009. Reprinted with the permission of Words without Borders.

Forugh Farrokhzad, "Sin," "Window," "Wind-Up Doll" and "Those Days." Translated by Sholeh Wolpé. From *Sin: Selected Poems of Forugh Farrokhzad*. Copyright 2007 by Sholeh Wolpé. Reprinted with the permission of the University of Arkansas Press, www.uapress.com.

Khalil Gibran, "The Future of the Arabic Language." Translated by Adnan Haydar from *Al-bad'I wa al-tara'if*. Translation copyright 2010 by Adnan Haydar. Published with the permission of the translator.

Houshang Golshiri, "My China Doll." Translated by Fatma Sinem Eryilmaz. From *Black Parrot Green Crow*. Published 2003 by Mage Publishers. Reprinted with the permission of the publisher.

Melisa Gürpınar, "The Bank Teller Tecelli Bey." Translated by Murat Nemet-Nejat. From *EDA: An Anthology of Turkish Poetry*, edited by Murat Nemet-Nejat. Published 2004 by Talisman House. Reprinted with the permission of the translator.

Yahya Haqqi, "The First Lesson." From *Good Morning! and Other Stories*. Translated by Miriam Cooke. Copyright © 1987 by Miriam Cooke. Reprinted with the permission of Lynne Rienner Publishers, Inc.

Haydar Haydar, "The Dance of the Savage Prairies." Translated by May Jayyusi and Anthony Thwaite. From *Modern Arabic Fiction: An Anthology*, edited by Salma Khadra Jayyusi. Published 2007 by Columbia University Press. Reprinted with the permission of the publisher.

Index of Works, Authors, and Translators

Abasıyanık, Sait Faik, 314
Abbas, Azra, 523
Abbas, Ghulam, 481
Abdulahad, Noel, 29, 30
Abu Salma, 176, 177, 178
Adonis, 184, 185, 188
A Dot Might Appear, 523
A dot might appear from somewhere, 523
After Twelve PM, 568
After Twelve PM, 568
Agamemnon I, 328
Agamemnon II, 337
Agamemnon III, 341
A gift is my rib, 597
Ahmad, Jalal Al-e, 389
Ahmad, Rukhsana, 521, 525, 526, 527
Ahmadi, Pegah, 562, 563, 565
A home without a woman lacks amity and affection, 114
al-Hakim, Tawfiq, 21
Alif, 595
Alizadeh, Ahmad, 389
Allen, Roger, 214
al-Mala'ika, Nazik, 584, 585, 588, 591
al-Nawwab, Mozaffar, 196
Alphabetical Formation, An, 595
al-Udhari, Abdullah, 182
Anday, Melih Cevdet, 322, 323

Aorta, The, 226
Aqsa Mosque, The, 32
Are We Going to Live Without Aging?, 323
Are You Intoxicated?, 29
'Arrar, 29, 30
Asfour, John Mikhail, 179, 180
At dawn, a throng came out, 323
At last half-promise of a spring has come—, 440
At the end, 608
Athens Airport, 182
Athens Airport boots us to other airports. The fighter said: "Where can, 182
August 1952, 440
Avery, Peter, 367
A window for seeing, 355
Azudi is just like, 428
Azudi lights his cigarette, 428

Ba, 595
Babilla, Assurbanipal, 550, 555
Baboon Whose Buffoon Was Dead, The, 367
Bakht, Baidar, 442, 443, 444, 448, 518
Bank Teller Tecelli Bey, The, 512
Baraheni, Reza, 427, 428, 430
Barakat, Ibtisam S., 591
Bardenstein, Carol, 196

Barefoot, 323
Battle of Kadesh, The, 322
Bayraqdar, Faraj, 595, 596, 597, 598
Beard, Michael, 185
Before the time of day—I am, 184
Behbahani, Simin, 424, 425
Behnam, Alireza, 607, 608
Being present myself, my impetuous
     tongue, 156
Beloved Palestine, how can I sleep, 177
Bezirgan, Basima, 584
Bird's Last Flight, The, 594
Black Book, The, 507
Black tulips in my heart, 179
Blasing, Randy, 58
Blind Owl, The, 89
Blockage, 605
Boy, The, 444
Bridge of Old Wonders, 196
Bury me, oh my country, under your
     pavements, 440
Bury Me Under Your Pavements, 440

Censorship, 526
Chaussee, G. A., 529, 530
Christie, Ruth, 328, 337, 341, 571
Chubak, Sadeq, 367
Chughtai, Ismat, 145
Cold Ashes, 109
Compromise, 442
Cooke, Miriam, 12
Costello, D. P., 89

Dammaj, Zayd Mutee', 578
Dance of the Savage Prairies, The, 233
Daneshvar, Simin, 399
Dark Room, The, 562
Darwish, Mahmoud, 179, 180, 182
Deserted Sheba, 164
Desirable Life of Mr. F, The, 555
Devadasi and Pujari, 158
Diary of a Country Prosecutor, 21
Doctor Azudi, the Professional, 428
Don't Read, 424
Don't read these deceptions made by the
     hands of Satan, 424
Do You Suppose It's the East Wind?, 532
Dreaming of Baghdad, 502

Drunk again!, 29
"Dying?," 568
"Dying?" you said, 568

Eban, Abba, 21
Ebru Diriker, 572
Elmusa, Sharif, 32, 176, 177, 178
Enemies, The, 214
Engin, Fuat, 56
Epic of Sheikh Bedreddin, The, 58
Eryilmaz, Fatma Sinem, 378
E'tesami, Parvin, 112, 114
Even more, oh yes, 357
Everywhere is closed, 605
Exodus I, 325

Faiz, Faiz Ahmed, 439, 440
False Dawn, 363
Far and Near, 158
Faraway Star, 365
Farrokhzad, Forugh, 354, 355, 357, 359
Fatima, Altaf, 532
Fernea, Elizabeth, 584
Finn, Robert P., 67
First Lesson, The, 12
First Morning, The, 435
For Freedom's Sake: A Memoir, 122
Formerly a woman in Iran was almost
     non-Iranian, 112
For one black mole the towns of Buqara
     and Samarqand!, 165
Four Views of a Private Orange, 565
Freedom's Dawn (August 1947), 439
From his window overlooking the roofs,
     325
From nights long gone, 109
From the temples' incense of bygone
     Babylon, 585
From town to town the tourist
     wandered, 160
Future of the Arabic Language, The, 6

Gharbzadegi, 389
Ghazoul, Ferial J., 585, 588
Gibran, Khalil, 6
Girl Sleeping on Top of Oil, The, 563
God's Command to the Angels, 157
Göknar, Erdağ, 294

Golshiri, Houshang, 378
Grand Lady of My Soul, The, 540
Grave for New York, 188
Gray Donkey, The, 67
Green, John, 389
Groans, 598
Gün, Güneli, 507
Gürpınar, Melisa, 512

Habib, M. A. R. , 163, 164, 165
Had to go. Had to wait. Had to look at
    men, vehicles, roads, 337
Halman, Talat Sait, 322, 323, 325
Hameed, Syeda, 145
Hanging from the Trees of Babylon, 608
Haqqi, Yahya, 12
Hasan, Khalid, 481
Has he finished . . . ?, 598
Haydar, Adnan, 6, 185
Haydar, Haydar, 233
Hazo, Samuel, 184
Heaven and the Priest, 156
Hedayat, Sadegh, 89
Here I am you alone, 598
Hikmet, Nâzım, 56, 58, 64
Honorable Prince! Before you stands a
    poet, 32
Hosseinzadeh, the Head Executioner, 428
Houri and the Poet, The, 155
Houshmand, Zara, 420
Husain, M. Hadi, 155
Hussein, Abdullah, 451
Hussein, Intizaar, 435

I Am an Underground Man, 427
I Am Listening to Istanbul, 325
I am listening to Istanbul with my eyes
    closed, 325
I Became a Tree, 322
Identity Card, 180
Idris, Yusif, 226
I Forgot, 160
I have sinned a rapturous sin, 354
I live, 603
I Love My Country, 56
I love my country:, 56
I Love You More, 178
I'm Dying, God, 568

I'm dying, God, 568
I'm still, 420
I'm Still Thinking of That Crow, 420
Inclination, 606
In my country, 518
In the City Court, 518
In the mirror images cry out, 365
In those times when the camera could
    not freeze tyranny forever, 526
Iqbal, Muhammad, 155, 156, 157
Iranian Women, 112
I shall keep on going like this, 443
Istanbul Boy: A Memoir, 37
Is This Home?, 495
It all, 560
It is we sinful women, 525
I want to know—, 529
I was going under a tree, 322

Jacobson, Joseph S., 37, 314
Jaeger, Kathleen Grant, 442, 443, 444, 448
Jafri, Ali Sardar, 447, 448
Jamal, Mahmood, 447
Jamalzadeh, Mohammad Ali, 78
Jamilah and Us, 584
Jamilah! Beyond the horizon, far beyond
    the borders of nations, 584
Jayyusi, May, 233, 578

Kanafani, Ghassan, 171
Kanık, Orhan Veli, 325
Karachi, 530
Karachi, 530
Karay, Refik Halit, 67
Karimi-Hakkak, Ahmad, 364, 365, 421,
    562, 563, 565
Kavukçu, Cemil, 572
Kemal, Yaşar, 277
Kha, 596
Kianush, Mahmud, 109, 110, 603, 605,
    606
Kiernan, V. G., 156, 439, 440
Kilpatrick, Hilary, 171
Konuk, Mutlu, 58
Koofa, 593

Lamp of Love's chamber, awake!, 163
Last Stop Before the Destination, The, 443

Leaves, asleep under wind:, 185
Leaving the ships to be scraped we
    trudged on, and reached a, 328
Le Gassick, Trevor J., 226
Let's go back to our own dusty moments,
    559
Letter from Gaza, 171
Levine, Leslie, 442, 443, 444
Life, they said, 588
Like the unbridled wind he winds after
    us, 591
Look, come see a dance, the dance, the
    undefiled dance of a, 158
Lover River, The, 591

Mafi, Maryam, 399
Mahfouz, Naguib, 247
Mahmud, 'Abd Al-Rahim, 32
Manouchehr Atashi, 559, 560
Manto, Sa'adat Hasan, 122
Mattawa, Khaled, 593, 594
McKane, Richard, 328, 337, 341
Memed, My Hawk, 277
Memon, Muhammad Umar, 122, 451,
    532
Milani, Farzaneh, 424, 425
Mind at Peace, A, 294
Miraji, 158, 160
Moayyad, Heshmat, 78, 112, 114
Mohammad, Zakaria, 495
Mountain Song, 560
Mrs. F Is a Fortunate Woman, 550
My China Doll, 378
My country is torrid, 527
My Country, I Will Build You Again, 425
My country, I will build you again, 425
My country! Live in safety, an Arab
    country, 176
My Country on Partition Day, 176
My heart drums a rhythm, 158
My Journey, 448
My kinsmen say: "Do, please repent, 30
My Kinsmen Say "Leave her!," 30
Myths, 588

Naderpour, Nader, 363, 364, 365
Naheed, Kishwar, 525, 526, 527
Naim, C. M., 523

Near the Window, 163
Nemet-Nejat, Murat, 325, 512, 567,
    568
Nesin, Aziz, 37
Nostalgia, 559
Now I am an underground man, 427
Nun, 597
Nye, Naomi Shihab, 32, 176, 177, 178

Oblivious to design, this tomorrow is
    baffled by intent, 597
Oil Merchants, 165
One arm hangs limp and empty, 523
One's throat must be like a garden, 606
On one of the banks of River Orontes,
    322
On the divan, Bursa silk in green-
    branching red boughs, 58
On the hills near villages in the east,
    444
O People!, 110
O people who are sitting, cheerful and
    laughing, 110
Our memories mix with leftover rains,
    the splendid Tree, 341

Pages of Day and Night, The, 184
Pamuk, Orhan, 507
Patel, Geeta, 158, 160
Peer, Basharat, 435
Perin, Deniz, 64
Persian Is Sugar, 78
Pirzad, Zoya, 550, 555
Playhouse, The, 399
Poem X, 569

Qom, 364
Quilt, The, 145
Quarter to Destruction, A, 603

Rahimi, Hamid Reza, 603, 605, 606
Rashed N. M., 163, 164, 165
Refugees, The, 451
Riaz, Fahmida, 518, 521
Rifat, Oktay, 328, 337, 341
Rise up!, 157
Robe of Flame, 447
Roditi, Edouard, 277

Rome, 529
Room with the Blue Light, The, 481
Route of the Crows, The, 572

Safa, Kaveh, 424, 425
Sahil, Zeeshan, 529, 530
Scott, Michael K., 495
Seventh Heaven, The, 247
Shah and Hosseinzadeh, The, 430
Shamloo, Ahmad, 420, 421
Sharpe, Patricia L., 518
Sheikh Says . . . , The, 29
She Is a Woman Impure, 521
She is a woman impure, 521
Simawe, Saadi A., 196
Sin, 354
Since I Was Thrown Inside, 64
Since I was thrown inside, 64
Solomon, head in his hands, and Sheba desolate, 164
Song of Abraham in Fire, The, 421
Sprachman, Paul, 78
St. John, David, 427, 428, 430
Stock, Raymond, 247
Such a Story, 314
suddenly a woman is sleepless in her dream, 428
Süreya, Cemal, 567, 568

Ta, 596
Tahir, Şehnaz, 569
Taleghani, Shareah, 595, 596, 597, 598
Tamir, Zakariyya, 214
Tanpınar, Ahmet Hamdi, 294
Taraghi, Goli, 540
Thal, 597
That's a mirror, 596
The beginning of wine is the shadow . . . , 596
The day will come, 448
The girl sleeping on top of oil, 563
The more I fight for you, the more I love you!, 178
There, sunset, 565
the Shah has granted full authority, 430
The Sheikh ordered me to repent, 29
The top part of this piece of writing, 323

They'd Love to See Me Dead, 182
They'd love to see me dead so they can say: he was one of us, he, 182
This Government, 567
This government, 567
This land is called "The daughter of the morning," 196
This leprous daybreak, dawn night's fangs have mangled—, 439
Those cavalry lights riding by the horse chestnuts, 569
Those Days, 359
Those days are gone, 359
Thousands of women, 364
Thwaite, Anthony, 233
Tingley, Christopher, 578
Today Was a Holiday, 523
Tonight the earth has bid all its sins, 363
Toorawa, Shawkat M., 188
To Poetry, 585
To the Masters of Countries with a Cold Climate, 527
To the Reader, 179

ul-Iman, Akhtar, 442, 443, 444
Under the bloody tumbling of twilight, 421
Until now, the Earth has been depicted in the shape of a pear, 188

Wall of Love, The, 571
Was it you or your loneliness, 571
We did not name it so that it would become a city, 593
We haven't yet finished the elegy for the century, 595
We Shall Return, 177
We Sinful Women, 525
What?, 607
What a war it is when the earth looks at "what," 607
Whenever I kissed her, the smell of cigarettes, 442
When I enter the earth's nest, 594
Who is that, 447
Window, 355
Wind-Up Doll, 357

Wolpé, Sholeh, 354, 355, 357, 359, 363, 540
Woman, A, 578
Woman's Place, A, 114
Wound, The, 185
Wrinkled summer, 562
Write down:, 180

Yah, 598
You Leave, I'll Stay, 425
You leave, I'll stay. You leave, I'll stay, 425

You neither relish wine nor even look at me, 155
You're not beginning . . . , 595
Youssef, Saadi, 593, 594
Yücel, Can, 569, 571
Yushij, Nima, 109, 110

Zadan! Nazadan!, 428
Zangana, Haifa, 502
Zara Houshmand, 559, 560
Ziad, Zeenut, 157

About Words without Borders

Words without Borders is a not-for-profit organization dedicated to the translation, publication, and promotion of the finest contemporary international literature. Every month, in our online magazine, we publish eight to ten new works by international writers. To date we have published well over a thousand pieces from 114 countries and 80 languages. In addition to producing the magazine, we partner with publishing houses to release print anthologies, of which *Tablet and Pen: Literary Landscapes from the Modern Middle East* is the fifth. Finally, Words without Borders is building an education program in order to expose students at both the high school and college levels to a broader spectrum of contemporary international literature. For more information on all our programs, please visit wordswithoutborders.org.

About the Editor

REZA ASLAN is associate professor of creative writing at the University of California, Riverside. His books include the international bestseller *No god but God* and *How to Win a Cosmic War* (published in paperback as *Beyond Fundamentalism*). He lives in Los Angeles.